PRAISE FOR EXODUS

"Tremendously exciting . . . A giant of a novel; one that takes a Tolstoyan grip on the struggle of the Jews for a homeland . . . Heartwarming."
—San Francisco Examiner

"A superlative story—superlative indeed—of a people in pursuit of a dream two thousand years old."
—Christian Herald

"A rich novel of Israel's birth . . . Written at white heat."
—Chicago Tribune

"Passionate summary of the inhuman treatment of the Jewish people in Europe, of the exodus in the nineteenth and twentieth centuries to Palestine and of the triumphant founding of the new Israel."
—The New York Times

LEON URIS SAYS:

Exodus is the story of the greatest miracle of
our times, an event unparalleled in the history
of mankind: the rebirth of a nation which
had been dispersed two thousand years before.

It tells the story of the Jews coming back after
centuries of abuse, indignities, torture, and
murder to carve an oasis in the sand
with guts and with blood.

All the cliché Jewish characters who
have cluttered up our American fiction—the
clever businessman, the brilliant doctor,
the sneaky lawyer, the sulking artist . . .

all those good folk who spend their chapters
hating themselves, the world, and all their
aunts and uncles . . . all those steeped
in self-pity . . . all those golden riders of the
psychoanalysis couch . . . all these have been
left where they rightfully belong,
on the cutting-room floor.

I have shown the other side of the coin, and
written about my people who, against a
lethargic world and with little else than courage,
conquered unconquerable odds.

Exodus is about fighting people, people who
do not apologize either for being born Jews
or the right to live in human dignity.

Their story was a revelation to me as I
discovered it in the farms and cities of Israel.

And . . . it has been a revelation to the
readers, Jewish and Gentile, alike.

BY LEON URIS

DUS

EXODUS

*A Bantam Book / published by arrangement with
Doubleday & Company, Inc.*

PRINTING HISTORY
*Doubleday edition published September 1958
30 printings through 1964*
Book-of-the-Month Club edition published September 1959
*Bantam edition / October 1959
57 printings through January 1981*

*Bantam Books are published by Bantam Books, Inc. Its trade-
mark, consisting of the words "Bantam Books" and the por-
trayal of a bantam, is Registered in U.S. Patent and Trademark
Office and in other countries. Marca Registrada. Bantam
Books, Inc., 666 Fifth Avenue, New York, New York 10103.*

PRINTED IN THE UNITED STATES OF AMERICA

66 65 64 63 62 61 60 59

Most of the events in *Exodus* are a matter of history and public record. Many of the scenes were created around historical incidents for the purpose of fiction.

There may be persons alive who took part in events similar to those described in this book. It is possible, therefore, that some of them may be mistaken for characters in this book.

Let me emphasize that all characters in *Exodus* are the complete creation of the author, and entirely fictional.

The exceptions, of course, are those public figures mentioned by name, such as Churchill, Truman, Pearson, and the rest who were related to this particular period.

CONTENTS

A NOTE OF THANKS

The space covered in my gathering of material for Exodus was nearly fifty thousand miles. The yards of recording tape used, the number of interviews, the tons of research books, and the number of film exposures and vanished greenbacks make equally impressive figures.

During the course of two years, tens of dozens of people gave me their time, energy, and confidence. I was twice blessed every foot of the way with uncommon co-operation and faith.

It is unfortunate, but the sheer weight of numbers precludes my thanking everyone here. Such listing would fill a volume in itself.

I would be less than grateful if I did not acknowledge the efforts of those two men who were truly instrumental in making Exodus a reality.

I hope I am not setting a dangerous precedent by publicly thanking my agent. Exodus evolved out of a conversation at lunch and became a tangible project because of the dogged persistence of Malcolm Stuart. He refused to give up the idea despite a dozen setbacks.

I most humbly thank Ilan Hartuv of Jerusalem. He made my arrangements, and traveled with me over every foot of Israel by train, plane, Vauxhall, and Austin, jeep and by foot. At times it was a pretty rough go. Mainly, I thank Ilan for sharing with me his vast knowledge of the subject.

BOOK 1

Beyond Jordan

Until the Lord have given rest unto your brethren, as
well as unto you, and until they also possess the
land which the Lord your God hath given them
beyond Jordan: and then shall ye return every man
unto his possession, which I have given you.

*The word of God as given to
Moses in Deuteronomy*

CHAPTER ONE

NOVEMBER 1946

WELCOME TO CYPRUS

WILLIAM SHAKESPEARE

The airplane plip-plopped down the runway to a halt before the big sign: WELCOME TO CYPRUS. Mark Parker looked out of the window and in the distance he could see the jagged wonder of the Peak of Five Fingers of the northern coastal range. In an hour or so he would be driving through the pass to Kyrenia. He stepped into the aisle, straightened out his necktie, rolled down his sleeves, and slipped into his jacket. "Welcome to Cyprus, welcome to Cyprus . . ." It ran through his head. It was from *Othello,* he thought, but the full quotation slipped his mind.

"Anything to declare?" the customs inspector said.

"Two pounds of uncut heroin and a manual of pornographic art," Mark answered, looking about for Kitty.

All Americans are comedians, the inspector thought, as he passed Parker through. A government tourist hostess approached him. "Are you Mr. Mark Parker?"

"Guilty."

"Mrs. Kitty Fremont phoned to say she is unable to meet you at the airport and for you to come straight to Kyrenia to the Dome Hotel. She has a room there for you."

"Thanks, angel. Where can I get a taxi to Kyrenia?"

"I'll arrange a car for you, sir. It will take a few moments."

"Can I get a transfusion around here?"

"Yes, sir. The coffee counter is straight down the hall."

Mark leaned against the counter and sipped a steaming cup of black coffee . . . "Welcome to Cyprus . . . welcome to Cyprus" . . . he couldn't for the life of him remember.

"Say!" a voice boomed out. "I thought I recognized you on the plane. You're Mark Parker! I bet you don't remember me."

Fill in one of the following, Mark thought. It was: Rome, Paris, London, Madrid (and match carefully); Jose's Bar, James's Pub, Jacques's Hideaway, Joe's Joint. At the time I was covering: war, revolution, insurrection. That particular night I had a: blonde, brunette, redhead (or maybe that broad with two heads).

The man stood nose to nose with Mark, gushing on all eight cylinders now. "I was the guy who ordered a martini and

3

they didn't have orange bitters. Now do you remember me?" Mark sighed, sipped some coffee, and braced for another onslaught. "I know you hear this all the time but I really enjoy reading your columns. Say, what are you doing in Cyprus?" The man then winked and jabbed Mark in the ribs. "Something hush-hush, I bet. Why don't we get together for a drink? I'm staying at the Palace in Nicosia." A business card was slapped into Mark's hand. "Got a few connections here, too." The man winked again.

"Oh, Mr. Parker. Your car is ready."

Mark put the cup down on the counter. "Nice seeing you again," he said, and walked out quickly. As he departed he dropped the business card into a trash basket.

The taxi headed out from the airport. Mark rested back and closed his eyes for a moment. He was glad that Kitty couldn't get to the airport to meet him. So much time had passed and there was so much to say and so much to remember. He felt a surge of excitement pass through him at the thought of seeing her again. Kitty, beautiful, beautiful, Kitty. As the taxi passed through the outer gates Mark was already lost in thought.

. . . Katherine Fremont. She was one of those great American traditions like Mom's apple pie, hot dogs, and the Brooklyn Dodgers. For Kitty Fremont was the proverbial "girl next door." She was the cliché of pigtails, freckles, tomboys, and braces on the teeth; and true to the cliché the braces came off one day, the lipstick went on and the sweater popped out and the ugly duckling had turned into a graceful swan. Mark smiled to himself—she was so beautiful in those days, so fresh and clean.

. . . and Tom Fremont. He was another American tradition. Tom was the crew-cut kid with the boyish grin who could run the hundred in ten flat, sink a basket from thirty feet out, cut a rug, and put a Model A together blindfolded. Tom Fremont had been Mark's best pal as long as he could remember for as far back as he could remember. We must have been weaned together, Mark thought.

. . . Tom and Kitty . . . apple pie and ice cream . . . hot dogs and mustard. The all-American boy, the all-American girl, and the all-American Midwest of Indiana. Yes, Tom and Kitty fitted together like the rain and springtime.

Kitty had always been a quiet girl, very deep, very thoughtful. There was a tinge of sadness in her eyes. Perhaps it was only Mark who detected that sadness, for she was joy itself to everyone around her. Kitty had been one of those wonderful towers of strength. She always had both hands on the rudder, always had the right words to say, always decent

4

and thoughtful. But that sadness was there. . . . Mark knew it if no one else did.

Mark often wondered what made her so desirable. Maybe it was because she seemed so unreachable to him. The iced champagne—the look and the word that could tear a man to pieces. Anyhow, Kitty had always been Tom's girl and the most he could do was envy Tom.

Tom and Mark were roommates at State University. That first year Tom was absolutely miserable being away from Kitty. Mark remembered the hours on end he would have to listen to Tom's mournful laments and console him. Summer came, Kitty went off to Wisconsin with her parents. She was still a high-school girl and her folks wanted to dampen the fervor of the affair with a separation. Tom and Mark hitchhiked to Oklahoma to work in the oil fields.

By the time school started again Tom had cooled down considerably. To remain in Mark's company one had to sample the field. The times between Tom and Kitty's letters lengthened and the times between Tom's dates on the campus shortened. It began to look like a strike-out for the college hero and the girl back home.

By their senior year Tom had all but forgotten Kitty. He had become the Beau Brummell of State, a role befitting the ace forward on the basketball team. As for Mark, he was content to bask in Tom's glory and generally make a name for himself as one of the worst journalism students in the university's history.

Kitty came to State as a freshman.

Lightning struck!

Mark could see Kitty a thousand times and it was always as exciting as the first. This time Tom saw her the same way. They eloped a month before Tom's graduation. Tom and Kitty, Mark and Ellen, a Model A Ford, and four dollars and ten cents crossed the state line and sought out a justice of the peace. Their honeymoon was in the back seat of the Model A, bogged down in the mud of a back road and leaking like a sieve in a downpour. It was an auspicious beginning for the all-American couple.

Tom and Kitty kept their marriage a secret until a full year after his graduation. Kitty stayed on at State to finish her pre-nursing training. Nursing and Kitty seemed to go together, too, Mark always thought.

Tom worshiped Kitty. He had always been a bit wild and too independent, but he settled down to very much the devoted husband. He started out as a very little executive in a very big public relations firm. They moved to Chicago. Kitty nursed in Children's Hospital. They inched their way up, typical American style. First an apartment and then a small home. A new car, monthly bills, big hopes. Kitty became pregnant with Sandra.

Mark's thoughts snapped as the taxi slowed through the outskirts of Nicosia, the capital city that sat on the flat brown plain beween the northern and southern mountain ranges. "Driver, speak English?" Mark asked.

"Yes, sir?"

"They've got a sign at the airport, Welcome to Cyprus. What is the full quotation?"

"As far as I know," the driver answered, "they're just trying to be polite to tourists."

They entered Nicosia proper. The flatness, the yellow stone houses with their red tiled roofs, the sea of date palms all reminded Mark of Damascus. The road ran alongside the ancient Venetian wall which was built in a perfect circle and surrounded the old city. Mark could see the twin minarets that spiraled over the skyline from the Turkish section of the old city. The minarets that belonged to St. Sophia's, that magnificent crusader cathedral turned into a Moslem mosque. As they drove along the wall they passed the enormous ramparts shaped like arrowheads. Mark remembered from his last visit to Cyprus that there was the odd number of eleven of these arrowheads jutting from the wall. He was about to ask the driver why eleven but decided not to.

In a matter of moments they were out of Nicosia and moving north on the plain. They passed one village after another, monotonously similar, made of gray mud-brick cottages. Each village had one water fountain which bore an inscription that it was built through the generosity of His Majesty, the King of England. In the colorless fields the peasants labored with the potato crop, working behind those magnificent beasts, the Cyprus mules.

The taxi picked up speed again and Mark sank back to his reveries.

. . . Mark and Ellen had gotten married a little after Tom and Kitty. It was a mistake from the first day. Two nice people not made for each other. Kitty Fremont's quiet and gentle wisdom held Mark and Ellen together. They both could come to her and pour their hearts out. Kitty kept the marriage intact long after time had run out. Then it broke wide open and they were divorced. Mark was thankful there had been no children.

After the divorce Mark moved East and began banging around from job to job, having matriculated from the world's worst journalism student to the world's worst newspaperman. He became one of those drifters who inhabit the newspaper world. It was not stupidity nor lack of talent, but complete inability to find his niche in life. Mark was a creative man and the business of routine reporting cut that creativity. Yet he had no desire to attempt the life of a creative writer. He knew that his personality would not take the demands on a novelist. So Mark hung in limbo, being neither fish nor fowl.

Each week there was a letter from Tom, and it would be filled with enthusiasm and the vigor of his climb to the top. The letters were also filled with Tom's love for Kitty and their baby girl, Sandra.

Mark remembered Kitty's letters. A calm appraisal of Tom's effervescence. Kitty always kept Mark posted on Ellen's whereabouts until Ellen remarried.

In 1938 the world opened up for Mark Parker. There was a post to be filled in Berlin with American News Syndicate, and Mark was suddenly transformed from a "newspaper bum" into the respectability of a "foreign correspondent."

In this capacity Mark proved to be a talented journeyman. He was able to fill part of his desire for creativity by developing a style that labeled him as an individual—as Mark Parker and no one else. Mark was by no means a world-beater but he did have that one great instinct of a crack foreign correspondent: an ability to smell out a story in the making.

The world was a lark. He covered Europe, Asia, and Africa from one end to the other. He had a title, he was doing work he liked, his credit was good at José's Bar, James's Pub, Joe's and Jacques's Hideaway, and he had an inexhaustible list of candidates for his blonde-, brunette-, or redhead-of-the-month club.

When the war broke out Mark chased all over Europe. It was good to settle back in London for a few days where a stack of mail from Tom and Kitty would be waiting.

Early in 1942 Tom Fremont enlisted in the Marine Corps. He was killed at Guadalcanal.

Two months after Tom's death, their baby, Sandra, died of polio.

Mark took emergency leave to return home, but by the time he arrived Kitty Fremont had disappeared. He searched for her without success until he had to return to Europe. To all intents she had disappeared from the face of the earth. It was strange to Mark, but that sadness that he always saw in Kitty's eyes seemed like a fulfilled prophecy.

The moment the war was over he returned to look for her again, but the trail had grown cold.

In November of 1945, American News Syndicate recalled him to Europe to cover the war-crimes trials in Nuremberg. By now Mark was an established craftsman and bore the title, "distinguished" foreign correspondent. He stayed on, turning in a brilliant series, until the top Nazis were hanged, only a few months back.

ANS granted Mark a much-needed leave of absence before transferring him to Palestine, where it appeared local war was brewing. To spend his leave in the accepted Mark Parker fashion, he chased down a passionate French UN girl he had met earlier, who had been transferred to the United Nations Relief in Athens.

It all happened from a clear blue sky. He was sitting in the American Bar, passing the time of day with a group of fellow newsmen, when the conversation somehow drifted to a particular American nurse in Salonika doing fabulous work with Greek orphans. One of the correspondents had just returned from there with a story on her orphanage.

The nurse was Kitty Fremont.

Mark inquired immediately and discovered that she was on vacation in Cyprus.

.The taxi began to move upwards, out of the plain, on a twisting little road that led through the pass in the Pentadaktylos Mountains. It was turning dusk. They reached the peak and Mark ordered the car to pull over to the side.

He stepped out and looked down at the magnificent jewel-like little town of Kyrenia nestled against the sea at the foot of the mountain. To the left and above him stood the ruins of St. Hilarion Castle, haunted with the memory of Richard the Lion-Hearted and his beautiful Berengaria. He made a mental note to come back again with Kitty.

It was nearing dark as they reached Kyrenia. The little town was all white plaster and red tiled roofs, with the castle above it and the sea beside it. Kyrenia was picturesque and remote and quaint to a point where it could not have been more picturesque or remote or quaint. They passed the miniature harbor, filled with fishing smacks and small yachts, set inside two arms of a sea wall. On one arm was the quay. On the other arm stood an ancient fortress rampart, the Virgin Castle.

Kyrenia had long been a retreat for artists and retired British Army officers. It was, indeed, one of the most peaceful places on earth.

A block away from the harbor stood the Dome Hotel. Physically the big building seemed outsized and out of place for the rest of the sleepy little town. The Dome, however, had become a crossroads of the British Empire. It was known in every corner of the world that flew a Union Jack as a place where Englishmen met. It was a maze of public rooms and terraces and verandas sitting over the sea. A long pier of a hundred yards or more connected the hotel to a tiny island offshore used by swimmers and sun bathers.

The taxi pulled to a stop. The bellboy gathered in Mark's luggage. Mark paid off his driver and looked about. It was November but it was warmish yet and it was serene. What a wonderful place for a reunion with Kitty Fremont!

The desk clerk handed Mark a message.

Mark darling:

I am stuck in Famagusta until nine o'clock. Will you ever forgive me??? Dying with anxiety. Love.

            Kitty

"I want some flowers, a bottle of scotch, and a bucket of ice," Mark said.

"Mrs. Fremont has taken care of everything," the room clerk said, handing a key to the bellboy. "You have adjoining rooms overlooking the sea."

Mark detected a smirk on the clerk's face. It was the same kind of dirty look he had seen in a hundred hotels with a hundred women. He was about to set the record straight but decided to let the clerk think anything he damned well pleased.

He gathered in the view of the sea as it turned dark, then he unpacked and mixed himself a scotch and water and drank it while he soaked in a steaming tub.

Seven o'clock . . . still two hours to wait.

He opened the door of Kitty's room. It smelled good. Her bathing suit and some freshly washed hosiery hung over the bathtub. Her shoes were lined up beside the bed and her make-up on the vanity. Mark smiled. Even with Kitty gone the empty room was full of the character of an unusual person.

He went back and stretched out on his bed. What had the years done to her? What had the tragedy done? Kitty, beautiful Kitty . . . please be all right. It was now November of 1946, Mark figured; when was the last time he saw her? Nineteen thirty-eight . . . just before he went to Berlin for ANS. Eight years ago. Kitty would be twenty-eight years old now.

The excitement and tension caught up with Mark. He was tired and he began to doze.

The tinkle of ice cubes, a sweet sound to Mark Parker, brought him out of a deep sleep. He rubbed his eyes and groped around for a cigarette.

"You sleep as though you were drugged," a very British

9

accent said. "I knocked for five minutes. The bellboy let me in. Hope you don't mind me helping myself tó the whisky."

The voice belonged to Major Fred Caldwell of the British Army. Mark yawned, stretched himself into wakefulness, and checked his watch. It was eight-fifteen. "What the hell are you doing on Cyprus?" Mark asked.

"I believe that is my question."

Mark lit a cigarette and looked, at Caldwell. He didn't like the major nor did he hate him. "Despise" was the suitable word. They had met before twice. Caldwell had been the aide of Colonel, later Brigadier, Bruce Sutherland, quite a good field officer in the British Army. Their first meeting had been in the lowlands near Holland during the war. In one of his reports Mark had pointed out a British tactical blunder that had caused a regiment of men to get cut to pieces. The second meeting had been at the Nuremberg war crimes trials which Mark was covering for ANS.

Toward the end of the war Bruce Sutherland's troops were the first to enter the Bergen-Belsen concentration camp in Germany. Both Sutherland and Caldwell had come to Nuremberg to give testimony.

Mark walked to the bathroom, washed his face with icy water, and fished around for a towel. "What can I do for you, Freddie?"

"CID phoned over to our headquarters this afternoón and told us you landed. You haven't been issued credentials."

"Christ, you're a suspicious bunch of bastards. Sorry to disappoint you, Freddie. I'm here on vacation en route to Palestine."

"This isn't an official call, Parker," Caldwell said; "just say we are a bit touchy over past relationships."

"You have long memories," Mark said, and began dressing. Caldwell mixed Mark a drink. Mark studied the British officer and wondered why Caldwell always managed to rub him the wrong way. There was that arrogance about him that stamped him as a member of that quaint breed, the Colonizer. Caldwell was a stuffy and narrow-minded bore. A gentleman's game of tennis, in whites . . . a bashing gin and tonic and damn the natives. It was Freddie Caldwell's conscience or the utter lack of it that bothered Mark. The meaning of right and wrong came to Caldwell through an army manual or an order. "You boys covering up some dirty work on Cyprus?"

"Don't be a bore, Parker. We own this island and we want to know what you want here."

"You know . . . that's what I like about you British. A Dutchman would tell me to get the hell out. You fellows always say, 'please go to hell.' I said I was on vacation. A reunion with an old friend."

"Who?"

"A girl named Kitty Fremont."

"Kitty, the nurse. Yes, smashing woman, smashing. We met at the governor's a few days back." Freddie Caldwell's eyebrows raised questioningly as he looked at the connecting door to Kitty's room, which stood ajar.

"Go give your filthy mind a bath," Mark said. "I've known her for twenty-five years."

"Then, as you Americans say—everything's on the up and up."

"That's right and from this point on your visit becomes social, so get out."

Freddie Caldwell smiled and set down his glass and tucked the swagger stick under his arm.

"Freddie Caldwell," Mark said. "I want to see you when that smile is wiped off your face."

"What in the devil are you talking about?"

"This is 1946, Major. A lot of people read the campaign slogans in the last war and believed them. You're a dollar short and an hour late. You're going to lose the whole shooting match . . . first it's going to be India, then Africa, then the Middle East. I'll be there to watch you lose the Palestine mandate. They're going to boot you out of even Suez and Trans-Jordan. The sun is setting on the empire, Freddie . . . what is your wife going to do without forty little black boys to whip?"

"I read your coverage of the Nuremberg trials, Parker. You have that terrible American tendency toward being overdramatic. Corny is the word, I think. Besides, old boy, I don't have a wife."

"You boys are polite."

"Remember, Parker, you are on vacation. I'll give Brigadier Sutherland your regards. Cheerio."

Mark smiled and shrugged. Then it came back to him. The sign at the airport. . . . WELCOME TO CYPRUS: WILLIAM SHAKESPEARE. The full quote was—"Welcome to Cyprus, goats and monkeys."

CHAPTER TWO: During the hours in which Mark Parker awaited his long-delayed reunion with Kitty Fremont, two other men awaited a reunion of a far different sort in a different part of Cyprus. Forty miles away from Kyrenia, north of the port city of Famagusta, they waited in a forest.

It was cloudy, socked-in with no light from the sky. The two men stood in utter silence and squinted through the dark toward the bay a half mile down the hill.

11

They were in an abandoned white house on the hill in the midst of a forest of pines and eucalyptus and acacias. It was still and black except for a wisp of wind and the muffled unsteady breathing of the two men.

One of the men was a Greek Cypriot, a forest service ranger, and he was nervous.

The other man appeared as calm as a statue, never moving his eyes from the direction of the water. His name was David Ben Ami. His name meant David, Son of My People.

The clouds began to break. Light fell over the still waters of the bay and on the forest and the white house. David Ben Ami stood in the window and the light played on his face. He was a man of slight build in his early twenties. Even in the poor light his thin face and his deep eyes showed the sensitivity of a scholar.

As the clouds swept away, the light crept over fields of broken marble columns and statuary that littered the ground about the white house.

Broken stone. The mortal remains of the once-great city of Salamis which stood mighty in the time of Christ. What history lay beneath this ground and throughout the fields of marble! Salamis, founded in times barely recorded by men, by the warrior Teucer on his return from the Trojan Wars. It fell by earthquake and it rose again and it fell once more to the Arab sword under the banner of Islam, never to arise again. The light danced over the acres and acres of thousands of broken columns where a great Greek forum once stood.

The clouds closed and it was dark again.

"He is long overdue," the Greek Cypriot forest ranger whispered nervously.

"Listen," David Ben Ami said.

A faint sound of a boat's motor was heard from far out on the water. David Ben Ami lifted his field glasses, hoping for a break in the clouds. The sound of the motor grew louder.

A flash of light streaked out from the water toward the white house on the hill. Another flash. Another.

David Ben Ami and the forest ranger raced from the white house, down the hill, and through the rubble and the woods till they reached the shore line. Ben Ami returned the signal with his own flashlight.

The sound of the motor stopped.

A shadowy figure of a man slipped over the side of the boat and began to swim toward the shore. David Ben Ami cocked his Sten gun and looked up and down the beach for signs of a British patrol. The figure emerged from the deep water and waded in. "David!" a voice called from the water.

"Ari," he answered back, "this way, quickly."

On the beach the three men ran past the white house and onto a dirt road. A taxi waited, hidden in the brush. Ben Ami thanked the Cypriot forest ranger, and he and the man from the boat sped off in the direction of Famagusta.

"My cigarettes are soaked," Ari said.

David Ben Ami passed him a pack. A brief flame glowed over the face of the man who was called Ari. He was large and husky, in complete contrast to the small Ben Ami. His face was handsome but there was a set hardness in his eyes.

He was Ari Ben Canaan and he was the crack agent of the Mossad Aliyah Bet—the illegal organization.

CHAPTER THREE: There was a knock on Mark Parker's door. He opened it. Katherine Fremont stood before him. She was even more beautiful than he remembered. They stared at each other silently for a long time. He studied her face and her eyes. She was a woman now, soft and compassionate in the way one gets only through terrible suffering.

"I ought to break your damned neck for not answering my letters," Mark said.

"Hello, Mark," she whispered.

They fell into each other's arms and clung to each other. Then for the first hour they spoke little but contented themselves with looking at each other, with quick smiles, occasional pressing of hands, and affectionate kisses on the cheek.

At dinner they made small talk, mostly of Mark's adventures as a foreign correspondent. Then Mark became aware that Kitty was steering all the conversation away from any talk of herself.

The final dish of cheeses came. Mark poured the last of his Keo beer and another of the many awkward silent periods followed. Now Kitty was obviously growing uncomfortable under his questioning stare.

"Come on," he said, "let's take a walk to the harbor."

"I'll get my stole," she said.

They walked silently along the quay lined with white buildings and onto the sea wall and out to the lighthouse which stood at the narrow opening of the harbor. It was cloudy and they could see but dim outlines of the little boats resting at anchor. They watched the lighthouse blink out to sea, guiding a trawler toward the shelter of the harbor. A soft wind blew through Kitty's golden hair. She tightened the stole over her shoulders. Mark lit a cigarette and sat on the wall. It was deathly still.

"I've made you very unhappy by coming here," he said, "I'll leave tomorrow."

"I don't want you to go," she said. She looked away out to the sea. "I don't know how I felt when I received your cable. It opened the door on a lot of memories that I have tried awfully hard to bury. Yet I knew that one day this minute would come . . . in a way I've dreaded it . . . in a way, I'm glad it's here."

"It's been four years since Tom got killed. Aren't you ever going to shake this?"

"Women lose husbands in war," she whispered. "I cried for Tom. We were very much in love, but I knew I would go on living. I don't even know how he died."

"There wasn't much to it," Mark said. "Tom was a marine and he went in to take a beach with ten thousand other marines. A bullet hit him and he died. No hero, no medals . . . no time to say, 'tell Kitty I love her.' Just got hit by a bullet and died . . . that's it."

The blood drained from her face. Mark lit a cigarette and handed it to her. "Why did Sandra die? Why did my baby have to die too?"

"I'm not God. I can't answer that."

She sat beside Mark on the sea wall and rested her head on his shoulder and sighed unevenly. "I guess there is no place left for me to run," she said.

"Why don't you tell me about it."

"I can't . . ."

"I think it's about time that you did."

A half dozen times Kitty tried to speak, but her voice held only short disconnected whispers. The years of terror were locked deep in her. She threw the cigarette into the water and looked at Mark. He was right and he was the only one in the world she could confide in.

"It was pretty terrible," she said, "when I got the telegram about Tom, I loved him so. Just . . . just two months after that Sandra died of polio. I . . . I don't remember too much. My parents took me away to Vermont and put me in a home."

"Asylum?"

"No . . . that's the name they give it for poor people . . . they called mine a rest home for a breakdown. I don't know how many months passed there. I couldn't remember everything. I was in a complete fog day and night. Melancholia, they call it."

Suddenly Kitty's voice became steady. The door had

14

opened and the torment was finding its way out. "One day the veil over my mind lifted and I remembered that Tom and Sandra were dead. A pain clung to me. Everything every minute of the day reminded me of them. Every time I heard a song, every time I heard laughter . . . every time I saw a child. Every breath I took hurt me. I prayed . . . I prayed, Mark, that the fog would fall on me again. Yes, I prayed I'd go insane so I couldn't remember."

She stood up tall and straight and the tears streamed down her cheeks. "I ran away to New York. Tried to bury myself in the throngs. I had four walls, a chair, a table, a swinging light bulb." She let out a short ironic laugh. "There was even a flickering neon sign outside my window. Corny, wasn't it? I'd walk aimlessly for hours on the streets till all the faces were a blur, or I'd sit and look out of the window for days at a time. Tom, Sandra, Tom, Sandra . . . it never left me for a moment."

Kitty felt Mark behind her. His hands gripped her shoulders. Out in the water the trawler was nearing the opening between the arms of the sea wall. She brushed her cheek against Mark's hand.

"One night I drank too much. You know me . . . I'm a terrible drinker. I saw a boy in a green uniform like Tom's. He was lonely and crew-cut and tall . . . like Tom. We drank together . . . I woke up in a cheap, dirty hotel room . . . God knows where. I was still half drunk. I staggered to the mirror and I looked at myself. I was naked. The boy was naked too . . . sprawled out on the bed."

"Kitty, for God's sake . . ."

"It's all right, Mark . . . let me finish. I stood there looking in that mirror . . . I don't know how long. I had reached the bottom of my life. There was no place lower for me. That moment . . . that second I was done. The boy was unconscious . . . strange . . . I don't even remember his name. I saw his razor blades in the bathroom and the gas pipe from the ceiling and for a minute or an hour . . . I don't know how long I stood looking down ten stories over the sidewalk. The end of my life had come but I did not have the strength to take it. Then a strange thing happened, Mark. I knew that I was going to go on living without Tom and Sandra and suddenly the pain was gone."

"Kitty, darling. I wanted so much to find you and help you."

"I know. But it was something I had to fight out myself, I suppose. I went back to nursing, plunged into it like crazy. The minute it was over in Europe I took on this Greek orphanage . . . it was a twenty-four-hour-a-day job. That's what I needed of course, to work myself to the limit. Mark

15

. . . I . . . I've started a hundred letters to you. Somehow I've been too terrified of this minute. I'm glad now, I'm glad it's over."

"I'm glad I found you," Mark said.

She spun around and faced him. ". . . so that is the story of what has become of Kitty Fremont."

Mark took her hand and they began walking back along the sea wall to the quay. From the Dome Hotel they could hear the sound of music.

CHAPTER FOUR: Brigadier Bruce Sutherland sat behind a big desk as military commander of Cyprus in his house on Hippocrates Street in Famagusta, some forty miles from Kyrenia. Except for small telltale traces—a slight roll around his middle and a whitening of the hair about his temples—Sutherland's appearance belied his fifty-five years. His ramrod posture clearly identified a military man. A sharp knock sounded on the door and his aide, Major Fred Caldwell, entered.

"Good evening, Caldwell. Back from Kyrenia already? Have a chair." Sutherland shoved the papers aside, stretched, and put his glasses on the desk. He selected a GBD pipe from the rack and dipped it into a humidor of Dunhill mix. Caldwell thanked the brigadier for a cigar and the two men soon clouded the room in smoke. The Greek houseboy appeared in answer to a buzz.

"Gin and tonic twice."

Sutherland arose and walked into the full light. He was wearing a deep red velvet smoking jacket. He settled into a leather chair before the high shelves of books. "Did you see Mark Parker?"

"Yes, sir."

"What do you think?"

Caldwell shrugged. "On the face of it we certainly can't accuse him of anything. He is on the way to Palestine . . . here to see that American nurse, Katherine Fremont."

"Fremont? Oh yes, that lovely woman we met at the governor's."

"So I say, sir, it all appears quite innocent . . . yet, Parker is a reporter and I can't forget that trouble he caused us in Holland."

"Oh, come now," Sutherland retorted, "we all made blunders in the war. He just happened to catch one of ours. Fortunately our side won, and I don't think there are ten people who remember."

The gin and tonics arrived. "Cheers."

Sutherland set his glass down and patted his white walrus mustache. Fred Caldwell wasn't satisfied.

"Sir," he persisted, "in case Parker does become curious and does decide to snoop around, don't you think it would be wise to have a couple of CID men watching him?"

"See here, you leave him alone. Just tell a newspaperman 'no' and you're apt to stir up a hornet's nest. Refugee stories are out of style these days and I don't believe he would be interested in their camps here. None the less we are not going to run the risk of arousing his curiosity by forbidding him to do anything. If you ask me I think it was a mistake for you to see him today."

"But, Brigadier . . . after that trouble in Holland . . ."

"Bring the chess table, Freddie!"

There was something absolutely final about the way Sutherland said "Freddie." Caldwell grumbled under his breath as they set up the chessmen. They made their opening moves but Sutherland could see that his aide was unhappy. He set down his pipe and leaned back.

"Caldwell, I have tried to explain to you that we are not running concentration camps here. The refugees at Caraolos are merely being detained on Cyprus until those blockheads in Whitehall decide what they are going to do with the Palestine mandate."

"But those Jews are so unruly," Caldwell said, "I'm certainly in favor of some good old-fashioned discipline."

"No, Freddie, not this time. These people are not criminals and they've got world sympathy on their side. It is your job and mine to see that there are no riots, no outbreaks, and nothing that can be used as propaganda against us. Do you understand that?"

Caldwell didn't understand. He damned well thought that the brigadier should be much tougher with the refugees. But no one wins an argument with a general unless he happens to be a bigger general and it was all so deep—so Caldwell moved a pawn forward.

"Your move, sir," he said.

Caldwell looked up from the board. Sutherland seemed completely withdrawn and oblivious of him. It was happening more and more lately.

"Your move, sir," Caldwell repeated.

Sutherland's face was troubled. Poor chap, Caldwell thought. The brigadier had been married to Neddie Sutherland for almost thirty years, and suddenly she had left him and run off to Paris with a lover ten years her junior. It was a scandal that rocked army circles for months, and Sutherland must still be taking it hard. Terrible blow for the brigadier. He had always been such a decent sort of chap. The white face of Sutherland was lined with wrinkles, and little red veins on his nose turned bright. At this moment he looked all of his fifty-five years and more.

Bruce Sutherland was not thinking about Neddie, as Caldwell believed. His mind was on the refugee camps at Caraolos.

"Your move, sir."

"*So shall your enemies perish, Israel . . .*" Sutherland mumbled.

"What did you say, sir?"

CHAPTER FIVE: Mark led Kitty back to the table, both of them breathless. "Do you know the last time I danced a samba?" she said.

"You're not so bad for an old broad."

Mark looked around the room filled with British officers in their army khakis and navy whites and their high and low English accents. Mark loved places like this. The waiter brought a new round of drinks and they clicked glasses.

"To Kitty . . . wherever she may be," Mark said. "Well ma'am, where do you go from here?"

Kitty shrugged, "Golly, I don't know, Mark. My work is finished at Salonika and I am getting restless. I've got a dozen offers I can take around Europe with the United Nations."

"It was a lovely war," Mark said. "Lots of orphans."

"Matter of fact," Kitty said, "I got a real good offer to stay right here on Cyprus just yesterday."

"On Cyprus?"

"They have some refugee camps around Famagusta. Anyhow, some American woman contacted me. Seems that the camps are overcrowded and they're opening new ones on the Larnaca road. She wanted me to take charge."

Mark frowned.

"That's one of the reasons I couldn't meet you at the airport. I went to Famagusta to see her today."

"And what did you tell her?"

"I told her no. They were Jews. I suppose Jewish children are pretty much like any others but I'd just rather not get mixed up with them. It seems that there's an awful lot of politics connected with those camps and they're not under UN auspices."

Mark was silent in thought. Kitty winked mischievously and waggled a finger under his nose. "Don't be so serious . . . you want to know the other reason I didn't meet you at the airport?"

"You're acting tipsy."

"I'm starting to feel that way. Well, Mr. Parker, I was in Famagusta seeing my boy friend off. You know me . . . one lover leaves by ship while another lands by airplane."

"As long as you brought it up . . . who was this guy you came to Cyprus with?"

"Wouldn't you like to know?"

"Uh-huh."

"Colonel Howard Hillings of the British Army."

"Anything dirty between you two?"

"Dammit, no. He was so proper it was disgusting."

"Where did you meet this guy?"

"Salonika. He was in charge of the British mission in the area. When I took over the orphanage we were short of everything . . . beds, medicine, food, blankets . . . everything. Anyhow, I went to him and he cut wads of red tape for me and we became friends for ever and ever and ever. He really is a dear man."

"Go on. It's getting interesting."

"He got notice a few weeks ago that he was being transferred to Palestine and he had leave coming and wanted me to spend it with him here. You know, I'd been working so hard I'd completely forgotten I haven't had a day off in eighteen months. Anyhow, they cut his leave short and he had to report to Famagusta to sail to Palestine today."

"Future prospects as Mrs. Hillings?"

Kitty shook her head. "I like him very much. He brought me all the way to Cyprus to find the right setting to ask me to marry him . . ."

"And?"

"I loved Tom. I'll never feel that way again."

"You're twenty-eight years old, Kitty. It's a good age to retire."

"I'm not complaining. I've found something that keeps me content. Mark, you're going to Palestine too. There are a lot of officers here leaving for Palestine."

"There's going to be a war, Kitty."

"Why . . . ? I don't understand."

"Oh, lots of reasons. Lot of people around the world have decided they want to run their own lives. Colonies are going out of vogue this century. These boys here are riding a dead horse. This is the soldier of the new empire," Mark said, taking a dollar bill from his pocket; "we've got millions of these green soldiers moving into every corner of the world. Greatest occupying force you've ever seen. A bloodless conquest . . . but Palestine . . . that's different again. Kitty, there's almost something frightening about it. Some people are out to resurrect a nation that has been dead for two

19

thousand years. Nothing like that has ever happened before. What's more, I think they're going to do it. It's these same Jews you don't like."

"I didn't say I didn't like Jews," Kitty insisted.

"I won't debate with you now. Think real hard, honey . . . since you've been on Cyprus. Have you heard anything or seen anything that might be, well, unusual?"

Kitty bit her lip in thought and sighed. "Only the refugee camps. I hear they are overcrowded and in deplorable condition. Why do you ask?"

"I don't know. Just say I've got an intuition that something very big is happening on Cyprus."

"Why don't you just say you're naturally nosey by profession?"

"It's more than that. Do you know a Major Fred Caldwell? He's aide to Brigadier Sutherland."

"Terrible bore. I met him at the governor's."

"He met me in my room before you got in. Why would a general's aide be sitting on my lap ten minutes after I landed on a matter that is seemingly trivial? Kitty, I tell you the British are nervous about something here. I . . . I can't put my finger on it, but five will get you ten it's tied up with those refugee camps. Look . . . would you go to work in those camps for me for a few weeks?"

"Certainly, Mark. If you want me to."

"Oh, the hell with it," Mark said, setting down his drink, "us two kids are on vacation. You're right . . . I'm nosey and suspicious by profession. Forget it, let's dance."

CHAPTER SIX: On Arsinos Street in Famagusta, facing the wall of the old city, sat a large and luxurious house belonging to a Greek Cypriot named Mandria, who was owner of the Cyprus-Mediterranean Shipping Company as well as owner of a great number of the island's taxicabs. Mandria and David Ben Ami waited anxiously as Ari Ben Canaan cleaned up and changed into dry clothing after his swim ashore.

They both knew that the appearance of Ari Ben Canaan on Cyprus meant a top-level mission for Mossad Aliyah Bet. British policy for many years had been to exclude or extremely limit the Jewish immigration to Palestine. They had the Royal Navy to execute this policy. The Mossad Aliyah Bet was an organization of Palestinian Jews whose business it was to help smuggle other Jews into Palestine. However, as fast as the British Navy caught the Mossad boats trying to run the blockade the refugees would be transferred to detention camps on Cyprus.

Ari Ben Canaan, in a fresh change of clothing, entered the room and nodded to Mandria and David Ben Ami. The Palestinian was a big man, well over six feet and well built. He and Ben Ami had long been intimate friends but they played a role of formality in front of Mandria, the Cypriot, who was not a member of their organization but merely a sympathizer.

Ari lit a cigarette and got right to the point. "Headquarters has sent me here to stage a mass escape from the detention camps. The reasons are obvious to all of us. What is your opinion, David?"

The thin young man from Jerusalem paced the room thoughtfully. He had been sent to Cyprus months before by the secret army of the Jews in Palestine called the Palmach. He and dozens of other Palmachniks smuggled themselves into the compounds of refugees without the knowledge of the British and set up schools, hospitals, and synagogues, built sanitation facilities, and organized light industry. The refugees who had been turned back from Palestine to Cyprus were hopeless people. The appearance of young Palestinians of the Jews' army infused new hope and morale. David Ben Ami and the other Palmachniks gave military training to several thousand men and women among the refugees, using sticks as rifles and rocks as grenades. Although he was but twenty-two years of age David was the Palmach commander in Cyprus. If the British had gotten wind that there were Palestinians inside the camps they kept quiet about it, for they did their guarding from the outside—having no desire to go into the hate-riddled compounds.

"How many people do you want to escape?" David asked.

"Three hundred, more or less."

David shook his head. "We have a few tunnels dug but those lead to the sea. As you know by coming in here tonight, the tides are treacherous and only strong swimmers can make it. Second, we move in and out through the garbage dumps. They are loosely guarded, but we could never get that many people through. Third, British uniforms and false papers . . . again, we can only get a few in and out at a time. Last, we crate some of our members up in boxes and send them to the docks. Mr. Mandria here owns the shipping company and his dock hands are on the alert for these crates. At this moment, Ari, I see no way to pull a mass escape."

"We will find a way," Ben Canaan said matter of factly, "but we only have a few weeks to complete this job."

Mandria, the Greek, arose, sighed, and shook his head.

"Mr. Ben Canaan, you have swum ashore tonight and asked us to do the impossible . . . in two weeks, yet. In my heart," Mandria said, touching his heart, "I say that it will be done, but! . . . in my head"—and Mandria tapped his skull with his forefinger—"it cannot be done." The Cypriot clasped his hands behind him and paced the dining room. "Believe me, Mr. Ben Canaan"—he swung around and made a bravado sweep of the arm—"you Palmach and Mossad people can count on the Greeks of Cyprus to back you to the last drop of blood. We are for you! We are with you! We are behind you! Nevertheless . . . ! Cyprus is an island and it is surrounded by water on all sides and the British are not stupid or asleep. I, Mandria, will do everything for you, but still you are not getting three hundred people out of Caraolos. There are ten-foot walls of barbed wire around those compounds and the guards carry rifles . . . with bullets in them."

Ari Ben Canaan arose and towered over the other two men. He had ignored much of Mandria's dramatics. "I will need a British uniform, papers, and a driver by morning. You can start looking for a boat, Mr. Mandria. Something between a hundred and two hundred tons. David, we will need an expert forger."

"We have a boy out in the children's compound who is supposed to be a real artist but he won't work. The rest of the stuff is primitive."

"I'll go out to Caraolos tomorrow and talk to him. I want to look over the camp, anyhow."

Mandria was elated. What a man of action Ari Ben Canaan was! Find a ship! Find a forger! Get me a uniform and a driver! Life was so exciting since the Mossad and Palmach had come to Cyprus, and he so loved being a part of the cat-and-mouse game with the British. He stood up and pumped Ari Ben Canaan's hand. "We Cypriots are with you. Your battle is our battle!"

Ben Canaan looked at Mandria disgustedly. "Mr. Mandria," he said, "you are being well paid for your time and efforts."

A stunned silence fell on the room. Mandria turned as white as a sheet. "Do you believe . . . do you dare believe, sir, that I, I, Mandria, would do this for money? Do you think I risk ten years in prison and exile from my home? It has cost me over five thousand pounds since I began working with your Palmach."

David stepped in quickly. "I think you had better apologize to Mr. Mandria. He and his taxi drivers and his dock hands take all sorts of risks. Without the help of the Greek people our work would be nearly impossible."

Mandria slumped into a chair deeply wounded. "Yes, Mr. Ben Canaan, we admire you. We feel that if you can throw the British out of Palestine then maybe we can do the same on Cyprus someday."

"My apologies, Mr. Mandria," Ari said. "I must be overtense." He recited the words completely without meaning.

A shrill sound of sirens outside brought the conversation to a stop. Mandria opened the french doors to the balcony and walked outside with David. Ari Ben Canaan stood behind them. They saw an armored car with machine guns leading a convoy of lorries up the street from the docks. There were twenty-five lorries, in all, surrounded by machine guns mounted on jeeps.

The lorries were packed with refugees from the illegal ship, *Door of Hope,* which had tried to run the British blockade from Italy to Palestine. The *Door of Hope* had been rammed by a British destroyer, towed to Haifa, and the refugees transferred immediately to Cyprus.

The sirens shrieked louder as the convoy swept close to the balcony of Mandria's home. The lorries passed one by one. The three men could see the jam of tattered, ragged misery. They were beaten people—at the end of the line— dazed, withered, exhausted. The sirens shrieked and the convoy turned at the Land Gate of the old wall and onto the road to Salamis, in the direction of the British detention camps at Caraolos. The convoy faded from sight but the shrieks of the sirens lingered on and on.

David Ben Ami's hands were tight fists and his teeth were clenched in a face livid with helpless rage. Mandria wept openly. Only Ari Ben Canaan showed no emotion. They walked in from the balcony.

"I know you two have much to talk over," Mandria said between sobs. "I hope you find your room comfortable, Mr. Ben Canaan. We will have your uniform, papers, and a taxi by morning. Good night."

The instant David and Ari were alone they threw their arms about each other. The big man picked the little man up and set him down as though he were a child. They looked each other over and congratulated each other on looking well and went into another bear hug.

"Jordana!" David said anxiously. "Did you see her before you left? Did she give you a message?"

Ari scratched his jaw teasingly. "Now let me see . . ."

"Please, Ari . . . it has been months since I have received a letter . . ."

Ari sighed and withdrew an envelope which David snatched from his hands. "I put it in a rubber pouch. The only thing I could think of tonight when I was swimming in was that you would break my neck if I got your damned letter wet."

David was not listening. He squinted in the half light and slowly read the words of a woman who missed and longed for her lover. He folded the letter tenderly and carefully placed it in his breast pocket to be read again and again, for it might be months before she could send another. "How is she?" David asked.

"I don't see what my sister sees in you. Jordana? Jordana is Jordana. She is wild and beautiful and she loves you very much."

"My parents . . . my brothers . . . how is our Palmach gang . . . what . . ."

"Wait a minute, wait a minute. I'll be here for a while—one question at a time."

David pulled out the letter and read it again, and the two men were silent. They stared out of the french doors at the ancient wall across the road. "How are things at home?" David whispered.

"Things at home? The same as always. Bombings, shootings. Exactly as it has been every day since we were children. It never changes. Every year we come to a crisis which is sure to wipe us out—then we go on to another crisis worse than the last. Home is home," Ari said, "only this time there is going to be a war." He put his arm on the shoulder of his smaller friend. "We are all damned proud of the work you have done in Caraolos with these refugees."

"I have done as well as can be expected, trying to train soldiers with broomsticks. Palestine is a million miles away to these people. They have no hope left. Ari . . . I don't want you antagonizing Mandria any more. He is a wonderful friend."

"I can't stand people patronizing us, David."

"And we can't do the job here without him and the Greek people."

"Don't be fooled by the Mandrias all over the world. They weep crocodile tears and they pay lip service to our millions of slaughtered, but when the final battle comes we will stand alone. Mandria will sell us out like all the others. We will be betrayed and double-crossed as it has always been. We have no friends except our own people, remember that."

"And you are wrong," David snapped back.

"David, David, David. I have been with the Mossad and the Palmach for more years than I care to remember. You are young yet. This is your first big assignment. Don't let emotion cloud your logic."

"I *want* emotion to cloud my logic," David answered. "I burn inside every time I see something like that convoy. Our people locked up in cages like animals."

"We try all sorts of schemes," Ari said; "we must keep a

clear head. Sometimes we are successful, sometimes we fail. Work with a clear mind, always."

Even now they could still hear the sound of sirens over the breeze. The young man from Jerusalem lit a cigarette and stood for a moment in thought. "I must never stop believing," he said solemnly, "that I am carrying on a new chapter of a story started four thousand years ago." He spun around and looked up at the big man excitedly. "Look, Ari. Take the place you landed tonight. Once the city of Salamis stood there. It was in Salamis that the Bar Kochba revolution began in the first century. He drove the Romans from our country and re-established the Kingdom of Judah. There is a bridge near the detention camps—they call it the Jews' Bridge. It has been called that for two thousand years. I can't forget these things. Right in the same place we fought the Roman Empire we now fight the British Empire two thousand years later."

Ari Ben Canaan stood a head taller than David Ben Ami. He smiled down at the younger man as a father might smile at an overenthusiastic son. "Finish the story. After the Bar Kochba revolution the legions of Rome returned and massacred our people in city after city. In the final battle at Beitar the blood of murdered women and children made a crimson river which flowed for a full mile. Akiva, one of the leaders, was skinned alive—and Bar Kochba was carried off to Rome in chains to die in the lions' den. Or was it Bar Giora who died in the lions' den in another revolution? I can get these revolutions mixed up. Oh yes, the Bible and our history are filled with wonderful tales and convenient miracles. But this is real today. We have no Joshua to make the sun stand still or the walls to come tumbling down. The British tanks will not get stuck in the mud like Canaanite chariots, and the sea has not closed in on the British Navy as it did on Pharaoh's army. The age of miracles is gone, David."

"It is not gone! Our very existence is a miracle. We outlived the Romans and the Greeks and even Hitler. We have outlived every oppressor and we will outlive the British Empire. That is a miracle, Ari."

"Well, David—one thing I can say about the Jews. We certainly know how to argue. Let's get some sleep."

CHAPTER SEVEN: "Your move, sir," Fred Caldwell repeated.

"Yes, yes, forgive me." Brigadier Sutherland studied the chessboard and moved his pawn forward. Caldwell brought out a knight and Sutherland countered with his own. "Dash

25

it!" the brigadier mumbled as his pipe went out. He relit it.

The two men glanced up as they heard the dim but steady shrill screams of sirens. Sutherland looked at the wall clock. That would be the refugees from the illegal ship, *Door of Hope.*

"*Door of Hope, Gates of Zion, Promised Land, Star of David,*" Caldwell said with a snicker. "I will say one thing. They do give those blockade runners colorful names."

Sutherland's brow furrowed. He tried to study out his next move on the board, but the sirens would not leave his ears. He stared at the ivory chessmen, but he was visualizing the convoy of lorries packed with agonized faces, machine guns, armored cars. "If you don't mind, Caldwell, I think I'll turn in."

"Anything wrong, sir?"

"No. Good night." The brigadier walked from the room quickly and closed the door of his bedroom and loosened his smoking jacket. The sirens seemed to screech unbearably loudly. He slammed the window shut to drown the noise but still he could hear it.

Bruce Sutherland stood before the mirror and wondered what was going wrong with him. Sutherland from Sutherland Heights. Another distinguished career in a line of distinguished careers that went on, the same as England itself.

But these past weeks on Cyprus something was happening. Something tearing him to pieces. He stood there before the mirror and looked into his own watery eyes and wondered where it had all begun.

Sutherland: Good fellow to have on your team, said the yearbook at Eton. *Right sort of chap, that Sutherland. Proper family, proper schooling, proper career.*

The army? Good choice, Bruce old man. We Sutherlands have served in the army for centuries. . . .

Proper marriage. Neddie Ashton. The daughter of Colonel Ashton was a clever catch. Fine stock, Neddie Ashton. Fine hostess, that woman. She always has the ear of the right person. She'll be a big help to your career. Splendid match! The Ashtons and the Sutherlands.

Where the failure, Sutherland wondered? Neddie had given him two lovely children. Albert was a real Sutherland. A captain in his father's old regiment already, and Martha had made herself a splendid marriage.

Bruce Sutherland opened the closet and put on his pajamas. He touched the roll of fat about his waist. Not too bad for a man of fifty-five. He still had plenty of punch left.

Sutherland had come up fast in World War II by comparison to the slow tedious advancements in the peacetime service. There had been India, Hong Kong, Singapore, and the Middle East. But it took a war to show what he was made of. He proved to be an exceptional infantry commander. V-E Day found him a brigadier.

He put on his bedroom slippers and sank slowly into a deep chair and dimmed the lamp and he was filled with remembering.

Neddie had always been a good wife. She was a good mother, a tremendous hostess, and a woman cut out for colonial service in the army. He had been very fortunate. When had the break come between them? Yes, he remembered. It was in Singapore so many years ago.

He was a major when he met Marina, the olive-skinned Eurasian woman. Marina—born and made for love. Each man has a Marina hidden deep in his inner thoughts, but he had his in the flesh and she was real. Laughter and fire and tears and passion. Being with Marina was like being in a bubbling volcano ready to erupt. He was insane for her—he desired her wildly, madly. He threw jealous tantrums before her only to half sob, begging forgiveness. Marina . . . Marina . . . Marina . . . the black eyes and the raven hair. She could torment him. She could delight him. She could spiral him to heights he never knew existed on this earth. Those precious, magnificent moments of their trysts . . .

His hands had clutched her hair and pulled her head back and he had looked at her deep red sensuous lips . . . "I love you, you bitch . . . I love you."

"I love you, Bruce," Marina had whispered.

. . . Bruce Sutherland remembered the stunned hurt look on Neddie's face as she confronted him with evidence of his affair.

"I won't say this hasn't hurt me deeply," Neddie said, too proud for tears, "but I am willing to forgive and forget. There are the children to think of. There is your career . . . and our families. I'll try to make a go of it with you, Bruce, but you must swear you'll never see that woman again and that you'll put in an immediate request for transfer from Singapore."

That woman—that woman, you call her, Bruce thought—is my love. She has given me something that you or a thousand Neddies never could or never will. She has given me something no man has a right to expect on this earth.

"I want your answer now, Bruce."

Answer? What could the answer be? A man can have a woman like Marina for a night, for a touch, but she is not real. There is only one Marina to a man . . . one to a lifetime. Answer? Throw away his career for a Eurasian girl? Bring scandal on the name of Sutherland?

"I will never see her again, Neddie," Bruce Sutherland promised.

27

Bruce Sutherland never saw her again but he never stopped thinking of her. Perhaps that is where it all started.

The sounds of the sirens were very faint now. The convoy must be quite near Caraolos, Sutherland thought. Soon the sirens would stop and he could sleep. He began thinking of the retirement that would be coming in another four or five years. The family house at Sutherland Heights would be far too big. A cottage, perhaps in the country. Soon it would be time to think about a pair of good hunting setters and gathering rose catalogues and building up his library. Time to start thinking about a decent club to join in London. Albert, Martha, and his grandchildren would indeed be a comfort in retirement. Perhaps . . . perhaps he would take a mistress, too.

It seemed strange that after nearly thirty years of marriage he would be going into retirement without Neddie. She had been so quiet, reserved, and distinguished all those years. She had been so sporting about his affair with Marina. Suddenly, after a lifetime of complete propriety Neddie burst out frantically to salvage her few years left as a woman. She ran off to Paris with a Bohemian chap ten years her junior. Everyone sympathized with Bruce, but it really didn't matter to him much. There had been no contact and little feeling for Neddie for many years. She could have her fling. They were quite civilized about it. Perhaps he would take her back later . . . perhaps a mistress would be better.

At last the sirens from the convoy stopped. There was complete silence in the room except for the muffled shushing of the surf breaking on the shore. Bruce Sutherland opened the window and breathed in the cool crisp November air. He went to the bathroom and washed and placed the bridge of four teeth in a glass of solution. Damned shame, he thought, losing those four teeth. He had said the same thing for thirty years. It was the result of a rugby game. He examined the other teeth to satisfy himself they were still in good shape.

He opened the medicine chest and studied the row of bottles. He took down a tin of sleeping powders and mixed a double dose. It was difficult to sleep these days.

His heart began racing as he drank down the solution. He knew it was going to be another one of those horrible nights. He tried desperately to lock out or stifle the thoughts creeping into his brain. He covered himself in bed and hoped sleep would come quickly, but it was already beginning to whirl around and around and around in his mind . . .

    . . . Bergen-Belsen . . . Bergen-Belsen . . . Bergen-Belsen . . . NUREMBERG . . . NUREMBERG! NUREMBERG! NUREMBERG!

28

"Take the stand and give your name."

"Bruce Sutherland, Brigadier General, Commander of . . ."

"Describe, in your own words . . ."

"My troops entered Bergen-Belsen at twenty minutes past five in the evening of April 15."

"Describe in your own words . . ."

"Camp Number One was an enclosure of four hundred yards wide by a mile long. That area held eighty thousand people. Mostly Hungarian and Polish Jews."

"Describe in your own words . . ."

"The ration for Camp Number One was ten thousand loaves of bread a week."

"Identify . . ."

"Yes, those are testicle crushers and thumbscrews used in torture . . ."

"Describe . . ."

"Our census showed thirty thousand dead in Camp Number One, including nearly fifteen thousand corpses just littered around. There were twenty-eight thousand women and twelve thousand men still alive."

"DESCRIBE . . . !"

"We made desperate efforts but the survivors were so emasculated and diseased that thirteen thousand more died within a few days after our arrival."

"DESCRIBE . . . !"

"Conditions were so wretched when we entered the camp that the living were eating the flesh of the corpses."

The moment Bruce Sutherland had completed his testimony at the Nuremberg war crimes trials he received an urgent message to return to London at once. The message came from an old and dear friend in the War Office, General Sir Clarence Tevor-Browne. Sutherland sensed it was something out of the ordinary.

He flew to London the next day and reported at once to that huge, ungainly monstrosity of a building on the corner of Whitehall and Great Scotland Yard which housed the British War Office.

"Bruce, Bruce, Bruce! Come in, come in, man! Good to see you. I followed your testimony at the Nuremberg trials. Nasty bit of business."

"I am glad it is over," Sutherland said.

"Sorry to hear about you and Neddie. If there is anything at all I can do . . ."

Sutherland shook his head.

At last Tevor-Browne led up to the reason for asking him to come to London. "Bruce," he said, "I called you here because a rather delicate assignment has come up. I must give a recommendation and I want to put your name up. I wanted to talk it over with you first."

"Go on, Sir Clarence."

"Bruce, these Jews escaping from Europe have posed quite a problem. They are simply flooding Palestine. Frankly, the Arabs are getting quite upset about the numbers getting into the mandate. We here have decided to set up detention camps on Cyprus to contain these people—at least as a temporary measure until Whitehall decides what we are going to do with the Palestine mandate."

"I see," Sutherland said softly.

Tevor-Browne continued. "This entire thing is touchy and must be handled with great tact. Now, no one wants to ride herd on a bunch of downtrodden refugees, and the fact is . . . well, they have a great deal of sympathy on their side in high quarters—especially in France and America. Things must be kept very quiet on Cyprus. We want nothing to happen to create unfavorable opinion."

Sutherland walked to the window and looked out to the Thames River and watched the big double-deck buses drive over the Waterloo Bridge. "I think the whole idea is wretched," he said.

"It is not for you and me to decide, Bruce. Whitehall gives the orders. We merely carry them out."

Sutherland continued looking out of the window. "I saw those people at Bergen-Belsen. Must be the same ones who are trying to get into Palestine now." He returned to his chair. "We have broken one promise after another to those people in Palestine for thirty years."

"See here, Bruce," Tevor-Browne said, "you and I see eye to eye on this, but we are in a minority. We both served together in the Middle East. Let me tell you something, man. I sat here at this desk during the war as one report after another of Arab sellouts came in. The Egyptian Chief of Staff selling secrets to the Germans; Cairo all decked out to welcome Rommel as their liberator; the Iraqis going to the Germans; the Syrians going to the Germans; the Mufti of Jerusalem a Nazi agent. I could go on for hours. You must look at Whitehall's side of this, Bruce. We can't risk losing our prestige and our hold on the entire Middle East over a few thousand Jews."

Sutherland sighed. "And this is our most tragic mistake of all, Sir Clarence. We are going to lose the Middle East despite it."

"You are all wound up, Bruce."

"There is a right and a wrong, you know."

General Sir Clarence Tevor-Browne smiled slightly and shook his head sadly. "I have learned very little in my years,

Bruce, but one thing I have learned. Foreign policies of this, or any other, country are not based on right and wrong. Right and wrong? It is not for you and me to argue the right or the wrong of this question. The only kingdom that runs on righteousness is the kingdom of heaven. The kingdoms of the earth run on oil. The Arabs have oil."

Bruce Sutherland was silent. Then he nodded. "Only the kingdom of heaven runs on righteousness," he repeated. "The kingdoms of the earth run on oil. You have learned something, Sir Clarence. It seems that all of life itself is wrapped up in those lines. All of us . . . people . . . nations . . . live by need and not by truth."

Tevor-Browne leaned forward. "Somewhere in God's scheme of things he gave us the burden of an empire to rule. . . ."

"Ours not to reason why," Sutherland whispered. "But I can't seem to forget the Arab slave markets in Saudi Arabia and the first time I was invited to watch a man have his hands amputated as punishment for stealing, and somehow I can't forget those Jews at Bergen-Belsen."

"It is not too good to be a soldier and have a conscience. I won't force you to take this post on Cyprus."

"I'll go. Of course I'll go. But tell me. Why did you choose me?"

"Most of our chaps are pro-Arab for no other reason than our tradition has been pro-Arab and soldiers are not in a position to do much other than follow policy. I don't want to send someone to Cyprus who will antagonize these refugees. It is a problem that calls for understanding and compassion."

Sutherland arose. "I sometimes think," he said, "that it is almost as much a curse being born an Englishman as it is being born a Jew."

Sutherland accepted the assignment on Cyprus, but his heart was filled with fear. He wondered if Tevor-Browne had known he was half Jewish.

That decision, that horrible decision he had made so long ago was coming back to haunt him now.

He remembered that afterward he began to find solace in the Bible. There were those empty years with Neddie, the painful loss of the Eurasian girl he loved, and it all seemed to plunge him deeper and deeper into a longing to find peace of mind. How wonderful for a soldier like him to read of the great campaigns of Joshua and Gideon and Joab. And those magnificent women—Ruth and Esther and Sarah . . . and . . . and Deborah. Deborah, the Joan of Arc, the liberator of her people.

He remembered the chill as he read the words: *Awake, awake, Deborah; awake, awake.*

31

Deborah! That was his mother's name.

Deborah Davis was a rare and beautiful woman. It was small wonder that Harold Sutherland was smitten with her. The Sutherland family was tolerant when Harold sat through fifteen performances of *The Taming of the Shrew* to watch the beautiful actress, Deborah Davis, and they smiled, benevolently as he went over his allowance on flowers and gifts. It was a boyish fling, they thought, and he'd get over it.

Harold could not get over Deborah Davis, and the family stopped being tolerant. She defied an edict they issued for her to appear at Sutherland Heights. It was then that Harold's father, Sir Edgar, traveled to London to see this amazing young woman who refused to travel to Sutherland Heights. Deborah was as clever and witty as she was beautiful. She dazzled Sir Edgar and completely won him.

Sir Edgar decided then and there that his son had been damned lucky. After all, the Sutherlands were known to have a tradition of inclining toward actresses and some of them had become the grandest dames in the family's long history.

There was, of course, the touchy business of Deborah Davis being a Jewess, but the matter was closed when she agreed to take instructions in the Church of England.

Harold and Deborah had three children. There was Mary, their only girl, and there was moody, irresponsible Adam. And there was Bruce. Bruce was the oldest and Deborah's favorite. The boy adored his mother. But as close as they were she never spoke of her own childhood, or of her parents. He knew only that she had been very poor and run away to the stage.

The years passed. Bruce took up his army career and married Neddie Ashton. The children, Albert and Martha, came. Harold Sutherland died, and Deborah moved along in age.

Bruce remembered so well the day that it happened. He was coming to Sutherland Heights for a long visit and bringing Neddie and the children. Deborah would always be in the rose garden or the conservatory or floating about gaily on her duties—smiling, happy, gracious. But this day as he drove up to Sutherland Heights she was not there to greet him nor was she anywhere about to be found. At last he discovered her sitting in darkness in her drawing room. This was so unlike Mother that it startled him. She was sitting like a statue, looking at the wall, oblivious to her surroundings.

Bruce kissed her on the cheek softly and knelt beside her. "Is something wrong, Mother?"

She turned slowly and whispered, "Today is Yom Kippur —the Day of Atonement."

Her words chilled Bruce to the bone.

Bruce talked it over with Neddie and his sister, Mary. They decided that since Father had died she had been alone too much. Furthermore, Sutherland Heights was too big for her. She should move into an apartment in London where she could be closer to Mary. Then, too, Deborah was getting old. It was hard for them to realize, because she seemed to them as beautiful as when they were children.

Bruce and Neddie went off for his tour of service in the Middle East. Mary wrote happy letters that Mother was getting along fine, and the letters from Deborah told of her happiness to be in London near Mary's family.

But when Bruce returned to England it was a different story. Mary was beside herself. Mother was seventy years old now and acting more and more strangely. A creeping on of senility. She could not remember something that had happened a day ago, but she would utter disconnected things about events that took place fifty years ago. It was frightening to Mary because Deborah had never spoken of her past to her children. Mary was most alarmed of her mother's strange disappearances.

Mary was glad that Bruce had returned. He was the oldest and Mother's favorite and he was so steady. Bruce followed his mother one day on one of her mysterious walks. It led to a synagogue in Whitechapel.

He thought it all over carefully and decided to leave her alone. She was old; he did not feel it proper to confront her with things that had happened over fifty years before. It was best to let it pass quietly.

At the age of seventy-five Deborah Sutherland lay on her deathbed. Bruce got back to England just in time.

The old woman smiled as she saw her son sitting on the edge of the bed. "You are a Lieutenant Colonel now . . . you look fine . . . Bruce, my son . . . I haven't too many hours left . . ."

"Hush now, Mother. You'll be up and about in no time."

"No, I must tell you something. I wanted to be your father's wife so badly. I wanted so much . . . so very very much to be the mistress of Sutherland Heights. I did a terrible thing Bruce. I denied my people. I denied them in life. I want to be with them now. Bruce . . . Bruce, promise that I shall be buried near my father and my mother . . ."

"I promise, Mother."

"My father . . . your grandfather . . . you never knew him. When . . . when I was a little girl he would hold me

33

on his lap and he would say to me . . . 'awake, awake, Deborah; awake, awake . . .' "

Those were the last words Deborah Sutherland spoke.

Bruce Sutherland sat in numb grief for a long hour beside the lifeless body of his mother. Then the numbness began to thaw under the nagging burn of a doubt that would not be kept out of his mind. Must he be bound by a promise he had made a dying woman? A promise he was forced to make? Would it be breaking the code of honor by which he had always lived? Wasn't it true that Deborah Sutherland's mind had been going on her bit by bit over the past years? She had never been a Jewess in life, why should she be one in death? Deborah had been a Sutherland and nothing else.

What a terrible scandal would be created if he were to bury her in a shabby run-down Jewish cemetery on the poverty side of London. Mother was dead. The living—Neddie, Albert and Martha and Mary's family and Adam would be hurt deeply. The living had to be served.

As he kissed his mother farewell and walked from her room he had made his decision.

Deborah was put to rest in the family vault at Sutherland Heights.

The sirens!

The sirens from the convoy of refugees!

The sirens shrieked louder and louder and louder until they tore through his eardrums. *Bergen-Belsen . . . Marina . . . Neddie . . . caged trucks . . . the camps at Caraolos . . . I promise, Mother . . . I promise, Mother . . .*

A burst of thunder rocked the house to its very foundation, and the sea outside became wild and waves smashed up the shore and raced nearly to the house. Sutherland threw off the covers and staggered about the room as though drunk. He froze at the window. Lightning! Thunder! The raging water grew higher and higher!

"God . . . God . . . God . . . God . . . !"

"Brigadier Sutherland! Brigadier Sutherland! Wake up, sir! Wake up, sir!"

The Greek houseboy shook him hard.

Sutherland's eyes opened and he looked about wildly. The sweat poured from his body and his heart pounded painfully. He gasped for breath. The houseboy quickly brought him a brandy.

He looked outside to the sea. The night was calm and the water was as smooth as glass and lapped gently against the shore.

"I'll be all right," he said. "I'll be all right. . . ."

"Are you sure, sir?"

"Yes."

34

The door closed.

Bruce Sutherland slumped into a chair and buried his face in his hands and wept and whispered over and over, ". . . my mother in he:ven . . . my mother in heaven . . ."

CHAPTER EIGHT: Brigadier Bruce Sutherland slept the sleep of the tormented and the damned.

Mandria, the Cypriot, twisted and turned in a nervous but exhilarated sleep.

Mark Parker slept the sleep of a man who had.accomplished a mission.

Kitty Fremont slept with a peace of mind she had not known in years.

David Ben Ami slept only after reading Jordana's letter so many times he knew it by memory.

Ari Ben Canaan did not sleep. There would be other times for that luxury, but not now. There was much to learn and little time to learn it in. All during the night he pored over maps and documents and papers, absorbing every fact about Cyprus, the British operation, and his own people there. He waded through the stacks of data with a cigarette or a coffee cup continuously at hand. There was a calm ease, a sureness about him.

The British had said many times that the Palestinian Jews were a match for anyone on matters of intelligence. The Jews had the advantage that every Jew in every country in the world was a potential source of information and protection for a Mossad Aliyah Bet agent.

At daybreak Ari awakened David, and after a quick breakfast they rode in one of Mandria's taxis out to the detention camp at Caraolos.

The compounds themselves stretched for many miles in an area that hugged the bay, midway between Famagusta and the ruins of Salamis. The garbage dumps were a contact point between the refugees and the Cypriots. The British guarded them loosely because the garbage detail was made up of "trusties." The garbage dumps became trading centers where leather goods and art work made in the camp were exchanged for bread and clothing. David led Ari through the dumps where the early morning bartering between Greeks and Jews was already going on. From here they entered their first compound.

Ari stood and looked at the mile after mile of barbed wire. Although it was November it was chokingly hot under a constant swirl of blowing dust. Compound after compound of tents were stretched along the bay, all set in an area of low-hanging acacia trees. Each compound was closed in by ten-to twelve-foot walls of barbed wire. On the corners there were searchlight towers manned by British guards armed with machine guns. A skinny dog began following them. The word "BEVIN" was painted on the dog's sides—a bow to the British Foreign Minister.

It was the same scene in each compound they visited: packed with miserable and angry people. Almost everyone was dressed in crudely sewn purple shorts and shirts made from cloth that had been torn from the inner linings of the tents. Ari studied the faces filled with suspicion, hatred, defeat.

In each new compound Ari would suddenly be embraced by a boy or girl in the late teens or early twenties who had been smuggled in by the Palestine Palmach to work with the refugees. They would throw their arms about him and begin to ask questions about home. Each time Ari begged off, promising to hold a Palmach meeting for the whole group in a few days. Each Palmach head showed Ari around the particular compound he or she was in charge of, and occasionally Ari would ask a question.

For the most part, he was very quiet. His eyes were searching the miles of barbed wire for some key that would help him get three hundred people out.

Many of the compounds were grouped together by nationalities. There were compounds of Poles and of French and of Czechs. There were compounds of Orthodox Jews and there were compounds of those who banded together with similar political beliefs. Most compounds, however, were merely survivals of the war, with no identity other than that they were Jews who wanted to go to Palestine. They all had a similarity in their uniform misery.

David led Ari to a wooden bridge that connected two main portions of the camp by crossing over the top of the barbed wire walls. There was a sign on the bridge that read: WELCOME TO BERGEN-BEVIN. "It is rather bitter irony, Ari, this bridge. There was one exactly like it in the Lodz ghetto in Poland."

By now David was seething. He berated the British for the subhuman conditions of the camp, for the fact that German prisoners of war on Cyprus had a greater degree of freedom, for the lack of food and medical care, and just for the general gross injustice. Ari was not listening to David's ranting. He was too intent on studying the structure and arrangement of the place. He asked David to show him the tunnels.

Ari was led to a compound of Orthodox Jews close to the bay. There was a row of outside toilets near the barbed wire wall. On the first toilet shack was a sign that read: BEVINGRAD. Ari was shown that the fifth and sixth toilets in the line of sheds were fakes. The holes under the seats led under the barbed wire and through tunnels to the bay. Ari shook his head—it was all right for a few people at a time but not suited for a mass escape.

Several hours had passed. They had nearly completed the inspection. Ari had hardly spoken a word for two hours. At last, bursting with anxiety, David asked, "Well, what do you think?"

"I think," Ari answered, "that Bevin isn't very popular around here. What else is there to see?"

"I saved the children's compound for last. We have Palmach headquarters there."

As they entered the children's compound Ari was once again pounced upon by a Palmachnik. But this time he returned the embrace with vigor and a smile on his face, for it was an old and dear friend, Joab Yarkoni. He whirled Yarkoni around, set him down, and hugged him again. Joab Yarkoni was a dark-skinned Moroccan Jew who had emigrated to Palestine as a youngster. His black eyes sparkled and a huge brush of a mustache seemed to take up half of his face. Joab and Ari had shared many adventures together, for although Joab was still in his early twenties he was one of the crack agents in the Mossad Aliyah Bet, with an intimate knowledge of the Arab countries.

From the beginning Yarkoni had been one of the wiliest and most daring operators in Mossad. His greatest feat was one which started the Jews of Palestine in the date-palm industry. The Iraqi Arabs guarded their date palms jealously, but Yarkoni had managed to smuggle a hundred saplings into Palestine from Iraq.

David Ben Ami had given Joab Yarkoni command of the children's compound, for it was, indeed, the most important place in the Caraolos camp.

Joab showed Ari around the compound, which was filled with orphans from infancy to seventeen years of age. Most of them had been inmates of concentration camps during the war, and many of them had never known a life outside of barbed wire. Unlike the other compounds, the children's section had several permanent structures erected. There was a school, a dining hall, a hospital, smaller units, and a large playground. There was a great deal of activity here in contrast to the lethargy in the other areas. Nurses, doctors, teachers, and welfare people from the outside, sponsored by money from American Jews, worked in the compound.

Because of the flow of outsiders, the children's compound was the most loosely guarded in Caraolos. David and Joab were quick to capitalize on this fact by establishing Palmach headquarters in the compound.

At night the playground was transformed into a military training camp for refugees. The classrooms were turned from standard schools into indoctrination centers in Arab psychology, Palestine geography, tactics, weapons identification, and a hundred other phases of warfare instruction.

Each refugee receiving military training by the Palmach had to stand trial by a kangaroo court. The pretense was that the refugee had got to Palestine and had been picked up by the British. The Palmach instructor would then put him through an interrogation to try to establish that the refugee was not in the country legally. The refugee had to answer a thousand questions about the geography and history of Palestine to "prove" he had been there many years.

When a "candidate" successfully completed the course, the Palmach arranged an escape, generally through the children's compound or the tunnels, to the white house on the hill at Salamis, whence he would be smuggled into Palestine. Several hundred refugees had been sent to Palestine that way, in groups of twos and threes.

British CID was not unaware of the fact that irregular things took place inside the children's compound. Time and again they planted spies among the outside teachers and welfare workers, but the ghetto and the concentration camps had bred a tight-lipped generation of children and the intruders were always discovered within a day or two.

Ari ended the inspection of the children's compound in the schoolhouse. One of the schoolrooms was, in fact, Palmach headquarters. Inside the teacher's desk was a secret radio and transmitter which maintained contact with Palestine. Under the floor boards weapons were hidden for the military training courses. In this room papers and passes were forged.

Ari looked over the forgery plant and shook his head. "This counterfeit work is terrible," he said. "Joab, you are very sloppy."

Yarkoni merely shrugged.

"In the next few weeks," Ari continued, "we are going to need an expert. David, you said there is one right here."

"That's right. He is a Polish boy named Dov Landau, but he refuses to work."

"We have tried for weeks," Joab added.

"Let me speak to him."

Ari told the two men to wait outside as he stepped into Dov Landau's tent. He looked over at a blond boy, undersized and tense and suspicious at the sudden intrusion. Ari knew the look—the eyes filled with hate. He studied the turned-down mouth and the snarling lips of the youngster: the expression of viciousness that stamped so many of the concentration-camp people.

"Your name is Dov Landau," Ari said, looking directly into his eyes. "You are seventeen years old and Polish. You have a concentration camp background and you are an expert forger, counterfeiter, and duplicator. My name is Ari Ben Canaan. I'm a Palestinian from Mossad Aliyah Bet."

The boy spat on the ground.

"Look, Dov, I'm not going to plead and I'm not going to threaten. I've got a plain out-and-out business proposition . . . let's call it a mutual assistance pact."

Dov Landau snarled, "I want to tell you something, Mr. Ben Canaan. You guys aren't any better than the Germans or the British. The only reason you want us over there so bad is to save your necks from the Arabs. Let me tell you—I'm getting to Palestine all right and when I do I'm joining an outfit that's going to let me kill!"

Ari did not change expression at the outburst of venom that erupted from the boy. "Good. We understand each other perfectly. You don't like my motives for wanting you in Palestine and I don't like yours for wanting to get there. We do agree on one thing: you belong in Palestine and not here."

The boy's eyes narrowed with suspicion. This Ben Canaan was not like the others.

"Let's take it a step further," Ari said. "You're not going to get to Palestine by sitting here on your arse and doing nothing. You help me and I'll help you. What happens after you get there is your business."

Dov Landau blinked with surprise.

"Here's the point," Ari said. "I need forged papers. I need piles of them in the next few weeks and these boys here can't forge their own names. I want you to work for me."

The boy had been thrown completely off guard by Ari's rapid and direct tactics. He wanted time to look for a hidden trick. "I'll think it over," he said.

"Sure, think it over. You've got thirty seconds."

"And what will you do if I refuse? You going to try to beat it out of me?"

"Dov, I said we need each other. Let me make myself clear. If you don't go along with this I'm going to personally see to it that you're the last person out of the Caraolos detention camp. With thirty-five thousand people ahead of you, you'll be too old and feeble to lift one of those bombs by the time you get to Palestine. Your thirty seconds are up."

"How do I know I can trust you?"

"Because I said you could."

A faint smile crossed the boy's face, and he nodded that he would go to work.

"All right. You get your orders from either David Ben Ami or Joab Yarkoni. I don't want you giving anyone a bad time. If you have any problems, you ask for me. I want you to report to Palmach headquarters in a half hour and look over their plant and let David know what special materials you'll need."

Ari turned and walked out of the tent to where David and Joab waited. "He'll report to work in a half hour," Ari said.

David gaped and Joab's mouth fell open in awe.

"How did you do it?"

"Child psychology. I'm going back to Famagusta," Ari said. "I want to see you two boys at Mandria's house tonight. Bring Zev Gilboa with you. Don't bother to show me out. I know the way."

David and Joab stared in fascination as their friend, the remarkable Ari Ben Canaan, crossed the playground in the direction of the garbage dumps.

That night in his living room Mandria, the Cypriot, waited, along with David, Joab, and a newcomer, Zev Gilboa, for the appearance of Ari Ben Canaan.

Zev Gilboa, also a Palestinian Palmachnik, was a broad-backed farmer from the Galilee. Like Yarkoni, he, too, wore a large brushlike mustache and was in his early twenties. Zev Gilboa was the best of the soldiers among the Palmach Palestinians working inside Caraolos. David had given Zev the task of heading military training for the refugees. With zest, with improvised weapons, and by using the children's playground at night he had taught his trainees nearly everything that could be taught without actual arms. Broomsticks were rifles, rocks were grenades, bedsprings were bayonets. He set up courses in hand-to-hand fighting and stick fighting. Mostly he instilled tremendous spirit into the spiritless refugees.

The hour grew very late. Mandria began pacing nervously. "All I know," he said, "I gave him a taxi and a driver this afternoon."

"Relax, Mr. Mandria," David said. "Ari may not be back for three days. He has strange ways of working. We are used to it."

Midnight passed and the four men began to sprawl out and make themselves comfortable. In a half hour they began to doze, and in an hour they were all asleep.

At five o'clock in the morning Ari Ben Canaan entered the room. His eyes were bleary from a night of traveling around the island. He had slept only in brief naps since he had landed on Cyprus. He and Zev Gilboa hugged each other in the traditional Palmach manner, then he set right to work without offering excuse or apology for being eight hours late.

40

"Mr. Mandria. Have you got us our boat yet?"

Mandria was aghast. He slapped his forehead in amazement. "Mr. Ben Canaan! You landed on Cyprus less than thirty hours ago and asked me for a boat. I am not a shipbuilder, sir. My company, Cyprus-Mediterranean Shipping, has offices in Famagusta, Larnaca, Kyrenia, Limassol, and Paphos. There are no other ports in Cyprus. All my offices are looking for a boat for you. If there is a boat on Cyprus you will know it, sir."

Ari ignored Mandria's sarcasm and turned to the others. "Zev, I suppose David has told you what we're going to do."

The Galilee farmer nodded.

"From now on you three boys are working for me. Find replacements for your jobs at Caraolos. Joab, how many healthy children are there in that compound between the ages of ten and seventeen?"

"Oh . . . probably around six or seven hundred."

"Zev. Pick out three hundred of the strongest. Get them in the peak of physical condition."

Zev nodded.

Ari arose. "It will be light in another half hour. I'll need a taxi to start out again, Mr. Mandria. I think that man I had yesterday is a little tired."

"I will drive you around, myself," Mandria said.

"Good. We'll leave just as soon as it turns light. Excuse me. I want to look over some papers in my room."

He left as suddenly as he had entered. Everyone began talking at once.

"Then the escape is going to be made by three hundred children," Zev said.

"It certainly appears so," Mandria said. "He is such a strange man. He expects miracles . . . he doesn't tell anything."

"On the contrary," David said, "he does not believe in miracles. That is why he works so hard. It seems to me that there is more to this than Ari is telling us. I have a feeling that the escape of three hundred children is only part of what is in his mind."

Joab Yarkoni smiled. "We all have known Ari Ben Canaan long enough not to try to second guess him. We also have known him long enough to know that he knows his business. We will learn, in due time, just what Ari is up to."

The next day Mandria drove Ari around Cyprus in what seemed to be an aimless chase. They drove from the sweeping Eastern Bay past Salamis and Famagusta clear to Cape Greco. In Famagusta he walked along the old wall and studied the harbor area. Ari barely spoke to Mandria the entire day, except to ask a pertinent question now and then. It seemed

41

to the Cypriot that the big Palestinian was the coldest human being he had ever met. He felt a certain hostility, but he could not help admiring Ari for his absolute concentration and seemingly superhuman stamina. He must, Mandria thought, be a tremendously dedicated man—but that was puzzling because Ben Canaan seemed to show no traces of human emotion.

From Cape Greco they drove along the Southern Bay on the underbelly of Cyprus and then into the high jagged mountains where the resorts prepared for the winter season of skiing and ice sports. If Ben Canaan had found anything of interest he certainly was not showing it. Mandria was exhausted when they arrived back in Famagusta after midnight, but there was another meeting held with Zev, David, and Joab. Then Ari went into another all-night session of study.

On the morning of the fourth day after Ari Ben Canaan had swum ashore onto Cyprus, Mandria received a call from his Larnaca office to the effect that a ship had just come in from Turkey that fitted his specifications and could be purchased. Mandria drove Ari to Caraolos to pick up David and Joab, and the four of them drove off for Larnaca.

Zev Gilboa was left behind, as he was already at work selecting the three hundred children and setting up special training courses for them.

Mandria was feeling quite proud of himself as they drove along the Famagusta-Larnaca road. At a halfway point Ari was suddenly attracted by some activity taking place in a large field off to the left of the road. He asked Mandria to stop the car and stepped outside for a look. There was feverish building going on in what appeared to be a military barracks.

"The British are building new detention compounds," David said; "they've reached the saturation point at Caraolos."

"Why wasn't I told about this?" Ari snapped.

"You didn't ask," Joab Yarkoni answered.

"The best we can figure," David said, "is that they'll begin transferring the overload from Caraolos in two or three weeks."

Ari returned to the car and they drove on. Joab Yarkoni, who declined to try to second guess his friend, could nevertheless see that Ari was definitely intrigued by the new compounds. Joab could almost hear the wheels grinding in Ari's brain.

The car entered the narrow bending streets of Larnaca and moved onto the waterfront road, lined with its neat two-storied white houses. They stopped before the Four Lanterns Tavern where the Turkish owner of the ship, a man named Armatau, awaited them. Ari insisted they forego the round

42

of drinks, the fencing for price, and general bartering that was so much a part of the normal business transactions. He wanted to see the ship immediately.

Armatau led them over the street to the long pier that jutted more than a half mile into the water. As they walked past a dozen or more trawlers, launches, and sailboats Armatau kept up a constant stream of talk over his shoulder. He assured them that the ship they were about to inspect was, indeed, a queen of the sea. They came to a halt near the end of the pier before an ancient wooden-hulled salvage tug that bore the faded name on her bow: *Aphrodite.*

"Isn't she a beauty?" Armatau said, glowing. Then he held his breath apprehensively as four pairs of cold eyes surveyed the old scow from stem to stern. "Of course," the Turk continued, "she is no racing cruiser."

Ari's practiced eye estimated the *Aphrodite* at a hundred and fifty feet in length and displacing around two hundred tons. By her general build and appearance she was in the neighborhood of forty-five years of age.

"Now just who was Aphrodite?" Joab Yarkoni asked.

"Aphrodite was the goddess of Love. She was washed up in the surf just a few miles from here—five thousand years ago," David answered.

"Well, this old girl has sure had her change of life," Joab said.

The Turk swallowed and tried to smile at the jibes. Ben Canaan spun around and faced him. "Armatau, I'm interested in one thing. It's two hundred miles to Palestine. She's got to make one run. Yes or no?"

Armatau threw up both arms. "On my mother's honor," he said, "I have made three hundred runs between Cyprus and Turkey. Mr. Mandria owns the shipping company. He knows."

"It is true," Mandria said. "She is old but reliable."

"Mr. Armatau, take my two friends aboard and show them the engines."

When the other three had gone below decks Mandria turned to Ari. "Armatau may be a Turk but he can be trusted."

"What kind of speed can we get out of this thing?" Ari asked.

"Probably five knots—with a gale in her back. The *Aphrodite* is in no hurry."

They went on deck and looked over the topside. She was half rotted away and long past the time it would have paid to repair her. Yet, despite the obvious qualifications there was something very sound about her. A solid feeling that she knew the tricks of the sea and had won many battles against it.

In a half hour David and Joab completed their inspection.

"This ship is an absolute abortion," David said, "but I am positive she'll make it."

"Can we get three hundred aboard?" Ari asked.

David rubbed his jaw. "Well . . . maybe, with a shoehorn."

Ari turned to Mandria. "We will have a lot of refitting to do. Of course it is necessary that we don't attract any attention."

Mandria smiled. He was in his glory now. "I have, as you may well know, very good connections. It is merely a matter of greasing the right palms and you can be sure that nothing can be seen, heard, or reported."

"David. Send a radio message to Palestine tonight. Tell them we need a captain and a two-man crew."

"Is a crew of three going to be enough?"

"I might as well tell you. You two boys and Zev are coming back to Palestine with me on this mud scow. We'll fill out the crew. Joab! You've always had a tendency toward mature women. Well, you've got one now. You're in charge of getting this thing refitted and stocked up." At last he turned to Armatau, who was still bewildered by Ari's rapid fire questions and commands. "O.K., Armatau, you can breathe easy, you've sold us this monstrosity—but not at your price. Let's go into the Four Lanterns and lock this up."

Ari jumped off the deck onto the pier and gave Mandria a hand. "David, you and Joab find your own way back to Famagusta. Mr. Mandria is driving me to Kyrenia after we finish our business."

"Kyrenia?" Mandria said, startled. "Doesn't that man ever get tired? Kyrenia is on the other side of the island," he protested.

"Is something wrong with your automobile?" Ari asked.

"No . . . no . . . we shall drive for Kyrenia."

Ari started off down the pier with Mandria and the Turk. "Ari!" David called, "what shall we name the old woman?"

"You're the poet," Ari called back. "You name her."

Joab and David watched the three men disappear at the end of the pier. Suddenly they broke out in smiles and threw their arms about each other. "That son of a gun Ari! He picks a fine way to tell us we are going home."

"You know Ari. The scorner of sentiment and emotion," David said.

They sighed happily, and for a moment both thought about Palestine. Then they looked about the *Aphrodite*. She certainly was a sorry old girl.

They walked around the deck examining the ancient hulk. "I've got a good name for her," Joab said, "why don't we call her the *Bevin*?"

"I've got a better name," David Ben Ami said. "From now on she will be known as the *Exodus*."

CHAPTER NINE: Mark pulled the rented car off the road and parked it. He had driven high up in the mountains directly over Kyrenia. An enormous jagged rock several hundred feet high rose to a peak before them. On the peak were the ruins of St. Hilarion Castle. It was a fairy castle, suggesting even in semicollapse the might and splendor of Gothic power.

Mark took Kitty's hand and led her over the field toward the peak, and they climbed the battlements until they stood on the lower wall and looked into the castle yards.

They picked their way through royal apartments and great halls and stables and the monastery and fortifications. It was deathly silent, but the grounds seemed to be alive and breathing, with ghosts of the past whispering of another day filled with love and hate and war and intrigue.

For almost an hour Mark and Kitty climbed slowly up the peak toward the summit. Then at last they stood on the very top, perspiring and breathless, dazzled at the breathtaking panorama below them. Below was a sheer cliff that fell nearly three thousand feet to Kyrenia. On the horizon they saw the coast line of Turkey, and to the left and right the lush green forests and terraced vineyards and houses hanging on cliff edges. Below, the olive orchards' leaves turned to a shimmering silver as zephyrs played through them.

Mark watched Kitty standing silhouetted against the sky as a cloud passed behind her. How very lovely she is, Mark thought. Kitty Fremont was the one woman in his world who was different. He had no desire to make love to her. Mark Parker honored little in the world. He wanted to honor Kitty. Moreover, she was the only woman he was absolutely comfortable with, for between them there was no pretense, no impression to make, no games to play.

They sat down on a huge boulder and continued to stare at the splendor all about them. The castle, the sea, the sky, the mountains.

"I think," Mark said at last, "this is the most beautiful vista in the world."

She nodded.

They had been wonderful days for both of them. Kitty seemed renewed since Mark's arrival. She had enjoyed the wonderful therapy of confession.

"I am thinking something terrible," Kitty said. "I am thinking of how glad I am that Colonel Howard Hillings was sent

45

off to Palestine and I have you all to myself. How long can you stay, Mark?"

"Few weeks. As long as you want me."

"I never want us to become far away from each other again."

"You know," he said, "everyone at the Dome is certain we're shacked up."

"Good!" Kitty said. "I'll put a sign on my door tonight in big red letters to read, 'I love Mark Parker madly.'"

They sat for another hour, then reluctantly began working their way down from the summit to descend before it turned dark.

After Mark and Kitty had returned to the hotel, Mandria drove his car into Kyrenia to the harbor and stopped on the quay. He stepped outside with Ari and they walked to the docks. Ari looked across the harbor to the tower of the Virgin Castle which stood on the sea's edge. They crossed over and climbed up inside the tower and from this vantage point could see the entire area perfectly. Ari studied in his usual silence.

The harbor had two sea walls. One ran out from the Virgin Castle and the tower where he now stood. Opposite him were the houses on the quay, and from that side the wall ran out to the sea so that the right and left arms of the sea wall formed a new circle, almost touching each other. There was a small break which was the entrance to the harbor. The inside of the harbor was tiny, not more than a few hundred yards in diameter. It was filled with small boats.

"Do you think we can get the *Aphrodite* inside the harbor here?" Ari asked.

"Getting it in won't be a problem," Mandria answered, "but turning it around and getting it out again will be."

Ari was silent in thought as the two men walked back toward the car. His eye was on the little harbor. It was beginning to turn dark as they reached the car.

"You might as well drive on back to Famagusta by yourself. I have to see someone at the Dome Hotel," Ari said, "and I don't know how long it's going to take. I'll find my own way back to Famagusta."

Mandria would have resented being dismissed like a taxi driver, but he was getting used to taking orders from Ben Canaan. He turned the ignition key and pressed the starter.

"Mandria. You have been a big help. Thanks."

Mandria beamed as Ari walked away. These were the first words of kindness he had heard from Ben Canaan. He was surprised and touched.

The dining room of the Dome Hotel was filled with the strains of a Strauss waltz playing softly over the drone of British voices, the clink of glasses, and the whisper of the sea outside. Mark sipped his coffee, wiped his lips with his napkin, and then stared over Kitty's shoulder intently at the figure who had entered the doorway. A tall man was whispering into the ear of the headwaiter, and the waiter pointed to Mark's table. Mark's eyes widened as he recognized Ari Ben Canaan.

"Mark, you look as though you've seen a ghost," Kitty said.

"I have and he's just about here. We are going to have a very interesting evening."

Kitty turned around to see Ari Ben Canaan towering over their table. "I see that you remember me, Parker," he said, taking a seat without invitation and turning to Kitty. "You must be Mrs. Katherine Fremont."

Ari's and Kitty's eyes met and held. Several awkward seconds of silence followed, then Ari looked around for a waiter and called him over. He ordered sandwiches.

"This is Ari Ben Canaan," Mark was saying, "he is a very old acquaintance of mine. I see that you seem to know Mrs. Fremont."

"Ari Ben Canaan," Kitty said. "What an odd name."

"It is Hebrew, Mrs. Fremont. It means 'Lion, Son of Canaan.' "

"That's quite confusing."

"On the contrary, Hebrew is a very logical language."

"Funny, it didn't strike me that way," Kitty said, with an edge of sarcasm.

Mark looked from one to the other. They had only met, and yet they were already engaged in the verbal fencing and maneuvering he himself so often played. Obviously Ben Canaan had struck either a sweet or a sour chord in Kitty, Mark thought, because she had her claws bared.

"Strange that it wouldn't strike you as logical," Ari was answering. "God thought Hebrew was so logical He had the Bible written in that language."

Kitty smiled and nodded. The orchestra changed to a fox trot. "Dance, Mrs. Fremont?"

Mark leaned back and watched Ben Canaan walk Kitty onto the floor, hold her, and lead her about with smooth gliding grace. For the moment Mark didn't like the spark that had obviously struck the second they met: it was hard to think of Kitty as a mere mortal playing mortals' games. They danced close to his table. There seemed to be a dazed look on Kitty's face and it was unnatural.

Then Mark began thinking of himself. He had had the feeling that something was brewing on Cyprus from the moment he landed. Now it was confirmed by Ben Canaan's appearance. He knew enough of the Palestinian to realize he was one of the top Mossad Aliyah Bet agents. He also knew that he was going to be approached for something, because Ben Canaan had sought him out. What about Kitty? Did he know of her only because she was with him or was there another reason?

Kitty was a tall girl but she felt lost in Ari Ben Canaan's arms. A strange sensation swept over her. The appearance of this strapping, handsome man had thrown her off guard. Now, in his arms only a moment after their meeting, she felt—unraveled. The sensation was attractive—it had been many, many years. But she felt rather foolish at the same time.

The music stopped and they returned to the table.

"I didn't think you Palestinians danced anything but a *hora*," Mark said.

"I've been exposed to too much of your culture," Ari answered.

His sandwiches arrived and he ate hungrily. Mark waited patiently for him to reveal the nature of his visit. He looked at Kitty carefully. She seemed to be regaining her composure, although she glanced at Ari from the corner of her eye as though she were wary and ready to strike.

At last Ari finished eating and said casually, "I have something I want to talk over with both of you."

"Here, in the middle of the British Army?"

Ari smiled. He turned to Kitty. "Parker didn't have a chance to tell you, Mrs. Fremont, that my employment is considered *sub rosa* in some quarters. Every so often the British even glorify us by calling us 'underground.' One of the first things I try to impress a new member of our organization with is the danger of making secret midnight rendezvous. I'd say there isn't a better place in the world to discuss this."

"Let's move the party up to my room," Mark said.

As soon as they had closed the door behind them Ari got right to the point. "Parker, you and I are in a position to do each other a good turn."

"Go on."

"Are you familiar with the detention camps at Caraolos?" Both Mark and Kitty nodded.

"I have just completed plans for three hundred children to make an escape. We are going to bring them over here and load them aboard a ship in the Kyrenia harbor."

"You boys have been smuggling refugees into Palestine for years. That isn't news any more, Ben Canaan."

"It will be news if you help make it news. You remember

48

the commotion over our illegal ship, the *Promised Land*?"

"Sure."

"The British looked pretty bad then. We feel that if we can create another incident as important as the *Promised Land* we stand a chance of breaking their immigration policy on Palestine."

"You just lost me," Mark said. "If you can pull a mass escape from Caraolos how are you going to get them to Palestine? If they do escape then where is the story?"

"That's the point," Ari said. "They aren't going any farther than boarding ship in Kyrenia. I have no intention of making a run for Palestine."

Mark leaned forward. He was interested, and there was obviously more to Ben Canaan's plan than first appeared.

"Let's say," Ari said, "that I get three hundred orphans out of Caraolos and on a ship in Kyrenia. Let's say the British find out and stop the ship from sailing. Now—let's say you have already written a story and it is sitting in Paris or New York. The minute those children board ship your story hits the headlines."

Mark whistled under his breath. Like most American correspondents he had sympathy for the refugee's plight. Mark would get the story, Ben Canaan would get the propaganda value. Was the story going to be big enough for him to become involved? There was no way he could seek instructions or talk it over. He alone had to evaluate and make the decision. Ari had thrown him just enough to whet his appetite. To question the Palestinian further could open the door to involvement. Mark looked at Kitty. She seemed completely puzzled by the whole thing.

"How are you going to get three hundred children from Caraolos to Kyrenia?"

"Do I take that to understand you are coming in?"

"Take it to understand I want to know. It doesn't commit me to a thing. If I decide against it you have my word that anything said will not leave this room."

"Good enough," Ari said. He balanced himself on the edge of the dresser and explained his escape plan step by step. Mark frowned. It was daring, audacious, even fantastic. Yet —there was an admirable simplicity about it. For his part, Mark had to write a report and smuggle it out of Cyprus to the ANS Paris or London bureau. By some prearranged signal the report would be published at the exact moment the escape was taking place. Ari finished and Mark digested the plan for many moments.

He lit a cigarette, paced the room, and fired a dozen questions at Ari. Ari seemed to have considered all the angles. Yes, there was a possibility of a sensational series of stories.

Now Mark tried to weigh the odds of Ari's wild scheme. There was no better than a fifty-fifty chance of success. Mark took into account the fact that Ari was an extremely clever man and he knew the British thinking on Cyprus. He also knew that Ari had the kind of people working with him who would be most likely to pull such a thing off.

"Count me in," Mark said.

"Good," Ari said, "I thought you'd see the possibilities." He turned to Kitty. "Mrs. Fremont, about a week ago you were offered a job working in the children's compound. Have you considered it?"

"I decided not to take it."

"Would you reconsider it now . . . say, to help Parker?"

"Just what do you have in mind for Kitty?" Mark asked.

"All of the teachers, nurses, and welfare people coming in from the outside are Jews," Ari said, "and we must go under the assumption they are suspect by the British."

"Suspect of what?"

"Co-operation with the Mossad. You are a Christian, Mrs. Fremont. We feel that someone of your background and religion could move about more freely."

"In other words, you want to use Kitty as a courier."

"More or less. We manufacture quite a few papers inside the camp that are needed outside."

Mark said, "I think I'd better tell you that I'm not too popular with the British. Sutherland's aide was sitting on my lap the minute I landed. I don't think this will affect me, but if Kitty goes to work at Caraolos it would be a cinch they'd suspect her of working with me."

"On the contrary. They would be dead certain you would not send her to work at Caraolos."

"Maybe you're right."

"Of course I'm right," Ari said. "Let us assume that the worst happens. Let us say Mrs. Fremont gets caught with forged papers. Absolutely nothing will happen to her except some embarrassment, an escort, and a free ticket away from Cyprus."

"Just a moment," Kitty said. "I've listened to you two divide me up. I am very sorry that I had to hear any of what went on here tonight. I am not going to work at Caraolos, Mr. Ben Canaan, and I am not getting mixed up in this scheme of yours."

Ari looked quickly to Mark, who merely shrugged. "She's a big girl."

"I thought you were a friend of Parker's."

"I am," Kitty said, "and I understand his interest."

"I don't understand your lack of it, Mrs. Fremont. This is the end of 1946. In a few months the war in Europe will

50

have been over for two years. We have people behind barbed wire under the most terrible conditions. There are children in Caraolos who have no idea there is a world outside barbed wire. If we don't break this British policy they can well be behind barbed wire the rest of their lives."

"That is just the point," Kitty fired back; "everything connected with Caraolos is neck deep in politics. I am certain that the British have their reasons. I don't wish to take sides."

"Mrs. Fremont. I was a captain in the British Army and I hold a Military Cross for valor. To coin an old cliché—some of my best friends are British. The fact is that we have dozens of British officers and soldiers who can't stomach what is happening in Palestine and who work with us twenty-four hours a day. This is not a case of politics but of humanity."

"I doubt your sincerity. Why would you risk the lives of three hundred children?"

"Most human beings have a purpose for living," Ari said; "there is no purpose in Caraolos. Fighting for your freedom is a purpose. We have a quarter of a million people in Europe who want to get into Palestine. Any one of them would board that ship in Kyrenia if given the choice."

"You are a very clever man, Mr. Ben Canaan. I cannot argue with you. I don't have your stock list of answers."

"I thought you were a nurse," he said sarcastically.

"The world is filled with suffering. I can give my services a thousand places just as needful as Caraolos, without the strings attached."

"Why don't you visit Caraolos and tell me that afterwards?"

"You're not going to trick me and you're not going to issue me challenges. I worked the night shift in a Cook County hospital, and more nights than not I've blotted up bodies off the receiving-room floor. You can't show me anything at Caraolos that I haven't seen before."

The room became quiet. Ari Ben Canaan blew a long breath and threw up his hands in defeat. "I am sorry," he said. "I'll be in touch with you in a few days, Parker." He turned for the door.

"Mr. Ben Canaan," Kitty said, "are you quite certain that I won't go telling this story to our mutual friends?"

Ari walked back and looked down into her eyes. She knew that instant he had said the wrong thing. A cruel little smile crossed his face. "I think you are just trying to be a woman and have the last word. I don't misjudge people very often. I can't afford to. I like Americans. Americans have consciences. As soon as yours begins to get the best of you, you can reach me at Mr. Mandria's and I'll be glad to show you around Caraolos."

"You are quite sure of yourself, aren't you?"

"Let us say," Ari answered, "that right this minute I am surer of myself than you are." Ari walked from the room.

It took a long time after Ari left for the impact of his visit to subside.

Kitty kicked off her shoes, at last, and sat back on the bed. "Well! You did say we were in for an interesting evening."

"I think you made a wise choice by staying out of this thing."

"And you?"

"It's a day's work. It could turn into something very big."

"Suppose you had refused him?"

"Oh, they'd get another correspondent somewhere in Europe to come over to Cyprus. They are very resourceful people. I just happened to be conveniently here."

"Mark," Kitty said thoughtfully, "did I make a fool of myself?"

"I don't suppose you made yourself any more foolish than a hundred other women have." Mark said it deliberately to let Kitty know she had been obvious about her attraction to Ari.

"He is a gorgeous man. When did you meet him?"

"The first time was in Berlin in the early part of 1939. That was my first ANS post. He had been sent over by Mossad Aliyah Bet to get as many Jews out of Germany as he could before the war started. He was in his early twenties then. I saw him again in Palestine. He was in the British Army . . . this was during the war. There was some kind of undercover assignment. I don't know exactly what it was. Since the war he has been heard of showing up all over Europe, buying arms, smuggling refugees into Palestine."

"Do you really think he can get away with this utterly fantastic plan of his?"

"He's a clever man."

"Well . . . I'll say one thing. This Ben Canaan doesn't act like any Jew I've ever met. You know what I mean. You don't particularly think of them in a capacity like his . . . or fighters . . . things of that sort."

"How do you think of them, Kitty? The good old Indiana version. The little Jew boy named Maury who's going to marry a little Jew girl named Sadie . . ."

"Oh, stop it, Mark! I've worked with enough Jewish doctors to know they are arrogant and aggressive people. They look down on us."

"With what? An inferiority complex?"

"I'd buy that if you were talking about Germany."

"What are you trying to say, Kitty—that we're pure?"

"I'm saying no American Jew would trade places with a Negro or a Mexican or an Indian for that matter."

"And I'm saying you don't have to lynch a man to rip his insides out. Oh sure, the American Jews have it good, but just enough of your thinking and enough of two thousand years of being a scapegoat has rubbed off on them. Why don't you argue it with Ben Canaan? He seems to know how to handle you."

Kitty shot off the bed angrily. Then both she and Mark began to laugh. They were Mark and Kitty and they could not really be angry.

"Exactly what is this Mossad Aliyah Bet?"

"The word *aliyah* means to arise, go up, ascend. When a Jew goes to Palestine it is always referred to as an *aliyah* . . . always going higher than he was. *Aleph* or the letter *a* was used to designate the legal immigration. *Bet* or the letter *b* for the illegal. Therefore Mossad Aliyah Bet means Organization for Illegal Immigration."

Kitty smiled. "My goodness," she said, "Hebrew is such a logical language."

For the next two days after Ari Ben Canaan's visit Kitty was perturbed and restless. She would not admit to herself that she wanted to see the big Palestinian again. Mark knew Kitty well and sensed her irritation, but he pretended to carry on as though Ben Canaan had never entered the scene.

She did not exactly know what was disturbing her, except that Ben Canaan's visit had left a strong impression. Was it that American conscience that Ben Canaan knew so well, or was she sorry about her anti-Jewish outburst?

Almost but not quite casually Kitty inquired when Mark expected to see Ari. Another time she made an unsubtle suggestion that it would be nice to go sight-seeing in Famagusta. Then again she would grow angry with herself and resolve to wipe out any thought of Ari.

On the third night Mark could hear Kitty's footsteps through the connecting door as she paced back and forth in her room.

She sat in the darkness in an overstuffed chair and puffed on a cigarette and decided that she would reason out the whole matter.

She did not like being drawn against her will into Ben Canaan's strange world. Her entire approach to life had been sane, even calculating. "Kitty is such a sensible girl," they always said of her.

When she fell in love with Tom Fremont and set out to win him it had all been a well-thought-out move. She ran a sensible home and served sensible meals on a sensible budget. She planned to give birth to Sandra in the springtime and that had been sensible too. She stifled spur-of-the-moment impulses in favor of planned decisions.

These past two days seemed to make no sense to her at all. A strange man appeared from nowhere and told her an even stranger story. She saw that hard handsome face of Ari Ben Canaan with his penetrating eyes that seemed to read her mind mockingly. She remembered the sensation in his arms, dancing with him.

There was no logic to this at all. For one thing Kitty always felt uncomfortable around Jewish people; she had admitted as much to Mark. Then why did this thing continue to grow?

Finally she knew that she would continue to be disturbed until she saw Ari again and saw the camp at Caraolos. She decided that the way to beat this whole idea was to see him again and assure herself she was not mystically involved but had merely been jolted by a sudden and brief infatuation. She would beat Ari Ben Canaan at his own game on his own ground.

At breakfast the next morning Mark was not surprised when Kitty asked him to make an appointment with Ben Canaan for her to visit Caraolos.

"Honey, I was happy with the decision you made the other night. I wish you'd stick to it."

"I don't quite understand this myself," she said.

"Ben Canaan called the shot. He knew you'd come around. Don't be a damned fool. If you go to Caraolos, you're in. Look . . . I'll pull out, myself. We'll leave Cyprus right away . . ."

Kitty shook her head.

"You're letting your curiosity throw you. You've always been smart. What's happening?"

"This sounds funny coming from me, doesn't it, Mark, but it almost feels as if some force were pushing me. Believe me, I'm going to Caraolos to end all this . . . and not to start something."

Mark told himself that she was hooked even though she was pretending she wasn't. He hoped that whatever lay ahead would treat her kindly.

CHAPTER TEN: Kitty handed her passes to the British sentry at the gate and entered Caraolos at Compound 57, which was closest to the children's compound.

"Are you Mrs. Fremont?"

She turned, nodded, and looked into the face of a young man who smiled and offered his hand. She thought that he was certainly a much friendlier-appearing person than his compatriot.

"I am David Ben Ami," he said. "Ari asked me to meet you. He will be along in a few moments."

"Now what does Ben Ami mean? I've taken a recent interest in Hebrew names."

"It means Son of My People," he answered. "We hope that you will help us in 'Operation Gideon.'"

"Operation Gideon?"

"Yes, that's what I call Ari's plan. Do you remember your Bible, Judges? Gideon had to select a group of soldiers to go against the Midianites. He picked three hundred. We have also picked three hundred to go against the British. I guess I may be stretching a point for the parallel and Ari does accuse me of being too sentimental."

Kitty had braced herself for a difficult evening. Now she was disarmed by this mild-appearing young man. The day was closing and a cool breeze whipped up a swirl of dust. Kitty slipped into her topcoat. On the other side of the compound she could make out the unmistakable towering figure of Ari Ben Canaan crossing over to meet her. She drew a deep breath and steadied herself to fight off the same electric sensation she had felt the first time she saw him.

He stopped before her and they nodded silently. Kitty's eyes were cold. She was letting him know, without a word, that she had come to accept a challenge and she had no intention of losing.

Compound 57 consisted mostly of the aged and very religious. They passed slowly between two rows of tents filled with dirty and unkempt people. The water shortage, Ben Ami explained, made bathing virtually impossible. There was also insufficient diet. The inmates appeared weak, some angry, some dazed, and all haunted by ghosts of the dead.

They stopped for a moment at an opened tent where a wrinkled old specimen worked on a wood carving. He held it up for her to see. It was a pair of hands, clasped in prayer and bound by barbed wire. Ari watched her closely for a sign of weakening.

It was squalid, filthy, and wretched here, but Kitty had prepared herself to accept even worse. She was beginning to be convinced that Ari Ben Canaan held no mysterious power over her.

They stopped once more to look into a large tent used as a synagogue. Over the entrance was a crudely made symbol of the Menorah, the ritual candelabra. She stared at the strange sight of old men swaying back and forth and reciting weird prayers. To Kitty it seemed another world. Her gaze became fixed on one particularly dirty, bearded old individual who wept and cried aloud in anguish.

She felt David's hand lead her away. "He is just an old man," David said. "He is telling God that he has lived a life of faith . . . he has kept God's laws, cherished the Holy Torah, and kept the covenants in face of unbelievable hardships. He asks God to kindly deliver him for being a good man."

"The old men in there," Ari said, "don't quite realize that the only Messiah that will deliver them is a bayonet on the end of a rifle."

Kitty looked at Ari. There was something deadly about this man.

Ari felt Kitty's disdain. His hands grabbed her arms. "Do you know what a *Sonderkommando* is?"

"Ari, please . . ." David said.

"A *Sonderkommando* is one who was forced by the Germans to work inside of their crematoriums. I'd like to show you another old man here. He took the bones of his grandchildren out of a crematorium in Buchenwald and carted them off in a wheelbarrow. Tell me, Mrs. Fremont, did you see one better than that at the Cook County Hospital?"

Kitty felt her stomach turn over. Then resentment took over and she fired back, eyes watering with anger. "You'll stop at nothing."

"I'll stop at nothing to show you how desperate we are."

They glared at each other wordlessly. "Do you wish to see the children's compound or not?" he said at last.

"Let's get it over with," Kitty answered.

The three crossed the bridge over the barbed-wire wall into the children's compound and looked upon war's merciless harvest. She went through the hospital building past the long row of tuberculars and into the other wards of bones bent with rickets and skins yellow of jaundice and festering sores of poisoned blood. She went through a locked ward filled with youngsters who had the hollow blank stares of the insane.

They walked along the tents of the graduation class of 1940-45. The matriculants of the ghettos, the concentration camp students, scholars of rubble. Motherless, fatherless, homeless. Shaved heads of the deloused, ragged clothing. Terror-filled faces, bed wetters, night shriekers. Howling infants, and scowling juveniles who had staved alive only through cunning.

They finished the inspection.

"You have an excellent staff of medical people," Kitty said, "and this children's compound is getting the best of the supplies."

56

"The British have given us none of it," Ari snapped. "It has come as gifts from our own people."

"You made the point right there," Kitty said. "I don't care if your facilities are manna from heaven. I came at the request of my American conscience. It has been satisfied. I'd like to go."

"Mrs. Fremont . . ." David Ben Ami said.

"David! Don't argue. Some people find just the sight of us repulsive. Show Mrs. Fremont out."

David and Kitty walked along a tent street. She turned slightly and saw Ari staring at her back. She wanted to get out as quickly as possible. She wanted to return to Mark and forget the whole wretched business.

A sound of uninhibited laughter burst from a large tent near her. It was the laughter of happy children and it sounded out of place at Caraolos. Kitty stopped in curiosity before the tent and listened. A girl was reading a story. She had a beautiful voice.

"That is an exceptional girl," David said. "She does fantastic work with these children."

Again laughter erupted from the children.

Kitty stepped to the tent flap and drew it open. The girl had her back to Kitty. She sat on a wooden box, bent close to a kerosene lamp. Circling her sat twenty wide-eyed children. They looked up as Kitty and David entered.

The girl stopped reading and turned around and arose to greet the newcomers. The lamp flickered from a gust of air that swept in from the open flap and cast a dancing shadow of children's silhouettes.

Kitty and the girl stood face to face. Kitty's eyes opened wide, registering shock.

She walked out of the tent quickly, then stopped and turned and stared through the flap at the astonished girl. Several times she started to speak and lapsed into bewildered silence.

"I want to see that girl . . . alone," she finally said in a hushed voice.

Ari had come up to them. He nodded to David. "Bring the child to the school building. We will wait there."

Ari lit the lantern in the schoolroom and closed the door behind them. Kitty had remained wordless and her face was pale.

"That girl reminds you of someone," Ari said abruptly. She did not answer. He looked through the window and saw the shadows of David and the girl crossing the compound. He glanced at Kitty again and walked from the room.

As he left, Kitty shook her head. It was mad. Why did she

57

come? *Why did she come?* She fought to get herself under command—to brace herself to look at that girl again.

The door opened and Kitty tensed. The girl stepped slowly into the room. She studied the girl's face, fighting off the urge to clutch the child in her arms.

The girl looked at her curiously, but she seemed to understand something and her gaze conveyed pity.

"My name . . . is Katherine Fremont," Kitty said unevenly. "Do you speak English?"

"Yes."

What a lovely child she was! Her eyes sparkled and she smiled now and held out her hand to Kitty.

Kitty touched the girl's cheek—then she dropped her hand.

"I . . . I am a nurse. I wanted to meet you. What is your name?"

"My name is Karen," the girl said, "Karen Hansen Clement."

Kitty sat on the cot and asked the girl to sit down, too.

"How old are you?"

"I'm sixteen now, Mrs. Fremont."

"Please call me Kitty."

"All right, Kitty."

"I hear that . . . you work with the children."

The girl nodded.

"That's wonderful. You see . . . I . . . I may be coming to work here and . . . and, well . . . I'd like to know all about you. Would you mind telling me?"

Karen smiled. Already she liked Kitty and she knew instinctively that Kitty wanted—needed—to be liked.

"Originally," Karen said, "I came from Germany . . . Cologne, Germany. But that was a long time ago . . ."

CHAPTER ELEVEN

COLOGNE, GERMANY, 1938

Life is quite wonderful if you are a young lady of seven and your daddy is the famous Professor Johann Clement and it is carnival time in Cologne. Many things are extra special around carnival time, but something that is always extra special is taking a walk with Daddy. You can walk under the linden trees along the banks of the Rhine or you can walk through the zoo that has the most magnificent monkey cages in the entire world or you can walk past the big cathedral and stare up at those twin towers over five hundred feet high that seem to push right through the sky. Best of all is walking through the municipal forest very early in the morning with Daddy and Maximilian. Maximilian is the most remarkable dog in Cologne, even though he looks kind of funny. Of course, Maximilian isn't allowed in the zoo.

Sometimes you take Hans along on your walks, too, but little brothers can be a nuisance.

If you are such a little girl you love your mommy, too, and wish she would come along with you and Daddy and Hans and Maximilian, but she is pregnant again and feeling rather grumpy these days. It would be nice if the new baby is a sister because one brother is just about as much as a girl can bear.

On Sunday everyone, except poor Maximilian, who has to watch the house, gets into the auto and Daddy drives along the Rhine River to Grandma's house in Bonn. Many of the aunts and uncles and bratty cousins gather every Sunday and Grandma has baked a hundred cookies, or maybe even more.

Soon, when summer comes, there will be a wonderful trip along the coast up north and through the Black Forest or to Brenner's Park Hotel at the springs at Baden-Baden. What a funny name—Baden-Baden.

Professor Johann Clement is a terribly important man. Everyone at the university doffs his cap and smiles and bows and says, "Good morning, Herr Doctor." At night there are other professors and their wives and sometimes fifteen or twenty students pack into Daddy's study. They sing and argue and drink beer all night along. Before Mommy's stomach started showing she used to like to joke and dance with them.

There are so many wonderful tastes and smells and feelings and sounds for a happy seven-year-old girl.

The best times of all were those nights when there would be no visitors and Daddy didn't have to work in his study or give a lecture. The whole family would sit before the fireplace. It was wonderful to sit on Daddy's lap and watch the flames and smell his pipe and hear his soft deep voice as he read a fairy tale.

In those years of 1937 and 1938 many strange things were happening you could not quite understand. People seem frightened of something and spoke in whispers . . . especially at a place like the university. But . . . these things seem quite unimportant when it comes to carnival time.

Professor Johann Clement had very much to think about. With so much utter insanity all about, a man had to keep a clear head. Clement reckoned a scientist could actually chart the course of human events as one would chart the tides and waves of the sea. There were waves of emotion and hate and waves of complete unreason. They'd reach a peak and fall to nothingness. All mankind lived in this sea except for a few who perched on islands so high and dry they remained always out of the reach of the mainstream of life. A univer-

sity, Johann Clement reasoned, was such an island, such a
sanctuary.

Once, during the Middle Ages, there had been a wave of
hatred and ignorance as the Crusaders killed off Jews. But
the day had passed when Jews were blamed for the Black
Death and for poisoning the wells of Christians. During the
enlightenment that followed the French Revolution the Christians themselves had torn down the gates of the ghettos. In
this new era the Jews and the greatness of Germany had been
inseparable. Jews subordinated their own problems to the
greater problems of mankind; they assimilated to the larger
society. And what great men came from this! Heine and
Rothschild and Karl Marx and Mendelssohn and Freud.
The list was endless. These men, like Johann Clement himself,
were Germans first, last, and always.

Anti-Semitism was synonymous with the history of man,
Johann Clement reasoned. It was a part of living—almost
a scientific truth. Only the degree and the content varied. Certainly, he felt, he was far better off than the Jews of eastern
Europe or those in semibarbaric condition in Africa. The
"humiliation oaths" and the Frankfurt massacre belonged to
another age.

Germany might be riding a new wave but he was not going
to turn around and run. Nor would he stop believing that the
German people, with their great cultural heritage, would
ultimately dispose of the abnormal elements which had temporarily got control of the country.

Johann Clement watched the blows fall. First there had
been wild talk and then printed accusations and insinua-
tions. Then came a boycott of Jewish business and professional people, then the public humiliations: beatings and beard
pullings. Then came the night terror of the Brown Shirts.
Then came the concentration camps.

Gestapo, SS, SD, KRIPO, RSHA. Soon every family in
Germany was under Nazi scrutiny, and the grip of tyranny
tightened until the last croak of defiance strangled and died.

Still Professor Johann Clement, like most of the Jews in
Germany, continued to believe he was immune to the new
menace. His grandfather had established a tradition at the
university. It was Johann Clement's island and his sanctuary.
He identified himself completely as a German.

There was one particular Sunday that you would never
forget. Everyone had assembled at Grandma's house in Bonn.
Even Uncle Ingo had come all the way from Berlin. All of
the children were sent outside to play and the door to the
living room had been locked.

On the way home to Cologne neither Mommy nor Daddy

spoke a single word. Grownups act like children sometimes. As soon as you reached home you and your brother Hans were bundled right off to bed. But more and more of these secret talks had been taking place, and if you stood by the door and opened it just a crack you could hear everything. Mommy was terribly upset. Daddy was as calm as ever.

"Johann, darling, we must think about making a move. This time it is not going to pass us by. It's getting so I'm afraid to go out into the street with the children."

"Perhaps it is only your pregnancy that makes you think things are worse."

"For five years you have been saying it is going to get better. It is not going to get better."

"As long as we stay at the university . . . we are safe."

"For God's sake, Johann. Stop living in a fool's paradise! We have no friends left. The students never come any more. Everyone we know is too terrified to speak to us."

Johann Clement lit his pipe and sighed. Miriam cuddled at his feet and lay her head on his lap and he stroked her hair. Nearby, Maximilian stretched and groaned before the fire.

"I want so much to be as brave and as understanding as you are," Miriam said.

"My father and my grandfather taught here. I was born in this house. My life, the only things I've ever wanted, the only things I've ever loved are in these rooms. My only ambition is that Hans will come to love it so after me. Sometimes I wonder if I have been fair to you and the children . . . but something inside of me will not let me run. Just a little longer, Miriam . . . it will pass . . . it will pass . . ."

NOVEMBER 19, 1938

> *200 synagogues gutted!*
> *200 Jewish apartment houses torn apart!*
> *8000 Jewish shops looted and smashed!*
> *50 Jews murdered!*
> *3000 Jews seriously beaten!*
> *20,000 Jews arrested!*

FROM THIS DAY ON NO JEW MAY BELONG TO A CRAFT OR TRADE!

FROM THIS DAY ON NO JEWISH CHILD MAY ENTER A PUBLIC SCHOOL!

FROM THIS DAY ON NO JEWISH CHILD MAY ENTER A PUBLIC PARK OR RECREATION GROUND!

A SPECIAL FINE OF ONE HUNDRED AND FIFTY MILLION DOLLARS IS HEREBY LEVIED ON ALL THE JEWS OF GERMANY!

It was hard to believe that things could get worse. But the
tide ran higher and higher, and the waves finally crashed
onto Johann Clement's island when one day little Karen ran
into the house, her face covered with blood and the words,
"Jew! Jew! Jew!" ringing in her ears.

When a man has roots so deep and faith so strong the destruction of his faith is an awesome catastrophe. Not only
had Johann Clement been a fool, but he had endangered the
life of his family as well. He searched for some way out, and
his path led to the Gestapo in Berlin. When he returned from
Berlin, he locked himself in his study for two days and two
nights, remaining there hunched over his desk, staring at the
document that lay before him. It was a magic paper the
Gestapo had presented him with. His signature on the paper
would free him and his family from any further harm. It
was a life-giving document. He read it over and over again
until he knew every word on its pages.

. . . I, Johann Clement, after the above detailed search and
the undeniable facts contained herein, am of the absolute
conviction that the facts concerning my birth have been falsi-
fied. I am not now or never have been of the Jewish religion.
I am an Aryan and . . .

Sign it! Sign it! A thousand times he picked up the pen to
write his name on the paper. This was no time for noble
stands! He had never been a Jew . . . Why not sign? . . . it
made no difference. Why not sign?

The Gestapo made it absolutely clear that Johann Clement
had but one alternative. If he did not sign the paper and continue his work in research his family could leave Germany
only if he remained as a political hostage.

On the third morning he walked from the study, haggard,
and looked into Miriam's anxious eyes. He went to the fireplace and threw the document into the flames. "I cannot do
it," he whispered. "You must plan to leave Germany with
the children immediately."

A terrible fear overtook him now for every moment that
his family remained. Every knock on the door, every ring of
the phone, every footstep brought a new terror he had never
known.

He made his plans. First, the family would go to live with
some colleagues in France. Miriam was nearly due and she
could not travel far. After the baby came and her strength
had returned they would continue on to England or America.

It was not all hopeless. Once the family was safe he could
worry about himself. There were a few secret societies

working in Germany which specialized in smuggling out German scientists. He had been tipped off to one working in Berlin—a group of Palestinian Jews who called themselves Mossad Aliyah Bet.

The trunks were all packed, the house closed down. The man and his wife sat that last night in silence, desperately hoping for some sudden miracle to give them a reprieve.

But that night—the day before departure—Miriam Clement began having her labor pains. She was not permitted into a hospital so she gave birth in her own bedroom. Another son was born. It had been a difficult and complicated delivery and she needed several weeks to convalesce.

Panic seized Johann Clement! He had visions of his family being trapped and never able to escape the approaching holocaust.

He frantically rushed to Berlin to Number 10 Meinekestrasse, the building which housed the Mossad Aliyah Bet. The place was a bedlam of people trying desperately to get out of Germany.

At two o'clock in the morning he was led into an office where a very young and very exhausted man met him. The man was named Ari Ben Canaan and he was a Palestinian in charge of the escape of the German Jews.

Ben Canaan looked at him through bloodshot eyes. He sighed. "We will arrange your escape, Dr. Clement. Go home, you will be contacted. I have to get a passport, a visa . . . I have to pay the right people off. It will take a few days."

"It is not for me. I cannot go, nor can my wife. I have three children. You must get them out."

"I must get them out," Ben Canaan mimicked. "Doctor, you are an important man. I may be able to help you. I cannot help your children."

"You must! You must!" he shrieked.

Ari Ben Canaan slammed his fist on his desk and jumped up. "Did you see that mob out there! They all want to get out of Germany!" He leaned over the desk an inch from Johann Clement. "For five years we have pleaded, we have begged you to leave Germany. Now even if you can get out the British won't let you into Palestine. 'We are Germans . . . we are Germans . . . they won't hurt us,' you said. What in God's name can I do!"

Ari swallowed and slumped down into his chair. His eyes closed a moment, his face masked in weariness. He picked up a sheaf of papers from his desk and thumbed through them. "I have obtained visas for four hundred children to leave Germany. Some families in Denmark have agreed to take them. We have a train organized. I will put one of your children on."

"I . . . I . . . have three children . . ."

"And I have ten thousand children. I have no visas. I have nothing to fight the British Navy with. I suggest you send your oldest who will be better able to take care of itself. The train leaves tomorrow night from Berlin from the Potsdam Station."

Karen clung drowsily to her favorite rag doll. Daddy knelt before her. In her half sleep she could smell that wonderful smell of his pipe.

"It is going to be a wonderful trip, Karen. Just like going to Baden-Baden."

"But I don't want to, Daddy."

"Well, now . . . look at all these nice boys and girls going along with you."

"But I don't want them. I want you and Mommy and Hans and Maximilian. And I want to see my new baby brother."

"See here, Karen Clement. My girl doesn't cry."

"I won't . . . I promise I won't . . . Daddy . . . Daddy . . . will I see you soon?"

"We'll . . . all try very hard . . ."

A woman stepped behind Johann Clement and tapped him on the shoulder. "I am sorry," she said. "It is time for departure."

"I'll take her on."

"No . . . I am sorry. No parents on the train."

He nodded and hugged Karen quickly and stood back biting his pipe so hard his teeth hurt. Karen took the woman's hand, then stopped and turned around. She handed her father her rag doll. "Daddy . . . you take my dolly. She'll look after you."

Scores of anguished parents pressed close to the sides of the train, and the departing children pressed against the windows, shouting, blowing kisses, waving, straining desperately for a last glimpse.

He looked but could not see her.

The steel train grumbled into motion. The parents ran alongside, screaming final farewells.

Johann Clement stood motionless on the fringe of the crowd. As the last car passed he looked up and saw Karen standing calmly on the rear platform. She put her hand to her lips and blew him a kiss as though she knew she would never see him again.

He watched her tiny figure grow smaller and smaller and smaller. And then she was gone. He looked at the little rag doll in his hand. "Good by, my life," he whispered.

CHAPTER TWELVE: Aage and Meta Hansen had a lovely home in the suburbs of Aalborg; it was just right for a little girl, for they had no children of their own. The Hansens were quite a bit older than the Clements; Aage was graying and Meta was nowhere as beautiful as Miriam but none the less Karen felt warm and protected from the moment they carried her drowsy little body into their car.

The train ride into Denmark had been bewildering. All she could remember was the stifled sobs of children all around her. The rest was a blur—standing in lines, being tagged, strange faces, strange language. Then waiting rooms, buses, more tags.

At last she was led alone into the room where Meta and Aage Hansen stood waiting anxiously. Aage knelt down and lifted her and carried her to the car, and Meta held her in her lap and fussed and petted her all the way to Aalborg, and Karen knew she was safe.

Aage and Meta stood back expectantly in the doorway as Karen tiptoed cautiously into the room they had prepared for her. It was filled with dolls and toys and books and dresses and records and just about everything one little girl could ever want. Then Karen saw the floppy little puppy on her bed. She knelt beside him and stroked him and he licked her face and she felt a wet nose against her cheek. She turned and smiled at the Hansens and they smiled back.

Those first few nights without her daddy and mommy were awful. It was surprising how much she missed her brother Hans. She nibbled at her food and just sat alone quietly in her room with the little dog she had named Maximilian. Meta Hansen understood. At night she lay beside Karen and held her and soothed her until her soft little sobs subsided into sleep.

During the next week a steady stream of visitors came with presents and made a great fuss over Karen and babbled in a language she still could not understand. The Hansens were very proud and she did her best to be nice to everyone. In a few more days she ventured out of the house.

Karen was terribly fond of Aage Hansen. He smoked a pipe like her daddy and he liked to take walks. Aalborg was an interesting place. Like Cologne, it had a river, called the Limfjorden. Mr. Hansen was a lawyer and very important and almost everyone seemed to know him. Of course, he wasn't as important as her daddy . . . but few people were.

"Well now, Karen. You have been with us for nearly three

65

weeks," Aage said one night, "and we would like to have a very important talk with you."

He clasped his hands behind him and paced back and forth and talked to her in a very wonderful way so that she understood. He told her that there was much unhappiness in Germany and her mommy and daddy thought it would be better if she remained with them for the time being. Aage Hansen went on to say that they knew they could never replace her own parents but because God had not let them have children of their own they were very happy to have her and wanted her to be happy too.

Yes, Karen understood it all and told Aage and Meta she didn't mind staying with them for the time being.

"And Karen, darling. Because we are borrowing you for a little while and because we love you so much, we wonder . . . would you mind borrowing our name?"

Karen thought about that. It seemed to her that Aage had other reasons. His question had that grown-up sound . . . like the sound of her mommy and daddy talking behind closed doors. She nodded and said that it would be fine with her too.

"Good! Karen Hansen it is, then."

They took her hands as they did every night and led her to her room and put on the low lamp. Aage played with her and tickled her, and Maximilian got mixed up in the fracas. She laughed until she couldn't stand any more. Then she got under the covers and said her prayers.

". . . God bless Mommy and Daddy and Hans and my new baby brother and all my aunts and uncles and cousins . . . and God bless the Hansens who are so nice . . . and God bless both Maximilians."

"I will be back in a few minutes to sit with you," Meta said.

"That's all right. You don't have to stay with me any more. Maximilian will take care of me."

"Good night, Karen."

"Aage?"

"Yes?"

"Do the Danish people hate the Jews too?"

My dear Dr. and Mrs. Clement,
Has it already been six weeks since Karen came to us? What an exceptional child she is. Her teacher tells us she is doing extremely well in school. It is amazing how quickly she is picking up Danish. I suppose that is because she is with children her own age. She has already gathered a large number of girl friends.
The dentist advised us to have one tooth pulled to make

66

*room for another. It was a small matter. We want to start
her on some sort of music lessons soon and will write more
about that.*

Every night in her prayers . . .

And there was a letter from Karen in big block print:

DEAR MOMMY, DADDY, HANS, MAXIMILIAN, AND MY NEW BABY
BROTHER: I MISS YOU MORE THAN I CAN TELL YOU. . . .

Wintertime is a time for ice skating on the frozen banks
of the Limfjorden and for building snow castles and for sled-
ding and for sitting before a blazing fire and having Aage
rub your icy feet.

But winter passed and the Limfjorden flowed again and
the countryside burst into wild bloom. And summertime came
and they all went away to the beach at Blokhus on the North
Sea and she and Meta and Aage took a sailboat a hundred
miles out.

Life was full and rich with the Hansens. She had a flock of
"best" girl friends, and she loved to shop with Meta at the
smelly fish market or stand beside her in the kitchen learning
to bake. And Meta was so good in so many things like sew-
ing or with studies, and she was a wonderful comfort at Karen's bedside if there was a sudden fever or sore throat.

Aage always had a smile and open arms and seemed nearly
as wise and gentle as her own daddy. Aage could be mighty
stern, too, when the occasion demanded.

One day, Aage told Meta to come into the office when
Karen was at her dancing lesson. He was pale and excited.

"I have just heard from the Red Cross," he said to his
wife. "They have all disappeared. Completely, no trace. The
entire family. I cannot get any information from Germany.
I've tried everything. . . ."

"What do you think, Aage?"

"What is there to think? They've all been put into a concentration camp . . . or worse."

"Oh, dear God."

They could not bring themselves to tell Karen that her entire family had disappeared. Karen was suspicious when the
letters stopped coming from Germany, but she was too frightened to ask questions. She loved the Hansens and trusted them
implicitly. Instinct told her that if they did not mention her
family there was a reason for it.

Then, too, a strange thing was happening. Karen missed
her family a great deal, but somehow the images of her
mother and father seemed to grow dimmer and dimmer.
When a child of eight has been removed from her parents

67

for such a long time, it gets harder and harder to remember. Karen felt bad sometimes that she could not remember more vividly.

At the end of a year she could hardly remember when she was not Karen Hansen and a Dane.

CHRISTMAS 1939

There was a war in Europe and a year had passed since Karen arrived at the Hansen house. Her bell-like voice carried a sweet hymn as Meta played the piano. After the hymns Karen went to the closet in her room where she had hidden the Christmas present she had made at school. She handed them the package proudly. It bore a label printed in her hand that read: TO MOMMY AND DADDY FROM YOUR DAUGHTER, KAREN.

APRIL 8, 1940

The night was filled with treachery. A misty dawn brought the chilling sound of marching boots to the frontiers of Denmark. Dawn brought barge after barge of gray-helmeted soldiers creeping through fog-filled inlets and canals. The German Army moved in silently with robot-like efficiency and dispersed over the length and breadth of Denmark.

April 9, 1940!

Karen and her classmates rushed to the window and looked up at a sky black with thundering airplanes, which one by one descended on the Aalborg airdrome.

April 9, 1940!

People rushed into the streets in confusion.

"This is the Danish State Radio. Today at 4:15 the German Army crossed our frontier at Saed and Krussa!"

Completely shocked by the lightning stroke and its masterful execution, the Danes clung desperately to their radios to await word from King Christian. Then the proclamation came. Denmark capitulated without firing a shot in her own defense. The crushing of Poland had taught them that resistance was futile.

Meta Hansen pulled Karen out of school and packed to flee to Bornholm or some other remote island. Aage calmed her and persuaded her to sit and wait it out. It would be weeks, even months, before the Germans got the government functioning.

The sight of the swastika and German soldiers opened a flood of memories for Karen, and with them came fear. Everyone was confused these first weeks, but Aage remained calm.

The German administration and occupation forces made

glowing promises. The Danes, they said, were Aryans like themselves. They were, indeed, little brothers, and the main reason for the occupation was to protect the Danes from Bolsheviks. Denmark, they said, would be allowed to continue to run her own internal affairs. She would become a model protectorate. Thus, after the initial shock had subsided, a semblance of normalcy returned.

The venerable King Christian resumed his daily horseback rides from the Amalienborg Palace in Copenhagen. He rode proudly alone through the streets, and his people followed his lead. Passive resistance was the order of the day.

Aage had been right. Karen returned to school and to her dancing lessons, and life resumed in Aalborg almost as though nothing had happened.

The year of 1941 came. Eight months of German occupation. It was becoming more obvious each day that tension was growing between the Germans and the people of their "model protectorate." King Christian continued to irritate the conquerors by snubbing them. The people, too, ignored the Germans as much as they could, or, worse, poked fun at their struttings and laughed at the proclamations. The more the Danes laughed the angrier the Germans became.

Any illusions the Danes had had at the beginning of the German occupation were soon dispelled. There was a place for Danish machinery and Danish food and Danish geography in the German master plan; Denmark was to become another cog in the German war machine. So with the example of their fellow Scandinavians in Norway before them, the Danes, by the middle of 1941, had established a small but determined little underground.

Dr. Werner Best, the German governor of Denmark, favored a policy of moderation for the "model protectorate," so long as the Danes co-operated peaceably. The measures against the Danes were mild by comparison to those of other occupied countries. None the less, the underground movement mushroomed. Although the members of the resistance could not hope to take on German troops in combat or to plan for a general uprising, they found a way to unleash their hatred for the Germans—*sabotage*.

Dr. Werner Best did not panic. He calmly went about organizing Nazi sympathizers among the Danes to combat this new threat. The German-sponsored HIPO Corps became a Danish terrorist gang for punitive action against their own people. Each act of sabotage was answered by an action by the HIPOS.

As the months and years of German occupation rolled by, Karen Hansen passed her eleventh and twelfth birthdays in faraway Aalborg, where life seemed quite normal. The reports of sabotage and the occasional sound of gunfire or an explosion were only momentary causes for excitement.

Karen began to blossom into womanhood. She felt the first thrills and despairs that come with caring deeply for someone other than parents or a girl friend. Young Mogens Sorensen, the best soccer player in the school, was Karen's beau, and she was the envy of every other girl.

Her dancing ability led her teacher to urge Meta and Aage to let her try out for the Royal Ballet in Copenhagen. She was a gifted child, the teacher said, and seemed to express through dance a sensitivity far beyond her years.

At the turn of 1943 the Hansens became more and more uneasy. The Danish underground was in communication with Allied Headquarters and was getting out vital information with regard to the location of essential war manufacturing plants and supply depots inside Denmark. They co-operated further by spotting these targets for the British RAF Mosquito bombers.

The HIPOS and the other German-sponsored terrorists stepped up reprisals. As the activity heightened, Aage began to ponder. Everyone in Aalborg knew of Karen's origin. Although no move had as yet been made against the Danish Jews, a sudden break could come. He could be fairly certain, too, that the facts concerning Karen had been relayed to the Germans by the HIPOS. At last Meta and Aage decided to sell their house in Aalborg and move to Copenhagen on the pretext that there was a better position for Aage there and that Karen could receive better instruction in ballet.

In the summer of 1943 Aage became affiliated with a law firm in Copenhagen, where they hoped they could become completely anonymous among its million inhabitants. A birth certificate and papers were forged for Karen to prove she was their natural child. Karen said her good bys to Mogens Sorensen, and suffered the pain of a badly broken heart.

The Hansens found a lovely apartment situated on the Sortedams Dosseringen. It was a tree-lined street looking out on the artificial lake and crossed by numerous bridges which led into the old town.

Once the strangeness of resettlement had worn off, Karen loved Copenhagen. It was a fairyland on earth. Karen, Aage, and Maximilian would walk for hours and hours to see the wonders of the town. There were so many wonderful places—around the port past the statue of the Little Mermaid, along the Langelinie or through the bursting gardens of the Citadel or the gardens at the Christiansborg Palace; there were the waterways and the narrow little alleys crammed with ancient five-story brick houses. There were the never-ending streams of bicycles and that wonderful fish market at Gammel Strand,

70

so vast and noisome it put the one in Aalborg to shame.

The crown jewel in that fairyland known as Copenhagen was the Tivoli—a maze of whirling lights and rides and theaters and restaurants and miles of flower beds—the children's band and the Wivex Restaurant and the fireworks and the laughter. Karen soon wondered how on earth she had ever managed to live away from Copenhagen.

One day Karen ran down her street, up the stairs, and threw open the apartment door. She flung her arms about Aage, who was trying to read his newspaper.

"Daddy! Daddy! Daddy!"

She pulled him from his seat and began to waltz around the room. Then she left him standing dazed in the center of the floor and began dancing over the furniture and back to him and threw her arms around him again. Meta appeared in the doorway and smiled.

"Your daughter is trying to tell you that she has been accepted by the Royal Ballet."

"Well now," Aage said, "that is pretty good."

That night, after Karen was asleep, Meta could at last pour out her pride to Aage. "They said she is one in a thousand. With five or six years of intensive training she can go right to the top."

"That is good . . . that is good," Aage said, trying not to show how very proud he was.

But not everything was fairylands and happiness in Copenhagen. Each night the earth was rocked by explosions caused by the underground, explosions that lit the skies, and dancing flames and the sounds of cracking rifles and stuttering machine guns filled the air.

Sabotage!

Reprisal!

The HIPOS began methodically to destroy places and things that were sources of pleasure for the Danes. The German-sponsored Danish terrorists blew up theaters and breweries and entertainment palaces. The Danish underground lashed back at places where the German war machine was being fed. Soon both the days and the nights were racked by the thunder of destruction and flying debris.

The streets were empty during German parades. Danes turned their backs on German ceremony. The streets were mobbed by silent mourners on every Danish national holiday. The daily horseback rides of the old King became a signal for hundreds upon hundreds of Danes to rally and run behind him shouting and cheering.

The situation seethed and seethed—and finally erupted! The morning of August 29, 1943, was ushered in with a blast heard across Zealand. The Danish fleet had scuttled itself in an effort to block the shipping channels!

The enraged Germans moved their forces on the government buildings and royal palace at Amalienborg. The King's guard fought them off. A furious pitched battle broke out, but it was all over rather quickly. German soldiers replaced the King's guard at Amalienborg. A score of German field generals, SS and Gestapo officials descended on Denmark to whip the Danes into line. The Danish Parliament was suspended and a dozen angry decrees invoked. The model protectorate was no longer a "model," if indeed it ever had been.

The Danes answered the Germans by stepping up their acts of sabotage. Arsenals, factories, ammunition dumps, bridges were blown to bits. The Germans were getting jittery. Danish sabotage was beginning to hurt badly.

From German occupation headquarters at the Hotel D'-Angleterre came the decree: ALL JEWS MUST WEAR A YELLOW ARM BAND WITH A STAR OF DAVID.

That night the underground radio transmitted a message to all Danes. "From Amalienborg Palace King Christian has given the following answer to the German command that Jews must wear a Star of David. The King has said that one Dane is exactly the same as the next Dane. He himself will wear the first Star of David and he expects that every loyal Dane will do the same."

The next day in Copenhagen almost the entire population wore arm bands showing a Star of David.

The following day the Germans rescinded the order.

Although Aage was not active in the underground the partners of his law firm were leading members, and from time to time he received information of their activities. At the end of the summer of 1943 he became terribly worried and decided that he and Meta must reach a decision concerning Karen.

"It is true," Aage told his wife. "In a matter of months the Germans will round up all the Jews. We just don't know the exact time the Gestapo will strike."

Meta Hansen walked to the window and stared blankly down at the lake and the bridge to the old town. It was evening and soon Karen would be coming home from ballet school. Meta's mind had been filled with many things she had been planning for Karen's thirteenth birthday party. It was going to be quite a wonderful affair—forty children—at the Tivoli Gardens.

Aage lit his pipe and stared at the picture of Karen on his desk. He sighed.

"I am not giving her up," Meta said.

"We have no right . . ."

"It is different. She is not a Danish Jew. We have records to show she is our child."

Aage put his hand on his wife's shoulder. "Someone in Aalborg may inform the Germans."

"They won't go to that trouble for one child."

"Don't you know these people by now?"

Meta turned around. "We will have her baptized and adopt her legally."

Aage shook his head slowly. His wife slumped into a chair and bit her lip. She clutched the arms of the chair so tightly her hand turned white. "What will happen, Aage?"

"They are organizing to get all the Jewish people up to the Zealand beaches near the straits. We are purchasing as many boats as we can to make runs over to Sweden. The Swedes have sent word that they will accept everyone and provide for them."

"How many nights I have lain awake and thought of this. I have tried to tell myself that she is in greater danger if she must flee. I tell myself over and over that she is safer here with us."

"Think of what you are saying, Meta."

The woman looked at her husband with an expression of anguish and determination he had never seen from her before. "I will never give her up, Aage. I cannot live without her."

Every Dane who was called upon co-operated in a gigantic effort. The entire Jewish population of Denmark was whisked secretly north to Zealand and smuggled to the safety of Sweden.

Later that month the Germans made a sweep of Denmark to catch the Jews. There were none to be caught.

Although Karen remained unharmed in Copenhagen with the Hansens the responsibility of the decision weighed heavily on Meta. From that second on the German occupation became a prolonged nightmare. A dozen new rumors would send her into a panic. Three or four times she fled from Copenhagen with Karen to relatives on Jutland.

Aage became more and more active in the underground. He was gone three or four nights a week now. These nights were long and horrible for Meta.

The Danish underground, now directed and co-ordinated, turned its energies against German transportation. Every half hour a rail line was bombed. Soon the entire rail network of the country was littered with the wreckage of blasted trains.

The HIPOS took their revenge by blowing up the beloved Tivoli Gardens.

The Danes called a general strike against the Germans.

They poured into the streets and set up barricades all over Copenhagen flying Danish, American, British, and Russian flags.

The Germans declared Copenhagen in a state of siege!

From German headquarters at the Hotel D'Angleterre, Dr. Werner Best shrieked in fury, "The rabble of Copenhagen shall taste the whip!"

The general strike was beaten down, but the underground kept up its acts of destruction.

SEPTEMBER 19, 1944

The Germans interned the entire Danish police force for failing to control the people and for overt sympathy with their actions against the occupation forces. The underground, in a daring raid, destroyed the Nazi record offices.

The underground manufactured small arms and smuggled fighters into Sweden to join Danish Free Forces. It turned its wrath on the HIPOS, dispensing quick justice to some of its members and to Danish traitors.

The HIPOS and the Gestapo went berserk in an aimless wave of reprisal murders.

Then German refugees began pouring over the border into Denmark. These were people bombed out by the Allies. They swarmed all over the country, taking food and shelter without asking; stealing and preying on the Danes. The Danes turned their backs on these refugees with utter contempt.

In April 1945 there were all sorts of rumors.

MAY 4, 1945

"Mommy! Daddy! The war is over! The war is over!"

CHAPTER THIRTEEN: The victors entered Denmark— the Yanks and the British and the Danish Free Forces. It was a great week—a week of retribution to the HIPOS and the Danish traitors, to Dr. Werner Best and the Gestapo. A week of din and delirious joy, climaxed by the appearance of creaking old King Christian to reopen the Danish Parliament. He spoke in a proud but tired voice which broke with emotion.

For Meta and Aage Hansen the week of the liberation was a time of sorrow. Seven years before they had rescued a child from grave danger and they had raised her into a blossoming young woman. What a lovely girl she was! Karen was grace and beauty and laughter. Her voice was pure and sweet and she danced with magic wings on her feet. Now: the Day of Judgment.

Once in a fit of anguish Meta Hansen had sworn she would

never give Karen up. Now Meta Hansen was becoming a victim of her own decency. There were no Germans left to fight now, only her own Christian goodness. And Aage would fall victim, as he had to, to his Danish sense of honor. Liberation brought upon them a fear of the haunted nights and the life of emptiness that lay ahead of them without Karen. The Hansens had aged badly during the last seven years. It was apparent the moment they were allowed to relax from the tension of war. No matter how trying things had been there had always been room for laughter, but now while Denmark laughed there was no laughter for them. The Hansens wanted only to look at Karen, hear her voice, spend the hours in her room in a desperate attempt to gather for themselves a lifetime of memories.

Karen knew it was coming. She loved the Hansens. Aage had always done what was right. She had to wait for him to speak first. For two weeks after the liberation the gloom thickened. At last, one evening after another wordless meal Aage rose from the table and put down his napkin. His kindly face was wrinkled and his voice a listless monotone. "We must try to find your parents, Karen. It is the thing to do." He walked from the room quickly. Karen looked to the empty doorway and then to Meta across the table.

"I love you," Karen said, and ran to her room and threw herself on the bed and sobbed, hating herself for bringing this sorrow on them. And now she was hating herself for another reason. She wanted to learn about her past. In a few more days they sought out the International Refugee Organization.

"This is my foster daughter," Aage said.

The case worker had been on her job only the few weeks since the liberation, but already she was becoming sick at the sight of couples like the Hansens and Karen. Day after day the woman was being forced to become a party to tragedy. In Denmark and Holland, in Sweden and Belgium and France, couples like the Hansens who had hidden and sheltered and raised children were now stepping forward to receive their bitter reward.

"You must be prepared for a long and difficult task. There are millions of displaced people in Europe. We have absolutely no idea how long it is going to take to reunite families."

They left with her all the known facts, a list of all the known relatives, and the letters. Karen had a large family and her father had been a prominent man. The woman gave them a little hope.

A week passed, and two, and then three. June—July. Months of torture for Aage and Meta. They would stand in the doorway of Karen's room more and more often. It was frilly and soft and it smelled good. There were her ice skates and her ballet slippers and pictures of classmates and prima ballerinas. There was a picture of her beau, the Petersen boy.

At last they were called to the Refugee Organization.

"We are faced with the fact," the woman said, "that all our initial inquiries have turned up nothing. This is not to be taken as conclusive. It means a long hard task. Were it my own decision I would absolutely forbid Karen to travel to Germany alone or even with Mr. Hansen. There is utter chaos inside Germany and you won't find a thing that we can't do from here." The woman looked squarely at the three of them. "I must warn you about one thing. We have been receiving more and more reports each day that something pretty hideous has happened. Many Jews have been put to death. It is beginning to look as though the numbers may run into the millions."

It was another reprieve for the Hansens, but what a ghastly thought! Were they to keep this girl only because over fifty members of her immediate family had been put to death? The Hansens were being pulled in two directions. The solution came from Karen herself.

Despite the love she had given and received from the Hansens, there had always been a strange, invisible barrier between them. Early in the German occupation when she was but eight years old Aage had told her she must never speak about being Jewish because it could endanger her life. Karen followed this order as she did all of Aage's decisions because she loved him and trusted him. But even though she obeyed it she could not keep from wondering why she was different from other people and exactly what this difference was that endangered her very life. It was a question she could never ask and therefore it was never answered. Furthermore, Karen had been completely isolated from any contact with Jews. She felt herself to be like other people and she looked like other people. Yet the invisible barrier was there.

Her question might well have died, but Aage and Meta kept it alive inadvertently. The Hansens were faithful to the traditions of the Danish Lutheran Church and were very devout. Each Sunday the three of them went to church together, and each night before bedtime Aage read from the Book of Psalms. Karen treasured the little white leather Bible the Hansens gave her on her tenth birthday and she loved the magnificent fairylike stories, especially those in Judges and Samuel and Kings, which were filled with all the wonderment of great loves and wars and passions. Reading the Bible was like reading Hans Christian Andersen himself!

But reading the Bible only led to confusion for Karen. So many times she wanted to talk it all over with Aage. Jesus was born one of these Jews, and his mother and all his disciples were Jews. The first part of the Bible, the most fascinating to Karen's mind, was all about Jews. Didn't it say over and over again that the Jews were people chosen by God Himself to carry out His laws?

If this was all true then why was it so dangerous to be Jewish and why were the Jews hated so? Karen probed deeper as she grew older. She read that God often punished the Jews when they were bad. Had they been very bad?

Karen was a naturally curious girl, and so long as these questions arose she became more and more perplexed by them. The Bible became her secret obsession. In the quiet of her room she studied its passages in the hope of finding some answers to the great riddle.

The more she read, the older she became, the more puzzled she was. By the time she was fourteen she was able to reason out many of the passages and their meanings. Almost everything that Jesus taught, all His ideas, had been set down before in the Old Testament. Then came the largest riddle of all. If Jesus were to return to the earth she was certain He would go to a synagogue rather than a church. Why could people worship Jesus and hate His people?

Another thing happened on her fourteenth birthday. At that age Danish girls are confirmed in the church with a great deal of ceremony and celebration. Karen had lived as a Dane and a Christian, yet the Hansens hesitated in the matter of her confirmation. They talked it over and felt that they could not take upon themselves a matter that had been decided by God. They told Karen the confirmation would be set aside because of the war and the uncertainty of the times. But Karen knew the real reason.

When she had first come to the Hansens she had needed love and shelter. Now her needs had expanded into a longing for identification. The mystery of her family and her past ran parallel with this mystery of being Jewish. In order to take her place forever as a Dane she had to close the door on these burning questions. She was unable to do so. Her life was based on something temporary, an invisible wall—her past and her religion—always stood between her and the Hansens.

As the war drew to a close Karen knew that she would be torn from them. Wisely she conditioned herself to the shock of the inevitable parting. Being Karen Hansen was merely playing a game. She made the need of becoming Karen Clement urgent. She tried to reconstruct threads of her past life; to remember her father, her mother, and her brothers.

Pieces and snatches came back to her in dim and disconnected hazes. She pretended over and over again how the reunion with them would be. She made her longing constant.

By the time the war was over, Karen had conditioned herself completely. One night a few months after the end of the war she told the Hansens that she was going away to find her parents. She told them she had seen the woman at the Refugee Organization and her chances of finding her family would be better if she moved to a displaced persons' camp in Sweden. Actually the chances were the same if she stayed, but she could not bear to prolong the Hansens' agony.

Karen cried for Aage and Meta far more than for herself. With promises to write and with the slim hope of another reunion with them, Karen Hansen Clement, aged fourteen, cast herself adrift in the stream of roamers of the backwash of war.

CHAPTER FOURTEEN: The dream was ruthless to the reality. The first month away from Denmark was a nightmare. She was frightened, for she had always been sheltered, but a dogged determination carried her on.

First to a camp in Sweden and then to a château in Belgium where there were armies of homeless, penniless drifters; inmates of concentration camps; those who fled and those who hid and were hidden and those who fought in the hills and forests as partisans and those legions of forced labor. Each day was riddled with rumors and new stories of horror. Each day brought a succession of new shocks to Karen. Twenty-five million people lay dead in the wake of war.

The trail led to the displaced persons' camp, La Ciotat, on the Gulf of Lions in southern France a few miles from Marseilles. La Ciotat seemed a morbid place packed with lusterless concrete-block barracks which seemed to slosh in a never-ending sea of mud. The numbers of refugees multiplied daily. It was overcrowded, short of everything, and the specter of death seemed to haunt the inmates. To them, all Europe had become a coffin.

Genocide! A dance of death with six million dancers! Karen heard the names of Frank and Mueller and Himmler and Rosenberg and Streicher and Kaltenbrunner and Heydrich. She heard the names of thousands of lesser ones: Ilsa Koch, who won infamy by making lampshades out of human tattooed skins, and of Dieter Wisliczeny, who played the role of stockyard goat leading the sheep to slaughter, or

78

Kramer, who sported in horsewhipping naked women and some of whose handiwork she saw. The name of the greatest killer of them all came up over and over again: Eichmann, the German Palestinian who spoke fluent Hebrew and was the master of genocide.

Karen rued the day she had opened that secret door marked *Jew*, for behind it lay death. One by one the death of an aunt or uncle or cousin was confirmed.

Genocide—carried out with the precision and finality of a machine. At first the efforts of the Germans had been clumsy. They killed by rifle. It was too slow. They organized their transport and their scientists for the great effort. Steel-covered trucks were designed to lock in and gas to death prisoners en route to burial grounds. But even the gas vans proved slow. Next came the crematoriums and the gas chambers capable of killing two thousand people in a half hour—ten thousand on a good day in a major camp. The organization and planning proved itself and genocide proceeded on an assembly-line basis.

And Karen heard of thousands of prisoners who threw themselves on the quick mercy of electrified barbed wire to cheat the gas chambers.

And Karen heard of hundreds of thousands who fell to disease and hunger, stacked-up emaciated corpses thrown into unmarked ditches, with logs placed between them and gasoline poured over them.

And Karen heard of the game of deception that was played to tear children away from their mothers under the guise of resettlement, and of trains packed with the old and feeble. Karen heard of the delousing chambers where prisoners were given bars of soap. The chambers were gas and the soap was made of stone.

Karen heard of mothers who hid children in their clothing, which was hung up on pegs before going into the chambers. But the Germans knew the ruse and always found the little ones.

Karen heard of thousands who knelt naked beside graves they had dug. Fathers holding their hands over the eyes of their sons as German pistols went off in the backs of their heads.

She heard of SS *Haupsturmfuehrer* Fritz Gebauer, who specialized in strangling women and children barehanded and who liked watching infants die in barrels of freezing water.

She heard of Heinen, who perfected a method of killing several people in a row with one bullet, always trying to beat his previous record.

She heard of Frank Warzok, who liked to bet on how long a human could live hanging by the feet.

She heard of *Obersturmbannfuehrer* Rokita, who ripped bodies apart.

She heard of Steiner, who bored holes into prisoners' heads and stomachs and pulled fingernails and gouged eyes and liked to swing naked women from poles by their hair.

She heard of General Franz Jaeckeln who conducted the massacre of Babi Yar. Babi Yar was a suburb of Kiev and in two days thirty-three thousand Jews were rounded up and shot—to the approval of many cheering Ukrainians.

She heard of Professor Hirts' Anatomical Institute at Strasbourg and of his scientists, and she saw evidences of the deformed women who had been subjects of their experiments.

Dachau was the biggest of the "scientific" centers. She learned that Dr. Heisskeyer injected children with t.b. germs and observed their death. Dr. Schutz was interested in blood poisoning. Dr. Rascher wanted to save the lives of German air crews and in his experiments high-altitude conditions were simulated and human guinea pigs frozen to death while they were carefully observed through special windows. There were other experiments in what the Germans referred to as "truth in science" which reached a peak, perhaps, in the attempted implantation of animal sperm in human females.

Karen heard of Wilhaus, the commander of the camp at Janowska, who commissioned the composer Mund to write the "Death Tango." The notes of this song were the last sounds heard by two hundred thousand Jews who were liquidated at Janowska. She heard other things about Wilhaus at Janowska. She heard his hobby was throwing infants into the air and seeing how many bullets he could fire into the body before it reached the ground. His wife, Otilie, was also an excellent shot.

Karen heard about the Lithuanian guards of the Germans who merely clubbed and kicked people to death and of the Croatian Ustashis and their violent killings of hundreds of thousands of prisoners too.

Karen wept and she was dazed and she was haunted. Her nights were sleepless and the names of the land tore through her brain. Had her father and mother and brothers been sent to Buchenwald or had they met death in the horror of Dachau? Maybe it was Chelmno with a million dead or Maidanek with seven hundred and fifty thousand. Or Belzec or Treblinka with its lines of vans or Sobibor or Trawniki or Poniatow or Krivoj Rog. Had they been shot in the pits of Krasnik or burned at the stake at Klooga or torn apart by dogs at Diedzyn or tortured to death at Stutthof?

The lash! The ice bath! The electric shock! The soldering iron! Genocide!

Was it the camp at Choisel or Dora or Neuengamme or

was it at Gross-Rosen or did they hear Wilhaus' "Death Tango" at Janowska?

Was her family among the bodies which were melted to fat in the manufacture of soap at Danzig?

Death lingered on and on at the displaced persons' camp at La Ciotat near Marseilles, France.

. . . and Karen heard more names of the land. Danagien, Eivari, Goldpilz, Vievara, Portkunde.

She could not eat and she could not sleep—Kivioli, Varva, Magdeburg, Plaszow, Szebnie, Mauthausen, Sachsenhausen, Oranienburg, Landsberg, Bergen-Belsen, Reinsdorf, Bliziny.

Genocide!

Fossenberg! Ravensbrück! Natzweiler!

But all these names were small beside the greatest of them all—*Auschwitz!*

Auschwitz with its three million dead!

Auschwitz with its warehouses crammed with eyeglasses.

Auschwitz with its warehouses crammed with boots and clothing and pitiful rag dolls.

Auschwitz with its warehouse of human hair for the manufacture of mattresses!

Auschwitz, where the gold teeth of the dead were methodically pulled and melted down for shipment to Himmler's Science Institute. Auschwitz, where an especially finely shaped skull would be preserved as a paperweight!

Auschwitz, where the bones of the cremated were broken up with sledge hammers and pulverized so that there would never be a trace of death.

Auschwitz which had the sign over the main entrance: LABOR LIBERATES.

Karen Hansen Clement sank deep in melancholy. She heard till she could hear no more. She saw until she could see no more. She was exhausted and confused, and the will to go on was being drained from her blood. Then, as so often happens when one reaches the end of the line, there was a turning upward and she emerged into the light.

It began when she smiled and patted the head of an orphan and the child sensed great compassion in her. Karen was able to give children what they craved the most, tenderness. They flocked to her. She seemed to know instinctively how to dry a runny nose, kiss a wounded finger, or soothe a tear, and she could tell stories and sing at the piano in many languages.

She plunged into her work with the younger children with a fervor that helped her forget a little of the pain within her. She never seemed to run out of patience nor of time for giving.

Her fifteenth birthday came and went at La Ciotat. Aside

from the fact that she was just plain stubborn, Karen clung to two great hopes. Her father had been a prominent man, and the Germans had kept one "prestige" camp where prisoners were neither tortured nor killed. It was the camp at Theresienstadt in Czechoslovakia. If he had been sent there, as well he might, he could still be alive. The second hope, a slimmer one, was that many German scientists had been smuggled out of the country even after being sent to concentration camps. Against these hopes she had the confirmed deaths of over half of her family.

One day several dozen new people entered the camp and the place seemed to transform overnight. The new people were Palestinians from the Mossad Aliyah Bet and the Palmach who had come to take over the interior organization.

A few days after they arrived, Karen danced for her youngsters—the first time she had danced since the summer. From that moment on she was in constant demand and one of the most popular figures in La Ciotat. Her renown spread even as far as Marseilles where she was invited to dance in an annual Christmas presentation of the *Nutcracker Suite*.

CHRISTMAS 1945

The pangs of loneliness of her first Christmas away from the Hansens were terrible. Half the children in La Ciotat had come to Marseilles to watch her dance in a special performance. Karen danced that night as she had never danced before.

When the performance was over a Palestinian Palmach girl named Galil, who was the section head at La Ciotat, asked Karen to wait until everyone had left. Tears streamed down Galil's cheeks. "Karen. We have just received positive confirmation that your mother and your two brothers were exterminated at Dachau."

Karen tumbled into a sorrow even deeper than before. The undaunted spirit which had kept her going vanished. She felt the curse of being born a Jewess had led her to the madness of leaving Denmark.

Every child in La Ciotat had one thing in common. Every one of them believed their parents were alive. All of them waited for the miracle which never came. What a fool she had been to believe!

When she was able to come to her senses several days later she talked it all over with Galil. She did not feel she had the strength to sit and wait until she heard that her father was dead also.

Galil, the Palestine girl, was her only confidante and felt that Karen, like all Jews, should go to Palestine. It was the only place a Jew could live with dignity, Galil argued. But, with her faith destroyed, Karen was about ready to close the door on Judaism, for it had brought her only misery and left her as Karen Hansen, a Dane.

At night Karen asked herself the same question that every Jew had asked of himself since the Temple in Jerusalem had been destroyed and the Jews were dispersed to the four corners of the earth as eternal drifters two thousand years before. Karen asked herself, "Why me?"

Each day brought her closer to that moment when she would write the Hansens and ask to return to them forever.

Then one morning Galil rushed into Karen's barrack and half dragged her to the administration building, where she was introduced to a Dr. Brenner, a new refugee at La Ciotat.

"Oh, God!" Karen cried as she heard the news. "Are you certain?"

"Yes," Brenner answered, "I am absolutely positive. You see, I knew your father in the old days. I was a teacher in Berlin. We often exchanged correspondence and met at conventions. Yes, my dear, we were in Theresienstadt together and I saw him last only a few weeks before the war ended."

CHAPTER FIFTEEN: A week later Karen received a letter from the Hansens stating that there had been inquiries from the Refugee Organization as to her whereabouts, as well as questions as to whether the Hansens had any information about her mother or brothers.

It was assumed that the inquiries came from Johann Clement or from someone in his behalf. Karen surmised from this that her father and mother had been separated and he was unaware of her death and the death of the brothers. The next letter from the Hansens stated that they had replied but the Refugee Organization had lost contact with Clement.

But he was alive! Every horrible moment of the months in the camps in Sweden, Belgium, and La Ciotat was worth it now! Once again she found the courage to search for her past.

Karen wondered why La Ciotat was being supported by money from Jews in America. After all, there was everything in the camp but Americans. She asked Galil, who shrugged. "Zionism is a first person asking money from a second person to give to a third person to send a fourth person to Palestine."

"It is good," Karen said, "that we have friends who stick together."

"We also have enemies who stick together," Galil answered.

The people at La Ciotat certainly looked and acted much like any other people, Karen thought. Most of them seemed just as confused by being Jewish as she was.

When she had learned enough Hebrew to handle herself she ventured into the religious compound to observe the weird rituals, the dress and prayer of those people who were truly different. The vastness of the sea of Judaism can drown a girl of fifteen. The religion was based on a complex set of laws. Some were written and some were oral. They covered the most minute of subjects, such as how to pray on a camel. The holiest of the holy were the five books of Moses, the Torah.

Once again Karen turned to her Bible. This time what she read seemed to throw new light and have new meaning for her and she would think for hours about lines like the cry of the prophet Isaiah: *"We grope for the wall like the blind, and we grope as if we had no eyes: we stumble at noon day as in the night; we are in desolate places as dead men. We roar like bears, and mourn sore like doves . . . we look for salvation, but it is far off from us."*

These words seemed to fit the situation at La Ciotat. Her Bible was filled with stories of bondage and freedom, and she tried to apply these things to herself and her family.

"Look from heaven and see how we have become a scorn and a derision among the nations; we are accounted as sheep and brought to the slaughter to be slain and destroyed or to be smitten and reproached. Yet, despite all this, we have not forgotten thy Name; we beseech thee, forget us not . . ."

And again the path would end in confusion. Why would God let six million of His people be killed? Karen concluded that only the experiences of life would bring her the answer, someday.

The inmates of La Ciotat seethed with a terrible desire to leave Europe behind them and get to Palestine. The only force that kept them from turning into a wild mob was the presence of the Palmachniks from Palestine.

They cared little about the war of intrigue that raged about them between the British and the Mossad Aliyah Bet. They did not care about British desperation to hold onto the Middle East or oil or canals or traditional co-operation with the Arabs.

For a brief instant a year earlier everyone's hopes had soared as the Labour party swept into power and with it promises to turn Palestine into a model mandate with open immigration. Talk was even revived of making Palestine a member of the British Commonwealth.

The promises exploded as the Labour Government listened to the voice of black gold that bubbled beneath Arab sand. The decisions were delayed for more study, more commissions, more talk, as it had been for twenty-five years.

But nothing could curb the craving of the Jews in La Ciotat to get to Palestine. Mossad Aliyah Bet agents poured all over Europe looking for Jewish survivors and leading them through friendly borders with bribes, forgery, stealing, or any other means short of force.

A gigantic game was played as the scene shifted from one country to another. From the very beginning France and Italy allied themselves with the refugees in open co-operation with the Mossad. They kept their borders open to receive refugees and to establish camps. Italy, occupied by British troops, was severely hampered, so France became the major refugee center.

Soon places like La Ciotat were bulging. The Mossad answered with illegal immigration. Every seaport of Europe was covered by Mossad agents who used the money sent them by American Jews to purchase and refit boats to run the British blockade into Palestine. The British not only used their navy but their embassies and consulates as counter-spying centers against the Mossad.

Leaky little boats of the Mossad Aliyah Bet, overloaded with desperate people, set out for Palestine, only to be caught by the British as soon as they entered the three-mile zone. The refugees would be interned in yet another camp, this one in Atlit in Palestine.

After Karen learned her father was alive she, too, became swept up in the desire to get to Palestine. It seemed natural to her that her father would come to Palestine also.

Although she was only fifteen she was drawn into the Palmach group, whose members held nightly campfires and told wonderful stories of the Land of Milk and Honey and sang wonderful oriental songs right out of the Bible. They joked and spun tall yarns all night long and they would call, "Dance, Karen, dance!"

She was made a section chief to take care of a hundred children and prepare them for the moment a Mossad boat would take them to run the blockade into Palestine.

The British quota for Palestine was only fifteen hundred a month, and they always took old people or those too young to fight. Men grew beards and grayed their hair to look old, but such ruses usually didn't work.

In April of 1946, nine months after Karen had left Denmark, Galil gave her the great news one day.

"An Aliyah Bet ship is coming in a few days and you and your section are going on it."

Karen's heart nearly tore through her dress.

"What is the name of it?"

"The *Star of David*," Galil answered.

CHAPTER SIXTEEN: British CID had a running acquaintance with the Aegean tramp steamer, *Karpathos*. They knew the instant the *Karpathos* was purchased in Salonika by the Mossad Aliyah Bet. They followed the movements of the eight-hundred-ton, forty-five-year-old tramp to Piraeus, the port of Athens where an American Aliyah Bet crew boarded her and sailed her to Genoa, Italy. They observed as the *Karpathos* was refitted into an immigrant runner and they knew the exact instant she left and sailed toward the Gulf of Lions.

The entire southern coast of France was alive with CID men. A twenty-four-hour watch was thrown around La Ciotat for signs of a large-scale movement. A dozen major and minor French officials were bribed. Pressure came from Whitehall to Paris to prevent the *Karpathos* from getting inside French territorial waters. But British pressure and bribes had no effect. French co-operation with Aliyah Bet remained solid. The *Karpathos* moved inside the three-mile zone.

The next stage of the game was set. A half-dozen trial runs were made from La Ciotat to trick and divert the British. Trucks were donated by the French teamsters and driven by French drivers. When the British were thoroughly confused the real break was made. Sixteen hundred refugees, Karen's section included, were sped out from La Ciotat to a secret rendezvous point along the coast. The entire area was blocked off from outside traffic by the French Army. The trucks unloaded the refugees on a quiet beach and they were transferred by rubber boats to the ancient *Karpathos,* which waited offshore.

The line of rubber boats moved back and forth all night. The strong hands of the American crew lifted the anxious escapees aboard. Palmach teams on board quickly moved each boatload to a predesignated section. A knapsack, a bottle of water, and an obsession to leave Europe was all the refugees had.

Karen's children, the youngest, were boarded first and given a special position in the hold. They were placed below deck near the ladder which ran to the deck. She worked quickly to calm them down. Fortunately most of them were too numbed with excitement and exhaustion and fell right off to sleep. A few cried, but she was right there to comfort them.

An hour passed, and two and three, and the hold began to get crowded. On came the refugees until the hold was so packed there was scarcely an inch to move in any direction.

Then they began filling up the deck space topside and when that was crammed they flooded over onto the bridge.

Bill Fry, an American and captain of the ship, came down the ladder and looked over the crush of humanity in the hold ˙ ˙ and whistled. He was a stocky man with a stubbly beard and an unlit cigar butt clenched between his teeth.

"You know, the Boston fire department would raise hell if they ever saw a room like this," Bill mumbled.

He stopped talking and began to listen. From the shadows a very sweet voice was singing a lullaby. He pushed his way down the ladder and stepped over the bodies and turned a flashlight on Karen, who was holding a little boy in her arms and singing him to sleep. For an instant he thought he was looking at the Madonna! He blinked his eyes. Karen looked up and motioned him to take the flashlight off her.

"Hey, kid . . . you speak English?" Bill's gruff voice said.

"Yes."

"Where is the section head of these kids?"

"I am the section head and I'll thank you to lower your voice. I've had enough trouble getting them quieted down."

"I'll talk as loud as I want. I'm the captain. You ain't no bigger than most of these kids."

"If you run your ship as well as I run this section," Karen snapped angrily, "then we will be in Palestine by morning."

He scratched his bearded jaw and smiled. He certainly didn't look like the dignified Danish ship's captains, Karen thought, and he was only pretending to be hard.

"You're a nice kid. If you need something you come up on the bridge and see me. And you be more respectful."

"Thank you, Captain."

"That's all right. Just call me Bill. We're all from the same tribe."

Karen watched as he climbed the ladder, and she could see the first crack of daylight. The *Karpathos* was crammed with as many people as she could hold—sixteen hundred refugees, hanging from every inch of her. The half-rusted anchor creaked up and slapped against the sides of her wooden hulk. The forty-five-year-old engines coughed and sputtered and reluctantly churned into action. A fog bank enshrouded them as though God Himself were giving cover, and the old ship chugged away from the shores of France at her top speed of seven knots an hour. In a matter of moments she was beyond the three-mile zone and into the waters of no man's land. The first round had been won by the Mossad Aliyah Bet! A blue and white Jewish flag was struck to the mast, and the *Karpathos* changed her name to the *Star of David*.

The boat bounced miserably. The lack of ventilation in the overjammed holds turned everyone pale. Karen worked with the Palmach teams feeding lemons and applying compresses to stave off a major epidemic of vomiting. When lemons failed, she went to work quickly with the mop. She found that the best way to keep things quiet was to sing and invent games and tell funny stories.

She had the children under control but by noon the heat worsened and the air grew more rancid, and soon the stench of sweat and vomit became unbearable in the semilit hold. Men stripped to shorts and women to their brassières, and their bodies glistened with sweat. An outbreak of fainting began. Only the unconscious were taken up on deck. There was simply no room for the others.

Three doctors and four nurses, all refugees from La Ciotat, worked feverishly. "Get food into their stomachs," they ordered. Karen coaxed, coddled, and shoved food down the mouths of her children. By evening she was passing out sedatives and giving sponge baths. She washed them sparingly, for water was very scarce.

At last the sun went down and a breath of air swept into the hold. Karen had worked herself into exhaustion, and her mind was too hazy to permit her to think sharply. She fell into only a half sleep with an instinctive reflex that brought her awake the second one of her children cried. She listened to every creak of the old ship as it labored for Palestine. Toward morning she dozed off completely into a thick dream-riddled sleep filled with annoying confusion.

A sudden roar brought her awake with a start. She looked up the ladder and it was daylight. Karen pushed her way up. Everyone was pointing to the sky where a huge four-engined bomber hovered over them.

"British! Lancaster Bomber!"

"Everyone return to your places and be calm," the loud-speaker boomed.

Karen rushed back to the hold where the children were frightened and crying. She began singing at the top of her voice urging the children to follow:

> Onward! Onward to Palestine
> In happiness we throng,
> Onward! Onward to Palestine
> Come join our happy song!

"Everyone keep calm," the loud-speaker said, "there is no danger."

By noontime a British cruiser, HMS *Defiance,* appeared on the horizon and bore down on the *Star of David,* blinker lights flashing. A sleek little destroyer, HMS *Blakely,* joined the *Defiance.* The two warships hovered about the old tramp as she chugged along.

"We have picked up our royal escort," Bill Fry said over the loud-speaker.

By the rules of the game the contest was over. Mossad Aliyah Bet had gotten another ship out of Europe and onto the high seas. The British had sighted the vessel and were following it. The instant the *Star of David* entered the three-mile limit off Palestine she would be boarded by a British landing party and towed off to Haifa.

On the deck of the *Star of David* the refugees hooted at the warships and cursed Bevin. A large sign went up which read: HITLER MURDERED US AND THE BRITISH WON'T LET US LIVE! The *Defiance* and the *Blakely* paid no attention and did not, as hoped, miraculously disappear.

Once her children were calmed, Karen had more to think about. Many of them were becoming quite sick from the lack of air. She went topside and inched her way through the tangle of arms, legs, and knapsacks up to the captain's bridge. In the wheel room Bill Fry was sipping coffee and looking down at the solid pack of humanity on deck. The Palmach head was arguing with him.

"Jesus Christ!" Bill growled. "One thing we get from Jews is conversation. Orders aren't made to be discussed. They are made to be obeyed. How in the hell you guys going to win anything if you've got to talk everything over? Now I'm the captain here!"

Bill's outburst hardly fazed the Palmach chief, who finished his argument and walked off.

Bill sat mumbling under his breath. He lit a cigar butt and then saw Karen standing rather meekly in the doorway.

"Hi, sweetheart," he said, smiling. "Coffee?"

"I'd love some."

"You look bad."

"I can't get too much sleep with the children."

"Yeah . . . how you getting along with them kids?"

"That's what I came to talk to you about. Some of them are getting quite sick, and we have several pregnant women in the hold."

"I know, I know."

"I think we should have a turn on deck."

He pointed down to the solid cluster of bodies. "Where?"

"You just find a few hundred volunteers to exchange places."

"Aw, look now, honey, I hate to turn you down, but I've got a lot on my mind. It just ain't that easy. We can't start moving people around on this can."

Karen's face retained a soft sweetness and her voice showed no anger. "I am going back down there and I am taking my

89

children on deck," she said. She turned her back and started for the door.

"Come back here. How did a sweet-looking kid like you get so ornery?" Bill scratched his jaw. "All right! All right! We'll get them brats of yours topside. Jesus Christ, all I get is arguments, arguments, arguments!"

That night Karen led her children to a place on the fantail of the ship. In the cool and wonderful air they fell into a deep and peaceful sleep.

The next day the sea was smooth as glass. Dawn brought more British patrol planes, and the now familiar escort, the *Defiance* and *Blakely,* were still there.

A tremor of excitement ran through the ship as Bill announced that they were less than twenty-four hours from Eretz Israel—Land of Israel. The mounting tension brought on a strange quiet that lasted far into the day. Toward evening the *Blakely* moved very close to the *Star of David.*

A booming British voice cut over the water from the *Blakely*'s loud-speaker. "Immigrant ship. This is Captain Cunningham of the *Blakely* here. I want to speak to your captain."

"Hello, *Blakely,*" Bill Fry's voice growled back, "what's on your mind?"

"We would like to send an emissary aboard to speak to you."

"You can speak now. We're all *mishpocha* here and we got no secrets."

"Very well. Sometime after midnight you will enter the territorial waters of Palestine. At that time we intend to board you and tow you to Haifa. We want to know if you are going to accept this without resistance?"

"Hello, Cunningham. Here's the picture. We've got some pregnant women and sick people aboard here and we would like you to accept them."

"We have no instructions. Will you accept our tow or not?"

"Where did you say?"

"Haifa."

"Well I'll be damned. We must be off course. This is a Great Lakes pleasure boat."

"We will be compelled to board you forcibly!"

"Cunningham!"

"Yes?"

"Inform your officers and men . . . you can all go to hell!"

Night came. No one slept. Everyone strained through the darkness for some sight of shore—the first look at Eretz Israel. Nothing could be seen. The night was misty and there were no stars or moon and the *Star of David* danced on brisk waves.

Around midnight a Palmach section head tapped Karen on the shoulder. "Karen," he said, "come up to the wheelhouse with me."

They threaded their way over the prone bodies to the wheelhouse, which was also packed with twenty of the crew and Palmach section heads. It was pitch black inside except for a bluish light from the compass. Near the wheel she could make out the husky outline of Bill Fry.

"Everyone here?"

"All accounted for."

"All right, pay attention." Bill's voice sounded in the darkness. "I've talked it over with the Palmach heads and my crew and we've reached a decision. The weather off Palestine is socking in solid . . . fog all over the coast. We are carrying an auxiliary motor aboard capable of boosting our speed to fifteen knots. In two hours we will be inside territorial waters. If this weather stays bad we've decided to make a run for it and beach ourselves south of Caesarea."

An excited murmur raced around the room.

"Can we get away from those warships?"

"They'll think this tub's the *Thunderbird* before I'm finished," Fry snapped back.

"How about radar? Won't they keep us on their screens?"

"Yeah . . . but they ain't going to follow us too close to shore. They're not going to risk beaching a cruiser."

"How about the British garrison in Palestine?"

"We have established contact with the Palmach ashore. They are expecting us. I'm sure they'll give the British an interesting evening. Now all of you section leaders have had special instructions at La Ciotat in beaching operations. You know what to expect and what to do. Karen, and you other two chiefs with children . . . better wait here for special orders. Any questions?"

There were none.

"Any arguments?"

There were none.

"I'll be damned. Good luck and God bless all of you."

CHAPTER SEVENTEEN: A wind-driven mist whistled around the ancient and abandoned port of Caesarea, Palestine, and its heaps of rubble, broken walls, and moss-covered harbor which was in use four hundred years before the Christian era.

For five long centuries Caesarea—built by Herod in honor of Caesar—had been the capital of Roman Palestine. All that was left was ruin. The wind howled and churned up the water into a swirling foam which dashed against rocks jutting far into the sea.

Here the revolution against Roman tyranny ended with the slaughter of twenty thousand Hebrews and their great sage, Rabbi Akiva, who had called his people to fight for freedom with Bar Kochba, met his martyrdom. The Crocodile River still flowed to the sea where Akiva was skinned alive.

A few yards south of the ruins were the first buildings of a collective Jewish fishing village named Sdot Yam (Fields of the Sea). This night no fisherman or his wife slept.

They were all crouched throughout the ruins and they silently, breathlessly strained their eyes to the sea. They numbered two hundred and were joined by two hundred more Palmach soldiers.

A flashlight signal blinked out from the ancient Tower of Drusus which jutted into the surf, and everyone tensed.

Aboard the *Star of David*, Bill Fry's teeth tightened on a cigar stub and his hands tightened on the wheel of the old ship. He zigzagged her in slowly, inching past treacherous reefs and shoals. On deck the refugees pressed toward the rail and steeled themselves.

The *Star of David* shuddered and creaked as her timbers slashed into a craggy boulder! A single flare spiraled into the air! The melee was on!

Everyone scrambled over the sides, diving into shoulder-high water, and began fighting foot by foot through the surf toward the shore line several hundred yards away.

As the flare burst, the fishermen and Palmachniks scrambled from their cover and waded out to meet the refugees. Many slipped and fell into potholes or were overturned by a sudden wave and went down on slimy rocks, but nothing could stop them. The two forces met! The strong hands from the shore grabbed the refugees and began dragging them in.

"Quick! Quick!" they were ordered. "Take off your clothing and change into these at once!"

"Throw away any identification papers!"

"Those dressed, follow us . . . move . . . move . . . move!"

"Quiet! No noise!"

"No lights!"

The refugees tore the drenched clothing from their bodies and put on the blue uniforms of the fishermen.

"Mingle . . . everyone mingle. . . ."

On deck of the *Star of David*, Karen handed children down to the Palmachniks one by one as fast as they could make a trip in and come back out. Strong, sure-footed men were needed to hold the children in the surf.

"Faster . . . faster . . ."

There were uninhibited cries of emotion from some who fell on the holy soil to kiss it.

"You will have plenty of time to kiss the ground later but not now . . . move on!"

Bill Fry stood on his bridge barking orders through a megaphone. Within an hour nearly everyone had abandoned the *Star of David* except for a few dozen children and the section chiefs.

Thirty kilometers to the north a Palmach unit staged a devastating assault on some British warehouses south of Haifa in an effort to divert the British troops in that area away from the beaching operation at Caesarea.

On the beach the fishermen and Palmachniks worked rapidly. Some of the refugees were taken into the village and others to trucks which sped them inland.

As the last of the children was handed over the rail of the *Star of David,* Bill Fry tore down the ladder to the deck and ordered the section heads over the side.

Karen felt the icy water close over her head. She balanced on her toes, treaded water for a moment, and found her direction. She swam in close enough to find footing. Ahead of her, on the beach, she could hear confused shouts in Hebrew and German. She came to a huge rock and crawled over it on all fours. A wave washed her back into the sea. Now she worked to solid ground and pushed in foot by foot against a driving undertow. Downed again on all fours she crawled closer to the shore.

A piercing sound of sirens!

An ear-splitting crackle of rifle fire!

On the beach everyone was dispersing!

Karen gasped for breath as she emerged into knee-high water, holding her side. Directly before her stood a half dozen khaki-clad British soldiers with truncheons in their hands.

"No!" she shrieked. "No! No! No!"

She hurled herself into the cordon screaming, clawing, and kicking with fury. A strong arm seized her from behind and she was wrestled into the surf. Her teeth sank into the soldier's hand. He yelled in pain and released her. She flung herself forward again fighting like a savage. A second soldier held his truncheon high and brought it down and it thudded against her head. Karen moaned, went limp, and rolled unconscious into the water.

She opened her eyes. Her head throbbed horribly. But she smiled as she looked up into the face of stubble-jawed, bleary-eyed Bill Fry.

"The children!" she screamed, and spun off the cot. Bill's hands grabbed her.

"Take it easy. Most of the kids got away. Some of them are here."

Karen closed her eyes and sighed and lay back on the cot again.

"Where are we?"

"British detention camp . . . Atlit. It was a wonderful show. More than half the people got away. The British are so damned mad they rounded everybody up and herded us off here. We got crew, fishermen, refugees . . . everybody mixed up in this mess. How do you feel?"

"I feel horrible. What happened?"

"You tried to whip the British Army singlehanded."

She pushed the blanket off and sat up again and felt the lump on the side of her head. Her dress was still damp. She stood and walked, a bit wobbly, to the tent opening. There were several hundred more tents and a wall of barbed wire. Beyond the barbed wire were British sentries. "I don't know what came over me," Karen said. "I've never struck anyone in my life. I saw those soldiers standing there . . . trying to stop me. Somehow the most important thing that ever happened, happened that moment. I had to put my foot on Palestine. I had to or I'd die . . . I don't know what came over me." She sat down beside him.

"Want something to eat, kid?"

"I'm not hungry. What are they going to do with us?"

Bill shrugged. "It will be light in a few hours. They'll start processing us and asking a lot of damned fool questions. You know the answers."

"Yes . . . I keep repeating that this is my country to whatever they ask."

"Yeah . . . anyhow, they'll keep you here a couple or three months and then they'll turn you loose. At least you're in Palestine."

"What about you?"

"Me? Hell, they'll throw me out of Palestine same as they did the last time. I'll get another Mossad ship . . . try another run on the blockade."

Her head began to throb and she lay back but she could not close her eyes. She studied Bill's grizzled face for many moments.

"Bill . . . why are you here?"

"What do you mean?"

"You're an American. It's different with Jews in America."

"Everybody is trying to make something noble out of me." He patted his pockets and pulled out some cigars. They were ruined by the water. "The Aliyah Bet came around and saw me. They said they needed sailors. I'm a sailor . . . been one all my life. Worked my way up from cabin boy to first mate. That's all there is to it. I get paid for this."

"Bill . . ."

"Yeah . . ."

"I don't believe you."

Bill Fry didn't seem to be convincing himself either. He stood up. "It's hard to explain, Karen. I love America. I wouldn't trade what I've got over there for fifty Palestines."

Karen propped up on an elbow. Bill began pacing the tent and groping to connect his thoughts. "We're Americans but we're a different kind of Americans. Maybe we make ourselves different . . . maybe other people make me different . . . I'm not smart enough to figure those things out. All my life I've heard I'm supposed to be a coward because I'm a Jew. Let me tell you, kid. Every time the Palmach blows up a British depot or knocks the hell out of some Arabs he's winning respect for me. He's making a liar out of everyone who tells me Jews are yellow. These guys over here are fighting my battle for respect . . . understand that?"

"I think so."

"Well, damned if I understand it."

He sat beside Karen and examined the lump on her head. "That don't look too bad. I told those Limey bastards to take you to a hospital."

"I'll be all right," she said.

Later that night the Palmach staged a raid on the Atlit camp and another two hundred of the refugees escaped through a gaping hole blown in the barbed wire. Karen and Bill Fry were not among the escapees.

When the full report of the *Star of David* episode reached Whitehall the British realized they had to change their immigration policy. To date, the illegal runners had brought in loads of a few hundred. This ship had carried nearly two thousand, and the greater part of them had escaped in the beaching at Caesarea and the subsequent raid on Atlit. The British were faced with the fact that the French government openly supported the Jews and that one out of every six Jews in Palestine had entered illegally.

And so the British were caught in a tangle. They were as far away from a final answer on the Palestine problem as they ever had been, and so it was decided that the Jews must be turned away from Palestine and not kept at Atlit. The camps on Cyprus were established as a direct result of the pressure of illegal immigration and specifically of the success of the *Star of David* expedition.

Karen Hansen Clement was sent to the island of Cyprus on a British prison ship and interned in the Caraolos camp. But even as the *Karpathos/Star of David* lay wedged in the rocks off the shore of Caesarea and the surf pounded her to bits, the Mossad Aliyah Bet speeded up their operations, planning for more ships and larger numbers of refugees to follow in the wake.

For six more months the young girl stayed in the swirling dust of Caraolos and worked among her children. Her time in the succession of DP and internment camps had done nothing to harden or embitter her. She lived only for the moment when she could once again see Palestine . . . Eretz Israel. . . . The magic words became an obsession for her too.

Many hours had passed when Karen finished telling her story to Kitty Fremont. During the telling a rapport had been established between them. Each detected the loneliness and the need for companionship of the other.

"Have you heard anything further about your father?" Kitty asked.

"No. Not since La Ciotat, and that was very long ago."

Kitty looked at her watch. "Goodness . . . it's past midnight."

"I didn't notice the time," Karen said.

"Neither did I. Good night, child."

"Good night, Kitty. Will I see you again?"

"Perhaps . . . I don't know."

Kitty stepped outside and walked away from the building. The thousands of tents were still now. A searchlight from the watchtower swept over the waves of canvas. Dust kicked up and blew around her feet and she tightened her coat. The tall figure of Ari Ben Canaan walked toward her and stopped. He handed her a cigarette, and they walked silently over the bridge out of the children's compound. Kitty stopped a moment and looked back, then continued on through the old people's area to the main gate.

"I will work for you on one condition," Kitty said, "that that girl does not go on the escape. She stays in this camp with me."

"Agreed."

Kitty turned and walked toward the sentry house quickly.

CHAPTER EIGHTEEN: The plan which David had romantically called Operation Gideon moved into action. At Caraolos a large batch of bills of lading and British army identification cards were forged by Dov Landau and given to Kitty Fremont. She carried them from the camp and turned them over to Ari Ben Canaan.

The delivery of the bills of lading enabled Ben Canaan to complete the first phase of his scheme. During his survey of Cyprus he had become familiar with a large British supply depot on the Famagusta road near Caraolos. It was a fenced-in area containing several acres of trucks and other rolling stock and a dozen enormous warehouses. During the war the depot had been a major supply base for the Allies in the Middle East. Now some of the stock was still being shipped to British forces in that part of the world. Other stock had been declared surplus and had been bought up by private consignees. There was always some measure of movement from the depot to the Famagusta harbor.

Mandria's Cyprus-Mediterranean Shipping Company was the agent for the British Army on Cyprus. In that capacity Mandria had a stock list and numbers of all the materials stored at the depot. He also had a very adequate supply of bills of lading.

On Thursday at 8:00 A.M., Ari Ben Canaan and thirteen Palmachniks, all dressed in British uniforms and carrying British papers, pulled to a halt before the main gate of the depot in a British truck. Zev Gilboa, Joab Yarkoni, and David Ben Ami were in the "working party."

Ari, who was carrying papers as "Captain Caleb Moore," presented a list of requisitions to the depot commander. Ari's "working party" had been detailed to gather the listed material and take it to the Famagusta docks for shipment aboard the SS *Achan*.

The forgeries were so perfect that the depot commander did not for a moment remember that Caleb was a spy for Moses in the Bible and that the *Achan*, a nonexistent ship, carried the same name as the man who stole the treasury at Jericho.

The first item the bills of lading called for was twelve trucks and two jeeps. They were rolled out of their parking area and checked out to "Captain Caleb Moore." The "working party" then moved from warehouse to warehouse, loading their twelve new trucks with everything that would be needed for the *Aphrodite/Exodus* to make her trip to Palestine with three hundred escapee children.

Joab Yarkoni, who was in charge of fitting the ship, had drawn up a list of things which included a late-model radio receiver and transmitter, canned foods, medical supplies, flashlights, small arms, water cans, blankets, air-conditioning units, a loud-speaker system, and a hundred other items. Joab was very sad because Ari had insisted he shave off his big black mustache. Zev's mustache met the same fate, for Ari feared this would identify them as Palestinians.

In addition to supplies for the *Exodus,* David took a few tons of the things most urgently needed in Caraolos.

Zev Gilboa nearly went to pieces when he saw the British arsenal. In all his years in the Palmach they had always needed arms, and the sight of so many lovely machine guns and mortars and carbines was almost more than he could stand.

The "working party" moved with clocklike precision. Ari knew from Mandria's lists where everything was located. Joab Yarkoni rounded out the afternoon's work by taking a few cases of scotch and a few of brandy and a few of gin and a few of wine—for medicinal purposes.

Twelve brand-new trucks crammed with supplies supposedly headed for the Famagusta harbor, where both supplies and trucks would be put aboard the SS *Achan.* Ari thanked the British commander for his excellent co-operation, and the "working party" left six hours after it had entered.

The Palmachniks were flushed with the ease of their initial victory, but Ari did not give them time to rest or be too proud of themselves. This was but a beginning.

The next stop of Operation Gideon was to find a base for the trucks and material they had stolen. Ari had the answer. He had located an abandoned British camp on the outskirts of Famagusta. It had apparently been used once by a small service unit. The fence was still up, two wooden office shacks and the outhouses remained. Electric wiring from the main line was still in.

During the night and for the next two nights all the Palmachniks from Caraolos came to this camp and labored feverishly pitching tents, cleaning the area, and generally making it appear to be once again in service.

The twelve trucks and two jeeps were painted the khaki color of the British Army. On the doors of each vehicle Joab Yarkoni drew an insignia which could be mistaken for any one of a thousand army insignias and the lettering: 23rd Transportation Company HMJFC.

The "company" office had enough actual and forged British papers and orders strewn about to give it an authentic look.

In four days the little camp with the twelve trucks looked quite natural and unimposing. They had taken enough British uniforms from the depot to dress the Palmachniks adequately as soldiers and enough of everything else to stock the camp completely.

As a finishing touch Joab Yarkoni put a sign over the entrance gate which read: 23rd Transportation Company HMJFC. Everyone sighed with relief as the sign raising officially dedicated the encampment.

Zev looked at the sign and scratched his head. "What does HMJFC stand for?"

"His Majesty's Jewish Forces on Cyprus . . . what else?" Joab answered.

The pattern of Operation Gideon was set. Ari Ben Canaan had had the utter audacity to form a fake unit of the British Army. Wearing a British uniform, he had established Mossad Aliyah Bet headquarters in broad daylight on the Famagusta road, and he was going to execute the final phases of his plan using British equipment. It was a dangerous game, yet he held to the simple theory that acting in a natural manner was the best cover an underground agent had.

The next phase of Operation Gideon became fact when three Americans from a merchant freighter landed in Famagusta and jumped ship. They were Mossad Aliyah Bet men who had received training during the war in the United States Navy. From another ship came two exiles of Franco Spain. Often former Spanish Loyalists worked Aliyah Bet ships. Now the *Exodus* had a crew, the balance of which would be filled out by Ari, David, Joab, and Zev.

Hank Schlosberg, the American skipper, and Joab set to the task of refitting the *Exodus* into an immigrant runner. Larnaca was a small port and Mandria certainly knew the right way to produce silence over any unusual activity around the *Aphrodite* at the end of the pier.

First the cabins, holds, and deck were stripped clean of cabinets, bins, shelves, furnishings, and trimmings. The ship was turned into a shell from stem to stern.

Two wooden shacks were constructed on deck to serve as toilets: one for the boys and one for the girls. The crew's mess hall was converted into a hospital room. There would be no formal mess hall or galley. All food would be eaten from cans. The galley was converted into an arsenal and storeroom. Crew's quarters were taken out. The crew would sleep on the small bridge. The loud-speaker system was hooked up. The ancient engine was overhauled thoroughly. An emergency mast and sail were constructed in case of engine failure.

There were Orthodox children among the three hundred, and this posed a particular problem. Yarkoni had to seek out the head of the Jewish community on Cyprus and have "kosher" food especially processed and canned for them according to dietary law.

Next an exact cubic measurement of the hold was taken, as well as a surface measurement of deck space. Shelves seventeen inches apart were built in the hold. These would serve as bunks and allow each child room to sleep on his stomach or back but not the luxury of rolling over. They computed an average height for the children and allotted four feet, eleven inches per child and marked it off down the shelves. The balance of the deck space in the hold and topside was also marked off, allowing a child just enough room to move an inch or two in each direction while asleep.

The lifeboats were repaired. Large holes were cut into the sides of the ship and wind pipes constructed so that air would be driven into the hold by electric fans. The air-conditioning units taken from the British depot were also fitted in. Air had to be circulated at all times in the packed quarters to prevent mass vomiting.

The work moved along smoothly. The sight of a half dozen men working on the old salvage tub appeared quite natural in the Larnaca harbor.

Loading supplies would pose another problem. Ari did not want to risk sending the khaki-colored trucks onto the dock, as he felt they were certain to attract attention. When the majority of the refitting had been completed the *Exodus* stole out of Larnaca each night to a rendezvous cove a few miles away in the Southern Bay. Here trucks from the 23rd Transportation Company HMJFC would come filled with supplies taken from the British depot. A constant stream of rubber boats moved from shore to ship all night until the *Exodus* was filled, inch by inch.

At the children's compound at Caraolos, Zev Gilboa carried out his part of Operation Gideon. He carefully screened three hundred of the strongest boys and girls and took them in shifts to the playground, where they were toughened up by exercises and taught how to fight with knives and sticks, how to use small arms and to throw grenades. Lookouts were posted all over the playground, and at sight of a British sentry a signal would change the games of war into games of peace. In three seconds the children could stop practicing gang fighting and start singing school songs. Groups not working out on the playground would be in the classroom learning Palestinian landmarks and the answers to mock questionings of "British Intelligence."

At night Zev would take them all to the playground and build a bonfire, and he and some of the Palmachniks would spin stories and tell the children how wonderful it would be for them in Palestine and how they would never live behind barbed wire again.

There was a hitch in Operation Gideon, but it developed among Ari's closest lieutenants: David, Zev, and Joab.

Although David was a sensitive boy and a scholar he feared no man when aroused. He was aroused now. The first expedition into the British depot had gone so well that he, Zev, and Joab felt it was sacrilegious to leave as much as a shoestring in it. He wanted to run 23rd Transportation Company trucks into the depot around the clock and take anything not nailed down. Zev envisioned even taking cannons. They had gone so long on so little that this windfall was too great a temptation.

Ari argued that greed could ruin the whole plan. The British were sleeping but not dead. Twenty-third Transportation Company trucks should appear from time to time for the sake of naturalness, but to attempt to drain the depot would be to hang them all.

None the less he could not hold them down. Their schemes began to sound wilder and wilder. Joab had got so cocky that he even went so far as to invite some British officers to the 23rd Transportation Company for lunch. Ari's patience ran out and he had to threaten to send them all back to Palestine in order to get them into line.

In a little over two weeks after the beginning of Operation Gideon everything was ready to go. The final phases of the plan—Mark Parker's story plus getting the three hundred children to Kyrenia—awaited word from the British themselves. The final move would be made when the British opened the new refugee camps on the Larnaca road and began transferring inmates from Caraolos.

CHAPTER NINETEEN: Caldwell, Sutherland's aide, went into the office of Major Allan Alistair, who was the Intelligence Chief on Cyprus. Alistair, a soft-spoken and shy-appearing man in his forties, gathered a batch of papers from his desk and followed Caldwell down the hall to Sutherland's office.

The brigadier asked Caldwell and Alistair to be seated and nodded to the intelligence man to begin. Alistair scratched the end of his nose and looked over his papers. "There has been a tremendous step-up of Jewish activity at Caraolos in the children's compound," he said in a half whisper. "We analyze it as a possible riot or breakout."

Sutherland drummed his fingers on the desk top impatiently. Alistair always made him nervous with his quiet, hush-hush ways and now he droned on through several more pages of information.

"Dear Major Alistair," Sutherland said when he had finished, "you have been reading to me for fifteen minutes and the theme of your story is that you suspect that some dire plot is being hatched by the Jews. During the past two weeks you have attempted to plant three men inside the children's compound and five men elsewhere inside Caraolos. Each one of your master spies has been detected within an hour and thrown out by the Jews. You have read to me two pages of messages which you have intercepted and which you cannot decode and you allege they are being sent from a transmitter you cannot locate."

Alistair and Caldwell glanced at each other quickly as if to say, "The old man is going to be difficult again."

"Begging the brigadier's pardon," Alistair said, leaning forward, "much of our information is always speculative. However, there has been concrete data handed down which has not been acted upon. We know positively that Caraolos is riddled with Palestinian Palmach people who are giving military training on the playground. We also know positively that the Palestinians smuggle their people into Cyprus at a place near the ruins of Salamis. We have every reason to suspect that the Greek chap, Mandria, is working with them."

"Blast it! I know all that," Sutherland said. "You men forget that the only thing that keeps those refugees from turning into a wild mob is the fact that these Palestinians are there. They run the schools, hospitals, kitchens, and everything else at that camp. Furthermore they keep discipline and they prevent escapes by letting only certain people go in and out. Throw the Palestinians out and we would be begging for trouble."

"Then hire some informers, sir," Caldwell said, "and at least know what they are planning."

"You can't buy a Jewish informer," Alistair said; "they stick together like flies. Every time we think we have one he sends us on a wild-goose chase."

"Then crack down on them," Caldwell snapped; "put the fear of God into them."

"Freddie, Freddie, Freddie," Sutherland said in dismay, lighting his pipe. "There is nothing we can do to frighten those people. They are graduates of concentration camps. You remember Bergen-Belsen, Freddie? Do you think we can do anything worse to them?"

Major Alistair was beginning to be sorry that he had asked Fred Caldwell to come in with him. He showed absolutely no latitude in his thinking. "Brigadier," Alistair said quickly, "we are all soldiers here. None the less I'd be less than honest if I reported to you that everything was peaceful at Caraolos and that I thought we'd be wise to continue to just sit and wait for trouble."

Sutherland rose, clasped his hands behind him, and began to pace the room thoughtfully. He puffed his pipe for several moments and tapped the stem against his teeth. "My mission here on Cyprus is to keep these camps quiet until our government decides what it intends to do with the Palestine mandate. We are not to risk anything that could bring adverse propaganda."

Fred Caldwell was angry. He simply could not understand why Sutherland chose to sit and let the Jews drum up trouble. It was beyond him.

Allan Alistair understood but did not agree. He favored a quick counterblow to upset any Jewish plans in Caraolos. None the less, all he could do was present the information; it was up to Brigadier Sutherland to act upon it. Sutherland, in his estimation, was being unreasonably soft.

"Is there anything else?" the brigadier asked.

"Yes, one more problem now, sir." Alistair thumbed through his papers. "I would like to know if the brigadier has studied the report on this American woman, Katherine Fremont, and the correspondent, Mark Parker?"

"What about them?"

"Well, sir, we are not certain if she is his mistress, but the fact that she has gone to work at Caraolos certainly coincides with his entry into Cyprus. From past experience we know that Parker has anti-British leanings."

"Rubbish. He is an excellent reporter. He did a splendid job at the Nuremberg trials. We made a costly blunder once in Holland and the man found it and reported it. That was his job."

"Are we correct in assuming, sir, that it is quite possible Mrs. Fremont's going to work in Caraolos may have something to do with helping Parker do an exposé of the camp?"

"Major Alistair, I hope that if you are ever brought to trial for murder the jury will not hang you on such evidence as you have just placed before me."

Little red patches dotted Alistair's cheeks.

"This Fremont woman happens to be one of the best pediatric nurses in the Middle East. She was cited by the Greek government for doing an outstanding job in an orphanage in Salonika. That is also in your report. She and Mark Parker have been friends since childhood. That is also in your report. It is also in your report that the Jewish welfare people sought her out. Tell me, Major Alistair . . . you do read your reports, don't you?"

"But . . . sir . . ."

"I haven't finished. Let us assume that the very worst of your suspicions are well founded. Let us assume that Mrs. Fremont is gathering information for Mark Parker. Let us say that Mark Parker writes a series of articles about Caraolos. Gentlemen, this is the end of 1946 . . . the war has been over for a year and a half. People are generally sick and tired of, and rather unimpressed with, refugee stories. What will impress people is our throwing an American nurse and newspaperman off Cyprus. Gentlemen, the meeting is concluded."

Alistair gathered his papers together quickly. Fred Caldwell had been sitting in cold and fuming anger. He sprang to his feet. "I say we kill a few of these sheenies and show them just who is running this show!"

"Freddie!"

Caldwell turned at the door.

"If you are so anxious I can arrange a transfer to Palestine. The Jews there are armed and they are not behind barbed wire. They eat little men like you for breakfast."

Caldwell and Alistair walked briskly down the hall. Freddie grumbled angrily under his breath. "Come into my office," Alistair said. Freddie flopped into a chair and threw up his hands. Alistair snatched a letter opener from his desk and slapped it in his open palm and paced the room.

"Ask me," Caldwell said, "they ought to give the old boy his knighthood and retire him."

Alistair returned to his desk and bit his lip hesitatingly. "Freddie, I've been thinking for several weeks. Sutherland has proven utterly impossible. I am going to write a personal letter to General Tevor-Browne."

Caldwell raised his eyebrows. "That's a bit risky, old boy."

"We must do something before this bloody island blows up on us. You are Sutherland's aide. If you back me up on this I'll guarantee there will be no repercussions."

Caldwell had had his fill of Sutherland. Alistair was a relative of General Tevor-Browne through marriage. He nodded. "And you might add a good word for me with Tevor-Browne."

A knock on the door brought in a corporal with a new batch of papers. He gave them to Alistair and left the office. Alistair thumbed through the sheets and sighed. "As if I didn't have enough on my mind. There is a ring of organized thieves on the island. They are so damned clever we don't even know what they are stealing."

General Tevor-Browne received Major Alistair's urgent and confidential report a few days later. His immediate reaction was to recall Alistair and Caldwell to London and to call them on the carpet for what amounted to mutiny; then he realized that Alistair would not have risked sending such a letter unless he was truly alarmed.

If Tevor-Browne was to follow the advice of Alistair and make a quick raid on Caraolos to upset any plans the Jews might have, he had to move quickly, for although he didn't know it, Ari Ben Canaan had set the day, hour, and minute for taking the children out of Caraolos.

The British announced that the new facilities near Larnaca

were ready and a general evacuation of many of the over-crowded compounds at Caraolos would begin in a few days. The refugees would be moved by truck at the rate of three to five hundred per day over a ten-day period. Ari chose the sixth day as the day.

No tunnels, no crates, no garbage dumps. Ari was just going to drive up to Caraolos and take the children out in British trucks.

CHAPTER TWENTY

DELIVER IN PERSON TO
KENNETH BRADBURY
CHIEF, ANS
LONDON BUREAU

Dear Brad:
This letter and enclosed report from Cyprus are being de-livered to you by F. F. Whitman, a pilot with British Inter-continental Airways.
D-Day on Operation Gideon is five days off. Cable me at once that you have received the report. I have used my own discretion on this thing. I feel that it can turn into something very big.
On D-Day I will send a cable to you. If my cable is signed MARK *that means that everything went off according to schedule and it is O.K. to release the story. If it is signed* PARKER *then hold off because that means something went wrong.*
I promised F. F. Whitman $500 for safe delivery of this to you. Pay the man, will you?

Mark Parker

MARK PARKER
DOME HOTEL
KYRENIA, CYPRUS

AUNT DOROTHY ARRIVED SAFELY IN LONDON AND WE WERE ALL HAPPY TO SEE HER. LOOKING FORWARD TO HEARING FROM YOU.

BRAD

Mark's story sat safely in the London ANS bureau, to be released on signal.

Kitty moved from the Dome Hotel to the King George in Famagusta when she went to work at Caraolos. Mark decided to stay put at the Dome in order to be on the spot in Kyrenia when the *Exodus* came in.

He had driven to Famagusta twice to see her. Both times she was out at the camp. Mandria confirmed what Mark suspected. The young refugee girl went to work as Kitty's aide. They were together all day long. Mark became worried. Kitty should have more sense than to try to bring her dead child to life through this girl. There seemed to him to be something unhealthy about it. In addition there was the business of her carrying forged papers out of Caraolos.

There were only a few days left until Operation Gideon moved into the final phase. The tension harassed Mark, and Kitty's strange behavior harassed him even more. He made a date to meet her at the King George in Famagusta.

As he drove to Famagusta his nerves were on edge. It had all gone too easily. Ben Canaan and his gang of bandits had run circles around the British. The British were aware that something was happening but they could not for the life of them seem to find the outside workers. Mark marveled at the finesse and skill of Ben Canaan and the courage of the Palmachniks. The outfitting of the *Exodus*, the training of the children had gone off perfectly. It would indeed be the biggest thing of his career, but because he was part of it all he was very worried.

He reached Famagusta and parked beside the King George Hotel, which was much like the Dome in that it sat on a beach with terraces overlooking the water. He found Kitty at a table looking out at the sea.

"Hello, Mark," she said, and smiled and kissed him on the cheek as he sat beside her.

He ordered drinks and lit a cigarette and one for Kitty. She was absolutely radiant. She seemed ten years younger than she had that first day in Kyrenia.

"I must say, you look the picture of happiness," she said in deference to his sour expression.

The drinks arrived.

"Are you on pins and needles for the big moment?"

"Sure, why not?" he snapped.

Their eyes met over the tops of their glasses. Kitty set hers down quickly. "All right, Mr. Parker. You are all lit up like a road sign. You'd better start talking before you explode."

"What's the matter? You mad at me? You don't like me any more?"

"For goodness' sake, Mark. I didn't think you were so thin skinned. I've been working very hard . . . besides, we agreed it would be best not to see too much of each other during the last two weeks, didn't we?"

"My name is Mark Parker. We used to be friends. We used to talk things over."

"I don't know what you're driving at."

"Karen . . . Karen Clement Hansen. A little refugee girl from Denmark via Germany."

"I don't think there is anything to discuss . . ."

"I think there is."

"She's just a lovely child I happen to like. She is my friend and I am her friend."

"You never could lie very well."

"I don't wish to talk about it!"

"You're asking for trouble. The last time you ended up naked with a marine in bed. This time I think you're going to have the strength to kill yourself."

Her eyes dropped away from Mark's glare. "Up to the past few weeks I've been so sane all my life," she said.

"Are you trying to make up for it all at once?"

She put her hand on his. "It has been like being born all over again and it doesn't make sense. She is such a remarkable girl, Mark."

"What are you going to do when she goes on the *Exodus*? Are you going to follow her to Palestine?"

Kitty squashed out her cigarette and drank her cocktail. Her eyes narrowed in an expression that Mark knew. "What have you done?" he demanded.

"She isn't going on the *Exodus*. That was my condition for going to work for Ari Ben Canaan."

"You damned fool . . . you damned fool, Kitty."

"Stop it!" she said. "Stop making something indecent out of this. I've been lonely and hungry for the kind of affection this girl has to give and I can give her the kind of understanding and companionship she needs."

"You don't want to be her companion. You want to be her mother."

"And what if I do! There's nothing wrong with that either."

"Look . . . let's stop yelling at each other . . . let's calm down. I don't know what you have figured out, but her father is probably alive. If he isn't, she has a family in Denmark. Exhibition number three . . . that kid is poisoned like they poison all of them. She wants Palestine."

Kitty's face became drawn and her eyes showed a return of sadness and Mark was sorry.

"I was wrong not to let her go on the *Exodus*. I wanted to have her for a few months . . . to gain her complete confidence . . . to let her know how wonderful it would be to go to America. If I could be with her a few months I'd be sure of myself. . . ."

"Kitty . . . Kitty . . . Kitty. She isn't Sandra. You've been looking for Sandra from the moment the war ended. You were looking for her in Salonika in that orphanage. Maybe that's why you had to take Ben Canaan's challenge, because there were children at Caraolos and you thought one of them might be Sandra."

"Please, Mark . . . no more."

"All right. What do you want me to do?"

"Find out if her father is alive. If he isn't, I want to adopt her and get her to the States."

"I'll do what I can," he said. He spotted Ari Ben Canaan, dressed as Captain Caleb Moore, coming through to their terrace. Ari walked quickly to their table and sat down. The Palestinian was his usual cold expressionless self. The instant Kitty saw him, her face lit up.

"David just contacted me from Caraolos. Something has come up that requires my immediate attention. I think under the circumstances that you had better come with me," he said to Kitty.

"What is it?" both Mark and Kitty said together.

"I don't know exactly. The Landau boy, the one who does our forgeries. He is now working on the transfer papers for getting the children out. He refuses to do any further work until he speaks to me."

"What do you want me for?" Kitty asked.

"Your friend, the little Danish girl Karen, is about the only person who can talk to him."

Kitty turned pale.

"We must have those papers completed in the next thirty-six hours," Ari said. "We may need you to talk to the boy through Karen."

Kitty stumbled from her chair and followed Ari blindly. Mark shook his head sadly, and his troubled glance remained on the empty doorway for many moments.

CHAPTER TWENTY-ONE: Karen stood in the classroom that was Palmach headquarters. She stared angrily at the boy with the soft face, blond hair, and sweet appearance. He was a little small for seventeen years and the softness was deceptive. A pair of icy blue eyes radiated torment, confusion, and hatred. He stood by a small alcove which held the papers and instruments he used for his forgeries. Karen walked up to him and shook a finger under his nose. "Dov! What have you gone and done?" He curled his lip and grunted. "Stop growling at me like a dog," she demanded. "I want to know what you have done."

He blinked his eyes nervously. No use arguing with Karen when she was angry. "I told them I wanted to talk with Ben Canaan."

"Why?"

"See these papers? They are forgeries of British mimeographed forms. Ben Ami gave me a list of three hundred kids here in our compound to be listed on these sheets for transfer to the new camp at Larnaca. They aren't going to the new camp. There's a Mossad ship out there someplace. It's going to Palestine."

"What about it? You know we don't question the Mossad or the Palmach."

"This time I do. Our name isn't listed. I'm not going to fix these papers unless they let us go too."

"You're not sure there is a ship. Even if there is and we don't go they have their reasons. Both of us have work to do right here in Caraolos."

"I don't care whether they need me or not. They promised to get me to Palestine and I'm going."

"Don't you think we owe these Palmach boys something for all they've done for us? Don't you have any loyalty at all?"

"Done for us, done for us. Don't you know yet why they're breaking their necks to smuggle Jews into Palestine? You really think they do it because they love us? They're doing it because they need people to fight the Arabs."

"And what about the Americans and all the others who aren't fighting Arabs? Why are they helping us?"

"I'll tell you why. They're paying for their consciences. They feel guilty because they weren't put into gas chambers."

Karen clenched her fists and her teeth and closed her eyes to keep herself from losing her temper. "Dov, Dov, Dov. Don't you know anything but hate?" She started for the door.

He rushed over and blocked her exit. "You're mad at me again," he said.

"Yes, I am."

"You're the only friend I've got, Karen."

"All you want to do is go to Palestine so you can join the terrorists and kill. . . ." She walked back into the room and sat down at a desk and sighed. Before her on the blackboard was this sentence chalked in block letters: THE BALFOUR DECLARATION OF 1917 IS THE BRITISH PROMISE OF A JEWISH HOMELAND IN PALESTINE. "I want to go to Palestine too," she whispered. "I want to go so badly I could die. My father is waiting there for me . . . I know he is."

"Go back to your tent and wait for me," Dov said. "Ben Canaan will be here soon."

Dov paced the room nervously for ten minutes after Karen had gone, working himself up to greater and greater anger.

The door opened. The large frame of Ari Ben Canaan passed through the doorway. David Ben Ami and Kitty Fremont followed him. David closed the door and locked it.

Dov's eyes narrowed with suspicion. "I don't want her in here," he said.

"I do," Ari answered. "Start talking."

Dov blinked his eyes and hesitated. He knew he couldn't budge Ben Canaan. He walked to the alcove and snatched up the mimeographed transfer sheets. "I think you have an Aliyah Bet ship coming into Cyprus and these three hundred kids are going on it."

"That's a good theory. Go on," Ari said.

"We made a deal, Ben Canaan. I'm not fixing these papers for you unless I add my name and the name of Karen Clement to this list. Any questions?"

Ari glanced at Kitty out of the corner of his eyes.

"Has it occurred to you, Dov, that no one can do your work and that we need you here?" David Ben Ami said. "Has it occurred to you that both you and Karen have more value here than in Palestine?"

"Has it occurred to you that I don't give a damn?" Dov answered.

Ari lowered his eyes to hide a smile. Dov was tough and smart and played the game rough. The concentration camps bred a mean lot.

"It looks like you're holding the cards," Ari said. "Put your name on the list."

"What about Karen?"

"That wasn't part of our deal."

"I'm making a new deal."

Ari walked up to him and said, "I don't like that, Dov." He towered over the boy threateningly.

Dov backed up. "You can beat me! I've been beaten by experts! You can kill me! I'm not afraid. Nothing you do can scare me after the Germans!"

"Stop reciting Zionist propaganda to me," Ari said. "Go to your tent and wait there. We'll give you an answer in ten minutes."

Dov unlocked the door and ran out.

"The little bastard!" David said.

Ari nodded quickly for David to leave the room. The instant the door closed Kitty grabbed Ari by the shirt. "She isn't going on that ship! You swore it! She is not going on the *Exodus*!"

Ari grabbed her wrists. "I'm not even going to talk to you unless you get control of yourself. We've got too much to cope with without a hysterical woman."

Kitty pulled her hands free with a fierce jerk.

"Now listen," Ari said, "I didn't dream this up. The finish of this thing is less than four days off. That boy has us by the throat and he knows it. We can't move unless he fixes those papers."

"Talk to him . . . promise anything, but keep Karen here!"

"I'd talk till I'm purple if I thought it would do any good."

"Ben Canaan . . . please . . . he'll compromise. He won't insist on Karen's going."

Ari shook his head. "I've seen hundreds of kids like him. They haven't left much in them that's human. His only link with decency is Karen. You know as well as I do he's going to be loyal to that girl. . . ."

Kitty leaned against the blackboard where the words: THE BALFOUR DECLARATION OF 1917 IS THE BRITISH PROMISE . . . were written. The chalk rubbed off on the shoulder of her dress. Ben Canaan was right; she knew it. Dov Landau was incorrigible but he did have a strange loyalty for Karen. Mark had been right. She had been a damned fool.

"There is only one way," Ari said. "You go to that girl and tell her the way you feel about her. Tell her why you want her to stay on Cyprus."

"I can't," Kitty whispered. "I can't." She looked up at Ben Canaan with a pathetic expression.

"I didn't want anything like this to happen," Ari said. "I am sorry, Kitty." It was the first time he had ever called her Kitty.

"Take me back to Mark," she said.

They walked into the hall. "Go to Dov," Ari said to David. "Tell him that we agree to his terms."

When Dov got the news he rushed over to Karen's tent and burst in excitedly. "We are going to Palestine," he cried.

"Oh dear," was all that Karen could say. "Oh dear."

"We must keep it quiet. You and I are the only ones among the children who know about it."

"When do we go?"

"A few more days. Ben Canaan is bringing some trucks up. Everyone will be dressed like British soldiers. They're going to pretend to be taking us to the new camp near Larnaca."

"Oh dear."

They went out of the tent, hand in hand. Dov looked out over the sea of canvas as he and Karen walked in and out among the acacia trees. They walked slowly toward the play-

111

ground, where Zev had a class of children practicing knife fighting.

Dov Landau walked on alone along the barbed-wire wall. He saw the British soldiers marching back and forth, back and forth. Down the long wall of barbed wire there was a tower and a machine gun and a searchlight.

Barbed wire—guns—soldiers——

When had he been outside of barbed wire? It was so very long ago it was hard to remember.

Barbed wire—guns—soldiers—— Was there a real life beyond them? Dov stood there and looked. Could he remember that far back? It was so long ago—so very long ago——

CHAPTER TWENTY-TWO

WARSAW, POLAND, SUMMER 1939
Mendel Landau was a modest Warsaw baker. In comparison with Dr. Johann Clement he was at the opposite end of the world—socially, financially, intellectually. In fact, the two men would have had absolutely nothing in common except that they were both Jews.

As Jews, each man had to find his own answer to the relationship between himself and the world around him. Dr. Clement clung to the ideals of assimilation up to the very end. Although Mendel Landau was a humble man he had thought out the problem, too, but had come to an entirely different conclusion.

Mendel Landau, unlike Clement, had been made to feel an intruder. For seven hundred years the Jews in Poland had been subjected to persecution of one kind or another, ranging from maltreatment to mass murder.

The Jews came to Poland originally to escape the persecution of the Crusaders. They fled to Poland from Germany, Austria, and Bohemia before the sword of "holy" purification.

Mendel Landau, like every Polish Jew, well knew what had followed the original flight of the Jews into Poland. They were accused of ritual murder and witchcraft and were loathed as business competitors.

An unbroken series of tribulations climaxed one Easter week when mobs ran through the streets dragging each Jew and his family from his home. Those who would not accept baptism were killed on the spot.

There was a Jew's tax. Jews were forced to wear a yellow cloth badge to identify themselves as a race apart. A thousand and one statutes and laws aimed at suppressing the Jews stood on the books. The Jews were moved into ghettos and

112

walled in to keep them isolated from the society around them.

In these ghettos something strange happened. Instead of dying slowly, the faith and culture of the Jews deepened and their numbers multiplied. Sealed off forcibly as they were from the outside world, the Jews turned more and more to the laws of Moses for guidance, and these laws became a powerful binding force among them. Inside the ghetto they governed themselves and developed closer-knit family and community ties which continued even after the ghettos were outlawed.

For those who ruled Poland the ghetto was only part of the answer of how to deal with the Jews. Jews were prevented by law from owning land or belonging to dozens of trades and crafts in which they might offer significant economic competition.

The Jews, locked in their ghettos, made ready scapegoats for any Polish disaster. Periodically mobs, goaded by blind hatred and fed on fear, tore into the ghettos and killed and whipped the Jews and smashed their homes and belongings until Jew beating became an accepted, if not honorable, pastime of the Poles.

Four centuries of Jew baiting came to a climax in 1648. During a Cossack uprising half a million Jews were slaughtered; the frenzy of the slaughterers was such that Jewish infants were often thrown into open pits and buried alive.

The Dark Ages, which came to an end in western Europe, seemed to linger on over the Polish ghettos. The enormous tragedy of 1648, together with hundreds of years of continuous persecution, created strange phenomena within the ghetto walls.

Throughout Jewish history, whenever events were black and hope all but vanished, a dozen or so self-styled "messiahs" would arise among the people and proclaim themselves their saviors. In this darkest of moments after the 1648 massacres a new group of "messiahs" stepped forward. Each claimed to have been sent in fulfillment of the prophecies of Isaiah. Each had a strong following.

With the messiahs came the Jewish mystics, a cult dedicated to finding Biblical explanations for the centuries of suffering. In their desperation for salvation the mystics concocted weird interpretations of the Bible based on mysticism, numerology, and just plain wishful thinking. They hoped through an involved system called the Cabala to find a way for God to lead them from the wilderness of death.

While the messiahs proclaimed themselves and the Cabalists looked for hidden meanings, a third sect arose in the ghettos: the Hasidim, who withdrew from the rigors of normal life and lived only for study and prayer. By submerging themselves in prayer they managed to lift themselves from the pain of reality into religious ecstasy.

Messiahs—Cabalists—Hasidim—all born of desperation.

Mendel Landau knew all this. He also knew there had been periods of enlightenment when the burden eased and the laws relaxed. Poland's own history was blood-marked. The Poles had struggled for freedom in a series of wars, revolutions, and plays of power. Parts of Poland's borders were torn away, and there was always an invasion—or the threat of invasion. During these Polish struggles the Jews took up arms and fought alongside the Poles, placing the cause of the larger nation above their own.

Much of what Mendel Landau knew was now ancient history. It was 1939 and Poland was a republic. He and his family no longer lived in a ghetto. There were over three million Jews in the country and they formed a vital part of the national life.

The oppression had not stopped with the formation of a republic. It only varied in degree. There was still unequal taxation for the Jews. There was still economic strangulation. The Jews continued to be blamed by most Poles for causing floods when it rained and drought when it was dry.

The ghetto was gone, but to Mendel Landau anywhere he lived in Poland was a ghetto. It was a republic, indeed, but since 1936 Mendel Landau had seen pogroms; and anti-Jewish rioting in Brzesc, Czestochowa, Brzytyk, Minsk Mazowiecki; and he knew the snarl of the hoodlums who specialized in smashing Jewish shops and cutting Jewish beards.

And so Mendel Landau and Johann Clement came to different conclusions. After seven centuries in Poland, Mendel Landau was still an intruder and he knew it.

He was a simple and rather modest man. Leah, his wife, was the plainest of women, a hard-working and devoted mother and wife.

Mendel Landau wanted something to give his children as a heritage. He did not have the fervor of the Hasidim for prayer, nor did he believe in messiahs or in the numerology of the Cabala.

Mendel retained only a measure of faith in his religion. He kept the Jewish holidays as most Christians keep Easter and Christmas. He accepted the Bible for its historical value as a story of his people rather than as a basis for worship. And so he could not offer his children even a deeply rooted religion.

What Mendel Landau gave his children was an idea. It was remote and it was a dream and it was unrealistic. He gave his children the idea that the Jews must someday return to Pales-

114

tine and re-establish their ancient state. Only as a nation could they ever find equality.

Mendel Landau worked hard as a baker. His world consisted of feeding a family and providing them with shelter, education, clothing, and love. He did not believe, in his wildest moments, that he would ever see Palestine, nor did he believe his children would ever see Palestine. But he did believe in the idea.

Mendel was not alone among the Polish Jews. Of Poland's three and a half million Jews, there were hundreds of thousands who followed the same star, and from them spouted the wellspring of Zionism. There were religious Zionists, labor Zionists, small militant Zionist groups, and middle-class merchant Zionists.

Because he was a trade unionist, Mendel's family belonged to a labor-Zionist group who called themselves the Redeemers. The entire social life of the Landaus revolved around the Redeemers. From time to time there were speakers from Palestine, there was recruiting work, there were books and pamphlets and discussions and songs and dances and endless hope to keep the idea alive. The Redeemers, like other Zionist groups, ran agricultural centers where boys and girls could be trained to work the land. And every so often the Redeemers sent a group to Palestine to cultivate newly purchased land.

There were six members of the Landau family. There were Mendel and his wife Leah. There was the oldest son, Mundek, who was a strapping boy of eighteen and a baker himself. Mundek was a natural leader and was a section head in the Redeemers. There were the two girls. Ruth, who was seventeen, was horribly shy as Leah had been. She was in love with Jan, who was also a leader of the Redeemers. Rebecca was fourteen, and there was little Dov, who was the baby of the family. He was ten and blond and wide-eyed and actually too young to be a member of the Redeemers. He idolized his big brother Mundek, who patronizingly allowed him to tag along to meetings.

SEPTEMBER 1, 1939

After manufacturing a series of border incidents the Germans invaded Poland. Mendel Landau and his eldest son Mundek went into the army.

The German Wehrmacht ripped Poland to shreds in a campaign that lasted only twenty-six days. Mendel Landau was killed in battle along with more than thirty thousand other Jewish soldiers who wore the uniform of Poland.

The Landaus were not allowed the luxury of prolonged sorrow for this was a time of peril. Mundek returned from the gallant but futile defense of Warsaw as head of the Landau family.

The same moment the Germans entered Warsaw, the Redeemers met to discuss a course of action. Most of Poland's Jews, being more hopeful than realistic, felt nothing would happen to them and adopted a "wait and see" attitude. The Redeemers and other Zionist groups throughout Poland were not so naïve. They were positive that grave danger lay ahead with Germans in occupation.

The Redeemers and many of the other Zionist groups decided to stay together and to take group action which would be binding on them all. Some groups chose to flee to the illusion of safety in the Soviet Union which had moved in to gobble up the eastern half of Poland when the Germans invaded. Other groups began an underground operation, and still others worked on the establishment of an "underground railway" for escape.

The Redeemers voted to remain in Warsaw and build up resistance inside the city and remain in contact with other Redeemer groups throughout Poland. Mundek was voted the military leader although he was not yet nineteen. Jan, Ruth's secret love, was made Mundek's second in command.

The moment the Germans established themselves in power and Hans Frank became governor, an immediate series of laws were levied against the Jews. Worship, forbidden; travel, limited; taxation, excessive. Jews were thrown out of public office, civil or elective. Jews were barred from bread-lines. Jews were barred from public places. Jews were taken out of schools.

There was talk of a revival of the ghetto.

With the restrictive laws the Germans embarked upon a campaign of "enlightenment" for the Polish population. This campaign fostered the already prevalent opinion that the Jews had started the war; and the Germans claimed further that the Jews were responsible for the German invasion, which was designed to save Poland from "Jewish Bolsheviks." Warsaw and the other cities were plastered with posters depicting bearded Jews violating nuns and other scenes of Jewish "depravity." Beard cutting, profaning synagogues, and public indignities against the Jews were encouraged.

BERLIN, GERMANY

In Berlin the top Nazi officials wrestled with the "Jewish problem." Several theories were advanced. Heydrich, the SD Chief, favored holding the Jews for ransom and then deporting them en masse. Schacht, the financial wizard, preferred a slow draining of the financial assets of the Jews. Many ideas were presented and discussed. An old plan of shipping all the Jews to the island of Madagascar was revived for consideration. Others would have preferred to send the Jews to Palestine, but the British blockade made that impossible.

SS Colonel Eichmann had long done "resettlement" work among the Jews. He had been born in Palestine and spoke fluent Hebrew and therefore seemed the most obvious man to be put in charge of the final solution of the Jewish problem. Headquarters were established at Kurfuerstenstrasse 46. The first thing that was apparent was that until a final solution was reached a mass resettlement program was called for. Most of the Nazis agreed that Poland was the natural place for resettlement. First, there were already three and a half million Jews in Poland. Second, they would encounter little or no public indignation as they would in western Europe.

Hans Frank, the German governor, objected to having more Jews dumped in Poland. He had tried to starve the Polish Jews and he had shot and hanged as many as he could. But Frank was overruled by the top planners in Berlin.

The Germans cast a dragnet all over Poland to catch the Jews. Raiding parties tore into villages and the smaller towns and rounded up the Jews at a moment's notice. They were packed onto freight trains, often without being able to take anything with them, and sent to the large population centers.

A few Jews learned of the roundups in advance and either fled or tried to buy their way into Christian homes. Very few Poles ran the risk of harboring a Jew. Others extorted every penny from the Jews and then turned them over to the Germans for a reward.

Once the Jews were "resettled," an edict was issued ordering every Jew to wear a white arm band bearing a Star of David.

Poland wasn't like Denmark. The Poles made no objection to the edict, and the Jews wore the arm band and the Star of David on their backs as well.

WARSAW, WINTER 1939

These were hard and bitter days for the Landau family. The death of Mendel Landau, renewed talk of reviving the ghetto, the resettlement program of the Germans, and the shortages made life very difficult.

One morning, early in 1940, there was a knock on the door of the Landau home. Polish Blue Police who worked with the Germans were outside. They abruptly informed Leah Landau that she had two hours to pack her belongings and move to another section of Warsaw which had been set aside for the Jews. There would be no compensation for the house and barely time to gather together what Leah had saved in over

117

twenty years of married life. The Landaus and all the rest of the Jews in Warsaw were resettled in an area in the center of the city near the main rail line.

Mundek and Jan moved quickly and were able to get an entire three-story building to serve as home and headquarters for over a hundred members of the Redeemers. The Landau family of five had a single room furnished with cots and a pair of chairs. The bathroom and kitchen were shared with ten other families.

The Jews were pressed into a tiny area that ran only twelve blocks in length from Jerozolimksa Street to the cemetery and was a bare six blocks wide. The Redeemers were situated in the Brushmakers' district on Leszno Street. Leah had managed to hoard a few jewels and valuables which might be useful later, although there was no immediate financial need, for Mundek continued to work as a baker and the Redeemers pooled their food resources in a common kitchen.

Jews from the provinces poured into Warsaw. They came in long lines, carrying all they were allowed to take in sacks or wheelbarrows or pushcarts. They unloaded in trainload after trainload at the siding near the Jews' quarters. The small area became packed. Jan's family moved in with the Landau family. There were nine now in the single room. The romance between Ruth and Jan became an open secret.

The Germans had the Jews set up a council to govern their area, but it quickly became an instrument for carrying out German orders. Other Jews who felt it better to "go along" with the Germans joined a special Jewish police force. The population in the compressed area swelled to over half a million people.

At the end of 1940, one year after the conquest of Poland, the Germans put many thousands of Jews into forced-labor battalions. A brick wall ten feet high was built around the Jewish area in Warsaw. Barbed wire was strung atop the wall. The fifteen exits were guarded by Polish Blues and by Lithuanians. *The ghetto had returned to Poland!* Almost all traffic from the ghetto outside the wall ceased. Mundek, who had held a job on the outside, was now unemployed. Rations inside the ghetto were cut to a level that could barely feed half the population. The only families who seemed to stand a chance of obtaining food were those who held "labor" cards and worked in one of the dozen forced-labor battalions or industries.

The creation of the ghetto brought panic. Some Jews began to trade their fortunes for food and some tried to escape to Christian homes. But most escape attempts ended in death or betrayal from the other side of the wall. Life inside the wall gradually became a day-to-day struggle to stay alive.

Mundek Landau emerged as a leader. Because of his importance among the Redeemers he obtained a license from the Jewish Council to run one of the few ghetto bakeries. Thus, through a continuation of united action, his group managed to keep alive and fed.

All was not blackness inside the ghetto. A very fine symphony orchestra gave weekly concerts, schools ran on schedule, little-theater groups were formed. There was always a choice of debates and lectures. A ghetto newspaper was printed and ghetto money became a legal means of exchange. Secret religious services were held. The Redeemers played a major part in keeping these services and activities going. Although little Dov wanted to be more active in the Redeemers, the rest of the Landau family forced him to get as much schooling as he could.

MARCH 1941

Eighteen months after the invasion of Poland, the final decision for a solution of the Jewish problem was handed down by Adolf Hitler. The order was verbal. Six weeks later SD Chief Heydrich announced the *Fuehrer*'s decision at a secret conference of SS, SD, and other Nazi officials at Gross-Wannsee.

The final solution was genocide.

SS Colonel Eichmann, the resettlement expert, was put in charge of eradicating the Jews from the face of Europe.

Within a few months the *Einsatzkommandos*—Action Commandos—were mobilized into *Einsatzgruppen*—Special Action Groups—and they swept into Poland, the Baltics, and occupied Russian territory on their mission of genocide. The initial efforts of the Special Action Groups followed a pattern. They rounded up Jews, took them to an isolated area, and forced them to dig their own graves. They stripped them and forced them to kneel beside their graves and shot them in the head.

The climax of the activities of the Special Action Commandos took place in the Russian city of Kiev in a suburb called Babi Yar where thirty-three thousand Jews were rounded up and shot over immense pits in a period of two days.

The *Einsatzgruppen* had a great measure of success because there was no opposition from the local population, which, to some degree, shared the Germans' feelings toward the Jews. The massacre of Babi Yar was carried out midst the cheers of many approving Ukrainians.

It became apparent that the methods of the *Einsatzkommandos* were not sufficient for the over-all plan of genocide. Shooting was slow and clumsy. Furthermore, the Jews were

119

not complying by starving to death in large enough numbers.

Eichmann, Paul Blobel, Himmler, Streicher, and dozens of other top Nazis worked out a huge master plan. The plan called for careful selection of secluded sites near railheads and population centers. Camps to be built on these sites would be designed by the best engineers at the lowest cost so that the executions could be carried out on an assembly-line basis.

Top personnel from old established concentration camps inside Germany would be promoted to take over the new establishments.

WINTER 1941

The Warsaw ghetto saw death in numbers that eclipsed even those in the pits at Babi Yar. People by the tens and hundreds and thousands starved or froze to death. Infants too weak to cry died by the hundreds, and old men died by the hundreds too weak to pray. Every morning the streets of the ghetto were strewn with new corpses. The sanitation teams walked through the streets with shovels and stacked the corpses onto pushcarts. Infants, children, women, men: piled up and wheeled off to the crematoriums to be burned.

Dov was now eleven years old. He quit school to prowl for food when Mundek's bakery was closed. Even groups like the Redeemers were in dire straits. Dov learned the tricks of staying alive in a ghetto. He moved about, listened, and acted with the cunning of a wily animal. The Landau kettle was empty for long periods of time. When none of the family or the Redeemers could get together a meal Leah traded off a piece of her hoarded jewelry for food.

It was a long and a cruel winter. Once, when they had gone for five days without food, the Landaus finally had a meal, but Leah's wedding band was missing from her hand. Then their fortunes took an upswing, for the Redeemers got hold of a horse. It was old and bony and forbidden by their religion as food, but it tasted wonderful.

Ruth was nineteen. When she married Jan that winter she was too thin to be really pretty. They spent their honeymoon in the single room they shared with the four other Landaus and three members of his family. But apparently the young couple was able to find some time alone somewhere, for in the springtime Ruth was pregnant.

One of Mundek's major responsibilities as leader of the Redeemers was keeping contact with the outside. Money could be used to bribe the Polish Blue Guards and the Lithuanians, but Mundek reckoned that the money should be saved for more important things. He set out to establish routes in and out of the ghetto "under the wall" through the sewers. It was

120

dangerous to go into Warsaw, for Polish hoodlum gangs were constantly on the lookout for escaped Jews to extort or turn in for reward money.

The Redeemers had lost five members who had been caught beyond the wall. The last one, captured by hoodlums and turned over to the Gestapo and subsequently hanged, was Ruth's husband, Jan.

Little Dov was wise to the ways of survival. He went to Mundek with the proposition that he be allowed to take up the job of courier through the sewers. Mundek would not hear of it at first but Dov persisted. His blond hair and blue eyes made him the least Jewish-looking of them all. He would be least suspect because of his age. Mundek knew that Dov was cagey and competent, but his heart would not let him let his younger brother do it. Then, when Mundek lost his sixth and seventh courier inside of a few days, he decided to let Dov have a try. Mundek reckoned that they all flirted with death each day anyhow. Leah understood and did not object.

Dov proved to be the best courier in the ghetto. He established a dozen alternate routes "under the wall." He became at home in the fetid, slimy, putrid waters that ran beneath Warsaw. Each week Dov took that journey in the blackness through shoulder-high filth. Once "under the wall" he made his way to an apartment at Zabrowska 99 to a woman he knew only as Wanda. After a meal he would return to the sewer, carrying with him pistols, ammunition, money, radio parts, and news from other ghettos and from the partisans.

When he wasn't making his weekly trip Dov liked to stay at Redeemer headquarters where Mundek and Rebecca spent most of their time. Rebecca's job was forging travel passes and passports. Dov liked to watch her and soon began working along with her. It was not long before it was discovered that Dov had a remarkable aptitude for copying and duplicating. His eye was sharp and his hand was steady, and at the age of twelve he was soon the best forger among the Redeemers.

LATE SPRING 1942

The Germans took a significant step toward the "final solution" of the Jewish problem by erecting several camps designed for the carrying out of mass exterminations. To handle the Jews from the Warsaw area, thirty-three acres were set aside in a place secluded from general view, called Treblinka. Two main buildings contained thirteen gas chambers. There were quarters here for workers and German personnel and there were enormous field plots for burning corpses. Treblinka, one of the first such camps, was a forerunner of more efficient models that followed.

July brought a day of mourning for all Jews. Those in the Warsaw ghetto and the other ghettos in Poland mourned perhaps more deeply than other Jews. It was the day of Tisha B'Ab, an annual Jewish holiday commemorating the destruction of the Temples by the Babylonians and Romans in Jerusalem. For the fall of Jerusalem to the Roman invaders nearly two thousand years before had signaled the end of the Jews as a nation. The Jews were thenceforth dispersed to the far corners of the earth. They were, from that day on, a Diaspora.

Tisha B'Ab 1942 coincided with major steps in the "final solution" of the Jewish problem.

As the Jews of Warsaw mourned both their ancient and present plight German patrols whisked into the ghetto and stopped before the building housing the Jewish Council. To all outward appearances the Germans seemed to be making another roundup for the forced-labor battalions. But this time something sinister was in the air. For the Germans wanted only old people and very young people. Panic swept through the ghetto as oldsters were herded in and the Germans sought out children, most of whom were torn from their mothers' arms.

Those rounded up were gathered at the Umschlagplatz and then marched off to Stawki Street near the rail sidings, where a long line of freight cars stood in readiness. Dazed and shocked crowds gathered. Some frantic parents were kept separated from their children at gun point, and several times the Germans shot to kill.

The children were laughing and singing. The German guards had promised them a picnic in the country. This was an event! Many of them could hardly remember being outside the ghetto.

As the train rolled off toward Treblinka the "final solution" was at hand. Tisha B'Ab—1942.

Two weeks later Dov Landau came back from Wanda's apartment at Zabrowska 99 with a shocking report. The report stated that those who had been rounded up on Tisha B'Ab and in five subsequent roundups had been sent off to death in gas chambers in a place called Treblinka. Further information from other ghettos around Poland reported the existence of other such camps: Belzec and Chelmno in the Cracow area, and Maidanek near the city of Lubin were in operation or being readied. It appeared, said the report, that a dozen more camps were under construction.

Mass murder in gas chambers? It did not seem possible! Mundek, as head of the Redeemers, met with half a dozen other Zionist groups in the ghetto and issued a joint decree for everyone to stage an immediate uprising and break through the wall.

The plea was emotional rather than practical. The Jews had nothing to fight with. Furthermore, everyone who held a card in a labor battalion had convinced himself that it was a passport to life.

The main reason that no uprising could be staged was that there was no support for it in Poland outside the ghetto. In France, the Vichy government had absolutely refused the Germans' demands that French Jews be turned over to them. In Holland, the unanimous feeling of all the citizens was to hide their Jews. In Denmark, the King not only defied German edicts but the Danes evacuated their entire Jewish population to safety in Sweden.

If the Poles did not agree to the extermination of their Jews, they did not disagree. If they disagreed, they did nothing to show it. Only a very small minority of Polish people would shelter an escaped Jew.

Inside the ghetto, each different organized group of Jews embraced a different philosophy. The religious and the labor people argued. The conservatives and the left-wingers argued. Jews liked to argue. In ghetto life argument and debate had always been a great pastime. But now the time of greatest peril had come. Mundek's Redeemers joined all the diversified groups in forming a unified command. The combined organizations carried the initials ZOB, and had the momentous task of saving the rest of the Jews in the ghetto.

Dov made one trip after another to Wanda's apartment at Zabrowska 99. On each trip through the sewers he carried a message from ZOB to the Polish underground begging for help and for arms. Most of the messages were never answered. The few answers that were received were evasive.

Throughout that horrible summer while the Germans continued rounding up Jews for Treblinka the ZOB worked desperately to stave off total annihilation.

One day early in September, Dov had a particularly dangerous trip into Warsaw. After leaving Wanda's he was spotted by four hooligans who chased him into a dead-end alley and demanded to see his papers proving he wasn't a Jew. The boy had his back to the wall, and his tormentors closed in on him to pull off his pants to see the circumcision, the sure identification of a Jew. As they set to pounce, Dov took out a pistol he was carrying back to the ghetto and with it killed one of the hooligans and chased the others off. He darted away and soon found the safety of the sewer.

Back at Redeemer headquarters the boy broke down under delayed shock. Mundek tried to comfort him. Dov always felt warm and wonderful with his brother near. Mundek was

123

almost twenty-one now, but he was gaunt and always tired-looking. He had been a good leader and he worked beyond the limits of exhaustion. He had kept almost the entire Redeemer group intact and had never let their fighting spirit flag. The brothers talked quietly. Dov calmed down. Mundek put his arm around Dov's shoulder and they walked from headquarters to their apartment. Mundek talked about Ruth's baby, which was due in a few weeks, and how wonderful it was going to be for Dov to be an uncle. Of course, everyone in the Redeemers would be aunt and uncle to the baby but Dov would be the real one. There had been many marriages in the group and there were already three babies—all new Redeemers. Ruth's baby would be the finest of them all. Things were bright, Mundek told Dov, because they had found another horse and there would be a real feast. Dov's trembling passed away. As they neared the top of the stairs Dov smiled at Mundek and told his brother that he loved him very much.

The instant they opened the door and saw the expression on Rebecca's face they knew disaster had struck. Mundek finally got his sister coherent enough to talk.

"Mother and Ruth," she cried. "They were taken out of the factory. Their work cards were invalidated and they were marched off to the Umschlagplatz."

Dov wheeled around for the door. Mundek grabbed him. The boy screamed and kicked.

"Dov! Dov! There is nothing we can do!"

"Momma! Momma! I want to go to Momma!"

"Dov! Dov! We can't look at her being taken away!"

Ruth, eight months pregnant, cheated the gas chambers of Treblinka. She died in the agony of childbirth and her baby died with her in a cattle car so packed it was impossible for her to lie down.

At Treblinka, SS Colonel Wirth, the commandant, was furious. There had been another breakdown in the mechanism at the main gas chambers and another trainload of Jews was en route from the Warsaw ghetto. Wirth had been proud that Treblinka had the best record for dispensing "special treatment" of all the camps in Poland. His engineers informed him that it would be impossible to get things into working order again before the train arrived from Warsaw.

To make matters worse, both SS Colonel Eichmann and Himmler himself were due on personal inspection tours. Wirth had planned to hold special gassings in their honor.

He was forced to round up all the old, obsolete gas vans he could find in the area and send them to the rail siding to meet the train. Generally the covered vans could accommodate only twenty people, but this was an emergency. By forcing the victims to hold their hands over their heads the Germans could make space for another six or eight Jews. The Germans discovered that there were still several inches between the tops of the heads and the ceiling of the van. In this space they packed another eight or ten children.

Leah Landau was in a daze of grief over Ruth's death as the train pulled to a siding near Treblinka. She and thirty others were taken from the cattle car and forced with whips, clubs, and dogs to get into one of the waiting vans and hold their hands high. When the van held an absolute maximum the iron door was shut. The truck started into motion, and in a matter of seconds the iron cage was filled with carbon monoxide. Everyone inside the van was dead by the time the trucks entered Treblinka and halted before the open pits where the bodies were unloaded and the gold extracted from the victims' mouths.

At least Leah Landau had cheated the Germans, for her gold teeth had been extracted long before and exchanged for food.

Winter was coming once again and the German roundups were becoming more and more frequent.

The entire ghetto moved into cellars, taking everything of value with them. The cellars expanded and some, like the Redeemers', became elaborate bunkers. Dozens, then hundreds, of bunkers sprouted and connecting tunnels began to weave through the earth.

The sweeps of the Germans and their Polish Blues and Lithuanians netted fewer and fewer Jews for Treblinka.

The Germans became angered. The bunkers were so well concealed they were nearly impossible to locate. At last the commander of Warsaw himself entered the ghetto one day to speak to the leader of the Jewish Council. He was angry and demanded that the Jewish Council assist the Germans in speeding up the resettlement program by locating the cowards who hid from "honest labor." For over three years the Jewish Council had been trapped and torn between carrying out German edicts on the one hand and trying to save their people on the other. Now, shortly after the German demand for assistance, the leader of the Jewish Council committed suicide.

It was winter in the ghetto again.

Mundek's Redeemers were assigned to plan the defense of a section of the Brushmakers' district. Dov spent his time either in the sewers or in the bunker forging travel passes. Actually his trips "under the wall" allowed him one or two decent meals a week at Wanda's. On his trips out of the ghetto he now led old people or others unfit for combat. On his trips in he carried arms and radio parts.

During the winter of 1943 the death rate became appalling. Out of an original five hundred thousand who had been put into the ghetto, only fifty thousand were alive by the end of the year.

One day in mid-January, Mundek and Rebecca took Dov aside before he was scheduled to descend into the sewer on a trip to Wanda's.

"It seems that we don't have much of a chance just to sit around and talk these days," Mundek said.

"Dov," Rebecca said, "we all talked it over here and took a vote while you were in Warsaw the last time. We have decided that we want you to stay on the other side of the wall."

"You have something special for me to do?" Dov asked.

"No . . . you don't understand."

"What do you mean?"

"We mean," Rebecca said, "that we have decided to send certain members out to stay."

Dov didn't understand it. He knew the Redeemers needed him. No one in the entire ZOB knew the sewer routes as well as he did. If the ZOB was preparing to stage a defense then he would be more valuable than ever. Besides, the papers and travel passes he forged had helped get over a hundred people out of Poland. Dov looked at his sister and brother questioningly.

Rebecca pressed an envelope into Dov's hands. "You have money there and papers. Stay with Wanda until she can find you a Christian family to live with."

"You didn't take a vote. This is your idea and Mundek's. I won't go."

"You will go and that is an order," Mundek said.

"It is not an order," Dov answered.

"It is an order from me as head of the Landau family!"

The three of them stood in the tiny earthen room in one corner of the bunker. It was very quiet. "It is an order," Mundek repeated.

Rebecca put her arms around Dov and stroked his blond hair. "You have grown up, Dov. We have not had much chance to spoil you, have we? I have watched you go into the sewers a hundred times and I have watched you bring us stolen food. We haven't given you much of a boyhood."

"It is not your fault."

"Dov," Mundek said. "Please don't deny Rebecca and me this one thing we want. We have not given you much. You must let us try to give you your life."

"Mundek, Rebecca. I don't care as long as I am with you."

"Please . . . please . . . understand us. One of the Landau family must live. We want you to live for us all."

Dov looked at the brother he worshiped. Mundek's eyes pleaded.

"I understand," Dov whispered. "I will live."

He looked at the package and slipped it into a canvas so that it wouldn't get wet in the sewers. Rebecca crushed his head against her bosom. "We will meet in Eretz Israel," she said.

"Yes . . . in the land of Israel."

"You have been a good soldier, Dov," Mundek said. "I am proud. *Shalom, l'hitraot.*"

"*Shalom, l'hitraot,*" Dov repeated.

Dov Landau spent his thirteenth birthday in the sewers beneath Warsaw wading to Wanda's apartment with a heart so heavy it nearly broke. In another day and another world it would have been his *bar mitzvah.*

JANUARY 18, 1943

Three days after Dov left the ghetto for the temporary safety of Wanda's apartment the Germans, Polish Blues, and Lithuanians converged on the ghetto. With only fifty thousand Jews left they began rounding up Jews for the final phase of the "final solution."

The Germans and their cohorts ran into a hail of bullets from ZOB defensive positions. They fled, leaving heavy casualties.

The news spread through Warsaw like wildfire!

The Jews were staging an uprising!

That night every ear in Warsaw was tuned to the secret ZOB radio which repeated this appeal over and over and over again:

"Fellow Poles! Today we struck a blow against tyranny! We ask all our brothers outside the ghetto to arise and strike against the enemy! Join us!"

The appeal fell on deaf ears. But from ZOB headquarters on Mila Street the flag of the Star of David was raised. Alongside it fluttered the flag of Poland. The Jews of the ghetto had chosen to fight to the death beneath a banner which had been denied them in life.

CHAPTER TWENTY-THREE: The Germans were chagrined at having been chased from the ghetto. Konrad, Gestapo chief of the ghetto security detail, reported to Hans Frank, the governor of Poland, that the matter would be cleared up in two or three days. The Polish people, who had been told previously that the Jews were cowards, were now told that the fighting had been the work of a few lunatics and sex deviates—the types who raped Polish girls.

ZOB assumed control of the ghetto and disposed of the Jewish Council. The fighters made a swift and merciless reprisal on all known collaborators and then moved into set defensive positions.

Hans Frank decided he would not play into ZOB's hand by making an attack on the ghetto. The Germans decided to laugh off the attack and minimize it. They cut loose with a propaganda barrage and asked the people of the ghetto to come forth for voluntary resettlement and guaranteed they would be given decent treatment in exchange for "honest labor."

ZOB issued an order informing the Jews remaining in the ghetto that they would be shot if they conformed with the German request. There would be no more evacuation.

After two weeks of quiet the Germans moved patrols in once again to round up Jews. This time they came heavily armed and moved with extreme caution. From carefully prepared positions the ZOB opened fire. Again the Germans fled beyond the wall.

The Germans decided to think it all over. Their press and radio were indignant over the Jewish Bolsheviks who were causing all the trouble. While the Germans wailed the ZOB tightened their defensive setups and desperately continued to plead for help from the Polish underground. They expanded their plea to the general public, but no arms came, no underground help came, and only a few dozen volunteers crossed into the ghetto "under the wall" to fight.

The German staff mapped one big crushing assault to wipe out the remains of the ghetto. The day they picked for the attack was the beginning of Passover, the Jewish holiday celebrated in commemoration of the exodus of the Jews from Egypt under the leadership of Moses.

At three o'clock in the morning, three thousand crack SS troops flanked with Polish Blues and Lithuanians threw a ring around the entire ghetto. Dozens of searchlights crisscrossed to pick out possible targets for German mortars and light artillery. The barrage lasted until daylight.

At dawn the SS launched their assault over the wall. Converging from several sides they penetrated deep into the heart of the ghetto without resistance.

From hidden barricades, from house tops, from windows, the ZOB—men and women—turned loose a barrage of small-arms fire at point-blank range against the trapped and surrounded Germans. For the third time the Germans scurried from the ghetto.

In blind fury the Germans came back into the ghetto with

tanks, and the tanks were met with a storm of gasoline-filled bottles which turned the iron monsters into flaming coffins. With the tanks disabled the German SS troops were forced to flee again; this time they left several hundred dead in the streets.

The ZOB fighters rushed out of hiding to take the German guns as well as their uniforms.

Konrad was dismissed and SS General Stroop was called in to take command. He was ordered to destroy the ghetto so thoroughly that no one would ever again dare challenge the power of the Nazis.

Stroop mounted attack after attack, day after day. Each new attack utilized a different strategy and hit from a different direction. Each attack and each patrol met the same fate. They were repulsed by the ZOB, whose members fought like madmen—house by house, room by room, step by step. They refused to be taken alive. Homemade land mines and booby traps, violent counterattacks, raw courage beat the Germans out of the ghetto every time they entered. Ten days passed and the Germans were desperate for a victory. They made a concerted attack on the ghetto's lone hospital—entered, shot every patient, blew up the building, and claimed they had destroyed ZOB headquarters.

ZOB teams dressed in uniforms of German soldiers they had killed and used this device to trick, trap, and ambush their enemy. They crossed out of the ghetto time and time again to hit the Germans from the rear by raiding their arsenals.

The Germans continued their attacks and soon, by the sheer weight of their numbers and arms, made themselves felt. The ZOB could not replace a fallen fighter; once a defensive position was destroyed there was no choice but to retrench; they could not replace ammunition as fast as they were expending it. Still, with the power on their side, the Germans were unable to get a foothold inside the ghetto. ZOB began calling upon many of the Jews not in fighting units to escape into Warsaw, for there were not enough rifles to go around.

Wearing a captured uniform, Mundek led an attack on the Pawiak Prison and freed all the inmates.

The three-day cleanup Konrad had promised had stretched into two weeks. On the fifteenth day after the first German assault Rebecca Landau was fighting in a building in the Brushmakers' district a few blocks from Redeemer headquarters. A direct mortar hit killed every defender but her. Under sustained mortar fire the walls of the building collapsed and she was forced into the street. As the Germans closed in on her and cut off all possibilities of retreat, she

129

reached beneath her dress and withdrew a hand grenade. Running at three Germans, she pulled the pin, and killed them and herself.

After three weeks Stroop was forced to change his tactics. He had drawn heavy casualties and the Nazis were unable to cover up the valiant action of the Jews with propaganda. Stroop pulled his troops back, reinforced the ring of men and armor surrounding the ghetto, and declared a state of siege. He brought in heavy artillery which blasted into the ghetto at near point-blank range in a determined effort to knock down all the buildings which the Jews had used so well as defensive positions. By night Heinkel bombers saturated the ghetto area with incendiary bombs.

Mundek returned to the Redeemer bunker after a staff meeting at ZOB headquarters. He and his fighters were half dead with exhaustion, hunger, and thirst. Many were badly burned. They gathered around him.

"German artillery has knocked down just about every building. What is standing is burning," he said.

"Have we been able to establish contact with the underground?"

"Oh yes . . . we've made contact, but they aren't going to help us. We cannot expect any more food, ammunition, or water than what we have on hand. Our communications are about ruined. In short, my friends, we can no longer fight according to a fixed plan. Each bunker is on its own. We will try to keep contact with ZOB through runners, but we will each plan and execute our own ambushes and encounters with the Germans when they come back."

"How long can we hold out like this, Mundek? We have only thirty people left and ten pistols and six rifles."

Mundek smiled. "All of Poland held out for only twenty-six days. We have done that well already." Mundek assigned his guards, rationed what little food was left, and mapped out a dawn patrol.

Ryfka, one of the girls, picked up a battered accordion and began playing a soft, slow tune. In that dank and slimy bunker ten feet beneath the earth the remaining Redeemers sang in a strange and wistful blend of voices. They sang a song that they had learned as children at Redeemer meetings. The song told them that the land in Galilee in Eretz Israel was beautiful and that wheat grew in the fields and the grain bent softly in the wind. In a bunker in the Warsaw ghetto they sang of the fields of Galilee that they knew they would never see.

"Alert!" a sentry called down as he spotted a lone figure weaving in and out of the flames and rubble.

The lights went out and the bunker became black and

silent. There was a knock in code. The door opened and closed and the lights were turned on again.

"Dov! For God's sake! What are you doing here?"

"Don't send me away again, Mundek!"

The two brothers embraced and Dov wept. It felt good to have Mundek's arms around him again. Everyone gathered about Dov as he relayed the final tragic news that the Polish underground definitely would not come in and that everyone else on the outside was being very quiet about the uprising.

"When I came back," Dov said, "the sewers were filled with people just lying in the muck. They are too weak to stand up. They have no place to go. No one wants them in Warsaw."

And so little Dov returned to the ghetto and a very strange thing happened. All over Warsaw and the surrounding countryside Jews who had managed to escape and live as Christians were beginning to return to the ghetto for the last-ditch stand. They had concluded that it was a privilege to be able to die with dignity.

MAY 1943

At last the furious bombardment stopped.

The fires went out.

Stroop moved his SS troops in once again, but this time they held all the cards. The Jews had no defensive positions or communications or fixed plans and almost no food, water, or arms. The Germans worked systematically, cutting off one section at a time and cleaning out bunkers one by one with cannon fire and flame throwers until the section was completely destroyed.

They tried hard to capture prisoners to torture into revealing the exact location of the bunkers, but the ZOB fighters preferred to burn alive rather than surrender.

They threw open the sewer lids and pumped the sewers full of poison gas, and soon the slimy waters were filled with bodies.

Still the ZOB fought on. They lashed out of their bunkers on swift and deadly raids when they could find a German patrol. Suicide squads hurled themselves into certain death. German casualties mounted until the number was in the thousands.

Stroop pressed on relentlessly. When the Jews became ineffective as a fighting force they kept going on instinct alone.

On May 14, Mundek held a meeting of the remaining twelve Redeemers in his group. He gave them two choices. One was to remain and fight to the last man. The second was to try the sewers where Dov might be able to lead them to safety and a remote chance of reaching a partisan unit.

Dov convinced Mundek he could work around the areas of the sewers that were being gassed.

He made his way in "under the wall," but as he approached Zabrowska 99 instinct told him something was wrong. He walked straight past the building. His sharp eye picked out a dozen men who were watching Zabrowska 99 from various vantage points. Dov did not know whether or not Wanda had been taken by the Gestapo but he did know the place was unsafe.

It was late at night when he returned to the ghetto. It was difficult even for him to locate the bunker, for there were no streets or buildings left, only rubble. As he approached he smelled the now familiar odor of burning flesh. He went beneath the ground and lit a candle he always carried in the sewer. Its flickering light bounced off the walls. Dov walked from one end of the bunker to the other and knelt low with his candle each time he came to a body. Direct hits from the flame thrower had charred the still smoking bodies so badly he could not identify them. Dov Landau wondered which of the burned corpses was his beloved brother, Mundek.

May 15, 1943. ZOB radio broadcast its last message: "This is the voice of the Warsaw ghetto! For God's sake, help us!"

May 16, 1943. Forty-two days had passed since the Germans had made their first attack. Four months had passed since the ZOB arose and chased the Germans out. As a last gesture SS General Stroop dynamited the Great Synagogue on Tlamatzka Street. It had long been the symbol of Judaism in Poland. As the Temple of Solomon once fell to the Romans, so had the Tlamatzka Synagogue fallen. The Germans announced that the problem of the Warsaw ghetto had reached its final solution.

The devastation had been absolute. Nothing stood in the entire area above a man's eye level. Stroop announced the capture of sixteen pistols and four rifles. Further, that the ruins of the buildings would make good material. There were no prisoners.

Even in this most meticulous of massacres there were ZOB fighters who refused to die. Even in the rubble the battle went on. The Jews who had somehow survived began to find each other, and in twos and threes they formed "rat packs" and attacked German patrols by night. The Germans and the Polish Blues swore the ghetto was haunted by ghosts.

Dov found six other Jews. They went from bunker to bunker until they were all armed. They moved from place to place but the stench and the sight of death was everywhere. At night Dov led them through the sewers "under the wall" where they made quick raids on food stores.

The Jews were rebelling in a dozen other places around Poland, but their risings all met with the same fate. Too little, too late, no support.

During all the daylight hours Dov and the six others remained below ground in a newly carved-out bunker. For five long and harrowing months neither Dov Landau nor any of his comrades saw the light of day. One by one they died —three on one raid in Warsaw, two by suicide, one of starvation.

Dov was the last one alive. At the end of the fifth month a German patrol found him close to death. His appearance was not even that of a human being. He was revived sufficiently to be dragged to Gestapo headquarters for questionings, which always ended in beatings. The Gestapo could get nothing from him. Dov Landau, age thirteen, ghetto rat, sewer rat, rubble rat, and expert forger, was marked for resettlement. Destination: Auschwitz!

CHAPTER TWENTY-FOUR: Dov Landau was put into an open gondola car with sixty other Jews. The Gestapo refused to believe that he had stayed alive without outside help for five months in the rubble of the Warsaw ghetto. The train moved southward over the icy countryside in the dead of winter toward Auschwitz.

BERLIN, GERMANY, 1940

SS Lieutenant Colonel Karl Hoess entered the office of SS Colonel Eichmann, who had been given the task of carrying out the final solution of the Jewish problem. Eichmann showed Hoess the master plan which was the culmination of the combined brainwork of all the top Nazi officials.

The entire continent of Europe was interlaced with concentration camps and political prisons. Every occupied country was well saturated with Gestapo establishments.

Another network of three hundred "combination" camps spanned Europe. Half of them were reserved for Jews.

SS Lieutenant Colonel Karl Hoess was impressed with the intricate planning that went into genocide.

Despite all these camps and their carefully chosen locations, the blueprinters felt they were going to run into a special problem, and this was why Hoess had been called to Berlin. The Nazis knew they would have tremendous difficulty trying to run extermination camps in western Europe. Furthermore, Poland was more or less centrally located in relation to the Balkans and western Europe. A final, major camp was needed, one that would serve as a "master model." In addition to Jews to dispose of there were Russian, French, and other prisoners of war, partisans, political enemies in occupied countries, religious fanatics, especially Christians of the Catholic faith, gypsies, criminals, Freemasons, Marxists, Bolsheviks, and Germans who talked peace, liberalism, trade unionism, or defeatism. There were suspected foreign agents, prostitutes, homosexuals, and many other undesirable elements. All these had to be eliminated to make Europe a fit place for Aryans to live.

Such a camp as Eichmann spoke of would handle all these people. Eichmann informed Hoess that he was to be rewarded for his years of faithful service as a Nazi by being given command of the new camp. Eichmann pointed on the map to a small Polish town near the Czech border. A town called Auschwitz.

The train bearing Dov Landau and heading south for Auschwitz rolled to a stop at Cracow, a rail center. At a siding on the outskirts many more cars were joined to the train. There were cattle cars holding Jews from France and Greece and coal cars holding Jews from Yugoslavia and Holland and there were open gondolas holding Jews from Italy for resettlement. It was bitter cold. The biting wind and the snow whipped through Dov in the open gondola and all that protected him against it was his torn shirt and some little warmth of bodies packed together.

BERLIN, GERMANY, 1940-41

When the Nazis selected Hoess to command the camp at Auschwitz, the major clearing house and extermination factory, they knew well the caliber of the man they had. Hoess had had a long career in the concentration-camp system beginning way back in 1934 when Hitler first rose to power. More recently he had been second in command of the concentration camp at Sachsenhausen. Hoess was a meticulous man and systematic and he carried out orders without questioning them. Furthermore, he was not bothered by hard work.

Twenty thousand acres of land were cleared of farms and villages in the Auschwitz area and fenced off. The best construction men, engineers, scientists, and transportation experts and the best of the elite storm troopers went to work on the massive project. An area called Birkenau, two miles from the main Auschwitz camp, was selected as the site of the gas chambers. Birkenau was well secluded and had its own rail sidings. The site was picked because of its accessibility by rail from western Europe, eastern Europe, and southern Europe. The little town of Auschwitz was completely undistinguished and lay in a basin of eternal mud at the entrance to the Silesian mining district. In erecting the camp system the Nazis had to overcome a major objection from their own colleagues.

The German Army needed all the railroads and rolling stock it could get its hands on to execute a war on the eastern front. They did not like this nonsense of using valuable rail space to cart Jews all over Europe. The Nazis were just as adamant that the final solution of the Jewish question was as important as running the war. The question was taken to Hitler, who sided with the SS, SD, Gestapo, and other Nazi elements against the German Army High Command.

Hoess assumed command of Auschwitz and traveled to Treblinka to study the methods of extermination. He concluded that Treblinka's commander, SS Colonel Wirth, was a clumsy amateur and said as much. The executions at Treblinka were carried out with carbon monoxide, which was inefficient; the machinery was always breaking down and it used up valuable petrol. Furthermore, Wirth was not systematic and he did not use any measure of deception, so that there were constant rebellions on the part of the Jews. Finally, Hoess felt, Treblinka had been poorly designed if only three hundred people could be executed at one time.

When the chambers of Birkenau were opened at Auschwitz, Hoess conducted extensive tests on the first "guests." He and his scientists concluded that Cyklon B, a crude prussic acid gas, did the job the best. He ordered huge quantities of it from the International Insecticide Company in Hamburg.

The Birkenau chambers were designed to hold three thousand people at one time, and with utmost efficiency ten thousand people a day could be exterminated, depending on weather conditions.

The train bearing Dov Landau was now nearly fifty cars long. It stopped at the town of Chrzanow, the last before Auschwitz. One out of five persons on the train was already dead. Other hundreds were frozen to the sides of the cars and unable to move without tearing off the flesh of arms or legs. Many women threw their children over the rail beds and screamed to the curious onlooking peasants to take them and hide them. The dead were removed and stacked in six new cars added on at the end of the train. Dov, though in very bad condition, was keen and alert. He knew exactly what to expect, and he knew that if he ever used his wits he must use them now. The train rolled on again. Auschwitz was an hour away.

Hoess worked to perfect the operation at Birkenau. First he worked out a system of deception that would keep the victims calm to the very end. Lovely trees, lawns, and flower beds were planted around the buildings which housed the gas chambers. There were signs everywhere in many languages which read: SANITATION CENTER. The main deception used was that the victims were going to be inspected and given a delousing shower before being issued new clothing and sent to labor camps at or around Auschwitz.

Under and around the gas chambers neatly laid-out dressing rooms had been built. There were pegs with numbers for hanging clothing. Everyone was told to "remember his number." Hair was cut for "delousing" and the victims were requested to remove their eyeglasses before entering the sanitation "shower."

Everyone was issued a bar of soap with a number on it. They were marched naked, three thousand at a time, down long corridors. A dozen mammoth doors ran along the corridors. The doors opened, revealing enormous "shower rooms."

Most of the guests were too numb to realize quite what was happening and entered the shower rooms quietly. Some began to examine the bar of soap and found it was made of stone. Others discovered the shower heads on the ceiling were fake and that there was no drainage for water.

Often a last-minute panic broke out but the Germans were ready now with storm troopers who clubbed and whipped the reluctant into the "shower rooms."

The iron doors were bolted shut.

A can or two of Cyklon B was dropped into each "shower room" and it was all over in ten or fifteen minutes.

Then came the *Sonderkommandos*. These were clean-up squads of inmates from Auschwitz. They emptied the gas chambers and removed the corpses to the crematoriums. Gold teeth were pulled and rings taken before the burnings. These would be melted down and sent to Berlin. Often a well-shaped skull would be taken for sale to the German guards as paperweights.

Little attention was given to pictures of families or love letters that were found in the clothing. The troopers were most interested in searching through the linings where jewelry was often hidden. Often an infant was found hidden in the clothes and designated for the next "shower."

Hoess was good to his troops. They worked hard when a large trainload came to Birkenau and were rewarded with extra rations and schnapps. His system worked with great efficiency and he never seemed fazed. He did not even get upset when Colonel Eichmann unloaded a quarter of a million Hungarian Jews on him practically without warning.

Hoess pressed his scientists and engineers for greater efficiency and lower costs. His architects had blueprinted elaborate expansion plans. One was for a gas chamber with a floor that could be lifted hydraulically like an elevator to another level where the crematorium was situated. Other plans were designed to increase the Birkenau capacity to forty thousand executions a day.

The greatest bottleneck at Birkenau was the disposal of corpses. At first they were taken directly from the gas chambers to open fields and buried in pits and covered with lime. The stench became unbearable. The SS troops forced the Jewish *Sonderkommandos* to dig up all the pits and burn bodies, then crush the bones. Again, open field burning proved too foul-smelling, so inside crematoriums had to be constructed.

The train bearing Dov Landau passed through Auschwitz and came to a halt at the siding at Birkenau.

CHAPTER TWENTY-FIVE: Dov was half dead with hunger and blue with cold, but his years of constant contact with danger and death had sharpened his instincts so that even in this state he was alert to survive. Dov knew that the next hour would spell life or death.

The doors of the cattle and freight cars were opened and those like him in open cars were ordered over the top with harsh guttural commands. The miserable victims dragged themselves onto a long platform and faced a line of storm troopers who stood in readiness with clubs, whips, pistols, and vicious dogs straining at their leashes. The whips cracked out in the cold air and brought screams of pain. The truncheons thudded against skulls, and pistols shot into the bodies of those too weak to walk.

A line was formed, four abreast down the length of the platform, and directed toward a huge station room. The line pressed to the room at a slow but steady pace.

Dov looked around him. To his left were the trains. Beyond the trains on the road outside the station room he could observe a line of waiting trucks. The trucks were not enclosed so they could not be gas vans, Dov assumed. To his right, past the line of guards, Dov could see the neatly groomed lawns and trees around the brick gas chambers of Birkenau.

137

He studied the shapes of the buildings and their conelike chimneys and he knew the area to his right held extermination chambers.

The line pressed on. A nausea born of fear racked him. A man staggered and fell, unable to arise. Two snarling dogs were turned loose and ripped the man to pieces. His shrieks set Dov to trembling. He fought to gain control; he knew that he must show no fear.

His line moved into the station room. The large line was split into four single lines, and each line moved toward a desk set up at the far end of the room. A German doctor sat behind each desk, and around each doctor stood a dozen guards and assistants. Dov fixed his attention on the desk ahead of him to try to find out what was happening.

The doctor quickly looked over every person as he or she stepped to the desk. The doctor would then order the person to go off in one of three directions.

The first way was out an exit on the right side of the room. Dov began counting; seven out of ten people were sent out that way. These people were old or children or appeared in bad condition. Since he assumed the buildings on the right were gas chambers, he came to the conclusion that those being sent out the right exit were going to be put to death immediately.

The second way was out an exit on the left side of the room. This exit led to the outside where the line of trucks was waiting. About two out of ten went that way and all of them appeared fit and well. Dov assumed they were being sent to the labor camp.

The right door meant death and the left door meant life!

There was also a third group. These people, one in ten or even more, were mostly young women, some quite beautiful. A few teen-age boys were ordered to join this group. Dov was certain the girls would be used as German field whores and the boys for homosexual activities with the German officers.

He drew in a dozen deep breaths as his line inched forward. He was a pack of bones and he knew he didn't stand much of a chance of being sent through the left exit to the labor camp.

In the next line a woman screamed and half a dozen guards converged on her and flung her to the ground and ripped away her skirts. The woman had been trying to hide an infant.

"Right . . . right . . . right . . . right . . ." the doctor kept ordering the victims.

Dov Landau stopped before the desk.

138

The doctor looked up and glanced at him. "Go to that exit on the right," he said.

Dov smiled softly. "You are making a mistake, Doctor," Dov said with infinite calm. "I am an expert forger and counterfeiter. Write your name down on that piece of paper and I'll show you."

The doctor sat back, stunned. Dov's coolness impressed him, for he obviously knew what awaited him. The youngster had put a sudden halt to the monotonous death march. The doctor caught his bearings and a smirk crossed his lips. Two guards grabbed Dov and began to drag him away.

"Wait!" the doctor commanded. He looked at Dov again and ordered him to turn around. For a second he became tired of the foolishness. The boy was making a clever bluff. He was about to order him out of the right exit, but his curiosity got the better of him. The doctor scribbled his name on a pad.

Dov wrote out six duplications of the signature and returned the pad. "Which one of those did you write?" Dov asked.

Half a dozen guards peeked over the doctor's shoulder and stared in amazement. The doctor looked at Dov again and then whispered to a guard who walked off.

"Stand over here to one side," the doctor snapped.

Dov stood by the desk and watched the line of people move toward him. He looked at them being condemned at the rate of four a minute.

Dov looked into the eyes of the guards and he looked at their truncheons and at the snarling dogs. He glanced at the right-hand exit and whistled a shaky tune half beneath his breath.

Five minutes passed. Ten minutes passed. The line coming in from the platform seemed never to end.

The guard returned with another man who was obviously a high-ranking officer, Dov thought, for his chest was filled with medals. The doctor handed the pad of signatures to the officer, who studied it for a full minute.

"Where did you learn this?" the officer snapped.

"In the ghetto at Warsaw."

"What kind of work do you do?"

"Passports, travel cards, any kind of paper. I can duplicate anything."

"Follow me."

Dov passed through the left-hand door. As he got into the car and drove off toward Auschwitz a Main he seemed to remember Mundek's words: "One of the Landaus must live through this." In a few moments the car passed through the main gate of Auschwitz. The sign over the entrance of the camp read: LABOR LIBERATES.

The main compound was set in an area that wallowed in mud. There was acre after acre of frame wooden barracks which were isolated from each other by high walls of electrified barbed wire.

These acres of barracks fed manpower into some thirty subsidiary slave-labor camps. Each inmate wore a black and white striped uniform and an identification color on his arm and left breast. A pink badge was worn by homosexuals, a black badge by field whores, a green badge by criminals, violet badges for clergymen, red for Russians and Poles, and the traditional Star of David for the Jews.

Dov received another badge at Auschwitz. It was a tattooed number on his left forearm. Dov Landau was now a black and white striped Jew number 359195.

LABOR LIBERATES. Dov Landau celebrated his fourteenth birthday in Auschwitz and his gift had been his life. He was quite fortunate for of all the tens of thousands of prisoners at Auschwitz, Dov's small group of forgers were among the elite. His particular section was given the task of engraving and printing counterfeit United States one- and five-dollar bills for use by German agents in western countries.

After a short time at Auschwitz Dov wondered if it would not have been better to have died at Birkenau.

Here the inmates were underfed, worked into living skeletons, and stacked on shelves for their five hours' sleep a night. Disease ran wild. Prisoners were tortured, driven insane, beaten, and degraded, and every known atrocity conceived by man was committed.

Here each morning found dozens of inmates who had hanged themselves by their own belts or thrown themselves on the quick mercy of the electric wire. The flogging blocks were in constant use and naked buttocks were lashed in public at roll calls.

Here the penal colony lived in single black cells and were fed only oversalted vegetables to induce unquenchable thirst.

Here in Block X, Nazi doctors Wirthe, Schumann and Clauberg kept the human raw material for their pseudo-scientific experiments. Polish prisoner Dr. Wladislaw Dering performed castrations and ovarectomies ordered by his German masters as part of their insane program to find a way to sterilize the entire Jewish race.

This was Auschwitz and this was Dov Landau's gift of life. LABOR LIBERATES.

"One of the Landaus must live through this," Mundek had said. What did Mundek look like? He could hardly remember. Or Ruth or Rebecca or his mother and father? He could not remember his father at all. The memories grew hazier and hazier until he could remember nothing but death and terror and he did not know that there was a life where death and terror did not exist.

A year passed. The trains came in and out of Birkenau. The deaths at the labor camps around Auschwitz from torture and disease and hunger were nearly as appalling as those at Birkenau. Somehow he managed to cling to his sanity and that animal instinct to survive.

Even in this blackest of pits there were some rays of hope. There was the prison orchestra. There was a flourishing underground and they had a radio receiver. Even here a man could find a way to get to a woman.

SUMMER 1944

There was a strange new stirring throughout Auschwitz. Dov could often look into the sky and see Russian bombers, and the secret radio began reporting German defeats. Hope, however dim, found its way through the muck and torture. Each new Allied victory sent the German guards into a murderous frenzy until the prisoners almost dreaded word of German defeats. At Birkenau activity speeded up until the gas chambers were in operation almost around the clock.

AUTUMN 1944

The feeling now was that Germany was going to lose the war. They were being beaten on all fronts. But as they lost on the battlefield the appetite for extermination grew. Colonel Eichmann threw every possible resource into finishing his mission of genocide.

OCTOBER 1944

The *Sonderkommandos* at Birkenau staged a wild uprising in which one of the crematoriums was blown up. Each day in new uprisings the *Sonderkommandos* snatched SS guards and their dogs and threw them into the crematoriums. At last every *Sonderkommando* was executed and a call went out for a new group from Auschwitz.

His back to the wall, Eichmann made a final gesture. Twenty thousand Jews, the cream of Jewry, who had been under guaranteed protection at the Czech camp of Theresienstadt, were ordered transferred to Birkenau for extermination.

The Jewish death toll at Birkenau mounted and mounted until the count reached nearly a million Poles, fifty thousand Germans, a hundred thousand Dutch, a hundred and fifty thousand French, fifty thousand Austrians and Czechs, fifty thousand Greeks, two hundred and fifty thousand Bulgarians, Italians, Yugoslavs, and Rumanians, and another quarter of a million Hungarians.

141

Each day during the macabre race for total annihilation came a call for more and more *Sonderkommandos*.

NOVEMBER 1944

The counterfeit shop was abruptly closed down in Auschwitz and everyone was sent to Birkenau to work as *Sonderkommandos*.

It was Dov's new job to wait in the corridor of the gas chambers until a gassing was over. He and other *Sonderkommandos* stood by until the shrieks of agony and the frantic pounding on the iron doors stopped. They waited another fifteen minutes for the gas to clear. Then the doors of the gas chambers would be opened. Dov had to go to work with ropes and hooks to untangle the hideous tangle of arms and legs and drag them out for reshipment to the crematorium. After the bodies were removed he had to enter the chamber and hose it down and get the room ready for the next batch of victims who were already in the dressing rooms, being prepared.

For three days Dov worked at this gory task. Every ounce of his strength was sapped, and now that stubborn, defiant will to live that had carried him through seemed to fade. He dreaded that instant when the iron chamber door opened and he was face to face with the tangle of corpses. He dreaded it worse than the thought of the ghetto or the sewers. He knew he would not be able to stand to see that horrible sight much more often.

Then a startling thing happened!

The Germans ordered the crematorium ovens dismantled and the gas chambers blown up! The Allies were advancing from the west and the Russians were coming from the east. Now the Nazis made frantic efforts to cover up their crimes. Pits of bodies were exhumed all over Poland and the bones crushed and scattered. Desperately needed transportation was used to get the Jews inside Germany.

JANUARY 22, 1945

The Russian Army entered Auschwitz and Birkenau and liberated them. The orgy of murder was over! Dov Landau, aged fifteen, was one of fifty thousand Polish Jews who had kept alive out of three and a half million. He had kept his promise to his brother.

CHAPTER TWENTY-SIX: The Russian army physicians who examined Dov were astonished that he had been able to live through the years of privation and punishment without incurring permanent damage. He was weak and under-sized and he would never have great stamina but with proper care he could be brought up to reasonable condition.

The injury to his mind was something else. The boy had been kept alive by an indomitable spirit. Now that he could relax after six years of constant strain a flood of memories surged through his brain day and night. He became morose and slipped into melancholia and his mental state approached the thin borderline that separates the sane from the insane.

The barbed wire was torn down and the chambers and the ovens were gone but the memories would never leave him. And the frightful smell seemed always to hang over him. As he looked at his arm with the blue tattooed number he relived that grotesque second when the doors of the gas chamber were flung open. Time and time and time again he saw his mother and his sister Ruth being removed from such a chamber at Treblinka. Time and time again he held that flickering candle close to the smoldering bodies in the bunker in the Warsaw ghetto and wondered which one was Mundek. Over and over again he saw the skulls the Germans used as paperweights as his mother and his sister.

The Jews remaining at Auschwitz huddled together in several barracks. Dov could not comprehend that there was a world of the living without depravity and torture. A world of food and warmth and love was beyond him. Even the news of the German surrender brought no scenes of joy at Auschwitz, for there was no joy in victory.

Dov Landau's memories festered into hate. He was sorry the gas chambers were gone for he could visualize lines and lines of German SS troopers and their dogs being marched into them.

The war was over but no one quite knew what to do or where to go. Warsaw? It was a hundred and sixty miles away and the roads were clogged with refugees. Even if he got to Warsaw, what then? The ghetto was rubble and his mother and father and sisters and Mundek were all gone—all of them were dead. Day after day Dov sat by the window without speaking a word. He stared out at the eternal pall that clung to the Silesian countryside.

One by one the Jews at Auschwitz ventured out to return to their homes. One by one they came back to Auschwitz with a final crushing disillusion. The Germans were gone but the Poles were carrying on for them. There were no cries of Poles for three and a half million murdered. Instead the cities were covered with posters and the people screamed, "The Jews brought this war on us . . . the war was started so that Jews could make a profit . . . the Jews

143

are the cause of all our troubles!" There were no tears for the dead but there was plenty of hatred for the few survivors. They smashed Jewish shops and beat up Jews who tried to return to their homes and property.

And so—those who ventured out of Auschwitz came back. They sat in the muck-filled compounds, shattered, half mad, and tragically waited to rot together. The memory of death never left them. The smell from Birkenau was always there.

SUMMER 1945

A man walked into Auschwitz and was greeted with suspicious snarls. This man was in his early twenties. He was husky and had a big black mustache and wore a snow-white shirt with the sleeves rolled up above the elbows. He walked with a wonderful step that seemed to tell everyone that he was a free man. An assembly was called on the grounds and they gathered about him.

"My name is Bar Dror, Shimshon Bar Dror," he called out. "I have been sent from Palestine to take you people . . . home!"

For the first time in the memory of many there was an outburst of happiness and tears of joy. Bar Dror was mobbed with a million questions. Many fell on their knees and kissed his hands and others just wanted to touch him, to hear him, and to see him. A free Jew—from Palestine! Shimshon Bar Dror—Samson, Son of Freedom—had come to take them home!

Bar Dror took charge of the compound with a vengeance. He told them that it would be some time before they could move out, but until the Mossad Aliyah Bet found a way for them they would do better to live like dignified human beings.

A new surge of life transformed the compound. Bar Dror organized committees to put the place into decent shape. School was started, a theatrical group organized, a small orchestra formed and dances held, a daily news bulletin printed, and endless discussion carried on about Palestine. Shimshon even started a model farm near the compound to begin agricultural training.

Once the new spirit had been instilled and the camp was self-governing, Shimshon Bar Dror set out on treks in search of other Jews to lead them to the base.

As Shimshon Bar Dror and other Mossad Aliyah Bet agents worked untiringly to gather the Jews together and get them out of Poland, another force was working just as hard to keep them in Poland.

Throughout Europe the British embassies and consulates put pressure on every government to keep their borders losed to these refugees. The British argued that it was all a plot of the world Zionists to force their own solution on the Palestine mandate.

As the undercover battle raged between the British and he Mossad Aliyah Bet, the Polish government issued an astonishing edict; it proclaimed that all Jews were to remain in Poland. The Polish government reasoned that if the few remaining Jews were allowed to leave they would confirm to the world that the Poles were continuing their persecution—as indeed they were—even after the German extermination program. Thus the Jews were locked in a country that did not want them and locked out of the country that did want them.

Winter came to Auschwitz and morale broke apart at the seams. All the good work of Bar Dror went for nought. The Palestinian held meetings to try to explain the political battle that raged around them, but the survivors would not listen. They did not care about politics.

In the dead of winter another Aliyah Bet man entered the camp, and he and Bar Dror made a gambling decision. The two men called the section leaders together and told them to prepare to abandon the camp.

"We are going to head for the Czech border," Bar Dror said. "It is not too long a journey but it will be difficult. We can only go as fast as the slowest man and we must stay off the main roads." Bar Dror opened a map and traced a route that would take them through the Carpathian Mountains and the Jablunkov Pass, a distance of seventy miles.

"What happens when we reach the border?" someone asked.

"We have Aliyah Bet men buying off the Polish border patrol. If we can get through to Czechoslovakia we will be safe for the time being. Jan Masaryk is a friend. He will not let them chase us out of Czechoslovakia."

They left Auschwitz in the middle of the night, striking off the main road—a tragic line of survivors streaming forth, with the strong holding up the weak and carrying the young. The straggling procession pushed over fields of snow, driving their beaten bodies for six harrowing days. Then they drove themselves up into the biting winds of the Carpathian Mountains, with the Palestinians miraculously keeping them all alive and moving them on and on closer to the border.

Along the frontier other Aliyah Bet men worked feverishly to spread bribe money among the Polish guards, and as the ragged caravan pressed to the boundary the guards, with their pockets stuffed, turned their backs and the Jews poured through into Czechoslovakia.

On they marched through the freezing cold until they

145

passed through the Jablunkov Pass and assembled at th
bottom, exhausted, feet bleeding, hungry, and in need of medi
cal attention. A special train had been chartered by the Mos
sad Aliyah Bet. The escapees were taken aboard to waitin
warmth, food, and attention. The first leg of the perilou
journey was over.

When a Jew entered Palestine legally he surrendered hi
passport to the Aliyah Bet so that it could be used agair
Five hundred such passports were distributed to the escapee
from Auschwitz. In addition to the passports the Aliyah Be
had collected visas for Venezuela, Ecuador, Paraguay, an
other South American countries. These "documents" woul
hold the British at bay for a while.

British CID got wind of the five hundred Jews who ha
crossed from Poland and relayed the news to the Foreig
Office at Whitehall. Whitehall sent an urgent dispatch to th
British ambassador in Prague to take the matter up with th
Czech Foreign Minister, Masaryk, and have the train stoppec
The British ambassador was granted an immediate meetin
with Masaryk and demanded that the Jews be returned t
Poland. He pointed out that the entire Mossad operatio
was illegal, contrary to Polish law, and had been sponsore
by the Zionists in an effort to force the issue over Palestine.

Masaryk smiled. "I do not know much about oil pipeline:
Mr. Ambassador," he said, "but I do know about huma
pipelines."

Masaryk was known to be outspoken in behalf of the Jew
The ambassador implied that British displeasure could be di
played in a more "practical" manner.

"Mr. Ambassador," Masaryk said, "I will not comply wit
this or any other British threat. So long as I am Foreig
Minister of Czechoslovakia the borders of my country ar
open to the Jews with or without visas and with or withou
passports."

The ambassador reported to Whitehall that the train coul
not be stopped. It rolled on toward Bratislava, the tow
where the borders of Hungary, Czechoslovakia, and Austri
came together.

Again the British attempted to stop it, but this time
crossed into Austria under the personal protection of a sym
pathetic American military commander.

In Vienna the travelers stopped for much-needed rest an
medical attention. They were issued clothing in a giant r
staging area that had been established by American Jews t
help the European survivors.

In Italy, the next stop, the Mossad Aliyah Bet had th
open co-operation of the public and the Italian officials, bu

146

movement was hampered by the fact that the country was occupied by the British.

Paradoxically some of the British occupation forces consisted of units of Palestinian Jews. The Palestine Brigade of the British Army and its units stationed all over occupied Italy had long been considered model troops by the British command. Aliyah Bet agents from Palestine integrated with these units, and soon the Palestinian soldiers were busy establishing refugee camps, helping with illegal ships, and the like. For formal purposes the Palestine units were commanded by army officers, but for practical purposes the units were under the command of the Aliyah Bet and Palmach. Shimshon Bar Dror had been an army sergeant in one such unit and used his British army papers to travel back and forth to Poland to round up refugees.

It was springtime when Dov's group of Auschwitz refugees embarked on another train that moved into the Austrian Alps and crossed into Italy through the Brenner Pass.

The train stopped near Lake Como outside Milan at a very isolated siding. Although the refugees had been warned that they would be met by men wearing British uniforms panic nearly broke out. The survivors could not comprehend men in fighting uniform wearing a Star of David on their arm. The Star of David had always been the insignia of the ghetto. No Jews, except in the ghetto uprisings, had fought under a Star of David for nearly two thousand years.

They debarked from the train apprehensively. The soldiers were kind and some spoke Yiddish and all spoke Hebrew and they were gentle but they seemed to be of a different breed of Jew.

A week after their arrival in Milan, Dov's group of a hundred people were taken from a small camp in the dead of night. They were transported in British trucks driven by members of the Palestine Brigade. The convoy dashed to a secret rendezvous point along the coast where it met another three hundred refugees who had assembled from other camps. From nearby La Spezia harbor a tiny vessel moved out to meet them.

The ship dropped anchor offshore and was loaded by rubber boat. It sailed and got out of the three-mile limit and was soon trailed by the ever alert British Navy.

There was something baffling about the *Gates of Zion*. Unlike all the other refugee ships, this one was not heading for Palestine. Its course, instead, was toward the Gulf of Lions on the southern coast of France. Neither the British nor the refugees aboard the *Gates of Zion* had the slightest idea the vessel was a part of a gigantic plot.

147

CHAPTER TWENTY-SEVEN: Bill Fry sat at a table at Miller Brothers' Restaurant in Baltimore, Maryland. He dropped a handful of oysterette crackers into a big steaming bowl of clam chowder and stirred it. He toyed with the soup for a moment but he had no appetite. "Jesus Christ," he thought. "I wonder if I can get that piss-pot across the Atlantic Ocean."

Bill Fry had earned a reputation as the most successful captain in the Mossad Aliyah Bet. His beaching of the *Star of David* at Caesarea had opened a new era in the illegal immigration war. It had forced the British to start the Cyprus detention camps. This had been a turning point, for the Mossad had run one shipload after another into Palestine as fast as the British turned them back, and now another crisis was brewing. Mossad Aliyah Bet had run in so many illegals that the camp in Cyprus was bursting.

Flushing with success and determined to break the British exclusion policy, the Mossad dreamed up a wild scheme and chose Bill Fry to execute it.

The largest of the illegal fleet to date had been his *Star of David*, which carried under two thousand passengers. Other ships carried from a few hundred to a thousand. The Mossad figured that if they could run the blockade with a ship holding upwards of five thousand refugees it would be a staggering blow for the British.

Bill was commissioned to find a ship that could do the job, outfit it, and take five thousand refugees from the big center at La Ciotat in southern France. It was felt that the ship should be purchased in the United States or South America where the British would not be suspicious. British CID simply had the European ports too well covered. Mossad agents covered South America while Bill himself searched the Gulf ports and the east coast. It became obvious that they weren't going to get much of a ship for the money they had to spend. So Bill had taken a gamble and now he was worried. He had purchased an overaged, obsolete steamship which had seen service only on the Chesapeake Bay in an overnight run between Baltimore and Norfolk. The ship, the *General Stonewall Jackson*, an oversized pleasure cruiser, had never sailed the ocean. The only thing Bill could think of that was decent about the ship was that it had been bought cheap.

The white-coated waiter hovered over Bill's table. "Is something wrong with the chowder, sir?"

"Huh? Oh, hell no . . . it's fine," he mumbled, and shoved a spoonful into his mouth.

Had the purchase of the obsolete bay liner been a mistake? At this moment it was being fitted in Newport News, Virginia, to hold 6850 refugees.

Bill sighed. There was the other side of the picture. Suppose he could get seven thousand refugees out of Europe at one crack! It would just about explode the British policy!

Bill shoved the bowl of chowder away and asked for the check. He picked up the dead cigar butt from the ash tray and relit it and once again read the telegram from Newport News: THE JACKSON IS READY.

At Newport News the next day Bill assembled his crew of Palestinian Palmach and Aliyah Bet, American Jews, sympathetic Spanish Loyalists, Italians, and French. He inspected the ship and ran a short shakedown cruise around the lower bay, then revved up her engines and made for the Atlantic Ocean.

Within three hours the *Jackson* developed engine trouble and had to return to Newport News.

During the next two weeks Bill made three more attempts. The moment the old ship got far from her natural habitat, she rebelled and had to be taken back to port.

Bill told the Aliyah Bet people he had made a mistake. The *Jackson* simply could not make it. They urged him to check her over in dock for another week and make one last try.

On the fifth attempt the entire crew held its collective breath as the obsolete steamer chugged past Cape Henry into deep waters of the Atlantic—and continued to chug.

Twenty-two days later the *Stonewall Jackson* wheezed up the Gulf of Lions to the French harbor of Toulon, which stood forty miles from Marseilles and only twenty miles from the big refugee camp of La Ciotat.

There had been a teamster strike in France, and the British CID who were watching La Ciotat relaxed for a moment, assuming that there would be no movement without trucks. Furthermore, there had been no reports of illegal ships coming from any European ports since the *Gates of Zion,* Dov's ship, had landed at Port-de-Bouc several weeks earlier.

The British were caught napping.

They had no advance notice of the *Jackson* because she had been purchased and fitted in the United States and to date no Aliyah Bet ship had been large enough to navigate the Atlantic. When the *Jackson* was due to arrive at Toulon the Aliyah Bet went to the head of the French Teamsters' Union and explained the situation. The Teamsters' head secretly rounded up drivers and trucks and during the middle of their strike they rushed in and out of La Ciotat transporting sixty-five hundred refugees to Toulon—among them Dov Landau.

British CID discovered the secret at the last moment and descended upon Toulon. They passed out enormous bribes to port officials to delay the departure of the *Jackson* long enough for them to contact London for instructions.

Mossad Aliyah Bet men made counterbribes to the officials to get the ship on the seas, and the *Jackson,* now renamed the *Promised Land,* ran the blue and white Star of David to her mast top in open challenge.

Hasty meetings took place at the Admiralty, Chatham House, and Whitehall. The implications of the situation for British policy were clear, and it was obvious that the *Promised Land* had to be stopped at all costs. The British issued angry threats to the French. British warships waited outside Toulon. The French answered by granting permission to the *Promised Land* to sail.

The *Promised Land* set out from Toulon mid the cheers of the refugees aboard her. The instant she passed the three-mile zone she was escorted by two waiting British cruisers, the *Apex* and *Dunston Hill.*

For the next three and a half days Bill Fry steered the *Promised Land* straight for Palestine. Her long thin smokestack puffed and her engines groaned and her decks bulged and her watchdog cruisers watched.

The *Apex* and *Dunston Hill* kept in constant radio contact with the Admiralty in London. As the *Promised Land* edged to within fifty miles of the Palestine coast, the British broke the rules of illegal blockade. The *Apex* came close to the steamer and sent a salvo over her ancient bows. The cruiser's bull horns blasted and her loud-speaker sent a voice over the water: "Illegal ship! Stand by to be boarded!"

Bill Fry bit his cigar. He grabbed a megaphone and stepped onto the bridge. "We are on the high seas," he shouted. "If you board us here it will be piracy!"

"Sorry, chaps, just following orders. Are you going to accept a boarding party peacefully?"

Bill turned to his Palmach chief who was standing behind him. "Let's give these bastards a reception."

The *Promised Land* turned on full steam in an attempt to sprint away from the cruisers. The *Apex* moved alongside her, then cut in sharply and her steel bow rammed the ancient steamer amidships. The blow splintered deep into the steamer's hull over the water line and she shuddered under the impact. The *Apex* sent out machine-gun fire to drive the refugees off the deck and make it clear for a landing party.

British marines, wearing gas masks and carrying small

150

arms, poured over the bow of the *Promised Land* and moved back to the superstructure. Palmachniks unrolled accordions of barbed wire in the path of the British and then loosed a barrage of rocks on them, followed by streams of water from pressure hoses.

The British were swept back to the bow by the attack. They fought off the Palmach with small arms and called for reinforcements. More marines boarded, this time with wire cutters. Another attack mounted toward the superstructure. Again the water hoses pushed them back and again the British returned, under cover of machine-gun fire from the *Apex*. They reached the barbed wire and cut it in time to receive scalding steam jets from the Palmach. Now the Palmachniks jumped to the attack and drove the British back. They overpowered the marines and threw them into the sea, one by one.

The *Apex* stopped the attack to fish their men out of the water, and the *Promised Land*, a huge hole in her side, chugged off once again. The *Dunston Hill* chased her down and pondered the advisability of another ram. The steamer might well go down with one more blow. It was too dangerous to risk. Instead, the *Dunston Hill* poured on heavy-caliber machine-gun fire that raked the decks clean of refugees and Palmach. The *Dunston Hill*'s boarding party came up amidships on ladders. A wild hand-to-hand brawl followed. With flailing clubs and an occasional pistol shot, the British pressed the attack toward the ladder leading up to the captain's bridge.

Meanwhile, the *Apex* recovered and raced to the scene again. The two cruisers boxed the steamship in. The *Apex* party boarded again behind a tear-gas barrage, and with the *Dunston Hill* marines pressing from the other direction the Palmach was driven back.

Dov Landau was in the fight. He and other refugees were guarding the top of the ladder near the captain's bridge. They pushed the British down the ladder half a dozen times until the tear gas and, finally, small arms drove them off.

The British had control of the deck now. They reinforced their position and held the refugees and Palmach off at gunpoint while another party stormed into the wheelhouse to gain command of the ship.

Bill Fry and five of his crew greeted the first three men who entered the wheelhouse with pistols and angry fists. Although he was completely cut off, Bill continued fighting until British marines dragged him from the wheelhouse and beat him unconscious with clubs.

After four hours of fighting, with eight of their men dead

and a score wounded, the British gained control of the *Promised Land*. Fifteen Jews were killed, among them the American captain, Bill Fry.

A general order for secrecy was issued at Haifa harbor in Palestine as the *Dunston Hill* towed the *Promised Land* in. The old steamship was listing badly. The entire Haifa dock area was flooded with British troops. The Sixth Airborne Division was there and they were armed to the teeth. But in their attempt at maintaining the secrecy, the British did not know that the Jews had broadcast a full account of the boarding of the *Promised Land* over their radio.

As the ships approached Haifa Bay, the Jews in Palestine called a general strike. Troops and tanks were required in the dock area to form a barrier between the refugees and Palestine's angry Jews.

Four British prison ships, *Empire Monitor, Empire Renown, Empire Guardian,* and the *Magna Charta* waited to effect an immediate transfer of the refugees from the *Promised Land*. But the very instant the Chesapeake Bay liner was towed into port, the harbor area and the entire city of Haifa shook under the impact of a mighty blast! The *Empire Monitor* was blown to pieces! This act was accomplished by Palmach frogmen who swam in and attached a magnetic mine to the ship's sides.

The *Promised Land* docked and the transfer operation began at once. Most of the refugees had had the fight knocked out of them. They went quietly to delousing sheds where they were stripped, sprayed, searched for weapons, and moved quickly on to the three remaining prison ships. It was a tragic procession.

Dov Landau and twenty-five others locked themselves into a hold, armed themselves with pipes, and defied the British to the very end. The hold was pumped full of tear gas; and Dov was carried from the *Promised Land* by four soldiers, still struggling, cursing, and fighting. He was thrown into a barred cell on the *Magna Charta*.

The prison ships were packed even more tightly than the *Promised Land* had been, and that same night they sailed from Haifa with the two cruisers, *Dunston Hill* and *Apex,* as escort.

If the refugees were sent on to Cyprus to the already crowded camps there, then the Jews would have won their point. Sixty-five hundred more Jews would have been taken out of Europe and added to the ever-growing numbers waiting on Cyprus to go to Palestine.

"The refugees from the so-called *Promised Land* on the *Empire Guardian,* the *Empire Renown,* and the *Magna Charta* are to be returned to their port of embarkation, Toulon,

France. Henceforth any other illegal blockade-runners that are caught will also be returned to their ports of origin."

The Palmachniks and Mossad Aliyah Bet people who were with the refugees on the three ships knew what they had to do. If they debarked and returned to Toulon and if the British rode out the storm, then there would be no more illegal immigration.

The order for secrecy went out in Toulon as the prison ships steamed into the Gulf of Lions and dropped anchor offshore.

Simultaneously the Palmach chiefs on each of the prison ships handed the British captains a message; each one was to the effect that "We will be taken ashore only by force."

The commander of the prison ships radioed to the Admiralty in London for instructions. Whitehall immediately turned on the toughest diplomatic pressure they could, short of breaking the Anglo-French alliance. They warned the French not to attempt to take sides with the Jews and to allow the British to carry out the debarkation by force. For four days messages and instructions flew between London and the prison ships and between Paris and London. Then the French government handed the British its dramatic decision.

"The government of France will not allow or be a party to the forcible removal of the refugees. If the refugees desire to return to France of their own free will, they are most welcome."

The French had taken a stand with the Jews, even at the risk of rupturing relations with the British. The refugees were exhilarated by the news. To a man, they renewed their vow to stay aboard the ships. The British, recovering from the shock, informed the refugees that they would either debark at Toulon or sit in the Gulf of Lions until they rotted.

Aboard the *Empire Guardian*, *Empire Renown*, and *Magna Charta*, the Jews dug in. The Palmachniks organized schools, taught Hebrew, compiled news, started a theater, and generally tried to keep things going. The French government kept up a daily stream of barges between the ships and Toulon to supply the refugees with good food and medical care. A dozen babies were born. At the end of a week, the refugees were holding fast.

On shore newsmen were getting curious about the three ships and were irate over the curtain of silence. One night an Aliyah Bet man swam ashore from the *Empire Guardian* and gave out the full story to the French press.

The story swept through France, Italy, Holland, and Denmark. Editorial insults were hurled at the British, in all four countries.

153

London braced itself against the onslaught of public resentment from the continent. They had expected it. They had, in fact, prepared for everything except the doggedness of the refugees. Conditions on the prison ships were of the worst. The atmosphere was sweltering and there was a good deal of sickness. Nevertheless, the refugees refused to come ashore. The British crews, who did not dare venture into the caged sections of the ship, were beginning to get uneasy. At the end of the second week the Jews were still holding fast and the clamor in the press was reaching a crescendo.

Three weeks passed. Four weeks passed.

At last the story began to lose its impetus. Then, the first Jew came ashore without being forced. He was dead. The whole issue was reignited. The captains of the three ships reported that the refugees seemed more determined than ever and the pressure on Whitehall mounted hourly. If more corpses were brought ashore it would be very bad.

The policy makers decided to take another tack. They asked that the refugees send in delegations to talk it all over. Their plan was to try to find a compromise that might let them out of the whole affair without losing face. From all three ships they received the same answer from the Palmach chiefs:

"We will settle for nothing more nor less than Palestine."

The affair went into its sixth week. When the second corpse was brought ashore the British issued an ultimatum to the Jews either to come ashore or suffer the consequences. It was not clear what those consequences were to be, but when the refugees again remained steadfast the British had to take direct action:

"The *Empire Guardian* and the *Empire Renown* will set sail from Toulon at once. The destination of these two ships will be Hamburg, Germany, in the British occupation zone. The inmates of these two ships will be removed peacefully or otherwise and be detained at Dachau until further notice."

As the two ships passed through the Straits of Gibraltar on the journey toward Germany, Mossad Aliyah Bet made feverish plans to load up two more ships with fifteen thousand refugees and make a run for Palestine. For as the *Renown* and *Guardian* landed on German soil, world opinion against the British reached a tidal peak. It was a somber victory for the Aliyah Bet.

As a last face-saving gesture the British let the third prison ship, *Magna Charta,* discharge its refugees at Cyprus, where they were sent to Caraolos. Dov Landau was fortunate to pass his sixteenth year at Caraolos rather than Dachau, but the boy was a study of hate.

154

CHAPTER TWENTY-EIGHT: Dov Landau spent his seventeenth birthday in yet another prison—Caraolos. He ushered in this birthday as he ushered in every day. He lay on his cot and stared at nothing and spent the day without uttering a word. He had not spoken to anyone since he had been dragged from the hold of the *Promised Land*. During the long weeks in Toulon harbor his hatred had grown.

At Caraolos a dozen welfare people and doctors and teachers and Palmachniks tried to reach him and break through his wall of bitterness, but Dov trusted no one and wanted no one near him.

By day he lay on his cot. By night he fought off sleep, for sleep always brought the recurring dream of that moment the doors of the gas chambers opened at Auschwitz. For hours on end Dov would stare at the blue tattooed numbers on his left forearm: 359195.

Across the path from his tent there lived a girl, and she was the most beautiful girl he ever remembered seeing. Of course, women could not be beautiful in the places he had been. She was in charge of many younger children and she always smiled when she saw him and she did not seem angry and aloof toward him as everyone else did. She was Karen Hansen Clement.

Karen saw Dov and made inquiries as to why he did not take part in school and other activities. She was warned to keep away from him, for he was said to be an "incurable" and maybe even dangerous.

Karen took this as a challenge. She knew Dov had been in Auschwitz, and her compassion seemed limitless. She had done amazing things with youngsters before, and although she knew it might be better to leave Dov alone her curiosity grew each time she went to her tent and looked over at his.

One day Dov lay on his cot, staring, and the sweat poured from him for it was very hot. He felt someone's presence and jumped up instinctively and tensed at the sight of Karen standing near him.

"I wonder if I could borrow your water bucket. Mine has a leak and the water trucks will be coming soon."

Dov stared and blinked his eyes nervously.

"I said I wonder if I could borrow your water bucket." Dov grunted.

"What does that mean? Yes or no? Can you talk?"

They stood and looked at each other like a pair of gamecocks. For that instant Karen was sorry she had come. She

155

took a deep breath. "My name is Karen," she said. "I am your neighbor."

Dov still did not answer. He glared.

"Well . . . may I use your bucket or not?"

"Did you come here to slobber over me?"

"I came here to borrow your bucket. You are certainly nothing to slobber over," she snapped.

He spun away and sat on the edge of his cot and chewed his fingernails. Her abruptness disarmed him completely. He pointed to his bucket on the floor and she picked it up. He glanced at her quickly out of the corner of his eye.

"What is your name? I'd like to be able to call you something when I bring your bucket back."

He did not answer.

"Well?"

"Dov!"

"Karen is mine. Perhaps you can call me that and we can say hello. At least till you learn to smile."

He turned very slowly but she was gone. He walked to the tent door and watched her moving toward the British water tanker which had just passed through the gate. She was beautiful.

It was the first time in many months that an outside event had been able to penetrate Dov Landau's absorption in himself. This Karen was completely different from the others who had come to see him. She was abrupt and snippy and afraid—yet there was a tenderness that radiated from her too. She did not gush over him or recite words she didn't feel. She was a prisoner at Caraolos but she did not complain or seem angry like all the others. Her voice was sweet, yet it was very stern.

"Good morning, Dov," Karen said. "Thank you for the use of your bucket."

He grumbled.

"Oh yes, you are the one who growls instead of talking. I have a little boy like you in my kindergarten class. But he pretends he is a lion."

"Good morning!" Dov shouted at the top of his lungs.

Dov knew what time she got up in the morning. He knew when she went to the wash racks and when she came and went from her classes. He slipped into her tent one day and looked around for her bucket and examined it. It had no hole in it at all. He would lie on his cot all day and wait anxiously for the sound of her footsteps coming down the catwalk. He would sneak to the tent door and steal a glance in her direction. Often, Karen would glance at his tent, too, and their eyes would meet for a brief instant. Then Dov would become angry with himself for being taken in and for showing weakness.

The days passed but they were different now. He was still silent and sullen but often his thoughts veered from death and hate and he could hear the children in the playground nearby and he could hear her voice speaking to them. It seemed strange to Dov. In all the time he was at Caraolos he had never heard the children playing until after he met her.

One night Dov stood by the barbed wire and watched the searchlights sweep through the tents. He often stood and looked, for he still did not want to sleep. On the playground the Palmach had built a campfire and there was singing and dancing. Once he used to sing and dance those songs at Redeemer meetings, but he did not want to hear them now. Mundek and Ruth and Rebecca had always been there.

"Hello, Dov."

He whirled around and saw the dim outline of Karen standing near him. Her long hair blew in the breeze and she tightened a ragged shawl about her shoulders. "Would you like to come to the campfire with me?" She pressed closer and he turned his back. "You like me, don't you? You can talk to me. Why don't you go to school and join our gang?"

He shook his head.

"Dov . . ." she whispered.

He spun around and faced her, watery-eyed. "Poor Dov!" he screamed. "Poor crazy Dov! You're just like all the rest of them! You just talk prettier!" Dov grabbed her and put his hands on her neck and tightened his fingers on her throat. "You leave me alone . . . you leave me alone . . ."

Karen looked him straight in the eye. "Take your hands off my throat . . . this instant."

He dropped his hands. "I was only trying to scare you," he said. "I wasn't going to hurt you."

"Well, you didn't scare me," she said, and walked off.

For a week after that Karen did not look at him or speak to him. He was seized with terrible restlessness. Dov was no longer able to spend the hours in sullen and morbid silence. He paced back and forth all day long. Why did he let the girl break into his thoughts! He had his memories and he had been alone with them! Now he could not think!

One evening Karen was on the playground when one of her children fell in a game and started to cry. She knelt beside him and put her arms about him and soothed away the boy's tears. For some reason she looked up and saw Dov standing over her. "Hello," he said very quickly, and walked away.

Despite the continued warnings of many to leave him alone,

157

Karen knew she had penetrated a great darkness. She knew the boy was desperate and trying to communicate and that his "hello" was his way of saying he was sorry.

A few evenings later she found a drawing on her bed. She held it to the candlelight and saw a picture of a girl kneeling and holding a child, and barbed wire was beyond her. She crossed the path to Dov's tent and when he saw her he turned his back.

"You are a very good artist," Karen said.

"I ought to be," he snapped. "I got plenty of practice. George Washington and Lincoln are specialties of mine."

He sat on his cot uncomfortably and bit his lip. Karen sat beside him. He felt funny, for he had never been so close to a girl other than his sisters before. Her finger touched the blue tattoo on his left arm. "Auschwitz?"

"Why do you bother with me?"

"Did you ever think that I might like you?"

"Like me?"

"Uh-huh. You are very good-looking when you aren't sneering, which is quite seldom, I must admit, and you have a very nice voice when you aren't growling."

His lips trembled. "I . . . like . . . you. You're not like the rest of them. You understand me. My brother Mundek used to understand me."

"How old are you?"

"Seventeen." Dov sprang to his feet and whirled around. "I hate these goddam British. They're no better than the Germans."

"Dov!"

His sudden explosion ended as quickly as it had started.

Yet, it was a beginning. He had blown off steam. It was the first time in well over a year that he had spoken more than one or two words. Karen watched him shrink back into that strange dark world of his.

Dov wanted to see Karen often because she was tender and she could listen to him and understand. He would talk quietly for a while and then burst forth with an impulsive short tirade of hate and then he would withdraw into himself.

Karen began to confide in him and tell him about how she was going to meet her father again in Palestine. Since she had left the Hansens she had always worked so long and hard with the youngsters she had never really formed a close friendship. Dov seemed proud that she would tell him all these things, and it was strange but she rather enjoyed talking to him.

And one day a great thing happened. Dov Landau smiled again.

158

When they spoke together he wanted to talk about nice things to her. The way she spoke . . . about the Hansens . . . the Danes . . . the children she loved . . . about her hope of reunion with her father . . . made him want to be able to talk like that too. But he could remember nothing nice, and before the war, 1939, was so long ago he could remember nothing about it at all.

Karen was careful with subjects that Dov did not mention. She never asked about Auschwitz or the ghetto.

After several weeks she came to him one day with a mission. "Dov, I have a favor to ask."

Immediately Dov turned suspicious.

"The Mossad people know you were in Auschwitz and they have also found out that you are an expert counterfeiter."

"So?"

"There is a new man here from Palestine. Joab Yarkoni tells me he wants to talk to you. His name is Ari Ben Canaan. He needs passports and documents and could use your services."

"So that's it! That's why you made friends! So you could get me to work."

"Oh, shut up, Dov. You don't even believe that yourself."

"Well," Dov grumbled, "if they want me so badly they can come and ask me themselves."

"How can anyone ask you anything when you won't even talk to them?"

"And why should I work for them?"

"Because they're working for you."

"Hell they are. They're working to save themselves."

"All right. Take your side of it. They are no worse than the Germans, and if you could make American dollars for *them* you can certainly make passports for the Mossad."

"You're always so damned smart with the answers."

"Dov. I've never asked a favor of you. What shall I tell them?"

"Tell them I might, but a lot of things have to be made clear."

Karen took his hand and smiled. "Why don't you make them clear? Ben Canaan is waiting for you."

"I'll see him here."

Dov secretly liked Ari Ben Canaan. He was direct and to the point and let Dov know that if he didn't work he was going to be the last Jew out of Caraolos. But more, Dov liked that quality of leadership in the man—the same quality Mundek had had. He went to work in the Palmach headquarters in one of the schoolrooms. Still, to everyone else in Caraolos but Karen, Dov Landau was incorrigible. He spoke only in anger. She was always called upon to calm his sudden eruptions.

She saw in him things that no other person saw—wonderful strength and pride. There were other things that she could not explain that made her like him very much.

Two and a half weeks after Ben Canaan's arrival on Cyprus, David Ben Ami gave Dov a list of three hundred names of children to be fixed on documents resembling British transfer orders. The three hundred were supposed to be moved from Caraolos to the new compounds near Larnaca. Dov knew that this was the escape! Neither his name nor the name of Karen was on the list of transferees.

Dov told David that he wanted to speak to Ben Canaan, and it was then that he put his demands to Ari that he and Karen be included in the escape. And Ari agreed to his demands.

CHAPTER TWENTY-NINE: The final steps in Operation Gideon were twenty-four hours away.

Ari Ben Canaan called a meeting of his chiefs in the home of Mandria, their Cypriot compatriot.

David Ben Ami gave Ari the transfer papers that Dov Landau had just completed. Ari looked them over and commented that the boy was a real artist. The papers could have fooled anyone. David reported that he had taken care of the hundred odds and ends, from security to putting kosher food on the ship for Orthodox children.

Joab Yarkoni, the Moroccan, reported that all the trucks were in ready condition and could be moved from the 23rd Transportation camp to Caraolos in twenty minutes. He gave the elapsed time of trial runs from Caraolos to Kyrenia by several alternate routes.

Zev Gilboa said that the three hundred and two children would be loaded on the lorries in a matter of minutes after the convoy arrived at Caraolos. He would brief the children as to what was going to happen a few minutes before the trucks departed.

Hank Schlosberg, the American skipper of the *Exodus,* said he would take the ship out of its Larnaca berth at dawn and steam up to Kyrenia and be there at least a full hour or two before the convoy was due to arrive.

Mandria reported that he had a system of lookouts posted along the escape route who could notify the convoy of any unusual British activity. He also had watchmen on a half dozen alternate routes. Mandria said that he would wait, as ordered, in Famagusta in his home. The minute the convoy passed through he would telephone Mark Parker in Kyrenia.

Ari rose and looked over his lieutenants. They were nervous, all of them. Even the usually placid Yarkoni was looking at the floor. Ari did not congratulate them or wish them luck. There was time for congratulations. As for luck, they'd make their own.

"I did not want to make the escape for three more days until the British themselves began moving children from the children's compound. Nevertheless we have received information that Major Alistair is suspicious of our activities. We even have reason to believe he has gone to London for instructions over Brigadier Sutherland's head. Therefore we must make our break at once. Our trucks arrive at Caraolos at nine o'clock. By ten o'clock I hope we have loaded the children and are passing your house here in Famagusta. The minute we turn off the Larnaca road we have two crucial hours. We have no reason to believe our convoy will be stopped. Our trucks are well known all over Cyprus. But . . . we must act under the assumption that we are under suspicion. Any further questions?"

David Ben Ami, the sentimentalist, could not let the occasion pass without proposing a toast. Ari tolerated the younger man's frivolity. "Le chaim," David said, raising his glass.

"Le chaim," the rest of them answered.

"I have heard that le chaim from you boys often," Mandria said. "What does it mean?"

"It means 'to life,' " David answered, "and to Jews that is no small request."

" 'To life,' " Mandria repeated. "That is nice."

Ari walked up to Mandria and hugged him in the Palmach manner. "You have been a friend," he said. "I must go meet Parker now."

Mandria stood there with tears streaming down his cheeks for he knew that this kind of affection was reserved for one of their own and to receive it from Ari Ben Canaan meant that he had been accepted fully as one of them.

A half hour later Ari, dressed as Captain Caleb Moore, met Mark on the terrace of the King George Hotel. Mark was a bundle of nerves.

Ari seated himself, refused a cigarette, and ordered a drink. "Well?" Mark asked impatiently.

"Tomorrow. We will be at Caraolos at nine."

"I thought you were going to wait until the British started cleaning out the children's compound."

"It would have been better but we can't wait. A friend at CID tells us that Alistair is on to something. But relax," Ari said. "It is almost over. The British still don't know what they're looking for. Now you understand everything."

Mark nodded. He would send a cable asking for an extension of his vacation. Bradbury in London would know by the signature, Mark, that Operation Gideon had been a success and would turn loose the story Mark had sent with a commercial pilot a week earlier.

"Suppose I don't get a phone call from Mandria at ten."

Ari smiled. "Then I'd suggest you get the hell off Cyprus unless you want to cover my hanging."

"That might be nice," Mark said. He finished his drink.

"By the way," Ari said, looking out to the water, "Kitty hasn't been in the camp since we were forced to put Karen on the *Exodus* list."

"That's right. She's with me at the Dome."

"How is she?"

"How in hell do you think she is? She's miserable. She doesn't want Karen to go on the *Exodus*. Do you blame her?"

"I don't blame her but I feel sorry for her."

"That's nice. I didn't know you felt sorry for anyone."

"I feel sorry that she has let her emotions get the best of her."

"I forgot. You don't know anything about human emotions."

"You're nervous, Mark."

Mark was angry at Ari's placidness. He remembered Kitty's anguish when she returned to Kyrenia and told him that Karen was going on the ship. "What do you want? Kitty has suffered more than one person has a right to suffer."

"Suffered?" Ari said. "I wonder if Kitty Fremont knows the meaning of the word."

"Damn you, Ben Canaan, damn you. What makes you think that Jews own a copyright on suffering?"

"Fortunately you're not being paid to like me and I couldn't care less."

"How could you? You see, I like people with human weaknesses."

"I never have them during working hours."

Mark stood up to leave. Ari grabbed Mark's arm in his powerful hand. For the first time Mark saw Ben Canaan shaken from his complacency. There was anger in Ari's eyes. "What the hell do you think this is? A tea party on the duchess's lawn? We're butting heads with the British Empire tomorrow."

He relased his grip on Mark's arm and regretted the short display of temper. At that instant Mark felt a tiny bit sorry for Ari. Perhaps he had a better way of disguising it but the pressure was beginning to tell on him too.

A few hours later Mark had returned to the Dome Hotel in Kyrenia. He knocked on Kitty's door. She managed to greet him with a half smile, but it could not disguise her red-rimmed eyes.

162

"Tomorrow."

Kitty froze an instant. "So soon?"

"They are afraid the British are on to something."

Kitty walked to the window and looked out at the pier and the island. It was a crystal-clear evening and she could even see the faint outline of the Turkish coast. "I've been trying to get up enough courage to pack up and leave Cyprus."

"Look," Mark said, "as soon as this blows over, you and I are going to head for the Riviera for a few weeks."

"To pick up the pieces? I thought you were supposed to go to Palestine."

"I doubt if the British will let me in after this. Kitty, I feel pretty rotten about dragging you into this thing."

"It isn't your fault, Mark."

"You read that line well but it's not quite true. Are you going to get over this?"

"Yes, I think so. I should have known better. You tried to warn me. At least I knew all the time that I was on thin ice. You know, Mark, it's funny, but we argued the night I met Ben Canaan. I told you there was something different about Jews. They aren't like us."

"They have an unlimited capacity for getting into trouble. It's their favorite sport," Mark said, spinning off the bed and rubbing his temples. "Well . . . one way or the other we might as well eat and I'm hungry."

Kitty leaned against the doorframe as Mark splashed his face with cold water. He groped for a towel. She handed him one.

"Mark. It's going to be very dangerous on the *Exodus*, isn't it?"

He hesitated a moment. There was no use trying to fool her at this point. "It's a floating bomb."

Kitty's heart sank. "Tell me the truth. Can they get away with this?"

"They have a fair chance with that mechanical monster, Ari Ben Canaan, running the show."

The sun went down and it was night.

Mark and Kitty sat wordlessly in her room.

"No use sitting up all night," he said at last.

"Don't go," Kitty said; "I'll just stretch out over the covers." She reached into the night stand and took out a couple of sleeping pills, turned off the light, and lay back.

Mark sat by the window and watched the surf slap against the shore.

Twenty minutes passed. He looked over at Kitty and saw

she had fallen into a restless and thrashing sleep. He walked to the bed and stood over her for several moments, then covered her with a blanket and returned to the chair.

At Caraolos, Dov and Karen sat on his cot, too excited to sleep. They spoke in whispers. They were the only ones among the children who knew what the new day would bring.

Karen tried to calm Dov. He kept whispering what he was going to do when he got to Palestine. How he was going to join the terrorists and kill British soldiers. She hushed him up as only she could and finally induced him to lie down.

As he closed his eyes Karen stood up and a strange sensation swept through her body. Odd and frightening. Dov meant more to her than she had realized until this moment. First it had been pity. Now Dov had a hold on her. She did not understand it. She wanted to be able to go and talk it over with Kitty. But Kitty was gone.

"Karen?"

"I am here, Dov."

The hours of darkness ticked by.

At the 23rd Transportation Company HMJFC three men lay on their cots wide-eyed.

Zev Gilboa dared think about springtime in Galilee for the first time in nearly a year. He thought of his wife and child and of the farm. His baby had been only a few months old when the Palmach sent Zev to Cyprus.

Joab Yarkoni thought of his farm too. It was different from Zev's, for it hugged the sea just a bit north of the Plain of Sharon. His farm was called Sdot Yam and it meant Fields of the Sea, for its main crop was fish. Yarkoni loved to walk for hours through the abandoned ruins of Caesarea and dig for antiquities, and he hoped that the Palmach might let him return there for a while. He would go out on his trawler fishing and he would see his brother and sister again.

. . . and David Ben Ami thought of his beloved Jerusalem. He loved Jerusalem almost as much as he loved Ari's sister Jordana. Now he would see them both again until they reassigned him to another mission. The rocky hills of Judea where his six brothers lived and the city rose out of stone. David propped on an elbow and reread the worn letter that Ari had brought him. Jordana! Jordana! His heart raced wildly. Jordana, my love!

The three men knew that their stay in Palestine might be brief because they belonged to the Palmach and Mossad and they might be needed anywhere in the world. But this night they thought of home. . . .

Brigadier Bruce Sutherland had another of his nightmares. He dressed and went out of his house alone and walked through Famagusta in the depth of night. He walked along the old wall of Famagusta and stared into the old city with its hundreds of churches and cathedrals and ruins of castles and memories of past glory. He walked until he came to Othello's Tower and he climbed it and looked down at the harbor. He was tired, very tired, and he wondered if there would ever be a night again in which he could close his eyes and fall into a peaceful sleep.

Major J. J. Alistair fell asleep over his desk. Most of the night he continued to pore through reports and bits and scraps of information in an attempt to put together exactly what the Jews were up to at Caraolos.

Mandria paced back and forth in the room where the Mossad and Palmach had held so many meetings. Yes, it had been only a few weeks since Ari Ben Canaan and David Ben Ami had stood on that balcony outside and watched a convoy of Jews being taken from their illegal runner, *Door of Hope*. Tomorrow he would stand on the balcony and another convoy would pass. This one would climax Ari Ben Canaan's fantastic scheme. The imagination of the Greek Cypriots had been tremendously stirred by the daring of the Mossad. Those of them, like Mandria, who worked with the Jews, were beginning to think in terms of an underground movement of their own against British rule on Cyprus.

One man slept soundly. Ari Ben Canaan slept like a well-fed baby without a care in the world.

A ray of light fell over Mark Parker's face. He opened his eyes and yawned. He had dropped off by the window with his feet propped on the sill. He was stiff and his mouth tasted foul from cigarettes and scotch. He glanced around and saw Kitty in a deep and quiet slumber on the bed. He pulled the window shade down and tiptoed from the room and shaved and spent several moments under an icy shower and he felt better. He dressed and returned to Kitty's room and sat gently on the edge of her bed and stroked her hair softly. She stirred and opened her eyes slowly. She smiled when she saw Mark and stretched and purred. Then her expression changed to one of fear.

At twenty minutes to nine, Ari Ben Canaan, dressed as Captain Caleb Moore, entered the lead jeep in the convoy of twelve trucks of the 23rd Transportation Company. Each truck had a Palmachnik dressed like a British soldier as driver. They sped out of their camp and twenty minutes later halted before the administration building at Caraolos, outside the barbed-wire compounds.

Ari entered the administration building and knocked on the door of the commanding officer, whose acquaintance he had carefully made during the past three weeks.

"Good morning, sir," Ari said.

"Good morning, Captain Moore. What brings you up here?"

"We received a special dispatch from headquarters, sir. It seems that they are getting the Larnaca camp ready faster than they expected. They want me to transfer some children today." Ari lay the forged papers on the officer's desk.

The CO thumbed through the sheets. "This isn't on the schedule of transfers," he said. "We didn't expect to start moving the children for three days."

"That's the Army for you, sir," Ari said.

The CO bit his lip and meditated and stared at Ari and looked through the transfer papers again. He reached for the phone. "Hello. Potter here. Captain Moore has orders to move three hundred children out of Compound 50. Dispatch a detail to help get them moved."

The CO picked up his pen and initialed the papers. He signed half a dozen other sheets authorizing entrance into the compound and removal of the children. "Move them along, will you, Moore? We have another load to be transferred in an hour and the roads could be clogged."

"Yes sir."

"Oh, uh . . . Moore. Many thanks, old man, for the whisky you sent up to the club."

"My pleasure, sir."

Ari gathered up the papers from the CO's desk. The CO sighed. "Jews come and Jews go," he said.

"Yes sir," Ari said. "They come . . . and they go."

The breakfast table was set in front of the window in Mark's room. He and Kitty nibbled at their food. Mark's ash tray brimmed over. "What time is it now?" Kitty asked for the fifteenth time.

"Almost nine-thirty."

"What would be happening?"

"If they're running on schedule they're loading the children aboard the trucks right now. Look," Mark said, pointing out to sea. The salvage trawler *Aphrodite/Exodus* turned and moved slowly toward the harbor entrance.

"Good Lord," Kitty said, "is that the *Exodus*?"

"That's her."

166

"My God, Mark. It looks like it's ready to fall apart."

"It is."

"But how on earth are they going to get three hundred children on her?"

Mark lit another cigarette. He wanted to pace the room but he did not wish to show Kitty how frightened he was.

Nine-thirty.

Nine-forty.

The *Exodus* passed between the lighthouse and the castle, through the narrow opening of the two arms of the sea wall, and into the Kyrenia harbor.

Nine-fifty.

"Mark, please sit down. You're making me nervous."

"We should be getting a call from Mandria soon. Any minute now . . . any minute."

Ten o'clock.

Five past ten.

Six past ten.

Seven past ten.

"Dammit! Where is that coffee I ordered? Kitty, phone from your room, will you. Tell them to get that coffee up here."

A quarter past ten. The fresh pot of coffee arrived.

Seventeen past ten. Mark's jitters abated. He knew that if he did not hear from Mandria in the next ten minutes something had gone wrong.

Ten-twenty. The phone rang!

Mark and Kitty looked at each other for an instant. Mark wiped the sweat from the palm of his hand, sucked in his breath, and lifted the receiver.

"Hello."

"Mr. Parker?"

"Speaking."

"Just a moment, sir. We have a call for you from Famagusta."

"Hello . . . hello . . . hello."

"Parker?"

"Speaking."

"Mandria here."

"Yes?"

"They have just passed through."

Mark replaced the receiver slowly. "He got them out of Caraolos, all right. They're moving down the road to Larnaca now. In about fifteen minutes they'll fork off and make a dash north. They've got about fifty miles, mostly flat country with only one mountain pass if they don't have to use alternate roads. They should be here a little after noon . . . if everything goes all right."

"I'm almost hoping that something will go wrong," Kitty said.

"Come on. No use waiting here."

He took his field glasses and walked with Kitty downstairs to the reception desk and asked for a cable blank.

KENNETH BRADBURY
CHIEF, AMERICAN NEWS SYNDICATE
LONDON

HAVING A BALL. REQUEST TWO WEEK EXTENSION OF MY VACATION. ADVISE.

MARK

"Send this through, urgent. How long will it take?"

The receptionist read it over. "It will be in London in a few hours."

They walked from the Dome toward the quay.

"What was that about?" Kitty asked.

"My story should be on the wires from London tonight."

They stood on the quay for several moments and watched the rickety salvage tug tie up at dockside. Mark led Kitty away. They crossed the harbor and climbed to the ramparts of the Virgin Castle. From here they could see both the harbor and far down the coastal road where the convoy was due to pass.

At eleven fifteen Mark focused his field glasses on the coast road. He slowly scanned the road that hugged the shore and wove in and out of the hills. The mountain pass was too far off to see. He froze! He had sighted a tiny trail of dust and a line of trucks which appeared as small as ants. He nudged Kitty and handed her the glasses. She held them on the trucks as they wove in and out the snake-like turns and inched toward Kyrenia.

"They are about half an hour away."

They came down from the rampart, crossed the harbor once again, and stood at the end of the quay, which was only five walking minutes from the Dome Hotel. As the convoy passed the hospital at the edge of town Mark took Kitty's hand and started back to the hotel.

In a phone booth at the Dome, Mark put in an urgent call to British Intelligence in Famagusta.

"I wish to speak to Major Alistair," Mark said, disguising his voice by putting a handkerchief over the mouthpiece and speaking with a British accent.

168

"Who is calling, please, and what do you wish to speak to Major Alistair about?"

"Look, old boy," Mark said, "three hundred Jews have escaped from Caraolos. Now just don't ask any damned fool questions and give me Alistair."

The phone on Major Alistair's desk rang.

"Alistair here," he said in his whispery voice.

"This is a friend," Mark said. "I am advising you that several hundred Jews have broken out of Caraolos and are boarding a ship in the Kyrenia harbor at this very moment."

Alistair clicked the receiver several times. "Hello . . . hello . . . who is this? I say . . . hello." He closed his own phone and opened it again. "Alistair here. I have a report of an escape of Jews. They are supposed to be boarding a ship at Kyrenia. Sound an alert, blue. Have the Kyrenia area commander investigate at once. If the report is true you'd better advise naval units to move for that area."

Alistair put down the receiver and rushed down the hall toward Sutherland's office.

The convoy rolled to a stop on the quay. Ari Ben Canaan got out of the lead jeep and its driver drove it off. One by one the lorries rolled up to the *Exodus*. The youngsters responded automatically as a result of Zev's training. They moved quickly and quietly from the truck to the ship. On board, Joab, David, and Hank Schlosberg, the captain, moved them into their places in the hold and on deck. The operation was effected calmly and wordlessly.

Along the quay a few curious onlookers stood and gaped. A few British soldiers shrugged and scratched their heads. As quickly as each truck was unloaded it was driven off toward the mountains around St. Hilarion to be abandoned. As of that moment the 23rd Transportation Company had fulfilled its purpose and was going out of existence. Joab left a note in his truck thanking the British for the use of their lorry.

Ari boarded the *Exodus* and went up to the wheelhouse. One by one the lorries discharged the children. It took only twenty minutes to load the boat. Zev, David, Joab, and Hank Schlosberg reported that the boarding had been completed. Ari gave the order to Hank and he cast off and started the engines.

"Get to the children," Ari said, "and tell them exactly what we are doing and what will be expected of them. Any child who feels he cannot go through with it will advise me in the wheelhouse and he will be returned to Caraolos. Explain to them that their lives are in danger if they stay.

169

There is to be no pressure from you or the children to induce others to remain who wish to go."

As the Palmachniks went down to brief the children the *Exodus* backed into mid-harbor and dropped anchor.

In an instant the entire Kyrenia area was alive with the shriek of sirens! Ari turned a pair of field glasses on the hills and coastal road and saw dozens of British lorries and jeeps converging on Kyrenia. He laughed out loud as he saw the trucks of the late 23rd Transportation Company rushing up the hills to be abandoned. They were rushing away from Kyrenia and passed the convoy of British soldiers coming in the opposite direction.

Ari looked below him. The children on deck were calm.

The British poured into the harbor area! Lorry after lorry of soldiers erupted onto the quay. Several officers were pointing at the *Exodus* and shouting orders. Soldiers began racing along both arms of the sea wall and setting up machine guns and mortars at the narrow harbor opening so that if the *Exodus* were to try it could not get out to sea.

More lorries poured into the area. The quay was roped off and curious spectators pushed back. Ari watched the British strength grow by the moment. Inside of an hour the harbor was swarming with five hundred fully armed soldiers. A pair of torpedo boats stationed themselves outside the harbor. On the horizon Ari could see a trio of destroyers rushing to the scene. The sirens shrieked on! The peaceful little town was turning into an armed camp! Then tanks rumbled onto the quay and artillery replaced the machine guns and mortars guarding the harbor entrance.

Another blaze of sirens brought a car bearing Brigadier Sutherland, Caldwell, and Alistair onto the quay. Major Cooke, the area commander of Kyrenia, reported to Sutherland.

"That's the ship out there, sir. It's loaded with Jews all right. It can't possibly get away."

Sutherland studied the harbor. "You've got enough here to fight a Panzer division," he said; "they must be insane on that boat. Get a public-address system hooked up right away."

"Yes, sir."

"If you asked me, we'd blow them out of the water," Caldwell said.

"I didn't ask you," Sutherland snapped. "Cooke . . . get this area cordoned off. Organize a boarding party. Tear gas, small arms, in case they won't come back by themselves. Freddie, hop over to the Dome and inform headquarters I want a news blackout."

170

Alistair had remained quiet and was studying the tugboat. "What do you make of it, Alistair?"

"I don't like it, sir," he said. "They aren't pulling a daylight escape like this unless they have something else in mind."

"Come now, Alistair. You're always looking for sinister plots."

Mark Parker pushed his way past the guards and approached the two officers.

"What's all the noise about?" Mark asked Alistair.

The instant Alistair saw Mark he knew his suspicion was correct. "Really, Parker," Alistair said, "do be a good sport and tell us. You know, old man, you ought to brush up on your British accent the next time you telephone me."

"I don't know what you're talking about, Major."

Brigadier Sutherland was beginning to catch on. He looked from the tug to Parker and to Alistair and he knew that the Mossad Aliyah Bet had caught him unprepared. He flushed. Major Cooke, the Kyrenia area commander, reported. "We'll have boarding parties formed in ten minutes, sir. Two hundred men and we'll commandeer some trawlers here to take them out." Sutherland did not even hear him.

"Where is the loud-speaker, damn it all!"

Ten minutes later Sutherland grabbed a microphone. A silence fell over the harbor. The boarding parties stood by to go out into the middle of the harbor after the *Exodus*.

"Hello, out there! This is Brigadier Bruce Sutherland, the commander of Cyprus, speaking," his voice shot out in a series of echoes. "Can you hear me out there?"

In the wheelhouse of the *Exodus*, Ari Ben Canaan opened his public-address system. "Hello, Sutherland," he said, "this is Captain Caleb Moore of the 23rd Transportation Company, His Majesty's Jewish Forces on Cyprus. You can find your lorries up at St. Hilarion."

Sutherland turned pale. Alistair's mouth dropped open.

"Hello, out there!" Sutherland's voice snapped angrily. "We are going to give you ten minutes to return to dockside. If you do not we are going to send out a heavily armed boarding party and bring you back."

"Hello, Sutherland! This is the *Exodus* speaking. We have three hundred and two children aboard this boat. Our engine rooms are loaded with dynamite. If one of your troops sets foot on this boat or if one round is fired from any of your guns we are going to blow ourselves up!"

At that instant Mark Parker's story was being cabled from London to every corner of the world.

Sutherland, Alistair, and the five hundred British soldiers on the quay stood speechless as a flag was run up on the mast of the *Exodus*. It was a British Union Jack and in its center was painted a huge Nazi swastika.

The battle of the *Exodus* was on!

CHAPTER THIRTY

EXCLUSIVE! DAVID VERSUS GOLIATH: MODEL 1946
BY AMERICAN NEWS SYNDICATE CORRESPONDENT
MARK PARKER
KYRENIA, CYPRUS: (ANS)

I am writing this story from Kyrenia. It is a tiny, jewel-like harbor on the northern coast of the British Crown Colony of Cyprus.

Cyprus has been rich in the pageantry of history. The island is filled with reminders of its vaunted past, from the ruins of Salamis to the cathedrals of Famagusta and Nicosia to the many castles of Crusader glory.

But none of this colorful history can match for sheer naked drama the scene that is being played at this very moment in this quiet, unknown resort town. For some months Cyprus has been a detention center for Jewish refugees who have tried to run the British blockade into Palestine.

Today, three hundred children between the ages of ten and seventeen escaped the British camp at Caraolos in an as-yet-undetermined manner, and fled across the island to Kyrenia where a converted salvage tug of about two hundred tons awaited them for a dash to Palestine.

Almost all the escapees were graduates of German concentration and extermination camps. The salvage tug, fittingly renamed the Exodus, was discovered by British Intelligence before it could get out of the harbor.

With its three hundred refugees the ship is sitting at anchor in the center of the harbor, which measures a mere three hundred yards in diameter, and has defied all British efforts to have the children debark and return to Caraolos.

A spokesman for the Exodus has announced that the hold of the boat is filled with dynamite. The children have joined in a suicide pact and they will blow up the boat if the British attempt to board her.

LONDON

General Sir Clarence Tevor-Browne dropped the copy of the newspaper on his desk. He lit a cigar and studied the reports. Mark Parker's story was creating a sensation not only in Europe but in the United States. Tevor-Browne had a request for instructions from Sutherland, who refused to take the responsibility of issuing an order to board the *Exodus*.

Tevor-Browne knew that part of the blame was his. He had chosen Bruce Sutherland for the job of commander himself, and he had failed to act on the letter from Alistair which had warned that something was going to happen unless Sutherland was replaced.

Humphrey Crawford entered Tevor-Browne's office. Crawford was a pasty-faced career man in the Middle East section of the Colonial Office, and served as liaison between the army and the policy makers at Whitehall and Chatham House. "Afternoon, Sir Clarence," Crawford said nervously. "It is time for our meeting with Bradshaw."

Tevor-Browne arose and gathered some papers together. "Mustn't keep old Cecil Bradshaw waiting."

Cecil Bradshaw's office was in the Institute of International Relations at Chatham House. For thirty years he had been one of the top men in formulating British Middle East policy.

At the end of World War I, Britain and France competed for influence in the Middle East. When the British got the Palestine mandate, Bradshaw had been one of those, with Winston Churchill, who had pushed for the creation of an Arab state out of half the mandate. The state they were instrumental in forming was Trans-Jordan. The entire purpose for bringing it into being was to turn it into a British military base. British subsidies made possible the establishment of Britain's Arab army, the "Arab Legion," and the choosing of a king for Trans-Jordan. He was the Hashimite Arab Abdullah, mortal enemy of Saud of Saudi Arabia.

At the end of World War II the Labour party swept into power with promises—among others—to help establish a Jewish homeland in Palestine and a refuge for the survivors in Europe. Cecil Bradshaw led that strong faction in Chatham House which convinced the new Foreign Minister that these promises were charming but not very practical and that Britain's interests lay with the Arabs. The Arabs' ten million square miles were rich in oil and included a vital canal.

General Sir Clarence Tevor-Browne and Humphrey Crawford were ushered into Cecil Bradshaw's office. The latter, a fat man in his sixties, stood looking at the wall with his back to them, his pudgy hands clasped behind him. Humphrey Crawford sat down nervously on the edge of a seat. Tevor-Browne made himself comfortable in a deep leather chair and lit a cigar.

Bradshaw talked to the wall. "Congratulations, gentlemen," he said in a voice filled with sarcasm and quivering with

173

anger. "I see we made the news today." He turned and patted his rotund stomach and smiled. "You expected to find me in a lather. No indeed, no indeed. Whitehall called this morning. As expected, the Minister has dumped this *Exodus* business into my lap." Bradshaw sat behind his desk, glanced at the reports, and snatched off his thick horn-rimmed glasses with a quick gesture. "Tell me, Sir Clarence . . . was your Intelligence staff dead or merely out for tennis? And I believe you have a bit of explaining to do about Sutherland. He was your idea."

Tevor-Browne refused to be bullied. "I believe the establishment of camps on Cyprus was your idea. What is your explanation?"

"Gentlemen," Crawford said quickly to avert a clash, "we are faced with a peculiar situation in this *Exodus* affair. This is the first time any publicity has carried into the American press."

Bradshaw laughed a wheezy laugh. His big apple cheeks reddened. "With all of Truman's talk the Americans have only allowed ten thousand Jewish refugees into the country since the end of the war. Certainly Truman is for Zionism . . . as long as Palestine isn't in Pennsylvania. Everyone talks idealistically but we are still the ones with a million Jews on our hands, a million Jews who could ruin our entire position in the Middle East." Bradshaw replaced his glasses. "*Star of David, Moses, Palmach, Gates of Zion, Door of Hope,* and now the *Exodus*. The Zionists are very clever people. For twenty-five years they have made us the villains in Palestine. They write words into the mandate articles and the Balfour Declaration that were never meant. They can argue a camel into thinking he is a mule. Good Lord . . . two hours with Chaim Weizmann and I'm about ready to join the Zionists myself." Cecil Bradshaw took off his glasses again. "We know *your* sympathies, Tevor-Browne."

"I resent the implications, Bradshaw. Perhaps I am one of a few hardheads who say the only way we are going to hold the Middle East is by building a powerful Jewish Palestine. I don't speak of Jewish interest but I speak of British interest."

Bradshaw interrupted. "Now let's get to this *Exodus* affair. The implications are absolutely clear. We gave in on the *Promised Land* but this time we will not give in. This boat is in our waters and not in French waters. We will not go on board, we will not send them to Germany, we will not sink them. They will sit in Kyrenia until they rot. Rot—do you hear that, Tevor-Browne?—rot." His hand began to shake as he grew angrier.

Tevor-Browne closed his eyes. "We cannot fight this out on moral grounds. We have no cause to keep three hundred

174

children who were raised in concentration camps from entering Palestine. Oil . . . canals . . . Arabs be damned! We have no cause! We made ourselves look ridiculous by sending the *Promised Land* refugees to Germany."

"I know your sympathies!"

"Gentlemen!"

Tevor-Browne stood up and leaned over Bradshaw's desk. "There is only one way we can win this *Exodus* affair. The Jews have planned this whole incident to create propaganda. Turn the tables on them. Let the *Exodus* sail this minute. That is what they don't want."

"Never!"

"Can't you see, sir, that we're playing right into their hands?"

"That ship will not sail as long as I am in Chatham House!"

CHAPTER THIRTY-ONE

MARK PARKER
DOME HOTEL
KYRENIA, CYPRUS

STORY GAINING MOMENTUM. KEEP THEM COMING.
                    KEN BRADBURY, ANS LONDON

KYRENIA, CYPRUS (ANS),
BY MARK PARKER

It is a ridiculous sight. One thousand armed soldiers, tanks, artillery, and a naval task force all looking helplessly out at an unarmed salvage tug.

The battle of the Exodus *ends week one in a draw. Both the British and the refugees are holding fast. To date no one has boarded the illegal runner which has threatened to blow itself up, but from the quay it is only a few hundred yards distant and a pair of field glasses bring the boat an arm's length away.*

The morale of the three hundred children on the Exodus *seems to be phenomenal. They spent the week in the harbor alternately singing and catcalling to the British troops on the quay and sea wall.*

Mark's reports went out daily, each new one adding new and interesting details.

When Cecil Bradshaw made the decision to make a test case of the *Exodus* he knew there would be a barrage of adverse criticism. The French press staged its usual uproar, although this time the insults were so terrible that the likes of them had not been heard in the history of the Anglo-French alliance. The story spread throughout Europe, and even the British press became split and questioned Whitehall's wisdom in not letting the *Exodus* sail for Palestine.

Bradshaw was a wise politician and he had weathered many storms. This one was a storm in a teacup and it would blow over, he was sure. He sent a trio of friendly journalists to Kyrenia to counter Parker's reports, and a half dozen experts worked full time to explain the British position. The British had a case and it was being presented well, but it was difficult to offset natural sentiment for a group of refugee children.

If the Zionists are so sincere, why are they endangering the lives of three hundred innocent children? The whole thing is a sinister and cold-blooded plot to create sympathy and becloud the real issues of the Palestine mandate. It is obvious we are dealing with fanatics. Ari Ben Canaan is a professional Zionist agitator with a record of years of illegal operations.

Newspapermen from half a dozen countries landed at the Nicosia airport and demanded permission to enter the Kyrenia area. Several large magazines also sent in teams. The Dome Hotel began to look like a small political convention headquarters.

In cafés in Paris the British were denounced.

In pubs in London the British were defended.

In Stockholm there were sermons.

In Rome there were debates.

In New York bookies were laying four to one that the *Exodus* would not sail.

At the end of the second week Ari granted Mark permission to board the ship. Mark picked what he believed to be the ripe moment and arranged it by preset signals. Since he was the first outsider to board the *Exodus* his next three reports were carried by every newspaper on the front page.

EXCLUSIVE INTERVIEW WITH EXODUS SPOKESMAN ARI BEN CANAAN:
KYRENIA, CYPRUS (ANS).

Today I became the first correspondent to interview Ari Ben Canaan, the spokesman for the children on the Exodus. *I confronted Ben Canaan with the barrage of British reports maintaining that he was a professional Zionist troublemaker and with other Whitehall accusations. We spoke in the wheelhouse of the boat, the only place aboard not teeming with*

176

humanity. Today the children seem still to be in top spirits but are starting to show physical effects of their two-week siege.

Ben Canaan, thirty, and a strapping six-footer with black hair and ice-blue eyes, could be mistaken for a movie leading man. He expressed his gratitude to well-wishers around the world and assured me the children were holding up fine. In reply to my questions he answered, "I don't care about the personal attacks on me. I wonder if the British added that I was a captain in their army during World War II. I admit I am a Zionist troublemaker and I will continue to be one until they keep their promises about Palestine. Whether my work is legal or not is a matter of opinion."

I pressed him about the British arguments and the importance of the Exodus. *"We Jews are blamed for many things and we are used to it. In anything concerning the Palestine mandate that cannot be explained logically and reasonably they drag out the old excuse that it is some sinister plot of Zionism. I am really amazed that they haven't blamed the Zionists for the trouble they are having in India. Fortunately for us, Gandhi is not Jewish.*

"Whitehall is using that tired whipping boy, the mysterious Zionists, to cover three decades of dirty work, lies to both Jews and Arabs, sellouts, double crosses, and betrayals in the mandate. The first promise they broke was the Balfour Declaration of 1917 which promised a Jewish homeland, and they have been breaking promises ever since. The latest double cross has come from the Labour party, which, before the elections, promised to open the doors of Palestine to survivors of Hitler's regime.

"I am astounded at Whitehall's crocodile tears over our victimizing of children. Every child on the Exodus *is a volunteer. Every child on th*e Exodus *is an orphan because of Hitlerism. Nearly every child has lived in either German or British concentration camps for six years.*

"If Whitehall is so concerned about the welfare of these children then I challenge them to throw open the gates of Caraolos to inspection of the newsmen. It is nothing more or less than a concentration camp. People are kept behind barbed wire at machine-gun point with insufficient food, water, and medical care. No charges have been brought against these people. But they are being forcibly detained in Caraolos.

"Whitehall talks of our trying to bully them into an unjust solution of the mandate. There are a quarter of a million Jews in Europe who survived out of six million.

"The British quota of Jews allowed into Palestine is seven hundred a month. Is this their 'just solution'?

177

"Finally, I argue the right of the British in Palestine. Have they more right to be there than the survivors of Hitler? Let me read you something."

With that, Ben Canaan took a Bible from the desk of the wheelhouse, opened it to Ezekiel, and read:

> "Thus saith the Lord God; When I shall have gathered the house of Israel from the people among whom they are scattered, and shall be sanctified in them in the sight of the nations, then shall they dwell in their land that I have given to my servant Jacob wherein your fathers abode and they shall abide therein and even they and their children and their children's children forever."

Ari Ben Canaan put the Bible down. "The gentlemen at Whitehall had better study their claims further. I say the same thing to the Foreign Minister that a great man said to another oppressor three thousand years ago—LET MY PEOPLE GO."

The day after his "Let my people go" report Mark followed up with the inside story of Operation Gideon, including details of how British trucks had been used in the escape. British prestige hit a low-water mark.

On Mark's advice, Ari allowed other newsmen to board the *Exodus* and they clamored to be let into the Caraolos camp.

Cecil Bradshaw had expected criticism, but he had not reckoned on the furor that had been created. Meeting followed meeting, as for that moment in time the eyes of the world focused on Kyrenia harbor. To allow the *Exodus* to sail would be completely disastrous now.

General Sir Clarence Tevor-Browne flew secretly to Cyprus to take command and see whether something could be done.

His plane landed in the small hours of the morning under security measures at the Nicosia airdrome. Major Alistair met him and they quickly entered a staff car and it whisked off toward Famagusta headquarters.

"I wanted to speak to you, Alistair, before I took over from Sutherland. Of course I received your letter and you are free to speak."

"Well, sir," Alistair said, "I would say that the strain has got Sutherland down. Something has happened to the man. Caldwell tells me he has one nightmare after another. He walks all night long, till dawn, and he spends most of his days reading the Bible."

"Damned shame," Tevor-Browne said. "Bruce has been a corking good soldier. I trust what is said will never leave this car. We must protect the man."

"Of course, sir," Alistair said.

KYRENIA, CYPRUS (AP)
EXCLUSIVE

General Sir Clarence Tevor-Browne of desert fame landed anonymously at Nicosia airdrome last night. Sir Clarence was dressed in civilian clothes and his arrival was marked by secrecy. Tevor-Browne's appearance on the scene confirms Whitehall's concern over the Exodus. *It could indicate a change in policy if not a change in command.*

Mark boarded the *Exodus* and asked that Karen be sent to the wheelhouse. He was worried as he pushed his way over the crowded deck. The children were looking gaunt and they smelled bad from the lack of water to wash with.

Ari was in the wheelhouse as placid as ever. Mark gave him cigarettes and a few bottles of brandy. "How's it going out there?" Ari asked.

"Doesn't look like any change in policy with Tevor-Browne in. The story is still tops all over. Bigger than I expected. Look, Ari, this thing has worked perfectly for you and me both. You've done what you started out to do, given the British a black eye. The word I got is that the British are not going to back down."

"What's the point?"

"The point is you can top this whole thing off by making a humanity move and taking the ship to dock. We'll make a big story when the British march them back to Caraolos. It will tear the people's hearts out."

"Did Kitty send you in with this?"

"Aw, cut it out, will you. Just look down there at those kids. They're starting to come apart."

"They knew what they were in for."

"There's another thing, Ari. I'm afraid we've hit the mark with this story. We're on top now, but tomorrow Frank Sinatra may unload a left hook on some columnist in a night club and we're off page one."

Karen entered the wheelhouse. "Hello, Mr. Parker," she said softly.

"Hello, honey. Here's a letter from Kitty and a package."

She took the letter and gave Mark one for Kitty. She refused the package as she had refused all the other packages.

"Christ, I haven't got the heart to tell Kitty she won't

179

take the packages for herself. That girl is sick. Did you see the circles under her eyes? You're going to have real trouble on this ship in another few days."

"We were speaking of maintaining public interest. Get one thing straight, Parker. We don't go back to Caraolos. There are a quarter of a million Jews in Europe waiting for an answer and we are the only ones who can answer them. Starting tomorrow we will declare a hunger strike. Anyone who passes out will be placed on deck for the British to look at."

"You ghoul . . . you stinking ghoul," Mark snarled.

"Call me what you want, Parker. Do you think I like starving a bunch of orphans? Give me something else to fight with. Give me something to shoot at those tanks and those destroyers! All we've got is our guts and what we believe in. We've had the hell knocked out of us for two thousand years. This is one fight we're going to win."

CHAPTER THIRTY-TWO

HUNGER STRIKE
CALLED ON EXODUS!
Children vow starvation rather than return to Caraolos.

After allowing the story to build up over a two-week period, Ari Ben Canaan fooled everyone by launching an offensive. It was no game of "wait and see" now; the children were forcing a decision.

A huge sign was tied to the sides of the *Exodus* with lettering in English, French, and Hebrew. The sign read:
Hunger Strike/Hour #1
Hunger Strike/Hour # 15
Two boys and a girl, aged ten, twelve, and fifteen, were brought on the forward deck of the *Exodus* and laid out, unconscious.
Hunger Strike/Hour #20
Ten children were stretched out on the forward deck.

"For Christ's sake, Kitty, stop pacing and sit down!"

"It's over twenty hours now. How much longer is he going to let this go on? I just haven't had the courage to go to the quay and look. Is Karen one of those children unconscious on deck?"

"I told you ten times she wasn't."

"They aren't strong children to begin with and they've been cooped up on that ship for two weeks. They have no stamina
180

left." Kitty pulled nervously at a cigarette and tugged at her hair. "That man is a beast. An inhuman beast."

"I've been thinking about that," Mark said. "I've been thinking about it a lot. I wonder if we really understand what is driving those people so hard. Have you ever seen Palestine? It's worthless desert in the south end and eroded in the middle and swamp up north. It's stinking, it's sunbaked, and it's in the middle of a sea of fifty million sworn enemies. Yet they break their necks to get there. They call it the Land of Milk and Honey . . . they sing about water sprinklers and irrigation ditches. Two weeks ago I told Ari Ben Canaan that the Jews don't have a patent on suffering but I'm beginning to wonder. I swear I wonder. I wonder how something can hurt so badly that can drive them so hard."

"Don't defend them, Mark, and don't defend those people."

"Try to remember one thing. Ben Canaan couldn't do this without the support of those kids. They're behind him one hundred per cent."

"That's what hurts," Kitty said, "this loyalty. This fantastic loyalty they have for each other."

The phone rang. Mark answered, listened, and hung up.

"What is it? I said what is it, Mark!"

"They've brought some more kids up on the deck unconscious. A half dozen of them."

"Is . . . is . . . Karen . . . ?"

"I don't know. I'm going to find out."

"Mark."

"What?"

"I want to go on the *Exodus*."

"That's impossible."

"I can't take it any more," she said.

"If you do this you're finished."

"No, Mark . . . it's different. If I knew she were alive and well I could bear it. I swear I could. I made myself know that. But I can't just sit idly and know she's dying. I can't do that."

"Even if I can get Ben Canaan to let you on the *Exodus* the British won't let you."

"You must," she said fiercely, "you must."

She stood with her back to the door and blocked his exit. Her face determined. Mark lowered his eyes. "I'll do what I can," he said.

Hunger Strike/Hour #35

Angry crowds in Paris and Rome demonstrated before the British embassies. Fierce oratory and placards demanded the release of the *Exodus*. Police clubs and tear gas were used in Paris to disperse the mob. In Copenhagen and in Stockholm and in Brussels and in The Hague there were other demonstrations. These were more orderly.

Hunger Strike/Hour #38

A spontaneous general strike swept over the island of Cyprus in protest against the British. Transportation stopped, businesses shut down, and ports closed, theaters and restaurants locked their doors. Famagusta, Nicosia, Larnaca, and Limassol looked like morgues.

Hunger Strike/Hour #40

Ari Ben Canaan stared at his lieutenants. He looked into the somber faces of Joab, David, Zev, and Hank Schlosberg.

Zev, the Galilee farmer, spoke up first. "I am a soldier. I cannot stand by and watch children starve to death."

"In Palestine," Ari snapped, "youngsters this same age are already fighters in Gadna."

"It is one thing to fight and it is another to starve to death."

"This is only another way of fighting," Ari said.

Joab Yarkoni had worked with Ari for many years and had served with him in World War II. "I have never gone against you, Ari. The minute one of these children dies this whole thing is liable to boomerang on us."

Ari looked over to Hank Schlosberg, the American captain. Hank shrugged. "You're the boss, Ari, but the crew is getting jittery. They didn't bargain for this."

"In other words," Ari said, "you want to surrender."

Their silence confirmed it.

"David, what about you? I haven't heard from you."

David, a scholar, was steeped in the Torah and in the holy books. He had a closeness to God that none of the rest of them had and they respected it.

"Six million Jews died in gas chambers not knowing why they died," he said. "If three hundred of us on the *Exodus* die we will certainly know why. The world will know too. When we were a nation two thousand years ago and when we rebelled against Roman and Greek rule we Jews established the tradition of fighting to the last man. We did this at Arbela and Jerusalem. We did this at Beitar and Herodium and Machærus. At Masada we held out against the Romans for four years and when they entered the fort they found us all dead. No people, anywhere, have fought for their freedom as have our people. We drove the Romans and the Greeks from our land until we were dispersed to the four corners of the world. We have not had much opportunity to fight as a nation for two thousand years. When we had that opportunity at the Warsaw ghetto we did honor to our tradition. I say if we leave this boat and willingly return to barbed-wire prisons then we will have broken faith with God."

"Are there any further questions?" Ari said.

Hunger Strike/Hour #42

In the United States, South Africa, and England mass prayer meetings were being held in synagogues, and in many churches there were prayers for the safety of the children on the *Exodus*.

Hunger Strike/Hour #45

The Jews in Argentina began to fast in sympathy with the children aboard the *Exodus*.

Hunger Strike/Hour #47

It was getting dark as Kitty boarded the *Exodus*. The stench was overpowering. All over the deck, in the lifeboats, on the superstructure she saw the crush of humanity. Everyone was lying down and absolutely motionless to conserve energy.

"I want to see those children who have passed out," she said.

David led her to the bow of the ship where there were three rows of unconscious children, sixty in number. David knelt and held his lantern close to the bodies as Kitty moved from one to the other, feeling their pulses and looking into the pupils of their eyes. Half a dozen times she thought she would faint as her heart pounded and she rolled over a child who looked like Karen.

David led her around the packed deck, stepping over the prostrate bodies. The children stared listlessly at her with dazed eyes. Their hair was matted and dirt caked their faces.

David led her down the steep ladder onto the hold. She nearly vomited as the stink enveloped her. In the half light she saw the ghastly sight of the children packed in shelves one atop the other.

On the deck of the hold they lay piled against each other. She found Karen in a corner, enmeshed in a tangle of arms and legs. Dov was asleep next to her. They lay on a pile of rags and the deck was slimy beneath them.

"Karen," she whispered. "Karen, it's me, Kitty."

Karen's eyes fluttered open. There were huge black circles beneath them and her lips were caked dry. She was too weak to sit up.

"Kitty?"

"Yes, it's me."

Karen held her arms open and Kitty held her tightly for many moments. "Don't leave, Kitty. I'm so frightened."

"I'll be near," Kitty whispered, releasing the girl.

She went to the hospital and examined the limited supply of drugs and sighed despondently. "There is very little that can be done," she said to David. "I'll try to make them as comfortable as possible. Can you and Joab work with me?"

"Of course."

"Some of those unconscious are in serious condition. We'll have to try to sponge them to get their fevers down. It is chilly up on deck. We'll keep them covered. Then I want everyone who is capable of working to get this ship clean."

Kitty labored feverishly for hours to ward off death. It was like trying to fill an ocean with a thimble. As soon as one child was brought under control three more became seriously ill. She hadn't the drugs, water, or other facilities to do very much. Food, the one weapon, could not be used.

Hunger Strike/Hour #81

Seventy children in coma lay on the deck of the *Exodus*.

On the quay of Kyrenia harbor there were angry grumbles of insubordination from the British ranks. Many of the soldiers could stand it no longer and asked to be removed, even at the risk of court-martial. The eyes of Cyprus fastened on Kyrenia.

Hunger Strike/Hour #82

Karen Hansen Clement was carried to the bow of the ship, unconscious.

Hunger Strike/Hour #83

Kitty walked into the wheelhouse and slumped exhausted into a chair. She had worked for thirty-five straight hours and her mind was muddled and dazed. Ari poured her a stiff brandy.

"Go on and drink," he said. "You aren't on strike."

She swallowed it down, and a second drink brought her to her senses. She stared at Ari Ben Canaan long and hard. He was a powerful man. He showed almost no effects of the siege. She looked into his cold eyes and wondered what thoughts, what plots, what tricks were running through his brain. She wondered if he was frightened or even knew fear. She wondered if he was sad or shaken.

"I was expecting you to come up here to see me much sooner," he said.

"I won't beg you, Ari Ben Canaan. Ben Canaan and God . . . in that order . . . isn't that right? Well, there are a dozen children on the verge of death. I am merely reporting to you like a good Palmachnik. They're going to die, Mr. Ben Canaan. How do you rule?"

"I've been insulted before, Kitty. It doesn't bother me. Is this humanity of yours so great that it cries out for all these children or does it appeal for the life of one child?"

"You have no right to ask that."

"You are begging for the life of one girl. I am begging for the lives of a quarter of a million people."

She rose. "I had better get back to work. Ari, you knew

184

why I wanted to come on board the *Exodus*. Why did you let me?"

He turned his back to her and looked from the window out to sea where the cruiser and destroyers stood watch. "Maybe I wanted to see you."

Hunger Strike/Hour #85

General Sir Clarence Tevor-Browne paced up and down Sutherland's office. The smoke from his cigar clouded the room. He stopped several times and looked out the window in the direction of Kyrenia.

Sutherland tapped out his pipe and studied the array of sandwiches on the tray on the coffee table. "Won't you sit down, Sir Clarence, and have a bite to eat and a spot of tea?"

Tevor-Browne looked at his wrist watch and sighed. He seated himself and picked up a sandwich, stared at it, nibbled, then threw it down. "I feel guilty when I eat," he said.

"This is a bad business to be in for a man with a conscience," Sutherland said. "Two wars, eleven foreign posts, six decorations, and three orders. Now I've been stopped in my tracks by a band of unarmed children. A fine way to end thirty years of service, eh, Sir Clarence?"

Tevor-Browne lowered his eyes.

"Oh, I know you've been wanting to talk to me," said Sutherland.

Tevor-Browne poured some tea and sighed, half embarrassed. "See here, Bruce. If it were up to me . . ."

"Nonsense, Sir Clarence. Don't feel badly. It is I who feel badly. I let you down." Sutherland rose and his eyes brimmed. "I am tired. I am very tired."

"We will arrange a full pension and have the retirement as quiet as possible. You can count on me," Tevor-Browne said. "See here, Bruce. I stopped over in Paris on my way here and I had a long talk with Neddie. I told her about your predicament. Listen, old boy, with some encouragement from you, you two could get together again. Neddie wants you back and you're going to need her."

Sutherland shook his head. "Neddie and I have been through for years. All we ever had between us that was meaningful was the Army. That's what held us together."

"Any plans?"

"These months on Cyprus have done something to me, Sir Clarence, especially these past few weeks. You may not believe this, but I don't feel that I've suffered a defeat. I feel that I may have won something very great. Something I lost a long time ago."

"And what is that?"

"Truth. Do you remember when I took this post? You told

185

me that the only kingdom that runs on right and wrong is the kingdom of heaven and the kingdoms of the earth run on oil."

"I remember it well," Tevor-Browne said.

"Yes," Sutherland said, "I have thought so much about it since this *Exodus* affair. All my life I have known the truth and I have known right from wrong. Most of us do. To know the truth is one thing. To live it . . . to create the kingdom of heaven on earth is another. How many times in a man's life does he do things that are repulsive to his morality in order to exist? How I have admired those few men in this world who could stand up for their convictions in the face of shame, torture, and even death. What a wonderful feeling of inner peace they must have. Something that we ordinary mortals can never know. Gandhi is such a man.

"I am going to that rotten sliver of land that these Jews call their kingdom of heaven on earth. I want to know it all . . . Galilee, Jerusalem . . . all of it."

"I envy you, Bruce."

"Perhaps I'll settle down near Safed . . . on Mount Canaan."

Major Alistair entered the office. He was pale and his hand shook as he gave Tevor-Browne a note to read. Tevor-Browne read it and reread it and could not believe his eyes. "Great God, save us all," he whispered. He passed the note to Bruce Sutherland.

URGENT

Ari Ben Canaan, spokesman for the Exodus, *announced that beginning at noon tomorrow ten volunteers a day will commit suicide on the bridge of the ship in full view of the British garrison. This protest practice will continue until either the* Exodus *is permitted to sail for Palestine or everyone aboard is dead.*

Bradshaw, with Humphrey Crawford and half a dozen aides, sped out of London to the quiet of a peaceful, isolated little house in the country. He had fourteen hours to act before the suicides on the *Exodus* began.

He had badly miscalculated the entire thing. First, the tenacity and determination of the children on the ship. Second, the powerful propaganda the incident created. Finally, he had not imagined that Ben Canaan would take the offensive and press the issue as he had. Bradshaw was a stubborn man but he knew when he was defeated, and he now turned his efforts to making a face-saving settlement.

Bradshaw had Crawford and his aides cable or phone a

186

dozen of the top Jewish leaders in England, Palestine, and the United States to ask them to intervene. The Palestinians, in particular, might possibly dissuade Ben Canaan. At the very least they could stall the action long enough to enable Bradshaw to come up with some alternate plans. If he could get Ben Canaan to agree to negotiate then he could talk the *Exodus* to death. Within six hours, Bradshaw had his answers from the Jewish leaders. They answered uniformly: WE WILL NOT INTERCEDE.

Next Bradshaw contacted Tevor-Browne on Cyprus. He instructed the general to inform the *Exodus* that the British were working out a compromise and to delay the deadline for twenty-four hours.

Tevor-Browne carried out these instructions and relayed Ben Canaan's answer back to England.

URGENT

> Ben Canaan informed us there is nothing to discuss. He says either the Exodus sails or it doesn't sail. He further states that complete amnesty to the Palestinians aboard is part of the conditions. Ben Canaan summarized: Let my people go.
>
> Tevor-Browne

Cecil Bradshaw could not sleep. He paced back and forth, back and forth. It was just a little over six hours before the children on the *Exodus* would begin committing suicide. He had only three hours left in which to make a decision to hand to the Cabinet. No compromise could be reached.

Was he fighting a madman? Or was this Ari Ben Canaan a shrewd and heartless schemer who had deftly led him deeper and deeper into a trap?

LET MY PEOPLE GO!

Bradshaw walked to his desk and flicked on the lamp.

URGENT

> Ari Ben Canaan, spokesman for the Exodus, announced that beginning at noon tomorrow ten volunteers a day will commit suicide . . .

Suicide . . . suicide . . . suicide . . .

Bradshaw's hand shook so violently he dropped the paper.

Also on his desk were a dozen communiqués from various European and American governments. In that polite language that diplomats use they all expressed concern over

187

the *Exodus* impasse. He also had notes from each of the Arab governments expressing the view that if the *Exodus* were permitted to sail for Palestine it would be considered an affront to every Arab.

Cecil Bradshaw was confused now. The past few days had been a living hell. How had it all begun? Thirty years of formulating Middle Eastern policy and now he was in his worst trouble over an unarmed salvage tug.

What queer trick of fate had given him the mantle of an oppressor? Nobody could possibly accuse him of being anti-Jewish. Secretly Bradshaw admired the Jews in Palestine and understood the meaning of their return. He enjoyed the hours he had spent arguing with Zionists around conference tables, bucking their brilliant debaters. Cecil Bradshaw believed from the bottom of his heart that England's interest lay with the Arabs. Yet the Mandate had grown to over half a million Jews. And the Arabs were adamant that the British were fostering a Jewish nation in their midst.

During all the years of work he had been realistic with himself. What was happening? He could see his own grandchildren lying on the deck of ·the *Exodus*. Bradshaw knew his Bible as well as any well-brought-up Englishman and like most Englishmen had a tremendous sense of honor although he was not deeply religious. Could it be that the *Exodus* was driven by mystic forces? No, he was a practical diplomat and he did not believe in the supernatural.

Yet—he had an army and a navy and the power to squash the *Exodus* and all the other illegal runners—but he could not bring himself to do it.

The Pharaoh of Egypt had had might on his side too! Sweat ran down Bradshaw's face. It was all nonsense! He was tired and the pressure had been too great. What foolishness!

LET MY PEOPLE GO!

Bradshaw walked to the library and found a Bible and in near panic began to read through the pages of Exodus and about the Ten Plagues that God sent down on the land of Egypt.

Was he Pharaoh? Would a curse rain down on Britain? He went back to his room and tried to rest, but a staccato rhythm kept running through his tired brain . . . let my people go . . . let my people go . . .

"Crawford!" he yelled. "Crawford!"

Crawford ran in, tying his robe. "You called?"

"Crawford. Get through to Tevor-Browne on Cyprus at once. Tell him . . . tell him to let the *Exodus* sail for Palestine."

BOOK 2

The Land is Mine

> ...for the land is mine: for ye are strangers
> and sojourners with me. And in all the land
> of your possession ye shall grant a redemption
> for the land.

The word of God as given to
Moses in Leviticus

CHAPTER ONE: The battle of the *Exodus* was over!

Within seconds, the words *"Exodus* to sail" were on the wires. Within minutes they blazed in headlines around the world.

On Cyprus the joy of the people was boundless and around the world there was one long sigh of relief.

On the *Exodus* the children were too exhausted to celebrate.

The British urged Ari Ben Canaan to bring the salvage tug to dockside so that the children could be given medical care and the ship restocked and inspected. Ben Canaan agreed, and as the *Exodus* pulled in, Kyrenia turned into a mad scramble of activity. A score of British army doctors swarmed onto the ship and quickly removed the more severe cases. A hastily improvised hospital was established at the Dome Hotel. Rations and clothing and supplies poured onto the dock. In addition, hundreds of gifts from the people of Cyprus deluged the ship. Royal engineers combed the ancient tug from stem to stern to patch leaks, overhaul the motor, and refit her. Sanitation teams made her spotless.

After an initial survey Ari was advised it would take several days to get the children strong enough and the ship fit enough to make the day and a half run to Palestine. The small Jewish community on Cyprus sent a delegation to Ari to appeal to him to allow the children to celebrate the first night of Chanukah, the Festival of Lights, on Cyprus before sailing; the holiday was to begin in a few days. Ari agreed.

Only after Kitty had been assured and reassured that Karen's condition was not serious did she allow herself the luxury of a steaming hot tub, a thick steak, a half pint of Scotch, and a magnificent, deep, seventeen-hour sleep.

Kitty awoke to a problem she could no longer avoid. She had to decide either to end the episode with Karen forever or to follow the girl to Palestine.

Late in the evening when Mark came into her room for tea she appeared none the worse for her ordeal. In fact, the long sleep had made her look quite attractive.

"Newsroom still hectic?"

"Matter of fact, no," Mark answered. "The captains and the kings are departing. The *Exodus* is day-old news now . . . the kind they wrap fish in. Oh, I suppose we can drum up a final page-one picture when the boat lands in Haifa."

"People are fickle."

"No, not really, Kitty. The world just has a habit of moving on."

She sipped her tea and sank into silence. Mark lit a cigarette and propped his feet on the window sill. He pretended his fingers were a pistol and pointed over his shoe tops out at the pier.

"What about you, Mark?"

"Me? Old Mark Parker has worn out his welcome in the king's domains. I'm going Stateside and then maybe take a crack at the Asian beat. I've had an itch to go there anyhow . . . I hear it runs crosswise."

"The British won't let you into Palestine?"

"Not a chance. I am held in very low esteem. In fact if they weren't proper Englishmen I'd say they hate my guts. Frankly, I don't blame them."

"Give me a cigarette."

Mark lit one and handed it to her. He bided his time, continuing to take target practice with his imaginary pistol.

"Damn you, Mark! I hate that smug way you have of reading my mind."

"You've been a busy little girl. You went to the British authorities to ask permission to enter Palestine. Being the gentlemen they are, they opened the door for you and bowed. You were just a clean-cut American girl doing her duty. Of course, CID doesn't know about your little rumrunning act for Aliyah Bet. Well . . . are you going or not?"

"God, I don't know."

"You mean you haven't talked yourself into it yet."

"I mean I don't know."

"So which side do you want me to take?"

"You could stop acting like a worldly Buddha looking down on the poor tormented mortals. And you could stop sniping at me, Mark."

Mark dropped his feet from the window sill. "Go on . . . go to Palestine. That's what you want to hear, isn't it?"

"I still don't feel right around Jewish people . . . I can't help it."

"You feel fine around that girl though, don't you? Does she still remind you of your daughter?"

"Not really, not any more. She is too much of herself to be anyone else. But I love her and want her, if that's what you mean."

"I've got a loaded question for you, Mrs. Fremont . . ."

"Go on."

"Are you in love with Ari Ben Canaan?"

Love Ari Ben Canaan? She knew that he affected her whenever he was near or spoke or looked at her or even when she thought of him. She knew she had never met another man exactly like him. She knew she had a certain fear of his dark quietness and his tremendous power. She knew she admired his daring and courage. She knew there were moments she loathed him as she had never loathed another human being. But love . . . ?

"I don't know," she murmured. "As much as I cannot walk into it . . . I can't seem to be able to walk away from it and I don't know why . . . I don't know why."

Later, Kitty spent over an hour with Karen in the hospital ward that had been set up on the second floor of the hotel. Karen had made a remarkable recovery. In fact, the doctors were amazed with the near magic effect the two words "Eretz Israel" had on all the children. It was more potent than any medicine. As Kitty sat with Karen she looked out over the faces of the children in the ward. Who were they? Where did they come from? Where were they going? What strange, strange people . . . what a strange, strange obsession they carried.

There were long periods of silence between Kitty and Karen in which neither of them dared broach the subject of her coming on to Palestine. At last Karen fell asleep. Kitty stared down at the girl. How lovely she was . . . how very lovely. She kissed Karen's forehead and stroked her hair and Karen smiled in her sleep.

She walked out to the corridor where Dov Landau was pacing back and forth. They both halted, stared at each other, and Kitty passed on wordlessly.

The sun was setting as Kitty walked out to the quay. Across the street Zev Gilboa and Joab Yarkoni were supervising the loading of materials aboard the salvage tug. She looked about quickly to catch a glimpse of Ari. He was not in sight.

"*Shalom*, Kitty!" they called to her.

"Hi!" she called back.

She walked on down the quay toward the lighthouse. It was getting chilly. She put on her sweater. "I must know . . . I must know . . . I must . . . I must" she repeated over and over to herself. Out on the edge of the sea wall sat young David Ben Ami. He seemed lost in thought, looking out over the water and flipping pebbles.

She came up alongside him and he looked up and smiled.

"*Shalom*, Kitty. You look rested."

She sat beside him. For several moments they admired the sea.

"Thinking of home?" she asked.

"Yes."

"Jordana . . . that's her name, isn't it . . . Ari's sister?"

David nodded.

"Will you see her?"

"If I am lucky we will have a little time."

"David."

"Yes."

"What is going to become of the children?"

"We will take good care of them. They are our future."

"Is there danger?"

"Yes, there is great danger."

Kitty was quiet again for many moments. . . .

"Are you sailing with us?" David asked.

She felt her heart skip a beat. "Why do you ask?"

"It is beginning to seem natural to have you around. Besides, Ari mentioned something or other about it."

"If . . . if Ari is interested then why doesn't he ask?"

David laughed. "Ari doesn't ask for anything."

"David," she said abruptly, "you must help me. I am terribly puzzled. You seem to be the only one who understands a little . . ."

"I will help you if I can."

". . . I haven't been around many Jews in my life. You people bewilder me."

"We bewilder ourselves even more," David said.

"Can I say something honestly? I feel so much like an outsider . . ."

"That is not at all strange, Kitty. Most people do. Even those few we call "friend," even though they have a loyalty bordering on fanaticism. Some, I believe, feel guilty for all the crimes committed against us. Others want to be Jews . . . although Lord only knows why. We are a confusing lot."

"But a man like Ari Ben Canaan. Who is he? Who is he really? Is he a real person?"

"Ari is quite real. He is the product of a historic abortion."

They began walking toward the hotel, for it was suppertime. "It is difficult to know where to begin," David said. "I suppose to really tell the story of Ari Ben Canaan we must start with Simon Rabinsky in the Jewish Pale. The Pale was an area in southwest Russia that included the Ukraine. I suppose we'd have to start before the turn of the century. I think the year of the great happening was 1884."

CHAPTER TWO

ZHITOMIR, RUSSIA, 1884

Simon Rabinsky was a bootmaker. His wife's name was Rachel. She was a good and a devout woman. Simon had two sons who were his greatest treasures.

Yakov, the younger, was fourteen years of age. He was a fiery lad with a whiplash tongue and a quick mind. He would argue at the slightest provocation.

Jossi, the older of the brothers, was sixteen. Jossi's appearance was distinctive. He was a powerful giant who stood over six feet tall and had a head of flaming red hair like his mother, Rachel. Jossi was as mild as Yakov was wild. Jossi was quiet and meditative and gentle; in fact, Yakov's fertile brain in Jossi's powerful body could well have created a superman.

The Rabinsky family was extremely poor. They lived in that part of western Russia which included Bessarabia, the Ukraine, the Crimea, and parts of White Russia and which was known as the Jewish Pale of Settlement. The boundaries of the Pale were established in 1804 as the only place in Russia where Jews could reside. It was, in fact, one enormous ghetto, with Moscow and Petrograd off limits except to those few wealthy Jews who could bribe their way into sending a son or a daughter beyond the boundaries.

Establishment of the Jewish Pale was merely one event in a long history of discrimination. Jews first settled in Russia in the Crimea area as far back as the first century. The Khazars who ruled in that area were so taken with Judaism that they adopted it as their own religion. The Khazars' kingdom was, in fact, a Jewish state. By the tenth century the Russians in the north had ascended to power and they swept down on the Khazars, dispersed them to oblivion, and began a sordid record against the Jews.

As Russia came to power, the flaming sword of Islam came up from the south. During those periods when the Moslems held parts of Russia the Jews knew their greatest times of peace and prosperity, for Jews had been a potent factor behind the rise of Islam.

With the final defeat of the Moslems, full power over all Russia went to the Czars and to the Greek Church. Jewish "heretics" were burned at the stake by the hundreds during the Middle Ages. The ignorant peasantry was well instructed in the fable that these Jews were magicians and witches and used Christian blood in their rituals.

Centuries of unrelieved abuse reached a climax during the reign of Catherine I. A series of pogroms—anti-Jewish riots—was unloosed against those who would not accept the Greek Orthodox religion. But attempts to convert the Jews failed utterly, so Catherine I expelled a million Jews from Russia. Most of them went to Poland.

After this came the era of war and conquest in which Poland was conquered and reconquered, partitioned and re-partitioned. Catherine II inherited a million of the Jews who had previously been expelled by Catherine I.

These events led directly to the establishment of the Jewish Pale. In 1827 Jews were driven ruthlessly from the smaller villages into the already overcrowded Jewish quarters in the larger cities. In the same year the Czar instituted a quota of Jewish youths to be turned over each year to the army for twenty-five years of military service.

Simon Rabinsky, the bootmaker of Zhitomir, his good wife Rachel, and his sons Yakov and Jossi were prisoners of the Pale and of a unique way of life. There was no social and very little commercial contact between these Jewish communities and the rest of the Russian people. The only regular visitor from the outside was the tax collector who might make off with anything from sacred candlesticks to beds and pillows and shoes. Frequent but less regular callers from the outside were the wild mobs of Cossacks and peasants and students who screamed for Jewish blood.

Divorced from the greater society, the Jews had little or no loyalty for "Mother Russia." Their spoken and written language was not Russian but Yiddish, which was a bastard German. Their language of prayer was ancient Hebrew. The Jews even dressed differently. They wore black hats and long gabardine coats. Although it was forbidden by law, many of them wore side curls, and it was a great sport among the Russians to catch a Jew and cut off his curls.

Simon Rabinsky lived the way his father and his father's father had been forced to live inside ghetto walls. Because they were so poor there was endless haggling over a few kopeks. Yet, despite the desperateness of their daily existence, Simon and all other Jews adhered to rigid codes of business ethics inside the ghetto. No man was allowed to infringe on the livelihood of his neighbor or to cheat or to rob.

Community life pivoted around the Holy Laws, the synagogue, and the rabbi, who was at once teacher, spiritual leader, judge, and administrator of the community. The rabbis of the Pale were all great scholars. Their wisdom was far-reaching and their authority rarely questioned.

Within the ghetto the Jews organized their own government under the over-all leadership of the rabbis. There were a hundred different lay offices and wardenships. There was a score of Biblical and Talmudic societies. There was an organization for the care of orphans and a society to pay the dowries of the poorer girls. There were societies to care for the sick, the aged, and the lame. There were administrators of marriage contracts and an elected synagogue summoner, as well as a dozen other synagogue posts. There was an ecclesiastical court, there were psalm readers, and administrators over the ritual baths. Indeed, the community moved as one for the existence of all.

The poor donated to the poorer. The poorer—to the poorer yet. Charity was the eleventh, the unwritten commandment. Leading scholars and religious leaders had to be cared for. Nothing was allowed to interfere with the pursuit of wisdom.

Many people said that Simon Rabinsky, the bootmaker, was second in wisdom only to the rabbi himself. In the Pale where nearly everyone was destitute the measure of man's wealth was his knowledge. Simon served as a deacon of his synagogue. Each year he was elected to one or two other high offices in the community. It was Simon's dream to fill his sons with the wonders of the conquest of the mind.

Jews called their Talmud a "sea." They claimed it was so vast that one could read it and study it for a lifetime without ever looking at another book and never swim from one side of the "sea" to the other. The Rabinsky brothers studied this great collection of laws and customs, which contained information on everything from social behavior to personal cleanliness.

In addition to studying the Talmud the Rabinsky brothers spent hours learning the Pentateuch, the first five books of Moses which make up the Torah and were considered the holiest of all works.

They learned the Bible. They learned the oral laws of the Mishnah. They learned the folk legends, wise sayings, and commentary on the Bible of the Midrash. They learned the Cabala, the book of mystics, and they learned the prayers and songs and customs and holidays.

Jossi and Yakov studied the great post-Talmudic scholars —Moses Maimonides and Rashi.

Although the Rabinsky family lived a grim existence it was not entirely a life without hope or joy. There was always talk and debate, a tempting scandal to discuss or a wedding or a death or a confirmation or a birth to celebrate. There were the holidays to look forward to. The matchmakers were constantly busy and there was the Sabbath.

On one night each week, Simon Rabinsky and every other ghetto Jew became a king. The traditional horn would sound in the ghetto, and Simon would lay down his tools and prepare for his day with God. How he loved the sound of the horn! It was the same sound that had called his people to prayer and to battle for four thousand years. Simon would go to the ritual bath while his good wife Rachel lit the Sabbath candles and recited a benediction.

He would dress in his Sabbath finery, a long black silk coat and a beautiful fur-rimmed hat. He would walk proudly to synagogue with Jossi on one arm and Yakov on the other.

At home there was traditionally a family poorer than his in to share the Sabbath meal. Over the candles and the blessed bread and wine he spoke a blessing and a few words of gratitude to God.

Rachel served stuffed fish and noodles and chicken broth, and in the evening they would stroll through the ghetto calling upon the sick or receiving visitors in their shop, as they had no parlor.

On Saturday, Simon Rabinsky prayed and meditated and spoke with his sons and reviewed their lessons and learnings and discussed religion and philosophy.

As the sun set ending the Sabbath, Simon sang the song of the ghetto with Rachel, Yakov, and Jossi: "Rejoice to Israel . . . banish despair."

With the day over he returned to the realities of his bitter life. In the dingy cellar he called home and shop, Simon Rabinsky would crouch over his workbench in the candlelight, with his wrinkled hands drive a knife deftly through leather. Simon then said the same lament that had been said by Jews since their captivity in Babylon. . . .

"If I forget thee, O Jerusalem, let my right hand forget her cunning . . . let my tongue cleave to the roof of my mouth, if I prefer not Jerusalem above my chief joy."

There was solace in prayer, and Simon Rabinsky was a believer among men. But even one so devout could not shut his eyes to the misery around and about him. "How long, O Lord . . . how long . . . ?" he would ask. "How long must we live in this abysmal darkness?" And then his heart would grow light and he would become exalted as he repeated his favorite passage of the Passover Prayer—*"Next year in Jerusalem."*

Next year in Jerusalem? Would it ever come? Would the Messiah ever come to take them back . . . ?

CHAPTER THREE: Yakov and Jossi walked home from the seminary. Jossi's head was bowed; he was deep in thought, wondering about the meaning of certain passages of the Torah he had studied that afternoon. Young Yakov danced around on his toes flinging rocks at various objects in the street. He always carried a pocket full of rocks in case they ran into some bullies.

As they approached the corner near home, Yakov grabbed Jossi's wrist. "There is going to be another meeting tonight in Hacohen's shop," he said.

"I heard all about it," Jossi said.

"Will you go this time?"

"No."

"You should go tonight," Yakov said; "there is going to be a real Bilu from Palestine to speak."

Jossi's heart pounded! A real Bilu from Palestine! How he would love to see and hear someone who had actually been to Palestine. Secretly Jossi envied his younger brother, who had been sneaking off to Lovers of Zion meetings. His curiosity was aroused by this new organization which spoke of the defense of the ghetto and a return to the Holy Land. A real Bilu! No—he would not yield to temptation—never so long as his father objected to the Lovers of Zion.

They turned the corner and entered the shop, first kissing the mezuzah, a tiny prayer scroll nailed to the doorpost. The place smelled strongly of leather. Simon looked up from his workbench and smiled.

"Hello, Papa," they both said quickly, and drew a curtain over the alcove which served as their bedroom in one corner of the shop. Simon knew by their manner that they had been discussing something in secret and he also knew full well what young Yakov had been up to, but he did not say a word. The boys must have their fling, Simon thought—I will not impose my will on them in this matter nor will I speak to them unless they speak to me first.

Simon could be considered among the more fortunate Jews of the ghetto. His family was in good health and he had a trade which allowed him to exist, however meagerly. The mortality rate of Jews in the Pale was more than twice that of the rest of the population of Russia.

Not only the Jews were near starvation. Most of Russia, especially the peasantry, hovered on the brink of destitution. The country wallowed in the backwash of feudalism, refused to industrialize, and was exploited by the aristocracy.

Bread, land, and reform movements sprang up all over the nation. Because their own plight was the worst, there were always Jews to be found in any organization which strived to alleviate the wretched conditions.

Unrest mounted throughout Russia. An undercurrent which spelled revolution was brewing. Only then did Czar Alexander II institute some long overdue reforms. His first move was to free the serfs and he relaxed some of the stringent anti-Jewish statutes. The new laws even allowed a limited number of professional and artisan Jews to live in Moscow. In Bessarabia a few Jews could purchase land. However, the reforms were mere crumbs.

In trying desperately to divert the people's attention from the real issue of tyranny, the masterminds behind the Czar found a new and convenient use for the old scapegoats, the Jews. Hatred for the Jew in Russia had been based on religious

199

bias, ignorance, and superstition, coupled with the peasants' blind hostility due to their inferior status. The Russian government decided to make anti-Semitism a deliberate political weapon. They launched a campaign in which the number of Jewish members in the Bread and Land movements was exaggerated and they claimed it was all a plot of Jewish anarchists out to seize the government for their own profit.

It was furthered as the Russian government secretly drummed up, sponsored, fostered, and condoned bloody pogroms in which ghettos of the Pale were sacked, the women raped, and blood flowed freely. As the mobs tore through the ghettos the Russian police either turned their backs or actively engaged in the affairs.

On March 13, 1881, an awesome catastrophe befell the Jews. Czar Alexander II was assassinated by a rebel's bomb, and one of the convicted revolutionaries was a Jewish girl!

This paved the way for years of horror.

The power behind the new Czar Alexander III was the sinister Pobiedonostsev. He handled the weak-minded new ruler like an infant. Pobiedonostsev regarded the principles of equality, bread, and democracy as extremely vulgar and set out to crush them ruthlessly.

As for the Jews, Pobiedonostsev had special plans. As procurator of the Holy Synod he received a silent nod from the Greek Church for his scheme which called for the elimination of the Jewish population. One third would go through government-sponsored pogroms, starvation, and other forms of murder. One third would go through expulsion and exile. One third would be converted.

Easter week, 1881. The coronation of Czar Alexander III was the signal to begin. Pobiedonostsev's pogroms erupted and spread to every city of the Pale.

After the first outbursts, Pobiedonostsev quickly had a dozen laws enacted that either eradicated any previous gains made by the Jews or aimed to destroy the rest of the Jewish population.

In the wake of the awful happenings of 1881 the Jews of the Pale groped desperately for an answer to their problems. A thousand ideas were advanced—each more impractical than the last. In many corners of many ghettos a new voice was heard by a group who called themselves Hovevey Zion —the Lovers of Zion.

Along with the Lovers of Zion came a document from the pen of Leo Pinsker which seemed to pinpoint the causes and solution of the Jewish plight. Pinsker's document called for auto-emancipation as the only way out for the Jews of the Pale.

Late in the year 1881 a group of Jewish students from

Romny bolted from the Pale and made for Palestine with the motto on their lips, "*Beth Yakov Leku Venelkha*—House of Jacob, let us go up!" This daring band of adventurers, forty in number, became known far and wide by the initials of their motto, which in transliteration became the "Bilu."

The Bilus started a small farming village in the Sharon Valley of Palestine. They named it Rishon le Zion: First to Zion.

The pogroms in the Pale increased in fury, reaching new heights of bloody destruction on Easter morning 1882 in the town of Balta.

As a result new groups of Bilus struck out for the Promised Land and the Lovers of Zion grew by leaps and bounds.

In the Sharon the Bilus founded Petah Tikva: the Gate of Hope.

In the Galilee they founded Rosh Pinna: the Cornerstone.

In Samaria they founded Zichron Yakov: the Memory of Jacob.

By the year 1884 a half dozen small, weak, and struggling Bilu settlements had been begun in the Holy Land.

Each night in Zhitomir and in every other city of the Pale there were secret meetings. Youths began to rebel and to be diverted from the old ways.

Yakov Rabinsky, the younger of the brothers, was swept up in the new ideology. Often during the night he lay awake, staring into the darkness in the alcove of the shop he shared with his brother Jossi. How wonderful it would be to be able to fight! How wonderful to strike out and really find the Holy Land! Yakov's head was filled with the past glory of the Hebrews. Often he pretended he fought alongside Judah "the Hammer" as the Maccabees swept the Greeks from Judea. He, Yakov Rabinsky, would be there as Judah Maccabee entered Jerusalem and rededicated the Temple.

Yakov Rabinsky would be there with Simon Bar Giora, who held Jerusalem against the might of Rome for eighteen long months. He would be there in chains alongside Giora as the proud Hebrew warrior was led off to Rome to the lions' den.

Yakov would be there with the greatest of them all—Bar Kochba, the scourge of the Romans.

He would be there at the stands at Herodium and Machaerus and Masada and Beitar, where they fought to the last man after several years of siege.

And of all his heroes, Yakov wanted most to be with Rabbi Akiva when he met his martyrdom at Caesarea, for Akiva was teacher, scholar, and fighter all in one.

When the Lovers of Zion came around to Zhitomir, Yakov

ran off to the meetings immediately. Their message of auto-emancipation was music to his ears. The Lovers of Zion wanted his brother Jossi because of his size and strength; but Jossi out of respect for his father as commanded by God was slow to move toward these radical ideas.

The day after the Bilu from Palestine spoke in Hacohen's candle shop, Jossi could stand it no longer. He wanted to know everything from Yakov—how the Bilu looked—every word he said—every gesture.

"I think, Jossi, the time has come for you to attend a meeting with me."

Jossi sighed. It would mark the first time in his life he had openly gone against his father's wishes. "Very well," he whispered, and all that day asked forgiveness for what he was about to do.

The brothers told their father they were going to say Kaddish, a mourner's prayer, for a friend who had recently died. They sped off to the shop of Hacohen, the candlemaker. It was a tiny basement shop like their own home. It smelled of wax and sweet scents. Curtains were drawn over the windows. Guards were posted outside on the street. Jossi was surprised at how many familiar faces he saw in the packed room. The speaker was a man from Odessa named Vladimir.

Vladimir neither looked nor acted like them. He had no beard or side curls. He wore boots and a black leather jacket. As he began to speak Yakov became entranced, and around the room a half dozen hecklers started up.

"Are you the Messiah who has come to lead us back?" someone called.

"Did you find the Messiah under your bed when you hid during the last pogrom?" Vladimir rejoined.

"Are you sure you are not one of the Czar's spies?"

"Are you sure you are not one of the Czar's next victims?" Vladimir retorted.

The room quieted down. Vladimir spoke softly. He reviewed the history of the Jews in Poland and in Russia and then expanded his summary to include Germany and Austria as well. Then he spoke of the expulsions from England and France—then of the massacres at Bray and York and Spires and Worms.

Vladimir spoke of how the Pope had called upon the Christians to regain the Holy Land from the Moslems and of how five Crusades over three hundred years were directed against the Jews in the name of God.

Vladimir spoke of one of the most horrible periods of all —the Spanish Inquisition, during which unbelievable atrocities against the Jews were committed in the name of the Church.

202

"Comrades, every nation on the face of this earth has derided us. We must arise again as a nation. It is our only salvation. Pinsker has seen it and the Lovers of Zion see it and the Bilus see it. We must rebuild the House of Jacob!"

Yakov's heart was pounding as the boys left the meeting. "See, Jossi! What did I tell you! You saw tonight that even Rabbi Lipzin was there."

"I must think about it," Jossi said defensively. But even as he spoke he knew that Vladimir was right and Yakov too. It was their only salvation. The street was quiet and dark and they walked briskly. They reached their home, quickly kissed the mezuzah, and went in.

A candle was burning on Simon's bench. He stood behind it in his long nightshirt with his hands clasped behind him.

"Hello, Papa," they said quickly, and tried to duck into their alcove.

"Boys!" Simon commanded. They walked slowly before his bench.

Their mother walked into the room and squinted. "Simon," she said, "are the boys home?"

"They are home."

"Tell them they shouldn't be on the streets so late."

"Yes, Mama," Simon said. "Go to sleep and I shall speak to them."

Simon looked from Yakov to Jossi and back to Yakov.

"I must tell Mrs. Horowitz tomorrow that her husband can surely rest in peace because my sons joined in a minyan for him tonight."

It was impossible for Jossi to lie to his father. "We weren't at minyan for Reb Horowitz," he mumbled.

Simon Rabinsky feigned surprise and held his hands aloft. "Oh . . . so! I should have known. You boys were courting. Just today Abraham, the matchmaker, was in the shop. He said to me, 'Simon Rabinsky,' he said, 'you have a fine boy in Jossi. Jossi will bring you a handsome dowry from the family of some very fortunate girl.' Can you imagine . . . he wants to make a *shiddoch* for you already, Jossi."

"We were not courting," Jossi gulped.

"Not courting? No minyan? Perhaps you went back to the synagogue to study?"

"No, Father," Jossi said almost inaudibly.

Yakov could stand it no longer. "We went to a Lovers of Zion meeting!"

Jossi looked up at his father sheepishly, bit his lip, and nodded red-faced. Yakov seemed glad it was in the open. He stood defiant. Simon sighed and stared at both his sons for a full five minutes.

"I am hurt," he announced at last.

"That is why we did not tell you, Father. We did not want to hurt you," Jossi said.

"I am not hurt because you went to a Lovers of Zion meeting. I am hurt because the sons of Simon Rabinsky think so little of their father they no longer confide in him."

Now Yakov squirmed too. "But if we'd told you," he said, "you might have forbidden us to go."

"Tell me, Yakov . . . when have I ever forbidden you to pursue knowledge? Have I ever forbidden a book? God help me . . . even the time you took the notion into your head that you wanted to read the New Testament? Did I forbid that?"

"No, sir," Yakov said.

"I think a talk is long overdue," Simon said.

The candlelight seemed to blend with the red of Jossi's hair. He stood half a head taller than his father and now as he spoke he did not falter. Although Jossi was slow in making up his mind, once it was made up he rarely changed it. "Yakov and I did not want to hurt you because we know how you feel about the Lovers of Zion and the new ideas. But I am glad I went tonight."

"I am glad you went too," Simon said.

"Rabbi Lipzin wants me to sign up for ghetto defense," Jossi said.

"Rabbi Lipzin departs from so many traditions I am beginning to wonder if he is a Jew," Simon said.

"That is just the point, Father," Jossi said. "You are afraid of the new ideas." It was the first time Jossi had ever spoken thus to his father and he was immediately ashamed.

Simon walked around the counter and put his hands on his sons' shoulders and led them into their alcove and bade them sit down on their beds. "Don't you think I know what is going through your minds? New ideas, indeed. There was exactly the same talk about auto-emancipation and ghetto defense when I was a boy. You are only coming to a crisis that every Jew comes to . . . to make your peace with the world . . . to know your place. When I was a boy I even thought once of converting . . . don't you think I know how it feels?"

Jossi was astonished! His father had thought of conversion!

"Why is it wrong for us to want to defend ourselves? Why is it made a sin by our own people to want to better our conditions?" Yakov demanded.

"You are a Jew," his father answered, "and being a Jew entails certain obligations."

"To hide under my bed while people try to kill me?"

"Don't raise your voice to Father," Jossi admonished.

"No one said it is easy to be a Jew. We were not born on this earth to live from its fruits. We were put here to guard the laws of God. This is our mission. This is our purpose."

"And this is our reward!" Yakov snapped back.

"The Messiah will come and take us back when He is good and ready," Simon said, unruffled, "and I do not believe it is for Yakov Rabinsky to question His wisdom. I do believe it is for Yakov Rabinsky to live by the laws of the Holy Torah."

There were tears of anger in Yakov's eyes. "I do not question the laws of God," he cried, "but I question the wisdom of some of the men who interpret those laws."

There was a brief silence. Jossi swallowed. Never had anyone spoken so harshly to his father. Yet he silently applauded his brother's courage, for Yakov was daring to ask the very questions he himself dared not ask.

"If we are created in the image of God," Yakov continued, "then the Messiah is in all of us and the Messiah inside me keeps telling me to stand up and fight back. He keeps telling me to make my way back to the Promised Land with the Lovers of Zion. That is what the Messiah tells me, Father."

Simon Rabinsky would not be shaken. "In our history we have been plagued with false messiahs. I fear you are listening to one of them now."

"And how do I recognize the true Messiah?" Yakov challenged.

"The question is not whether Yakov Rabinsky recognizes the Messiah. The question is whether the Messiah will recognize Yakov Rabinsky. If Yakov Rabinsky begins to stray from His laws and listens to false prophets, then the Messiah will be quite certain that he is no longer a Jew. I suggest to Yakov Rabinsky that he continue to live as a Jew as his father and his people are doing."

CHAPTER FOUR: "Kill the Jews!"

A rock smashed through the seminary window. The rabbi hurried the students out through the back to the safety of the cellar. In the streets, Jews scampered wildly for cover ahead of a frenzied mob of over a thousand students and Cossacks.

"Kill the Jews!" they screamed. "Kill the Jews!"

It was another pogrom inspired by Andreev, the humpbacked headmaster of a local gymnasium—high school—and foremost Jew hater in Zhitomir. Andreev's students swaggered down the streets of the ghetto, smashing up store fronts and dragging any Jews they could find into the streets and beating them mercilessly.

"Kill the Jews . . . kill the Jews . . . kill the Jews!"

Yakov and Jossi raced from the seminary. Using a route

through back alleys, they sped over deserted cobblestone streets to reach their home and protect their parents. They ducked frequently for cover and worked away from the sounds of hoofbeats of Cossack horses and from the blood-curdling screams of the students.

They turned the corner into their street and ran head on into a dozen hoodlums wearing university caps—disciples of Andreev.

"There go two of them!"

Yakov and Jossi turned around and fled, leading the pack of pursuers away from their own home. The students howled with glee as they sprinted after the brothers. For fifteen minutes they wove in and out of streets and alleys until the students trapped them against a dead-end wall. Jossi and Yakov stood with their backs to the wall, dripping sweat and panting for breath as the students formed a semicircle and closed in on them. His eyes gleaming, the leader stepped forward with an iron pipe and swung on Jossi!

Jossi blocked the blow and snatched up the student, spun him around, lifted him over his head, and hurled him at the rest of his companions. Yakov, whose pocket full of rocks was for just such occasions, bounced two stones off the heads of two students, sending them to the ground unconscious. The other students scattered in flight.

The boys dashed home and flung open the door of the shop.

"Mama! Papa!"

The shop was a shambles.

"Mama! Papa!"

They found their mother cowering in a corner in a state of hysteria. Jossi shook her hard. "Where is Papa?"

"The Torah!" she shrieked. "The Torah!"

At that instant, six blocks away, Simon Rabinsky staggered into his burning synagogue and fought his way gagging to the end of the room where the Holy Ark stood. He threw back the curtains with the Ten Commandments inscribed on them and pulled down the Sefer Torah, the Scroll of the Laws of God.

Simon pressed the holy parchment against his breast to protect it from the flames and staggered back to the door. He was badly burned and choking. He staggered outside and fell onto his knees.

Twenty of Andreev's students were waiting for him.

"Kill the Jew!"

Simon crawled a few yards and collapsed, covering the Sefer Torah with his body. Clubs smashed his skull. Hob-nailed boots ripped his face. . . .

"Kill the Jew!"

In mortal agony Simon Rabinsky screamed out . . . "Hear, O Israel . . . the Lord is our God . . . the Lord is one!"

When they found Simon Rabinsky he was beyond recognition. The Sefer Torah, the laws which God had given Moses, had been burned by the mob.

The entire Zhitomir ghetto mourned his passing. He had died in the noblest way a Jew could meet death—protecting the Sefer Torah. Simon was put to rest along with a dozen others who had been murdered in Andreev's pogrom.

For Rachel Rabinsky, the death of her husband was but another tragedy in a life which had known little else but sorrow. But this time her strength and will were gone. Even her sons could not comfort her. Rachel was taken off to live with relatives in another town.

Jossi and Yakov went to synagogue twice each day to say Kaddish for their father. Jossi remembered how his father had wanted to live as a Jew so that the Messiah would recognize him. His whole mission in life had been to protect God's laws. Perhaps his father had been right—perhaps it was not theirs to live from the fruits of the earth but to serve as the guardians of God's laws. In his sorrow Jossi probed to find a reason for his father's brutal death.

Yakov was different. His heart was full of hatred. Even as he went to say the mourners' prayers, his soul demanded revenge. He seethed and smoldered—he was restless and angry. He muttered time and again that he would avenge his father's death.

Jossi, knowing his brother's state of mind, barely let him out of his sight. He tried to soothe and comfort Yakov but Yakov was inconsolable.

A month after the death of Simon Rabinsky, Yakov slipped from the shop in the middle of the night as Jossi slept. He took from his father's bench a long sharp knife and hid it in his belt and ventured from the ghetto toward the school where Andreev the Jew hater lived.

Jossi awoke instinctively a few minutes later. The instant he saw Yakov was gone he dressed hurriedly and ran after him. He knew where his brother would be going.

At four o'clock in the morning, Yakov Rabinsky pulled the brass knocker on the door of Andreev's house. As the demented hunchback opened the door, Yakov sprang from the shadows and plunged the knife deep into his heart. Andreev emitted one short shriek and rolled to the ground, dead.

A few moments later Jossi rushed onto the scene to find his brother standing hypnotized over the body of the slain man. He pulled Yakov away and they fled.

All the next day and night they hid in the cellar of Rabbi

Lipzin's house. Word of Andreev's murder spread quickly throughout Zhitomir. The elders of the ghetto met and came to a decision.

"We have reason to fear that you two were spotted," the rabbi said when he returned. "Your red hair, Jossi, was seen by some students."

Jossi bit his lip and did not reveal that he had only been trying to prevent the crime. Yakov showed no remorse for his deed. "I would do it again, gladly," he said.

"Although we understand well what drove you to this deed," said the rabbi, "it cannot be forgiven. You may well have started another pogrom. On the other hand . . . we are Jews and there is no justice for us in a Russian court. We have reached a decision you are to abide by."

"Yes, Rabbi," Jossi said.

"You are to cut off your curls and dress like goyim. We will give you food and money enough to travel for a week. You must leave Zhitomir at once and never return."

In 1884, Yakov and Jossi Rabinsky, aged fourteen and sixteen, became fugitives. They used the roads only by night and hid during the day, moving east to Lubny, a distance of a hundred-odd miles from Zhitomir. At Lubny they found the ghetto immediately and sought out the rabbi, only to learn that their notoriety had preceded them. The rabbi and the elders of Lubny met and agreed to give the boys enough food and money for another week's travel. This time their destination was Kharkov, some two hundred miles away, where the search for them might not be so intense. Advance word was sent to the Kharkov rabbi that the Rabinsky boys were on the way.

The entire countryside was on the alert for the Rabinsky brothers. It took twenty days of cautious moving for them to get to Kharkov.

Their fame had spread throughout the Pale, and their capture was being turned into a holy mission. For two weeks they hid in the clammy basement beneath the synagogue in Kharkov, their presence known only to the rabbi and a few elders.

At last the Rabbi Solomon came to them. "It is not safe, even here," he said. "It is only a matter of time until you boys are discovered. Already the police have been prowling around asking questions. But with winter coming on it will be near impossible to move."

The rabbi sighed and shook his head. "We have also tried to get you papers to enable you to travel beyond the Pale, but I am afraid that is impossible. You are too well known by the police."

He paced back and forth. "We have decided there is but one thing to do. There are some Jewish families in this district who have passed as gentiles and who own small farms. We feel it would be the safest plan for you to hide with one of them until spring at least."

"Rabbi Solomon," Jossi said, "we are very thankful for everything that has been done for us, but my brother and I have made a plan of our own."

"What is that?"

"We are going to Palestine," Yakov said.

The good rabbi looked stunned. "To Palestine? How?"

"We have a route in mind. God will help us."

"No doubt God will help you but let us not press Him for a miracle. It is over three hundred hard cold miles to the port of Odessa. Even if and when you reach Odessa you cannot get a boat without papers."

"We are not going by way of Odessa."

"But there is no other way."

"We intend to walk."

Rabbi Solomon gasped.

"Moses walked for forty years," Yakov said; "it will not take us that long."

"Young man, I am well aware that Moses walked for forty years. That does not explain how you are going to walk to Palestine."

"I'll tell you our plan," Jossi said. "We will go south. The police won't be looking for us so strenuously in that direction. We will cross out of the Pale into Georgia and then over the Caucasus Mountains into Turkey."

"Madness! Insanity! It cannot be done! Do you mean to tell me you will walk over two thousand miles, through the cold of winter, across strange lands and fifteen-thousand-foot mountain ranges without papers . . . without knowledge of the country . . . with the police after you? Why, you are but little more than children!"

Yakov's eyes were burning with passion; he looked at the rabbi. *"Fear not for I am with thee. I will bring thy seed from the east and gather thee from the west. I will say to the north, give up and to the south, keep not back; bring my sons from far, and my daughters from the ends of the earth."*

And so it came to pass that the Rabinsky brothers who were wanted for murder fled from Kharkov and moved to the east and to the south through an inhumanly bitter winter.

They trudged through waist-high snow during the night, bending their young bodies against howling winds and fighting off the numbness of frostbite. Their bellies rumbled with hunger. They stole from the countryside and in the hours of daylight they hid in the forests.

209

Through those tortured nights it was Yakov who filled Jossi with the spirit of their mission. It was Yakov who urged another step and another and yet another when all strength was gone. It was Jossi with his powerful body who held his younger brother up. Between their two strengths they somehow managed to keep alive and moving.

Many a night Jossi had to carry Yakov on his back for eight hours because the younger brother's feet were raw and bleeding and he could not walk. Many a day Jossi had to sleep on top of Yakov to pass his warmth on to his weaker brother. Often they crawled the last few yards to a hiding place.

Over the ice and the snow they staggered south with but cloth wrappings around their feet—yard after yard—mile after mile—week after week.

In the spring they reached Rostov and collapsed.

They found the ghetto and were taken in and fed and sheltered. Their rags were exchanged for new clothing. They had to rest several weeks before they were fit enough to continue the journey.

Late in the spring they went on again, fully recovered from their winter's flight.

Although they did not now have to contend with the elements they had to move with greater caution, for they had left the Pale behind and could no longer depend on protection, food, and shelter from the Jewish communities. They skirted the Black Sea south of Rostov and moved deep into Georgia. All their food now was stolen from the fields —they never let themselves be seen by daylight.

As winter came on again they were faced with a tremendous decision. To hole up in Georgia, to try to get through the Caucasus Mountains in winter, or—to attempt a boat across the Black Sea.

Each plan had its dangers. Although trying the mountains in winter seemed the most foolhardy their urge to leave Russia behind was so great that they decided to risk it.

At Stavropol at the base of the mountains they staged a series of robberies which completely outfitted them with clothing and food for the assault over the mountains. Then they fled into the Caucasus toward Armenia with the police on their track.

Through another brutal winter they moved deep into the mountains, walking by day, climbing the treacherous passes in the dark, and pillaging the countryside. The first year had hardened them and made them wise—the obsession to get to Palestine was greater than ever and drove them onward. Yakov would babble passages from the Bible by the hour to

210

drive their bodies forward. They made the last part of their push instinctively, in a numbed daze.

And in spring they received their second miracle of re-birth. One day they stood up and for the first time breathed free air—as they left "Mother Russia" behind them forever. As Yakov passed the border marker into Turkey he turned and spat into Russia.

Now they could move in daylight, but it was a strange land with strange sounds and smells and they had no passports or papers. All of eastern Turkey was mountainous and the going was slow. They went to work in the fields in places where they could not steal food, but twice that spring they were caught and thrown into prison briefly.

Jossi reckoned they would have to give up thievery, for it was too dangerous being caught; they might be sent back to Russia.

In the middle of summer they passed the base of Mount Ararat where the Ark of Noah had landed. They pressed on to the south.

In each village they asked, "Are there Jews here?"

In some there would be Jews and they would be fed and clothed and sheltered and sent along their way.

These Jews were different from any they had known. They were peasants filled with ignorance and superstition, yet they knew their Torah and kept the Sabbath and the Holy Days.

"Are there Jews here?"

"We are Jews."

"Let us see your rabbi."

"Where are you boys going?"

"We are walking to the Promised Land."

It was the magic password. "Are there Jews here?"

"There is a Jewish family in the next village."

Never once were they refused hospitality.

Two years went by. The brothers pressed on doggedly, stopping only when exhaustion overcame them or they had to work for food.

"Are there Jews here?"

They pressed over the Turkish border into the province of Syria and another strange land.

In Aleppo they received their first taste of the Arab world. They passed through bazaars and dung-filled streets and heard Moslem chants from the minarets——

They walked on until the blue-green of the Mediterranean Sea burst suddenly before them and the howling winds and cold of the past years were exchanged for a blistering heat of one hundred and twenty degrees. They plodded down the Levantine coast wearing Arab rags.

"Are there Jews here?"

Yes, there were Jews, but again they were different. These Jews looked and dressed and spoke like Arabs. But yet they knew the Hebrew language and the Torah. Like the Jews of the Pale and the Jews of Turkey, the Arab-like Jews took the Rabinsky brothers in without question and shared their homes and their food. They blessed the brothers as they had been blessed before for the sacredness of their mission.

On into Lebanon they walked—through Tripoli and the wildness of Beirut—they neared the Promised Land.

"Are there Jews here?"

The year was 1888. Forty months had passed since that night Yakov and Jossi fled the Zhitomir ghetto. Jossi had grown into a lean and leathery giant six feet three inches tall with a frame of steel. He was twenty years of age and he wore a flaming red beard.

Yakov was eighteen and also hardened by the more than three years of travel but he was still of medium height with dark sensitive features and was filled with the same intenseness he had had from childhood.

They stood upon a hill. Below them was a valley. Yakov and Jossi Rabinsky stared down at the Huleh in northern Galilee. Jossi Rabinsky sat down upon a rock and wept. Their journey was over.

"But the Lord liveth," Yakov said, *"which brought up and led the seed of the house of Israel out of the north country and from all the countries whither I had driven them, and they shall dwell in their own land."*

Yakov put his hand on Jossi's shoulder. "We are home, Jossi! We are home!"

CHAPTER FIVE: From the hill they looked down onto the land. Across the valley in Lebanon rose the towering snow-capped peak of Mount Hermon. Below them stretched the Huleh Lake and marshes. There was an Arab village nestled in the hills to their right. Jossi Rabinsky experienced the greatest exaltation he had ever known! How beautiful the Promised Land looked from here!

He vowed to himself, as young men will at such times, that he would return someday and from this very spot would look down on his very own land.

They stayed there for a day and a night and the next morning began the descent in the direction of the Arab village. The white-colored mud houses clumped together in a saddle of the hill were dazzling in the morning sun. The farmlands and olive orchards sloped from the village toward the swamp of the Huleh Lake. In the fields a donkey pulled a wooden plowshare. Other donkeys carried small harvest upon their backs. In the vineyards the Arab women labored among the grapes. The village was as it must have been a thousand years before.

The distant beauty of the village faded with each step they took nearer and was soon replaced by an overwhelming stench. Suspicious eyes watched the brothers from the fields and the houses of the village as they entered the dirt street. Life moved in slow motion in the blistering sun. The road was filled with camel and donkey excrement. Swarms of giant flies engulfed the brothers. A lazy dog lay motionless in the water of the open sewer to cool himself. Veiled women ducked for cover into squalid one-room houses made of mud; half the huts were in a state of near collapse and held a dozen or more people, as well as pigs, chickens, mules, and goats.

The boys stopped at the village water well. Straight-backed girls balanced enormous urns of water on their heads or were busy kneeling and scrubbing clothing and exchanging gossip.

The appearance of the travelers brought immediate silence.

"May we have some water?" Jossi asked.

No one dared answer. Haltingly they drew a bucket of water, splashed their faces, filled their canteens, and made off quickly.

Further on they came upon a dilapidated shack which served as a coffeehouse. Listless men sat or lay around on the ground as their wives tilled the fields. Some played backgammon. The air was foul with the mixed aroma of thick coffee, tobacco, hashish smoke, and the vile odors of the rest of the village.

"We would like directions," Jossi said.

After several moments one of the Arabs pulled himself off the ground and bade them follow. He led them out of the main area to a stream; on the other side of the stream was a small mosque and a minaret. On their side was a nicely built stone house set in the shade, and near it a room which served as the village reception room. They were taken to the room, told to enter and be seated. The high walls of the room were whitewashed, and thick, well-placed windows made it quite cool. A long bench ran around the walls. The bench was covered with bright pillows. On the walls hung an assortment of swords and trinkets and pictures of Arabs and visitors.

At last a man in his mid-twenties entered. He was dressed in an ankle-length striped cloth coat and a white headdress with a black band. His appearance immediately indicated that he was someone of wealth.

"I am Kammal, muktar of Abu Yesha," he said. He clapped his ringed hands together and ordered fruit and coffee to be brought to the strangers. As his brothers went off to carry out the order a cold half silence pervaded the room as the village elders filed in one by one.

To the boys' surprise, Kammal spoke some Hebrew.

"The site of this village is the traditional burial place of Joshua," he told them. "You see, Joshua is a moslem prophet as well as a Hebrew warrior."

Then, following the Arab custom of never asking a direct question, Kammal set out to find out who the visitors were and what their mission was. At last he suggested that perhaps the boys were lost—for no Jews had ventured into the Huleh before.

Jossi explained that they had entered the country from the north and sought the nearest Jewish settlement. After another half hour of roundabout questions Kammal seemed satisfied that the two Jews were not scouting for land in the area.

Then Kammal seemed to relax a bit; he confided that he was not only the muktar and owned all the land in Abu Yesha but the spiritual leader as well and the only literate person in the village.

Jossi somehow liked this man—for what reason, he did not know. He told Kammal about their pilgrimage from Russia and their desire to settle down and farm in the Holy Land. When the last of the fruit had been eaten, Jossi asked his leave.

"You will find Jews thirty kilometers south. You can walk the distance by nightfall if you stay on the road. The place is called Rosh Pinna."

Rosh Pinna! How exciting! He had heard the name many times in the Pale.

"Rosh Pinna is halfway between the Huleh Lake and the Sea of Galilee. On the way you will pass a large *tel*. Beneath the *tel* lies the ancient city of Hazor. . . . May God protect you on your journey."

The road took them past the fields of Abu Yesha and skirted the forbidding Huleh swamplands. Jossi looked back over his shoulder. He could see the spot from which they had crossed earlier that day. "I'll be back," he said to himself. "I know I'll be back——"

At midday they came upon the large man-made hill Kammal had described. As they climbed upward they realized that beneath them lay buried the ancient city of Hazor. Jossi was elated. "Do you realize that Joshua may have been standing on this very spot when he conquered the city from the Canaanites!" Jossi went about collecting bits of broken pottery which were strewn all about. Since his very first sight of the Holy Land, Jossi had been in such a state of joy that he was completely unaware of the bad mood that had been overtaking Yakov. Yakov did not want to spoil his brother's happiness so he remained silent, but his sullenness grew by the minute.

At dusk they reached Rosh Pinna, the Cornerstone, the farthest northern settlement of Jews. Their arrival produced a great furor. In a small building which served as the meeting room they were eagerly questioned. But it was forty months since they had left Zhitomir and they could only say that the pogroms that had started in 1881 were getting progressively worse.

Although both boys concealed their feelings, Rosh Pinna was a terrible disappointment. Instead of flourishing farms they found a rundown village. There were but a few dozen Jews living midst conditions not much better than those of the Arabs of Abu Yesha.

"Sometimes I think it would have been better to have stayed in Russia," one of the Bilus opined. "At least in the ghetto we were among Jews. We had books to read, music to hear, and people to speak to . . . there were women. Here, there is nothing."

"But all those things we heard at the Lovers of Zion meetings——" Jossi said.

"Oh yes, we were filled with ideals when we arrived. One soon loses them in this country. Look at it . . . so ruined that nothing can grow. What little we do have is stolen by the Bedouins, and the Turks take what the Bedouins leave. If I were you boys I'd keep on going to Jaffa and get on the next boat to America."

An outlandish idea, Jossi thought.

"If it were not for the charity of Rothschild, De Hirsch, and De Schumann we would all have starved long ago."

They left Rosh Pinna the next morning and set out to cross the hills to Safed. Safed was one of the four holy cities of the Jews. It sat on a beautiful cone-shaped hill at the entrance to the Huleh area of the Galilee. Here, Jossi thought, their dejection would soon fade because here there were second-, third-, and fourth-generation Jews who lived and studied the Cabala, the book of mystics. The shock of Rosh Pinna was repeated in Safed. They found a few hundred aged Jews who lived in study and from the alms of co-religionists around the world. They cared nothing about the rebirth of the House of Jacob—but wanted only to live quietly, studiously, and in poverty.

The Rabinsky brothers set out again from Safed the next morning, and crossed to nearby Mount Canaan, and stopped to get their bearings. From Mount Canaan the vista was magnificent. From here they could look back at Safed on its cone-shaped hill and beyond it to the Sea of Galilee. To the north they could see the rolling hills of the Huleh from whence they had come. Jossi loved this view—for before him was the land he had first trod. Yes, he vowed again that someday—someday it would be his.

Yakov's bitterness began to show. "All our lives, all our prayers . . . and look at it, Jossi."

Jossi put his hand on his brother's shoulder. "Look how beautiful it appears from here," he said. "I tell you, Yakov, someday we will make it look just as beautiful from the bottom of the hill as it does from the top."

"I don't know what to believe any more," Yakov whispered. "All through those winters as we walked through the mountains blue with cold . . . all through those blistering summers."

Jossi said, "Now cheer up. Tomorrow we begin our journey to Jerusalem."

Jerusalem! The magic word caused Yakov's flagging spirits to soar.

The next morning they came down from Mount Canaan and moved south along the Sea of Galilee into the Genossar Valley, past Arbel and the Horns of Hattin on the plains where Saladin the Kurd had once crushed the Crusaders in mortal combat.

But as they trudged on, even Jossi became dismayed. Their Promised Land was not a land flowing with milk and honey but a land of festering stagnated swamps and eroded hills and rock-filled fields and unfertile earth caused by a thousand years of Arab and Turkish neglect. It was a land denuded of its richness. It was a land that lay bleeding and fallow.

After a while they came to Mount Tabor in the center of the Galilee, and climbed up this hill which had played such a great part in the history of their people. It was here that the Jewish Joan of Arc, Deborah, and her General Barak hid with their armies and swooped down to crush the invading host. Atop Tabor they could see for miles in every direction. Around them stood Crusader ruins and a tiny monastery; it was here that Jesus was transfigured and held communion with Moses and Elijah.

From Tabor they could see the entire sorrowful picture. A fruitless, listless, dying land.

. . . and they trudged on with heavy hearts. The seeds of the past were all around them. They passed Mount Gilboa where Saul and Jonathan fell in battle and where Gideon lies—and they passed Bethel and Jericho——

As they moved into the hills of Judea their spirits rose again! The ancient terraces still stood from the time when hundreds of thousands of Jews took richness from the earth. There was no richness left, the hills were eroded, but the elation of the Rabinsky brothers could not be dimmed as they ascended higher and higher and higher.

Arriving at the peak of the ridges, Jossi and Yakov saw the City of David!

Jerusalem! Heart of their hearts—dream of their dreams! In that second all the years of privation and all the bitterness and suffering were erased.

They entered the old walled city through the Damascus Gate and wended their way through the narrow streets and bazaars to the mighty Hurva Synagogue.

"If only Father were with us now," Jossi whispered.

"If I forget thee, O Jerusalem . . ." Yakov prayed the lament of the captives.

From the synagogue they went to the one remaining wall of their great ancient temple. It stood on the site of the Mosque of Omar, the Dome of the Rock. This wall was the holiest place in all Jewry.

When at last they sought hospitality from the Jews they lost their illusions. The Jews in Jerusalem were Hasidim, ultra-Orthodox fanatics whose interpretations of the Laws were so strict they could be lived up to only by complete withdrawal from the civilized world. Even in the Pale these groups had separated themselves from the rest of the ghetto.

For the first time since they left Zhitomir, Jossi and Yakov were refused the hospitality of a Jewish home. The Jerusalem Jews did not like the Bilus, and the Lovers of Zion were berated for their ungodlike ideas.

The boys then saw themselves as intruders in their own land. They walked away from Jerusalem shrouded in sadness—down from the hills of Judea toward the port of Jaffa.

This ancient port, which had been in constant use since Phoenician times, was another version of Beirut, Aleppo, or Tripoli—narrow alleys, filth, degradation. However, there were a few Jewish settlements nearby at Rishon le Zion, Rehovot, and Petah Tikva. In Jaffa itself there was some Jewish commerce as well as an agency for Jewish immigrants. Here they learned the full story. There were but five thousand Jews in the entire Palestine Province of the Ottoman Empire. Most of these were ancients who lived in study and prayer in the four holy cities of Safed, Jerusalem, Hebron, and Tiberias. The dozen or so agricultural colonies established by Jews were all in dire straits. They were kept going through the philanthropy of wealthy European Jews, the Barons de Hirsch, Rothschild, and the Swiss multimillionaire De Schumann. Much of the idealism of the Bilus had disappeared. It was one thing to speak of rebuilding the House of Jacob from a cellar in the Pale—it was another to face the realities of the hardships and the complete disintegration that had befallen Palestine. The Bilus were all inexperienced in agriculture. The philanthropists sent over experts to help them, but it was a matter of using cheap Arab labor and settling on two or three crops for export: olives, grapes, and citrus. No attempt at self-labor had been tried nor were there attempts to balance the agriculture. The Jews, in fact, had become overseers.

Both the Arabs and the ruling Turks stole from the Jews mercilessly. Crops were taxed to the limit—there were all sorts of restrictive stumbling blocks. The roving bands of Bedouins looked upon the Jews as "Children of Death" because of their refusal to defend themselves.

There were, however, a few hundred Jewish boys like the Rabinsky brothers who stayed around Jaffa, and these kept the spark of the Bilu movement alive. They talked night after night in the Arab cafés. The task of regenerating this miserable land seemed nearly impossible, but it could be done if there were only more Jews with a fighting spirit. Jossi reckoned that more Jews had to come to Palestine sooner or later, for there were bound to be more and worse pogroms in Russia and the entire Pale was stirring. Everyone recognized that something was missing that was not in the Talmud or the Torah or the Midrash or the Mishna. Most of the boys, like Yakov and Jossi, had escaped from Russian military service or had fled out of misery or poverty or some idealistic hopes. The Jews already in Palestine treated them as "outsiders." Further—they were stateless wanderers.

It took a year for an answer to come back from Rabbi Lipzin. They learned that their mother had died of incurable and bottomless grief.

For the next four or five years Yakov and Jossi grew to manhood. They worked around the docks in Jaffa and in the fields of the Jewish settlements either as laborers or overseers. When the Jews began moving out of the old walled city in Jerusalem with the aid of the British Jewish philanthropist, Moses Montefiore, they worked as stonemasons. Everything in Jerusalem was being built of that hauntingly beautiful limestone quarried from the hills of Judea.

They lived from job to job. Little by little they lost contact with their deep religious training which had been the dominating force of ghetto life. Only on the high holy days did

218

they travel to Jerusalem. Only on the Day of Atonement, Yom Kippur, did they search their souls and their lives—and, too, on the Day of Judgment, Rosh Hashana—the new year. Yakov and Jossi Rabinsky became typical of a new type of Jew. They were young and strong and they were free men tasting of a freedom they had never known in the Pale. Yet they longed for a purpose and they longed for contact with the Jews of Europe.

The years 1891, 1892, and 1893 came and went.

A few more settlers straggled in to burden the pocketbooks of the philanthropists.

But as Yakov and Jossi lived in apparent aimlessness in Palestine, dramatic events were taking place in another part of the world which were to shape their destiny and the destiny of every Jew for all time.

CHAPTER SIX

FRANCE 1894-97

The Jews of France and of most of western Europe were better off than the Jews of eastern Europe. After the massacres and expulsions of the Middle Ages, the vicious side of Jew-hating abated in both France and England.

A great day came for the Jews with the French Revolution. After fifteen hundred years there was at last a country in Europe which accepted them as equal human beings. France was the first country in Europe to grant Jews the full rights of citizenship without qualification. Their position was further enhanced by Napoleon, according to whom Judaism was a religion, not a nationality. So long as French Jews regarded it only as a religion and gave their loyalty to France, they ought to be granted full and equal status.

The early 1800s were the beginning of a golden era for the Jews of France. The Jewish community produced a host of brilliant doctors, lawyers, scientists, poets, writers, musicians, and statesmen who seemed to justify the Napoleonic concept of assimilation.

There were discreet forms of anti-Semitism in France, of course. But the unpleasantnesses associated with being Jewish were at a minimum there. Never before had Jews in Europe known such freedom or held such a position in society. By the middle of the 1800s they were well integrated into all walks of French life and had formed the powerful Universal Alliance as their voice and philanthropic arm.

Jew hating is an incurable disease. Under certain democratic conditions it may not flourish well. Under other conditions the germ may even appear to die, but it never does die even in most ideal climate.

In France there lived a young career army captain. He came from a well-to-do family. In the year 1893 he was hauled into a military court on trumped-up charges of selling secrets to the Germans. The trial of this man shook the world, and became an irremediable blotch on the cause of French justice. The man was found guilty of treason and sentenced to life on Devil's Island.

His name was Alfred Dreyfus.

In the bitter winter of 1894 Alfred Dreyfus stood in disgrace in a courtyard. In a ceremony of public ostracism the epaulets were cut from his shoulders, his cheeks were slapped, his sword broken, and the buttons pulled from his cloak. He was denounced above an ominous drum roll as a traitor to France. As he was taken off to begin life in a penal hell he cried, "I am innocent! Long live France!"

Alfred Dreyfus was a Jew.

The dormant disease of anti-Semitism erupted in France. Goaded on by Édouard Drumont, the arch Jew hater, mobs of Frenchmen ran through the streets of Paris screaming the age-old cry—"Death to the Jews!"

In later years the great novelist Émile Zola took up the case of Dreyfus. In an open letter to the President of France he branded the horrible miscarriage of justice in immortal prose.

A certain man witnessed Dreyfus' hour of disgrace in the Paris courtyard. Although Dreyfus was freed, this man could not forget the cry, "I am innocent!" Moreover he could not forget the Parisian mobs screaming, "Death to the Jews!" It haunted him day and night.

The man who could not forget was Theodor Herzl.

Theodor Herzl was also a Jew. He was born in Hungary, but his well-to-do family moved to Austria and he grew up in Vienna. His training in formal Judaism was superficial. He and his family firmly believed in the prevalent theories of assimilation.

Herzl was a brilliant essayist, playwright, journalist. Like so many creative men of his school he was hounded by an incessant restlessness. He was married to a good woman but one completely incapable of giving him the compassion and understanding he needed. Fortunately for Herzl his restless ventures were well financed by a generous family allowance.

Herzl drifted to Paris and eventually became Paris correspondent for the powerful Viennese *New Free Press*. He was relatively happy. Paris was a carefree city and his job was good and there was always that wonderful intellectual exchange.

What had brought him to Paris, really? What unseen hand guided him into that courtyard on that winter's day? Why Herzl? He did not live or think as a devout Jew, yet when he heard the mobs beyond the wall shout, "Death to the Jews!" his life and the life of every Jew was changed forever.

Theodor Herzl pondered and thought, and he decided that the curse of anti-Semitism could never be eradicated. So long as one Jew lived—there would be someone to hate him. From the depths of his troubled mind Herzl wondered what the solution could be, and he came to a conclusion—the same conclusion that a million Jews in a hundred lands had come to before him—the same conclusion that Pinsker had written about in his pamphlet about auto-emancipation. Herzl reasoned that only if the Jews established themselves again as a nation would all Jews of all lands finally exist as free men. They had to have a universal spokesman—they had to command respect and dignity as equals through a recognized government.

The paper in which he set down these ideas was called "The Jewish State."

Galvanized into action by this sudden calling, Herzl drove himself unmercifully to gather support for his ideas. He went to those enormously wealthy philanthropists who were supporting the colonies of Jews in Palestine. They ridiculed the Jewish state idea as nonsense. Charity was one thing—as Jews they gave to less fortunate Jews—but talk of rebuilding a nation was madness.

But the Jewish state idea caught on and spread through a hundred lands. Herzl's idea was neither novel nor unique, but his dynamic drive would not let it die.

Important support began to gather around him. Max Nordau a transplanted Hungarian in Paris with an international reputation as a writer, rallied to his support, as did Wolfsohn in Germany and De Haas in England. Many Christians in high places also expressed their approval of the idea.

In the year 1897 a convention of leading Jews throughout the world was called in the town of Basle, Switzerland. It was, indeed, a parliament of world Jewry. Nothing like it had happened since the second Temple had been destroyed. Assimilationists were there and Lovers of Zion were there. Orthodox Jews were there and Socialists were there. No matter what their leanings, they all had a common bond, and to a man they were prepared to stage a rebellion against two thousand years of unspeakable persecution. The Basle convention called for a return of Jews to their ancient historic homeland, for only through the establishment of a Jewish state could all Jews of all lands achieve freedom.

They called the movement Zionism.

As blood riots against the Jews were increasing in Russia, Poland, Rumania, Austria, and Germany and as Jew baiting was reborn in France, the Basle convention made its historic proclamation:

THE AIM OF ZIONISM IS TO CREATE A HOMELAND FOR THE JEWISH PEOPLE IN PALESTINE SECURED BY PUBLIC LAW.

Theodor Herzl wrote in his diary, "In Basle I established a Jewish State. If I were to say that aloud today, universal laughter would be the response. Maybe in five years, certainly in fifty, everybody will recognize it."

After the formal declaration of Zionism, Theodor Herzl plunged into the arduous work like a man possessed. He was a dynamic leader and inspired all those around him. He consolidated his support, gained new adherents, raised funds, and built an organization.

Herzl's immediate objective, however, was to obtain a charter or some other legal basis upon which Zionism could be built.

There was a split within Jewry itself. Herzl was constantly harassed by an element which considered his "political" Zionism impure. Many of the old Lovers of Zion balked. A part of the religious element decried him as a false Messiah, just as another segment had praised him as the true Messiah. But the Herzl train would not and could not be derailed. Hundreds of thousands of Jews carried an imprinted "shekel" in their pockets as proof of membership.

Still without a charter, Herzl began visiting heads of state to obtain a hearing for his ideas.

Herzl worked beyond his capacities. He depleted his personal finances, neglected his family, and impaired his health. Zionism had become a great obsession with him. At last he obtained an interview with the Sultan of the crumbling Ottoman Empire, Abdul Hamid II, "Abdul the Damned." The aging old despot fenced with Herzl and gave half promises to consider a charter for Palestine in exchange for desperately needed money. Abdul was a corrupt human being. His vast holdings in the Middle East ran from the Mesopotamian Province and included Syria, Lebanon, Palestine, and much of the Arabian Peninsula. He tried to play the Zionist proposal off against better gains and finally refused Herzl's appeal. It was a terrible setback.

In the year 1903 matters reached a new low in Russia. In the city of Kishinev the Jews were charged once again with using Christian blood for their rituals, and on Easter of that year the government secretly spurred on a wanton slaughter that left the ghetto of Kishinev in ruins.

Finally England lent a sympathetic ear. At the turn of the century the British were expanding their influence in the Middle East and were already becoming a challenge to the failing Ottomans. They were entrenched in Egypt as well as in half a dozen sheikdoms on the Arabian Peninsula, and they were anxious to gain the favor of world Jewry in order to further their own aspirations. They offered the Zionists a part of the Sinai Peninsula for Jewish immigration and colonization. It was the understanding that this area stood at the door of the Promised Land and the door would open when the British took over. The plan was vague and ill advised and Herzl still hoped to gain a charter for Palestine, so the plan collapsed.

More attempts to gain a charter failed. The pogroms were overrunning a great part of Europe. Herzl became certain that a temporary haven had to be obtained to ease the situation. The British came forth with a second proposal. They offered the African territory of Uganda to the Zionists for Jewish colonization. Herzl desperately agreed to take it up before the next convention.

When the Uganda plan was proposed by Herzl, a fierce opposition developed, led by the Russian Zionists. The basis of their resistance was the fact that they could find no mention of Uganda in the Bible.

Twenty-five solid years of pogroms in Russia and in Poland were now causing the Jews to pour out from eastern Europe by the thousands. By the turn of the century fifty thousand had found their way to Palestine. Abdul Hamid II saw this influx of Jews as potential allies of the British and decreed that no more Jews from Russia, Poland, or Austria would be allowed.

However, the Sultan's empire was rotten to the core. The Zionists had a world headquarters in England and a growing bank to back them up. Zionist bribe money kept the door of Palestine open for all who would enter.

This was the First Aliyah of the Jewish exodus!

Along with the return of the exiles to their Promised Land another event was taking place in the Arab world. After centuries of subjugation there was a rankling of unrest among the Arabs that spelled the beginnings of Arab nationalism. In all the Arab world there existed not a single independent or autonomous state.

Arab nationalism sprang first from liberal elements in

Lebanon as a progressive movement bent on instituting long overdue reforms. The ideas grew until a first conference was held in Paris and the call was given for the sleepers to awake.

These ideas not only frightened the colonials but they frightened the oppressors within the Arab world, and the well-meaning movement was grabbed up by tribal leaders, sheiks, religious leaders, and effendi landowners, under whose influence the original ideals degenerated into hate-filled dogma as each maneuvered to gain control of the dying Ottoman Empire.

The twentieth century!

Chaos in the Middle East. Zionism! Arab nationalism! The Ottoman's decline and the British ascent! All these elements stewing in a huge caldron were bound to boil over.

Theodor Herzl's comet streaked over the sky with blinding light and speed. It was a mere ten years from the day he had heard Alfred Dreyfus cry, "I am innocent!" to the day he dropped dead of a heart attack at the age of forty-four.

CHAPTER SEVEN: By the time the Zionist movement came into being the Rabinsky brothers were old-timers in Palestine. They knew almost every corner of the land and had worked at almost every job. They had lost most of their illusions.

Yakov was restless and bitter.

Jossi tried to find a measure of contentment in his existence. He appreciated his relative freedom. Moreover, he never stopped dreaming of the land in the Huleh Valley above Safed.

Yakov held both the Arabs and Turks in contempt. He looked upon them as enemies as he had looked upon the Cossacks and students of the gymnasium. It was quite true that the Turks would not tolerate murder, but everything else against the Jews seemed justified. Many a night Yakov and Jossi sat up arguing.

"Certainly we should obtain land through legal purchase but where are we going to get farmers and what is going to make the Bedouins and Turks leave us alone?"

"We will get farmers when the pogroms get bad enough again," Jossi answered. "As for the Turks . . . you can buy them. As for the Arabs, we must learn to live side by side with them in peace. This will happen only if we understand them."

Yakov shrugged. "One thing an Arab understands"—and

he held up his fist and shook it—"he understands this."

"Someday they will hang you on the gallows," Jossi said.

The brothers grew further and further apart. Jossi maintained his desire for peace and understanding and Yakov continued to be a proponent of direct action to counter the injustices against the Jews.

At the beginning of the new century Yakov joined a group of fifteen men who set out on a daring venture. One of the philanthropic funds purchased a small piece of land deep in the Jezreel Valley where no Jews had penetrated for centuries. Here the fifteen pioneers established an agricultural training center and experimental farm. The place was called Sde Tov, Field of Goodness. Their position was extremely dangerous, for they were locked in on four sides by Arab villages and at the mercy of Bedouin tribes who would not hesitate to murder for anything of value.

By 1900 there were fifty thousand Jews in Palestine and a bit more social life for Jossi. Most of those who fled the pogroms wanted nothing to do with the floundering agricultural colonies but were content to become merchants or tradesmen in Jaffa. A few of them settled in the tiny port town of Haifa. However, there were too many coming in for all of them to be absorbed as merchants and there were too many who owned just the clothes they wore; soon there was a good deal of talk of land redemption.

The Zionists opened their first land-buying office, the Zion Colonizing Society, in a dingy run-down hotel in Jaffa which was the local headquarters for Jewish itinerants. Rothschild's Palestine Investment Corporation and the De Schumann Foundation also stepped up land-buying operations to open new villages for the "returnees."

In the middle of 1902 the De Schumann Foundation contacted Jossi Rabinsky and offered him a job as their chief buyer of land. He knew the country as well as any Jew and was noted for his courage in going into Arab territory. Further, he was wise enough to deal with the Turks, for land buying by Jews was severely restricted. Also, one had to be shrewd to trade with the Arab effendis, or landowners. Jossi had his doubts about the new colonies. Living by means of philanthropy and using the fellaheen labor did not seem to him to be the way to redeem the Promised Land, but the opportunity of obtaining land for Jews made him decide to accept the job.

There were other motives behind Jossi's decision. He could get to see Yakov more often this way. He could also learn every inch of the land. Jossi never tired of steeping himself in past glories, and every bit of Palestine held another ghost of the former Jewish greatness. Finally Jossi wanted to be able to travel beyond Rosh Pinna, the last Jewish settlement, to see again the land of the Huleh near Abu Yesha.

Jossi was indeed a handsome figure on his white Arabian stallion. He was a man of thirty now, tall, lean, and muscular. His fiery beard set off the white robes and Arab headdress he was wearing. There were bandoleers of bullets across his shoulders and a bull whip at his side as he rode deep up into the Hills of Samaria and through the Plains of Sharon and into the Galilee to search out land.

Most of the land throughout Palestine was owned by a few dozen powerful effendi families. They charged the fellaheen rent amounting to from half to three quarters of all their crops, and they did absolutely nothing for these poor miserable souls.

Jossi and buyers from the other foundations could obtain land only at outrageous prices. The effendis sold the worst properties—unproductive swamps—to the Jews. They did not believe that anything could or would ever be done with this land, and at the same time the "Hebrew gold" was a windfall.

Jossi took many trips beyond the last Jewish settlement of Rosh Pinna, often to visit Kammal, the muktar of Abu Yesha. The two men became friends.

Kammal was a few years older than Jossi and a rarity among the effendis. Most of the effendis lived as absentee landlords in pleasure spots such as Beirut and Cairo.

This was not so with Kammal. He owned all the land in and around Abu Yesha and he was absolute monarch within its boundaries. As a youth he had had a tragic love affair with the daughter of a poverty-stricken fellah. His father had ignored his pleas to provide medical care for the girl; she was suffering from trachoma. Kammal's father reasoned that his son could have four wives and innumerable concubines, so why trouble himself with one miserable fellah woman. The girl went blind of the dread disease and died before her eighteenth birthday.

This event made Kammal a hater of his own class. It cut a scar so deep in his heart that he developed a social conscience. He went off to Cairo, not to enjoy its wild pleasures, but to study advanced farming methods, sanitation, and medicine. When his father died he returned to Abu Yesha determined to live among his people and to better their wretched conditions.

Kammal fought a losing battle. The Turks would not give him a school or medical facilities or any social services. Conditions in the village were just about as they had been a thousand years before. Most heartbreaking for the Arab was the fact that he was unable to translate what he had learned into practical applications for his villagers; they were so illiterate

226

and so backward that they simply could not comprehend.

Since he had become muktar, Abu Yesha had fared better than any Arab village in the Galilee, but conditions there were still primitive.

Kammal was puzzled by the strange coming of the Jews to Palestine. Because he wanted to learn its meaning, he intentionally cultivated the friendship of Jossi Rabinsky.

Jossi tried to get Kammal to sell him a parcel of land which was not being worked to begin a colony, but Kammal balked. These Jews confused him. He did not know whether they could be trusted or not, for certainly they were not all like Jossi Rabinsky. Besides, he was not going to be the first effendi to sell land in the Huleh Valley.

Just as Kammal learned from Jossi, so Jossi learned from Kammal. Despite Kammal's enlightenment he was heart and soul an Arab. He never spoke of his three wives, for the servitude of woman was traditional. Kammal was always polite, but he was a great man to bicker when bartering. Jossi watched him exercising his authority. Although he had compassion for his people he could not comprehend any means of rule that was not absolute. On occasion Kammal even consulted Jossi in some typical double-dealing scheme which seemed perfectly legitimate to the Arab.

Through Kammal, Jossi Rabinsky learned about the magnificent and tragic history of the Arab people.

In the seventh century the dogma of Islam had erupted upon the wild semicivilized Bedouin tribes in the deserts. Inspired by Mohammed's divine teachings, they swept out of the sand and with fire and sword spread their gospel from the doorsteps of China to the gates of Paris. During a hundred years of holy persuasion, hundreds of millions of the world's peoples had gathered to the banner of Islam. The heart and soul of Islam were the Arabs, who were bound together by a common language and a common religion of submission to God's will. During the meteoric rise of Islam, Jews held the highest positions of esteem in the Arab-speaking world.

A magnificent civilization arose from the deserts. It was the light of all mankind while the Western world wallowed in the morass of the Dark Ages and feudalism. Bagdad and Damascus became the Athens of their day. The Moslem culture was dazzling. For five hundred years the most advanced thinking, the greatest scientific efforts, the most magnificent artisans belonged to the Arab-speaking world.

Then came the Holy Wars of the Crusaders, who sacked and raped and killed in the name of the very same God who was shared by Moslem and Christian.

After the Crusaders came a century—one hundred unrelieved years—of Mongol invasions. The Mongols swooped in from Asia and the wars were so cruel and so bloody that they defied any known bounds of brutality. Pyramids of Arab skulls stood as the monuments of the Mongols.

The Arabs so exhausted themselves in ten decades of fighting that their once mighty cities were decimated and a dry rot fell on the flowering oases. The beautiful islands of fruit and plenty were eaten up by seas of sand and erosion. The Arabs turned more and more against themselves and a bitter and desperate struggle ensued in which blood feuds pitted brother against brother. Divided against themselves, their land ruined, and their culture all but destroyed, they were unprepared to defend themselves against the final disaster.

This time it was brought about by fellow Moslems as the mighty Ottomans gobbled up their lands. Five centuries of corruption and feudalism followed.

A drop of water became more precious than gold or spices in the unfertile land. The merest, most meager existence was a series of tortured, heartbreaking struggles from birth to death. Without water the Arab world disintegrated into filth; unspeakable disease, illiteracy, and poverty were universal. There was little song or laughter or joy in Arab life. It was a constant struggle to survive.

In this atmosphere cunning, treachery, murder, feuds, and jealousies became a way of life. The cruel realities that had gone into forming the Arab character puzzled outsiders.

Cruelty from brother to brother was common. In parts of the Arab world thousands of slaves were kept, and punishment for a thief was amputation of a hand, for a prostitute, amputation of ears and nose. There was little compassion from Arab to Arab. The fellaheen who lived in abysmal filth and the Bedouin whose survival was a day-to-day miracle turned to the one means of alleviating their misery. They became Moslem fanatics as elements of the Jews had become fanatics in their hour of distress.

It was small wonder that the Arabs mistrusted all outsiders. The restless movement for freedom originated with the ruling classes, for the Bedouins and fellaheen were far too demoralized even to comprehend freedom and better conditions. The masses were but pawns in the schemes of the effendis and sheiks. They could be stirred into religious hysteria at the least provocation and were thus useful as a political weapon.

Jossi Rabinsky became fascinated by the many-sided Arab character. He could stand for hours around the shops in Jaffa and watch the endless bickering and boisterous trading. He observed as the Arab ran his life as though it were a game of chess. Every move was made with an astuteness designed to

228

outfox those he was dealing with. In the cafés and dens Jossi watched violent passions erupt. During his land-buying expeditions he observed the unscrupulous ethics of the Arab. Yet he enjoyed entering an Arab home where hospitality was unsurpassed. He was confounded by the fantastic reasoning that condoned every crime short of murder. He thought the position of women intolerable; they were held in absolute bondage, never seen, never heard, never consulted. Women often sought quick and vicious revenge by dagger or poison. Greed and lust, hatred and cunning, shrewdness and violence, friendliness and warmth were all part of that fantastic brew that made the Arab character such an enormous mystery to an outsider.

Kammal introduced Jossi Rabinsky to the Koran, the Holy Book of Islam. Jossi learned that Abraham was the father of the Arabs as well as of the Jews. From Ishmael, the cast-out son of Hagar, came the seed of the Arabs.

Jossi learned that Moses, the Jews' great lawgiver, was also the chief prophet of the Moslems, and that all of the prophets of the Bible were also prophets of the Koran. Even many of the great rabbis were looked upon as holy men in Islam.

Kammal eyed the return of the Jews to the Promised Land with suspicion. The Jews puzzled him, for they had come in peace, purchased their land legally, and spoke only in lofty terms of redemption. Kammal, in understanding the basic drive behind the "return," admitted to himself that it was a just and true move—but yet his mind could not believe that the newcomers would not eventually engulf and exploit the Arabs as all the others before them had done.

Yakov left Sde Tov. The experimental farm had not been a success. In much the same state he had been in before, Yakov continued to wander around from one end of the country to the other trying to find his niche.

In the year 1905 the revolution long brewing in Russia took place. It was crushed.

The failure of the 1905 revolution was a signal for new pogroms. These were so fearful that the entire civilized world stood aghast. Leo Tolstoy was so moved that he wrote a blistering condemnation of the Czar, his Minister of the Interior Count Plehve, and of the Black Hundreds whose specialty was murdering Jews. The Black Hundreds, protected by the Russian secret police, continued the pogroms until hundreds of thousands of Jews poured out of Russia. Most of them fled to America. Some went to Palestine.

Those who came to the Promised Land were of a new breed. They were not refugees like the Rabinsky brothers nor were they of a mind to become merchants. These were youngsters indoctrinated in Zionism and filled with idealism and a determination to redeem the land.

The year 1905 ushered in the Second Aliyah of the exodus.

CHAPTER EIGHT: The need for idealism in Palestine was satisfied by the coming of the Second Aliyah. These newcomers were not content to be merchants in Jaffa nor did they wish to live off the alms of coreligionists. They were fired with a mission to redeem the land.

They set out in groups for the land the effendis had sold and tried to dry up the swamps. It was terrible work. To many of the old-timers the thought of Jews laboring in the fields like Arabs was unbelievable. In Palestine they had been the overseers. In the Old Country they did not work the land at all. Of all the gifts the Second Aliyah brought with them the greatest, perhaps, was the pronouncement of self-labor and the conquest of labor. Through their chief spokesman, A. D. Gordon, labor was made something dignified. Gordon was an older man and a scholar but he gave up scholarship for the greater task of working the soil with his own hands.

These were stimulating days for Yakov. He went out to another new experimental farm in the Galilee called Sejera. In Sejera the excitement never died as the young Jews of the Second Aliyah got down to work. One day Yakov came into Jaffa to see Jossi and he was filled with excitement over a new idea.

Yakov spoke with that fiery exuberance that was his own. "As you know, the Bedouin tribes use extortion to get our settlements to hire them as guards . . . against themselves. Well . . . they tried it at Sejera. They came in and made threats of what they'd do unless he hired them . . . and we didn't. And we've defended ourselves very well. It was precarious for a while, but we set a trap and killed their leader and they haven't come back since.

"We have talked it over," Yakov continued. "If we can defend one settlement we can defend them all. We have made plans to form a roving guard and we want you to take over one of the units."

A Jewish guard! What an astonishing idea! Jossi was excited but he answered in his usual way: "I will have to think it over."

"What is there to think over?"

"You are making it too black and white, as usual, Yakov. First of all the Bedouins are not going to give up this important source of income without a fight. Then there are the

Turks. They will make it nearly impossible for us to carry arms."

"I'll be blunt," Yakov said. "We wanted you, Jossi, because no one knows the country better and no one has had more experience in dealing with both Arabs and Turks."

"Oh," Jossi mocked, "so all of a sudden my dear brother realizes that my years of friendship with the Arabs hasn't been a complete waste of time."

"What do you say, Jossi?"

"I say I'll consider it. Our own farmers may need a lot of convincing to let us guard them. And one thing that really annoys me . . . if we carry loaded guns it may be interpreted to mean we are looking for a fight."

Yakov threw up his hands. "Challenging a fight by defending your own property! After twenty years in Palestine you still think like a ghetto Jew."

Jossi refused to be rattled. "We came in peace. We have purchased our land legally. We have built our settlements without disturbing anyone. Now if we start to arm, it will be a compromise with the basic idealism of Zionism and don't pretend there is no risk in that."

"But he stood in the midst of the ground, and defended it . . . and the Lord wrought a great victory."

"Still quoting . . ."

"You make me sick," Yakov snapped. "Sure, Jossi . . . redeem the land under the magnanimous protection of the Bedouin cutthroats. Very well. I shall tell them my brother is deep in meditation. With or without you the Guardsmen are forming. The unit we want you to command is leaving next week for our base camp."

"Where?"

"On Mount Canaan."

Mount Canaan! Jossi's heart skipped a beat. He wetted his lips and tried to conceal his excitement. "I will think it over," he said.

Jossi did think it over. He was tired of buying land for the De Schumann Foundation and of establishing more colonies to live on charity.

A dozen armed Jews who were as hotheaded as Yakov could cause a great deal of trouble. Restraint and wisdom were needed in an armed guard. But the thought of living around Mount Canaan with the chance to spend time in the Huleh Valley proved too great a temptation.

Jossi resigned from the De Schumann Foundation and joined the new group as they arrived at Mount Canaan. They called themselves Hashomer: the Guardsman.

Jossi's company was to work in a circle from Mount Canaan

from Rosh Pinna in the north to the Genossar Valley along the Sea of Galilee in the south and west to Safed and Meron.

Jossi knew that it would be only a matter of time until trouble broke out. As soon as the Bedouins learned they had lost their jobs they were certain to strike. He concocted a plan designed to avert trouble. The most troublesome of the Bedouin tribes in the area was led by an old renegade and smuggler named Suleiman whose encampments were generally in the hills above Abu Yesha. Suleiman extorted one fourth of Rosh Pinna's crops in return for "protection." The day after his arrival, before the Arabs were aware of the presence of the Guardsmen, Jossi rode out alone and unarmed to find Suleiman's camp.

He located it late in the evening beyond Abu Yesha, near Tel Hai on the Lebanon side. The camp consisted of goatskin tents scattered about the browned-out hills. These eternal nomads considered themselves the purest and freest of all Arabs. They looked down contemptuously at the lowly fellaheen and the city dwellers. Life was indeed hard for the Bedouin but he was a free man with strong tribal ties, fiercest of the Arab fighters, and the most cunning of the Arab traders.

The sight of the giant red-bearded stranger caused a general alarm. The women, dressed in black Bedouin robes with chains of coins forming masks over their faces, hastened for cover as Jossi rode in.

When he had ridden halfway through the camp a Negro Arab, obviously from the Sudan, came toward him. The Negro introduced himself as Suleiman's personal slave and led him to the largest of the tents near the largest flock of goats.

The old brigand stepped outside his tent. The Arab wore black robes and black headdress. Two magnificent silver daggers hung from his waist. He was blind in one eye and his face was scarred from many battles with men armed with knives and women armed with claws. Suleiman and Jossi sized each other up quickly.

Jossi was ushered into the tent. The earthen floor was covered with rugs and cushions. The two men made themselves comfortable. Suleiman ordered his slave to bring fruit and coffee to the guest. The two men smoked from a long-stemmed water pipe and exchanged meaningless amenities for half an hour. Dishes of curried rice and lambs' testicles were served and they had melons for dessert as they maneuvered the conversation for another hour. Suleiman realized Jossi was no ordinary Jew and on no ordinary mission.

At last he asked Jossi the purpose of his visit and Jossi informed him that Hashomer was taking up his guarding duties. He thanked Suleiman for his past loyal services. The

Arab received the news without batting his good eye. Jossi requested a handshake upon a pact of friendship. Suleiman smiled and offered his hand.

Late that night Jossi rode into Rosh Pinna and called a meeting of farmers. Everyone was terrified by the whole idea of the Guardsmen. They were certain that Suleiman would slit their throats when he heard about it. The appearance of Jossi Rabinsky and his promise to remain at Rosh Pinna did much to calm them down.

In the rear of the meeting room a new girl of twenty watched and listened to Jossi Rabinsky. She had only arrived from Silesia in Poland a short time before. Her name was Sarah. She was as tiny as Jossi was huge, and her hair was as black as his was red. She was absolutely entranced as she watched him and listened to him talk.

"You are new here," he said after the meeting.

"Yes."

"I am Jossi Rabinsky."

"Everyone knows of you."

Jossi remained at Rosh Pinna for a week. He was certain that Suleiman would make a call but he knew the Bedouin was crafty enough not to be reckless. Jossi was in no hurry for the Arab to come, because he was greatly taken by Sarah. But in her presence he became tongue-tied and shy, for he had had little or no experience with Jewish girls in his adult life. The more Sarah teased and prodded, the more he turned into a shell. Everyone in Rosh Pinna, except Jossi, knew that he was a marked man.

On the ninth day a dozen Arabs slipped into Rosh Pinna in the middle of the night and made off with several hundred pounds of grain. Jossi was standing guard and saw them coming and observed every move they made. He could easily have caught them red-handed, but it was no crime to catch a Bedouin stealing. Jossi had a different strategy in mind.

The next morning Jossi rode off once more for Suleiman's camp. This time he was armed—with his ten-foot bull whip. He galloped into the camp at full speed and made directly for Suleiman's tent and dismounted. The Sudanese slave came out and smiled sweetly and welcomed Jossi and invited him to enter. Jossi hit the slave with the back of his hand as though he were flicking a fly from his arm and sent him sprawling to the ground.

"Suleiman!" his big voice boomed out for the whole camp to hear. "Step outside!"

A dozen kinsmen appeared from nowhere with rifles in their hands and surprise on their faces.

"Outside!" Jossi roared again.

The old brigand took a long time to make his appearance.

He stepped from the tent and put his hands on his hips and smiled menacingly. Ten feet of ground separated the two.

"Who is it who howls outside my tent like a sick goat?" Suleiman asked. The tribesmen were seized by a fit of laughter. Jossi did not take his eyes off the Arab for a second.

"It is Jossi Rabinsky who howls like a sick goat," he said, "and says that Suleiman is a thief and a liar!"

The smile on Suleiman's lips turned into an ugly scowl. The Bedouins tensed and waited for the signal to pounce on the Jew and devour him.

"Go on," Jossi challenged softly, "call all your nephews. Your honor is no greater than a pig's and I hear you have no more courage than a woman."

No more courage than a woman! This was the deadliest insult he could hear. Jossi had issued him a personal challenge.

Suleiman raised his fist and shook it. "Your mother is the biggest whore in the world."

"Go on, woman . . . keep talking," Jossi answered.

Suleiman's very honor was at stake. He drew one of his silver daggers and with a bloodcurdling shriek charged at the red-bearded giant.

Jossi's bull whip whistled out!

It wrapped around the Arab's feet, picked him up, and sent him smashing to the earth. Jossi was at him like a cat. He brought the whip down on Suleiman's back with such terrifying speed and strength that the snap echoed through all the hills.

"We are brothers! We are brothers!" Suleiman cried for mercy at the end of five lashes.

Jossi pointed at his frantic foe. "Suleiman, you gave me your hand in a bargain of honor and you lied. If you or your kinsmen ever again set foot in our fields I will cut your body apart with this whip and feed the pieces to the jackals."

Jossi turned and his eyes pierced the astonished Bedouins. They were all too stunned to move. Never had they seen a man so powerful and fearless and angry. Showing utter disdain for their rifles, Jossi turned his back on them, walked to his horse, mounted, and rode off.

Suleiman never touched a Jewish field again.

The next morning when Jossi mounted up to rejoin his company at Mount Canaan, Sarah asked when he would be back. He mumbled something about getting to Rosh Pinna each month or so. As he swung onto his horse, saluted, and galloped off, Sarah thought her heart would burst apart. There was never a man like Jossi Rabinsky—Jew, Arab, Cossack, or king! She swore as she saw him ride away that she would dedicate the rest of her life to loving him.

234

For a year Jossi commanded his Guardsman company in their territory with such skill that little or no trouble occurred. He never had to resort to firearms. When there was trouble he would go to the Arabs for a friendly consultation and warning. If it happened again—the bull whip. The bull whip of Jossi Rabinsky became as well known through the northern Galilee as his red beard. The Arabs called it "lightning."

All this proved too dull for Yakov. He was bored with the lack of action. After six months in the Guardsman he left again to go on the prowl, hoping somehow to fill the constant void in his life.

Jossi was neither sad nor happy as a Guardsman. It gave him more pleasure than buying land and it established an important principle by demonstrating that the Jews could and would defend themselves and were no longer "children of death." He looked forward to his northern swing so that he could have a visit with his friend Kammal and then travel up to his hill to keep his dream alive.

Secretly he eagerly anticipated those moments when he rode into Rosh Pinna. He would straighten up to look even more elegant and gallant on his white steed, and his heart would beat more quickly for he knew that Sarah, the dark-eyed girl from Silesia, was watching. But when it came to conversation or action, Jossi was lost.

Sarah was perplexed. She simply could not break down Jossi's shyness. If it had been the Old Country the matchmaker would have gone to Jossi's father and arranged everything. Here there was not only no matchmaker but not even a rabbi.

This went on for a year.

One day Jossi rode into Rosh Pinna unexpectedly. It was all he could do to ask Sarah if she would like to ride with him to see the country north of the settlement in the Huleh Valley.

How thrilling! No Jew but Jossi Rabinsky dared wander up that far! They galloped past Abu Yesha, on up the road, and then into the hills. The trail ended atop his hill.

"I crossed into Palestine right here," he said softly.

As Jossi looked down into the Huleh Valley he did not need to say another word. Sarah knew how deeply he loved this earth. The two of them stood and gazed for ever so long. Sarah barely reached his chest.

A warm flood of love passed through her. This was Jossi's only way of sharing his most intimate longing.

"Jossi Rabinsky," Sarah whispered, "would you please, please marry me?"

Jossi cleared his throat and stammered, "Ahem . . . uh . . . how strange of you to mention it. I was about to say something of the sort myself."

There had never been a wedding in Palestine to compare with Jossi's and Sarah's. They came from all over the Galilee and even from as far away as Jaffa, even though it was a two-day journey to Safed. The Guardsmen came and Yakov came and the settlers of Rosh Pinna came and Turks came and Kammal came and even Suleiman came. Everyone watched as Jossi and Sarah stood beneath the canopy and exchanged vows and drank the blessed wine. Jossi crushed the wine-glass beneath his foot in remembrance of the bitterness of the fall of the Temple. There was food enough for an army and there was dancing and gaiety and celebration that lasted nearly a week.

When the last guest had gone home Jossi took his bride to his tent on the side of Mount Canaan and consummated their marriage.

Jossi took his bride down from Mount Canaan to Jaffa where there was much work to be done for the Zionists. His fame left him well equipped to take charge of settling newcomers and to deal with the many intricacies of this strange land. He signed on with the Zionists as one of the chief men in the Zion Settlement Society.

In the year 1909, Jossi was consulted in a very important matter. Many of the Jews of Jaffa's growing community wanted better housing, sanitation, and a cultural life that the ancient Arab city could not offer. Jossi was instrumental in purchasing a strip of land north of Jaffa, which consisted mostly of sand and orange groves.

On this land the first all-Jewish city in two thousand years was built. They called it the Hill of Spring: Tel Aviv.

CHAPTER NINE: The agricultural colonies were failing miserably.

There were many reasons. Apathy and lethargy and complete lack of idealism, for one. They still planted only export crops and continued to use the cheaper Arab labor. Despite the influx of Jews and the desire of these Jews to work the land the Zionists could barely convince the colonies to use them.

The over-all situation was discouraging. Palestine was not much better off than it had been when the Rabinsky brothers came twenty years before. There was a measure of culture

236

around Tel Aviv, but all other progress was too small to be measured.

The energy and idealism which had come in with the Second Aliyah was going to waste. Like Yakov and Jossi, the immigrants drifted from place to place without cause and without putting down roots.

As the Zion Settlement Society purchased more and more land it became increasingly obvious that some drastic change in the entire thinking about colonization was necessary.

Jossi and others had long concluded that individual farming was a physical impossibility. There was the matter of security, there was the ignorance of the Jews in farming matters, and, worse, there was the complete wastage of the land.

What Jossi wanted with this new land was villages whose inhabitants would work the soil themselves, plant balanced crops to become self-sustaining, and be able to defend themselves.

The first principle involved was to keep all land in the name of the Zion Settlement Society—all-Jewish land for all the Jewish people. Only self-labor would be allowed on the land: the Jew had to do the work himself and could hire no other Jew or Arab.

The next dramatic step was taken when Jews of the Second Aliyah pledged to work only for the redemption of the land and build a homeland with no thoughts of personal gain or profits or ambition. Their pledge, in fact, came close to later communal farming ideas. The communal farm was not born of social or political idealism. It was based on the necessities of survival; there was no other way.

The stage was set for a dramatic experiment. The year was 1909. The Zion Settlement Society purchased four thousand *dunams* of land below Tiberias at a point where the Jordan River flowed into the Sea of Galilee. Most of it was swamp or marshland. The society staked twenty young men and women to a year's supplies and money. Their mission was to reclaim the land.

Jossi traveled out with them as they pitched their tents at the edge of the marshland. They named their place Shoshanna after the wild roses which grew along the Sea of Galilee.

The Shoshanna experiment on national land could well be the key to future colonization and was the most important single step taken by the Jews since the exodus.

Three clapboard sheds were erected. One was a communal dining and meeting hall. One was a barn and tool shed. The third served as a barracks for the sixteen men and four women.

In the first winter the sheds collapsed a dozen times in the winds and floods. The roads were so muddy they became isolated from the outside world for long stretches. At last they were forced to move into a nearby Arab village to wait it out till springtime.

In the spring Jossi returned to Shoshanna as the work began in earnest. The marshlands and swamps had to be rolled back foot by foot. Hundreds of Australian eucalyptus trees were planted to soak up the water. Drainage ditches were carved out by hand; the work was backbreaking. They labored from sunup till sundown, and a third of the members were always bedridden with malaria. The only cure they knew was the Arab method of cutting the ear lobes and draining blood. They worked in waist-deep muck through the terrible heat of the summer.

By the second year there was some reclaimed land to show for their toil. Now the rocks had to be dragged from the fields by donkey teams and the thick brush hacked down and burned.

In Tel Aviv, Jossi continued to fight to continue support for the experiment, for he was discovering an amazing thing. He was discovering that the drive to build a homeland was so great that there were at least twenty people willing to do this thankless, backbreaking work without pay.

The hardships endured at Shoshanna never ceased, but by the end of two years enough land had been readied to lay in a crop. This was a crucial stage, for most of the group did not know how to farm or what to farm or the difference between a hen and a rooster. They worked by trial and error, and the results were mostly errors. They did not know how to sow or plow in a straight line or how to get milk from cows or how to plant trees. The earth was a gigantic mystery.

They attacked the problem of farming with the same dogged determination with which they had attacked the swampy land. With the swamp water drained off, irrigation water had to be brought in. At first it was carried from the river in water cans on donkey back. Next came an experiment with an Arab water wheel, and after that several attempts at wells. Finally they put in irrigation ditches and built a network of dams to trap the winter rains.

Little by little the land yielded its secrets. On many of his visits Jossi held his breath and wondered and marveled at the morale at Shoshanna. They had nothing but what they wore on their backs and even that belonged to the community. They ate the meagerest of meals in a community dining hall, had common showers and toilets, and slept everyone under the same roof. The Arabs and Bedouins watched the slow steady growth of Shoshanna with amaze-

238

ment. When the Bedouins saw several hundred acres of land under cultivation they set out to dislodge the Jews.

All work in the fields had to be done under cover of armed guards. Along with sickness, overwork—security became a problem. After a torturous day in the fields the tired farmers had to stand guard throughout the night. But they carried on at Shoshanna through isolation and ignorance and threats of attack and swamps and murderous heat and malaria and a dozen other calamities.

Yakov Rabinsky came to Shoshanna to try his luck there.

Joseph Trumpledor arrived. Trumpledor had been an officer in the Russian Army and was famous for his valor in the Russo-Japanese War during which he lost an arm. The call of Zionism brought Trumpledor to Palestine and the path led to Shoshanna. With Trumpledor and Yakov handling security the Bedouin raids soon ceased.

There were more problems in communal living than they had imagined.

There was the governing of the community. This was completely democratic, but Jews were traditionally independent and no two Jews ever agreed on any given subject. Would the governing turn into endless conversation and haggling?

There was the division of work. There was community responsibility for health, welfare, and education. And what of the members who could not or would not do a full day's work? What of those who were disgruntled over their assignments? What of those who objected to the cooking or to living in such tight quarters? What of the clash of personalities?

One thing seemed to overrule all else. Everyone in Shoshanna had a violent hatred for the things which had made him a ghetto Jew. They were going to destroy those things and they were going to build a homeland. Shoshanna had its own code of ethics and its own social laws. They made the marriages and the divorces by common consent. They ran the village in such a way as not to be bound by the old traditions. They threw off the shackles of their past.

So long had their oppression been and so great their desire that here at Shoshanna was the birth of a true free Jewish peasantry. They dressed like peasants, and they danced the *hora* by firelight. The earth and the building of the homeland had become a noble cause for existence. As time went on flowers and trees and shrubs and lawns were set in and new and fine buildings were erected. Small cottages were built for the married couples and a library was begun and a full-time doctor was hired.

Then came the rebellion of the women. One of the four original women settlers was a stocky unattractive girl named

Ruth. She was the leader of the women's rebellion. She argued in the community meetings that the women had not ventured from the Pale and from Poland and certainly not to Shoshanna to become domestics. They demanded equality and responsibilities on the farm. They broke down the old taboos one by one and joined the men in all phases of the work, even plowing the fields. They took over the chickens and the vegetable fields and proved equal in ability and stamina to the men. They learned how to use weapons and stood guard during the nights.

Ruth, the ringleader of the women's uprising, really had her eye on the five-cow dairy herd. She wanted very badly to have the cows. But the votes of the men squashed that ambition. The girls were going too far! Yakov, the most boisterous of the men, was sent into battle with Ruth. Surely she must know that the cows were too dangerous for women to handle! Besides, those five cows were the Shoshanna's most prized and spoiled possessions.

Everyone was astounded when Ruth coyly quit her fight. It was so unlike her! She did not mention another word about it for another month. Instead she slipped out of Shoshanna at every opportunity to the nearby Arab village to learn the art of milking. In her spare time she studied everything she could get her hands on concerning dairy farming.

One morning Yakov went into the barn after a night of guard duty. Ruth had broken her word! She was milking Jezebel, their prize cow.

A special meeting was called to chastise comrade Ruth for insubordination. Ruth came armed with facts and figures to prove that she could increase the milk yield with proper feed and common sense. She accused the men of ignorance and intolerance. They decided to put her in her place by letting her take charge of the herd.

Comrade Ruth ended up as permanent keeper of the cows. She increased the herd twenty-five times over and became one of the best dairy farmers in all of Palestine.

Yakov and Ruth were married, for it was said that she was the only person in the world who could win an argument with him. They loved each other very much and were extremely happy.

The greatest crisis came at Shoshanna with the birth of the first children. The women had fought for equality and gained it and in so doing had become important in the farm's economy. Many of them held key positions. The point was argued and discussed. Should the women quit their jobs and become domestics? Could some other way be found to keep a family going? The members of Shoshanna argued that because they had a unique way of life they could find a unique way to handle the children.

Children's houses came into existence. Certain members of Shoshanna were chosen for the job of raising the children under supervision during the day. This allowed the women to be free to work. In the evenings the families stayed together. Many outsiders cried that this would destroy family life, which had been the saving factor of the Jewish people through centuries of persecution. Despite the detractors, the family ties at Shoshanna became as powerful as those in any family anywhere.

Yakov Rabinsky had found happiness at last. Shoshanna grew until it had a hundred members and over a thousand *dunams* of the land reclaimed. Yakov did not have money or even clothing to call his own. He had a snippy, sharp-tongued woman who was one of the best farmers in the Galilee. In the evenings, when the day's labor was done, he and Ruth would walk over the lawns and through the flower gardens or to the knoll and look down at the lush green fields—and Yakov was content and fulfilled.

Shoshanna, the first *kibbutz* in Palestine, seemed to be the long-awaited answer for Zionism.

CHAPTER TEN: Jossi came home one evening from a special meeting of the Vaad Halashon and he was steeped in thought. Because of his position in the community they had made a special appeal to him.

Sarah always had tea ready for Jossi, no matter what time of day or night he returned from his meetings. They sat on the balcony of their three-room flat on Hayarkon Street overlooking the Mediterranean. From here Jossi could look down the curve of coastline to Jaffa which joined Tel Aviv.

"Sarah," he said at last, "I have come to a decision. Tonight I was at the Vaad Halashon and they have asked me to take a Hebrew name and speak Hebrew exclusively. I heard Ben Yehuda speak tonight. He has done a tremendous job in modernizing Hebrew."

"Such nonsense," Sarah replied. "You told me yourself that never in the history of the world has a language been revived."

"And I have come to think that never before have a people tried to revive a nation as we are doing. When I see what has been done at Shoshanna and the other *kibbutzim* . . ."

"Speaking of Shoshanna . . . you only want to take a Hebrew name because your brother, the former Yakov Rabinsky, has done so."

"Nonsense."

"Just what do we call the former Yakov Rabinsky now?"

"Akiva. He named himself after his childhood idol . . ."

"And maybe you want to call yourself Jesus Christ after a boyhood idol."

"You are impossible, woman!" Jossi snorted and stomped in from the balcony.

"If you ever went to a synagogue any more," Sarah said, following him, "you would know that Hebrew is for communication with God."

"Sarah . . . I sometimes wonder why you bothered to come from Silesia. If we are to think like a nation, we had better speak like a nation."

"We do. Yiddish is our language."

"Yiddish is the language of exiles. Yiddish is the language of the ghetto. Hebrew is the language of all the Jews."

She pointed her finger up at her giant of a husband. "Don't recite Zionist propaganda to me, Jossi. You will be Jossi Rabinsky to me till the day I die."

"I have made the decision, Sarah. You had better study your Hebrew because that is what we will be speaking from now on."

"Such stupidity, your decision!"

Jossi had been slow in agreeing with Ben Yehuda and the others. Hebrew had to be revived. If the desire for national identity was great enough a dead language could be brought back. But Sarah was set in her ways. Yiddish was what she spoke and what her mother had spoken. She had no intention of becoming a scholar so late in life.

For a week Sarah locked Jossi out of the bedroom. He refused to break down. Then for three weeks he spoke to Sarah only in Hebrew and she answered him in Yiddish.

"Jossi," she called one night, "Jossi, come here and help me."

"I beg your pardon," Jossi said. "There is no one in this house by the name of Jossi. If you happen to be speaking to me," he continued, "my name is Barak. Barak Ben Canaan."

"Barak Ben Canaan!"

"Yes. It took much thought to select a proper name. The Arabs used to call my whip 'lightning,' and that is what Barak is in Hebrew—lightning. It is also the name of Deborah's leading general. I call myself Canaan because I happen to like Mount Canaan."

The door slammed.

Jossi shouted through it. "I was happy living on Mount Canaan! I did not have a hardheaded woman then! Get used to it, Sarah Ben Canaan . . . Sarah Ben Canaan!"

Jossi, now Barak, was again locked out of his bedroom. For a solid week neither adversary spoke.

One night, a month after their warfare had started, Barak returned from a grueling three-day meeting in Jerusalem. He came in late at night, exhausted, and looked around, hoping that Sarah might be up to talk things over and have a cup of tea. The door to her room was closed. He sighed and pulled off his shoes and lay back on the sofa. He was so large his legs hung over the arm. He was tired and wished he could sleep in his own bed and was sorry for starting the whole business. He began to doze but was awakened by a crack of light under the bedroom door. Sarah tiptoed to him and knelt by his huge frame and put her head on his chest.

"I love you, Barak Ben Canaan," she whispered in perfect Hebrew.

Life was busy for Barak Ben Canaan in the brand-new city of Tel Aviv. As the community grew the Jews of Palestine became known by the literal definition of the term— the Yishuv—and Hebrew was revived as the language of the Yishuv. Barak Ben Canaan had risen high among the Zionists and in the Zion Settlement Society. His life was a constant round of meetings and delicate negotiations with the Turks and Arabs. He wrote many papers of importance in the formulation of policy and he and Sarah traveled many times to London to Zionist headquarters and to Switzerland to the international conferences. Yet Barak did not know the true happiness that his brother Akiva had found at Shoshanna. Barak's heart was always north of Mount Canaan in the land of the Huleh Valley. Sarah was a wise and devoted wife. She wanted badly to compensate for his hunger for the land by trying to give him children. This ended in sadness. For five consecutive years she lost children through early miscarriages. It was indeed bitter, for Barak was already in his mid-forties.

Briefly in 1908 there was a rebellion of the Young Turks, who deposed the corrupt old tyrant and despot Abdul Hamid II. The entire Zionist movement was hopeful as he was replaced by Mohammed V as Sultan of the Ottomans and spiritual head of the Moslem world.

They soon learned that the rebellion would have no effect on the granting of a charter. Mohammed V had inherited a collapsing empire, and was known to the world as the "sick man of Europe."

From the very beginning, the British had shown the greatest sympathy for the Zionists. Barak felt that Jewish interests and British interests could be brought together, while

243

there was no basis for co-operation with the Turks. The British had offered both Sinai and Uganda for settlement. Many high British officials spoke openly in support of a Jewish homeland. England itself was the headquarters for the Zionists; and further, Dr. Chaim Weizmann, a Russian-born Jew, had become the world spokesman for the Zionist movement.

With the rise of the British in the Middle East and the obvious eclipse of the Ottomans, Barak and the Yishuv and the Zionists became openly pro-British.

Mohammed V had lost a series of costly Balkan wars. His position as the "Shadow of God," the Moslem spiritual leader, was slipping and the five-century-old Ottoman reign was tottering as the empire came close to economic collapse.

For centuries the Czars of Russia had dreamed of having warm-water ports on the Mediterranean. It had been their eternal ambition to break through the Bosporus and the Dardanelles. With the collapse of the Ottomans at hand, Russia concocted a gigantic power play to carry this out at last. Russia goaded Turkey in an attempt to line her up on the side of Germany. Russia wanted a war with Turkey and she made the ownership of Constantinople the condition of entering that war on the side of the Allied powers. Mohammed V was well aware of what Russia was up to and he studiously avoided a fight. He realized that not only were the Russians going to grab Constantinople but the British, French, and Italians were impatiently waiting to pounce on the empire and split it up among themselves.

World War I erupted!

Mohammed V did not oblige either the Russians or the British by collapsing. Indeed, the Turks showed more fight than anyone had bargained for. The Russian Army was stopped dead trying to cross the Caucasus Mountains; and in the Middle East the Turks lunged out of Palestine, crossed the Sinai Desert, and stood at the very artery of the British Empire, the Suez Canal.

McMahon, the British commissioner in Egypt, began making promises to the Arabs if only the Arabs would rebel against the Ottomans. The British promises implied independence for the Arabs in return for their aid. British agents worked desperately to drum up an Arab revolt against the Turks. They went to the leading Arab prince, Ibn Saud, the powerful Wahabite of Arabia. Ibn Saud decided to wait until he was certain which way the wind was blowing. The balance of the Arab world either fought alongside the Turks or played a game of waiting.

On the Ottoman side, Mohammed V, titular head of all the Moslems, sent out hysterical calls for the entire Moslem world to rise against the British in a "holy war." His appeals were met with silence.

The British concluded that the only way to get Arab allies was to buy them. British gold was consequently spread about liberally as bait to hook support. The bait was snapped at. The position of sherif of Mecca was a semi-independent job within the Ottoman rule. The sherif was officially "Keeper of the Holy Places of Medina and Mecca." The job was inherited and held for a lifetime by those in the direct line of descent from Mohammed.

The sherif of Mecca was indeed a little man in the Arab world. Further, he was the arch enemy of Ibn Saud. When the British approached him he saw the opportunity to seize power over the entire Arab world if Mohammed V and the Ottomans should fall. So the sherif of Mecca went over to the British, at the price of several hundred thousands of pounds sterling. The sherif had a son named Faisal who was a rarity among Arab leaders, a man who had a social conscience and vision. He agreed to assist his father in getting Arab tribes to "rebel" against the Ottomans.

The Yishuv in Palestine did not have to be bribed or coddled or bought. The Jews were solidly behind the British. When the war broke out they placed themselves in great peril as avowed friends of the enemies of the Ottomans.

In a swift move, Jemal Pasha the Turk took command of the Palestine province and clamped a reign of terror on the Jewish community.

Barak Ben Canaan had only six hours' warning to flee Palestine. Both he and his brother Akiva were on the extermination rolls of the Turkish police. The Zionist Settlement Society had been forced to close its offices and most Jewish activity had stopped.

"How soon, darling?" Sarah asked.

"We must be gone by daybreak. You are only to pack one small handbag. We must leave everything behind."

Sarah slumped against the wall and rubbed her hand over her belly. She was six months pregnant and could feel the life in her body as she had never felt it in any of the previous pregnancies. . . . Five miscarriages, she thought. . . .

"I can't go," she said. "I can't go."

Barak turned and faced her. His eyes narrowed and his red beard seemed to blaze in the candlelight. "Come now, Sarah . . . we have not time for that."

She spun around. "Barak . . . oh, Barak"—and she ran into his arms—"I'll lose this child too . . . I can't, I can't . . . I can't."

He sighed deeply. "You must come with me. God knows what will happen if the Turks get you."

"I will not lose this baby."

Barak packed his handbag slowly and shut it.

"Get up to Shoshanna right away," he said. "Ruth will take care of you . . . stay away from her blessed cows . . ." He kissed his wife's cheek gently, and she stood on her tiptoes and clung to him.

"*Shalom*, Sarah. I love you." He turned and walked out quickly.

Sarah made the perilous journey from Tel Aviv to Shoshanna by donkey cart and there, with Ruth, awaited the birth of her child.

Akiva and Barak fled to Cairo where they met their old friend Joseph Trumpledor, the one-armed fighter. Trumpledor was busy forming a unit of Palestinian Jews to fight in the British Army.

Trumpledor's unit, the Jewish Mule Corps, joined the Anzacs in a mammoth operation. Barak and Akiva were there as the British landed at Gallipoli and vainly attempted to open the Dardanelles and march on Constantinople from the south. In the retreat and debacle that followed the landing, Akiva was wounded in the chest.

The Jewish Mule Corps was disbanded after the Gallipoli disaster. Akiva and Barak continued on to England where Zev Jabotinsky, an ardent Zionist, was busy forming a larger Jewish fighting unit, the 38th, 39th, and 40th Royal Fusiliers, comprising a brigade known as the Judeans.

Akiva had not fully recovered from his wounds and was sent to the United States to lecture in the cause of the Jewish homeland under the sponsorship of the American Zionists, whose leader was Justice Brandeis of the Supreme Court.

When it was discovered that Barak Ben Canaan was among the Fusiliers he was pulled from the ranks at once. Dr. Weizmann, the world spokesman for Zionism, reckoned that Barak was too important a figure to carry a rifle.

Barak entered the Zionists' negotiation team in time to hear about a further British disaster in the Middle East. General Maude had launched an attack on the eastern flank of the Ottoman Empire. Using Mesopotamia as a jumping-off point, he planned to come down on Palestine from the north. The route of conquest was to be the Tigris-Euphrates Valley into Bagdad, and then he would wheel and strike for the sea. Maude's legion pressed forward with ease as long as the opposition was Arab troops. The campaign was termed "brilliant." Then, at Kut, the British ran into a Turkish division and their forces were beaten to the ground.

The British were reeling! The Ottomans sat on the edge of the Suez Canal and the Germans had torn the Russian first-line army to shreds. British efforts to stir up an Arab revolt against the Ottomans had fallen flat.

Then came the final blow! The Arabs suspected that a secret British-French agreement was in the wind to carve up and subjugate the Arab world.

Dr. Weizmann and the Zionists felt the time was ripe to score a point for the Jewish homeland. England desperately needed sympathy and help. In Germany, Jews were fighting for their fatherland as they were in Austria. In order for the Zionists to gain the support of the Jews of the rest of the world, especially those in America, a dramatic decision was needed.

As the negotiations between the Zionists and the British were brought to a close, Lord Balfour, the British Foreign Minister, wrote a letter to Lord Rothschild with the revelation:

His Majesty's Government view with favour the establishment in Palestine of a national home for the Jewish people, and will use their best endeavours to facilitate the achievement of this object.

Thus was born the Balfour Declaration, the Magna Charta of the Jewish people!

CHAPTER ELEVEN: Jemal Pasha's police found Sarah Ben Canaan at the Shoshanna *kibbutz* just two weeks before her baby was due. Till then, Ruth and the members of the *kibbutz* had guarded her carefully and seen to it that she had rest and comfort to protect the baby.

The Turkish police were not so considerate. Sarah was dragged from her cottage in the middle of the night, locked in a covered van, and driven over a bumpy, muddy road to the black basalt rock police station in Tiberias.

She was grilled without respite for twenty-four solid hours. *Where is your husband? . . . how did he make his escape? . . . how are you communicating with him? . . . you are smuggling out information and we know it . . . you are spying for the British. Come now, your husband wrote these papers in behalf of the British, you cannot deny it . . . what Jews in Palestine do you contact? . . .*

Sarah answered the questions directly and without being ruffled. She admitted that Barak had fled because of his British sympathies, for it was no secret. She insisted she had remained only to deliver her child. She made no further admissions to their charges. At the end of twenty-four hours Sarah Ben Canaan was the calmest person in the inspector's office.

They began to make threats, and still Sarah remained calm and direct. At last she was grabbed and pulled into a forbidding-looking room with thick basalt walls and no windows. One small light burned over a wooden table. She was stretched out on her back, pinned down by five policemen, and her shoes were removed. The bottoms of her feet were lashed with thick branches. As they beat the soles of her feet they repeated the questions. Her answers were the same.

Spy! How do you get information out to Barak Ben Canaan? Speak! You are in touch with other British agents ... who are they?

The pain was excruciating. Sarah stopped speaking altogether. She clenched her teeth and the sweat poured from her. Her courage fed the Turks' anger. The whip ripped open the soles of her feet and blood spurted out.

"Speak!" they screamed. "Speak!"

She quivered and writhed in agony. . . .

"Jew! Spy!"

At last she fell unconscious.

A bucket of water was thrown at her face. The beating and the questioning continued. She passed out again and they revived her again. Now they held her arms apart and placed red hot stones in her armpits.

"Speak! Speak! Speak!"

For three days and three nights the Turks tortured Sarah Ben Canaan. Even the Turks were awed by the woman's endurance. At last they let her go as a token to her courage, for they had never seen anyone endure pain with such dignity. Ruth, who had been waiting and pleading in the station anteroom, carried Sarah back to Shoshanna on a donkey cart.

With the first labor pains she allowed herself the luxury of screaming in anguish. She shrieked for all the times the Turks could not make her cry. Her battered body rebelled convulsively.

Her cries grew dimmer and weaker. No one believed she was going to live through it.

A son was born and Sarah Ben Canaan lived.

She hung between life and death for weeks. Ruth and the farmers of Shoshanna lavished every affection and care upon her. The remarkable courage that had kept the little black-eyed Silesian alive under Turkish torture and the pain of childbirth kept her alive now. Her will to see Barak again was so strong that death could not intervene.

It took over a year for her to mend. Her recovery was slow

and filled with pain. It was months before she was able to stand and walk on her battered feet. There was a limp that would never go away.

The child was strong and healthy. Everyone said he would grow up to be another Barak, for already he was lean and tall, although he had Sarah's dark features. With the torment over, Sarah and Ruth awaited their men.

From Cairo to Gallipoli to England to America the brothers wandered. Each day they were tormented with fear for the lives of Sarah and Ruth. They were aghast at the tales being brought from Palestinian refugees of the terror of Jemal Pasha.

Early in 1917 the British Army swept out of Egypt and pushed the Turks back over the Sinai Peninsula to the doorstep of Palestine. At Gaza they were stopped cold. General Allenby then took command of the British forces and under him the British renewed the offensive. By the end of 1917 they had slashed into Palestine and captured Beersheba. On the heels of this victory the ancient gates of Gaza were stormed and Gaza fell. The British knifed up the coast to capture Jaffa.

With Allenby's successful campaign, the long-overdue, much-heralded, very costly, and highly overrated Arab revolt began. Faisal, son of the sherif of Mecca, brought in a few tribes from the desert when it was obvious that the Turks were losing. With the Ottomans on their backs, the Arabs dropped their cloak of neutrality so that they could share in the coming spoils. Faisal's "rebels" made a good deal of noise and hacked up an unguarded rail line but never put it out of commission. Never once did Arab "rebels" engage in a major or minor battle.

At the ancient city of Megiddo the forces of Allenby and those of the Turks set for a battle. Here was the testing ground for a hundred conquering armies over five thousand years—Megiddo, where the stables of Solomon were to be found and where it was said that the second coming of Christ would take place. Megiddo commanded a ravine to the north which was a natural passageway. It had been the route of conquest since man had begun to record time.

Megiddo fell to Allenby!

By Christmas, less than a year after Allenby assumed command, he led his British forces into liberated Jerusalem!

The British rolled on to Damascus until the Turks were scattered and driven to oblivion. The fall of Damascus was the death knell of the Ottomans.

The Czar of Russia, who had wanted so badly to start a war with the Turks, never lived to realize his dream of a Russian Constantinople. The Russian people rebelled against centuries of suppression, and he and his entire family were shot by a firing squad.

Although his empire was completely crushed and stolen and he had lost his position as the "Shadow of God" to a billion Moslems, Mohammed V was enjoying life in his harem as the war ended.

Barak Ben Canaan and his brother Akiva came home. The roses were in bloom and the land was alive and green and the waters of the Jordan plunged into the Sea of Galilee as they entered the gates of Shoshanna.

There was white in the great red beard of Barak and there was white in the black hair of Sarah as they stood before each other at the door to her cottage. He held her in his arms very softly, and in that moment all the hardships of the past few years faded away. His little Sarah took him by the hand. She limped slightly as she led him into the cottage. A scrappy, strapping, bright-eyed three-year-old boy looked up at him curiously.

Barak knelt before the boy and held him up in his powerful hands.

"My son," Barak whispered, "my son."

"Your son . . . Ari," she said.

CHAPTER TWELVE: The Balfour Declaration was ratified by fifty nations.

During World War I the Yishuv population had been cut in half by the Turkish terror. In the wake of the war a new rash of pogroms broke out in eastern Europe.

The times that followed were exciting and vital for the Yishuv. The Third Aliyah was pouring in to escape persecution and filling the decimated ranks of the Yishuv.

For years the Zion Settlement Society had had its eye on the Jezreel Valley which made up the entire southern Galilee. It was mostly swampland with but a few poverty-stricken Arab villages. Most of the Jezreel belonged to a single effendi family, the Sursuks, who lived in Beirut. The Turks would not permit the Jews to buy into the Jezreel, but with the coming of the British and the lifting of land restrictions Barak Ben Canaan and two other land buyers traveled to Beirut and purchased an area from Haifa to Nazareth. The great Jezreel purchase was the first land deal of such magnitude in Palestine and the first one backed entirely by the funds of world Jewry. The Jezreel opened great opportunities for the establishment of more *kibbutzim*.

Old-time *kibbutzniks* unselfishly left their farms to help

found new *kibbutzim*. Akiva and Ruth, and their newborn daughter Sharona, left the relative comfort of their beloved Shoshanna to help build a new *kibbutz* just north of Rosh Pinna. The settlement was named Ein Or, the Fountain of Light.

At last the Jews shared part of Barak Ben Canaan's dream. Land was purchased deep in the Huleh Valley near the Syrian and Lebanese borders. They even farmed at his hill and built a *kibbutz*, the village of Giladi, close by. Barak's old friend and comrade, Joseph Trumpledor, went up to Kfar Giladi to handle security.

Along with the growth of farming, Tel Aviv and the other cities grew. Jews began buying homes in Haifa above the city on Mount Carmel. In Jerusalem there was building beyond the old Walled City as the needs of the Yishuv called for larger headquarters and the religious elements joined with the Zionists in the spirit of redemption.

The British administration made many reforms. Roads were built. Schools and hospitals were erected. Justice came to the courts. Balfour himself traveled to Jerusalem and on Mount Scopus lay the cornerstone of a new Hebrew university.

To govern the Yishuv, the Jews elected a representative body. The Yishuv Central was a quasi-government to speak for the Jews, deal with the Arabs and British, and serve as a link to the Zion Settlement Society and to the world's Zionists. The Yishuv Central and the Zion Settlement Society both moved to the new headquarters in Jerusalem.

Barak Ben Canaan, a senior respected citizen, was elected to the Yishuv Central, a position he held along with his work with the Zionists.

But there were ominous signs. Palestine was becoming the center of a gigantic power play.

The first act of this play was the publication of the secret Sykes-Picot Agreement, by which the French and the British sought to divide the Middle East between themselves. The paper was first discovered in the files of the Czar by Russian revolutionaries and published to embarrass the British and French.

The Sykes-Picot Agreement directly contradicted earlier British promises to grant independence to the Arabs. The Arabs felt betrayed. Despite British efforts to soothe the situation, Arab fears proved justified later when, at the San Remo Conference, England and France cut the Middle East pie and England grabbed for herself the lion's share. France snatched the Syrian province and a pipeline from the oil-rich Mosul fields.

Under Ottoman rule the Syrian province had also included

Palestine and Lebanon. France felt she was entitled to northern Palestine. The British were adamant. They too wanted a terminal from the Mosul oil fields at Haifa, and they argued that because of the Balfour Declaration and the unique position of Palestine as a promised Jewish homeland it should stay under British rule.

As a result, the French hired several tribes of Syrian Arabs to stir up trouble in Palestine and grab up as much of northern Palestine as possible until fixed boundaries were set.

Those Jews who had ventured into the Huleh to Kfar Giladi were caught in the trap. The French-hired Arabs, in an effort to dislodge them in order to fortify French border claims, attacked Tel Hai, the very hill that Barak and Akiva had crossed to come into Palestine.

Joseph Trumpledor, the legendary Jewish soldier of fortune, made a valiant stand at Tel Hai. He himself was killed but Tel Hai held and the Jews remained at Kfar Giladi and the Huleh Valley remained within the British mandate.

The next of France's troubles came from Faisal, son of the sherif of Mecca and leader of the alleged Arab revolt in World War I. Faisal arrived in Damascus, sat himself down, and declared himself king of a new greater Arab state and the new head of the Moslems. The French chased him out of Syria. Faisal moved on to Bagdad where the British accorded him better treatment. They rewarded their faithful servant by creating a new state out of the Mesopotamian Province. They called the country Iraq and proclaimed Faisal king.

Faisal had a brother named Abdullah who had to be rewarded too. The British, without authorization from the League of Nations, formed another "country" from part of the Palestine mandate and named Abdullah its king. This country they called Trans-Jordan.

Both Faisal and Abdullah were arch enemies of Ibn Saud, who had refused to help the British in World War I.

So—the British fared well. They had their puppets in Iraq and Trans-Jordan—two creations. They had Egypt, the Suez Canal, the Mosul oil fields, and the Palestine mandate. In addition they had a dozen "protectorates" and sheikdoms around the Arabian Peninsula.

The British knew about Arab hate feuds and employed the proved method of "divide and rule." Their Arab puppets were kept happy with the latest automobiles and with well-stocked harems.

Palestine was a different problem. It could not be governed by British puppets. The Balfour Declaration had been ratified by the entire world. The articles of mandate further bound the British to create a Jewish homeland. Further, the Jews had presented them with a democratically elected quasi-

252

government, the Yishuv Central, the only democratic body in the entire Middle East.

Barak Ben Canaan, Dr. Chaim Weizmann, and a dozen other Zionist leaders entered into a historic negotiation with Faisal, then leader of the Arab world. A mutual friendship pact was signed between Jews and Arabs in which each agreed to respect the aspirations of the other. The Arabs welcomed the return of the Jews and appreciated their historic rights to Palestine and their humanitarian rights to a homeland. Further, the Arabs stated openly that they welcomed the culture and the "Hebrew gold" the Jews were bringing in. Further, the Arabs in many quarters had proclaimed the Jews as redeemers.

In Palestine as elsewhere in the Arab world, there was no representative Arab government. When the British asked the Arabs to present their government, the usual inner-Arab squabble ensued. The various alliances of effendi families spoke for a small percentage of Arabs.

The most powerful effendi family was the El Husseini clan which owned land in the Jerusalem area. They were so feared by the other effendis that a power block was formed against them that made impossible any form of Arab representation.

The leader of the dreaded El Husseinis was the most vile, underhanded schemer in a part of the world known for vile, underhanded schemers. His name was Haj Amin el Husseini. Haj Amin had once fought on the side of the Turks. Now he saw the demise of the Ottoman Empire as a chance to gain power, just as a dozen Arab leaders in a dozen parts of the Arab world saw it. El Husseini was backed by a clan of devils.

Haj Amin's first move was to grab Palestine. He saw his opening through the position of Mufti of Jerusalem. Jerusalem was second only to Mecca and Medina as a holy Moslem city. Under Ottoman rule the job of Mufti was mostly honorary. Constantinople as head of Islam was the true ruler of all Moslems. With the Ottomans gone and a Christian power ruling Palestine the position of Mufti suddenly became important. Enormous funds poured in from Moslems all over the world for the retention of holy places. Once these funds had been administered by Constantinople but now they would be at the discretion of the Mufti. If Haj Amin could seize the position he could use this money to further his own aspirations. There was another reason why he wanted to be Mufti. The Palestinian fellaheen were ninety-nine per cent illiterate. The only means of mass communication was the pulpit. The tendency of the fellaheen to become hysterical at the slightest provocation might become a political weapon.

One thing stood in the way of Haj Amin's desire to become Mufti of Jerusalem. Moslem law declared the position could be held only by someone in the direct blood line of Mohammed. Haj Amin dodged this requirement by marrying a girl in the Mohammed line and holding this as valid enough fulfillment of the prerequisite.

When the old Mufti died, an election was held for the position. The effendis knew of Haj Amin's ambitions and he came in fourth. This did not disturb him, for the El Husseini clan was busy terrorizing the three men who had drawn more votes and "persuaded" them to withdraw from office.

Haj Amin el Husseini became Mufti of Jerusalem by default.

He saw the return of the Jews as the greatest block to his plans.

On the Moslem holy day which celebrated the birth of Moses, Haj Amin el Husseini whipped up a mob of fellaheen with hatred for the Jews. The mob became hysterical and a pogrom was on!

They did not become so hysterical as to turn their wrath on the cities and *kibbutzim* where the Jews were able to defend themselves. Instead they slaughtered pious old defenseless Jews in the holy cities of Safed, Tiberias, Hebron, and Jerusalem.

Ruth was in Tiberias on her way back to Ein Or from a visit to Shoshanna when the rioting broke out. She and her daughter Sharona were caught and murdered.

Akiva was inconsolable. No one had ever seen a man with such grief. Barak rushed up to Ein Or and took his brother home to Tel Aviv; and as he had done as a boy, he maintained a day-and-night watch. It was months before Akiva came out of his grief. But it left a scar so ugly and deep within him it would never heal.

Many of the settlements had given up their arms to the British when they took over the mandate. Had the Arabs chosen to attack these settlements there would have been a slaughter. The British were responsible for maintaining order and the Yishuv waited for them to bring the Arabs under control and lead the culprits to justice. Such a thing would not have happened under the Turks, for as corrupt as they were they would not tolerate murder.

A commission of inquiry found Haj Amin el Husseini at fault. He was pardoned!

Immediately after the pardon the British Colonial Office issued a White Paper, or declaration of policy, limiting Jewish immigration to "economic absorption." It was then that Winston Churchill became instrumental in taking over half the mandate and creating Trans-Jordan from it. For the Yishuv it was the end of an era.

The bubble of British benevolence burst. The Yishuv Central and the Zion Settlement Society called a secret meeting in Tel Aviv which fifty of the leading members of the Yishuv attended.

Dr. Chaim Weizmann flew in from London to attend. Barak was there and Akiva, still in a state of bereavement, was there. Itzak Ben Zvi was there. A stocky, short, bushy-browed young leader in the second Aliyah named David Ben Gurion was there. Many felt that this fiery, Bible-quoting Zionist was destined to lead the Yishuv.

Avidan, a bald, block-like man of the Third Aliyah, was there. Avidan had come to Palestine after a momentous war record in the Russian Army. He was second in reputation as a fighter only to the martyr Trumpledor, and it was said he was destined to lead Jewish defense.

The meeting was called to order by Barak Ben Canaan. The cellar room was grim and tense as he spoke. A great crisis had fallen. Barak recalled the personal misfortune that all of them had suffered for being born Jews. Now, in the one place they sought freedom from persecution, a pogrom had occurred.

Dr. Chaim Weizmann led a group that argued that the British were the recognized authority and had to be dealt with legally and openly. Defense was a British responsibility.

Another group, ultra-pacifists, felt it would only invite trouble from the Arabs to arm the Jews.

At the other extreme, there were the activists led by Akiva, who demanded nothing less than swift and ruthless retribution. They argued that British protection and well meaning was an illusion; the British acted only in self-interest. Haggling, guilt documents, and the like would never take the place of a gun in an Arab's mind.

The debate raged far into the night, never exhausting that endless capacity of Jews to argue. The British were damned and the British were praised. The pacifists begged caution while the activists called Palestine the "Twice Promised Land" —once to the Jews and once to the Arabs.

Between the two extremes in thinking, Ben Gurion, Ben Canaan, Avidan, and many of the others suggested a realistic middle course. While they recognized need to arm themselves, they wanted to further the Jewish position by legal means.

These men, on behalf of the Yishuv, decided to arm themselves quietly and train a militia in secret. This armed force would be used for one purpose and one purpose alone—defense. While this force existed, the official agencies of the Yishuv were to disclaim all knowledge of it publicly and privately co-operate with its growth. With this silent arm, the Jews would have an unseen partner in restraining the Arabs and in negotiating with the British.

Avidan, the fighter, was voted to head this new secret organization.

They called it Haganah, the Army of Self-Defense.

CHAPTER THIRTEEN: The Third Aliyah penetrated the newly purchased Jezreel, the Sharon Valley, and Samaria and into the hills of Judea and the Galilee and even south toward the desert, and called the earth back from its long-naked slumber. They brought in heavy machinery and introduced intensive agriculture through crop rotation and fertilization and irrigation. In addition to the grape, citrus, and olive export crops they raised grain and vegetables, and fruits and flax and poultry and dairy herds.

They experimented with anything and everything to find new crops and increased the yield of the old ones.

They penetrated to the Dead Sea. They went after alkaline land which had not produced a living thing for forty thousand years and they brought it back and made it produce.

They dug fishponds and farmed fish as a crop.

By the mid-1920s over fifty thousand Jews in a hundred colonies worked better than a half million *dunams* of redeemed land. Most of them wore the blue of the *kibbutz*.

A million trees were planted. In ten—twenty—thirty years the trees would fight off soil erosion. Tree planting became an obsession of the Yishuv. They left a trail of budding forests behind them wherever they went.

Many of the new *kibbutzim* and other settlements adopted the name of the Biblical site they occupied. Many new names sprang up over the ancient land and they had the sound of music. Ben Shemen, Son of Oil; and Dagania, the Cornflower on the Sea of Galilee; and Ein Ganim, the Fountain of the Gardens; and Kfar Yehezkiel, the Village of the Prophet Ezekiel; and Merhavia, which means the Wide Spaces of God; and Tel Yosef, the Hill of Joseph. There was Ayelet Hashahar, the Morning Star, which stood at the entrance to Barak's beloved Huleh Valley. There was Gesher, the Bridge; and Givat Hashlosha, the Hill of the Three; and there were more and more being built every month.

The *kibbutz* movement, that unique child of necessity, became the key to all settlement. The *kibbutzim* could absorb vast numbers of new arrivals.

Yet not everyone could adapt to life on a *kibbutz*. Many women who fought for their independence didn't like it once they had it. Others objected to the lack of privacy and others to the children's houses. Although the entire Yishuv subscribed to the idea of national land and the conquest of self-labor, the main reason some could not stand *kibbutz* life was the lack of personal identification with a piece of land one could call one's own. A splinter group broke off from the *kibbutz* movement. It was called the *moshav* movement. In a *moshav* each man had his own piece of land to work and his own house instead of the communal arrangement. As on the *kibbutz* all the civic functions were centrally run and all the heavy machinery was owned by the entire *moshav*. Certain base crops were farmed by the entire community and there was a central agency which did all the marketing and purchasing.

The main difference was the measure of individual freedom and the fact that a man's family was in his own house and he ran his own farm in the way he saw fit. The first *moshav* was in the Jezreel Valley and was named after its Biblical site, Nahalal, the Heritage. The Nahalal pioneers faced the toughest swamp and did a miraculous job of redemption.

The drawback of the *moshav* movement in the over-all scheme was the working for personal profit and the inability of the *moshav* to absorb the numbers of new arrivals the *kibbutz* could; but both movements flourished and grew.

As the Yishuv grew, so did the complexities of the community. Barak Ben Canaan, a respected elder citizen, was never at rest. Zionism had a bulky machinery and there were a dozen different political philosophies inside the Yishuv. The dealings with the Arabs became more delicate after the riots and the dealings with the British became more confusing after their sudden departure from the Balfour Declaration and the articles of mandate. Barak's wise council was sought in every quarter. Although there were no more outbreaks against the Jews, the atmosphere was one of uneasy calm. Every day there was a new story of an ambush, a sniping, or a theft. The tirades from the Moslem pulpit never ended. There was always tension in the air, for the sinister Mufti, Haj Amin el Husseini, lurked in the shadows.

One day in 1924 Barak returned to Tel Aviv after a particularly difficult week at the Yishuv Central in Jerusalem. He was always happy to come home to his three-room flat on Hayarkon Street overlooking the Mediterranean. This time he was delighted and surprised to see his old friend, Kammal, the muktar of Abu Yesha, awaiting him.

257

"For many years I have been meditating to try to solve the perplexing riddle of how to help my people. It grieves me to say this but there are no greater exploiters than the Arab effendis. They do not want things better for the fellaheen ... it may endanger their own pleasures."

Barak listened intently. This was a tremendous confession on the part of an Arab and one so enlightened as Kammal.

"I have watched the Jews come back and perform miracles on the land. We have nothing in common in religion or language or outlook. I am not even sure the Jews will not eventually take all the land. Yet ... the Jews are the only salvation for the Arab people. The Jews are the only ones in a thousand years who have brought light to this part of the world."

"I know this is difficult for you to say, Kammal ..."

"Let me continue, please. If we can live side by side in peace although our worlds are far apart then we must eventually prosper from what you have done. I see no other way for the Arab people, Barak, and I don't know if it is right or wrong."

"We have never given you reason to doubt our sincerity in wanting peace ..."

"Yes ... but there are powers greater than you and I who could bring us into conflict against our will."

How true ... how very true, Barak thought.

"Barak, I am going to sell the Zion Settlement Society that land by the Huleh Lake you have always wanted."

Barak's heart began to beat fast.

"It is not merely benevolence. I have conditions. You must allow the Arabs of Abu Yesha to learn your farming and sanitation methods. This can only be done slowly over a period of time. I want a portion of the village's more deserving boys to be able to attend your school to learn to read and write."

"That will all be done," Barak said.

"There is one more condition."

"And what is that?"

"You must come too."

Barak rose and rubbed his great beard. "Me? Why me?"

"As long as you are there I know the conditions will be kept and that we will be able to live in peace. I have trusted you from the first day you entered Abu Yesha as a boy over thirty years ago."

"I will think it over," Barak said.

"And what will you tell Kammal?" Sarah asked.

Barak shrugged. "What is there to say? We can't go, of course. What a shame. For years I have been trying to get

258

him to sell that land. Now if I don't go up there we will never get it."

"It is a pity," Sarah agreed and poured some tea.

Barak paced the floor unhappily. "After all, Sarah," he mumbled, "we must face facts. I am needed at the Yishuv Central and the Settlement Society. It isn't as if I was running a candy store on Allenby Road."

"Of course not, dear," Sarah said sympathetically. "You are vital in your work. The entire Yishuv needs you."

"Yes," he said, pacing again, "and we aren't children any longer. I am past fifty and the land is going to be very very hard to redeem."

"You are right, Barak. We are too old to pioneer. You have done your share in building this country."

"Right! I'll turn Kammal down."

He sank into a chair and sighed deeply. He had not succeeded in convincing himself. Sarah stood over him and smiled. "You are mocking me, woman," he said softly. "What's the use?"

She sat on his lap and was almost lost in his greatness. His huge hands were amazingly gentle as they stroked her hair.

"I was thinking of you and Ari. It will be brutal work and the hardships will be great."

"Shhhh . . . drink your tea."

Barak resigned his position with the Zion Settlement Society, sold his apartment in Tel Aviv, and led twenty-five pioneer families out to the Huleh swamplands to build a *moshav*. They called it Yad El, the Hand of God.

They pitched tents below the fields of Abu Yesha and mapped out their task. No pioneers yet had faced a job so difficult. The Huleh swamp was deep, and full of forbidding tangles of thickly matted unyielding brush and papyrus which towered to heights of fifteen feet. The muck was alive with poisonous snakes, scorpions, and rats and a hundred other creatures. Wild boars and wolves lurked near the isolated base camp. Everything had to be brought in on muleback, including drinking and washing water.

Sarah was in charge of the base camp, the hospital tent, and the kitchen. Barak headed the work gangs which took to the swamps daily with shovels and picks.

In that first scorching summer they worked day after day, week after week, and month after month in hundred-degree heat, in waist- and neck-high water, slogging away the muck to start drainage channels. With machetes they hacked at the jungle growth until they couldn't raise their arms. The women worked right in the swamps along with the men. Young Ari

Ben Canaan, ten years of age, one of the three children in the settlement, ran off the pails of sludge and ran in drinking water and food to the workers. The workdays were seven each week. The work hours were sunrise to sunset. Still each night they found the energy to sing a few songs of the fields and dance a *hora* before their six or seven hours of sleep.

At night there was the usual guard against robbers and animals.

It was a race to get the channels in before the winter rains. If the water didn't drain off, the summer's work would be wasted. Hundreds of Australian eucalyptus trees were put in to suck up water. Every *kibbutz* and *moshav* in the area sent over as many workers as they could spare each day to help the pioneers.

At night, by candlelight, Sarah and Barak took turns schooling Ari and the other two children.

The winter downpours came and all but swept the base camp into the swamp. After each downpour they rushed to the channels to keep the slush from blocking the runoff.

Even a man so strong and resolute as Barak Ben Canaan was beginning to wonder if they hadn't attempted too much this time. Each time he looked at Ari and Sarah his heart bled. They were always covered with bug bites or suffering from dysentery or hunger or thirst.

And worse was the ravaging malaria. In that first summer and winter Sarah had five attacks and Ari four. The chills and fevers and deliriums all but killed them. Ari, like Sarah, took his pain in silence.

The swamp broke many of the families. Half the original group quit to return to the city to find an easier way.

And soon—Yad El had a graveyard. Two members died of malaria.

Yad El: the Hand of God. It may have been the hand of God that led them there but it was going to be the hands of men that licked the swamp.

For three solid years they beat back the swamp!

At last there was enough land to make twenty-five farms of two hundred *dunams* each. There was no time to gloat, for there were crops to be planted and homes to be built.

Young Ari Ben Canaan had shaken off the effects of malaria and the other illnesses and had become as sturdy as a rock. At the age of fourteen he could do a man's day's work.

When they moved into their cottage and the fields had been plowed and planted Barak was given a reward for his years of toil. Sarah told him she was pregnant again.

At the end of the fourth year two momentous things happened to Barak Ben Canaan. Sarah presented him with a baby daughter who had flaming red hair like his own. The second occasion was the harvest of the first crop at Yad El.

At last the weary pioneers stopped their labor and took time to celebrate. What a celebration it was! *Kibbutzniks* and *moshavniks* from all over the area who had lent a hand at Yad El came to join in the celebration. Arabs from Abu Yesha came. There was gaiety for a week, each night ending at dawn as weary *hora* dancers collapsed with joy. Everyone came to look at Barak's and Sarah's new daughter. She was named Jordana after the river which flowed past the edge of Yad El.

As the celebration continued, Barak took his son Ari and saddled two horses and they rode up to Tel Hai to that place where he had crossed into the Promised Land from Lebanon forty years before. Tel Hai, the death place of Joseph Trumpledor, was a shrine of the Yishuv. Barak looked down from the hill to Yad El as he had sworn he would long ago.

"I took your mother up here before we were married," he said to Ari. He put his arm around his son's shoulder. "Someday there will be two dozen settlements in this valley and it will be green all the year around."

"Look how beautiful Yad El is from here, Father."

The irrigation sprinklers were whirling and a school was under construction. They could see an enormous shed where the community had put a dozen pieces of heavy machinery. There were paths of rose bushes and flowers and lawns and trees.

There was sadness, too, for the Yad El cemetery had already claimed five members.

As Kammal had hoped, the establishment of Yad El had a tremendous effect upon the Arabs of Abu Yesha. The creation of the *moshav* was in itself a startling revelation. Barak was true to his agreement and set up special schools for the Arabs to teach them sanitation, the use of heavy machinery, and new farming methods. Their school was open to any Arab youngster of Abu Yesha who would attend. The Yad El doctor and nurse were always at the call of the Arabs.

Kammal's favorite son was a youngster named Taha who was a few years younger than Ari. From the time of his birth Kammal had ingrained into Taha his own great desire to better the conditions of the fellaheen. As the coming muktar of Abu Yesha, Taha spent more time at Yad El than in his own village. He was the personal ward of the Ben Canaan family. Taha and Ari became close friends.

While Yad El and Abu Yesha lived in peace and proved Arab and Jew could exist side by side despite their cultural differences a slow mantle of fear was falling over many of the other effendi families in Palestine. They were becoming

261

frightened at the spirit and progress of the Third Aliyah.

In the beginning the effendis had sold the Jews worthless swamps and rock-filled and eroded hills, eager to get their hands on Jewish gold and certain the land would continue its dormancy. The Jews turned around and performed miracles of redemption. Not only had the farms grown, but cities were springing up all over Palestine.

The example of the Jews could be disastrous. What if the fellaheen began demanding education, sanitation, and medical facilities? What if the fellaheen, God forbid, were to take a fancy to the way the Jews governed themselves by equal votes of both men—and women! It could well wreck the perfect feudal system of the effendis!

To counter the progress of the Jews, the effendis harped on the ignorance, fears, and religious fanaticism of the fellaheen. They pounded the theme that the Jews were invaders from the West out to steal their fellaheen's lands—even though the effendis had themselves sold this land. They maintained tension so that the fellaheen would not come into too close contact with the new ideas.

After many years without a major incident Haj Amin el Husseini moved again. This time he concocted a cold-blooded fraud aimed at driving the Arabs wild. The year was 1929.

The site of the Dome of the Rock or the Mosque of Omar in Jerusalem was worshiped as holy ground by the Moslems as the point where their prophet Mohammed ascended to heaven. On this very site stood the one remaining wall of the Great Jewish Temple which had been destroyed for a second time in A.D. 76 by the Romans. This wall of the Temple was the holiest of all Jewish holy places. Pious Jews gathered before the wall to pray and to weep for the past glory of Israel. From their tears it became known as the "Wailing Wall."

The Mufti circulated faked pictures showing Jews at the Wailing Wall preparing to "desecrate" the Arab holy place of the Dome of the Rock. The fanatic Moslem fellaheen started another outbreak supported by effendi and Husseini Jew baitings. Again the riots hit the defenseless old Jews of the holy cities. The slaughter was far greater than the Mufti-inspired riots of a decade before. The rioting spread against some of the weaker settlements and on to the roads, and casualties mounted into the thousands on both sides. The British again appeared helpless to stop the slaughter.

They sent a commission of inquiry. The commission squarely placed the blame on Arab shoulders. Then, by great paradox, they completely ignored the Balfour Declaration and the articles of mandate and suggested that Jewish land buying and immigration be restricted to "soothe Arab fears."

CHAPTER FOURTEEN: In the same year as the riots, 1929, the farmers of Yad El made an agreement with the grain miller of the Arab village of Aata, some ten kilometers away.

Barak gave Ari the job of going to Aata to have their grain milled. Sarah objected to sending a fourteen-year-old boy out on the roads alone with the tension of the riots all around. Barak was adamant on the subject. "Neither Ari nor Jordana is going to live in fear like ghetto Jews."

Ari felt very proud of the trust as he jumped onto the seat of the donkey cart. It was loaded with a dozen bags of grain. He set out down the road for Aata.

He was spotted the instant he entered the village by a dozen Arab boys who were lying around near the coffeehouse. They waited till he turned the corner, then trailed him to the miller's.

Ari went about his business, flushed with his own importance. He carried on his transactions in perfect Arabic, which he had learned from his good friend Taha. The grain was crushed to flour. Ari watched closely to make certain that the sacks were filled full and with the same grain, not inferior Arab wheat. The miller, hoping to gain a sack on the deal, was perplexed by the youngster's sharpness. Ari headed back toward Yad El.

The Arab boys who had been waiting quickly made a deal with the miller to steal all Ari's wheat and sell it to him. The boys scampered out of Aata by a short cut and set up an ambush and road block.

In a few moments Ari rode along the road right into the trap. They sprang out from cover, hurling stones at him. Ari whipped the donkey but moved only a few feet before the road block stopped him. He was stoned from the cart and knocked half senseless to the ground. Four of the attackers pounced on him and pinned him down while the others pulled the grain from the cart and made off with it.

The boy returned to Yad El late that night.

Sarah opened the door, took one look at his blood-streaked face and torn clothing, and screamed. He stood there wordless for a moment, then clenched his teeth and pushed past his mother and went into his room and locked the door.

He refused to open it despite her pleas until Barak returned home later from a *moshav* meeting.

He stood before his father. "I let you down . . . I lost the wheat," he said through puffed and distorted lips.

"It is I who have let you down, son," Barak said.

Sarah rushed over to Ari and threw her arms around him. "Never, never, never send this boy out alone . . ." She led him off to clean him up. Barak did not answer.

The next morning after breakfast, before Barak headed for the fields, he took Ari by the hand and led him out to the barn. "I have neglected some of your education," Barak said, and pulled down his old bull whip from a peg.

Barak built a dummy and nailed it to the fence. He showed Ari how to judge distance, aim, and swing. With the sound of the first crack Sarah came running from the house with Jordana in her arms.

"Have you gone mad teaching a boy like that to use a bull whip?"

"Shut up, woman!" Barak roared in a tone she had never heard in over twenty years of marriage. "The son of Barak Ben Canaan is a free man! He shall never be a ghetto Jew. Now get out of here . . . we have business."

From morning to night Ari practiced using the bull whip. He cut the dummy to shreds. He aimed at rocks and tins and bottles until he could whirl around and split them with a flick of the wrist. He threw the whip so often that by the end of each day he could barely lift his arm.

At the end of two weeks, Barak loaded up the donkey cart with another dozen bags of grain. He put his arm around his son's shoulder and led him to the cart and handed him the bull whip. "Take the grain to Aata and have it milled."

"Yes, Father," Ari said softly.

"Remember one thing, son. You hold in your hand a weapon of justice. Never use it in anger or revenge. Only in defense."

Ari jumped onto the cart and started for the gate of Yad El toward the main road. Sarah went into her bedroom and wept softly as she watched her son disappear down the road.

Barak did something he had not done for many, many years. He sat down and read the Bible.

The Arab ambush struck again when Ari was a mile outside Aata on his way back to Yad El. This time Ari's eyes were sharp and his body alerted for danger. Remembering his father's words, he remained cold, calm. As the first rocks flew at him he leaped from the cart, spotted the Arab leader, and with a lightning flick sent the mighty bull whip whistling through the air and wrapped it around the boy's neck and flung him to the ground. Then Ari unwrapped the whip and brought down a lash that snapped so sharply it tore his foe's flesh apart. It was all over that quickly.

Barak Ben Canaan's face paled as the sun began to set and Ari had still not come back. He stood trembling by the gate of Yad El. Then he saw the donkey cart coming down the road and his face broke into a large smile. Ari stopped for his father.

"Well, Ari. How was your trip?"

"Fine."

"I'll unload the flour. You had better go right in and see your mother. She was worried for some reason or the other."

By 1930 the riots had died down. Abu Yesha and Yad El stayed out of trouble altogether. The majority of villages out of the Mufti's sphere of influence did not participate in the disturbances.

Ari Ben Canaan was not only built like his father but acted very like him too. He was deep within himself and he had Barak's quiet, stubborn ways. He saw the value of learning about his Arab neighbors. Taha was always one of his closest friends and he treated all other Arabs with understanding and compassion.

Ari fell in love with a girl named Dafna whose family had a farm half a mile away. No one was quite sure when it had happened but everyone was quite sure that Ari and Dafna would marry someday, for they had eyes only for each other.

Little redheaded Jordana was a spirited and rebellious girl. In many ways Jordana typified the children being born to the settlers of Palestine. Their parents who had lived in ghettos and had known the fear and degradation of being Jews were determined to purge this horror from the new generation. They bent over backward to give the children freedom and to make them strong.

At the age of fifteen Ari was a member of Haganah, the secret Army of Self-Defense. At the age of thirteen, Dafna could handle half a dozen weapons. For if this was a new generation and a new type of Jew it was also a generation born with a mission even greater than the missions of the Second and Third Aliyah.

The Haganah had grown strong enough to be a restraining force on the Mufti-inspired disturbances, but they were unable to erase the cause of these riots—only the British could do that.

Again British commissions of inquiry came and again the Arabs were whitewashed.

British timidity caused the Mufti to grow bolder.

Shortly after the riots abated, Haj Amin el Husseini called a conference of Moslem leaders to Jerusalem. They arrived from all over the world. He formed a federation, with himself as head, and advertised his fight to save Islam from the British and Jews.

The early friendships, the fact that the Jews had raised the standard of living of the entire Arab community, and the fact that Palestine had lain neglected and unwanted for a thousand years in fruitless despair until the Jews rebuilt it was all forgotten in the face of the Mufti's tirades. The destruction of the Jewish homeland was made a "holy" mission of Pan-Arabism.

The British were subjected to the next tirade. They had lied about granting independence to the Arabs. They supported the Jews against Arabs. And as the Arab demagogues ranted and raged the British took it all in silence.

In the year of 1933 another great calamity befell the Jews as Adolf Hitler and the Nazis ascended to power. Hitler moved first against the Jewish "professional" people. The wiser ones among them left Germany immediately and many sought sanctuary in Palestine.

Once again the need for a national home and for Zionism were confirmed. Jew baiting could flare up in any part of the world at any time. Herzl had known it and every Jew knew it.

The German Jews who fled Hitler were different from the ghetto and eastern European Jews. They were not devout Zionists but had largely been assimilated into German society. They were not pioneers and merchants but doctors and lawyers and scientists and artisans.

In 1933 the Arab leaders called a general strike of all Arabs to protest the new Jewish immigration. There was an attempt to stir up more rioting. But both efforts failed. Most Arabs who had done business with the Jews continued to do so for they were economically dependent on one another and many communities like Yad El and Abu Yesha lived in close harmony with each other. Furthermore, the Haganah stood ready to halt a repetition of the 1929 disturbances.

The British solution to the general strike was more talk and more commissions of inquiry. In outright appeasement of the Arab threats the British this time definitely limited immigration and land selling by the Jews. At the very moment when the Yishuv needed open immigration so desperately the British forgot their promises.

The Yishuv Central through the Haganah fought back in the only way they could . . . Aliyah Bet.

The Mufti maintained his pressure on the British until the

British sent the Royal Navy out to stop Aliyah Bet runners and to set up a blockade of the Palestinian coast.

The strength of Haj Amin el Husseini grew every day. He found a powerful ally for himself—Adolf Hitler. For the Germans, who had their own aspirations in the Middle East, the situation was perfect. What could be more fortunate for the German propaganda machine than to be able to pump the theme that the Jews of Palestine were stealing the Arab lands just as they had tried to steal Germany. Jew hating and British imperialism—what music to the Mufti's ears! The Germans were in luck. And Haj Amin el Husseini saw at long long last the instrument for seizing control of the Arab world.

German money showed up in Cairo and Damascus. The Germans are your friends! Arab lands for Arab people! Throw out the British and their Jewish henchmen! In many high places in Cairo and Bagdad and in Syria the Arabs clasped hands with Nazis in friendship.

As the storm gathered the Yishuv still held one trump card—the Haganah! Although this secret army was officially divorced from the Yishuv Central its existence and strength was an open secret. The Jews pretended it was not there but the British knew it existed. More important, the Mufti knew it existed.

It had grown from nothing to a force of over twenty-five thousand men and women. It was almost entirely a militia with but a few dozen "paid" full-time leaders. It had a small but deadly efficient intelligence service, which not only had the open co-operation of many British officers but could purchase Arab spies for next to nothing. Every city, village, *kibbutz,* and *moshav* had its Haganah setup. A secret code word could send a thousand men and women to hidden arms caches within minutes.

Avidan, the bald-headed square-built ex-soldier who headed Haganah, carefully built it up in a decade and a half under the noses of the British. The efficiency of the organization was terrifying; they ran a secret radio, carried on the Aliyah Bet immigration, and their intelligence network spread throughout the world where agents purchased arms to smuggle back to the Yishuv.

Arms were smuggled into Palestine in a hundred ways. Hiding them in heavy building equipment was a favorite method. The roller of a steam roller as often as not contained a hundred rifles. Every crate, piece of machinery, and even food tins and wine bottles coming into Palestine were potential munitions carriers. It was impossible for the British to halt the smuggling without inspecting every item, and many

267

British were turning their backs at the docks to let the arms through.

The entire Yishuv was behind the arms-smuggling movement, but even so they could not bring in heavy weapons or sufficient numbers of first-class small arms. Most of what came in were old rifles and pistols discarded or outmoded in other countries. No arsenal in the world contained the conglomeration of weapons the Haganah had. Every known rifle and pistol was represented in some numbers. A thousand ingenious varieties of mortars, Sten guns, and grenades were manufactured in secret. The Haganah arsenal even included walking canes which could fire a single shot.

Once inside Palestine every desk, chair, table, icebox, bed, and sofa was a potential hiding place for weapons. Every Jewish home had at least one false-bottom drawer, hidden closet, trap door, or trick wall.

Arms were moved about inside the spare tires of buses and in market baskets and under donkey carts. The Haganah played on British "respectability" by having the children run weapons and by using the best hiding place of all—under women's skirts.

In the building of the Haganah the *kibbutz* proved not only the answer to redemption but the answer to Jewish arms. Because of the communal character of the *kibbutz* it was the best place to train young soldiers. A dozen or two dozen could be slipped in easily among three or four hundred members and absorbed by the community. The *kibbutz* was the best place to hide the larger arms caches and the best place to manufacture small arms. It was also the best place to absorb newly arrived illegal immigrants. From the *kibbutzim* came the majority of the outstanding Haganah leaders.

The one great strength of the Haganah lay in the fact that its authority was accepted without question by the entire Yishuv. A Haganah command was a positive order. Avidan and the other Haganah leaders were very careful to use their army only in self-defense. When the 1933 general strike broke out Avidan warned that the Haganah would not try to conquer the Palestine Arabs. "Palestine will be conquered with our sweat." It was an army of restraint.

There were many in the Haganah who felt that it should not be held in such restraint. These were activists who demanded swift retribution.

Akiva was one of these. Officially he was a dairy farmer in the *kibbutz* of Ein Or but in reality he was a high man in the Haganah in charge of all defense in the Galilee.

The years had aged Akiva far more than his brother Barak. His face looked tired and his beard was nearly gray. He never fully recovered from the death of Ruth and Sharona.

It was a bitterness he carried with him every day of his life.

He was the unofficial leader of the fringe element within the Haganah who demanded more action. As time went on and the trouble heightened, Akiva's group became very militant. Outside Palestine, splinter groups formed from the main Zionist body to support them.

When the British threw the blockade along the coast of Palestine, Akiva could stand it no longer. He called a rump session of his supporters within the Haganah. They were all angry men like himself and they reached a decision that rocked the Yishuv to its core.

In the spring of 1934 Barak received an urgent call from Avidan to come to Jerusalem.

"A terrible thing has happened, Barak," Avidan said. "Your brother, Akiva, has withdrawn from the Haganah and taken dozens of our top men with him. Hundreds of rank-and-file people are beginning to follow."

When the initial shock had passed, Barak sighed. "He has threatened to do that for years. I have been amazed at the restraint he has shown till now. Akiva has been smoldering for decades, ever since our father was killed. He has never recovered from his wife's death."

"You know," Avidan said, "that half my work in the Haganah is to hold our boys back. If we let them, they'd make war on the British tomorrow. Your feelings, my feelings, and Akiva's feelings are the same, but he can destroy us all. One reason we have been able to achieve what we have in Palestine is that despite our differences we have acted in unison in our outside dealings. The British and the Arabs have always had to negotiate as though with a single person. Now Akiva has a hot-tempered gang of activists. If they start terror tactics the entire Yishuv will have to answer for his actions."

Barak traveled back north to Ein Or, which was not far from his own *moshav* of Yad El. Ein Or, like most of the older *kibbutzim*, had been turned into a veritable garden. As senior member and one of the founders Akiva had a separate little two-room cottage of his own which was filled with books. He even had his own radio and toilet—a rarity in *kibbutz* life. Akiva loved Ein Or as he had loved Shoshanna before it. Barak had wanted him to live with them at Yad El after the death of Ruth and his daughter but Akiva loved *kibbutz* life and remained, unhealthily, with their ghosts.

Barak talked softly to his brother. Akiva had heard all the arguments before. He was nervous and restless at the prospect of a showdown with his brother.

"So, the gentlemen of Yishuv Central have sent you around

to cry for them. They are becoming experts at appeasement."

"I would have come without their invitation when I heard what an insane thing you have done," Barak said.

Akiva paced the room again. Barak studied him. He was alive with the same angry fire he had had as a boy. "All I am doing is something the Yishuv Central recognizes and is afraid to do. Sooner or later even they are going to have to face the facts of life. The British are our enemy."

"We do not believe that, Akiva. All told we have done very well under British rule."

"Then you are a fool."

"I have been wrong before. The British represent the constituted government of Palestine."

"While they cut our throats," Akiva mocked. "The gentlemen of the Yishuv Central carry their brief cases to conferences and read their little notes and findings and bow and scrape while the Mufti and his cutthroats run wild. Do you see the Arabs negotiating?"

"We will achieve our aims legally."

"We will achieve our aims by fighting for them!"

"Then if we must fight, let us fight as a unified people. You put yourself in the category of the Mufti by starting a band of outlaws. Have you ever thought of the consequences if the British leave Palestine? No matter how bitter your feelings . . . and mine . . . the British are still our greatest instrument for achieving statehood."

Akiva waved his hand in disgust. "We will achieve statehood the same way we redeemed this land . . . with our sweat and blood. I refuse to sit around and wait for British handouts."

"For the last time, Akiva . . . don't do this thing. You will only give our enemies an opportunity to point their fingers at us and increase their lies."

"Aha!" Akiva cried. "Now we have come to the guts of the matter! Jews must play the games by the rules. Jews cannot be wrong! Jews must beg and appeal! Jews must turn their cheeks!"

"Stop it!"

"God no!" Akiva cried. "Whatever you do, don't fight! You wouldn't want the Germans and the Arabs and the British to think you are bad boys."

"I said stop it."

"Ghetto Jew Barak. That is what you are and that is what the Yishuv Central is. Well, let me tell you something else, dear brother. Here is one Jew who may be wrong but intends to live. So let us be wrong in the eyes of the whole damned world."

Barak trembled with rage. He sat motionless to try to hide

his anger. Akiva ranted on. Was Akiva really wrong? How much pain and degradation and betrayal and suffering must a man take before fighting back?

Barak got out of his chair and walked to the door.

"Tell Avidan and the gentlemen of the Yishuv Central and all the little negotiators that Akiva and the Maccabees have a message for the British and the Arabs . . . 'an eye for an eye and a tooth for a tooth!' "

"You are never to set foot in my house again," Barak said.

The two brothers glared at each other for many moments. Tears welled in Akiva's eyes. "Not set foot in your house?" Barak was frozen.

"We are brothers, Barak. You carried me to Palestine on your back."

"And I have lived to regret it."

Akiva's lips trembled. "I am a Jew who loves Palestine no less than you do. You condemn me for following the dictates of my conscience . . ."

Barak stepped back into the room. "It is you, Akiva, and your Maccabees who have turned brother against brother. Since we were children I have heard your convenient quotations from the Bible. Well . . . perhaps you had better read again about the Zealots who turned brother against brother and divided Jewish unity and brought on the destruction of Jerusalem by the Romans. Maccabees you call yourselves. I call you Zealots." Barak again walked to the door.

"Remember one thing, Barak Ben Canaan," Akiva said. "Nothing we do, right or wrong, can ever compare to what has been done to the Jewish people. Nothing the Maccabees do can even be considered an injustice in comparison to two thousand years of murder."

CHAPTER FIFTEEN: Yad El blossomed into a Garden of Eden. The *moshav* continued to push back the swamps so that its cultivable land was increased to bring in another hundred families. There were two dozen pieces of heavy machinery and an experimental station. The entire *moshav* worked the fishponds as a joint crop.

The streets of Yad El were green all year round and there was a blaze of colors in the spring and autumn. Yad El had a primary and secondary school, large community center with a swimming pool, library and theater, and a small hospital with two full-time doctors.

The greatest event of all occurred when electricity was brought in! The celebration throughout the Huleh Valley settlements made all other celebrations look small as the

271

lights went on in Ein Or and Kfar Giladi and Ayelet Hashahar and Yad El simultaneously.

In the same year, the Jews of Yad El helped bring tap
water to Abu Yesha, making it the first Arab village in all of
Palestine to have it. Yad El extended some of the electric
irrigation pumps into Abu Yesha fields to show the Arabs
how to farm intensively through irrigation.

To show his gratitude, Kammal gave several *dunams* of a
hillside site to the Zion Settlement Society when he learned
the Jews were looking for land in the area for a youth village.

Ari Ben Canaan was the pride of his father's heart. By the
age of seventeen he was six feet tall and had the strength of
a lion. Besides Hebrew and English he mastered Arabic,
German, French, and Yiddish, which Sarah slipped back to
in moments of anger or excitement.

Ari loved farming.

He and Dafna and most of the *moshav*'s youngsters belonged to a youth group, as did most of the young people in
the Yishuv. They would tramp the length and breadth of
Palestine to the sites of ancient battles and tombs and cities.
They climbed the mountain at Masada where the Hebrews
held out against the Roman siege for over three years and
they tramped through the desert over the route of Moses
and the twelve tribes. They wore the traditional blue
shirts and shorts and they were always filled with the songs
and dances and ideals of the redemption of the homeland.

Dafna had developed into a buxom, earthy, attractive
girl filled with love for the son of Barak Ben Canaan. It
appeared that Ari and Dafna would marry at an early age.
They would either open a new farm at Yad El or travel out
with a youth group to begin a new *moshav* or *kibbutz* as was
sometimes the tradition after schooling. But as the troubles
mounted in Palestine, Ari and Dafna had less and less time
to spend together. Ari had shown remarkable skill and leadership within the Haganah and despite his tender age was
considered by Avidan one of the most promising soldiers in
all of Palestine. In fact, most of the outstanding soldiers
were in their late teens.

By the age of seventeen Ari had set up defenses at Yad
El, Ein Or, and half a dozen *kibbutzim* and had done so well
that he went into Haganah work almost full time.

When the illegal immigration war with the British began,
Ari was called to duty at the sites where Aliyeh Bet ships
beached. Ari worked at getting the illegal immigrants hidden
in *kibbutzim* and at collecting the visas and passports of
"tourists" who had entered Palestine.

When he had a day or two free he would often phone

272

Yad El and Dafna would hitchhike to Tel Aviv to meet him. They could hear the new philharmonic symphony which had been formed largely with German musicians and whose initial concert was conducted by Toscanini—or they could go to the art exhibits or lectures at the Youth Headquarters—or merely walk along Ben Yehuda Street and Allenby Road where crowds sipped coffee in the sidewalk cafés. Or perhaps they would stroll along the quiet beaches north of Tel Aviv. Each separation became more and more difficult. Ari did not wish to marry until he could get a parcel of land and build a home. With trouble constant and his services more and more in demand it seemed as though that time would never come. They loved each other very much. By the time she was seventeen and he was nineteen she had given herself to him. Now in their rendezvous they spent their few hours discovering the wonder of each other.

The tension which began with the German Aliyah in 1933 hit a peak in the year 1935 when the Jews succeeded in bringing in more immigrants than ever before, legally and illegally. Just as the Second Aliyah brought ideals and leaders and the Third Aliyah brought the pioneers—the German Aliyah resulted in a tremendous cultural and scientific spurt in the Yishuv.

The effendis who were watching the continued progress of the Jews became frantic—frantic enough, in fact, to unite their dissident political groups for the first time and as a unified body make definite demands on the British that all selling of land to Jews and all Jewish immigration be stopped.

Early in 1936 Yishuv Central requested several thousand visas from the British to conform with the growing anxiety of the Jews in Germany. Under violent Arab pressure the British granted less than a thousand visas.

The Mufti, seeing the growing British weakness, made his move at last for control of Palestine. In the spring of 1936 he stirred up a new series of riots. They began in Jaffa with the fable that the Jews were snatching all the Arabs in Tel Aviv and murdering them, and they spread from city to city. As usual, the majority of the victims were defenseless old Orthodox Jews in the holy cities. Immediately after the first outbursts Haj Amin announced the formation of a Higher Arab Committee, with himself as head, for the purpose of "directing" another Arab general strike in protest against the "pro-Jewish" British policies.

This time the Mufti moved after careful preparation. The instant the Higher Arab Committee was announced, the El Husseini mob, flanked by hired thugs, fanned out throughout the Arab community to "enforce" the general strike, and to see that a full boycott was carried out. A wanton rash of assassinations began systematically to wipe out any known Arab opponent of the Mufti. Although the rebellion was supposedly directed against the Jews and the British, its major objective was to kill off all the Mufti's political opponents.

Kammal, the long-time friend of Barak Ben Canaan, and the muktar of Abu Yesha, was made to pay for his friendship with the Yishuv. Husseini's henchmen found the aging muktar kneeling at prayer in the little mosque by the stream in his village—and they slit his throat.

Taha, the son, was whisked away into Yad El to live in the Ben Canaan home where he would be safe. The Mufti's blood orgy continued to enforce the general strike and the boycott of the Jews. Without a market the Arab crops rotted in the fields. The port of Jaffa and the commerce around it ground to a near halt. The strike was paralyzing the Arab population, but they were helpless against the Mufti. Haj Amin el Husseini again used his pulpit to twist the blame upon the Jews; and as the Arab hardship heightened, so did their desperation and anger. Soon the Arabs began to dare to attack settlements and burn fields and steal crops. When an isolated and unarmed Jew was found his murder was always followed by decapitation, dismemberment, eye gouging, and the most primitive brutalities.

As the atrocities increased, Avidan called upon the Yishuv to exercise self-restraint. The Arab population was being victimized, he declared, and no good would come of returning their cruelties.

It was a different story with Akiva and the Maccabees. Soon after the Maccabees broke from the Haganah the British outlawed them and forced them underground. The British, to some extent, turned their backs on the Haganah because they knew about the policy of self-restraint and the fact that the Haganah fought only in self-defense. Furthermore, the Haganah never fought against the British. Not so the Maccabees. They were avowed enemies of the British and they had no intention of exercising restraint. The Maccabees, therefore, had to move into the cover of the three major cities: Tel Aviv, Jerusalem, and Haifa.

Akiva's followers tried to trade terror for terror but they were not large or effective enough to keep pace with the Mufti's thugs. Although they were officially disclaimed by the Jewish leadership, many of the Yishuv were happy over the Maccabee actions.

Once Haj Amin el Husseini had his hands on Palestine's throat, he moved ahead with the next phase of his plan. He sent out a fanatically worded appeal for all Arabs of all nations to join the common struggle to liberate Palestine from the clutches of British imperialism and Zionism.

Husseini gangsters entered Arab villages and demanded fighters for attacks on Jewish settlements. Most of the beleaguered fellaheen had absolutely no desire to fight but they were too terrified of the Mufti to refuse.

From outside of Palestine came an answer to the Mufti's appeal. An Iraqi army officer named Kawukji saw the Palestine "revolt" as his long awaited chance to seize power and make a fortune as the Mufti's military arm. Kawukji was obsessed with himself; his egomania knew no bounds. He purchased many fine new uniforms with all types of fancy decorations and declared himself generalissimo of the army of liberation. With money extorted from the Palestinian Arabs by the Mufti, Kawukji went about recruiting his army outside the country. He got together a band of thieves, dope runners, white slavers, and the like with the lure of the many Jewish women they could rape and the "Hebrew gold" they could loot. They were as vicious, degenerate, and brutal a gang as had ever been assembled. Under Generalissimo Kawukji they poured in from Lebanon to save the great Islam martyr, Haj Amin el Husseini.

Kawukji used safe and simple tactics. He would set up a road ambush after first having made certain of an avenue of retreat. When a bus, unarmed vehicle, or party small enough not to fight passed by, the Arabs would spring, loot, and flee.

Soon Kawukji and the Mufti's gangs had the entire country terrorized. The Arab community was defenseless, the British were inept and reluctant to fight, and the Jews would fight only in self-defense.

Instead of moving to stamp out the Arab attacks, the British were nearly comical in their efforts. A few times they swept in on suspected bandit hide-out villages and assessed collective fines, and once or twice they even destroyed a few villages. But they went into a defensive shell. They built over fifty enormous concrete police forts that encircled all of Palestine. Each fort was capable of holding from a few hundred up to several thousand troops. Each fort was to control its own immediate area. They were designed by a man named Taggart and built by the Jews.

The Taggart forts that ringed besieged Palestine were a system as old as the land itself. In Biblical days the Jews used twelve mountains. A fire from one could be seen by the next and relayed to the next. The Crusaders adhered to the same theory by erecting fortified castles each within sight of the next castle or walled town. Even the Jews now put each new agricultural settlement within sight of a neighbor.

At night the British buttoned up in their Taggart forts and stayed put. By day their raids were ineffective. The moment a convoy was spotted leaving a fort the word was passed along the countryside. Every Arab in every field was a potential spy. By the time the British reached their objective, the opposition had disappeared into thin air.

Yet, under this unbelievable pressure, the Jews continued to smuggle in immigrants and build new settlements for them. On the first day of a new settlement several hundred farmers and builders from all the neighboring settlements would gather on the breaking grounds at sunrise. Between sunup and sundown they quickly constructed a tower with searchlight facilities and generator and a small stockade around it. By night of the same day it would be completed and they would disappear to their own settlements, leaving the new settlers inside the stockade with a small guard of Haganah men.

Ari Ben Canaan, just over twenty years of age, became an expert on the "tower and blockade" settlements. He generally commanded the Haganah unit which stayed behind to teach the new settlers the trick of handling Arab infiltrators and attackers and how to use their weapons. Almost every new settlement underwent an Arab attack. The presence of the Haganah and their ability ultimately to repulse the attackers was a steadying influence upon the newcomers. Not Ari or any other Jewish leader ever lost a "tower and stockade" settlement. At the end of a few weeks in one place, Ari would take his unit on to the next new "tower and stockade" settlement under construction.

The settlers worked out from the stockades slowly, opening up their land a bit at a time. They erected permanent buildings and slowly expanded into full-fledged villages. If the settlement was a *kibbutz* the first building would be the children's house. It was always built in the inner line of defense so that it would be the last building that could be reached by attackers.

Avidan said that the "tower and stockade" farms were a fulfillment of the Biblical story of the rebuilding of Jerusalem with one hand on the spear and one hand on the trowel. The prophet Nehemiah had said . . . "half my servants wrought in the work and the other half held the spears." And so it was that they worked their land and built their homes with a rifleman behind every plow and every carpenter.

The Arabs became so bold that even the British could not go on ignoring the terror. Haj Amin and Kawukji had made them all look like jackasses. At last they plunged into action and broke up the Higher Arab Committee and issued a warrant for the arrest of Haj Amin. The Mufti fled ahead of

British police into the Mosque of Omar, the holiest Moslem shrine in Palestine.

The British balked and dared not enter the mosque for fear of inciting a "holy" uprising on the part of the entire Moslem world. After a week of hiding out, Haj Amin, dressed as a woman, fled and escaped to Jaffa, where a boat carried him to Lebanon.

Everyone breathed a great sigh of relief as the Mufti of Jerusalem left Palestine—especially the Arab community. The riots and attacks abated and the British again renewed their commissions of inquiry and investigations.

The Arabs boycotted the British inquiries except to send a few of their most fanatical members in to read prepared speeches. Although Haj Amin had left the scene, the El Husseinis were still on hand. At the commissions of inquiry the Arabs made more and more outrageous claims against the Jews, who paid eighty-five per cent of all the taxes despite the fact that the Yishuv was smaller than the Arab community.

And so, after another survey of the situation, the British took a new tack and recommended that Palestine be divided into two separate states. The Arabs were to get the lion's share and the Jews a strip of land from Tel Aviv to Haifa and those parts of the Galilee they had reclaimed.

The Yishuv Central, the world Zionists, and the Jews in Palestine were tired of the continued bloodshed, the growing Arab fanaticism, and the ever more apparent British betrayal. Once the mandate for the Jewish homeland had included both sides of the Jordan River—now the British were offering but an iota. Yet, despite everything, the Jews decided to accept the proposal.

The British pointed out to the Arabs that it would be wise to accept, because the area allotted to the Jews couldn't hold many more immigrants. But the Arabs wanted nothing more or less than that every Jew be thrown into the sea. Haj Amin el Husseini was the treasure of Islam and the martyred victim of British and Zionist injustice. From Beirut he renewed the rebellion.

Taggart, who had built the British system of forts, erected an electrified barbed-wire wall along the Lebanese border to stop the Mufti's thugs and arms runners. At intervals he constructed more blockhouse forts to interlace with the wall.

One of the forts on the Taggart wall was erected above Abu Yesha and Yad El at the site believed to be the burial ground of Queen Esther. It became known as Fort Esther.

The Taggart wall slowed the Arab infiltration but could not stop it.

The Haganah, which had contained itself so long, became very restless and the Yishuv began to wonder when the Yishuv Central would let the Haganah fight. Under this growing pressure, Ben Gurion finally agreed to listen to a plan advanced by Avidan. In turn the Zion Settlement Society purchased a piece of land on the northern extremity of the Galilee, right on the Lebanese border, at a point where Haganah intelligence suspected most of the Arab infiltration to be taking place.

Shortly after the land purchase Ari Ben Canaan and two other top young men in Haganah were called to Tel Aviv to Avidan's secret headquarters.

The bald-headed leader of Jewish defense unfolded a map and pointed out the new parcel of land. Its importance to the continuation of the Arab revolt was obvious.

"I want you three boys to take command of a unit to go up to this land and build a *kibbutz* there. We are carefully picking eighty of our top men and twenty women to go with you. I don't have to tell you what to expect."

They nodded.

"We know the Mufti is going to stop everything else in an effort to run you out. This is the first time we have picked a spot for a *kibbutz* because of its strategic value."

Sarah Ben Canaan was sick at heart. For years she had not seen her son without a whip or a gun near at hand. Now she feared this mission as she had feared none of the others. A hundred of the best members of the Yishuv were being put into a suicidal position. Ari kissed his mother and brushed away her tears and in his simple way said that it would be all right. He shook his father's hand and said nothing, for the understanding between them was complete.

Dafna knocked on the door and they said good-by to her too.

Dafna and Ari walked out the gates of Yad El and turned to look back briefly at the fields and at the friends who had gathered. Barak sighed and put his arm on Sarah's shoulder as the younger couple disappeared down the road.

"They want so little from life," Sarah said. "How long . . . how long must we go on giving him?"

Barak shook his great head and his eyes narrowed to catch a last glimpse of his boy and Dafna.

"God asked Abraham to give his son in sacrifice. I suppose we of the Yishuv live in that shadow. We must keep giving Ari so long as God wills it."

A hundred of the finest young men and women of the Yishuv went up to the border of Lebanon and placed themselves in the path of thieves and murderers. Ari Ben

278

Canaan, at twenty-two years of age, was second in command.
They called the place Ha Mishmar, the Guardpost.

CHAPTER SIXTEEN: Ten trucks carrying a hundred Haganah boys and girls and their equipment sped along the coastal road past the last Jewish settlement at Nahariya in northern Galilee and penetrated into territory where no Jew had gone before. A thousand pairs of Arab eyes watched the convoy as it moved up into the foothills of the mountains on the Lebanese border below the Taggart wall.

They stopped, set out guards, and unloaded the trucks quickly. The trucks rushed back to Nahariya before dark. The hundred were alone. Above them the hills were filled with Arab marauder gangs. Behind them were a dozen hostile Arab villages.

They erected a small stockade, dug in, and waited out the night.

By next morning the word had spread from Hebron to Beirut . . . "The Jews have moved into the hills!" Haj Amin el Husseini in Beirut was enraged. It was an open challenge. He swore by the beard of Allah that the Jews would be thrown into the sea.

During the next few days the Haganah force worked themselves to exhaustion tightening the defenses of the base camp at the bottom of the hill against the attack that had to come. Each night when they weren't standing guard, Dafna and Ari fell into exhausted slumber in each other's arms.

On the fourth night the attack came!

The Jews had never undergone anything like it. A thousand Arab riflemen flanked with machine guns poured a steady tattoo of fire into the Jews' stockade for five consecutive hours from the top of the hill. For the first time the Arabs used mortar fire. Ari and his forces lay low and waited for the Arabs to try an assault.

The attack came when Arab thugs began slithering along the ground with knives between their teeth.

Suddenly——

Half a dozen searchlights darted out from the stockade and swept the field. The light caught the Arabs in close. The Jews poured on a deadly counterfire and in the very first burst shot sixty Arabs dead.

The Arabs were paralyzed with fear. Ari led half the Haganah force out from the cover of the stockade in a fierce counterattack which littered the field of battle with Arab dead and wounded. Arabs who survived fled back to high ground screaming in terror.

279

The Arabs did not attack again for a week. Nothing the Mufti could say or do could make them attack. Kawukji could not make them attack.

In that first night three Haganah boys and one girl were killed in the fighting. One of them was the commander. Ari Ben Canaan stepped up to assume command.

Each day the Haganah moved up the hill a few feet, consolidated the position, and waited out the night. The Arabs watched from their positions above but never attacked during the daylight hours. By the end of a week Ari abandoned the first base camp and had established a second camp midway up the hill.

The Arabs resumed their attacks, but the lesson of the first night was still fresh. They did not try a direct assault but were content to fire at the camp from long distances.

While the Arabs remained indecisive, Ari decided to take the offensive. At the end of the second week at dawn he made his move. He waited until the Arabs were tired from firing all night and their guard was lax. He led twenty-five crack men and ten women in a dawn attack that threw the sleepy Arabs off the top of the hill. The Jews dug in quickly while the Arabs got their bearings and reassembled for a counterattack. Ari lost five soldiers but he held his position.

Quickly he fortified a lookout post on the top of the hill which commanded a view of the entire area. By daylight they worked feverishly to build their foothold into a fortress.

The Mufti was nearly insane with rage! He changed commanders and assembled another force of a thousand men. They attacked, but as soon as they came into close range they broke and fled.

For the first time Jews commanded a hilltop position and the Arabs were not going to dislodge them.

Although the Arabs would not fight at close quarters and would therefore not be able to run the Haganah out, they did not intend to make life easy for the Jews. Ari's troops were constantly harassed by Arab rifles. His force was completely isolated from the rest of the Yishuv. The closest settlement was Nahariya. All supplies and even water had to come in through hostile territory by truck, and once there everything had to be carried up the hill by hand.

Despite the hardships, Ha Mishmar held fast. A few crude huts were erected inside the stockade and a road was started to the bottom of the hill. Ari began night patrols along the Taggart wall to catch infiltrators and arms runners. The Mufti's underground highway into Palestine was being squeezed shut.

Ninety per cent of the Haganah force were from either *kibbutzim* or *moshavim*. Redemption was so much a part of them that they could not stay long in one spot without trying to grow something. They began farming at Ha Mishmar! The place had been opened in the guise of a *kibbutz,* and by God they were going to make it one. Hillside farming was a new venture for them—and it was especially difficult when there was no natural water except the sparse rainfall. None the less they went at the task with the same vigor with which they had redeemed the swamplands of the Jezreel Valley and the eroded Plain of Sharon. They terraced the hillsides and petitioned the Zion Settlement Society for money for farm tools.

The Yishuv Central and the Haganah were so delighted over the success of the dogged youngsters at Ha Mishmar that they decided that from then on some new settlements would be selected for their strategic value in choking off the Arab revolution.

A second group of pioneers set out for another trouble-some spot. This time they were Orthodox Jews. They moved deep into the Beth Shean Valley and built a *kibbutz* at the juncture of the Syrian and Trans-Jordan borders. Their *kibbutz* was called Tirat Tsvi, the Castle of the Rabbi Tsvi. It stood in the midst of a dozen hostile Arab towns and villages. Again the Mufti attempted to dislodge them. But this force of religious Jews was not of the same ilk as the old pious Jews of the holy cities. As at Ha Mishmar, the Arabs could not defeat the Jews of Tirat Tsvi.

Ari was sound asleep in his tent.

"Ari . . . come quickly."

He threw off his blanket, grabbed his rifle, and ran after them to the south fields which were being terraced for grape-vines. There was a gathering. Everyone turned silent as they saw Ari approach. He pushed through and stared at the ground. It was blood-spattered. Parts of a blue blouse were on the ground. A trail of blood led off to the hills. Ari looked from face to face. No one spoke.

"Dafna," he whispered.

Two days later her body was dumped near their camp. Her ears, nose, and hands had been amputated. Her eyes had been gouged out. She had been raped over a hundred times.

No one saw Ari Ben Canaan weep or even raise his voice.

After Dafna's murder he would disappear for hours at a time, returning chalky-faced and shaken. But he never displayed passion or hatred or even great anger. He never mentioned her name to anyone again. Ari accepted this tragedy in the same way that the Yishuv had learned to accept such things—not by being stirred to violence, but only by deepening his determination not to be thrown from the land. Ari

Ben Canaan was all soldier. Half a dozen Arab villages near Ha Mishmar cringed and awaited a revenge attack—but it never came.

The Jews hung on at Ha Mishmar and at Tirat Tsvi and half a dozen other strategically placed settlements. The new tactic was hampering the Mufti's revolt but not stopping it.

Into this hodgepodge came an English major named P. P. Malcolm.

Major P. P. Malcolm had been transferred to British intelligence in Jerusalem at the outbreak of the Mufti's revolt. He was a loner. P.P. dressed sloppily and scorned military tradition. He thought protocol ridiculous. He was a man who could express his feelings openly and violently if need be, and he was also a man given to deep meditation for days on end, during which he might neither shave nor comb his hair. His periods of detachment came at odd times—even in the middle of the formal parades, which he hated and believed a waste of time. P. P. Malcolm had a tongue like a lash and never failed to startle those around him. He was eccentric and looked upon as an "off horse" by his fellow officers.

Physically P.P. was tall and thin and bony-faced and had a slight limp. He was, all told, everything that a British officer should not be.

When Malcolm arrived in Palestine he was pro-Arab because it was fashionable for the British officers to be pro-Arab. These sympathies did not last long. Within a short period of time P. P. Malcolm had turned into a fanatic Zionist.

Like most Christians who embrace Zionism, his brand was far more intense and rabid than a Jew's. Malcolm learned Hebrew from a rabbi and spent every spare minute reading the Bible. He was certain it was in God's scheme for the Jews to rise again as a nation. Malcolm made detailed studies of the Biblical military campaigns and of the tactics of Joshua, David, and especially Gideon, who was his personal idol. And finally—he became obsessed with the notion that his coming to Palestine had been divinely inspired.

He, P. P. Malcolm, had been chosen by God Himself to lead the children of Israel in their noble mission.

Malcolm drove around Palestine in a battered secondhand jalopy and he hiked on his gimpy leg where there were no roads. Malcolm visited every site of every battle of Biblical times to reconstruct the tactical events. Often Jew and Arab alike were stunned to see this strange creature limping along a road singing a Psalm at the top of his voice and oblivious to everything worldly.

It was often asked why the British command tolerated Malcolm. General Charles, the commander of Palestine, recognized quite simply that Malcolm was a genius and one of those rare types of military rebels who pops up every so often. Malcolm laughed at the British handbooks on war, had nothing but disdain for their strategy, and for the most part thought the entire British Army was a waste of money. No one ever seemed to win an argument with him for he never appeared to be wrong and he was convinced of his own infallible judgment.

One day toward evening P. P. Malcolm abandoned his car when it blew two tires at once and hiked along the road toward Yad El. As he entered the defense perimeter half a dozen guards headed in on him. He smiled and waved at them. "Good work, chaps," he called. "Now be dear lads and take me to Barak Ben Canaan."

Malcolm paced up and down Barak's living room. His appearance was even more slovenly than usual. For a solid hour he lectured Barak Ben Canaan about the glory and beauty of Zionism and the destiny of the Hebrew nation.

"I like Jewish soldiers," Malcolm said. "The Hebrew warrior is the finest, for he fights and lives close to ideals. This land is real to him. He lives with great glories all around him. Your chaps in the Haganah probably constitute the most highly educated and intellectual as well as idealistic body of men under arms in the entire world.

"Take the British soldier," Malcolm continued. "He is a stubborn fighter and that is good. He responds to discipline and that is good. But it ends right there. He is a stupid man. He drinks too much. He would sleep with a pig and often does. Ben Canaan, that is what I have come to see you about. I am going to take your Haganah and make a first-class fighting organization out of it. You've got the best raw material I've ever laid eyes on."

Barak's jaw dropped!

Malcolm looked out the window. He could see the water sprinklers whirling in the fields and in the distance he could see Abu Yesha nestled in the hills below the Taggart fort, Fort Esther.

"See that fort up there—Esther, you call it—stupidity, I call it. All the Arabs have to do is walk around it. The British will never learn." Malcolm began humming Psalm 98 and singing the words softly in Hebrew. "I have the Psalms memorized up to a hundred and twenty-six. It comforts me."

"Major Malcolm. Just what is the nature of this visit?" Barak said.

"Everyone knows that Barak Ben Canaan is fair and nonpartisan. Frankly, most Jews like to talk too much. In my Jewish army they won't have ten words to say. I'll do all the talking."

"You have made me quite aware that you like to do all the talking," Barak said.

"Humph," Malcolm grunted, and continued to look at the lush fields of Yad El through the window. Suddenly he swung around and his eyes were ablaze with the same intensity Barak had often seen in his brother Akiva.

"Fight!" Malcolm cried. "That is what we must do . . . fight! The Jewish nation is destiny, Ben Canaan, destiny."

"You and I are in certain agreement about the destiny of the homeland . . . I don't need refreshing."

"Yes you do . . . all of you do . . . so long as you stay buttoned up in your settlements. We must go there and start punishing those infidels. If an Arab comes out of his coffeehouse and takes a pot shot at a *kibbutz* from a thousand yards distant he thinks he is a brave man. The time has come to test these bloody heathens. Hebrews, that's what I want . . . Hebrew soldiers. You arrange an appointment with Avidan for me at once. Englishmen are too stupid to understand my methods."

As suddenly as this strange man had appeared at Yad El, he left. P. P. Malcolm limped through the gates singing a Biblical Psalm at the top of his voice and left Barak Ben Canaan scratching his beard and shaking his head.

Barak later phoned Avidan and they spoke in Yiddish in case the line was being tapped.

"Who is this man?" Barak asked. "He walked in like the Messiah and began preaching Zionism at me."

"We have reports on him," Avidan said. "Frankly, he is so odd we don't know what to make of him."

"Can he be trusted?"

"We don't know."

Major P. P. Malcolm now spent all his free hours among the Jews. He candidly observed that British officers were idiots and bores. In a matter of months he was known by the entire Yishuv. Although he moved in the highest circles most of the leaders treated him like a harmless eccentric. "Our mad Englishman," he was called with affection.

Soon it became apparent that P. P. Malcolm was not mad. In close discussion Malcolm had the persuasive power to talk the devil out of his horns. Members of the Yishuv came away from his home certain they had been under a magic spell.

After nearly six months of evasions, Malcolm burst into Ben Gurion's office in the Yishuv Central building in Jerusalem one day, unannounced.

"Ben Gurion," he snapped. "You are a God-damned fool. You waste all your time talking to your enemies and you haven't five minutes to spare for a friend."

With that blunt announcement he turned and walked out.

Malcolm's next appointment was with General Charles, the military commander. He argued to convince the general to let him work out some of his theories on Arab warfare with the use of Jewish troops. General Charles was pro-Arab as was most of his staff, but the Mufti's rebellion was beginning to make him look ridiculous. Little by little the British had trained and armed their own Jewish police and had ignored the Haganah arms which supplemented their own forces. The British had failed so badly he decided to let Malcolm go ahead.

Malcolm's jalopy showed up at Ha Mishmar where guards took him up the hill to Ari. The strapping Haganah commander studied the scrawny Englishman before him with puzzlement.

Malcolm patted his cheek. "You look like a good boy," he said. "Listen to me, obey my orders, observe what I do, and I'll make a first-class soldier out of you. Now, show me your camp and fortifications."

Ari was perplexed. By mutual arrangement the British had stayed out of Ha Mishmar and turned their backs on Ari's patrols. Yet they had every legal right to enter Ha Mishmar. Major Malcolm completely ignored Ari's suspicions and obvious attempt to show him only half the layout.

"Where is your tent, son?"

In Ari's tent, P. P. Malcolm stretched out on the cot and meditated.

"What do you want here?" Ari demanded.

"Give me a map, son," he said, ignoring Ari's question. Ari did so. P. P. Malcolm sat up, opened the map, and scratched his scraggly beard. "Where is the key Arab jump-off base?"

Ari pointed to a small village some fifteen kilometers inside Lebanon.

"Tonight we shall destroy it," Malcolm said calmly.

That night a patrol of eight men and two women crossed over from Ha Mishmar into Lebanon with Malcolm in command. The Jews were astounded at the speed and stamina with which he could push his fragile body through the steep and tortuous hills. He never once stopped for rest or to check directions. Before they left, Major Malcolm had heard someone sneeze and had said he could not go—and that anyone who did not keep up with the pace would be thrashed

285

within an inch of his life. He led them in singing a Psalm and lectured them on the nobility of their mission.

As they neared their objective, Malcolm went up ahead to reconnoiter the village. He returned in half an hour.

"As I suspected, they have no security up. Here is what we shall do." He drew a hasty map to pinpoint what he believed to be the three or four huts belonging to the smugglers. "I will take three of you chaps into the village and we will open fire from short range and give them a blast or two of grenades to loosen the party up a bit. Everyone will flee in wild disarray. My force will drive them to the edge of the village here where you, Ben Canaan, shall establish an ambush. Be so good as to bring a pair of prisoners, for this area is obviously loaded with arms caches."

"Your plan is foolish. It will not work," Ari said.

"Then I suggest you begin walking back to Palestine," Malcolm retorted.

That was the first and the last time Ari ever questioned the wisdom of P. P. Malcolm. The man's certainty was gripping.

"Never question my judgment again, young man," he said.

Malcolm's plan was executed. The major led a four-man squad right up to the suspected headquarters. Four grenades were lobbed into the huts and followed by rifle fire. According to Malcolm's prediction, there was a panic. He coolly drove the thugs right at Ari's ambush. It was all over within ten minutes.

Two prisoners were taken to the major.

"Where are your guns hidden?" he asked the first one in Arabic. The Arab shrugged.

Malcolm slapped the Arab's face and repeated the question. This time the Arab pleaded his innocence as Allah was his judge. Malcolm calmly took out his pistol and shot the Arab through the head. He turned to the second prisoner. "Where are your guns hidden?" he asked.

The second Arab quickly revealed the location of the arms.

"You sons and daughters of Judea have learned many valuable lessons this night," Malcolm said. "I will explain them to you in the morning. One thing, never use brutality to get information. Get right to the point."

The news of Malcolm's raid had a sobering effect on all of Palestine. For the Yishuv it marked a historic occasion. For the very first time the Jews had come out of their settlements to make an offensive action. Many thought it was long overdue.

The British were in an uproar. Most of them demanded that P. P. Malcolm be removed at once. General Charles was not so sure. British methods of fighting Arabs were sorely

286

lacking, and he felt Malcolm had most of the answers.

For the Mufti's thugs and the Husseinis and the Moslem fanatics it was a day of reckoning. No longer could they rove at will and pick their places for attack without expecting retribution.

Ari went out with P. P. Malcolm on a dozen more raids deep into Lebanon. Each raid was more successful than the last. The marauder gangs, the thugs and the gun runners and Kawukji's mercenaries, were shaken from their complacency, for their activities were no longer profitable or safe against the swift merciless raids of the Haganah. The Mufti placed a reward of a thousand pounds sterling on P. P. Malcolm's head.

After Malcolm and his Haganah boys and girls at Ha Mishmar succeeded in quieting down the Taggart line, he moved his headquarters to the *kibbutz* of Ein Or. Malcolm requested from the Haganah a hundred and fifty top soldiers; he specifically wanted Ari Ben Canaan, whom he greatly favored. At *kibbutz* Ein Or, Malcolm formed his Raider Unit.

When the hundred and fifty soldiers had assembled from all over the Yishuv, Major Malcolm led them on a long hike to Mount Gilboa at the traditional site of the grave of the great Hebrew judge and warrior, Gideon, who was Malcolm's idol. At Gideon's grave he stood before his charges and opened his Bible and read in Hebrew.

" . . . *so Gideon, and the hundred men that were with him, came unto the outside of the camp in the beginning of the middle watch; and they had but newly set the watch: and they blew the horns, and brake the pitchers that were in their hands. And the three companies blew the horns, and brake the pitchers, and held the lamps in their left hands, and the horns in their right hands to blow withal; and they cried, The sword of the Lord and of Gideon. And they stood every man in his place round about the camp; and all the host ran, and cried, and fled."*

Malcolm closed the Bible. He walked back and forth with his hands clasped behind him and seemed to look off into space as he spoke. "Gideon was a smart man. Gideon knew the Midianites were an ignorant and a superstitious people. Gideon knew he could play on their primitive fears and that they could be frightened by noise and by the night. Gideon knew it . . . and so do we."

The Arabs never knew where or when the Raider Unit would strike next. Their old reliable spy system simply did not work against Malcolm. He would send three units out in three different directions to confuse them. He would pass an

Arab village and double back and strike it. He would send a convoy of trucks down a road and drop men off one at a time. During the day they lay hidden in the ditches at the roadside and at night they would assemble.

Every attack that came sounded like a thousand men. He never failed to send his enemy into a panic.

He elaborated on something his Jews already knew—the terrain of Palestine. He taught them the strategic as well as the historic value of every wadi and hill and tree by pointing out how the ancient Hebrew generals had used the land and the knowledge of it to great military advantage.

Ari Ben Canaan became a devoted disciple of this eccentric Englishman, as did all of the Raiders. He went alongside Malcolm in a hundred raids against the enemy and never once was Malcolm guilty of error. It was almost as though he were divinely guided as well as divinely inspired. He created a flawless text on Arab fighting. He demanded iron discipline and fanatical and unquestioning devotion in payment for victory after victory.

The Raider Unit put a fear into the Arabs which was even greater than that of the Husseinis. With a hundred and fifty men he ripped the rebellion to shreds. The marauders began to flee and Kawukji's grand army of liberation raced back to Lebanon. In floundering desperation the Mufti turned his fire on the oil line which ran from the Mosul fields to Haifa.

"Twenty thousand of those dunderheaded Englishmen could not defend that pipeline," Malcolm said. "We will do it with our Raider Unit. Our plans are simple. Each time there is a break in the line the nearest Arab village to that break will be attacked and flattened by the Raider Unit. This will teach the Arab villages to guard the lines against marauders in the interest of their own safety and it will teach them not to shelter those thugs. Reprisal . . . remember that, for the Jews are outnumbered . . . we must use the principle of reprisal."

Every time the Arabs moved they got it right back in the teeth. Reprisal, from then on, became the key to Jewish defense.

The Arab revolt petered out and died. It had been a miserable and costly failure. The Arabs had bankrupted their entire community and murdered their foremost spokesmen. Three years of riots and bloodshed had put them on the brink of destitution. In all that time they did not displace a single Jewish settlement or keep some fifty new ones from going up.

With the death throes of the Arab uprising Whitehall made a clean sweep of their government in the mandate.

Major P. P. Malcolm was told he must leave Palestine, for

his continued consorting with the Jews now would cause them nothing but embarrassment. Malcolm had been the greatest single instrument in breaking the backs of the Arabs. The Jews he trained were the nucleus of a greater new army—his brilliant tactics their military Bible.

For the last time Major P. P. Malcolm stood before his Jews at Ein Or. The Raider Unit honored by red badges on their blue farmer's clothing stood at attention, and there were tears in the eyes of many.

Malcom opened his Bible. ". . . *Gird thy sword upon thy thigh O. most mighty, with thy glory and thy majesty. And in thy majesty ride prosperously because of truth and meekness and righteousness.*"

He walked away quickly to the waiting car. His heart was broken. The Yishuv had bestowed upon him the greatest honor they could give a non-Jew. They called him "the Friend."

Ari Ben Canaan returned to Yad El after the Raider Unit was disbanded. His heart seemed always on a lonely hill on the Lebanese border where Dafna lay in eternal sleep alongside twenty other Haganah boys and girls who had fallen for Ha Mishmar.

With things quiet and safer, Taha left Yad El, where he had lived all this time under the protection of the Ben Canaan family, to assume the job of muktar of Abu Yesha. Both Barak and Sarah realized that in the eighteen months Taha had lived with them he had fallen in love with Jordana, who was now past her thirteenth birthday. Love of a younger girl was not uncommon among Taha's people. Both of the parents never spoke a word about it and hoped that the boy would get over it without too much pain.

The new British administration, under the command of General Haven-Hurst, came to Palestine. They soon rounded up the Raider Unit men. The latter were hauled into court and thrown into jail for terms of six months to five years! The charge—illegal use of arms!

Ari and a hundred other Haganah members of Malcolm's Raider Unit were locked in the dungeon-like Acre jail. Many of them regarded their plight as rather humorous and spent their days frustrating the British guard by singing Haganah marches and songs of the fields from morning to night. It was a thick-walled old castle—clammy and monstrous and filled with lice and rats and slime and darkness.

Ari was released in the spring of 1939. He returned home to Yad El pale and gaunt.

Sarah cried in the sanctity of her room after she had seen him. What had her son had from birth but a whip and a gun and tragedy? His Dafna was dead and so many of his comrades were dead—how long would it go on? Sarah vowed she would keep her boy at Yad El forever.

With Haven-Hurst commanding Palestine with an iron fist and open anti-Jewish sentiments the stage was set for the final British betrayal. . . .

There was another commission of inquiry. The three years of Mufti-inspired bloodshed were blamed on Jewish immigration.

Whitehall and Chatham House and Neville Chamberlain, their Prime Minister and renowned appeaser, shocked the world with their pronouncement. The British Government issued a White Paper on the eve of World War II shutting off immigration to the frantic German Jews and stopping Jewish land buying. The appeasers of Munich who had sold Spain and Czechoslovakia down the river had done the same to the Jews of Palestine.

CHAPTER SEVENTEEN: The Yishuv was rocked by the White Paper, the most staggering single blow they had ever received. On the eve of war the British were sealing in the German Jews.

The Maccabees, who had been dormant, suddenly sprang to life. The White Paper brought Jews into the Maccabees by the hundreds. They lashed out in a series of raids, bombing a British officers' club in Jerusalem and terrorizing the Arabs. They raided a British arsenal and they ambushed several convoys.

General Haven-Hurst completely reversed all previous policies of semi-co-operation with the Jews. The Jewish police were disbanded and the Haganah was driven underground. Leaders of the Yishuv Central and more former Raider men were hauled into court and then thrown into Acre jail.

Ben Gurion again called upon the Yishuv to show the same wisdom and restraint they had shown in the past. He publicly denounced the terror tactics. But even as he spoke there were elements within Haganah who wanted to come into the open and fight. Fearing a showdown would lead to its destruction, Avidan was again forced to hold his army in check.

Barak Ben Canaan was sent to London to join Dr. Chaim Weizmann and the other Zionist negotiators in trying to force a reversal of the White Paper. But the men in Whitehall were determined not to revoke it and thereby incite the Arabs.

In Palestine the Husseini mob was busy again. Despite the

fact that Haj Amin was still in exile the rest of the clan was still handling opposition through assassination. The Higher Arab Committee was grabbed by the Mufti's nephew, Jemal Husseini.

Within Germany the Jewish situation was beyond despair. The Zionists' organizations were on the verge of collapse as even the most complacent German Jews panicked to get out of the country.

The British were making it as difficult for certain Jews to leave Palestine as for Jews to get in from Germany. They realized that anyone with a Haganah and Aliyah Bet background was a potential agent. When Ari left Palestine on orders from Avidan he had to slip over the Lebanese border at Ha Mishmar and hike to Beirut on foot. He carried the passport and visa of a Jew who had recently arrived in Palestine as a "tourist." In Beirut, Ari caught a boat for Marseilles. In another week he showed up in Berlin at Zionist headquarters at Number 10 Meinekestrasse.

His orders were: "Get as many Jews out as possible."

When he arrived in Berlin, Zionist headquarters was a scene of panic and chaos.

The Germans were playing the visa market for all it was worth. The more desperate the Jews became, the higher the price for their freedom. Many families turned over entire fortunes for the privilege of being able to escape from Germany. Visas were forged and stolen—visas were life. The first cruel fact of life was that few countries of the world wanted the German Jews. They simply closed their doors. If they did give visas it was with the understanding that the Jews would not come to their countries.

Ari was faced with the decision of deciding who got the visas and who didn't. Each day he was the victim of threats or the object of bribes and desperate pleas. The Zionist rule of thumb was to get the children out. For five years the Jews had appealed to their German numbers to leave Germany.

Along with the children there were essential scientists, doctors, professionals, and artisans, the very cream of the society.

Ari and the Aliyah Bet were moving them in mere hundreds, while thousands were being trapped.

He decided on a desperate gamble in an attempt to get several thousand visas at one time. That way, Ari reckoned, he could at least move the "essentials" and many children out. He alerted Aliyah Bet in France to be prepared either to receive these thousands—or to expect his own disappearance to a concentration camp.

Ari then went into negotiations with high Nazis to sell them the idea of issuing exit permits in larger numbers. He

291

argued with a strange but fascinating logic. Britain and Germany were both trying to win Arab favor; Ari pointed out that the more Jews who got to Palestine, the more embarrassed the British would be.

How paradoxical that the Aliyah Bet was teaming up with the Nazis in an effort against the British. Ari quickly had training farms set up in the Berlin area under Gestapo protection.

In addition to all the visas he could buy, steal, bribe, and otherwise wangle, Ari built an underground railroad right under the Germans' noses for getting out the top-priority Jews; but these people, mostly scientists, escaped only in twos and threes. During the fear-filled summer of 1939 he worked around the clock as the time ran out.

Meanwhile in London, Barak Ben Canaan and the other negotiators worked the clock around too. They spoke to members of Parliament, Ministers, or anyone who would listen to them. But do what they might, the British would not budge from their immigration policy.

In mid-August, Ari received an urgent message from Aliyah Bet in France: LEAVE GERMANY AT ONCE.

Ari ignored the cable and continued his work, for each day now seemed a race against death.

Another cable came. This time it was a Haganah order for him to leave.

Ari gambled on just seventy-two hours more, for he was working on a stack of visas to get a trainload of children into Denmark.

A third cable came—and a fourth.

As the trainload of children crossed the Danish frontier, Ari Ben Canaan made his own escape. He left Germany forty-eight hours before Hitler's Wehrmacht rolled into Poland and ushered in World War II.

Ari and Barak Ben Canaan returned to Palestine from their separate missions. Both men were exhausted and both of them were crushed by despair.

At the outbreak of war it took only ten minutes for the Jewish leaders to announce their course of action. Ben Gurion urged the Yishuv to come forth for duty in the British Army to fight the common enemy.

There was additional encouragement from the Haganah which saw this as an opportunity to train its men legally.

General Haven-Hurst, the Palestine military commander, raised strong objections with the War Office about letting Palestinian Jews into the British Army. "If we train Jews now and give them combat experience we will only be spiting ourselves, for surely we will have to fight the very same Jews later on."

Within a week after the war began one hundred and thirty thousand men and women—one out of four in the entire Yishuv—had signed up at Yishuv Central to volunteer for the British Army.

As for the Arabs, most of the Arab world looked upon the Germans as their "liberators" and waited for them.

It was impossible for the British to ignore the Yishuv's offer. It was also impossible not to heed General Haven-Hurst's warning. The War Office decided upon the middle road of accepting Palestinian Jews but keeping them out of front-line assignments so that they could not get actual weapons training and combat experience. The Palestinians were turned into service units, transportation and engineering battalions. Yishuv Central protested angrily against the discrimination and demanded equal opportunities fighting the Germans.

The Yishuv had presented a solid front, except for the dissenting Maccabees. Avidan decided to swallow his pride and through a chain of underground contacts asked for a meeting with Akiva.

The two men met in a cellar beneath Frankel's Restaurant on King George Road in Jerusalem. It was filled with cases of canned food and bottled goods stacked halfway to the ceiling, and it was dark except for the light from a single light bulb.

Avidan offered no handshake as Akiva entered, flanked by two Maccabees. It had been five long years since the two men had seen each other.

Akiva looked in his sixties and more. The long hard years of building two *kibbutzim* and the more recent years of underground living had turned him into an old man.

The room was cleared of Maccabee and Haganah guards. The two men faced each other.

At last Avidan spoke. "I have come, quite simply, to ask you to call a truce with the British until the war is over."

Akiva grunted. He spat out his contempt for the British and their White Paper and his anger at the Yishuv Central and Haganah for their failure to fight.

"Please, Akiva," Avidan said, holding his temper. "I am aware of all your feelings. I know exactly what differences there are between us. Despite them, Germany is a far greater enemy and threat to our existence than the British."

Akiva turned his back on Avidan. He stood in the shadows thinking. Suddenly he spun around and his eyes blazed as of old. "Now is the time to get the British to revoke the White Paper! Now—right now—declare our statehood on both sides of the Jordan! Now! Hit the damned British when they're down!"

"Is statehood so important to us that we must gain it by contributing to a German victory?"

"And do you think the British will hesitate to sell us down the river again?"

"I think we have only one choice—to fight Germany."

Akiva paced the cement floor like a nervous cat. Tears of anger welled up in his eyes. He grunted and mumbled to himself—and at last he spoke with trembling softness. "Even as the British blockade our coast against desperate people . . . even as the British create a ghetto inside their army with our boys . . . even as they have sold us out with the White Paper . . . even as the Yishuv puts its heart and soul into the war effort while the Arabs sit like vultures waiting to pounce . . . even with all this the British are the lesser of our enemies and we must fight with them. Very well, Avidan . . . the Maccabees will call a truce."

The air was filled with Akiva's hostility as the two men finally shook hands. Akiva wet his lips. "How is my brother?"

"Barak just returned from conferences in London."

"Yes . . . conferences . . . that would be Barak. And Sarah and the children?"

Avidan nodded. "You can be proud of Ari."

"Oh yes, Ari is a fine boy . . . a fine boy . . . how . . . how . . . does Ein Or look these days?"

Avidan lowered his eyes. "Ein Or and Shoshanna show the love and the sweat of the men who built them." Avidan turned and walked toward the ladder to the trap door.

"Zion shall be redeemed with judgment," Akiva cried from the shadows of the cellar, *"and the destruction of the transgressors and of the sinners shall be together and they that forsake the Lord shall be consumed.* Our day with the British will come!"

Ari had changed. He was melancholy all the time. It was difficult to say exactly what had been the breaking point for him. He had carried arms since he was a boy. The "tower and stockade" days—Ha Mishmar—the Raider Unit—the Acre prison. The heartbreaking work for Aliyah Bet in Berlin. And the death of Dafna. Ari lived at Yad El and farmed and wanted to be left alone. He scarcely spoke a word.

Even when the war broke out Ari remained at Yad El. Most of his spare time was spent at the Arab village of Abu Yesha with his boyhood friend, Taha, who was now the muktar.

One day, several months after the war had begun, Ari returned one evening from the fields to find Avidan himself waiting to see him. After dinner Ari, Avidan, and Barak retired to the living room to talk.

"I suppose you know why I came," Avidan said.

"I can imagine."

"Let me get right to the point. There are a few dozen of our boys that we feel should join up. The British have contacted Haganah half a dozen times and asked for you. They are willing to give you an officer's commission."

"I'm not interested."

"They want you badly, Ari. I'm sure we can put you into a position—say, Arab intelligence—where you could be of great value to the Haganah too."

"That's very nice. I thought they'd have me shoveling garbage with the rest of the Yishuv troops. It's good to know I'm one of the good Jews."

"Don't make me issue this to you as an order."

"You may be surprised if you do."

Avidan, who was an iron disciplinarian, was somewhat taken aback. Ari Ben Canaan had been as reliable and unquestioning a soldier as any in the Haganah.

"I'm glad this is in the open," Barak said. "This boy has been eating his heart out since his return from Berlin."

"Ari . . . I'm afraid we are going to have to insist upon it."

"Why should I wear a British uniform? So they can throw me into prison again for bearing arms for them."

Barak threw up his hands.

"All right, Father . . . if you want it in the open. Five years ago Uncle Akiva had the courage to name our enemy."

"You are not to mention his name in this house!" Barak roared.

"It's about time it was mentioned. I might even have joined the Maccabees except that I would not go against you."

"But Ari," Avidan said quickly, "even Akiva and the Maccabees have called a truce with the British."

Ari turned and started for the door. "I'll be playing backgammon at Taha's house. Call me if the Germans invade."

The German avalanche thundered across Europe. The British suffered one debacle after another. Dunkirk! Crete! Greece! London underwent merciless bombing.

Even as the Yishuv poured its energy into the British war effort it was forced to swallow degradation by the British. A series of unbelievably horrible events occurred which rankled in the hearts of even the most benevolent Jews.

A pathetic, fifty-foot Danube river boat named the *Struma* crept into Istanbul loaded with nearly eight hundred frantic Jews trying to escape from Europe. The boat was unsafe and the people in dire straits. Yishuv Central literally begged the British for visas. The British refused. In fact, they turned heavy diplomatic pressure on the Turkish government to get the *Struma* out of Istanbul. Turkish police boarded the *Struma* and towed it through the Bosporus and cut it adrift in the Black Sea without food, water, or fuel. The *Struma* sank. Seven hundred and ninety-nine human beings drowned. One survived.

Two battered steamers reached Palestine with two thousand refugees and the British quickly ordered them transferred to the *Patria* for exile to Mauritius, an island east of Africa. The *Patria* sank off Palestine's shores in sight of Haifa, and hundreds of refugees drowned.

And so it went—the British clung to the White Paper— the Arabs had to be kept calm!

The war continued badly for the British. By the end of 1941 Palestinian Jews had made their way into fighting units despite General Haven-Hurst's forebodings, for the British were desperate and they were getting no manpower at all from the Arabs. As the Arabs sat, fifty thousand of the cream of the Yishuv wore British uniforms.

With western Europe crushed, German barges waited in the English Channel to invade. England had her back to the wall! And this was the moment of English glory! The Germans, who had beaten the Russians and the Greeks and the Yugoslavs, stood and balked at the showdown with those pale, scrawny wonders—the dogged Englishman. They feared the English as they feared no others.

As England had carved up the Ottoman Empire, so now the Germans prepared to carve up the British Empire. Rommel's powerful Afrika Korps was building toward a series of strikes that would throw the British out of the Middle East and open a gateway to the Orient and India.

Haj Amin el Husseini moved from Lebanon in search of greener pastures. He landed in Bagdad, Iraq, nominally a British ally but in not much more than name. In Bagdad he was greeted as a great martyr of Islam. He staged a coup with a gang of Iraqi army officers to deliver Iraq to the Germans. The plot failed. But only at the last moment did the British prevent it from succeeding by sending the Arab Legion in to control the country.

Haj Amin fled again. This time he went to Germany where Adolf Hitler greeted him personally as a brother. The two madmen could work through each other for mutual personal profit. The Mufti saw in Germany's military plans a new opportunity to seize power over the entire Arab world. Hitler needed the Mufti to show what a warm and tender friendship could exist between Arab and German. As a Nazi agent, Haj Amin broadcasted over and over again from

Berlin to the Arab world; what he had to say he had said many, many times before.

"O, Arabs, rise and avenge your martyrs . . . I, Mufti of Palestine, declare this war as a holy war against the British yoke of tyranny. . . . I know the hatred you feel for them . . . I know you Moslems are convinced the British and the Jews are enemies of Islam and plot against the precepts of the Koran . . . the Jews will take our holy Islamic institutions . . . they even now claim a Temple occupies the site of our most holy Mosque of Omar and surely they will desecrate it as they have tried before . . . kill Jews wherever you find them for this pleases God, history, and religion. This saves your honor . . . God is with you . . . perish Judea!"

As the Mufti spoke, the Arab world seemed to heed his words.

Syria and Lebanon were in the hands of Vichy French, and German matériel was pouring in to pave the way for an invasion of Palestine and Egypt.

The Egyptian chief of staff sold secrets to the Germans. King Farouk of Egypt refused to give the British a single soldier for the defense of Egypt against Rommel. Further plots hatched in Iraq.

The only avowed friend of the Allies was the old despot, Ibn Saud, who had been bought with American dollars. But Ibn Saud did not so much as offer a single camel to the British Eighth Army, which was fighting for its life.

In all the Middle East the Allied Powers had but one true fighting friend—the Yishuv!

Rommel, flushed with victory in Libya, stood poised to break through to Alexandria where German flags were being prepared to welcome the "liberators."

On the Russian front, the Wehrmacht stood before the gates of Stalingrad!

This was the Allies' darkest hour.

The prime target of the Germans was the Suez Canal, Egypt, and Palestine—the solar plexus of the British Empire. A break-through at Stalingrad could form another arm of a pincer movement to sweep through the Caucasus Mountains and open the doors of India and the Orient.

At last the British came to Yishuv Central and asked the Jews to form guerrilla units to cover the retreat of the British and harass the German occupation. This guerrilla force was called the Palmach. It was later to become the striking arm of the Haganah.

Ari Ben Canaan sat down for supper one evening.

"I enlisted in the British Army today," he announced quietly.

The next day Ari reported to *kibbutz* Beth Alonim, House of the Oaks, where youths from all over Palestine had assembled to organize the Palmach.

CHAPTER EIGHTEEN: *Kibbutz* Beth Alonim stood at the foot of Mount Tabor in the center of the Jezreel Valley. Ari was given a commission in the British Army and placed in charge of operations of the guerrilla units of boys and girls, most of whom were in their teens. Most of the officers were "old-timers" in their mid-twenties like Ari.

Many of the former Raider Unit men joined the Palmach to indoctrinate the youngsters in the methods of Major P. P. Malcolm.

The troops wore no uniforms nor was there rank below the officers, and boys and girls were treated exactly the same. They were trained with the same sense of Biblical destiny that Malcolm had given his fighters.

Two of the soldiers showed such promise and leadership that they were advanced to lead units directly under Ari. One was a heavy-set *kibbutznik* from Galilee. His name was Zev Gilboa. He wore a big black mustache which later became the badge of a male Palmachnik. The other was a small intense young student from Jerusalem named David Ben Ami. Neither David nor Zev was yet twenty.

One day they were paid a visit by General Haven-Hurst. He was a tall thin blond man in his early fifties. As he inspected the camp he was aware of the coldness which greeted his presence. After the inspection, Haven-Hurst asked Ari to report to the camp's headquarters.

As Ari entered the office, the two men nodded stiffly, neither concealing his dislike for the other.

"Sit down, Lieutenant Ben Canaan," Haven-Hurst said. "You are to be commended on your work here with these Palmach troops."

"Thank you, sir."

"Matter of fact, I've been studying your record . . . or your case history, if you will. You've been a busy chap."

"The conditions of my environment and the unfortunate circumstances of my birth have dictated it," Ari said. "I am a farmer at heart."

Haven-Hurst took the rebuff without showing it.

"My main purpose for coming to Beth Alonim today was to ask you to volunteer for a special assignment. I know that when you enlisted it was on the proviso that you could train Palmach troops, but we feel this is urgent enough to alter that."

"I am a soldier in the British Army, General Haven-Hurst. I will accept any assignment given me."

"Good. Briefly, here is what it consists of. There has been a large German build-up in Syria. We feel they may attempt an invasion of Palestine this spring."

Ari nodded.

"We are not at war with the Vichy French and we cannot invade Syria, but we do have sufficient Free French forces to do the job, provided we get flawless intelligence. We have selected you for this job because you know Syria and Lebanon from your Ha Mishmar days, and also because of your mastery of Arabic. We want you to reassemble those lads who were at Ha Mishmar with you and return there to use it as a reconnoitering base. When the invasion begins there will also be special assignments. There will be a captain's rank in this for you."

"I see one problem, sir."

"Yes?"

"A great number of my comrades from Ha Mishmar have been thrown into jail by the British."

Haven-Hurst's face turned crimson. "We will arrange releases."

"Yes, sir. One more thing, sir. I have two men here who are exceptional soldiers. I would like to take them to Ha Mishmar with me and have them transferred into the British Army."

"Very well," Haven-Hurst said, "take them with you."

Ari walked to the door. "An invasion of Syria at this time is excellent strategy, sir. It will give the British Eighth Army plenty of room to retreat to India."

Haven-Hurst glared at the Jew. "I suppose it is unnecessary to say, Ben Canaan, that you and I will be on opposite sides of the fence one day."

"We already are, sir."

Ari left Beth Alonim with Zev Gilboa and David Ben Ami as his sergeants and returned to Ha Mishmar on the hill which held such bitter memories for him. Fifty of the original Haganah gang were assembled—some from many parts of the world where they had been serving in the British forces.

Using Ha Mishmar as headquarters, Ari's patrols worked all the way up to Damascus. Extreme caution was needed, for the invasion was to be a complete surprise. Ari's basic method was simple. Most of his people spoke fluent Arabic and were familiar with the territory. He sent them out during the day, dressed as Arabs, and they merely walked along the roads gathering information. Although his intelligence was

299

proving flawless, Ari wanted to get right inside Damascus and Beirut. This was a touchy job, and Ari reckoned it called for an individual foray. The one selected had to be able to move perfectly without raising suspicion. Ari checked with Haganah and they sent him a seventeen-year-old boy named Joab Yarkoni.

Yarkoni was a Moroccan Jew born in Casablanca and could indeed pass for an Arab anywhere. He was small, with saucer-like flashing black eyes and an overabundant sense of humor.

In Casablanca he and his family had lived in a *mellah,* the Oriental-African version of a ghetto. These Oriental and African Jews had little in common culturally with their Russian or German counterparts. Most of them were descendants of ancestors who had fled the Spanish Inquisition. Many still had Spanish names.

In some Arab lands the Jews were treated with a measure of fairness and near equality. Of course, no Jew could be entirely equal to a Moslem. A thousand years before, when Islam swept the world, Jews had been among the most honored of the Arab citizens. They were the court doctors, the philosophers, and the artisans—the top of the Arab society. In the demise of the Arab world that followed the Mongol wars, the demise of the Jews was worse.

There were Jews in Bagdad and Cairo and Damascus and Fez and Kurdistan and Casablanca, throughout the coast of Africa and deep into countries of the Middle East.

The Moslems never went to the extremes of the Christians in the matter of killing Jews. Arab riots were always kept within reasonable bounds—a few dozen murders at a time.

Joab Yarkoni and his family had escaped the *mellah* of Casablanca when he was but a youngster. His family settled down in a *kibbutz* in Samaria that hugged the sea. It was at Caesarea and called Sdot Yam, Fields of the Sea. Many illegal boats beached near Caesarea and it was here that Joab first went to work for Aliyah Bet as a gun runner when he was only twelve years of age.

When he was fifteen he took it upon himself to try a daring feat that spread his fame throughout the Yishuv. Joab walked from Sdot Yam with a donkey to Bagdad. There he stole some of the precious Iraqi date-palm saplings and smuggled them into Palestine. The saplings were sent to Shoshanna *kibbutz* on the Sea of Galilee and were instrumental in opening an entire new export crop for the Yishuv.

Ari's job was easy for young Joab. He walked to Damascus to Beirut to Tyre and returned to Ha Mishmar within three weeks. His information confirmed everything they already knew and further located Vichy strength nearly to a man.

Free French Forces moved quietly into Palestine, to the Galilee, and deployed for the invasion.

Ari's fifty men were bolstered by a special hand-picked group of forty Australians, experts in mines, automatic weapons, and explosives.

This ninety-man force was split into three units of thirty each. Each unit was given a special assignment to cross into Lebanon and Syria ahead of the invasion, advance and hold key roads and bridges against a counterattack until the main body could reach them.

Ari's force had the most dangerous of the missions. He was to lead his thirty men right up along the Lebanese coast, penetrate close to a Vichy garrison, and keep them from getting to half a dozen vital mountain bridges which could halt the Free French advance. Ari took Joab, Zev, and David with him. He had sixteen more Jews and ten Australians.

His unit moved out twenty-four hours before the invasion and sped up the coast with beautiful ease, for they knew every inch of the way. They passed the six crucial bridges one by one.

They stopped three miles from the Vichy garrison of Fort Henried and in a mountain pass mined the roads, set in their machine guns, and waited for the invasion to reach them.

As so often happens in a large-scale battle, an error was made. How, why, who made it is not so important after it occurs. The eastern arm of the invasion crossed from Trans-Jordan into Syria twelve hours ahead of H-Hour. As they moved toward Damascus they tipped off the entire operation.

For Ari it meant he would have to hold his mountain pass for twelve hours plus the additional three or four hours it would take for the main body to reach him.

Within a few hours after the error was made the Vichyites had massed two battalions with tanks and artillery at Fort Henried and started down the coastal road to blow up the mountain bridges.

As soon as Ari saw them coming he realized something had gone wrong. Quickly he dispatched David and Zev back to Palestine to bring help.

The Vichy troops marched blindly into the pass and were pulverized by explosions and crossfire from both sides of the hill. They fell back, reassembled, and sent artillery fire into the pass.

Six unbelievable hours passed before David and Zev came back with a battalion of Free French troops.

All the bridges were intact. There was no break-through. The pass was littered with over four hundred dead Vichyites who had tried to break Ari's position.

Five men of Ari's force were alive when help arrived. Ari Ben Canaan himself was at death's door. His back was filled with shrapnel, two bullets were lodged in his body, and his leg and nose were broken.

The Free French went on to complete the invasion of Syria.

For Ari Ben Canaan the war was over. He was taken back to Palestine for a long slow recovery. The British promoted him to major and he was decorated for his stand at the mountain pass.

Ari had played his role for Allied victory. So had the Yishuv.

Members of the Yishuv were in suicide squads that helped capture Tobruk and Bardia. Later a battalion of Palestinians was at the epic defense of Tobruk.

They fought in Italy and in Greece and in Crete and in the Lowlands. They numbered thousands in the Royal Air Force. They ran the "death" patrol along the Mediterranean coast. The home guard kept the Arabs under control within Palestine. They fought in the desert in the captures of Sidi Barrani, Sollum, and Fort Capuzzo.

Jewish suicide units were picked for their valor in the campaigns in Eritrea and Ethiopia. Three thousand of the Yishuv joined the Free Forces of Czechoslovakia, Holland, France—and even Poland. A suicide force of Jews went out to destroy the oil refinery at Tripoli. Every member perished. Jews were used by the British for special spying missions. German Jews were dressed in German uniforms and worked right in Rommel's headquarters. Jews guarded the Mosul oil fields against continued Arab attempts to disrupt production.

When the British needed spies in the Balkans they turned to the Jews and trained them as parachutists. They reasoned that any Jew would be protected by the rest of the Jews in the country where he was dropped. Several were parachuted —few returned. One girl, Hanna Senesh, from Joab Yarkoni's *kibbutz* was dropped into Hungary and captured. She became a martyr by refusing to her death to break under the cruelest Nazi torture.

The Yishuv covered itself with glory. Just as in World War I the British glorified the Arab revolt—so they tried to hide the efforts of the Yishuv in World War II. No country gave with so much vitality to the war. But the British Government did not want the Jews to use this as a bargaining point for their homeland aspirations later on. Whitehall and Chatham House kept the Yishuv's war effort one of the best secrets of the war.

Rommel never reached Alexandria—they never broke the defenses of Stalingrad.

As the tide turned in favor of the British the Arabs no longer looked for the Germans to liberate them. Quickly they "declared war" on Germany. The main purpose behind the Arab declarations of war was to gain a vote at the peace conferences and block the Zionists who had no vote but only the blood of their sons to show for their efforts.

Despite the Yishuv's magnificent record the British did not revoke the White Paper. Despite the Arab treachery and the fact that they did not raise a finger for victory they did not revoke it. Even with the ghastly news of the murder of six million Jews the British would not allow the survivors in.

The Haganah grew restless. Its ranks were filled with experienced soldiers. But it was the Maccabees who called off the truce! A series of terror bombings shook Palestine from end to end and again sent the British into their Taggart forts. The Maccabees, now numbering in the thousands, blew up one British installation after another.

General Haven-Hurst went after the Maccabees. With surprising swiftness he snared and deported several hundred Maccabee leaders to the Sudan. But Akiva's avenging warriors were not deterred.

Haven-Hurst ordered newly captured Maccabees to be lashed. The Maccabees retorted by catching British soldiers and whipping them in public.

Maccabees were hanged. British soldiers were caught and hanged. A dozen Maccabee bullets and grenades found their mark on a dozen of the more outspoken anti-Jewish officers.

Violent and sordid murders were perpetrated by the Arabs in answer to the Maccabees. The Holy Land reeled under the terror.

Haj Amin el Husseini was placed on the list of war criminals by the Yugoslav government. He had made himself spiritual head of the Yugoslav Moslems who had fought for the German Army. He was placed under arrest in France. The British, however, wanted El Husseini alive and ready to stir up trouble when they needed him, so they helped him escape to Egypt where he was welcomed as a Moslem hero. In Palestine his nephew Jemal seized control of the Arab community.

A new phase of history was bringing the United States into focus as the new power in the Middle East. In addition, since most of the European Jewish communities had been wiped out, by mere process of elimination Jews and others in the United States became the world leaders of the Zionist movement.

With America's rise, the British proposed a joint Anglo-

American inquiry into the Palestine situation. This joint committee made another exhaustive survey of the Arabs and the Yishuv. They went to Europe to the DP camps. They came to the only human conclusion possible—"100,000 JEWS MUST BE ALLOWED INTO PALESTINE AT ONCE."

The British balked.

It would only be considered if the Haganah and Palmach were disbanded at once! Preposterous! The British found a dozen more reasons not to follow the commission's recommendations.

The Arabs were as relentless as the Maccabees. Throughout the Arab world there were riots and protests against the Anglo-American commission.

At last the Yishuv Central had had enough. They sent the Palmach and Haganah on a series of damaging raids on British positions.

The British poured in tens of thousands of front-line troops and turned the country into a police state. In a massive roundup they arrested several hundred prominent leaders of the Yishuv and threw them into Latrun prison.

In a masterful countermove, the Haganah blew up every frontier bridge in and out of Palestine in a single night.

The Aliyah Bet was putting more and more pressure on the British blockade.

Finally the British Foreign Minister burst forth with an anti-Jewish tirade and proclaimed all further immigration stopped.

The answer to this came from the Maccabees. The British had their main headquarters in the right wing of the King David Hotel in Jerusalem. This hotel was in the new city with its rear and gardens facing the wall of the old city. A dozen Maccabees, dressed as Arabs, delivered several dozen enormous milk cans to the basement of the hotel. The milk cans were placed under the right wing of the hotel beneath British headquarters. The cans were filled with dynamite. They set the timing devices, cleared the area, and phoned the British a warning to get out of the building. The British scoffed at the idea. This time the Maccabees were playing a prank. They merely wanted to make fools of the British. Surely they would not dare attack British headquarters!

In a few minutes there was a blast heard across the breadth of Palestine. The right wing of the King David Hotel was blown to smithereens!

CHAPTER NINETEEN: The *Exodus* was declared fit and ready for the run to Palestine.

Ari set the sailing time as the morning after the Chanukah party which the management of the Dome Hotel had arranged on the hotel terrace.

Three hundred places were set. The small Jewish community of Cyprus and the crew of the *Exodus* sat at a long head table. There was tremendous gaiety as the children rushed to the terrace dressed in new clothing and were deluged with gifts from the people of Cyprus and soldiers from the garrison. The children took one gift each for themselves and marked the rest for the detention camps at Caraolos. The tables were bulging with food and the children squealed with delight. The terrible ordeal of the hunger strike was behind them; they had carried their burden like adults and now they could act like happy children with complete abandon. All around the terrace dozens of curious Greeks and British soldiers watched the celebration.

Karen looked around frantically for Kitty and lit up when she saw her some distance away, standing with Mark Parker by the rail.

"Come on, Kitty," Karen called, "There is a place for you here."

"It's your party," Kitty answered. "I'll just watch."

When everyone had opened his present, David Ben Ami stood at the head table. The terrace became very still as he began to speak. Only the steady shush of the sea could be heard behind him.

"Tonight we celebrate the first day of Chanukah," David said. "We celebrate this day in honor of Judah Maccabee and his brave brothers and his band of faithful men who came from the hills of Judea to do combat with the Greeks who enslaved our people."

Some of the youngsters applauded.

"Judah Maccabee had a small band of men and they had no real right fighting so large and powerful an enemy as the Greeks, who ruled the entire world. But Judah Maccabee had faith. He believed that the one true God would show him the way. Judah was a wonderful fighter. Time and again he tricked the Greeks; his men were the greatest of warriors, for the faith of God was in their hearts. The Maccabees stormed Jerusalem and captured it and drove out the Greeks of Asia Minor, who ruled that area of the world."

A riot of applause.

"Judah entered the Temple and his warriors tore down the idol of Zeus and again dedicated the Temple to the one true God. The same God who helped us all in our battle with the British."

As David continued with the story of the rebirth of the

Jewish nation, Kitty Fremont listened. She looked at Karen and at Dov Landau—and she looked at Mark and she lowered her eyes. Then she felt someone standing alongside her. It was Brigadier Bruce Sutherland.

"Tonight we will light the first candle of the Menorah. Each night we will light another candle until there are eight. We call Chanukah the feast of lights."

David Ben Ami lit the first candle and the children said "oh" and "ah."

"Tomorrow night we shall light the second Chanukah candle at sea and the night after we shall light the third one in Eretz Israel."

David placed a small skullcap on his head and opened the Bible. " *'He will not suffer thy foot to be moved; he that keepth thee will not slumber.'* "

Kitty's eyes came to rest on the head table. She looked at them—Zev Gilboa the farmer from the Galilee, and Joab Yarkoni the Moroccan Jew, and David Ben Ami, the scholar from Jerusalem. Her eyes stopped at Ari Ben Canaan. His eyes were rimmed with weariness now that he had had a chance to relax from his ordeal. David set the Bible down and continued to speak from memory.

" *'Behold!'* " David said, " *'he that keepeth Israel shall neither slumber nor sleep.'* "

An icy chill passed through Kitty Fremont's body. Her eyes were fixed on the tired face of Ari Ben Canaan. *"Behold . . . he that keepeth Israel shall neither slumber nor sleep."*

The ancient motors of the *Exodus* groaned as she slid back into the center of Kyrenia Harbor and she turned and pointed out to sea in the direction of Palestine.

At dawn of the second day everyone sighted land at once. "Palestine!"

"Eretz Israel!"

A hysteria of laughing and crying and singing and joy burst from the children.

The little salvage tug came within sight of land and the electrifying news spread through the Yishuv. The children who had brought the mighty British Empire to its knees were arriving!

The *Exodus* sputtered into Haifa Harbor amid a blast of welcoming horns and whistles. The salute spread from Haifa to the villages and the *kibbutzim* and the *moshavim* and all the way to Jerusalem to the Yishuv Central building and back again to Haifa.

Twenty-five thousand Jews poured onto the Haifa dock to cheer the creaky little boat. The Palestine Philharmonic

Orchestra played the Jewish anthem—"Hatikvah," the Hope.

Tears streaked down the cheeks of Karen Hansen Clement as she looked up into Kitty's face.

The *Exodus* had come home!

BOOK 3

An Eye for an Eye

> ... thou shalt give life for life, eye for eye, tooth
> for tooth, hand for hand, foot for foot, burning
> for burning.

*The word of God as given to
Moses in Exodus*

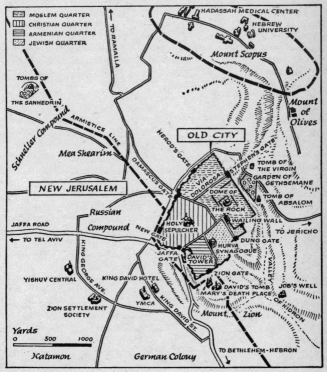

MOSLEM QUARTER
CHRISTIAN QUARTER
ARMENIAN QUARTER
JEWISH QUARTER

HADASSAH MEDICAL CENTER
HEBREW UNIVERSITY

TO RAMALLA

Mount Scopus

TOMBS OF THE SANHEDRIN

ARMISTICE LINE

Schneller Compound

Mea Shearim

DAMASCUS GATE

HEROD'S GATE

OLD CITY

Mount of Olives

NEW JERUSALEM

STEPHEN'S GATE

TOMB OF THE VIRGIN

GARDEN OF GETHSEMANE

VIA DOLOROSA

DOME OF THE ROCK

TOMB OF ABSALOM

Russian

Compound

JAFFA ROAD

NEW GATE

HOLY SEPULCHER

WAILING WALL

TO JERICHO

← TO TEL AVIV

KING GEORGE AVE.

JAFFA GATE

DAVID'S TOWER

HURVA SYNAGOGUE

DUNG GATE

VALLEY OF KIDRON

YISHUV CENTRAL

KING DAVID HOTEL

ZION GATE

JOB'S WELL

ZION SETTLEMENT SOCIETY

YMCA

KING DAVID ST.

DAVID'S TOMB

MARY'S DEATH PLACE

Mount Zion

Yards
0   500   1000

Katamon

German Colony

TO BETHLEHEM-HEBRON

CHAPTER ONE: A line of silver and blue buses from the Palestine bus co-operative, the "Egged" Company, awaited the children on the docks. The official celebration was kept to a quick minimum. The children were loaded aboard the buses and whisked out of the harbor area, convoyed by British armored vehicles. The band played and the crowd cheered as they rolled out of sight.

Karen tugged her window open and shouted to Kitty, but Kitty could not hear her over the din. The buses disappeared and the crowd dispersed. In fifteen minutes the dock was deserted except for a gang of longshoremen and a few British soldiers on guard duty.

Kitty stood motionless by the rail of the *Exodus*, stunned by the sudden strangeness. It was hard to realize where she was. She looked at Haifa. It was beautiful, with that special beauty that belonged to cities built on hills and around a bay. Close to the waterfront was the Arab sector with crowded clusters of buildings. The Jewish sector sprawled all over the long fingerlike slope of Mount Carmel. Kitty looked to her left, just past Haifa, and saw the futuristic shape of the tank and chimney buildings of the immense Haifa oil refinery, the terminus of the lines from the Mosul fields. At a nearby dock she saw a dozen dilapidated, rickety ships of the Aliyah Bet which, like the *Exodus,* had managed to reach Palestine.

Zev, David, and Joab interrupted Kitty's thoughts as they said good-bys and offered thanks and hope that they would see her again. And then they, too, were gone and Kitty was alone.

"Pretty town, isn't it?"

Kitty turned around. Ari Ben Canaan was standing behind her. "We always bring our guests into Palestine through Haifa. It gives them a good first impression."

"Where are the children going?" she asked.

"They will be dispersed to a half dozen Youth Aliyah Centers. Some of the centers are located on a *kibbutz.* Other centers have their own villages. In a few days I will be able to tell you where Karen is."

"I'll be grateful."

"What are your plans, Kitty?"

She laughed sardonically. "I was just asking myself the same thing, along with a dozen other questions. I'm a stranger in town, Mr. Ben Canaan, and I feel a little foolish at the moment, asking myself how I got here. Oh, Good Nurse Fremont has a solid profession in which there is always a shortage. I'll find a place, somewhere."

"Why don't you let me help you get situated?"

"I suppose you're rather busy. I'm always able to get along."

"Listen to me, now. I think Youth Aliyah would be perfect for you. The head of the organization is a close friend of mine. I'll arrange an appointment for you in Jerusalem."

"That's very kind but I don't want to impose."

"Nonsense. It's the very least . . . If you can tolerate my company for a few days I will be happy to drive you to Jerusalem. I must go to Tel Aviv on business first, but it's just as well . . . it will give me a chance to set your appointment."

"I don't want you to feel that you are obligated to do this."

"I'm doing it because I want to," Ari said.

Kitty wanted to give a sigh of relief. She *was* nervous about being alone in a strange land. She smiled and thanked him.

"Good," Ari said. "We will have to stay in Haifa tonight because of the road curfew. Pack one bag with what you will need to keep you for a few days. If you carry too much with you the British will be going through your suitcases every five minutes. I'll have the rest of your things sealed and held at customs."

After clearances Ari ordered a taxi and drove up Mount Carmel into the Jewish section, which spread through the hills on the mountainside. Near the top they stopped at a small pension set in a pine grove.

"It's better to stay up here. I know too many people and they won't let me alone for a minute if we stay in the center of town. Now you rest up. I'll go down the hill and scare up an auto. I'll be back by dinner."

That evening Ari took Kitty to a restaurant on the very top of the Carmel, commanding a view of the entire area. The sight beneath was breath-taking. The whole hillside was alive with green trees and half-hidden brownstone houses and apartment buildings, all done in a square Arabic style. The weird-looking oil refinery appeared to be but a dot from this height, and as it turned dark a golden string of lights ran down the twisting road from Har Ha-Carmel into the Arab section by the waterfront.

Kitty was flushed with excitement and pleased with Ari's sudden show of attention. She was surprised by the modernness of Jewish Haifa. Why, it was far more modern than Athens or Salonika! Much of the strangeness went away when she was addressed in English by the waiter and a half dozen people who knew Ari and stopped at their table to exchange greetings.

312

They sipped brandy at the end of the meal and Kitty became solemn, intent on the panorama below.

"Are you still wondering what you are doing here?"

"Very much. It doesn't seem quite real."

"You will find that we are quite civilized and I can even be charming—sometimes. You know, I never have properly thanked you."

"You don't have to. You are thanking me very nicely. I can only remember one other place so lovely as this."

"That must be San Francisco?"

"Have you been there, Ari?"

"No. All Americans say that Haifa reminds them of San Francisco."

It was fully dark and lights twinkled on all over the Carmel hillside. A small orchestra played some light dinner music and Ari poured Kitty another brandy and they touched glasses.

Suddenly the music stopped. All conversation halted.

With startling speed a truckload of British troops pulled to a stop before the restaurant and the place was cordoned off. Six soldiers led by a captain entered and looked around. They began to move among the tables, stopping at several and demanding to see identification papers.

"This is just routine," Ari whispered. "You'll get used to it."

The captain in charge of the detail stared at Ari's table, then walked over to it. "If it isn't Ari Ben Canaan," the captain said sarcastically. "We haven't had your picture on the boards for a long time. I hear you've been making mischief elsewhere."

"Evening, Sergeant," Ari said. "I'd introduce you if I could remember your name."

The captain grinned through clenched teeth. "Well, I remember yours. We're watching you, Ben Canaan. Your old cell at Acre jail is lonesome for you. Who knows, maybe the high commissioner will be smart this time and give you a rope instead." The captain gave a mock salute and walked on.

"Well," Kitty said, "what a lovely welcome to Palestine. He was certainly a nasty person."

Ari leaned close to Kitty and spoke into her ear. "He is Captain Allan Bridges. He is one of the best friends the Haganah has. He keeps us advised on every Arab and British move in the Haifa area. That was all for appearance."

Kitty shook her head, bewildered. The patrol left with two Jews whose papers didn't appear in order. The orchestra harassed them with a chorus of "God Save the King."

The lorry drove away and in a moment it was as though nothing had happened, but Kitty was a little dazed by the suddenness of it and astonished by the calm of the people.

"You learn to live with tension after a while," Ari said, watching her. "You'll get used to it. It is a country filled with angry, emotional people. After a while you won't know what to do when you get one of those rare weeks of peace and quiet. Don't be sorry you came just when you are getting . . ."

Ari's speech was cut off by a shock wave that ran through the restaurant, rattling the windows and jarring some dishes from the tables. In a second they saw a huge orange ball of flame push angrily into the sky. Another series of explosions followed, shaking the place to its foundations.

Shouts arose: "The oil refinery!" . . . "They've got the refinery!" . . . *"Maccabee raid!"*

Ari grabbed Kitty's hand. "Let's get out of here. In ten minutes the whole Carmel Valley will be crawling with British soldiers."

The café was emptied in seconds. Ari led Kitty out quickly. Below them oil was flaming madly. The entire city screamed with the frantic siren shrieks of speeding fire trucks and British patrols.

Kitty lay awake half the night trying to comprehend the sudden violent things she had seen. She was glad that Ari had been with her. Would she get used to living with this? She was too bewildered to think about it, but at the moment she felt her coming to Palestine was a sorry mistake.

The next morning the oil refinery was still blazing. A pall of thick smoke hung over the entire Haifa area. The information spread that the raid was Maccabee terrorist work. It had been led by Ben Moshe—Son of Moses—the Maccabee field commander under Akiva, and formerly a professor at the Hebrew University before he rose in Maccabee ranks. The raid was part of a double-pronged Maccabee action. The other strike was against the Lydda airdrome in another part of Palestine, where the terrorists destroyed six million dollars' worth of Spitfire fighter planes on the ground. The action was the Maccabees' own way of welcoming the *Exodus*.

Ari had been able to acquire a small Italian Fiat, a 1933 model. The drive to Tel Aviv took only a few hours under normal conditions. Inasmuch as he had never known conditions to be normal he suggested they depart Haifa early. They drove down from the Carmel and took the coastal road along the edge of Samaria. Kitty was impressed by the greenness of the fields of the *kibbutzim* near the sea. Their color showed more brilliantly by contrast to the drabness of the hills and the dulling glare of the sun. A few minutes' drive from Haifa they met the first roadblock. Ari had warned Kitty to expect it. She watched his reactions. He was apparently not at all annoyed, despite the fact that many of the soldiers knew him and taunted him with the reminder that his amnesty was only temporary.

Ari left the main road and drove to the Caesarea ruins on the sea. A lunch had been packed for them at the pension and they ate it on the ancient sea wall. Ari pointed to the Sdot Yam—Fields of the Sea—*kibbutz* where Joab Yarkoni lived and where he had spent much time with the Aliyah Bet when they beached the illegal runners during the 1936-39 riots. Ari showed Kitty how the Arabs had built their town on ruins, some Roman, some Crusader. The Arabs were experts in building on other people's civilizations and had, in fact, constructed only one wholly new city in all of Palestine in a thousand years. Some of the magnificent Roman statuary and columns had been dragged off from Caesarea and could be found in Arab homes throughout the Samarian and Sharon districts.

After lunch they continued south toward Tel Aviv. The traffic was light. There was only an occasional bus load of either Arabs or Jews or the ever-present donkey cart. Every now and then a speeding, siren-screaming British convoy raced past them. As they passed Arab sections Kitty noticed the contrast of these villages and lands. The Arab woman toiled in the fields and the Arab fields were stony and drab. The women walked along the roadside encased in cumbersome robes with enormous loads balanced on their heads. The coffeehouses along the road were filled with listless men sitting motionless or lying down playing backgammon. Below Zichron Yakov—Memory of Jacob—they passed the first barbwire-enclosed ominous-looking Taggart fort. At Hadera, a bit farther, they came to another, and thereafter they seemed to pop up at every town and crossroad.

Beyond Hadera the land around the Plain of Sharon was even more lush and fertile. They drove between enormous archways of Australian eucalyptus trees.

"Everything you see was waste just twenty-five years ago," Ari said.

In the afternoon they entered Tel Aviv—the Hill of Spring.

Along the Mediterranean coast arose this city so white it dazzled the eye in the afternoon sun. Tel Aviv was like frosting on a cake. Ari drove on broad, tree-lined boulevards between rows of ultramodern apartment houses. The city was alive with bustle and movement. Kitty liked Tel Aviv the instant she saw it.

On Hayarkon Street, right on the sea, Ari checked into Gat Rimon Hotel.

In late afternoon all the shops reopened after the siesta period. Ari and Kitty strolled down Allenby Road. Kitty had to change some currency, purchase a few things, and satisfy a lot of curiosity. Beyond the Mograbi Theater and plaza the road was filled with small shops, the honking and rushing of buses, cars, and people. Kitty had to see every last shop. There were a dozen or more book stores, and she paused to gaze at the cryptic Hebrew letters. They walked and walked, up to Rothschild Boulevard past the main business district. Here was the older town where Tel Aviv had begun as an outgrowth of Jaffa. The closer they came to the Arab city the more run-down the buildings and shops became. Walking along the streets connecting the two cities, Kitty felt as though she were walking back in time. The surroundings grew dirtier and more odorous and the shops grew smaller and shabbier with each step. They circled back to Tel Aviv through a market place common to both Jews and Arabs. The narrow street was a mass of haggling people crowded around the stalls. They returned down the opposite side of Allenby Road, back to the Mograbi plaza and turned into another wide, tree-lined street. This was Ben Yehuda Street and it was filled with sidewalk cafés. Each café had its own distinctive flavor and its own distinctive clientele. There was a café for the gathering of lawyers and there was a café of the socialist politicians and a café of artists and a businessmen's café. There was a café where fellow travelers of the terrorists hung out and there was a café of old retired folk playing never-ending chess games. All the cafés of Ben Yehuda Street were filled and were bursting with chatter and arguments.

The news hawkers of the tiny, four-page newspapers shouted out in Hebrew of the Maccabee raids on Lydda and the Haifa refinery and of the arrival of the *Exodus*. There was a steady stream of people flowing by. There were Orientals in mideastern habit and there were well-groomed women in the latest of fashions from a dozen European countries. Mostly, there were native men in khaki pants and white shirts opened at the necks. They wore thin chain necklaces with a Star of David or some Hebrew pendant. Most of them sported the black mustache which was a trademark of the native born. They were a rugged lot. Many were in the blue of a *kibbutz* with sandaled feet. The native women were tall, angular, and high breasted in plain dresses or slacks or shorts. There was an aggressiveness and pride about them, even in their walk.

Then Ben Yehuda Street became quiet.

It was the same sudden quiet that Kitty remembered from the night before at the restaurant in Haifa.

A British armored sound truck inched down the middle of Ben Yehuda Street. Tight-lipped Tommies manned machine guns on the car.

316

"ATTENTION ALL JEWS. THE COMMANDING GENERAL HAS ORDERED A CURFEW. ALL JEWS MUST BE OFF THE STREET BY DARK. ATTENTION ALL JEWS. THE COMMANDING GENERAL HAS ORDERED A CURFEW. ALL JEWS MUST BE OFF THE STREET BY DARK."

A ripple of applause and laughter broke out from the onlookers.

"Watch it, Tommy," someone called. "The next intersection is mined."

When the trucks had passed, the scene quickly returned to normal.

"Let's get back to the hotel," Kitty said.

"I told you you'll get so that you won't be able to live without excitement inside a month."

"I'll never get used to it, Ari."

They returned to the hotel with their arms filled with Kitty's purchases. After cocktails in the small quiet bar there was dinner on the terrace overlooking the sea. Kitty could see the sweep of the coast line where the new city of Tel Aviv ran into the ancient city of Jaffa, the oldest port in the world.

"Thank you for a very nice day, British patrols and roadblocks notwithstanding."

"You'll have to forgive me," Ari said. "I must leave after dinner for a while."

"What about the curfew?"

"That only applies to Jews," Ari said.

Ari left Kitty and drove from Tel Aviv to the adjoining suburb town of Ramat Gan—the Hill Garden. It was a contrast to the apartment-house city of Tel Aviv in that it was a town of individual homes set in lawns and trees and gardens. The houses were of stucco with red tiled roofs, and they ranged from cottages to huge villas. Ari parked the car and walked about for more than a half hour to make certain he was not being followed.

He came to Montefiore Street 22, a large villa owned by a Dr. Y. Tamir. Dr. Tamir answered the knock, greeted Ari with a warm handshake, and led him downstairs to the basement.

The home of Tamir was Haganah headquarters.

The cellar held munitions and arms, and a printing press which ground out leaflets in Arabic warning the Arabs to remain calm and keep the peace. In another section of the basement a girl spoke in Arabic into a tape recording machine, repeating the warning of the leaflets. The tape would later be transmitted over the secret mobile radio station, Kol Israel—the Voice of Israel. The manufacturing of hand grenades and the assembly of homemade Sten guns were also among the activites of the underground headquarters.

All activity stopped as Dr. Tamir appeared with Ari. The latter was surrounded and congratulated on the *Exodus* affair; questions were fired at him from all sides.

"Later, later," Dr. Tamir pleaded.

"I must see Avidan," Ari said.

He made his way past the stacked cases of rifles to the door of a secluded office and knocked upon it.

"Yes?"

Ari opened the door and stood before the bald-headed, squat farmer who commanded the underground army. Avidan looked up from the papers on his rickety desk and burst into a smile. "Ari! *Shalom!*" He sprang up and threw his arms around Ari's neck, shoved him into a chair, closed the door, and slapped Ari on the back with the force of a pile driver. "So good to see you, Ari! You did a first-class job on the British. Where are the boys?"

"I sent them home."

"Good. They deserve a few days. Take a few days yourself."

This was an impressive reward from Avidan, who had not taken a day off for himself in a quarter of a century.

"Who is the girl you came in with?"

"An Arab spy. Don't be so nosy."

"Is she one of our friends?"

"No, she isn't a friend. Not even a fellow traveler."

"A shame. We could use a good American Christian."

"No, she's just a nice woman who looks at Jews as though she were looking into a cage at a zoo. I'm running her up to Jerusalem tomorrow to see Harriet Saltzman about getting her a place in Youth Aliyah."

"Something personal, maybe?"

"Good Lord, no. Now turn your Jewish curiosity somewhere else."

The room was stuffy. Avidan pulled out a large blue kerchief and mopped the sweat from his bald pate.

"That was quite a welcome we got yesterday from the Maccabees. I hear the refinery will be burning for a week. Wrecked production."

Avidan shook his head. "They did a good job yesterday—but what of the day before yesterday and what of the day after tomorrow? They are making three bad raids to every good one. Every time they resort to brutality or indiscriminate murder the whole Yishuv suffers. We are the ones who have to answer for Maccabee actions. Tomorrow General Haven-

318

Hurst and the high commissioner will be at Yishuv Central. They'll be pounding their fists on Ben Gurion's desk demanding we use the Haganah to apprehend them. I swear I don't know what to do sometimes. So far the British haven't really turned on the Haganah but I am afraid if Maccabee terror continues . . . they've even taken up bank robbery to finance their operations."

"British banks, I hope." Ari lit a cigarette and stood up and paced the tiny office. "Perhaps the time has come to stage a few good raids of our own."

"No . . . we just can't risk the Haganah. We are the ones who must defend all the Jews. Illegal immigration . . . that is the way we will fight them for now. One thing like the *Exodus* is more important than blowing up ten Haifa refineries."

"But the day must come that we commit ourselves, Avidan. We have an army or we don't."

Avidan took some sheets of paper from his desk drawer and pushed them over toward Ari. Ari thumbed through them: ORDER OF BATTLE, 6TH AIRBORNE DIVISION.

Ari looked up. "They have three parachute brigades?"

"Keep reading."

ROYAL ARMORED CORPS WITH KING'S OWN HUSSARS, 53RD WORCESTERSHIRE, 249TH AIRBORNE PARK, DRAGOON GUARDS, ROYAL LANCERS, QUEEN'S ROYAL, EAST SURREY, MIDDLESEX, GORDON HIGHLANDERS, ULSTER RIFLES, HERTFORDSHIRE REGIMENT—the list of British troops in Palestine ran on and on. Ari threw the papers down on Avidan's desk. "Whom are they fighting, the Russian Army?"

"You see, Ari? Every day I go through it with some young hotheads in the Palmach. Why don't we raid? Why don't we come out and fight? Do you think I like it? Ari . . . they have twenty per cent of the combat strength of the British Army here. One hundred thousand troops, not counting the Trans-Jordan Arab Legion. Sure, the Maccabees run around shooting up everything, grabbing the limelight, accusing us of hiding." Avidan slammed his fist on the desk. "By God, I'm trying to put an army together. We haven't even got ten thousand rifles to fight with and if the Haganah goes, we all go with it.

"You see, Ari . . . the Maccabees can keep mobility and hide with a few thousand blowhards. We have got to stall and keep stalling. We can't have a showdown. We can't get Haven-Hurst angry, either. One British soldier here for every five Jews."

Ari picked up the list of British troops again and studied it in silence.

"The British dragnets, cordons, screenings, raids get worse

every day. The Arabs are building strength while the British turn their backs."

Ari nodded. "Where do I go from here?"

"I am not going to give you a command, yet. Go on home, take a few days' rest then report to Palmach at Ein Or *kibbutz.* I want you to assess our strength in every settlement in the Galilee. We want to know what we can expect to hold . . . what we are going to lose."

"I've never heard you talk like this, Avidan."

"Things have never been so bad. The Arabs have refused even to sit at the same conference table and talk with us in London."

Ari walked to the door.

"My love to Barak and Sarah and tell Jordana to behave herself with David Ben Ami home. I am sending him and the other boys to Ein Or."

"I'll be in Jerusalem tomorrow," Ari said. "Do you want anything?"

"Yes, dig me up ten thousand front-line troops and the arms to outfit them."

"*Shalom,* Avidan."

"*Shalom,* Ari. It is good to have you home."

Ari grew morose as he drove back to Tel Aviv. Long ago in Cyprus he had told young David Ben Ami that many things are tried in the Haganah and Palmach and Aliyah Bet. Some plans work and some fail. A professional should do his work and not become entangled emotionally. Ari Ben Canaan was a machine. He was an efficient, daring operator. Sometimes he won, sometimes he lost.

But once in a while Ari Ben Canaan looked at it all with realism and it nearly crushed him.

Exodus, the Haifa refinery, a raid here, a raid there. Men died to smuggle in fifty rifles. Men were hanged for smuggling in a hundred frantic survivors. He was a little man fighting a giant. He wished, at that moment, he could have David Ben Ami's faith in divine intervention, but Ari was a realist.

Kitty Fremont waited in the little bar off the lobby for Ari's return. He had been so decent that she wanted to wait up for him and talk some more and have a nightcap or two. She saw him walk into the lobby and go to the desk for his key.

"Ari!" she called.

His face showed the same deep concentration it had showed that first day she saw him on Cyprus. She waved to him but he did not even seem to see or to hear her. He looked directly at her, then walked upstairs to his room.

CHAPTER TWO: Two buses carrying fifty of the *Exodus* children drove past the *tel* of the ruins of Hazor and into the Huleh Valley. All during the drive from Haifa through the Galilee the travelers had been hanging out of the window cheering and waving and pointing in wonder at the sights of their long-promised land.

"Dov! Everything is so beautiful!" Karen cried.

Dov's grumble Karen interpreted as meaning that he didn't see so much to make a fuss about.

They drove deep into the Huleh to Yad El, the home of Ari Ben Canaan. Here a road branched from the main road and ran up into the hills toward the Lebanese border. The children saw the road sign pointing to Gan Dafna; they nearly exploded with anticipation, with the lone exception of the morose Dov Landau. The buses worked up the winding road and soon the Huleh expanded into full vista, carpeted with green fields of the *kibbutzim* and *moshavim*. The rectangular fishponds made a dozen small lakes around the larger swamplands of Huleh Lake.

They slowed as they entered the Arab village of Abu Yesha halfway up the mountains. There was none of the coldness or hostility at Abu Yesha the children had noted in the other Arab villages. They were greeted with friendly waving.

Past Abu Yesha they climbed beyond the two-thousand-foot elevation marker and then on to the Youth Aliyah village of Gan Dafna—the Garden of Dafna. They stopped before green lawn measuring fifty by a hundred yards in the center of the village. The whole place sat on a large plateau. The center green was surrounded by administration buildings and was the hub of the village, which ran off in all four directions. Flowers and trees and green were everywhere. As the *Exodus* children debarked the village orchestra greeted them with a rousing march.

In the center of the green stood a life-sized statue of Dafna, the girl after whom the village was named. The figure was cast in bronze with a rifle in her hands, looking down on the Huleh, much the same as that day at Ha Mishmar when the Arabs had killed her.

The village founder, a tiny man with a slight humpback named Dr. Lieberman, stood by the statue of Dafna, smoking a large-bowled pipe as he welcomed the new youngsters. He briefly told them that he had left Germany in 1934 and founded Gan Dafna in 1940 on this land which had been generously given to Youth Aliyah by Kammal, the late muktar of Abu Yesha. Dr. Lieberman went to each youngster to speak a few personal words of welcome in a half dozen languages. As Karen watched him she had a feeling that she had seen him before. He looked and acted like the professors at Cologne when she was a baby . . . but it was so long ago she could not really remember.

Each new child was attended by a member of the village.

"Are you Karen Clement?"

"Yes."

"I am Yona, your new roommate," said an Egyptian Jewess a bit older than Karen. The two girls shook hands. "Come, I will show you to our room. You will like it here."

Karen called to Dov that she would see him later and she walked beside Yona past the administration buildings and the schoolrooms to an area of cottages set in a shrubbed pathway. "We are lucky," Yona said. "We get the cottages because we are seniors."

Karen stopped a moment before the cottage and looked at it with disbelief, then entered. It was very simple but Karen thought it the most wonderful room that she had ever seen. A bed, a desk, a wardrobe and a chair—her own, her very own.

It was evening before Karen had a free moment. After dinner the children were to be given a welcoming show at the outdoor theater.

Karen met Dov on the green near the statue of Dafna. For the first time in weeks and weeks she felt like dancing. The air was so crisp and wonderful and the village was heaven! Karen trembled with happiness. She stood by Dov and pointed to the white clustered houses of Abu Yesha below them in a saddle of the hill. Above them was the Taggart fort, Fort Esther, on the Lebanese border, and down at the floor of the valley were the fields belonging to the village, adjoining the fields of the *moshav* of Yad El. Along the hilltops at the far end of the Huleh was Tel Hai, where Trumpledor fell, and across the valley was Mount Hermon and Syria.

Karen was dressed in olive-drab slacks and high-collared peasant's blouse and she wore new sandals on her feet. "Oh, Dov! This is the most wonderful day of my life," she cried. "Yona is lots of fun and she was telling me that Dr. Lieberman is the nicest man on earth."

She rolled in the grass and looked up in the sky and sighed. Dov stood over her, wordless. She sat up and took his hand and tugged at him to sit beside her.

"Cut it out," he said.

She persisted and he sat down. He became nervous as she

322

squeezed his hand and lay her head on his shoulder. "Please be happy, Dov . . . please be happy."

He shrugged and pulled away from her.

"Please be happy."

"Who cares about it?"

"I care," Karen said. "I care for you."

"Well . . . care for yourself."

"I care for myself, too." She knelt in front of him and gripped his shoulders. "Did you see your room and your bed? How long has it been since you've been in a room like that?"

Dov flushed at the touch of her hands and lowered his eyes. "Just think, Dov. No more displaced persons' camps . . . no more La Ciotats, no more Caraolos. No more illegal ships. We are home, Dov, and it is even more beautiful than I dreamed."

Dov got to his feet slowly and turned his back. "This place is fine for you. I got other plans."

"Please forget them," she pleaded.

The orchestra played and the music drifted over the green.

"We had better get to the theater," Karen said.

Once Ari and Kitty left Tel Aviv and drove past the huge British camp at Sarafand she felt the tension of Palestine again. They passed through the all-Arab city of Ramle on the road to Jerusalem and felt angry Arab eyes on them. Ari seemed oblivious of the Arabs and oblivious of Kitty. He had not spoken a dozen words to her all day.

Beyond Ramle the car turned into the Bab el Wad, a snaking road that twisted up into the Judean hills. Young forests planted by the Jews pushed up from the earth on ravines on either side of the road. Deep into the hills stood ancient terracing that stood out from the denuded earth like ribs of a starving dog. Once these very hills and terraces supported hundreds of thousands of people. Now it was completely eroded. The hilltops held Arab villages clustered in white clumps above them.

Here in the Bab el Wad the magic pull of Jerusalem gripped Kitty Fremont. It was said that none could pass through the Judean hills for the first time and escape the haunting power of the City of David. It seemed strange to Kitty that she should feel it so intensely. Her religious training had been in matter-of-fact midwestern Protestantism. It had been approached with a basic sincerity and a lack of intensity. Higher and higher they drove and the anticipation became greater. She was with the Bible now, and for the first time, in these silent and weird hills, came the realization of what it was to be in the Holy Land.

In the distance a dim outline of the citadels of Jerusalem jutted on the horizon and Kitty Fremont was filled with a kind of exaltation.

They entered the New City built by the Jews and drove down Jaffa Road, the principal commercial spine that passed crowded shops, toward the wall of the Old City. At the Jaffa Gate, Ari turned and drove along the wall to King David Avenue and in a few moments stopped before the great King David Hotel.

Kitty stepped from the car and gasped at the sight of the right wing of the hotel sheared away.

"It was once British headquarters," Ari said. "The Maccabees changed all that."

The hotel was built of Jerusalem stone. It was grandiose in the overburdened European manner, with its lobby an alleged duplication of King David's court.

Kitty came down to lunch first. She waited on the terrace in the rear of the hotel that looked over a small valley to the Old City wall. The terrace was opposite David's Tower and was set in a formal garden. A four-piece orchestra behind her played luncheon music.

Ari walked out to the terrace and stopped in his tracks. Kitty looked lovely! He had never seen her like this before. She wore a flouncy and chic cocktail dress and a wide-brimmed hat and white gloves. At that moment he felt far away from her. She was all the lovely women in Rome and in Paris and even Berlin who belonged to a world in which women acted in a way he could not quite understand. It was a light year from Kitty to Dafna but she was beautiful, indeed.

He seated himself. "I have spoken to Harriet Saltzman. We will see her right after lunch."

"Thanks. I'm very excited about Jerusalem."

"She has mysterious powers. Everyone is excited on his first visit. Take David Ben Ami . . . David never gets over Jerusalem. Matter of fact he will be sight-seeing with you tomorrow. It is the Sabbath. He wants to take you into the Old City."

"He is sweet to think of me."

Ari looked at her closely. She seemed even prettier now than when he entered the terrace. He turned his eyes away and signaled for a waiter, then stared off into space after giving the order. Kitty had the feeling now that Ari had committed himself and was anxious to complete his obligation. No word passed between them for ten minutes.

She picked at her salad. "Do I bore you?"

"Of course not."

"Since you came back from your engagement last night you've acted as though I haven't existed."

"I'm sorry, Kitty," he said without looking at her. "I guess I have been rather bad company today."

"Is there something wrong?"

"There's a lot wrong but it doesn't concern you or me or my bad manners. Let me tell you about Harriet Saltzman. She's an American. She must be well over eighty years old now. If we conferred sainthoods in the Yishuv, she would be our first saint. See that hill beyond the Old City?"

"Over there?"

"That's Mount Scopus. Those buildings make up the most modern medical center in the Middle East. The money comes from American Zionist women that Harriet organized after the first world war. Most of the hospital and medical centers in Palestine come from her Hadassah organization."

"She sounds like quite a girl."

"Yes, she is. When Hitler came to power Harriet organized Youth Aliyah. She is responsible for saving thousands of youngsters. They maintain dozens of youth centers all over Palestine. You'll get along fine with her."

"Why do you say that?"

"Well, no Jew who has lived in Palestine can ever go without leaving his heart here. It's the same way with Americans, I think. Harriet has been here for years but she's still very much an American."

The orchestra stopped playing.

A silence fell over Jerusalem. They could hear the faint cry of a Moslem muezzin calling his people to prayer from a minaret in the Old City. Then it became quiet again with a stillness that Kitty had never experienced.

The bells from the carillon in the YMCA tower over the street played a hymn and the tones flooded the hills and the valleys. And then—again it became still. It was so peaceful it would have been sacrilegious to speak. All life and all time seemed to stand still in one moment.

"What an utterly wonderful sensation," Kitty said.

"Those kinds of moments are rarities these days," Ari said. "I am afraid that the calm is deceptive."

Ari saw a small olive-skinned man standing at the terrace door. He recognized the man as Bar Israel, the contact for the Maccabees. Bar Israel nodded to Ari and disappeared.

"Will you excuse me for a moment?" Ari said. He walked into the lobby to the cigarette stand and purchased a pack and then thumbed through a magazine. Bar Israel walked up alongside him.

"Your Uncle Akiva is in Jerusalem," Bar Israel whispered. "He wants to see you."

"I have to go to the Zion Settlement Society but I will be free shortly after."

"Meet me in the Russian compound," the contact man said, and hastened through the lobby.

King George Avenue was a wide boulevard in the New City and was lined with administrative buildings and schools and churches. The Zion Settlement Society, a large, four-storied rambling affair, stood on a corner. A long driveway led to the main entrance.

"*Shalom*, Ari!" Harriet Saltzman said, prancing from behind her desk with an agility that belied her years. She stood on her toes, put her arms around Ari's neck, and kissed his cheek heartily. "Oh, what a job you did on them at Cyprus. You are a good boy."

Kitty watched quietly in the doorway. The old woman turned to her.

"So this is Katherine Fremont. My child, you are very lovely."

"Thank you, Mrs. Saltzman."

"Don't make with the 'Mrs. Saltzman.' Only Englishmen and Arabs call me that. It makes me feel old. Sit down, sit down. I'll order tea. Or perhaps you would rather have coffee."

"Tea is fine."

"So you see, Ari . . . this is what an American girl looks like." Harriet made a gesture of tribute to Kitty's beauty with mischief twinkling in her eyes.

"I am certain that not all American girls are as pretty as Kitty . . ."

"Stop it, both of you. You are embarrassing me."

"You girls don't need me. I have a few things to do, so I'll just beat it. Kitty, if I'm not back for you would you mind taking a taxi back to the hotel?"

"Go already," the old woman said. "Kitty and I are going to have dinner together at my flat. Who needs you?"

Ari smiled and left.

"That's a fine boy," Harriet Saltzman said. "We have lots of good boys like Ari. They work too hard, they die too young." She lit a cigarette and offered Kitty one. "And where do you hail from?"

"Indiana."

"San Francisco, here."

"It is a lovely city," Kitty said. "I visited it once with my husband. I always hoped to go back someday."

"I do too," the old woman said. "It seems that I miss the States more every year. For fifteen years I have sworn I would go back for a while, but the work never seems to stop here. All these poor babies coming in. But I get homesick. Senility is creeping up on me, I guess."

"Hardly."

"It is good to be a Jew working for the rebirth of a Jewish nation but it is also a very good thing to be an American and don't you ever forget that, young lady. Ever since the *Exodus* incident started I've been very anxious to meet you, Katherine Fremont, and I must say I am tremendously surprised and I don't surprise easily."

"I am afraid that the reports overromanticized me."

Behind Harriet Saltzman's disarming friendliness functioned a shrewd brain, and even though Kitty was completely at ease she realized how carefully the old woman was estimating her. They sipped their tea and chatted, mostly about America. Harriet became nostalgic. "I go home next year. I will find an excuse. Maybe a fund-raising drive. We are always having fund-raising drives. Do you know that the American Jews give us more than all Americans give to the Red Cross? So why should I bore you with these things? So you want to go to work for us?"

"I am sorry that I don't have my credentials with me."

"You don't need them. We know all about you."

"Oh?"

"Yes. We have a half dozen reports already on file."

"I don't know whether to be pleased or offended."

"Don't be offended. It is the times. We must be sure of everyone. You will find that we are really a small community here and very little happens that doesn't come back to these ancient ears. As a matter of fact I was reading our files on you before you came this afternoon and I was wondering why you have come to us."

"I am a nurse and you need nurses."

Harriet Saltzman shook her head. "Outsiders don't come to us for that reason. There must be another one. Did you come to Palestine for Ari Ben Canaan?"

"No . . . of course I am fond of him."

"A hundred women are fond of him. You happen to be the woman he is fond of."

"I don't think so, Harriet."

"Well . . . I am glad, Katherine. It is a long way from Yad El to Indiana. He is a *sabra* and only another *sabra* could really understand him."

"*Sabra?*"

"It is a term we use for the native born. A *sabra* is the
327

fruit of a wild cactus you will find all over Palestine. The *sabra* is hard on the outside ... but inside, it is very tender and sweet."

"That is a good description."

"Ari and the other *sabras* have no conception of American life, just as you have no conception of what his life has been.

"Let me be very candid. When a gentile comes to us, he comes as a friend. You are not a friend, you are not one of us. You are a very beautiful American girl who is completely puzzled by these strange people called Jews. Now why are you here?"

"It's not that mysterious. I am very fond of a young girl. She came over on the *Exodus*. We met earlier in Caraolos. I am afraid her attempts to reunite with her father may end very unhappily. If she is unable to find her father I want to adopt her and take her to America."

"I see. Well, you are on the level. Let us talk turkey. There is an opening for a head nurse in one of our Youth Villages in the northern Galilee. It is a lovely place. The director is one of my oldest and dearest friends, Dr. Ernest Lieberman. The village is called Gan Dafna. We have four hundred children there and most of them are concentration-camp bred. They need help badly. I do hope you will take this assignment. The pay and the facilities are very good."

"I ... I ... would like to know about ..."

"Karen Hansen?"

"How did you know?"

"I told you we were a small community. Karen is at Gan Dafna."

"I don't know how to thank you."

"Thank Ari. He is the one who arranged it all. Ari will take you up there. It is very close to his home."

The old woman emptied her teacup and leaned back in her chair. "Could I give you one last piece of advice?"

"Of course."

"I have been working with orphans since 1933. The attachment they form for Palestine may be something very difficult for you to understand. Once they have breathed the air of freedom ... once they are filled with this patriotism it is extremely difficult for them to leave, and if and when they do most of them never become adjusted to living away from Palestine. Their devotion is a fierce thing. Americans take so many things about America for granted. Here, a person wakes up every morning in doubt and tension—not knowing if all he has slaved for will be taken from him. Their country is with them twenty-four hours a day. It is the focal point of their lives, the very meaning of their existence."

"Are you trying to say I may not be able to persuade the girl to leave?"

"I am trying to make you aware that you are fighting tremendous odds."

There was a knock on the door.

"Come in."

David Ben Ami entered. "*Shalom*, Harriet. *Shalom*, Kitty. Ari told me that I could find you here. Am I interrupting anything?"

"No, we've finished our business. I am sending Katherine to Gan Dafna."

"Splendid. I thought that it would be a good idea to show Kitty around Mea Shearim when the Sabbath starts."

"An excellent idea, David."

"Then we had better get started. Will you come with us, Harriet?"

"Lug these old bones around? Not on your life. You have Katherine at my flat for dinner in two hours."

Kitty stood up and shook hands with the old woman and thanked her and then turned to David. He stared at her.

"Is something wrong, David?" Kitty asked.

"I have never seen you dressed up. You look very beautiful." He looked at himself awkwardly. "Perhaps I am not dressed well enough to walk around with you."

"Nonsense. I was just trying to show off for my new boss."

"*Shalom*, children. I will see you later."

Kitty was pleased that David had come for her. She felt more comfortable around him than with any of the other Jews. They walked from the Zion Settlement Society and crossed to the Street of the Prophets. Kitty took his arm, but it seemed as though David was the one who was the sightseer. He was rediscovering everything about Jerusalem and he was as delighted as a child. "It is so good to be home again," he said. "How do you like my city?"

"Are there words? It is overwhelming and a little frightening."

"Yes, that is the way I have always felt about Jerusalem ever since I was a boy. It never fails to thrill me and to haunt me."

"It was very kind of you to take time away from your family."

"We are not all assembled yet. I have six brothers, you know. Most of them are in the Palmach. I am the baby of the family so there will be a reunion. All of us except one . . . I will have to see him alone later."

"Is he ill?"

"He is a terrorist. He is with the Maccabees. My father

will not permit him to enter our house. He is with Ben Moshe, a leader of the Maccabees. Ben Moshe was once my professor at the Hebrew University." David stopped and pointed to Mount Scopus beyond the Hadassah Medical Center and beyond the Valley of Kidron. "There is the university."

"You miss it very much, don't you?"

"Yes, of course. Someday I will have the chance to go back."

The froggy sound of a horn blasted as it turned dusk.

"Sabbath! Sabbath!" a call went up along the streets.

All over Jerusalem the sound of the ancient horn could be heard. David put on a small skull cap and led Kitty to the street of Mea Shearim—the Hundred Gates of the ultra-Orthodox.

"Here in Mea Shearim you will be able to look into the synagogues and see the men pray in many different ways. Some of the Yemenites pray with a swaying motion as though they were riding on a camel. This was their way of getting even, as Jews were not allowed to ride camels because it would make their heads higher than a Moslem's."

"I am impressed."

"Take the descendants of Spanish Jews. . . . During the Inquisition they were forced to convert to Catholicism on pain of death. They said their Latin prayers aloud but at the end of each sentence they whispered a Hebrew prayer under their breaths. They still pray in silence at the end of each sentence."

Kitty was speechless when they turned into Mea Shearim. The street comprised connected two-story stone dwellings, all displaying iron grillwork on their balconies.

The men were bearded and wore side curls and fur-brimmed hats and long black satin coats. There were Yemenites in Arabic dress and Kurds and Bokharans and Persians in riotous-colored silks. Everyone walked from the ritual bath with a quick-paced bobbing motion, as though swaying in prayer.

In a few moments the street emptied into the synagogues, small rooms for the most part and several on each block. There were congregations from Italy and Afghanistan and Poland and Hungary and Morocco. The Mea Shearim was filled with the chanting of prayers and Sabbath songs and weeping voices of anguished Hasidim who whipped themselves into a furor. Women were not permitted to enter rooms of prayer, so David and Kitty had to content themselves with peeking through iron-grilled windows.

What strange rooms—what strange people. Kitty watched near-hysterical men cluster about the Sefer Torah wailing and moaning. She saw the angelic faces of Yemenites who sat cross-legged on pillows, softly praying. She saw old men weaving back and forth emitting a stream of Hebrew in monotone read from decrepit prayer books. How different and how far away they all were from the handsome men and women of Tel Aviv.

"We have all kinds of Jews," David Ben Ami said. "I wanted to bring you here because I know that Ari wouldn't. He and many of the *sabras* despise them. They do not farm the land, they do not bear arms. They shove an ancient brand of Judaism down our throats. They are a force of reaction against what we are trying to do. Yet, when one lives in Jerusalem as I have, we learn to tolerate them and even appreciate the horrible things in the past that could drive men to such fanaticism."

Ari Ben Canaan waited near the Greek Church in the Russian compound. It turned dark. Bar Israel appeared from nowhere. Ari followed the contact man into an alley where a taxi waited. They got in and Bar Israel produced a large black handkerchief.

"Must I submit to this?"

"I trust you, Ari, but orders are orders."

The blindfold was tied over Ari's eyes and Ari was made to lie on the floor and was covered by a blanket. For a long twenty minutes the taxi moved in zigzags and circuitous routes to confuse Ari, then headed toward the Katamon district near the former German colony. The taxi stopped. Ari was quickly led into a house and into a room and was told he could remove the kerchief.

The room was bare except for a single chair, a single table which held a single flickering candle and a bottle of brandy and two glasses. It took a full moment for Ari's eyes to adjust to the darkness. His uncle, Akiva, stood opposite him by the table. Akiva's beard and his hair had turned snow white. He was wrinkled and bent. Ari walked to him very slowly and stopped before him.

"Hello, Uncle," he said.

"Ari, my boy."

The two men embraced, and the older man had to fight back choking emotion. Akiva lifted the candle and held it close to Ari's face and he smiled. "You are looking well, Ari. It was a good job you did in Cyprus."

"Thank you."

"You came with a girl, I hear."

"An American woman who helped us. She is not a friend, really. How are you feeling, Uncle?"

Akiva shrugged. "As well as I can be expected to feel living in the underground. It has been too long since I have

331

seen you, Ari . . . too long. Over two years now. It was nice when Jordana was studying at the university. I saw her once each week. She must be nearly twenty now. How is she? Does she still care for that boy?"

"David Ben Ami. Yes, they are very much in love. David was with me at Cyprus. He is one of our most promising young people."

"His brother is a Maccabee, you know. Ben Moshe used to teach him at the university. Perhaps I can meet him someday."

"Of course."

"I hear Jordana is in the Palmach."

"Yes, she is in charge of training the children at Gan Dafna and she works on the mobile radio when it transmits from our area."

"She must be around my *kibbutz* then. She must see a lot of Ein Or."

"Yes."

"Does she . . . does she ever say how it looks?"

"It is always beautiful at Ein Or."

"Perhaps I can see it one day again." Akiva sat down at the table and poured two brandies with an unsteady hand. Ari took a glass and they touched them. *"Le chaim,"* he said.

"I was with Avidan yesterday, Uncle. He showed me the British battle order. Have your people seen it?"

"We have friends in British Intelligence."

Akiva stood up and began to pace the room slowly. "Haven-Hurst means to wipe out my organization. The British are dedicated to the destruction of the Maccabees. They torture our prisoners, they hang us, they have exiled our entire command. It is not bad enough that the Maccabees are the only ones with the courage to fight the British, we must also fight the betrayers among our own people. Oh, yes, Ari . . . we know the Haganah has been turning us in."

"That is not true," Ari gasped.

"It is true!"

"No! Just today at Yishuv Central, Haven-Hurst demanded that the Jews destroy the Maccabees and they again refused."

Akiva's pacing quickened and his anger rose. "Where do you think the British get their information if not from the Haganah? Those cowards at Yishuv Central let the Maccabees do the bleeding and the dying. Those cowards betray and betray. Cleverly, yes! But they betray! Betray! Betray!"

"I won't listen to this, Uncle. Most of us in the Haganah and the Palmach are dying to fight. They restrain us until we burst, but we cannot destroy everything that has been built."

"Say it! We destroy!"

Ari gritted his teeth and held his tongue. The old man

ranted, then suddenly he stopped and flopped his arms to his sides. "I am a master at creating arguments when I don't mean to."

"It is all right, Uncle."

"I am sorry, Ari . . . here, have some more brandy, please."

"No, thank you."

Akiva turned his back and murmured, "How is my brother?"

"He was well when I saw him last. He will be going to London to join the conferences."

"Yes, dear Barak. He will talk. He will talk to the end." Akiva wetted his lips and hesitated. "Does he know that you and Jordana and Sarah see me?"

"I think so."

Akiva faced his nephew. His face reflected the sorrow within him. "Does he . . . does he ever ask about me?"

"No."

Akiva gave a hurt little laugh and sank into the chair and poured more brandy for himself. "How strange things are. I was always the one who angered and Barak was always the one who forgave. Ari . . . I am getting very tired. A year, another year, I don't know how long it will be. Nothing can ever undo the hurt that we have brought to each other. But . . . he must find it in his heart to break this silence. Ari, he must forgive me for the sake of our father."

CHAPTER THREE: A hundred church bells from the Old City and the Valley of Kidron and the Mount of Olives and Mount Zion pealed in chorus to the YMCA carillon. It was Sunday in Jerusalem, the Christian Sabbath.

David Ben Ami took Kitty into the Old City through the ornate Damascus Gate and they walked along the Via Dolorosa—the Way of the Cross—to Stephen's Gate which looked over the Kidron Valley and the tombs of Zacharias and Absalom and Mary and to the Mount of Olives, the scene of the Ascension.

They walked through the narrow streets, through the Arab bazaar and the tiny shops and the scenes of wild bartering. At the Dome of the Rock, the Mosque of Omar, a thousand pairs of shoes covered the steps. Ancient, bearded Jews stood and wept before the Wailing Wall of their great temple.

How strange this place is, again Kitty Fremont mused. Here, so far away in these barren hills, the merging point of a hundred civilizations in its thousands of years. Of all the earth, why this place, this street, this wall, this church? Romans and Crusaders and Greeks and Turks and Arabs and

Assyrians and Babylonians and British in the city of the maligned Hebrews. It is holy, it is sacred, it is damned. Everything strong and everything weak, all that is good in man and all that is evil in him are personified. Calvary and Gethsemane. The room of the Last Supper. The last supper of Jesus, a Jewish Passover Seder.

David took Kitty to the Holy Sepulcher, the site of the crucifixion and the tiny chapel lit with ornate hanging lamps and perpetually burning candles over the marble tomb of Jesus Christ. Kitty knelt beside the tomb and kissed it as it had been kissed thin by a million pilgrims.

The next morning Ari and Kitty left Jerusalem and continued northward into the Galilee. They drove through the timeless Arab villages into the fertile carpet of the Jezreel Valley, which the Jews had turned from swamp into the finest farmland in the Middle East. As the road wound out of the Jezreel toward Nazareth again, they moved backwards in time. On one side of the hill the lush lands of the Jezreel and on the other, the sun-baked, dried-out, barren fields of the Arabs. Nazareth was much as Jesus must have found it in His youth.

Ari parked in the center of town. He brushed off a group of Arab urchins, but one child persisted.

"Guide?"

"No."

"Souvenirs? I got wood from the cross, cloth from the robe."

"Get lost."

"Dirty pictures?"

Ari tried to pass the boy but he clung on and grabbed Ari by the pants leg. "Maybe you like my sister? She is a virgin."

Ari flipped the boy a coin. "Guard the car with your life."

Nazareth stank. The streets were littered with dung and blind beggars made wretched noises and barefoot, ragged, filthy children were underfoot. Flies were everywhere. Kitty held Ari's arm tightly as they wound through the bazaar and to a place alleged to be Mary's kitchen and Joseph's carpenter shop.

Kitty was baffled as they drove from Nazareth: it was a dreadful place.

"At least the Arabs are friendly," Ari said. "They are Christians."

"They are Christians who need a bath."

They stopped once more at Kafr Kanna at the church where Christ performed His first miracle of changing water to wine. It was set in a pretty and timeless Arab village.

Kitty was trying to digest all that she had seen in the past few days. It was such a small land but every inch held ghosts of blood or glory. At certain moments the very sacredness of it was gripping; at other moments exaltation turned to revulsion. Some of the holy places struck her speechless with awe and others left her with the cold suspicion of one watching a shell game in a carnival. The wailing Jews of Mea Shearim and the burning refinery. The aggressive *sabras* of Tel Aviv and the farmers of the Jezreel. The old and the new jammed together. There were paradoxes and contradictions at every turn.

It was very late afternoon when Ari turned into the gates of Yad El. He stopped before a flower-bedecked cottage.

"Ari, how lovely it is," Kitty said.

The cottage door opened and Sarah Ben Canaan ran from it. "Ari! Ari!" She was swept into his arms.

"Shalom, ema."

"Ari, Ari, Ari . . ."

"Now don't cry, *ema* . . . shhhh, don't cry, don't cry."

Kitty saw the massive Barak Ben Canaan rush out and throw his arms about his son.

"Shalom, abba, shalom."

The old giant clung to his son and slapped his back again and again, repeating, "You look good, Ari, you look good."

Sarah studied her son's face. "He is tired. Can't you see how tired he is, Barak?"

"I'm fine, *ema*. I have company. I want you to meet Mrs. Katherine Fremont. She is going to work at Gan Dafna tomorrow."

"So you are Katherine Fremont," Barak said, taking her hand in his two giant paws. "Welcome to Yad El."

"Ari, you're such a fool," his mother said. "Why didn't you telephone and say you were bringing Mrs. Fremont? Come in, come in . . . you'll take a shower, you'll change your clothes, I'll make a little to eat and you'll feel better. You're such a fool, Ari." Sarah put her arm around Kitty's waist and led her toward the cottage. "Barak! Bring Mrs. Fremont's luggage."

Jordana Ben Canaan stood before the newly arrived *Exodus* children in the outdoor theater. She was tall and straight, with a statuesque carriage and long shapely legs. Jordana, with red hair hanging free below her shoulders, had a striking and classic beauty. She was nineteen years of age and had been in the Palmach since leaving the university. The Palmach assigned Jordana to Gan Dafna to head the Gadna unit which gave military training to all children in the village over fourteen years. Gan Dafna was also one of the prime places for hiding arms and smuggling them to the Huleh settlements. Jordana also worked on the mobile Voice of Israel secret radio when it transmitted in the Huleh. Jordana lived at Gan Dafna, right in her office.

"I am Jordana Ben Canaan," she said to the *Exodus* children. "I am your Gadna commander. In the next weeks you will learn spying, messenger work, arms cleaning and firing, stick fighting, and we will have several cross-country hikes. You are in Palestine now and never again do you have to lower your head or know fear for being a Jew. We are going to work very hard, for Eretz Israel needs you. Tomorrow we will have our first hike. We will go over the hills north to Tel Hai. My father came to Palestine through Tel Hai nearly sixty years ago. It is the place where our great hero, Joseph Trumpledor died. Trumpledor is buried there, and a great stone lion near the graveyard looks down upon the Huleh just as the statue of Dafna looks upon the Huleh. On the lion are written the words . . . 'It is good to die for one's country.' I might add to that: it is good to have a country to die for."

As Jordana entered the administration building later she was called to the telephone. She lifted the receiver, "*Shalom,* Jordana here."

"*Shalom!* This is *ema!* Ari is home!"

"Ari!"

Jordana ran from her office to the stable. She mounted her father's white Arab stallion and spurred him through the gates of Gan Dafna. She galloped bareback down the road toward the village of Abu Yesha with her scarlet hair waving in the wind behind her.

She galloped full speed into the main street of the Arab village, sending a dozen people scurrying for safety. The men at the coffeehouse turned and sneered. What a disrespectful prostitute this red-headed bitch was to dare ride through their streets wearing shorts! It was fortunate for her that she was the daughter of Barak and the sister of Ari!

Ari took Kitty's hand and led her through the door. "Come along," he said, "I want to show you some of the farm before it turns dark."

"Did you have enough to eat, Mrs. Fremont?"

"I'm ready to burst."

"And the room is comfortable?"

"I'm just fine, Mrs. Ben Canaan."

"Well, don't be too long, dinner will be ready when Jordana gets down from Gan Dafna." Sarah and Barak stared after them, then looked at each other. "She is a beautiful woman. But for our Ari?"

"Stop being a *Yiddische* momma. Don't go making a *shiddoch* for Ari," Barak said.

"What are you talking, Barak? Can't you see the way he looks at her? Don't you know your own son yet? He is so tired."

Ari and Kitty walked through Sarah's garden on the side of the house to the low rail fence. Ari put his foot up on the rail and looked out over the fields of the *moshav*. The water sprinklers were whirling a cooling spray and the orchard trembled lightly in the evening breeze. The air was scented with the fragrance of Sarah's winter roses. Kitty watched Ari as he looked out at his land. For the first time since she had known Ari Ben Canaan he seemed to be at peace. They *are* rare moments for him, Kitty thought, remembering that brief period of peace in Jerusalem.

"Not much like your Indiana, I'm afraid," Ari said.

"It will do."

"Well . . . you didn't have to build Indiana out of a swamp." Ari wanted to say much more to Kitty. He wanted to talk about how much he longed to be able to come home and work on his land. He wanted to beg her to understand what it was for his people to own land like this.

Kitty was leaning over the fence gazing at the beauty and proud achievement that Yad El represented. She looked radiant. Ari was filled with a desire to take her in his arms and hold her, but he did nothing and said nothing. They turned away together and walked along the fence until they came to the barn buildings, where the cackle of chickens and the honk of a goose met their ears. He opened the gate. The hinge was broken.

"That needs fixing," he said. "A lot of things need fixing. I'm away all the time and Jordana is gone too. My father is away at conferences so much. I'm afraid the Ben Canaan farm has become a village liability. The whole *moshav* has the responsibility. Someday we are all going to be home together . . . then you'll really see something." They stopped by a hogpen where a sow lay panting in the mud as a dozen gluttonous pigs fought to get at her teats. "Zebras," Ari said.

"If I wasn't an old zebra expert I'd swear I was looking at pigs," Kitty answered.

"Shhh . . . not so loud. There might be someone from the Land Fund eavesdropping. We aren't supposed to raise . . . zebras . . . on Jewish national land. Up at Gan Dafna the children call them pelicans. At the *kibbutz* they are more realistic. They are spoken of as comrades."

They walked beyond the barn, chicken house and machinery shed to the edge of the fields.

"You can see Gan Dafna from here." Ari stood behind her and pointed to the hills near the Lebanese border.

"Those white houses?"

"No, that's an Arab village called Abu Yesha. Now look to the right of it and farther up where those trees are, on the plateau."

"Oh yes, I see it now. My, it's really up in the air. What is that building behind it on top of the hill?"

"Fort Esther, a British border station. Come along. I have something else to show you."

They walked through the fields as it began to turn dusk, and the sun played strange tricks of coloring on the hills. They came to a wooded area on the edge of the fields where a stream rushed past toward the Huleh Lake.

"Your colored people in America sing very pretty spirituals about this stream."

"Is this the Jordan?"

"Yes."

Ari moved close to Kitty and they looked solemnly at each other. "Do you like it? Do you like my parents?"

Kitty nodded. She waited for Ari to take her in his arms. His hands touched her shoulders.

"Ari! Ari! Ari!" a voice shouted from a distance. He released Kitty and spun around. A horse and rider were racing toward them, framed by the dying red sun. Soon they could make out the figure, the straight back, and the flaming hair.

"Jordana!"

She pulled the frothing horse to a halt, threw up both her arms and screamed for joy and leaped down on Ari so hard they both crashed to the ground. Jordana climbed on top of Ari and smothered his face with kisses.

"Cut it out," he protested.

"Ari! I love you to pieces!"

Jordana began to tickle him and they rolled over wrestling. Ari was forced to pin her down to hold her still. Kitty watched with amusement. Suddenly Jordana saw her and her expression froze. Ari, remembering Kitty's presence, smiled sheepishly and helped Jordana to her feet.

"My overwrought young sister. I think she mistook me for David Ben Ami."

"Hello, Jordana," Kitty said, "I feel as though I know you, from David . . ." She extended her hand.

"You are Katherine Fremont. I have heard of you, too."

The handshake was cold and Kitty was puzzled. Jordana turned quickly and picked up the reins of her horse and led him back toward the house as Ari and Kitty followed.

"Did you see David?" Jordana turned and asked Ari.

"He is in Jerusalem for a few days. He told me to say he would phone you tonight and he will be here by the end of the week, unless you want to go to Jerusalem."

"I can't with those new children at Gan Dafna."

Ari winked at Kitty. "Oh," he continued to Jordana, "by the way, I saw Avidan in Tel Aviv. He did mention something or the other about . . . now let me see . . . yes, about transferring David to the Galilee Brigade at Ein Or."

Jordana turned. Her blue eyes widened and for an instant she was unable to speak. "Ari, you mean it? You're not teasing me!"

Ari shrugged. "Silly girl."

"Oh, I hate you! Why didn't you tell me?"

"I didn't know it was that important."

Jordana was about to jump on Ari and wrestle with him again, but Kitty's presence obviously restrained her. "I am so happy," she said.

Another dinner was forced upon Kitty, who did her best by it when it became apparent that refusal would come close to creating an international incident. When dinner was done Sarah brought out tables full of snacks for the company that would be arriving.

That evening almost everyone at Yad El came to the Ben Canaan home to welcome Ari and to satisfy curiosity about the American woman. There was, in discreet Hebrew, excited speculation. They were a rugged and friendly lot of people and they went out of their way to make Kitty feel like visiting nobility. Ari hovered near her during the evening with the intent of protecting her from a torrent of questions but marveled at the ease with which Kitty was able to handle the pressing group.

As the evening wore on Jordana became more obvious in the coldness she had shown Kitty earlier. She was hostile and Kitty knew it. She could almost read Jordana's thoughts . . . "What kind of a woman are you who wants my brother?"

It was exactly what Jordana Ben Canaan was thinking as she watched Kitty perform perfectly, charming the curious farmers of Yad El. Kitty looked like all the soft, white, useless wives of English officers who spent their days at tea and gossip around the King David Hotel.

It was very late when the last guest left and Ari and Barak were alone and able to speak. They talked at length about the farm. It was running well despite their absences. The *moshav* saw to it that little was neglected during the protracted leaves of Ari, Jordana, and Barak.

Barak looked around the room for a cognac bottle with something left in it amid the shambles of the welcome-home gathering. He poured his son a glass and one for himself. Both of them settled down and stretched their long legs out and relaxed.

"Well, what about your Mrs. Fremont? We are all bursting with curiosity."

"Sorry to disappoint you. She is in Palestine in the interest of a girl who came over on the *Exodus*. I understand she is anxious to adopt the child later. We have become friends."

"Nothing more?"

"Nothing."

"I like her, Ari. I like her very much, but she is not our kind. Did you see Avidan in Tel Aviv?"

"Yes. I will be staying in the Huleh Palmach at Ein Or most likely. He wants to do an assessment of the strength of each village."

"That is good. You have been away so much it will do *ema* good to be able to fuss over you for a while."

"What about you, Father?"

Barak scratched his red beard and sipped his cognac. "Avidan has asked me to go to London for the conferences."

"I imagined he would."

"Of course we must keep stalling and fighting to gain a political victory. The Yishuv can't take a military showdown, so I'll go to London and add my bit. I hate to say it but I am finally coming to the conclusion that the British are going to sell us out completely."

Ari arose and began pacing the room. He was almost sorry that Avidan hadn't sent him away on another assignment. At least when he was working the clock around to complete a mission he did not have time to think of the realities ready to crush the Yishuv.

"Son, you had better go to Abu Yesha and see Taha."

"I was surprised he wasn't here tonight. Is something wrong?"

"Just what is wrong with the whole country. We have lived in peace with the people of Abu Yesha for twenty years. Kammal was my friend for a half a century. Now . . . there is a coldness. We know them all by first names, we have visited their homes, and they have attended our schools. We have celebrated weddings together. Ari, they are our friends. Whatever is wrong must be righted."

"I will see him tomorrow after I take Mrs. Fremont to Gan Dafna."

Ari leaned against the bookcases filled with classics in Hebrew, English, French, German, and Russian. He ran his fingers over them a moment and hesitated, then spun around and faced Barak. "I saw Akiva in Jerusalem."

Barak stiffened as though he had been struck. In reflex his lips parted for an instant, but he stopped the words that would have asked how his brother was. "We will not discuss him under my roof," Barak said softly.

"He has grown old. He cannot live too much longer. He begs for you to make peace with him in the name of your father."

"I do not want to hear it!" Barak cried with a quiver in his voice.

"Isn't fifteen years of silence long enough?"

Barak stood up to his towering height and looked into the eyes of his son. "He turned Jew against Jew. Now his Maccabees are turning the people of Abu Yesha against us. God may forgive him but I never will . . . never."

"Please listen to me!"

"Good night, Ari."

The next morning Kitty said good-by to the Ben Canaan family and Ari drove her from Yad El to the mountain road leading to Gan Dafna. At Abu Yesha, Ari stopped for a moment to have someone inform Taha he would be back in an hour or so.

As their car moved high into the hills Kitty grew more and more eager to see Karen, but at the same time she was apprehensive about Gan Dafna. Was Jordana Ben Canaan playing the role of a jealous sister or was she the forerunner of a kind of people who would be hostile because of their differences? Harriet Saltzman had warned her she was a stranger with no business in Palestine. Everyone and everything seemed to point out this difference. Jordana unsettled her. Kitty had tried to be sociable to everyone but perhaps underneath she was drawing lines and too thinly disguising the fact. I am what I am, Kitty thought, and I come from a place where people are judged for what they are.

As they drove into isolation she felt alone and glum.

"I must leave right away," Ari said.

"Will we be seeing each other?" Kitty asked.

"From time to time. Do you want to see me, Kitty?"

"Yes."

"I will try then."

They turned the last corner and the plateau of Gan Dafna spread before them. Dr. Lieberman, the village orchestra, the staff and faculty, and the fifty children from the *Exodus* were all clustered around the bronze statue of Dafna on the center green. There was a warm and spontaneous welcome for Kitty Fremont, and in that moment her fears vanished. Karen rushed up to her and hugged her and handed her a bouquet

341

of winter roses. Then Kitty was engulfed by "her" *Exodus* children. She looked over her shoulder long enough to see Ari disappear.

When the welcoming ceremony was over Dr. Lieberman and Karen walked with Kitty into a tree-studded lane holding the neat little two- and three-room cottages of the staff. They came to a halt halfway down the dirt road before a white stucco house which was deluged in blooms.

Karen ran up on the porch and opened the door and held her breath as Kitty walked in slowly. The combination living room and bedroom was simple but tasteful. The draperies and the spread over the couch-bed were of the thick Negev linen weave and the room was almost buried under fresh-cut flowers. A paper cutout was strung from one side to the other: "SHALOM KITTY," it read, and it was from her children of the *Exodus*. Karen ran to the window and pulled the draperies back and revealed a panoramic view of the valley floor two thousand feet below. There was another small room, a study, and a pullman kitchen and bath. Everything had been prepared beautifully. Kitty broke into a smile.

"Shoo, shoo, shoo," Dr. Lieberman said, whisking Karen out of the door. "You will see Mrs. Fremont later . . . shoo, shoo."

"Good-by, Kitty."

"Good-by, dear."

"You like it?" Dr. Lieberman asked.

"I will be very comfortable here."

Dr. Lieberman sat on the edge of the couch. "When your children from the *Exodus* heard you were coming to Gan Dafna they worked day and night. They painted the cottage, they made the drapes. They brought in plants . . . all the plants in Gan Dafna are on your lawn. They made a big fuss. They love you very much."

Kitty was very touched. "I don't know why they should."

"Children are instinctive about knowing who their friends are. You would like to see Gan Dafna now?"

"Yes, I'd love to."

Kitty stood a head taller than Dr. Lieberman. They strolled back toward the administration buildings. He walked with his hands alternately clasped behind him and patting his pockets, searching for matches to light his pipe.

"I came from Germany in 1933. I guess I knew quite early what was going to happen. My wife passed away shortly after we arrived. I taught humanities at the university until 1940 when Harriet Saltzman asked me to come up here and found a Youth Aliyah village. Actually, I had been longing to do just that for many years. This entire plateau was given to us by the late muktar of Abu Yesha, a most generous man.

If only our relations could be a model for all Jews and Arabs . . . Do you have a match?"

"No, I'm sorry, not with me."

"Never mind, I smoke too much."

They came to the center green where the view of the Huleh Valley was the best. "Our fields are down on the floor of the valley. The land was given to us by the Yad El *moshav*."

They stopped before the statue. "This is Dafna. She was a girl from Yad El who died in the Haganah. The sweetheart of Ari Ben Canaan. Our village is named for her."

Kitty felt a flash of—yes, jealousy. The power of Dafna was there even in sculpture. Kitty could see in the bronze that rugged earthiness of a Jordana Ben Canaan and the other farm girls who were in the Ben Canaan home last night.

Dr. Lieberman waved both hands. "In all directions we are surrounded by history. Across the valley you see Mount Hermon and near it is the site of ancient Dan. I could go on for an hour . . . it is filled with the past." The little hunchback looked fondly around at his creation and took Kitty's arm and led her on.

"We Jews have created a strange civilization in Palestine. In every other place in the world the culture of its people has almost always come from the large cities. Here, it is just the reverse. The eternal longing of the Jewish people to own land is so great that this is where our new heritage comes from. Our music, our poetry, our art, our scholars and our soldiers came from the *kibbutz* and the *moshav*. See these children's cottages?"

"Yes."

"You will notice how all windows face the fields of the valley so their land will be the first thing they see in the morning and the last thing they see at night. Half of the schooling here is in agriculture. From this village, groups have gone out and started or joined in four new *kibbutzim*. We are self-sustaining in food. We own our own dairy and poultry and cattle. We even weave much of our own cloth. We make our own furniture and we repair our farm machinery in our own shops. All this is done by the children and they govern themselves and very well, too."

They reached the far end of the green. Just before the administration building the beautiful lawn was abruptly broken by a long trench that circled the entire area. Kitty looked around and sighted more trenches and a bomb shelter.

"It is very ugly," Dr. Lieberman said, "and there is too much worship of fighters among our children. I am afraid that condition will last until we win our independence and can base existence on something more human than arms."

They walked along the trench. Kitty became intrigued by

343

an odd phenomenon. The trench works ran past a few scraggly trees. One of the trenches had been dug close to the root system of one of the trees and the roots were bared. The trench revealed layers of solid stone under the topsoil. Sandwiched between the rock there were thin layers of earth, some only a few inches thick. The tree was stunted from trying to grow in such ground but the roots fought a stubborn fight. They ran over and under and about the rock in thin veins, thickening wherever they found a little life-giving soil between the rock strata.

"Look how that tree fights to live," Kitty said. "Look how it tries to dig its roots into rock."

Dr. Lieberman observed thoughtfully for a moment. "That tree is the story of the Jews who have come back to Palestine," he said.

Ari stood in the high-ceilinged living room of Taha, the muktar of Abu Yesha. The young Arab, his lifelong friend, nibbled on a piece of fruit from a large bowl and watched Ari begin pacing.

"There is enough double talk going on at the conferences in London," Ari said. "I think that you and I can talk straight."

Taha flipped the fruit down. "How can I explain it, Ari? Pressure is being put on me. I have resisted it."

"Resisted it? Taha, you're talking to Ari Ben Canaan."

"Times are changing."

"Now wait a minute. Our people have lived together through two sets of riots. You went to school in Yad El. You lived in my home under the protection of my father."

"Yes, I existed because of your benevolence. Now you ask my village to exist the same way. You arm yourselves. Are we not allowed to arm ourselves? Or don't you trust us with guns as we have trusted you?"

"This isn't even you talking."

"I hope that I never live to see the day that you and I must fight, but you know that passiveness is a thing of the past for all of us."

Ari spun around angrily. "Taha! What has gotten into you? All right, then. Maybe you'd better hear it again. These stone houses in your village were designed and built by us. Your children can read and write because of us. You have sewers because of us and your young don't die before the age of six because of us. We taught you how to farm properly and live decently. We have brought you things that your own people would not give you in a thousand years. Your father knew this and he was big enough to admit that no one hates or exploits an Arab worse than another Arab. He died because he knew your salvation was with the Jews and he was man enough to stand for it."

Taha arose. "And will you guarantee me that the Maccabees will not come into Abu Yesha tonight and kill us?"

"Of course I can't guarantee it but you know what the Maccabees stand for just as you know what the Mufti stands for."

"I will never lift my hand against Yad El, Ari. You have my word."

Ari left, knowing that Taha meant what he said, but Taha was not the man of the strength that his father, Kammal, had been. Even as they promised peace to each other a breach had come between Yad El and Abu Yesha, just as breaches were coming to all the Arab and Jewish villages that had lived together in peace.

Taha watched his friend leave the house and walk to the road near the stream and the mosque. He stood motionless long after Ari disappeared. Each day the pressure grew and there were even voices of dissent in his own village. He was told that he was an Arab and a Moslem and he had to choose his side. How could he turn on Ari and Barak Ben Canaan? Yet, how could he still the voices around him?

He was a brother of Ari. Or was he? This was the tormenting question. From childhood his father had groomed him to lead his village. He knew the Jews had built the great cities and the roads and the schools and they had redeemed the land and they were the enlightened ones. Was he really their equal? Or was he a second-class citizen in his own land, riding on coattails, picking up the crumbs, living in the shadows of Jewish achievement?

Yes, he had benefited from the Jews. His people had benefited more because his father had realized the Jews could give greater benefits than his own Arabs. Yet, was he a partner? Was his equality a real thing or merely a phrase? Was he being tolerated rather than accepted?

Was he really the brother of Ari Ben Canaan or the poor cousin? Taha asked himself this question more often each day. Each time the answer was more certain. He was a brother in name only.

What of this equality the Jews preached? Could he as an Arab ever declare that he had loved Jordana Ben Canaan quietly and with the heartache that comes with long silence? He had loved her since he had lived under their roof and she was but a child of thirteen.

How far did their equality extend? Would they ever accept Taha and Jordana as man and wife? Would all the democracy-preaching members of the *moshav* come to their wedding?

345

What would happen then if Taha were to go to Jordana and tell her of his love? She would spit on him, of course.

In his heart he felt an inferiority and it tore him apart, despite the fact that the distinction was far less than that between a landowning effendi and the slave fellaheen.

He could not lift his hand against Ari and he could never declare his love for Jordana. He could not fight his friends nor could he resist the force around him which told him he was an Arab and an enemy of the Jew and he had to fight them whether it was right—or it was wrong.

CHAPTER FOUR: Dr. Ernest Lieberman, the funny little hunchback, was able to translate his tremendous love of people into a living thing at Gan Dafna. The atmosphere was as casual as a summer camp. The children were given complete freedom of movement and thought. School classes were held outdoors, and the children dressed in shorts and lay about on the grass so that even their academic study was close to nature.

Dr. Lieberman's children had come from the stink pits of the earth, the ghetto and the concentration camp. Yet, there was never a serious disciplinary problem at Gan Dafna. Disobedience did not exist, thievery was unheard of, and promiscuity between sexes was rare. Gan Dafna was life itself to the children, and they governed and policed themselves with a pride and dignity that reflected their reaction to being loved.

The range of learning and thinking was vast at Gan Dafna; it was difficult to believe the participants were merely teenagers. The library ran from St. Thomas Aquinas to Freud. No book was barred, no subject seemed too broad. The children possessed a political awareness beyond their years.

The primary principle the staff and faculty was able to inculcate upon these children was that their lives had a purpose.

Gan Dafna had an international staff, with teachers from twenty-two countries ranging from Iranians to the rugged *kibbutz*-bred *sabras*. Kitty was the only gentile as well as the only American and this proved to be a paradox. She was looked upon with both reserve and affection. Her early fears of hostility proved unfounded. There was an air of intellectualism which seemed to make Gan Dafna more like a university than an orphanage. Kitty was welcomed as a part of a team whose prime concern was the welfare of the children. She became very friendly with many of the staff and was completely at ease in their company. The problem of the Jewishness of the village also proved smaller than she had expected. Judaism at Gan Dafna was founded upon a fierce kind of nationalism rather than upon any religious basis. There was no formal religious training or even a synagogue.

They managed to keep tension and fear out of Gan Dafna despite reports of growing violence all over Palestine. The village was physically isolated enough to form some shelter from the realities of the bloodshed. Yet, it was not completely free of the signs of danger. The border was above them. Fort Esther was always in sight. Trenches, shelters, arms, and military training were in evidence.

The medical department building was in the administration area on the edge of the center green. The building had a clinic and a well-equipped twenty-bed hospital and operating room. The doctor was shared with the Yad El *moshav* and came daily. There was a dentist and four trainee nurses under Kitty and a full-time psychiatrist.

Kitty ran her clinic and hospital with machinelike efficiency after completely overhauling the system. She put sick calls and hospital rounds and the dispensation of treatment on a rigid schedule. She demanded and received a respect for her position that created a ripple of talk in the village. She kept a discreet professional distance from her assistants and she refused to operate her section with the informality of the rest of the village. She discouraged the familiarity which most of the teachers encouraged. This was all strange to Gan Dafna. There was a reluctant admiration of her, for the medical section was the most efficient department the village had. In their desire to foster freedom the Jews often leaned too far back from the discipline that Kitty Fremont knew. She was not disliked for the way she ran her department. When Kitty took off her uniform she was the most sought-after companion in Gan Dafna.

If she was firm in running her section, she was the opposite when it came to "her" children. The fifty *Exodus* youngsters at Gan Dafna continued to keep their identification and Kitty Fremont was always to be identified with them. She was "Mother of the *Exodus*." It seemed a natural step that she become personally involved in the cases of some of the more disturbed children from the *Exodus*. She volunteered to work with the psychiatrist in psychotherapy. With the disturbed children Kitty completely dropped her coldness and gave to them all the warmth she was capable of giving. Gan Dafna and Palestine had tremendous curative powers but the horrors of the past still brought on the nightmares, the insecurity, and the hostility that required patience and skill and love.

Once a week Kitty went down to Abu Yesha with the doctor to hold morning clinic for the Arabs. How pathetic the dirty little Arab children were beside the robust youngsters of Gan Dafna. How futile their lives seemed in contrast to the spirit of the Youth Aliyah village. There seemed to be no laughter or songs or games or purpose among the Arab children. It was a static existence—a new generation born on an eternal caravan in an endless desert. Her stomach turned over as she entered the one-room hovels shared with chickens, dogs, and donkeys. Eight or ten people on the same earth floor.

Yet Kitty could not dislike these people. They were heart-warming and gracious beyond their capacity. They too, longed for better things. She became friendly with Taha, the young muktar who was always present on clinic days. Many times Kitty felt that Taha wanted to speak to her about things other than the health problem of the village. She felt an urgency about him. But Taha was an Arab: a woman could only be confided in on certain matters and he never revealed his constant fears to her.

The days passed into the late winter of 1947.

Karen and Kitty had grown inseparably close. The young girl who had found some measure of happiness in the most abysmal places fairly bloomed at Gan Dafna. She had become overnight one of the most popular children in the village. Karen became more dependent on Kitty's guidance through the complex stages of early maturity. Kitty was aware that each day at Gan Dafna would tend to draw Karen farther away from America. She kept America alive in the girl's interest while the search for Karen's father continued.

Dov Landau was a problem. Several times Kitty was tempted to step in between the boy and Karen—their relationship seemed to be deepening. But Kitty, recognizing the possibility of driving them closer together, stayed out of it. Karen's devotion to the boy perplexed her, for Dov gave nothing in return. He was morose and withdrawn. He did talk a little more, but for practical purposes Karen was still the only one who could reach him.

Dov became obsessed with a desire to learn. His education had been almost nothing and now he seemed to want to try to make up for it with a passion. He was excused from both Gadna military training and agriculture. Dov crammed as much into himself as he could absorb. He read and studied day and night. He concentrated upon his natural gift of art with studies of anatomy and drawing and architecture and blueprinting. Occasionally a painting would furnish an escape valve and his drive would come out in effects that displayed his talent and energy. Sometimes he came near breaking through and joining into Gan Dafna society, only to withdraw again. He lived by himself, he engaged in no activities, and he saw only Karen outside classes.

Kitty took the problem to Dr. Lieberman. He had seen many boys and girls like Dov Landau. Dr. Lieberman had observed that Dov was an alert and intelligent human being who showed great talent. He felt any attempts to force attention on him would work the opposite way: so long as the boy remained harmless and grew no worse, he should be left alone.

As the weeks passed Kitty was disappointed that she did not hear from or see Ari. The statue of Dafna and the Yad El *moshav* below always seemed to remind her. From time to time when she had occasion to pass Yad El she dropped in on Sarah Ben Canaan, until the two women became quite friendly. Jordana learned of it and made no effort to disguise her dislike for Kitty. The beautiful young redheaded hellion made it a point to be rude whenever she spoke to Kitty.

One evening Kitty came to her cottage to find Jordana standing before the mirror, holding one of her cocktail dresses in front of her. Kitty's sudden appearance did not bother Jordana. "It is pretty, if you like this sort of thing," Jordana said hanging the dress back in the closet.

Kitty walked to the stove and put on some water for tea. "To what do I owe the honor of this call?"

Jordana continued to look about Kitty's cottage, at the little touches of her femininity. "There are some Palmach troops training at the Ein Or *kibbutz*."

"I've heard something about it," Kitty said.

"We have a shortage of instructors. We have a shortage of everything, anyhow. I was asked to ask you if you would come to Ein Or once a week to give a course in first aid and field sanitation."

Kitty pulled back the drapes and kicked off her shoes and settled back on the studio bed. "I would prefer not to do anything that would bring me into contact with troops."

"Why not?" Jordana pressed.

"Well, I suppose there is no graceful way of refusing you, and I would like it better if the Palmach understood why."

"What's to understand?"

"My personal feelings. I don't wish to become involved."

Jordana laughed coldly. "I told them at Ein Or it would be a waste of time to speak to you."

"Is it impossible for you to respect my feelings?"

"Mrs. Fremont, you can work anywhere in the world and

349

remain neutral. This is a strange place for you to come to work if you want to stay out of trouble. Why are you really here?"

Kitty sprang off the bed angrily. "None of your damned business!"

The teakettle whistled. Kitty snapped it off.

"I know why you are here. You want Ari."

"You're an insolent young lady and I think I've taken just about all I am going to from you."

Jordana remained unmoved. "I've seen the way you looked at him."

"If I wanted Ari, you would be the last thing in my way."

"Tell yourself you don't want him but don't tell it to me. You are not Ari's kind of woman. You don't care for us."

Kitty turned and lit a cigarette. Jordana came behind her.

"Dafna was Ari's kind of woman. She understood him. No American woman ever will."

Kitty turned around. "Because I don't run around in shorts and hike up the sides of mountains and shoot cannons and sleep in ditches doesn't make me one ounce less a woman than you. You or that precious statue. I know what's the matter with you—you're afraid of me."

"That's funny."

"Don't tell me what makes a woman—you don't know, you aren't one. You're Tarzan's mate and you behave as though you belong in a jungle. A brush and comb wouldn't be a bad start at fixing what's wrong with you." Kitty pushed past Jordana and threw open her closet. "Take a good look. This is what women wear."

Tears of anger welled in Jordana's eyes.

"The next time you wish to see me you may come to my office," Kitty said coldly. "I am not a *kibbutznik* and I like my privacy."

Jordana slammed the door so hard it shook the cottage.

Karen came to Kitty's office after the dinner sick call and flopped into a chair.

"Hi," Kitty said. "How did it go today?"

Karen grabbed two imaginary cow teats and made a milking motion. "Weak hands. I am a lousy milker," she opined with teen-age sadness. "Kitty, I am truly broken-hearted. I must, must, must, talk to you."

"Shoot."

"Not now. We have a Gadna meeting. We are cleaning some new Hungarian rifles. What a mess!"

"The Hungarian rifles can wait a few minutes. What is troubling you, dear?"

"Yona, my roommate. Just when we are getting to be intimate friends. She's going to join the Palmach next week."

Kitty felt a stab of dismay. How much longer until Karen came to her and told her she was going to do the same thing? Kitty shoved her papers aside. "You know, Karen, I have been thinking that there is a real shortage of good nurses and medical aides . . . I mean, in the Palmach as well as in the settlements. You've had lots of experience working with the youngsters in the DP camps and I've taken on quite a crowd of the disturbed ones. Do you suppose it would make sense if I asked Dr. Lieberman to let you come to work with me and let me train you as my assistant?"

"Would it!" Karen broke into a broad grin.

"Fine. I'll try to arrange it so you skip the agriculture work and report right to my office after school."

Karen sobered. "Well, I don't know. It doesn't seem quite fair to the others."

"As we say in American, they won't be losing a farmer, they'll be gaining a nurse."

"Kitty, I have a terrible confession to make. Don't tell the Youth Aliyah, the Zion Settlement Society, or the Central Kibbutz Movement but honest, I'm the worst farmer at Gan Dafna and I'd just love to be a nurse."

Kitty got up and walked to Karen and put her arm about the girl's shoulder. "Do you suppose that with Yona gone you would like to move into my cottage and live with me?"

The instantaneous look of happiness on Karen's face was all the answer that Kitty needed.

Kitty left Dr. Lieberman's cottage early to give Karen the good news. Dr. Lieberman had considered their duty to dispense love and not rules and decided the cause would not be hurt with one less farmer and one more nurse.

When she left Karen she crossed the center green and stopped before the statue of Dafna. She felt that she had hurt Dafna tonight, she had won a victory. With Karen near her she could keep the child from becoming an aggressive, angry *sabra* girl. It was good to live with a purpose, Kitty knew. But too much purpose could destroy womanliness. She had hit Jordana in a weak spot and she knew it. Since birth Jordana had been given a mission to carry out without question, at the price of her own personal happiness, career, and femininity. Jordana did not know how to compete with the elegant women coming into Palestine from the Continent and from America. She hated Kitty because she wanted to be more like Kitty and Kitty knew it.

"Kitty?" A voice called out in the darkness.

"Yes?"

"I hope I didn't startle you."

It was Ari. As he came near her she felt that same now-familiar sensation of helplessness.

"I'm sorry I haven't been able to get up to see you. Jordana gave you my messages?"

"Jordana? Yes, of course," Kitty lied.

"How are you getting along?"

"Fine."

"I came up to ask you if you would care to take the day off tomorrow. A Palmach group is going to climb Mount Tabor. It is something that should not be missed. Would you come with me?"

"Yes, I'd love to."

CHAPTER FIVE: Ari and Kitty arrived at the *kibbutz* of Beth Alonim—the House of the Oaks—at the foot of Mount Tabor, shortly after dawn. It was the *kibbutz* which gave birth to the Palmach during the war and the place Ari had trained troops.

Tabor was odd: not high enough to be a real mountain but far too high to be a hill. It stood in the middle of flatlands arising suddenly in the shape of a thumb poking through the earth.

After breakfast at the *kibbutz* Ari rolled a pair of packs with rations, canteen, and blankets and drew a Sten gun from the arsenal. He planned to hike up ahead of the rest of the group during the morning hours when it was cool. The air was crisp and invigorating and Kitty was charged with the spirit of adventure. They passed through the Arab village of Dabburiya at the opposite base of Tabor from Beth Alonim and took up a narrow dirt path. Within moments they could see Nazareth in the hills several kilometers away. It stayed cool and their progress was fast, although Kitty realized her first view was deceptive. Tabor rose to more than two thousand feet; it was going to be a long day. Dabburiya grew smaller and began to look quaint as they put distance between themselves and the village.

Suddenly Ari stopped, and tensed.

"What is it?"

"Goats. Can you smell them?"

Kitty sniffed. "No, I don't smell anything."

Ari's eyes narrowed. He scanned the path ahead. It circled out of sight and there was a very gentle slope off to the blind side.

"Probably Bedouins. There was a report about them at the *kibbutz*. They must have moved in since yesterday. Come on."

Around the turn they saw a dozen haired goatskin tents along the hillside and a flock of little black goats grazing around them. Two rifle-bearing nomads came up to them.

Ari spoke to them in Arabic, then followed them to the largest of the tents, which obviously belonged to the sheik. Kitty looked around. They seemed the dregs of humanity. The women were encased in black robes—and layers of dirt. She was not able to smell the goats but she was able to smell the women. Chains of Ottoman coins formed veils over their faces. The children wore dirty rags.

A grizzled individual emerged from the tent and exchanged greetings with Ari. They conversed a moment, then Ari whispered to Kitty. "We must go in or he will be insulted. Be a good girl and eat whatever he offers you. You can throw it up later."

The inside of the tent stank even more. They sat down on goat-hair and sheep-wool rugs and exchanged amenities. The sheik was impressed that Kitty came from America and relayed the information that he once owned a photograph of Mrs. Roosevelt.

Courses of food came. A greasy lamb leg was thrust into Kitty's hand together with marrow mixed with rice. Kitty nibbled, the sheik watched expectantly. She smiled weakly and nodded to convey how delicious it was. Unwashed fruits were served, and the meal was ended with thick, sickeningly sweet coffee in cups so filthy they were crusted. The diners wiped hands on trousers and mouths with sleeves, and after a bit more conversation Ari begged leave.

They left the camp behind. Kitty emitted a long and loud sigh. "I feel sorry for them," she said.

"Please don't. They are quite sure they are the freest men on earth. Didn't you ever see *The Desert Song* when you were a girl?"

"Yes, but now I know the composer never saw a Bedouin camp. What were you two men gabbing about?"

"I told him to behave tonight and not try to collect any rings and watches from the Palmach."

"And what else?"

"He wanted to buy you. He offered me six camels."

"Why, that old devil. What did you tell him?"

"I told him that anyone could see you were a ten-camel girl." Ari glanced at the rising sun. "It's going to get hot from now on. We'd better get out of these heavy clothes and pack them."

Kitty wore a pair of the traditional blue shorts from the Gan Dafna stores.

"Damn, you look just like a *sabra*."

They followed the trail which wove along the southern face of Tabor. Both of them perspired as the sun beat down. The trail broke in frequent places and they were forced to climb. Ari's strong hands led Kitty up the steep inclines. By late afternoon they had passed the two-thousand-foot mark.

The entire top of Tabor was a large, rounded plateau. The south edge of the plateau opened the entire Jezreel Valley to their eyes. It was a staggering sight. Kitty could follow the Jezreel, the square-cut fields, the splashes of green around the Jewish settlements, and the white clusters of Arab villages all the way to Mount Carmel and the Mediterranean. In the other direction was the Sea of Galilee, so that the entire width of Palestine was below them. Through field glasses Kitty followed Ari's pointing out Ein Dor where Saul met the witch and the bald top of Mount Gilboa where Gideon was buried and Saul and Jonathan fell in battle to the Philistines.

"Ye mountains of Gilboa, let there be no dew, neither let there be rain, upon you nor fields of offerings: for there the shield of the mighty is vilely cast away, the shield of Saul . . ."

Kitty lowered the glasses. "Why Ari, you are poetic."

"It is the altitude. Everything is so removed from up here. Look over there—Beth Shean Valley. Beth Shean *tel* holds the oldest civilized city in the world. David knows more about these than I do. There are hundreds of *tels* around Palestine. He says that if we were to start excavating them now our modern cities would be ruins by the time we are finished. You see, Palestine is the bridge of history here and you are standing on the center of the bridge. Tabor has been a battleground since men made axes out of stone. The Hebrews stood against the Romans here and between the Crusaders and the Arabs it changed hands fifty times. Deborah hid here with her army and swooped down on the Canaanites. The battleground of the ages . . . You know what we say? . . . that Moses should have walked the tribes for another forty years and found a decent place."

They walked over the plateau through a pine forest with relics of Roman, Byzantine, Crusader, and Arab all around. Mosaics, pottery, a wall here, a stone there.

Two abbeys, one Greek Orthodox and one Roman Catholic, stood near the grounds believed to be the place Christ was transfigured and spoke to Moses and Elijah.

Beyond the forest they reached the highest point of Tabor. Ruins of a Crusader fort and Saracen castle occupied the site. They picked their way over the rubble and the walls until they had climbed the eastern rampart which hung over the mountain side and was called Wall of the East Winds. Here the Sea of Galilee came into full view with the Horns of Hattin where Saladin the Kurd demolished Crusader forces.

The wind blew through Kitty's hair as she stood on the wall and the air began to cool again. They sat for over an hour with Ari pointing out the countless points of Biblical history. Finally they retreated to that point on the edge of the forest where it met the castles, and changed back to their warmer clothing. Ari spread their blankets and Kitty stretched out and grunted with a weary happiness. "It has been a wonderful day, Ari, but I am going to ache for a week."

Ari propped himself up on an elbow, watched her. Again he felt a desire for her but he held his silence.

By dusk, parties of threes and fours and fives began reaching the summit. There were dark and olive-skinned Orientals and Africans and there were blonds who had immigrated to Israel. There were many girls, most of them straight and high breasted. There were the *sabras* with their large mustaches and the stamp of aggressiveness. It was a reunion. Palmach groups had to train in small units in different *kibbutzim* to remain hidden. This was a chance for both friends from the city and from the same settlements to see each other again and for sweethearts to meet. The greetings were warm, with affectionate hugs and back slaps and kisses. They were a lively bunch of youngsters in their late teens and early twenties.

Joab Yarkoni and Zev Gilboa had come when they learned Kitty would be there, and she was delighted.

David and Jordana came also, and Jordana was provoked by David's attention to Kitty, but she remained quiet to avoid creating a scene.

By dusk nearly two hundred of the young Palmach soldiers had gathered. A pit was dug near the castle wall, while some of them turned to gathering wood for an all-night fire. Three lambs were prepared and spitted for roasting. The sun plunged down behind the Jezreel Valley, the fire was lit with a single bursting blaze, and the lambs were placed over their pits and couples joined in a huge circle around the fire. Kitty, the visiting dignitary, was forced into the place of honor with Joab, Zev, and Ari around her.

Soon the plateau atop Mount Tabor rang with songs. They were the same songs that Kitty had heard the children sing at Gan Dafna. They told of the wonder of the water sprinklers that redeemed the land and they told of the beauty of the Galilee and Judea. They sang of how haunted and lovely was the Negev Desert and they sang the spirited marches of the old Guardsman and the Haganah and the Palmach. They sang a song that said that David the King still walked the land of Israel.

Joab sat cross-legged with his tambour before him. It was a clay drum with goatskin head. With his fingertips and the heels of his hand he beat a rhythm to a reed flute playing an ancient Hebraic melody. Several of the Oriental girls danced in the same slow, swaying, sensuous gyrations that must have been danced in the palace of Solomon.

With each new song and each new dance the party quickened.

"Jordana!" someone called. "We want Jordana!"

She got into the ring and a cheer went up. An accordion played a Hungarian folk tune and everyone clapped in beat and Jordana whirled around the edge of the ring pulling out partners for a wild *czardas*. One by one she danced her partners down, with her red hair flying wildly in her face, framed against the leaping fire. Faster the accordion played and faster the onlookers clapped until Jordana herself stopped in exhaustion.

A half dozen came to the center and started a *hora*, the dance of the Jewish peasants. The *hora* ring grew larger and larger until everyone was up and a second ring formed outside the first. Joab and Ari pulled Kitty into the circle. The circle moved in one direction, then stopped as the dancers made a sudden leap and changed directions.

They had been singing and dancing for four hours and there was no indication of slowing up. David and Jordana slipped away quietly to the Saracen castle and wandered through the rooms until the sounds of the music and the tambour nearly vanished. They came upon a tiny cell set in the Wall of the East Winds and now the sound of the wind from the Jezreel Valley was all that they could hear. David spread his blanket on the earth and they embraced and caressed and loved each other.

"David! David!" Jordana cried, "I love you so!"

The wind died and they could hear wild music . . .

"David . . . David . . . David . . ." she whispered over and over as her lips pressed his neck . . .

And David repeated her name over and over.

His hand felt for the smoothness of her body. She took the clothing from her to ease his way and they pressed against each other and she asked to be taken and they blended into one.

After their love, Jordana lay in his arms. His fingertips traced over her lips and her eyes and through her hair.

"Jordana." His whisper thrilled her through her body and soul.

"Do you remember the first time, David?"

"Yes."

"*I am the rose of Sharon and the lily of the valleys. . . .*" she whispered. "*For lo, the winter is past, the rain is over and gone; the flowers appear on the earth; the time of the singing of birds is come, and the voice of the turtle is heard in our land.*"

It became so still that each could hear only the other's uneven breathing and the other's heart beating.

"*Take us the foxes, the little foxes, that spoil the vines: for our vines have tender grapes. My beloved is mine and I am his.* Oh, David . . . tell me, tell me."

David whispered with his lips touching her ear, "*Behold thou art fair, my love; behold, thou art fair; thou has doves' eyes within thy locks . . . thy lips are like a thread of scarlet . . .*"

She squeezed his hand that rested upon her breast and he kissed her breast . . . "*Thy two breasts are like two young roes that are twins, which feed among the lilies. . . .*"

And he kissed her lips . . . "*And the roof of thy mouth like the best wine for my beloved, that goeth down sweetly, causing the lips of those who are asleep to speak.*"

David and Jordana fell into a bliss-filled sleep, locked tightly in each other's arms.

At four o'clock in the morning the lamb was served, with hot Arabic coffee. Kitty was honored with the first cut. The fervor of song and dance had slowed a little; many of the couples lay in each other's arms. The lamb tasted wonderful.

Joab played his tambour, and the reed flute behind him made a tune as ancient as the land itself. One of the girls who had been born in distant Yemen sang in a voice filled with the mystic and melancholy of the Hebrew, right from the pages of the Bible. Her haunting voice sang a Psalm of David.

Kitty Fremont looked at the faces in the dying firelight.

What kind of army was this? What kind of army without uniform or rank? What kind of army where the women fought alongside their men with rifle and bayonet? Who were these young lions of Judea?

She looked at the face of Ari Ben Canaan and a chill passed through her body. An electrifying revelation hit her.

This was no army of mortals.

These were the ancient Hebrews! These were the faces of Dan and Reuben and Judah and Ephraim! These were Samsons and Deborahs and Joabs and Sauls.

It was the army of Israel, and no force on earth could stop them for the power of God was within them!

CHAPTER SIX

Chatham House
Institute Of International Relations
London

Cecil Bradshaw, the dumpy expert on the Middle East, had been studying the survey reports from a variety of sources. For three days he had been digesting the summaries. The Colonial Office, the Ministry and even Number 10 Downing Street were all bringing pressure on him. The Palestine mandate was in a muddle. A clean-cut new policy had to be formulated. Bradshaw was a man of thirty-seven years' experience in the area. During that time he had gone through a hundred conferences with the Zionists and the Arabs. Bradshaw believed, as most of the officialdom believed, that Britain's interests lay with the Arabs. Time and again he was able to cover up Arab blackmail and threats. This time they had gone completely wild. The current London Conferences were ending in a fiasco.

It is completely obvious that Haj Amin el Husseini, the Mufti, is running the Palestine Higher Arab Committee from exile in Cairo. Our failure to prosecute the Mufti as a war criminal for fear of religious outbursts has now come back to haunt us. The Arab attitude has reached complete unreason. They refuse to sit at the same table with the Jews unless pre-imposed conditions are agreed upon.

Cecil Bradshaw had been at the San Remo Conference when the Middle East was divided between the British and French and he had been there when the Articles of Mandate were drawn and when the Balfour Declaration was issued. Bradshaw worked on Churchill's group that took half the Palestine mandate and created the kingdom of Trans-Jordan. In all the years, in all the Mufti's riots, they had never been up against a band of fighters in the class of the Maccabees. The Jewish terrorists fought with a fearsome conviction.

We have time and again demanded from the Yishuv Central and the Jewish community that they assist British authorities in stamping out the gangster elements who go under the name of the Maccabees. Whereas the Yishuv claims no authority over these people and they publicly condemn their actions it is known that a large segment of the

*Jews secretly approve the gangster actions. We have received
no co-operation in this matter. Maccabee activities have
reached such proportion that we deem it necessary to evacuate all nonessential British personnel and families from
Palestine.*

Bradshaw read over the reports of the stepped-up terrorist
raids which rocked the Holy Land from one end to another.

*In addition to the costly gangster raids on the Haifa re-
finery which stopped production for two weeks, and the
raid on the Lydda airdrome, which destroyed a squadron of
fighter planes, ten major road ambushes and fifteen major
raids on British installations have taken place. There is increasing evidence that the Haganah and its striking arm, the
Palmach, is becoming restless and may even be partaking in
some of the recent raids.*

The leaky tubs, the floating slums of Aliyah Bet, brought
loads of illegal immigrants into the shores of Palestine.

*Despite increased naval patrol forces there has been a
marked step-up in Aliyah Bet activity since the* Exodus *incident. The* America, San Miguel, Ulloa, Abril, Susannah, *and*
San Filipo *have carried eight thousand illegals from European displaced-persons camps. We have reason to believe
two other ships were successful in breaking the blockade and
beached. Our embassies and consulates in the Mediterranean
countries report that at least five more ships are being outfitted by Aliyah Bet to attempt immigrant runs on Palestine
in the near future.*

The British command had powerful forces in Palestine.
Fifty-two vaunted Taggart forts spread an interlocking network over the tiny country. In addition, there were border
forts such as Fort Esther and there was a regular police
force in every town and there was the powerful Arab Legion
from Trans-Jordan. Besides the Taggarts the British maintained large bases at Atlit in the Haifa area, the Schneller
Barracks in Jerusalem, and the immense Sarafand camp outside Tel Aviv.

*We have, in recent months, launched Operations Noah,
Ark, Lobster, Mackerel, Cautious, Lonesome, Octopus, Can-
tonment, and Harp to keep constant pressure upon the Yishuv.
These operations basically are for continued screening for
illegals, cordons, and arms searches, and counterattacks
where our forces have been attacked. Our success has been*

limited due to the hundred per cent organization and co-operation of every Jew in the Yishuv in their efforts. Arms are hidden in flower boxes, file cabinets, stoves, refrigerators, false table legs, and a thousand other ingenious places, making arms seizure a near impossibility. Arms are transported by women and small children who readily engage in this practice. Our efforts to obtain Jewish informers has met with total failure. On the other hand, the Jews are able not only to purchase Arab spies but are getting information from sympathetic people within the British command. The Jews are manufacturing weapons of improvised nature, and the Sten guns, land mines, and grenades are continually improving in quality and ingenuity. In a recent attempt to uncover a manufacturing plant on a kibbutz the women poured scalding water on our soldiers . . .

Bradshaw was not only having his trouble in controlling the mandate. Other outside factors were increasing the pressure. In England, the people were living under the hardships of austerity and the economy was failing badly. The cost of maintaining the Palestine garrison was enormous. The English were sick of the bloodshed, too. On the world political scene the American Zionists had definitely caught the ear of Truman and had in him a sympathetic ally.

Since our failure to follow the recommendation of the Anglo-American Committee to allow a hundred thousand Jews to enter Palestine, our prestige has fallen greatly among our allies. Also damaging our prestige is the manner of humiliation by the Maccabee terrorist operation. British authority has never been so badly flaunted as in the recent kidnaping of a British judge who passed sentence on a Jewish terrorist.

Cecil Bradshaw took off his horn-rimmed glasses, wiped his red eyes, and shook his head. What a mess! He thumbed through the reports once more. Jemal Husseini, the Mufti's nephew, was again wiping out Arab opposition within Palestine through assassination. The Haganah through Aliyah Bet and the Maccabees under Akiva had made things impossible. British officers had been horsewhipped in public streets and British soldiers were hung in reprisals. The Jews who had preached and obeyed the rules of self-restraint during the two sets of prewar riots were showing less and less restraint against the Arab acts of aggression.

It was said in official circles that Cecil Bradshaw had lost his stomach for fighting the Jews after the *Exodus* incident.

The Palestine mandate was nearing its twelfth hour. The little country occupied a position of tremendous economic and strategic importance. It was the pivot of the empire itself. The Haifa naval base and refinery and the position in relation to the central artery of the Suez made it imperative that it be held.

The intercom buzzer went off on Bradshaw's desk.

"General Tevor-Browne has arrived."

Bradshaw and Tevor-Browne mumbled cold greetings. Tevor-Browne was one of the few pro-Jews in official circles. It was he who had predicted the end of the mandate in this very office at the onset of the *Exodus* incident and had pleaded that the *Exodus* be allowed to sail before the hunger strike. Tevor-Browne had always felt that the Jews and not the Arabs deserved British support for the reason that the Jews were faithful allies and could be depended upon and the Arabs could not. He had been for the building of a Jewish Commonwealth nation out of Palestine.

General Tevor-Browne's thinking could not sway Bradshaw and the Chatham House crowd or the Colonial Office. Even at this hour they did not have the courage to reverse their drastic mistake but were standing ready to sink with it. The fear of Arab blackmail over the oil fields and the Suez Canal prevailed.

"I have been reading the summaries," Bradshaw said.

Tevor-Browne lit a cigar. "Yes, very interesting. The Jews certainly aren't obliging us by marching backwards into the sea."

Bradshaw tapped his pudgy fingers on the desk top, resenting the general's "I told you so," attitude. "I must give a recommendation in a few weeks."

"I don't want your needling implications, Sir Clarence. I wanted to speak over the advisability of retaining Haven-Hurst. I think the time has come to get tougher with the Jews."

"Haven-Hurst is fine for what you want—unless you wish to obtain the services of some SS generals in the war crimes prisons. We still maintain a civil government in Palestine, you know . . . we do have a high commissioner."

Bradshaw turned crimson under the insults. He managed to hold his temper, a temper which was growing shorter and more violent each day. "I think the time has come to place greater authority with Haven-Hurst." He handed a sheet of paper over the desk to Tevor-Browne.

It was a letter addressed to the British commander in Palestine, General Sir Arnold Haven-Hurst, KBE, CB, DSO, MC. "The situation has degenerated to such a state that unless

361

means can be recommended for immediate stabilization by you I will be compelled to suggest the matter be turned over to the United Nations."

"Well said, Bradshaw," Tevor-Browne said. "I am certain Haven-Hurst will have some rather interesting suggestions if you are a devotee of horror stories."

SAFED, PALESTINE

The retirement order came through for Brigadier Bruce Sutherland quickly and quietly after the *Exodus* affair. He moved to Palestine and settled down on Mount Canaan near Safed, the ancient city at the entrance to the Huleh Valley in northern Galilee.

At long last Bruce Sutherland seemed to find a bit of peace and some respite from the years of torment since the death of his mother. For the first time he was able to sleep at night without fear. Sutherland purchased a magnificent small villa on Mount Canaan three miles from Safed proper. The air was the purest in Palestine and a constant fresh breeze kept summer's heat from fully penetrating the area. His home was of white plaster with red tiled roof and granite floor. It was open and breezy and tastefully furnished in Mediterranean décor. Beyond his rear patio there was a terraced hillside of four full *dunams* of land which he converted into a lush garden crowned with four hundred Galilee rosebushes.

The rear garden afforded a breath-taking view of Safed across the valley. From here the city appeared to be a perfect cone in shape. At the wide base of Safed's hill were the beginnings of winding roads which fought up the peak to the acropolis on top, some three thousand feet in the air. Like so many of the hilltops in Palestine, the acropolis of Safed had once been a citadel in the revolutions of the Hebrews against the Greeks and Romans.

He spent his days puttering in his rose garden, considered to be the finest in Palestine, on trips to the holy places, in studying Hebrew and Arabic, or in just wandering through the maze of crooked and aimless alleys that made up Safed. The town was a constant fascination. It was pressed against the hillside with its narrow oriental streets circling up toward the acropolis in no fixed plan, and the houses were jammed together equally haphazardly. These each with its own special design, grillwork, odd-shaped windows, doors, and balconies cluttered the strangled passageways to add up to a strange sort of charm.

The Jewish quarter, a tenth of the city, was inhabited by the poverty-stricken pious who were content to live off the meager offerings of coreligionists. Safed was the center of the Cabala, the Jewish science of mysticism. The ancient ones here spent their lives in study and prayer and were as colorful as the town itself. They ambled along the rows of tiny shops dressed in outlandish oriental costumes and tattered remains of once majestic silks. They were a gentle and peaceful lot, and for this reason the Cabalists of Safed had suffered the most at the hands of the Mufti's riots for they were least able to defend themselves.

Their history in Palestine was one of the longest unbroken records of Jewish habitation of the Holy Land. The Crusaders banished the Jews, but after their defeat the Cabalists returned to Safed and had remained ever since. The cemetery held graves of the great Cabalist scholars with tombs dating back four and five hundred years. The Cabalists all believed that anyone buried in Safed would go straight to Gan Eden—the Garden of Eden—so pure was the air in Safed.

Sutherland never tired of walking through the tortuous lanes crowded with tiny synagogues and watching the people or filling himself with the folklore and legend of the rabbis and of the Cabala itself.

The Arab section of Safed held the usual broken-down hovels that are found in every Arab city and town in the world. However, the wonderful climate and scenic beauty of Safed attracted many effendi families to build splendid and spacious homes. Mount Canaan had many homes and resorts for the Jews, Arab Safed had the same for wealthy Arabs. Sutherland had friends in both places.

Consistent with the Arab renown for building atop ruins there were, in the Arab quarters of Safed, remains of medieval buildings converted into contemporary housing. The most beautiful example of the architecture was the Mosque of the Daughters of Jacob on the ruins of a Hungarian Crusader convent.

The crown jewel of Safed was the acropolis. The paths that wound up to the hilltop passed the old Knights Templar castle and the ruins of a Hebrew fort. The very peak stood in a pine forest amid a carpet of wild flowers and commanded a view from the Sea of Galilee on the south to the Huleh Lake in the north where one could follow the winding course of the Jordan River. On the horizon was Mount Hermon, and all the valleys and hills of the Galilee were visible beyond Meron on the western side.

On this hill the ancient Hebrews came once each year to light a fire. The signal would be seen and transmitted from hill to hill to indicate the start of the Holy Days. In the days before calendars the Holy Days were determined by calculations of the chief rabbis, and the fires burned on the hilltops from Jerusalem to Tabor to Gilboa to Safed and on to Babylon to where the Jews lived in captivity.

One discordant note jarred the otherwise perfect beauty and visual poetry: a large, ugly concrete Taggart fort stood outside Safed on the road up Mount Canaan and was visible from Sutherland's villa.

Sutherland ventured north to look at the *tel* of Hazor and along the Lebanese border to see the burial places of Esther at the fort and Joshua at Abu Yesha. It was by chance that he happened into Gan Dafna and friendship with Dr. Lieberman and Kitty Fremont. For Kitty and Sutherland the renewal of the brief acquaintance made at Cyprus was a welcoming thing. Sutherland was happy to develop into a patron saint of the children. Kitty prevailed upon him to let some of the more disturbed children come with her to visit his villa and Safed. In a short time the two formed a fast friendship.

One afternoon Sutherland returned from Gan Dafna and was surprised to find his former aide, Major Fred Caldwell, awaiting him.

"How long have you been in Palestine, Freddie?"

"I arrived just a bit ago."

"Where are you serving?"

"Headquarters, Jerusalem, in Intelligence. I'm doing liaison with the Criminal Investigation Division. They've had a shake-up recently. Seems that some of our chaps have been working with the Haganah and even with the Maccabees, if you can imagine that."

Sutherland could imagine it quite easily.

"Actually, sir, this visit is only partly social, although I certainly intended to drop up and see how you've been getting on. General Haven-Hurst asked me to see you personally because I had worked under you in the past."

"Oh?"

"As you know we are now in the process of carrying out Operation Polly, the evacuation of nonessential British from Palestine."

"I've heard it referred to as Operation Folly," Sutherland said.

Freddie smiled politely at the jibe and cleared his throat. "General Haven-Hurst wanted to know what you planned to do."

"I don't plan to do a thing. This is my home and this is where I am going to remain."

Freddie's fingers drummed impatiently on the table top. "What I mean, sir, is that General Haven-Hurst wants it understood that once the nonessentials are gone he cannot assume responsibility for your safety. If you remain here it could pose a problem to us."

Caldwell's speech held obvious devious connotations: Haven-Hurst knew of Sutherland's leanings and was afraid of his working with the Haganah. He was, in effect, advising him to get out.

"Tell General Haven-Hurst I am grateful for his concern and I fully realize his exact position."

Freddie wanted to press the matter. Sutherland arose quickly and thanked Caldwell for the visit and walked him to the driveway, where a sergeant waited with a staff car. He watched the car drive down toward the Taggart fort. As usual, Freddie had botched his assignment. His delivery of Haven-Hurst's warning had been clumsy, indeed.

Sutherland walked back to the villa and thought it over. He was in physical danger. The Maccabees could easily take exception to a retired British brigadier with Arab friends living alone on Mount Canaan, although the Maccabees would certainly think twice about doing him in. There was no danger from the Haganah. He had a loose contact with them and they were not only discriminate but did not go in for assassination. On the other side there was no telling what Husseini was likely to do: Sutherland had friends among the Jews. Some of them could well have been Maccabees unbeknownst to him.

Bruce Sutherland walked to his gardens. They were bursting with the early spring roses. He looked beyond the valley to Safed. He had found peace and comfort here. The hideous dreams were gone. No, he would not leave tomorrow—or ever.

Caldwell's car entered the Taggart fort a few moments after he left Sutherland. The four outside walls held the offices and barracks. The inner court served as the assembly ground and parking lot for vehicles. He was met and asked to report to CID.

"Are you going back to Jerusalem tonight, Major Caldwell?" the Criminal Investigation Division inspector asked.

Freddie looked at his watch. "Yes, I plan to. We can make it back before evening if I leave right now."

"Good. I have a Jew here I want taken back to CID in Jerusalem for questioning. Maccabee prisoner . . . dangerous one. There is a chance that the Maccabees know we are holding him here and will be watching for a convoy to transfer him. That is why it will be safer if he goes in your car."

"Happy to do it."

"Bring the Jew boy in."

Two soldiers dragged in a boy of fourteen or fifteen years of age manacled with heavy chains on hands and feet. A taped gag was over his mouth. His face was bruised from a CID third degree. The inspector walked up to the prisoner. "Don't let Ben Solomon's angel face fool you. He's a ruddy little bastard."

"Ben Solomon? Ben Solomon? I don't remember seeing his name."

"Just got him last night. Raid on the Safed police station. They were trying to steal arms. He killed two policemen with a grenade. Yes, indeed, you're a mean little sheeny, aren't you?"

Ben Solomon stood calm with his eyes blazing contempt at the inspector.

"Don't take his gag off, Major Caldwell, or he'll start singing Psalms for you. He's a fanatic little bastard."

The inspector became annoyed at the boy's steady withering glare. He took a step toward Ben Solomon and smashed him in the mouth, sending him crashing to the floor, bloody and tangled in his chains.

"Get him out of here," the inspector snapped in a nervous voice.

The boy was shoved on the floor in the back of the car. One armed soldier sat in back with him and Caldwell sat in front next to the driver. They drove out of the Taggart fort.

"Dirty little bastard," the driver mumbled. "Ask me, Major Caldwell, they ought to turn us loose on these Jews 'ere a few weeks. That's what we should do, by rights."

"Cobber of mine got it last week," the guard in the back said, "and a fine bloke he was, too. 'Ad a wife and a new baby. Them Maccabees give it to him right through the 'ead, they did."

As they drove into the Beth Shean Valley the three men relaxed; they were now in all-Arab territory and the danger of attack was gone until they reached the Jerusalem area.

Caldwell turned around and looked at the prisoner on the floor. The juices of hatred churned in his stomach. He detested Bruce Sutherland. He knew in his heart that Sutherland was helping the Haganah. Sutherland was a Jew lover. Sutherland had intentionally let the catastrophe on Cyprus occur.

Caldwell remembered standing near the barbed wire at the Caraolos camp and a fat Jewish woman spitting out on him.

He looked back at the boy on the floor. The guard sat in the middle of the seat. One heavy boot was planted on Ben Solomon's head and he snickered with amusement.

"Dirty Jew!" Caldwell mumbled under his breath.

He could see a parade of them. The bearded characters in London's Whitechapel and he could smell the smell of pickles.

The line of pawn shops—they sat hunched over their benches mumbling prayers. Caldwell could see the little boys on their way to Jew school with the black caps on their heads.

They drove toward the all-Arab city of Nablus.

Caldwell smiled as he remembered the officers' club and the sheeny jokes. He could see his mother leading him into the office of an arrogant Jew doctor.

And they think Hitler was wrong, Caldwell thought. Hitler knew what the score was. It was bloody well too bad that the war ended before he could do them all in. Caldwell remembered entering Bergen-Belsen with Sutherland. Sutherland was sick at what he saw. Well, Caldwell wasn't sick. The more Jews dead, the better.

They passed into an Arab village with a record of known hostility toward the Yishuv. It was an Husseini strong point.

"Stop the car," Caldwell ordered. "Now you two men listen to me. We are throwing this kike out."

"But, Major, they'll murder him," the guard said.

"I admits I'm put out at the Jews, sir," the driver said, "but we got a responsibility to deliver our prisoner, we has."

"Shut up!" Caldwell barked, half hysterically. "I said we are throwing him out. Both of you are to swear he was taken by Maccabees who roadblocked us. If you open your mouth otherwise you'll end up in ditches. Am I clear?"

The two soldiers merely nodded as they saw the mad look in Caldwell's eyes.

Ben Solomon was unchained from the floor. The car slowed near the coffeehouse. The boy was hurled into the street and they sped away for Jerusalem.

It worked just as Caldwell knew it would. Within an hour Ben Solomon had been killed and mutilated. He was decapitated. The bodyless head was held up by the hair and photographed with twenty laughing Arabs around it. The picture was sent out as a warning of what was going to happen to all the Jews sooner or later.

Major Fred Caldwell made a disastrous mistake. One of the Arabs in the coffeehouse who saw the boy thrown from the car was a member of the Maccabees.

General Sir Arnold Haven-Hurst, KBE, CB, DSO, MC was infuriated. He paced the office of his headquarters in the Schneller compound in Jerusalem, then snatched Cecil Bradshaw's letter from his desk and read it again.

The situation has degenerated to such a state that unless means can be recommended for immediate stabilization by you I will be compelled to suggest the matter be turned over to the United Nations.

The United Nations, indeed! The tall blond man snorted and crumpled the letter and threw it to the floor. A week before Haven-Hurst had ordered a boycott on all Jewish places of business.

This was to be his thanks after fighting the Jews for five years. He had warned the Home Office in World War II not to take these Jews into the British Army but no, they wouldn't listen. Now, lose the Palestine mandate. Haven-Hurst went to his desk and began working on an answer to Bradshaw's letter.

I propose immediate adoption of the following points, which in my opinion will stabilize Palestine.

1. Suspension of all civil courts with fines and punishments and prison terms to be dispensed by the military commander.

2. Dissolve the Yishuv Central, disband the Zion Settlement Society and all other agencies of the Jews.

3. Cessation of all Jewish newspapers and publications.

4. Swift, quiet elimination of some sixty top Yishuv leaders. Haj Amin el Husseini has proved this method successful against his political opposition. This phase could be carried out by Arab confederates.

5. Complete use of the Arab Legion of Trans-Jordan.

6. Imprisonment of several hundred secondary leaders in the Yishuv and their subsequent quick banishment to some remote African colonies.

7. Grant the military commander the right to destroy any kibbutz, moshav, village, or part of a city found with arms. Institute a nationwide screening with all illegals to be deported at once.

8. Impose collective fines against the entire Jewish population for every act of Maccabee terror, and place these fines so high the Jews will begin to co-operate in the apprehension of these gangsters.

9. Offer larger rewards for information on key Maccabee terrorists, Aliyah Bet agents, Haganah heads, etc.

10. Hang or execute every apprehended Maccabee gangster on the spot.

11. Institute a series of boycotts on Jewish business, farm products, and halt all Jewish imports and exports. Keep complete control on all the movements of all Jewish vehicles.

12. Destroy the Palmach by armed attacks on kibbutzim known to be harboring them.

My forces have been compelled to operate under most difficult circumstances. We have been made to follow the rules and restrain ourselves from the widest and most effective use of our powers. On the other hand the Maccabees, Haganah, Palmach, and Aliyah Bet observe no rules and, indeed, attack

368

our restraint as a weakness. If I am allowed to use my power I assure that order will be restored in short time.

General Sir Arnold Haven-Hurst
KBE, CB, DSO, MC

CHATHAM HOUSE, INSTITUTE OF FOREIGN RELATIONS, LONDON

Cecil Bradshaw's color was a sickly gray when General Tevor-Browne finally reached his office.

"Well, Bradshaw, you asked Haven-Hurst for his ideas. You have them now."

"Has the man gone mad? Good Lord, his report reads iike Adolf Hitler's 'Final Solution.'"

Bradshaw picked up the twelve-point "Haven-Hurst Report" and shook his head. "God knows we want to keep Palestine, but murder, burning villages, hangings, starvation? I cannot recommend this beastly thing. Even if I did I don't know whether you have enough men in the British Army who could carry it out. I've been for the Empire all my life, Sir Clarence, and many's the time we've had to take harsh and unfair measures in our own behalf. But I also believe in God. We're just not going to hold Palestine this way. I wash my hands of the matter. Let someone else endorse Haven-Hurst . . . I won't."

Cecil Bradshaw took the "Haven-Hurst Report" and crumpled it. He put it in his large ash tray and put a match to it and watched it burn. "Thank God, we've got the courage to answer for our sins," he whispered.

The question of the Palestine mandate was thrown open to the United Nations.

CHAPTER SEVEN: Now it was the late spring of 1947 and Ari Ben Canaan disappeared from Kitty Fremont's life. She did not see or hear from him after Mount Tabor. If Ari had given any messages to Jordana, Jordana had not delivered them. The two women scarcely spoke a word to each other. Kitty tried to be tolerant but Jordana made even that difficult.

The Palestine mandate issue was handed over for the United Nations to attempt to unscramble it. United Nations machinery was in the process of forming a committee of small, neutral nations to investigate the problem and come up with recommendations for the General Assembly. The Yishuv Central and the World Zionists accepted mediation of the problem by the United Nations. On the other side, the Arabs used threats, boycotts, blackmail, and any other pressure they could find to keep the Palestine issue away from an impartial judgment.

At Gan Dafna the Gadna military training speeded up. The Youth Village became a chief arms depot. Rifles were brought in to be cleaned by the children and then smuggled in village trucks to Huleh settlements and the Palmach. Time and again Karen was called upon to go out on arms-smuggling missions. The assignments were accepted by her and the other children without question. Kitty's heart was in her mouth every time Karen went out, but she had to keep her silence.

Karen doggedly continued to press the search for her father without success. The once bright promise at La Ciotat faded.

The girl retained contact with the Hansens in Denmark. Karen wrote each week, and each week a letter and often a package arrived from Copenhagen. Meta and Aage Hansen had given up all hope of ever getting her back. Even if Karen did not find her father there was something in the girl's letters that indicated she was lost to them. Karen's identification with Palestine and being Jewish became a nearly complete thing. The only qualification was Kitty Fremont.

Dov Landau was taking strange turns. At times he would appear to be breaking out of his reclusion, and in those moments he and Karen added a deeper dimension to their relationship. Then the very audacity of his coming into the clear light would force Dov back into his shell. Whenever he was able to reason about his role he disliked himself for what he felt he was doing to Karen. Then loyalty to him produced self-pity and he at once hated and loved her. He felt he must not contaminate Karen with himself, yet he did not wish to cut off his only link with humanity. The times he would sink back again into bitterness he often stared at the blue tattoo number on his arm by the hour. He would turn to his books and his painting with a savage concentration and close out all living things. Just as he neared the bottom, Karen would succeed in pulling him out of it. His bitterness never quite grew so deep that he could turn on her.

In the time that Kitty Fremont had been at Gan Dafna she had made herself one of the most important persons in the village. Dr. Lieberman leaned on her more each day. Looked upon as a sympathetic outsider, she was frequently able to exert the needed extra influence of someone "outside the family." Dr. Lieberman's friendship was becoming one of the most rewarding she had ever known. She was completely integrated into the life of Gan Dafna; she did splendid work with disturbed children. Yet a barrier still remained. She knew that she was partly responsible for it but she wanted it that way.

370

Kitty was far more at ease with Bruce Sutherland than she was with the people of Gan Dafna. With Sutherland she was in her own element and she looked forward with increasing impatience to those free days that she and Karen could spend at his villa. When she was with Sutherland it renewed her awareness of the difference between herself and the Jews.

Harriet Saltzman came to Gan Dafna two times. On both occasions the old woman pleaded with Kitty to take charge of one of the new Youth Aliyah Centers in the Tel Aviv area. Kitty was a wizard at organization and a stickler for routine. This, plus her over-all experience and ability was badly needed at places not so well run as Gan Dafna. Harriet Saltzman wisely calculated that the "outside" influence of a Kitty Fremont would be a tremendous asset to a Youth Aliyah Center.

Kitty refused. She was settled at Gan Dafna and Karen was completely at home. She did not seek a career in Youth Aliyah and had no aspirations.

The main reason, however, was that she did not want to be placed in a capacity where she would have to answer for Gadna activities and arms smuggling. This would put her into the category of a participant. Kitty clung to her neutrality. Her work was going to remain professional and not political.

To Karen Clement, Kitty Fremont was like an older sister who was raising her without the help of parents. Kitty made herself indispensable to the girl. The Hansens in Denmark faded from her life and there had been no progress in finding her father. This left only Dov and Dov gave nothing. Kitty encouraged this condition of dependence—she wanted Karen to need her. She wanted Karen to need her so much the need would defeat the hidden foe, the power of Eretz Israel.

With the passing of the weeks holidays came and left Gan Dafna.

There had been Tuv b'Shevat in the late winter, an arbor day, to perpetuate the fanatical tree planting of the Jews.

Late in the month of March came Hero's Day. Jordana Ben Canaan led the Gadna troops on a hike along the border ridges to Tel Hai where Barak and Akiva had entered Palestine from Lebanon. It was now hallowed ground. At Trumpledor's grave soldiers of the Palmach and the young soldiers of Gadna gathered to pay homage to the new heroes.

The glorious festival of Purim came. Gan Dafna erupted with Mardi gras- and Halloween-like costumes and floats and decorations that turned it into a carnival. The Purim story was told—of how Queen Esther saved the Jews, then in the Persian Empire. The evil Haman, the Amalekite, plotted to have the Jews annihilated but Esther unmasked Haman and

371

saved her people. The grave of Esther was on the border of Fort Esther, where part of the celebration took place. The Purim story was a real thing to the children of Gan Dafna, for almost all of them had been victims of a later-day Haman named Adolf Hitler.

Passover came and went.

The holiday of Lag Ba Omer occurred on the full moon thirty days after the end of Passover and in time became a memorial to the second uprising of the Hebrews against the Romans. Homage was paid to the great sages buried in the city of Tiberias and in Safed and in Meron. There were the graves of Moses Maimonides, the immortal philosopher and physician, and of the rabbis, Hiya, Eliezer, and Kahana and of the great revolutionary, Rabbi Akiva. There was the grave of Rabbi Meir the Miracle Maker. All these were in Tiberias where the festival started and whence it moved to Safed. From Safed the pious moved in a great gathering body to Meron and to the graves of Johanan the Sandal Maker and Hillel and Shammai. The ancient synagogue still stood in part at Meron with its door which was supposed to welcome the return of the Messiah.

Of all the rabbis praised on Lag Ba Omer, Simon Bar Yohai received the greatest reverence. Bar Yohai defied the Roman edicts which banned Judaism and he fled to the village of Peki'in where he lived in a cave and where the Lord provided him with a carob tree for food and a stream for water. He lived in hiding for seventeen years. One day each year he came to Meron to teach the forbidden Torah to his disciples. It is said by both Mohammedans and Christians that they owe the life of their religions to those rabbis who kept Judaism alive in hiding. Without Judaism and the Holy Torah neither Christianity nor Islam could have survived, for their roots were in the Torah and their very life and air and blood were the doctrines of Judaism.

While in hiding Bar Yohai wrote the *Zohar*—the Brightness —which was the standard work of the mystic Cabala. Hasidic and Oriental celebrants converged on the holy cities of Tiberias and Safed from all corners of Palestine and continued on to Meron to spend several days and nights in prayer and song and dance and praise of Simon Bar Yohai.

When the month of May came the rains were gone and the Huleh Valley and the hills of Syria and Lebanon turned a rich green and the valleys filled with carpets of wild flowers and the buds on the spring roses of Galilee burst into magnificent reds and whites and oranges and once again Gan Dafna prepared for a holiday. It was time for Shavuot to celebrate the bringing of the first fruits of the new year.

All holidays concerned with farming were particularly close to the hearts of the Jews of Palestine. Shavuot at Gan Dafna had become traditional for the coming of delegations from the Huleh settlements to the children's village to share in the celebration.

Again Gan Dafna took on the air of a carnival as truckloads of farmers arrived from the Yad El *moshav*. Sarah Ben Canaan came.

They arrived from the border *kibbutzim* of Kfar Giladi up on the Lebanon border. They came from Ayelet Hashahar *kikkutz* on the lake and from Ein Or. They came from Dan on the Syrian border and from Manara on the mountaintop.

Dr Lieberman expressed his disappointment to Harriet Saltzman and Kitty that the Arab delegation from Abu Yesha was only half the usual size and that Taha was missing. The meaning was obvious and saddening.

Kitty managed to see each truck as it arrived. She hoped that Ari Ben Canaan would come and she was unable to mask her disappointment. Jordana in turn watched Kitty, with a cynical smirk.

Some soldiers came from Fort Esther. These were among the "friends" who always tipped off the village when an arms search was on the way.

The day was filled with merriment. There were athletic contests and open house in the classrooms and laboratories. There was *hora* dancing on the center green, and outdoor tables bent under the weight of food.

At sundown everyone moved to the outdoor theater cut into a hillside, set in the middle of a stand of pine trees. The theater filled to overflowing; hundreds more lay about on the surrounding lawns. As it turned dark multi-colored lights came on, strung through the pines.

The Gan Dafna orchestra played "Hatikvah"—the Hope— and Dr. Lieberman spoke a brief welcome and signaled the parade of Shavuot to begin. He returned to his seat with Kitty, Sutherland, and Harriet Saltzman.

Karen led the parade. The instant Kitty saw her she felt fear. Karen sat astride a large white horse and balanced the staff of the flag with the white field and the blue Star of David. She wore dark blue slacks and an embroidered peasant's blouse and sandals on her feet. Her thick brown hair was done in pigtails and hung to her small breasts.

Kitty gripped the arms of her chair. Karen looked the very spirit of the Jews!

Have I lost her? Have I lost her? The wind whipped the flag and her horse broke for a second, but Karen turned it into line quickly. She is gone from me as she is from the Hansens, Kitty thought.

Harriet Saltzman was looking at Kitty and Kitty lowered her eyes.

Karen passed out of the spotlight and the parade continued. The five tractors of Gan Dafna were polished and shined. Each pulled a flatcar loaded with fruits and vegetables and grains grown at the village farm.

Jeeps and trucks and station wagons buried under flowers from the gardens passed by. Trucks passed by filled with children in peasants' clothing holding rakes and hoes and scythes and power tools.

The livestock was passed in review, led by the cows, which were decked in ribbons and flowers, and the horses were shiny with manes and tails braided. The sheep and goats were herded past and then the pet dogs and cats and a monkey and white rats and hamsters were led or carried in affectionate display.

Children passed holding cloth of material they had grown, spun, and woven and newspapers they had printed and their art work and baskets and pottery. Their athletic teams marched by.

When the parade was done there was a final rousing cheer from the audience.

Dr. Lieberman's secretary slipped alongside him and whispered into his ear.

"Excuse me, please," he said, "I have an important phone call."

"Hurry back," Harriet Saltzman called after him.

The lights in the trees were turned off, plunging the place into darkness for a moment before a spotlight shone on the stage. The curtain opened and the tambour beat and a reed flute played an ancient melody. The children began to enact the Song of Ruth. It was done in pantomime against the plaintive sound background of the two instruments.

Their costumes were authentic. The dances were the slow and sensuous movements of the days of Ruth and Naomi. Then came performers who danced with wild leaps and a passion like that of the dancers Kitty saw on top of Tabor.

How they lived for the re-creation of their past, Kitty thought. How dedicated they were to regaining the glory of Israel.

Karen stepped onto the stage and commanded an instant expectant hush. Karen danced the part of Ruth. Her movements told the simple and beautiful story of the Moabite girl and her Hebrew mother-in-law who traveled to Beth Lehem —the House of Bread. The story of love and of one God had been retold at Shavuot since the days of the Maccabees.

Ruth had been a gentile in the land of the Jews. Yet Ruth was an ancestor of King David.

Kitty's eyes were glued to Karen as she enacted Ruth's words to Naomi that she would come to the land of the Hebrews with her.

"Whither thou goest I will go; and where thou lodgest I will lodge. Thy people shall be my people and thy God my God."

Kitty was dismayed as never before. Could she get Karen away from this? Kitty Fremont was the stranger. She would always be a stranger. The gentile among the Hebrews, but she could not say as Ruth had said, *"Thy people shall be my people."* Would this mean losing Karen?

Dr. Lieberman's secretary tapped Kitty's shoulder. "Would you come to Dr. Lieberman's office at once?" she whispered.

Kitty excused herself and slipped from her seat. She walked up to the top of the theater and looked back for a moment to see the children dancing the dance of the reapers and to watch Karen go to sleep at the feet of "Boaz." She turned and left the theater.

The path was dark and she had to be careful of trenches. Kitty turned her pocket flashlight on the ground. She crossed the center green and passed the statue of Dafna. Behind her she could hear the beat of the tambour and the cry of the flute. She walked quickly to the administration building, led by the single light.

She opened the door to Dr. Lieberman's office.

"Good Lord," she said, startled at the sight of him, "what's the matter? You look as though . . ."

"They have found Karen's father," he whispered.

CHAPTER EIGHT: Bruce Sutherland drove Kitty and Karen to Tel Aviv the next day. Kitty used the pretext that she had to do some overdue shopping and wanted to give Karen her first look at the big city. They arrived slightly before the noon hour and checked into the Gat Rimon Hotel on Hayarkon Street, on the Mediterranean. After lunch Sutherland excused himself and left. The shops were closed during the midday hours so Kitty and Karen romped along the sandy beach below the hotel, then cooled off from the heat with a refreshing swim.

At three o'clock Kitty ordered a taxi. They drove to Jaffa where one of the faculty at Gan Dafna had recommended some great buys in Arab and Persian brass- and copperware. Kitty wanted some things for the cottage. The taxi took them into a narrow, twisting street in the center of the Jaffa flea market. A row of shops were indentations in a Crusader wall. They stopped before one of the holes in the wall guarded by

375

a fat individual sitting asleep in the doorway, with a red fez tipped over his eyes. Kitty and Karen studied the shop. It was five feet wide and not much deeper and a mess of hanging pots, pans, plates, jugs, vases, urns, candlesticks, and what not. The floor had not been swept for at least ten years.

The fat Arab sensed the presence of customers and awakened from his sleep. He gallantly gestured to the women to enter his domain. He shoved some brassware off two boxes and offered them as seats, then ran outside and called for his oldest son to get some coffee for the honored guests. The coffee arrived. Kitty and Karen sipped it and politely exchanged smiles with the shopkeeper. The son stood by the door, a portrait in stupidity. A half dozen spectators gathered on the outside to observe the proceedings. The attempts to converse soon proved frustrating. There were grunts, gestures, and hand wavings in place of a common language. Whereas Karen spoke Danish, French, German, English, and Hebrew and Kitty spoke English, Spanish, and a smattering of Greek, the Arab was versed only in Arabic. He sent his son out once again to find the flea market interpreter and in another few minutes the intermediary was produced. The interpreter's English was of a pidgin variety, but he was conscientious and the shopping commenced.

Kitty and Karen browsed around the shop blowing dust off encrusted antiques, some with a hundred years' coating of dirt and tarnish to testify to their authenticity. After forty tense minutes of womanly thoroughness, every piece in the shop had been handled by one or the other shopper. They settled on a pair of vases, three long-spouted Arab coffee pots of exquisite delicacy, and an enormous Persian plate with thousands of hand-engraved figures depicting an entire legend. Kitty asked the price for the entire lot, cleaned, polished, and delivered to her hotel. The crowd on the outside pressed closer as the interpreter and the proprietor went into a huddle.

The interpreter turned and sighed. "Mr. Akim, him heart broke. These treasures to depart. Plate, he swear by Allah, three hundred years."

"Just how much is it going to take to mend Mr. Akim's broken heart?" Kitty asked.

"Because lady, your daughter here, so beautiful, Mr. Akim make special bargain. Take all, sixteen pounds sterling."

"It's a steal," Kitty whispered to Karen.

"You can't pay him what he asks," Karen said with exasperation. "Do you want to ruin his day by not bartering?"

"I'm taking it and running," Kitty whispered. "That plate alone would cost three or four hundred dollars in the States."

"Kitty! Please!" Karen cried in disgust. She stepped in front of Kitty and the smile disappeared from Akim's face. "Nine pounds sterling and not a *grush* more," Karen announced firmly.

The interpreter reported the counter-offer to Mr. Akim. Mr. Akim was offended. He went into wails of anguish. He had a large family to feed. Again his kind heart was being taken advantage of. The items picked by these sharp-eyed women they knew were antiques . . . on his honor, his father's honor, and by Allah's beard. Thirteen pounds.

"Twelve and that's final."

Akim sobbed that he was being cheated but he was a poor Arab so what could he do. He was putty in the hands of these clever women. Twelve and a half.

It was a deal.

The bartering was over and smiles bloomed within and without the shop. There was an extended handshaking ceremony. Akim blessed Kitty and Karen and all their subsequent offspring. She left the name of her hotel and advised Akim he would be paid when the cleaned and polished goods were delivered. She tipped the interpreter and the stupid son and they left.

They walked through the flea market amazed by the amount that could be jammed into the tiny shops and the degree of filth one street could collect. As they approached the end of the street a man who looked like a *sabra* stepped up to Karen and exchanged several words in Hebrew and walked away quickly.

"What did he want?"

"He saw by my uniform I was a Jew. He wanted to know if you were English. I told him who you were and he advised us to return to Tel Aviv. There might be trouble."

Kitty looked down the street but the man was gone.

"He must have been a Maccabee," Karen said.

"Let's get out of here."

Kitty's heart was in her mouth until they were out of Jaffa. They drove to the intersection of Allenby Road and Rothschild Boulevard. Allenby Road was filled with new shops, and Rothschild was a wide street with a center parkway lined with ultramodern three-storied white apartment houses. It was a striking contrast to the flea market of Jaffa. Cars and buses moved in a steady flow and people walked with the big-city gait, all in a hurry.

"It is so thrilling," Karen said. "I'm glad I was able to come. It is hard for me to realize that everyone here, bus drivers and waiters and salespeople, are all Jews. They built this whole city . . . a Jewish city. You don't understand what that means, do you . . . a city in which everything belongs to the Jews."

Karen's words annoyed Kitty.

"In America we have many important Jews, Karen, and they are very happy and very much American."

"But it's not the same as a Jewish country. It's not the same as knowing that wherever you go and whatever you do there is still one corner of the earth where you are wanted and that belongs to you."

Kitty fished in her purse quickly and took out a piece of paper. "Where would this address be?"

Karen looked at the paper. "Two blocks down. When are you going to learn to read Hebrew?"

"Never, I'm afraid," Kitty said, then added quickly, "I chipped two teeth trying to say some words yesterday."

They found the address. It was a dress shop.

"What are you going to get?" Karen asked.

"I'm going to buy you a decent wardrobe. It's a surprise from Brigadier Sutherland and me."

Karen stopped dead. "I couldn't," she said.

"What's the matter, dear?"

"There is nothing wrong with what I'm wearing."

"It is fine for Gan Dafna . . ." Kitty said.

"I have all the clothing I need," Karen insisted.

Sometimes she sounds like Jordana Ben Canaan, Kitty thought. "Karen, let's not forget that you are a young lady. You won't be betraying the cause if you dress up in something nice once in a while."

"I am quite proud of . . ."

"Oh, quiet!" Kitty said with finality. "You sound more like a *sabra* every day. When you are away from Gan Dafna with me you are going to make me and Bruce proud of you."

Kitty appeared angry and sounded adamant. Karen bit her lip and retreated. She peeked out of the corner of her eye at the full-skirted mannequins in the window. "It isn't fair to the rest of the girls," she said in a final effort.

"We'll hide the dresses under the rifles if it will make you happy."

A few moments later she was bouncing before the mirror, happily staging a one-woman fashion show and terribly pleased that Kitty had been insistent. It did feel so wonderful and look so wonderful! How long had it been since she wore nice things? Denmark . . . so long ago that she had almost forgotten. Kitty was as delighted as she watched Karen transform herself from peasant to *soignée* teen-ager. They walked the length of Allenby Road, still shopping, and turned into Ben Yehuda Street at the Mograbi Square, loaded with packages. They plopped down at a table at the first sidewalk café. Karen gobbled an ice-cream soda and watched the panorama of passing people with wide eyes.

She shoved a spoonful of ice cream in her mouth. "This is

378

the nicest day I can remember," she said. "It would be perfect if Dov and Ari were here."

She was adorable, Kitty thought. Her heart was so filled with goodness she wanted only to give to others.

Karen meditated as she sipped from the bottom of the glass. "Sometimes I think we have picked a pair of lemons."

"We?"

"You know . . . you and Ari. Me and Dov."

"I don't know what on earth gives you the impression there is something between Mr. Ben Canaan and myself, but you are quite, quite, quite mistaken."

"Ha, ha, ha," Karen answered. "Is that why you twisted your neck watching every truck that came in the gate before the Shavuot celebration yesterday? Just who were you looking for if not Ari Ben Canaan?"

"Humph," Kitty grunted, and sipped her coffee to cover her guilty confusion.

Kitty shrugged as she wiped at her lips. "Gosh, anyone could tell you are sweet on him."

Kitty narrowed her eyes and glared at Karen. "You listen to me, Miss Smarty . . ."

"Deny it and I'll run up and down the street and shout it in Hebrew."

Kitty threw up her hands. "I can't win. Someday you'll realize a man can be very attractive to us older women of thirty without there being the least bit of seriousness attached to it. I like Ari, but I'm sorry to have to dispel your romantic notions."

Karen looked at Kitty with an expression that clearly said she was simply not convinced. The girl sighed and leaned close to Kitty and held her arm as though she were going to impart a deep dark secret. Karen's mien took on the earnest sincerity of the teen-ager. "Ari needs you, I can tell that."

Kitty patted Karen's hand and adjusted a loose strand of hair in the girl's pigtail. "I wish I were sixteen again and things were so pure and uncomplicated. No, Karen, Ari Ben Canaan comes from a breed of supermen whose stock in trade is their self-reliance. Ari Ben Canaan hasn't needed anyone since the day he cut his teeth on his father's bull whip. His blood is made up of little steel and ice corpuscles and his heart is a pump like the motor in that bus over there. All this keeps him above and beyond human emotions."

She sat silent and very still and her eyes looked beyond Karen.

"You do care for him."

"Yes," Kitty sighed, "I do, and what you said is right. We've got a pair of lemons. We'd better get back to the hotel. I want you to dress up for me and make yourself look like a princess. Bruce and I have a surprise for you. We'll take the pigtails down."

Karen indeed looked like a princess when Sutherland picked them up for dinner. The surprise was attendance at a touring French ballet company's staging of *Swan Lake* at the Habima National Theater, accompanied by the Palestine Philharmonic Orchestra.

Karen leaned forward and sat on the edge of her seat during the entire performance, concentrating intently on the steps of the prima ballerina as she floated her way through the fairy tale. The overpowering, haunting beauty of the score filled her brain.

How beautiful it all was, Karen thought. She had almost forgotten things like ballet were still in the world. How lucky she was to have Kitty Fremont. The stage was bathed in blue light and the music swelled into the finale with the storm and Siegfried defeating the evil Von Rotbart and the beautiful swan maidens turning into women. Tears of happiness fell down her cheeks.

Kitty watched Karen more than she watched the ballet. She sensed that she had awakened something dormant in the girl. Maybe Karen was rediscovering that there was something in the world she once had that was as important as the green of the fields of the Galilee. Kitty resolved again to keep this thing alive in Karen always; as much as the Jews had won her over there was still much of her they could never get.

Tomorrow Karen would see her father and her world would move on in another direction. Kitty won something this day.

They returned to the hotel late. Karen was bursting with happiness. She flung the hotel door open and danced through the lobby. The British officers raised their eyebrows. Kitty sent her up to get ready for bed and repaired to the bar with Sutherland for a nightcap.

"Have you told her about her father yet?"

"No."

"Do you want me to go with you?"

"I'd rather . . . alone."

"Of course."

"But please be there afterwards."

"I'll be there."

Kitty stood up and kissed Sutherland on the cheek. "Good night, Bruce."

Karen was still dancing in their room when Kitty arrived. "Did you see Odette in the last scene?" she said, imitating the steps.

"It's late and you're a tired Indian."

"Oh, what a day!" Karen said, flopping into her bed.

Kitty walked into the bathroom and changed. She could hear Karen humming the melodies of the ballet. "Oh God," Kitty whispered. "Why does this have to happen to her?" Kitty held her face in her hands and trembled. "Give her strength . . . please give her strength."

Kitty lay wide-eyed in the darkness. She heard Karen stir and looked over to the girl's bed. Karen arose and knelt beside Kitty's bed and lay her head on Kitty's bosom. "I love you so much, Kitty," Karen said. "I couldn't love my own mother more."

Kitty turned her head away and stroked Karen's hair. "You'd better go to sleep," Kitty said shakily. "We have a busy day tomorrow."

Kitty stayed awake smoking one cigarette after the other and occasionally pacing the floor. Each time she looked at the sleeping child her heart tightened. Long past midnight she sat by the window listening to the waves and looking at Jaffa on the bend of the coast line. It was four o'clock before Kitty fell into a restless, thrashing sleep.

In the morning she was heavy with depression, her face drawn and her eyes showing rings of sleeplessness beneath them. A dozen times she tried to broach the subject. Breakfast on the terrace was in silence. Kitty sipped her coffee.

"Where is Brigadier Sutherland?" Karen asked.

"He had to go out on business. He'll see us later this morning."

"What are we going to do today?"

"Oh, a little of this and a little of that."

"Kitty . . . it's something about my father, isn't it?"

Kitty lowered her eyes.

"I guess I really knew all along."

"I didn't mean to deceive you, dear . . . I . . ."

"What is it . . . please tell me . . . what is it?"

"He is very, very sick."

Karen bit her finger and her mouth trembled. "I want to see him."

"He won't know you, Karen."

Karen straightened up and looked off to the sea. "I've waited so long for this day."

"Please . . ."

"Every night since I knew the war was ending over two years ago I've gone to sleep with the same dream. I lay in bed and pretended we were meeting each other again. I'd know just how he would look and what we are going to say to each other. At the DP camp in Caraolos and in Cyprus all those months I dreamed about it every night . . . my father and me. See . . . I always knew he was alive and . . . kept going over and over it."

"Karen . . . stop it. It's not going to be the way you dreamed."

The girl trembled from head to foot. The palms of her hands were wet. She sprang from her chair. "Take me to him."

Kitty took her arms and gripped her tightly. "You must prepare for something terrible."

"Please . . . please, let's go."

"Try to remember . . . no matter what happens . . . no matter what you see . . . that I'm going to be right there. I'll be with you, Karen. Will you remember that?"

"Yes . . . I'll remember it."

The doctor sat before Karen and Kitty.

"Your father was tortured by the Gestapo, Karen," the doctor said. "In the early part of the war they wanted him to work for them and they made things very hard. They finally gave up. He was unable to work for them even upon threat of danger to your mother and brothers."

"I remember now," Karen said. "I remember the letters stopped coming to Denmark and how I was afraid to ask Aage about my family."

"He was sent to Theresienstadt in Czechoslovakia, and your mother and brothers . . ."

"I know about them."

"They sent him to Theresienstadt in hope he would change his mind. After the war he found out about your mother and brothers first. He felt guilty because he had waited too long to leave Germany and had trapped your mother and brothers. When he learned what had happened to them, on top of the years of torture, his mind snapped."

"He will get better?"

The doctor looked at Kitty. "He has a psychotic depression . . . extreme melancholia."

"What does that mean?" Karen asked.

"Karen, your father is not going to get well."

"I don't believe you," the girl said. "I want to see him."

"Do you remember him at all?"

"Very little."

"It would be far better to keep what you can remember than to see him now."

"She must see him, Doctor, no matter how difficult it is going to be. This question cannot be left open," Kitty said.

The doctor led them down a corridor and stopped before a door. A nurse unlocked it. He held the door open.

Karen walked into a cell-like room. The room held a chair, a stand, and a bed. She looked around for a moment and then she stiffened. A man was sitting on the floor in a corner. He was barefooted and uncombed. He sat with his back against the wall and his arms around his knees and stared blankly at the opposite wall.

Karen took a step toward him. He was stubble-bearded and his face was scarred. Suddenly the pounding within Karen's heart eased. This is all a mistake, she thought . . . this man is a stranger . . . he is not my father . . . he cannot be. It is a mistake! A mistake! She was filled with the urge to turn around and scream out . . . *you see, you were wrong. He is not Johann Clement, he is not my father. My father is still alive somewhere and looking for me.* Karen stood before the man on the floor to assure herself. She stared into the crazed eyes. It had been so long . . . so very long, she could not remember. But the man she had dreamed about meeting again was not this man.

There was a fireplace and the smell of pipe tobacco. There was a big moppy dog. His name was Maximilian. A baby cried in the next room. "Miriam, see to Hans. I am reading a story for my girl and I cannot be disturbed."

Karen Hansen Clement slowly knelt before the hulk of mindless flesh.

Grandma's house in Bonn always smelled of newly-baked cookies. She baked all week getting ready for the family on Sunday.

The insane man continued to stare at the opposite wall as though he were alone in the room.

Look how funny the monkeys are in the Cologne Zoo! Cologne has the most wonderful zoo. When will it be carnival time again?

She studied the man from his bare feet to his scarred forehead. Nothing . . . nothing she saw was like her father . . .

"Jew! Jew! Jew!" the crowd screamed as she ran into her house with the blood pouring down her face. "There, there, Karen, don't you cry. Daddy won't let them hurt you."

Karen reached out and touched the man's cheek. "Daddy?" she said. The man did not move or react.

There was a train and lots of children around and they were talking of going to Denmark but she was tired. "Goodby, Daddy," Karen had said. "Here, you take my dolly. He will watch after you." She stood on the platform of the train and watched her Daddy on the platform and he grew smaller and smaller.

"Daddy! Daddy!" Karen cried. "It's Karen, Daddy! I'm your girl. I'm all grown up now, Daddy. Don't you remember me?"

The doctor held Kitty in the doorway as she shook from head to foot. "Let me help her, please," Kitty cried.

"Let it be done," he said.

And Karen was filled with remembering—"Yes! Yes! He is my father! He is my father!"

"Daddy!" she screamed and threw her arms around him. "Please talk to me. Please say something to me. I beg you . . . beg you!"

The man who was once the living human person of Johann Clement blinked his eyes. A sudden expression of curiosity came over his face as he became aware of a person clutching at him. He held the expression for a tense moment as though he were trying, in his own way, to allow something to penetrate the blackness—and then, his look lapsed back into lifelessness.

"Daddy!" she screamed. "Daddy! Daddy!"

And her voice echoed in the empty room and down the long corridor—"Daddy!"

The strong arms of the doctor pried her loose, and she was gently dragged from the room. The door was closed and locked and Johann Clement was gone from her—forever. The girl sobbed in anguish and crumpled into Kitty's arms. "He didn't even know me! Oh, my God . . . God . . . why doesn't he know me? Tell me, God . . . tell me!"

"It's all right, baby, it is all right now. Kitty is here. Kitty is with you."

"Don't leave me, don't ever leave me, Kitty!"

"No, baby . . . Kitty won't ever leave you . . . ever."

CHAPTER NINE: The news of Karen's father had spread through Gan Dafna before she and Kitty returned. It had a shattering effect on Dov Landau. For the first time since his brother Mundek had held him in his arms in a bunker beneath the Warsaw ghetto, Dov Landau was able to feel compassion for someone other than himself. His sorrow for Karen Clement was, at last, the ray of light that illuminated his black world.

She was the one person he could trust and care for. Why of all people on earth did it have to happen to her? How many times in that stinking camp on Cyprus had Karen expressed her simple, all-powerful faith to him? Now Karen was hurt and her despair was deep pain to him.

What did she have left? Himself and Mrs. Fremont. What was he to her? He was a millstone—a nothing. There were times he wanted to hate Mrs. Fremont but he couldn't because he knew that she was good for Karen. With Karen's father out of the way perhaps Mrs. Fremont would take her to America.

He stood in the way. He knew Karen wouldn't leave him. In Dov's mind there was only one thing to do.

A youth named Mordecai was a secret recruiter for the Maccabees at Gan Dafna. From him Dov succeeded in discovering where and how to make contact with the underground organization. The cottages of the faculty were never locked at Gan Dafna. He waited one evening until they were all at dinner, then rifled several cottages. He stole a few objects of gold jewelry and fled to Jerusalem.

Bruce Sutherland went directly to Dr. Lieberman and got him to urge Kitty to bring Karen to Sutherland's villa for a week or two to allow her to recover from the shock.

Karen bore her grief with the same dignity and courage that had carried her through a life filled with tragedy. Kitty Fremont was wise. She never left the girl's side.

The fate of Karen's father along with the disappearance of Dov Landau added up to a grim victory for Kitty. She felt that in time she would be able to get Karen to America. Kitty thought about it constantly at Sutherland's villa, detesting herself at times for finding consolation in Karen's tragedy, but she could not stop her thoughts. Since she had first seen Karen in the tent at Caraolos her entire life had revolved around the girl.

One day after lunch Ari Ben Canaan came to Sutherland's villa. He waited in the study while the servant fetched Sutherland from the terrace patio. Bruce excused himself and left the girls sunning. The two men spoke for nearly an hour, transacting their business.

"I have a friend of yours here," Sutherland said after they had concluded their discussion. "Kitty Fremont is spending a fortnight here as my house guest with the young Clement girl."

"I heard you two had become great friends," Ari said.

"Yes, I think Katherine Fremont is one of the finest women I have ever met. You should run up to Gan Dafna and see what she has done with some of those children. There was a boy who didn't even talk six months ago who now has not only opened up but is starting to play a bugle for the school band."

"I've heard about that too," Ari said.

"I insisted she come here and bring the Clement girl. The child found her father. Poor chap is completely and incurably insane. It was a terrible shock, needless to say. Come on out to the garden."

"I'm sorry. I have some other things to attend to."

"Nonsense, won't hear of it." He took Ari's arm and led him out.

Kitty had not seen Ari since the Mount Tabor affair. She was startled by the first sight of him. Ari had been neglecting himself.

She thought that Ari was amazingly gentle in his conveyance of condolence to Karen. He showed her a tenderness that he apparently reserved for his own people. He had never treated Kitty that way. Was this because Ari accepted Karen as one of them, Kitty wondered? Then she grew angry at herself. It seemed to her that she was beginning to categorize every word and situation on its meaning in relation to Karen's Jewishness. Now perhaps she was creating meanings that did not even exist.

Kitty and Ari walked through Sutherland's rose garden.

"How is she?" Ari asked.

"She is a very strong and courageous child," Kitty said. "It was a shocking experience but she is doing remarkably well."

Ari looked back to where Karen and Sutherland were playing checkers. "She is a lovely girl," he said sincerely.

His words surprised Kitty. She had never heard that tone of appreciation from him before and she had wondered if things of beauty even reached him. They stopped at the end of the path where a low stone wall ran around the edge of the garden. Beyond the wall the valley lay at the bottom of the hill with Safed beyond. Kitty sat on the wall and stared out at the Galilee, and Ari lit a cigarette for himself and one for her.

"Ari, I've never asked a personal favor of you. I am about to do so."

"Of course."

"Karen is going to get over her father in time, but there is another thing that she may not get over. Dov Landau has run away from Gan Dafna. We assume he has gone to Jerusalem to join the Maccabees. As you know, she has taken the boy as a personal crusade. The loss of her father has magnified the loss of Dov. She is eating her heart out for him. I want you to find him for us and bring him back to Gan Dafna. I know you have the connections which can locate him. He would come back if you could convince him that Karen needs him."

Ari blew a stream of smoke and looked at Kitty with curiosity. "I don't think I understand you at all. The girl belongs to you now. He is the one possible person who stands in your way and he has removed himself."

Kitty looked at him evenly. "I should be offended by what you say but I'm not because it's true. The fact is that I can't build my own happiness on her misery. I can't take her away to America with this thing with Dov unresolved."

"That is very commendable."

"It isn't honorable intent, Ari. Karen is a wise girl about everything but that boy. We all have our weak spots, I suppose. She will get over him far more quickly if he is at Gan Dafna. With him away in the Maccabees she will magnify his image until it is beyond proper proportion."

"Forgive me for thinking in simple terms, Kitty. You are shrewd."

"I love that girl and there's nothing sinister or devious about it."

"You're making sure she has no place to go but with you."

"I'm making certain that she knows she has a better place to go. Perhaps you don't believe this, but if I knew it was better for her to stay in Palestine, this is where she would stay."

"Maybe I do believe that."

"Can you in all honesty tell me that I am doing something wrong by wanting to take her to America?"

"No . . . it is not wrong," Ari said.

"Then help me get Dov back."

There was a long silence, then Ari snuffed out his cigarette on the wall. He peeled the paper, unconscious of his action and scattering the loose tobacco and balling the paper into a tiny knot which he put into his pocket. P. P. Malcolm had taught him never to leave traces of a cigarette. Cigarette butts were glaring signposts to Arabs in search of enemy troops.

"I can't do it," Ari said.

"You can. Dov respects you."

"Sure, I can find him. I can even force him back to Gan Dafna and say, 'Stay put little boy, the ladies don't want you to get hurt.' Dov Landau has made a personal decision that every Jew in Palestine has got to make with his own conscience. The feeling about this is very intense. My father and my uncle haven't spoken to each other for fifteen years over it. Every fiber of Dov Landau's being shrieks out for revenge. He is being driven with an intensity that only God or a bullet can stop."

"You sound as though you condone the terrorists."

"Sometimes I am in complete sympathy with them. Sometimes I detest them. Yet I would not want to be the judge of their actions. Who are you and I to say that Dov Landau is not justified? You know what they've done to him. You are wrong about something else. If he is brought back he can only bring more pain to that girl. Dov must do what he must do."

Kitty got down from the wall and brushed her skirt and they walked toward the gate. "Ari," she said at last, "you are right."

Sutherland joined them as they walked outside to his car. "Are you going to be around long, Ben Canaan?" he asked.

"I have a few things to attend to in Safed. I better get them done."

"Why don't you come back and join us for dinner?"

"Well, I . . ."

"Please do," Kitty said.

"Very well. Thank you."

"Good. Come on back up just as soon as you are through in Safed."

They waved as he drove down the hillside, past the Taggart fort and out of sight.

"*He who guards Israel shall neither rest nor sleep,*" Kitty said.

"Good Lord, Kitty. Have you gotten around to Biblical quotations?"

They opened the gate and walked back toward the patio.

"He looks exhausted."

"I think he looks fine," Sutherland said, "for a man who works a hundred and ten hours a week."

"I've never seen such dedication . . . or would you call it fanaticism? I was surprised to see him here, Bruce. I didn't know you were mixed up in this business."

Sutherland stuffed a pipe full of tobacco. "I'm not really actively engaged. The Haganah came to me and asked me to make an appraisal of the Arab armies' strength outside Palestine. They simply want a professional, nonpartisan point of view. See here, Kitty, don't you think it is time you became honest with yourself in this matter?"

"I told you I'm not going to be partial to either side."

"Kitty, I'm afraid you're acting like an ostrich. You're sitting in the middle of a battlefield and saying 'Don't hit my house, my blinds are drawn.' "

"I'm getting out, Bruce."

"Then you'd better do it quickly. If you believe you can stay on much longer the way you have then you are living in a fool's paradise."

"I can't bring myself to it just yet. I must have a little more time until Karen has recovered from this."

"And is that the only reason?"

Kitty shook her head. "I guess I'm afraid of a showdown. There are times when I am sure I have beaten this thing of her and Palestine—and other times, like right now, I'm terrified of putting it to a test."

From Sutherland's villa before dinner they could see the enormous full moon hanging over the city.

" *'Three great gifts hath the Lord granted Israel, but every one of them will be won by suffering. One of them is the*

Land of Israel,' " Sutherland said. "Those are the words of Bar Yohai two thousand years ago. I would say he was a wise man."

"Speaking of wise men, I am going to the Sea of Galilee tomorrow. Have you been there yet, Kitty?" Ari asked.

"No, I'm afraid my travel has been rather restricted."

"You should see it for sure. You'd better go soon. It will be too hot in a few weeks."

"Why don't you take her?" Karen said quickly.

There was an embarrassed silence.

"That . . . that's really a good idea," Ari said. "I could work my schedule around to take a few days off. Why don't we all go, the four of us?"

"I don't care to," Karen said. "I've hiked there twice already with the Gadna."

Bruce Sutherland picked up Karen's cue. "Not me, old chap, I've seen the lake a dozen times."

"Why don't you go with Ari?" Karen said.

"I think I'd better stay here with you," Kitty answered.

"Nonsense," Sutherland pressed. "Karen and I will get on just fine by ourselves. As a matter of fact it will be a pleasure to get rid of you for a few days, not to mention the fact that Ari looks as though he could stand a bit of a rest."

Kitty laughed. "Ari, I smell an underhanded plot. It appears we have a pair of matchmakers trying to make a *shiddoch.*"

"Listen to her!" Karen cried in excitement.

"Shucks, I'm just a *sabra* at heart. It looks as though you're trapped, Ari."

"That suits me fine," he said.

CHAPTER TEN: Early the next morning Ari and Kitty drove to the Sea of Galilee. They entered the Genossar Valley which ran along its northern shores. Across the lake the browned-out hills of Syria loomed over this low point on the earth and the warm, sultry air hung still.

This is God's own sea, Kitty thought. Once again she was alone with Ari Ben Canaan and once again she felt the timelessness of the land close in on her as she had felt it in the Judean hills. Why was she more affected when she was with Ari, she wondered?

At the edge of the sea he took her to the ruins of the synagogue of Capernaum. Here, Jesus walked and taught and healed. Words came to Kitty's mind that she thought she had forgotten. *Jesus walked by the Sea of Galilee and saw two brethren, Simon called Peter and Andrew his brother cast-*

ing a net into the sea . . . And they went into Capernaum and straight away on the Sabbath He entered into the synagogue and taught.

It was as though He had never left. On the water's edge fishermen cast their nets into the sea and a small flock of black goats grazed and the ages had not passed.

From there Ari took her to the church which marked the place of the miracle of the multiplication of loaves and fishes a short distance from Capernaum. The floor of the church held a Byzantine mosaic depicting cormorants and herons and ducks and other wild birds which still inhabited the lake.

And then they moved on to the Mount of Beatitudes to a little chapel on the hill where Jesus preached the Sermon on the Mount.

Blessed are they which are persecuted for righteousness' sake: for theirs is the kingdom of heaven. Blessed are ye, when men shall revile you, and persecute you, and shall say all manner of evil against you falsely, for my sake. Rejoice, and be exceeding glad: for great is your reward in heaven: for so persecuted they the prophets which were before you.

These were His words spoken from this place. As she saw the Christian holy places the thought came to confuse her that Ari Ben Canaan and David Ben Ami and her own Karen seemed to live with a closeness to all this that she could never attain.

They sped past the sleeping Arab village of Migdal, the birthplace of Mary Magdalene, and then beneath the Horns of Hattin, which held the tomb of Jethro, the father-in-law of Moses and the chief prophet of the Druses, but Kitty's attention was distracted by her mental turmoil.

Then the car turned away from the plains of Hattin and into a flat field where a burst of scarlet hit their eyes. The field was a red carpet of wild flowers.

"How red it is," Kitty said. "Stop the car for a moment, Ari."

He pulled over to the side of the road and Kitty got out. She picked one of the flowers and as she looked at it her eyes narrowed. "I've never seen anything like this," she whispered in a shaky voice.

"The ancient Maccabees lived in caves around here. It is the only place in the world this flower grows. It is called Blood of the Maccabees."

Kitty examined the red bloom closely. It did look like little droplets of blood. She dropped the flower quickly and rubbed her hand on her skirt.

This land and everything about it was closing in on her! Even the wild flowers will not let you forget for a moment. It creeps into you from its very earth and its very air and it is damning and tormenting.

Kitty Fremont was frightened. She knew that she would have to leave Palestine at once: the more she resisted the place the harder it struck back at her. It was all around her and above her and beneath her and she felt stifled and crushed.

They entered Tiberias from the north through the modern Jewish suburb of Kiryat Shmuel—the Village of Samuel—and drove past another large Taggart fort and descended from the hills to the water level, into the Old City. The buildings were mostly of black basalt rock and the hills were filled with the graves and caves of ancient Hebrew greats.

Beyond the city they turned into the Galilean Hotel on the sea. It was very hot in the midday. Kitty nibbled her lunch of Galilee catfish and barely spoke a word. She wished she had not come.

"I haven't yet shown you the holiest of the holy," Ari said.

"Where is that?"

"Shoshanna *kibbutz*. That's where I was born."

Kitty smiled. She suspected that Ari knew she was disturbed and was trying to cheer her up. "And just where is this great shrine?"

"A few miles down the road where the Jordan River runs into the sea. Although I do hear I was almost born in the old Turkish police station in town here. This place is full of tourists in the winter. It's a little late in the season. Anyhow, we have the whole lake to ourselves. Why don't we take a swim?"

"That sounds like a really good idea," Kitty said.

A long pier of basalt rock jutted out beyond the hotel for some forty yards into the lake. Ari was on the pier first after lunch. Kitty found herself looking at his body as she walked from the hotel. He waved to her. Ari had a lean build and looked hard and powerful.

"Hi," she called. "Have you been in yet?"

"I've been waiting for you."

"How deep is it from the end of the pier?"

"About ten feet. Can you swim as far as the raft?"

"You've asked for a race."

Kitty dropped her robe and put on her bathing cap. Ari inspected her frankly just as she had measured him. Her body had not the angular sturdiness of a *sabra* girl. She was more of the softness and roundness one would expect from an American woman.

Their eyes met for an instant and both of them looked a little abashed.

She ran past him and dived into the water. Ari followed.

391

He was surprised to find that it was all he could do to catch her and get a few strokes ahead. Kitty swam with a graceful crawl and a steady stroke that pressed him to the utmost. They climbed on the raft breathless and laughing.

"You pulled a fast one on me," he said.

"I forgot to mention it but . . ."

"I know, I know. You were on the girls' swimming team in college."

She lay on her back and took a deep breath of contentment. The water was cool and refreshing and seemed to wash her bad spirits away.

It was late in the afternoon before they returned to the hotel for cocktails on the veranda and then retired to their rooms to rest before dinner.

Ari, who had had little rest in recent weeks, was asleep the instant he lay down. In the next room Kitty paced the floor. She had recovered from much of the agitation of the morning but she was tired of this emotional drain and she was still actually a little frightened of the mystical power that this land held. Kitty longed to return to a normal, sane, planned life. She convinced herself that Karen needed the same therapy more than anything else. She made up her mind to face the issue with Karen without further delay.

By evening it had turned pleasantly cool. Kitty began to dress for dinner. She opened her closet and considered the three dresses hanging there. Slowly she took down one of them. It was the same dress that Jordana Ben Canaan had picked from her closet the day of their argument. She thought of Ari's look on the pier today. Kitty had liked it. The dress was a strapless sheath which clung to her body and emphasized her bosom.

Every male eyebrow in the hotel lifted as Kitty drifted by, and nostrils twitched with the scent of her perfume. Ari stood like a man stunned, watching her cross the lobby. As she came up to him he suddenly became aware of the fact that he was staring at her and quickly found his voice.

"I have a surprise for you," he said. "There is a concert at the Ein Gev *kibbutz* across the lake. We will go right after dinner."

"Will this dress be all right to wear?"

"Uh . . . yes . . . yes, it will be excellent."

Most of the full moon of the night before was left for them. Just as their motor launch left the pier it rose from behind the Syrian hills, unbelievably huge, sending a great path of light over the motionless waters.

"The sea is so still," Kitty said.

"It is deceptive. When God gets angry He can turn it into an ocean in minutes."

In a half hour they had crossed the water and landed at the docks of the *kibbutz* of Ein Gev—the Spring of the Mountain Pass. Ein Gev was a daring experiment. The *kibbutz* sat isolated from the rest of Palestine and directly below the mountains of Syria. A Syrian village hung above it and its fields were plowed to the border markers. It had been founded by immigrants of the German Aliyah in the year of 1937 and strategically commanded a view of the Sea of Galilee.

The *kibbutz* was set near a basin formed by the Yarmuk River, the border between Syria and Trans-Jordan, and the basin was the site of a cradle of man. Everyday the farmers plowed up evidences of human life, some prehistoric. They had found crude plows and pottery thousands of years old, proving the area had been farmed and there had been community life even there.

Right on the border between Ein Gev and the Syrian hills stood a small mountain shaped like a column. It was called Sussita—the Horse. Atop Sussita were the ruins of one of the nine Roman fortress cities of Palestine. Sussita still dominated the entire area.

Many of the German pioneers had been musicians in former life and they were an industrious lot. In addition to farming and fishing they hit upon another idea to augment the *kibbutz* income. They formed an orchestra and bought a pair of launches to bring the winter tourists of Tiberias across the lake for concerts. The idea proved successful and the tradition grew until Ein Gev drew every artist who visited Palestine. A large outdoor auditorium was built into a natural woodland setting on the edge of the lake, and additional plans called for a covered building in years to come.

Ari spread a blanket on the grass at the edge of the auditorium and the two of them lay back and looked up into the sky and watched the enormous Lag Ba Omer moon grow smaller and higher and make room for a billion stars. As the orchestra played a Beethoven concert the tension within Kitty passed away. This moment was perfection. No more beautiful setting could have been created. It seemed almost unreal and she found herself hoping that it would go on and on.

The concert ended. Ari took her hand and led her away from the crowds, down a path along the lake. The air was still and filled with a pine scent, and the Sea of Galilee was like a polished mirror. At the water's edge there was a bench made of three slabs of stone from an ancient temple.

They sat and looked over at the twinkling lights of Tiberias. Ari brushed against her and Kitty turned and looked at him. How handsome Ari Ben Canaan was! Suddenly she wanted to hold him and to touch his cheek and stroke his hair. She wanted to tell him not to work so hard. She wanted to tell him to unlock his heart to her. She wanted to say how she felt when he was near and to beg not to be a stranger and to find something for them to share. But Ari Ben Canaan *was* a stranger and she dare not ever say what she felt.

The Sea of Galilee stirred and lapped against the shore. A sudden gust of breeze caused the bulrushes at the water's edge to sway. Kitty Fremont turned away from Ari.

A tremor passed through her body as she felt his hand touch her shoulder. "You are cold," Ari said, holding her stole for her. Kitty slipped it over her shoulders. They stared long at each other.

Ari stood up suddenly. "It sounds like the launch is returning," he said. "We had better go."

As the launch pushed off, the Sea of Galilee turned from smooth to choppy with the suddenness of which Ari had spoken. Wisps of spray broke over the bow and whipped back on them. Ari put his arm about Kitty's shoulder and brought her close to him to protect her from the water. All across the lake Kitty rested her head on his chest with her eyes closed, listening to the beat of his heart.

They walked from the pier hand in hand along the path to the hotel. Kitty stopped beneath the willow tree whose branches spread like a giant umbrella, bending clear down into the lake. She tried to speak but her voice trembled and the words would not come out.

Ari touched her wet hair and brushed it back from her forehead. He held her shoulders gently, and the muscles of his face worked with tenseness as he drew her close. Kitty lifted her face to him.

"Ari," she whispered, "please kiss me."

All that had smoldered for months burst into flames of ecstasy, engulfing them, in this first embrace.

How good he feels! How strong he is! Kitty had never known a moment like this with any man—not even Tom Fremont. They kissed and they kissed again and she pressed against him and felt the power of his arms. Then they stood apart and walked in quick silence to the hotel.

Kitty stood awkwardly before the door of her room. Ari moved toward his door but she took his hand and turned him around. They stood facing each other wordlessly for a moment. Kitty nodded, and turned and entered her room quickly and closed the door behind her.

She undressed in the dark and slipped into a nightgown and walked toward her balcony, where she could see the light from his room. She could hear him pacing the floor. His light went off. Kitty fell back into the shadows. In a moment she saw him standing on her balcony.

"I want you," Ari said.

394

She ran into his arms and held him tightly, trembling with desire. His kisses fell over her mouth and cheeks and neck and she exchanged kiss for kiss, touch for touch, with an abandon she had never known. Ari swept her up in his arms and carried her to the bed and placed her on it and knelt beside her. Kitty felt faint. She gripped the sheets and sobbed and writhed.

Ari lowered the shoulder strap of her nightgown and caressed her breast.

With violent abruptness Kitty spun out of his grasp and staggered from the bed. "No," she gasped.

Ari froze.

Kitty's eyes filled with tears and she cringed against the wall, holding herself to stop the trembling. She sagged into a chair. Moments passed until the quaking within her abated and her breathing became normal. Ari stood over her and stared down.

"You must hate me," she said at last.

He did not speak. She looked up at his towering figure and saw the hurt on his face.

"Go on, Ari . . . say it. Say anything."

He did not speak.

Kitty stood up slowly and faced him. "I don't want this, Ari. I don't want to be made. I guess I was just overcome by the moonlight . . ."

"I shouldn't have thought I was making love to a reluctant virgin," he said.

"Ari, please . . ."

"I don't have time to indulge in games and words. I am a grown man and you are a grown woman."

"You state it so well."

His voice was cold. "I will leave by the door if you don't mind."

Kitty winced with the sharp crack of the door closing. She stood for a long time by the french doors and looked out at the water. The Sea of Galilee was angry and the moon faded behind a sinister black cloud.

Kitty was numb. Why had she run from him? She had never felt so strongly for anyone and she had never lost control of herself like this. Her own recklessness had frightened her. She reasoned that Ari Ben Canaan did not really want her. Beyond a night of love he had no need of her, and no man had treated her this way before.

Then it came to her that she had been fleeing from this very feeling she had for him, this new desire for Ari which could lead her to stay in Palestine. She must never let it happen again. She was going to leave with Karen and nothing was going to stop her! She knew that she was afraid of Ari:

Ari could defeat her. If he were to show the slightest signs of really caring she might not have the strength—but the thought of his steely coldness strengthened her determination to resist, leaving her reassured and yet, perversely, at the same time resentful.

Kitty threw herself onto the bed and fell into an exhausted sleep, with the wind from over the water beating against her window.

In the morning it was calm again.

Kitty threw back the covers and jumped from bed and all the events of the night before came to her. She blushed. They did not seem so terrible now but she was embarrassed. She had created a scene and there was no doubt Ari had thought it pretty melodramatic as well as childish. The whole thing had been her doing; she would set it right by making up with him, sensibly and forthrightly. She dressed quickly and went down to the dining room to await Ari. She thought of the words she would use to apologize.

Kitty sipped coffee and waited.

A half hour passed. Ari did not come down. She snuffed out her third cigarette and walked out to the front desk.

"Have you seen Mr. Ben Canaan this morning?" she asked the clerk.

"Mr. Ben Canaan checked out at six."

"Did he say where he was going?"

"Mr. Ben Canaan never says where he is going."

"Perhaps he left a message for me?"

The clerk turned around and pointed to the empty key box.

"I see . . . well . . . thank you very much."

CHAPTER ELEVEN: Dov Landau found a room in a dilapidated fourth-rate hotel on the Street of the Chain in the Old City of Jerusalem. As instructed, he went to the Saladin Café on the Nablus Road near the Damascus Gate and left his name and hotel to be given to Bar Israel.

Dov pawned the gold rings and bracelets he had stolen from the faculty at Gan Dafna and turned to the job of studying Jerusalem. To the ghetto rat and past master of thievery Jerusalem was simple. Within three days Dov knew every street and alley in the Old City and the immediate business districts around it. His sharp eye appraised and his deft hands lifted enough objects of value to keep him sustained. The matter of escape through the narrow alleyways and crowded bazaars was ridiculously easy for him.

Dov spent much of his money for books and art material.

He walked along Jaffa Road searching the many bookstores for texts on art, draftsmanship, and architecture.

He locked himself in his room with his books and art material, some dried fruits and bottled soft drinks, and waited for contact from the Maccabees. Dov studied by candlelight. He was unaware of the pageantry that took place outside his window on the Street of the Chain which ran between the Jewish and Moslem quarters to the Dome of the Rock and the Wailing Wall. He would read until his eyes burned and he could read no more, then he would lay the book on his chest and stare at the ceiling and think of Karen Clement. Dov had not realized how badly he would miss her nor that missing her could cause an actual physical pain. Karen had been with him for so long he had forgotten what it was like to be away from her. He remembered every moment with her. Those days at Caraolos and on the *Exodus* when she lay in his arms in the hold of the ship. He remembered how happy she was and how beautiful she looked that first day at Gan Dafna. He remembered her kind, expressive face and her gentle touch and her sharp voice when she was angry.

Dov sat on the edge of his bed and sketched a hundred pictures of Karen. He drew her in every way he remembered her but crumpled each picture and threw it on the floor, for no picture could show how beautiful she was to Dov.

Dov stayed in his room for two weeks, leaving only upon necessity. At the end of the second week he needed some more money and he left his room with some rings to pawn. As he reached the entrance to the building he saw a man standing in the shadows. Dov wrapped his hand around his pistol and walked past, poised to spin around at the first sound.

"Don't move, don't turn," a voice from the shadows commanded.

Dov froze in his tracks.

"You made inquiries for Bar Israel. What do you want?"

"You know what I want."

"What is your name?"

"Landau, Dov Landau."

"Where do you come from?"

"Gan Dafna."

"Who sent you?"

"Mordecai."

"How did you get into Palestine?"

"On the *Exodus*."

"Keep walking out to the street and don't look around. You will be contacted later."

Dov became restless after the contact was made. He rose to the point of chucking it all and returning to Gan Dafna. He missed Karen terribly. He started a half dozen letters and

397

tore each one up. Let's get it over with . . . let's get it over with, Dov said to himself again and again.

He lay in his room reading and began to doze. Then he roused himself and lighted fresh candles: if he fell asleep and the old nightmare came he did not want to awaken in a dark room.

There was a sharp knock on his door.

Dov sprang to his feet, picked up his pistol, and stood close to the locked door.

"It is your friends," a voice said from the hallway. Dov recognized it as the same voice that had spoken to him from the shadows. He opened the door. He could see no one.

"Turn around and face the wall," the voice commanded from the darkness. Dov obeyed. He felt the presence of two men behind him. A blindfold was tied over his eyes and two pairs of hands led him down the stairs to a waiting car where he was shoved on the back floor and covered and driven from the Old City.

Dov concentrated on sensing where he was being driven. The car screeched into King Solomon Street, followed the Via Dolorosa to Stephen's Gate. It was child's play to Dov Laudau, who knew his way through a hundred alternate routes in the blackness of the sewers under Warsaw.

The car shifted into a lower gear to make a hill. They must be driving past the Tomb of the Virgin toward the Mount of Olives, Dov calculated. The road became smooth. Now Dov knew they were driving past the Hebrew University and Hadassah Medical Center on Mount Scopus.

They drove another ten minutes and stopped.

Dov accurately pinpointed their position in the Sanhedriya section near the Tombs of the Sanhedrin, the ancient supreme court of Hebrew rabbis, almost to the precise part of the block.

He was led into a house and into a room filled with cigarette smoke where he was made to sit. He sensed at least five or six people. For two hours Dov was grilled. Questions were fired at him from around the room until he began to perspire nervously. As the questioning continued he began to piece it together. The Maccabees had learned through their infallible intelligence sources that Dov had extraordinary talent as a forger, and it was badly needed by them. He had obviously been brought before some of the highest members in the Maccabees, perhaps the commanders themselves. At last they had satisfied themselves that Dov's qualifications and security checked.

"There is a curtain in front of you," a voice said. "Put your hands through it."

Dov pushed his hands through the cloth. One of his hands

398

was placed on a pistol and the other on a Bible. He repeated the oath of the Maccabees:

"I, Dov Landau, do give my body, my soul, my being, without reservation or qualification, to the Freedom Fighters of the Maccabees. I will obey any and all orders without question. I will subordinate myself to the authority over me. Under torture, even to death, I will never divulge the name of a fellow Maccabee or the secrets entrusted to me. I will fight the enemies of the Jewish people unto the last breath of life in my body. I will never cease in this sacred battle until realization of a Jewish state on both sides of the Jordan River, which is the natural historical right of my people. My creed to mine enemies shall be: Life for life, eye for eye, tooth for tooth, hand for hand, burning for burning. All this I swear in the name of Abraham, Isaac and Jacob, Sarah, Rebecca, Rachael and Leah and the prophets and of all the Jews who have been slaughtered and all my gallant brothers and sisters who have died in the name of freedom."

The blindfold was taken from Dov's eyes and the candles on the Menorah before him were blown out and the lights went up in the room. Dov looked into the eyes of six grim men and two women. They shook hands with him and introduced themselves. Old man Akiva himself was there and Ben Moshe, their field leader, who had lost a brother fighting for the British in the war and a sister with the Palmach. Nahum Ben Ami was one of seven brothers. The other six were in the Palmach. These men and women banded together because they were neither capable or desirous of the self-restraint of the Yishuv.

Old Akiva stepped up before Dov. "You will be of value to us, Dov Landau. That is why we took you without the usual training."

"I did not join to draw pictures," Dov snapped.

"You will do what you are told to do," Ben Moshe answered.

"Dov, you are a Maccabee now," Akiva said. "You are entitled to take a name of a Hebrew hero. Do you have such a name in mind?"

"Giora," Dov said.

There was some laughter about the room. Dov gritted his teeth.

"Giora, is it?" Akiva said. "I am afraid there are others ahead of you."

"How about Little Giora," Nahum Ben Ami said, "until Dov can become Big Giora?"

"I will become Big Giora soon enough if you give me the chance."

"You will set up a forgery plant," Ben Moshe said, "and

399

travel with us. If you behave and do as you are told we may let you go out on a raid with us now and again."

Major Fred Caldwell played bridge in the main lounge of the British Officers' Club at Goldsmith House in Jerusalem. Freddie was finding it difficult to concentrate on card playing. His mind kept wandering back to the CID Headquarters and on the captured Maccabee girl they had been interrogating for some three days. Her name was Ayala and she was in her early twenties and fetchingly pretty. She had been a music major at the university. At least she was pretty before the questioning started. Ayala had been another tough Jewess and she had spit defiance at the CID. Like most of the captured Maccabees she spent her time quoting biblical passages, predicting their eternal damnation, or proclaiming the righteousness of her cause.

This morning their patience had run out and Ayala began to get the third degree.

"Your play, Freddie," his partner said across the table.

Fred Caldwell looked at his cards quickly. "Forgive me," he said, and played a bad card. His mind was on the inspector standing over Ayala and flailing her with a rubber hose. He heard it thud into the girl's face time and again until her nose was broken and her eyes blacked and swollen almost shut and her lips puffed and distorted. But Ayala would not break.

Freddie considered that he didn't give a damn if Ayala never broke: the thought of the smashing of her Jewish face delighted him.

An orderly walked up alongside the table.

"I beg your pardon, Major Caldwell. There is a telephone call for you, sir."

"Excuse me, chaps," Freddie said throwing his cards face down and walking off to the phone on the other side of the lounge. He picked up the receiver. "Caldwell here."

"Hello, Major. This is the sergeant of the guard at CID, sir. Inspector Parkington asked me to phone you right away, sir. He says the Maccabee girl is ready to talk and thought you'd best come over to headquarters right away."

"Righto," Freddie said.

"Inspector Parkington has already sent a car for you, sir. It will be there in a few minutes."

Caldwell returned to the card players. "Sorry, chaps. Have to leave. Duty calls."

"Bad luck, Freddie."

Bad luck, hell, Freddie thought. He was looking forward to it. He walked outside Goldsmith House. The guards saluted. A car pulled up to a stop and a soldier jumped from behind the wheel, walked to Caldwell and saluted.

"Major Caldwell?"

"Here, boy."

"Your car from CID, sir."

The soldier held the rear door open. Freddie got into the back seat and the soldier ran around, got behind the wheel and they drove off. Two blocks beyond Goldsmith House he pulled the car over to a curb at an intersection. In a second the doors were flung open and three men jumped into the car, slammed the doors, and the car picked up speed again.

Caldwell's throat closed with fear. He shrieked and tried to leap across Ben Moshe. The Maccabee in the front seat turned around and slapped him with a pistol barrel and Ben Moshe snatched his collar and jerked him back into his seat. The Maccabee driver took off the military cap and looked up in the mirror.

Caldwell's eyes bugged in terror.

"I demand to know what this is all about!"

"You seem upset, Major Caldwell," Ben Moshe said coldly.

"Stop this car and let me out immediately, do you hear?"

"Shall we let you out the same way you threw out a four-teen-year-old boy named Ben Solomon in an Arab village? You see, Major Caldwell, Ben Solomon's ghost called out to us from his grave and asked us to make retribution against the guilty."

The sweat poured into Caldwell's eyes. "It's all a lie . . . a lie . . . a lie . . ."

Ben Moshe flipped something on Caldwell's lap and shined his flashlight on it. It was a photograph of the decapitated boy, Ben Solomon.

Caldwell began to sob for mercy. He doubled over and vomited in fear.

"It appears that Major Caldwell is in a mood to talk. We had better take him to headquarters and let him give out with his information before settling Ben Solomon's account."

Caldwell blurted out all he knew about the British army plans and CID's operations and afterwards signed a confession of the murder of the boy.

Three days after his abduction Major Fred Caldwell's body was found on Mount Zion at the Dung Gate of the Old City. Pinned to his body was a picture of Ben Solomon and a photostat of Caldwell's confession and across it were scribbled the words: *An eye for an eye and a tooth for a tooth.*

Major Fred Caldwell received the same fate that Sisera, the Canaanite, met at the hands of Jael when he fled from the scene of his battle with Deborah and Barak.

CHAPTER TWELVE: The revenge murder of Major Fred Caldwell had a shattering effect. No one seemed to question its justification, but the Maccabee method was more than many could condone.

In England people had become disgusted with the entire situation and were bringing pressure on the Labour government to give up the mandate. Inside Palestine the British garrison was at once enraged and worried.

Two days after Caldwell was found by the Dung Gate, a Maccabee prisoner, the girl named Ayala, died of internal hemorrhages from the beatings she had received during questioning. When the Maccabees learned of Ayala's death, there were fourteen days of wrathful retribution. Jerusalem reeled under the impact of terrorist raids. On the last days the raids were climaxed by an audacious daylight attack on Criminal Investigation Division headquarters.

During "Hell's Fortnight," as the Maccabee's wrath came to be designated, Dov Landau had displayed a reckless courage that awed even the toughest of the terrorists. Dov went out four times on raids, the last time as one of the leaders of the final assault against the CID. During Hell's Fortnight a legend of "Little Giora" was born, in which his name became synonymous with wild fearlessness.

Palestine held its breath waiting for the next blow to fall. General Arnold Haven-Hurst was stunned at first but retaliated against the Yishuv with martial law, cordons, searches, raids, and even executions in a campaign that slowed normal industry and commerce to a crawl. His all-encompassing Operation Squid encircled Palestine.

Caldwell's murder, Hell's Fortnight, and the final raid on CID were obvious mockeries of British authority. As the Maccabees erupted, the Aliyah Bet brought three more illegal ships into Palestine waters. While the illegal immigration runs were not so spectacular they were just as damaging as the activities of the terrorists. British troops patrolled the streets of Jewish cities and the highways with the taut expectancy of ambush any moment.

The United Nations delegation was arriving shortly. Haven-Hurst determined to cripple the Yishuv before they came. The general obtained a list of officers and men who were known for overt anti-Jewish actions. He screened the list personally and selected six of the most vicious: two officers and four enlisted men. The six were brought to his quarters in the Schneller Barracks and sworn in on an ultrasecret mission.

For five days the affair was plotted. On the sixth day, Haven-Hurst launched his last-ditch effort.

The six men were disguised as Arabs. A pair of them drove along King George Avenue in a truck loaded with two tons of dynamite. The truck made for the Zion Settlement Building. It stopped catercorner from the building, headed at the long driveway that led into the main entrance. The driver in Arab costume locked the steering wheel, put the truck in gear, and opened the throttle; the two men jumped clear and disappeared.

The truck tore over the street, through the open gate and down the driveway. It swerved for an instant, then careened off the curbing and hit just off the main entrance. A thunderous explosion occurred. The building was demolished.

At the same moment another pair of men in another truck filled with dynamite tried the same maneuver at the Yishuv Central building just two blocks away. A meeting was in session and the building held almost the entire Yishuv leadership.

The truck bore down on the second building. At the last instant it had to jump a curb. In hitting the curb the truck was thrown far enough off course to miss the building and blow up an adjoining apartment house.

The four soldiers were scooped up in two escape cars driven by the last two of the picked team. The cars fled toward the sanctuary of British-controlled Trans-Jordan.

General Arnold Haven-Hurst had attempted in one blow to wipe out the Yishuv leadership and representation. One hundred people died at the Zion Settlement Society. None was killed at Yishuv Central. Among the dead was Harriet Saltzman, the eighty-year-old leader of Youth Aliyah.

Within moments after the explosions, Haganah and Maccabee Intelligence went into action to comb Palestine for the culprits. By the end of the day both of the organizations had identified the six "Arabs" as British soldiers. They were further able to trace the action directly to Arnold Haven-Hurst, although with no usable proof. Instead of destroying Yishuv leadership, Haven-Hurst's desperate gamble had a reverse effect. It united the Jews of Palestine in a way they had never before been united and it drove together the two armed forces, the Haganah and Maccabees. The Haganah had obtained a copy of the "Haven-Hurst Report." With the evidence behind the bombings they knew the general was out to destroy them if they had not known it before. Avidan dispatched Zev Gilboa to Jerusalem to seek out Bar Israel to arrange a meeting between himself and the Maccabee commanders. The procedure was almost unique: the only precedent had been at the beginning of World War II when Avidan asked Akiva to abstain from terror for the duration.

The meeting was held at one o'clock in the morning in an open field on the road from Jerusalem on the site of what was once the Tenth Roman Legion camp. There were four men present: Akiva and Ben Moshe for the Maccabees, Avidan for the Haganah, with Zev Gilboa representing the Haganah's striking arm, the Palmach. There were no handshakes or amenities between the two organizations' representatives. They stood facing each other in the darkness, filled with mutual distrust. The late-night air was cold despite the coming of summer.

"I have asked this meeting with you to see if there is some basis for closer co-operation between our forces," Avidan said.

"You mean you want us to come under your jurisdiction?" Ben Moshe asked suspiciously.

"I have long given up the idea of trying to control your group," Avidan said. "I merely think the times call for a maximum effort. You have strength inside the three cities and are able to operate with a greater degree of freedom than we can."

"So that's it," Akiva snapped. "You want us to do your dirty work."

"Hear him out, Akiva," his field commander said.

"I don't like the whole idea. I didn't approve of this meeting, Ben Moshe. These people have betrayed us in the past and they'll do it again."

Avidan's bald head turned crimson under the old man's words. "I choose to listen to your insults tonight, Akiva, because there is too much at stake. I count on the fact that despite our differences you are a Jew and you love Eretz Israel." He handed a copy of the "Haven-Hurst Report" to Akiva.

The old man gave it to Ben Moshe, who turned his flashlight on the paper.

"Fourteen years ago I said the British were our enemy. You didn't believe me then," Akiva whispered.

"I won't argue politics with you. Will you or won't you work with us?" Avidan demanded.

"We will try it out," Ben Moshe said.

After the meeting liaison groups went to work to plot out a joint Haganah-Maccabee action. Two weeks after the explosions the British received their answer for the destruction of the Zion Settlement Society building and the attempted destruction of the Yishuv Central.

In one night the Haganah completely wrecked the railroad system, stopping all rail traffic to and from Palestine.

The next night the Maccabees broke into six British embassies and consulates in ˉMediterranean countries and destroyed records used in the fight against Aliyah Bet.

The Palmach branch of the Haganah wrecked the Mosul oil pipelines in fifteen places.

With this done, the final measure was plotted by the Maccabees—the elimination of General Sir Arnold Haven-Hurst. Maccabees observed the Schneller compound twenty-four hours a day. They charted all movement in and out, logged each car and truck, and diagramed the entire compound.

After four days it began to look like an impossible task. Haven-Hurst was locked in the center of a fortress surrounded by thousands of troops. No one but British personnel was allowed anywhere near his quarters. When Haven-Hurst did move out of the compound it was in secrecy and he was guarded by convoys so heavy the Maccabees would lose a hundred men by attacking it.

Then the first flaw was spotted.

A civilian automobile was logged as leaving the Schneller compound area between midnight and one o'clock in the morning about three times each week, returning to the compound just before daylight. There was only a driver in the car and he was dressed as a civilian. The regularity of the movement of this automobile during such unusual hours made it automatically suspect.

The Maccabee team went to work to find the registry of the owner, who turned out to be a wealthy Arab family. Thereupon the Maccabees decided that the car must belong to someone working with the British on the Arab side and gave it up as a possible device for getting to Haven-Hurst.

Meanwhile reports on Arnold Haven-Hurst's personal background, conduct, and habits were compiled and studied. The Maccabees knew he was an ambitious man who had made an important marriage. The marriage gave him station as well as money and he had never endangered it. Haven-Hurst was considered the epitome of a proper gentleman in his social life; he was considered, in fact, a rather dull bore.

Probing beneath this apparent circumspect surface, the Maccabees discovered that Haven-Hurst had had not one, but several, extramarital affairs. In the Maccabees were people who had served in the British Army under Haven-Hurst years before. Camp rumors always had him with a mistress.

A theory developed that Haven-Hurst could well have been very lonely locked in the compound. Because of his marriage and position he would not dare to bring a woman into the camp. He could possibly be going out to a mistress. The idea was put forward that Haven-Hurst was an unseen passenger in the mystery car and was regularly traveling between the compound and a woman.

It seemed preposterous even to the Maccabees, yet until the mystery car was properly identified it could not be cast away. Who could the mistress of Arnold Haven-Hurst be? There were no rumors to be checked upon. If he had a love nest he had concealed it with great skill. No Jewess would risk living with him, and there were no Englishwomen available. This left only an Arab woman.

To attempt to follow the car would have risked detection and alerting of the quarry. It would have been possible for the Maccabees to waylay the single car traveling late at night, but the command decided that if there were the least chance that Haven-Hurst was a passenger it would be better to discover his destination and catch him at an indiscretion.

They worked from the other direction, the owner of the car. In this family of Arab effendis was a young woman who in beauty, education, and background could qualify as an attraction for a man like Haven-Hurst. The pieces of the puzzle were beginning to fit together.

The Maccabees watched the Arab family house and constantly trailed the girl. On the second night, their persistence paid off. The girl left her home at midnight and made for a house in the rich Arab El Baq'a section of Jerusalem near the Hebron-Bethlehem Road. A half hour after she arrived the mystery automobile pulled up and the Maccabees were able to catch a fleeting glimpse of General Arnold Haven-Hurst rushing from the back of the car to keep his rendezvous.

At three o'clock that same morning Haven-Hurst was awakened by a voice in the darkness which shouted out a bloodcurdling quotation, *"Praise ye the Lord for the avenging of Israel!"*

He leaped from the bed. The Arab woman shrieked as Maccabee bullets raked the room.

Later that morning British headquarters received a phone call from the Maccabees. The British were advised where they could find their late commander. They were further advised that the demise of Arnold Haven-Hurst had been well photographed. If the British brought undue retribution against the Yishuv, the Maccabees would publish the pictures.

Headquarters speculated on the effect of the scandal of one of their generals being murdered in the bed of his Arab mistress. They decided to cover up the entire affair with public announcements that he had died in an automobile accident.

The Maccabees agreed that Haven-Hurst indeed was the victim of an automobile accident.

With the general gone from the scene the terrorist activity

dwindled. The pending arrival of the United Nations committee lay an uneasy calm over the land.

In late June of 1947, the United Nations Special Committee on Palestine, known as UNSCOP, arrived in Haifa. The neutrals represented Sweden, the Netherlands, Canada, Australia, Guatemala, Uruguay, Peru, Czechoslovakia, Yugoslavia, Iran, and India.

The odds were long against the Jews. Iran was a Moslem country. India was partly Moslem and its delegate was a Moslem as well as representing a British Commonwealth nation. Canada and Australia were also of the British Commonwealth. Czechoslovakia and Yugoslavia, in the Soviet bloc, had a traditional history of anti-Zionism. The South American representatives, Uruguay, Peru, and Guatemala, were Catholic in predomination and could possibly be influenced by the Vatican's lukewarm feeling toward Zionism. Only Sweden and the Netherlands could be considered fully nonpartisan.

None the less, the Yishuv welcomed UNSCOP.

The Arabs opposed the presence of the United Nations. Inside Palestine a general strike of the Arabs was called, demonstrations were held, and the air was filled with oaths and threats. Outside of Palestine the Arab countries began riots and blood pogroms against their Jews.

Barak Ben Canaan, the old warrior and negotiator, was once again pressed into service by the Yishuv. He joined Ben Gurion and Dr. Weizmann on the advisory committee to UNSCOP.

CHAPTER THIRTEEN: Kitty and Karen returned to Gan Dafna. Kitty waited for the right moment to have it out with Karen. When the letter from Dov Landau arrived, she decided to delay it no longer.

Kitty poured a lemon rinse over Karen's head and wrung out her long, thick brown hair and rubbed the girl's head briskly with a big towel.

"Phew," Karen said, taking a corner of the towel to wipe the soap from her eyes.

The water boiled in the teakettle. Karen got up and tied the towel around her head and brewed a pot of tea. Kitty sat at the kitchen table filing her fingernails. She began to paint them carefully with polish.

"What's bothering you?" Karen said disarmingly.

"Good Lord, I'm not even allowed the privacy of my own thoughts."

"Something is wrong. Something's been wrong since you came back from your trip to the Sea of Galilee. Did something happen between you and Ari?"

"Plenty happened between me and Ari but that's not what is disturbing me. Karen, we have to have a talk about us, and our futures. I guess we'd better do it right now."

"I don't understand."

Kitty waved her hands to dry her fingernails. She stood up and lit a cigarette awkwardly. "You know how much you mean to me and how much I love you?"

"I think so," the girl whispered.

"Since that first day at Caraolos I've wanted you to be my girl."

"I've wanted it that way too, Kitty."

"Then you'll believe that I have thought this all out carefully and what I want to do is for your own good. You must have faith in me."

"I do . . . you know that."

"What I am about to say will be hard for you to appreciate fully. It is hard for me to come to this, too, for I am very fond of many children here and I have grown quite attached to Gan Dafna. Karen, I want to take you home to America with me."

The girl stared at Kitty as though she had been slapped. For a moment she did not even understand or believe she had heard it right.

"Home? But . . . but this is my home. I have no other home."

"I want your home to be with me—always."

"I want that too, Kitty. I want it more than anything. It is so strange."

"What is, dear?"

"When you said home, in America."

"But I am an American, Karen, and I miss my home."

Karen bit her lip to keep from crying. "That's funny, isn't it? I thought we would go on like we were. You would be at Gan Dafna and . . ."

"And you would go off into the Palmach . . . and then to some *kibbutz* out on a border?"

"I guess that's what I thought."

"There are many things I have learned to love here, but this is not my country and these are not my people."

"I guess I have been selfish," Karen said. "I never thought of you as getting homesick or wanting anything for yourself."

"That is the nicest thing anyone has ever said to me."

Karen poured two cups of tea and tried to think. Kitty was everything to her . . . but leave?

"I don't know how to say it, Kitty, but ever since I was old enough to read in Denmark I've asked myself the question about being Jewish. I still don't know the answer. I only know that I have something here that is mine . . . no one is going to take it from me. Whatever it is, it's the most important thing in the world. Someday I might know the words for it—but I can't leave Palestine."

"Whatever you have, you will still have it. Jews in America and I suppose Jews everywhere have this same belonging that you have. Going away won't change that."

"But they are exiles."

"No, baby . . . don't you understand that Jews in America love their country?"

"The Jews of Germany loved their country too."

"Stop it!" Kitty cried suddenly. "We are not that kind of people and I will not listen to those lies they fill you with!" She caught herself quickly. "There are Jews in America who love their country so much they would prefer death to ever living to see what happened to Germany come to America." She walked up behind the girl's chair and touched her shoulder. "Don't you think I know how difficult this is for you? Do you believe I would do anything to hurt you?"

"No," Karen whispered.

Kitty faced Karen and knelt before her chair. "Oh, Karen. You don't even know the meaning of peace. In all your life you have never been able to walk in the light of the sun without fear. Do you think it will be any better here? Do you think it will ever be better? Karen, I want you to go on being a Jew and I want you to go on loving your land, but there are other things I want for you too."

Karen turned her eyes away from Kitty.

"If you stay here you'll spend your whole life with a gun in your hands. You'll turn hard and cynical like Ari and Jordana."

"I guess it isn't fair of me to have expected you would stay."

"Come with me, Karen. Give us both a chance. We need each other. We've both had enough suffering."

"I don't know if I can leave . . . I don't know . . . I just don't," she said with a shaky voice.

"Oh, Karen . . . I want so much to see you in saddle shoes and pleated skirts, going out to a football game in a cut-down Ford. I want to hear the phone ringing and you giggling and talking to your boy friend. I want you full of delicious nonsense as a teen-age girl should be—not carrying a gun in your hands or smuggling ammunition. There are so many things that you are missing. You must at least find out what they are in the world before you make your final decision. Please, Karen . . . please."

Karen was pale. She walked away from Kitty. "What about Dov?"

Kitty took Dov's letter from her pocket and handed it to

Karen. "I found this on my desk. I don't know how it got there."

Mrs. Fremont:
This letter is being written by someone who knows more better how to say in English than I do but I copy it to show it is my writing. This letter must be sent to you in a special way for reasons you know of. I am very busy these days. I am with friends. My friends are the first I have in a long time and they are real good friends. Now that I am perma-nent situated, I want to write to you and to say how glad I am not to be at Gan Dafna no more where everybody makes me sick, including you and Karen Clement. I write to say I won't see Karen Clement no more as I am too busy and with real friends. I don't want Karen Clement to think I am going to come back and take care of her. She is nothing but a kid. I have a real woman of my own age and we live together and everything. Why don't you go with Karen Clement to Amer-ica because she doesnt belong here.

Dov Landau

Kitty took the letter from Karen's hand and ripped it to shreds. "I will tell Dr. Lieberman that I am resigning. As soon as we can straighten up matters here we will book passage to America."

"All right, Kitty. I'll go with you," Karen said.

CHAPTER FOURTEEN: Every few weeks the Maccabee high command changed its headquarters. After "Hell's Fort-night" and the assassination of Arnold Haven-Hurst, Ben Moshe and Akiva thought it would be best to get out of Jeru-salem for a while. The Maccabees were a small organization, a few hundred full-time members and a few thousand part-time with a few thousand more sympathizers. Because they had to remain constantly on the move the headquarters com-mand group carried no more than a half dozen of the top men. Now the pressure was so great that the command split up and only four persons went to Tel Aviv. There was Akiva and Ben Moshe and Nahum Ben Ami, the brother of David, and there was Little Giora—Dov Landau. Dov had become a personal favorite of Akiva. He had gained the inner circle of the Maccabee command by his fame in the raids and by the usefulness of his talents in forgery.

The four moved into a basement apartment owned by a fellow Maccabee, located on Bene Berak Road near the Cen-tral Bus Station and the old market, where there was great activity. Maccabee lookouts were posted around the apartment house and an escape route was worked out. It looked ideal—and could have been worse.

For nearly fifteen years Akiva had frustrated CID and British Intelligence. There was a period of amnesty during World War II when Akiva was free, but for the rest of that time he was wanted. He had always evaded them and had escaped many traps that had been set for him. Akiva was the biggest prize in Palestine with the price on his head running to several thousand pounds sterling.

It was coincidence that the CID was observing the activities of another apartment house on Bene Berak Road just three houses away from the new Maccabee headquarters. The suspects were a ring of smugglers who had been storing goods got past customs in the Jaffa port. The alert CID men watching from an observation point in a building across the street spotted the suspicious picket of watchmen regularly near the basement headquarters. With a telescopic lens camera they photographed all the lookouts and identified two as known Maccabees. While stalking smugglers, they had stumbled onto a Maccabee hangout. Their long experience with the Maccabees induced them to raid at once. They organized quickly and moved to effect complete surprise. They still had no idea they were going into Maccabee headquarters itself.

Dov was in one of the three rooms of the basement apartment forging an El Salvador passport. Only Akiva was with him. Nahum and Ben Moshe had gone out to meet Zev Gilboa, the liaison for the Haganah and Palmach. Akiva came into the room.

"Well, well, Little Giora," Akiva said, "how did you manage to talk Ben Moshe out of taking you along on today's business?"

"I must finish this passport," Dov grumbled.

Akiva looked at his watch and then stretched out on a cot behind Dov. "They should be returning shortly."

"I don't trust the Haganah," Dov said.

"We have no choice but to trust them for the time being," the old man said.

Dov held the passport paper up to the light to study his erasures and see if they could be detected through the water marks and seal. It was a good job. Not even an expert could spot where he had worked over the name and description of the former owner. Dov bent close to the paper and etched in the signature of an El Salvador official, then put the pen down. He got up and paced the tiny room restlessly checking frequently to see if the ink was dry, then resuming his walking, back and forth, snapping his fingers.

"Don't be so impatient, Little Giora. You will find that waiting is the worst part of underground life. Waiting for what, I often wonder?"

"I've lived underground before," Dov said quickly.

"So you have." Akiva sat up and stretched. "Waiting, waiting, waiting," Akiva said. "You are very young, Dov. You should learn not to be quite so serious and quite so intense. That was always one of my faults. I was always too intense. Worked day and night for the cause."

"That sounds strange coming from Akiva," Dov said.

"An old man begins to see many things. We wait for a chance to wait. If they get us, the best we can expect is exile or life in prison. The hanging and the torture is getting to be standard procedure these days. That's why I say . . . don't be so serious. There are many nice Maccabee girls who would love to meet our Little Giora. Have fun while there is time."

"I am not interested," Dov said firmly.

"Ah, hah," the old man teased, "perhaps you already have a girl you have been holding out on us."

"I had a girl once," Dov said, "but no more."

"I must tell Ben Moshe to find you a new one and you will go out and enjoy yourself."

"I don't want one and I'll stay in headquarters. It is the most important place to be."

The old man lay back again and he meditated. At length he spoke. "How wrong you are, Little Giora. How very wrong you are. The most important place to be is awakening in the morning and looking out at your fields, working in them —and coming home at night to someone you love and who loves you."

The old man is getting sentimental again, Dov thought. He tried the paper and found it dry. He fitted the passport photo into place. As Akiva dozed on the cot, Dov began his pacing again. It was worse now that he had sent the letter to Mrs. Fremont. He wanted to go on raids. Another raid and another and another. Sooner or later the British would get him and hang him and it would be all over with. They didn't know that his bravery came from the fact that he didn't care. He almost begged to be hit by enemy gunfire. The dream was bad these days and Karen was not there to stand between him and the gas-chamber door. Mrs. Fremont would take her to America now. That would be good. And he would keep on going on raids until they got him, because it was no good to live without Karen.

Outside of the apartment fifty plain-clothed British police intermingled with the crowds near the bus station. They moved quickly, picking up the Maccabee lookouts and whisk-

412

ing them out of the area before they could give a warning.
Then they cordoned off the entire block.

Fifteen police armed with shotguns, tear gas, axes, and
sledge hammers slipped down to the basement apartment and
stationed themselves around the door.

There was a knock.

Akiva's eyes fluttered open.

"That must be Ben Moshe and Nahum. Let them in, Dov."

Dov slipped the chain latch into place and opened the
door a crack. A sledge hammer crashed into the door, rip-
ping it open.

"British!" Dov screamed.

Akiva and Little Giora captured!

The word was on every lip in Palestine! The legendary
Akiva who had eluded the British for more than a decade was
now theirs!

"Betrayal!" cried the Maccabees. They placed the blame on
the Haganah. Ben Moshe and Nahum Ben Ami had been
meeting with Zev Gilboa. Either Gilboa or some other Haganah person had followed them to learn the Maccabee headquarters. How else could it have been found? The two factions
were again at odds. The Maccabees voiced accusations. A
hundred rumors circulated purporting to reveal how the
Haganah had managed its alleged sellout.

The British High Commissioner for Palestine moved for
an immediate trial to produce a quick sentence which would
further demoralize the Maccabees. He felt that swift justice
for Akiva would restore British authority and curtail the Maccabee activities, since the old man had long been the spiritual
force behind the terrorists.

The high commissioner arranged a secret trial. The name of
the judge was withheld for his own safety. Akiva and Little
Giora were sentenced to be hanged within a fortnight of their
capture.

They were both incarcerated in the impenetrable Acre jail.

In his eagerness the high commissioner had made a disastrous mistake. Newsmen had been barred from the trial, and
in the United States in particular the Maccabees had powerful friends and financial aid. The guilt or innocence of Akiva
and Little Giora were lost sight of in the passionate outbursts
that followed. Like the *Exodus* incident, the sentencing of the
pair was being turned into a focus for violent protest of the
British mandate. Dov's background of the Warsaw ghetto and
Auschwitz was dug up and published, producing a wave
of public sympathy all over Europe. There was indignation
over the secrecy of the trial. Pictures of the eighty-year-old
Akiva and eighteen-year-old Little Giora, the prophet and the

disciple, captured the imagination of readers. Newsmen demanded to see the pair.

Cecil Bradshaw was in Palestine with UNSCOP. Having seen what could happen in the case of the *Exodus* he quickly went into a conference with the high commissioner and applied to the Home Office for instructions. The incident was creating ill will for the British at a delicate time, when the United Nations Committee was in Palestine. Instead of halting Maccabee activity the affair might trigger a new rash of terror. Bradshaw and the high commissioner decided to move quickly to show the world that British justice was merciful. Using the extreme ages of Dov and Akiva as an excuse they announced that they would allow the sentenced pair to make petitions for mercy and spare their lives. Their action put a halt to the storm of protest.

The high commissioner and Bradshaw themselves went to the Acre prison to see Akiva and Dov and tell them the good news. The latter were brought into the warden's office where the two officials bluntly explained the proposal.

"We are reasonable people," the commissioner said. "We have arranged these petitions for you to sign. Officially they are petitions for mercy. However, off the record it is merely a formality . . . a loophole, if you will."

"Now you sign these petitions," Bradshaw said, "and we will give you a fair compromise. We'll take you two out of the country. You'll serve a short term in one of the colonies in Africa and in a few years it will have all blown over."

"I don't quite understand you," Akiva said. "What are we serving a sentence in Africa for? We have committed no crime. We are merely fighting for our natural and historical rights. Since when has it been a crime for a soldier to fight for his country? We are prisoners of war. You have no right to pass any sentence on us. We are an occupied country."

The high commissioner broke into a sweat. The old man was going to be stubborn. He had heard Maccabee fanatics recite that theme before. "See here, Akiva. This is beyond arguing politics. It is your life. Either you sign these petitions for mercy or we will carry through the sentences."

Akiva looked at the two men, whose anxiety was fully apparent. He was quite aware that the British were trying to gain an advantage or undo a mistake.

"You there, boy," Bradshaw said to Dov. "You don't want to hang on the gallows, do you? You sign and Akiva will sign afterwards."

Bradshaw shoved the petition across the desk and took out his pen. Dov looked at the document a moment.

He spit on it.

Akiva looked at the two frustrated, half-frightened Eng-

414

lishmen. *"Thine own mouth condemneth thee,"* he snapped.

The rebuff by Akiva and Little Giora of the mercy petitions was carried in headlines as a dramatic protest against the British. Tens of thousands in the Yishuv who had formerly had little regard for the Maccabees were inspired by the action. Overnight the old man and the boy became the symbol of Jewish resistance.

Instead of damaging the Maccabees, the British were well on their way toward creating a pair of martyrs. They had no choice now but to set the hanging date, ten days away.

Every day the tension grew in Palestine. The raids of the Maccabees and the Haganah had stopped, but the country knew it was sitting on a short-fused powder keg.

The all-Arab city of Acre stood at the northern end of an arced bay with Haifa on the southern end. Acre jail was a monstrosity built on Crusader ruins. It ran along a sea wall that stretched from the prison at the northern outskirt of the town to the opposite end of the city. Ahmad el Jazzar—the Butcher—had turned it into an Ottoman fortress and it had stood against Napoleon. It was a conglomeration of parapets, dungeons, tunnels, towers, dried-up moats, courtyards, and thick walls. The British converted it into one of the most dreaded prisons in the Empire's penal system.

Dov and Akiva were placed in tiny cells in the north wing. The walls, ceiling, and floors were made of stone. The cells' dimensions were six feet by eight feet. The outside wall was sixteen feet thick. There was no light and no toilet. A stink of mustiness was present continuously. Each door was a solid sheet of iron with a tiny peephole for viewing, covered from the outside. The only other opening in the cells was a slit two inches wide and twelve inches high cut through from the outside wall, that allowed in a thin ray of light. Through it Dov could see the tops of some trees and the rim of Napoleon's Hill, which marked the farthest advance point in the drive to conquer India.

Akiva fared badly. The ceilings and walls dripped, and the clammy damp penetrated his ancient inflamed joints and put him in agonizing pain.

Two or three times each day British officials came to plead for some sort of compromise to prevent the hanging. Dov merely ignored them. Akiva sent them out with quotations from the Bible ringing in their ears.

Six days remained before the hanging. Akiva and Dov were moved to the death cells adjoining the hanging room. These were conventional barred cells in another wing of the prison: four concrete walls, a deep hole under the floor, and a trap door under a steel-beamed rigging to hold the rope. A sandbag of the weight of a man was used in testing; the guards pulled the lever to release the trap door and let the sandbag fall with a crunching thud.

Dov and Akiva were dressed in scarlet pants and shirts, the traditional English hanging dress.

CHAPTER FIFTEEN: It was one o'clock in the morning. Bruce Sutherland dozed in his library with his head bowed over a book. He sat up quickly, awakened by a sharp knocking. His servant ushered Karen Clement into the room.

Sutherland rubbed his eyes. "What the devil are you doing here this time of night?"

Karen stood before him, trembling.

"Does Kitty know you are here?"

Karen shook her head.

Sutherland led her to a chair. Karen was white and tense. "Have you eaten, Karen?"

"I'm not hungry," she said.

"Bring her a sandwich and some milk," Sutherland ordered his servant. "Now see here, young lady, what is all this about?"

"I want to see Dov Landau. You are the only one I know who can help me."

Sutherland snorted and paced the room with his hands clasped behind him. "Even if I can help you this can only hurt you more. You and Kitty will be leaving Palestine in a few weeks. Why don't you try to forget him, child?"

"Please," she pleaded. "I know all the reasons why. I have thought of nothing else since he was captured. I must see him once more. Please help me, General Sutherland, please."

"I'll do what I can," he said. "First, let me call Kitty and tell her you are here. She is probably half out of her mind. You had no business traveling through Arab country as you did."

The next morning Sutherland called Jerusalem. The high commissioner was quick in granting the request. The British were still trying to get Dov and Akiva to change their minds and were willing to grab at any straws. There was a possibility that Karen's visit could break the armor of Dov's defiance. It was arranged quickly. Kitty left Gan Dafna and was picked up in Safed by Sutherland, whence the three drove to Nahariya on the coast. There from the police station an escort took them directly into Acre jail, where they were taken to the warden's office.

Karen had been in a daze all the way to Acre. Now, in the prison, it seemed even more unreal to her.

The warden came in.

"All right, young lady."

"I'd better go with you," Kitty said.

"I want to see him alone," Karen said firmly.

A pair of armed guards waited for Karen outside the warden's office. They led her through a series of iron doors and into a huge stone courtyard surrounded by barred windows. Karen could see the eyes of the prisoners leering at her. Some catcalls echoed in the hollow yard. She looked straight ahead. They walked up narrow steps into the death wing. They passed through a barbed-wire machine gun emplacement, then came to another door where two soldiers stood with fixed bayonets on their rifles.

She was ushered into a tiny cell. The door was closed behind her and a soldier stood near. He opened a slot in the wall measuring a few inches wide and a few inches high.

"You'll talk to him through that slot there, girlie," the guard said.

Karen nodded and looked into it. She could see the two cells on the other side of the wall. She saw Akiva in the first and Dov in the other, his scarlet dress. Dov lay on his back, staring at the ceiling. Karen could see a guard enter and unlock his cell door.

"Up, Landau," the guard barked. "Somebody to see you."

Dov picked up a book from the floor and opened it and read.

"You've got a visitor."

Dov turned a page in the book.

"I said you've got a visitor."

"I'm not in for any of your good-will ambassadors. Tell them I said to go . . ."

"It ain't one of ours. It's one of yours. It's a girl, Landau."

Dov's hands tightened on the book and his heart raced. "Tell her I'm busy."

The guard shrugged and walked to the slot in the wall. "He says he don't want to see nobody."

"Dov!" Karen called. "Dov!"

Her voice echoed in the death cell. "Dov! It's me, Karen!"

Akiva looked tensely to Dov's cell. Dov gritted his teeth and turned another page.

"Dov! Dov! Dov!"

"Talk to her, boy," Akiva shouted. "Don't go to your grave in the silence my brother has condemned me to. Talk to her, boy."

Dov set the book down and rolled off the cot. He motioned the guard to open his cell door. He walked to the slot and looked into it. He could see only her face.

Karen looked into his cold, blue, angry eyes.

"I don't want no more tricks," he said acidly. "If they sent you here to beg, just turn around and get out. I'm not asking for mercy from these bastards."

"Don't talk like that to me, Dov."

"I know they sent you."

"I swear no one asked me to come. I swear it."

"Then what are you doing here?"

"I just wanted to see you once again."

Dov clenched his teeth and kept his control. Why did she have to come? He nearly died with wanting to touch her cheek.

"How do you feel?"

"Fine . . . just fine."

There was a long silence.

"Dov . . . did you really mean what you wrote to Kitty or did you say it just because . . ."

"I meant it."

"I wanted to know."

"Well, you know now."

"Yes, I know. Dov . . . I . . . I'll be leaving Eretz Israel soon. I'm going to America."

Dov shrugged.

"I guess I shouldn't have come. I'm sorry I bothered you."

"That's all right. I know you was just trying to be nice. I would really like to see my girl but she's a Maccabee and she can't come. She's my own age, you know."

"I know."

"Anyhow. You're a nice kid, Karen . . . and . . . uh . . . you uh . . . get to America and forget about all this business here. And good luck."

"I guess I had better go," Karen whispered.

She stood up. Dov's expression did not change.

"Karen!"

She turned quickly.

"Uh . . . just to show that we are friends . . . uh . . . we could shake hands if the guard says it's all right."

Karen put her hand through the opening and Dov pressed it between his own and pressed his forehead against the wall and closed his eyes.

Karen grasped his hand and pulled it back to her side of the wall.

"No," he said, "no . . ." but he could not resist.

She kissed his hand and pressed it against her cheek and her lips and he felt the tears from her eyes. And then she was gone.

His cell door clanged behind him. Dov flopped on his bed. In all of his lifetime he could not remember shedding tears.

But now nothing could stop them. He turned his back to the door so the guards and Akiva could not see his face and he wept softly from his heart.

Barak Ben Canaan was one of the Yishuv advisors who traveled with the UNSCOP as it inspected Palestine and made its various inquiries. The Yishuv showed its proud record of land reclamations, rehabilitation for the homeless—the progress of the *kibbutzim* and factories and the cities they had built. The UNSCOP delegates were impressed by the contrast of the Jewish and Arab communities. After the inspection tours formal inquiries were opened in which each side was allowed to present its case.

Ben Gurion, Weizmann, Barak Ben Canaan, and the other Yishuv leaders argued with tremendous skill the morality and justice of the Jewish case.

On the Arab side, the Higher Arab Committee, steered by the Husseini family stirred up bitter demonstrations against the United Nations. They barred the committee from many of the Arab towns where the squalor and primitive factory conditions would turn the strongest stomach. When the inquiries opened, the Arabs officially boycotted it.

It became obvious to the UNSCOP that there could be no middle road in Palestine. On a basis of strict justice the United Nations would have to recommend a settlement in favor of the Jews, but there was the weight of Arab threats to consider.

The Jews had long accepted the theory of compromise and partition, yet they were fearful of the creation of a land ghetto like the Pale.

With the tour of Palestine and the inquiries concluded, the UNSCOP prepared to leave and retire to Geneva to analyze their findings while a subcommittee studied the displaced-persons camps in Europe, which still held a quarter of a million desperate Jews. They would then present recommendations to the General Assembly of the United Nations. Barak Ben Canaan once again accepted a commission to travel to Geneva and continue his advisory capacity.

He returned to Yad El a few days before departure for Geneva so that he might spend some time with Sarah, who, despite his many departures, had never quite got used to them. Neither did she ever get used to Jordana's and Ari's being away.

Ari and David Ben Ami were at the nearby Ein Or *kibbutz,* at Palmach headquarters for the Huleh. They came to Yad El and Jordana came down from Gan Dafna for a farewell dinner.

Barak was preoccupied through the entire evening. He

spoke little of the UNSCOP, the coming trip, or of the pressing politics. It was a grim reunion.

"I suppose you've heard that Mrs. Fremont is leaving Palestine," Jordana said at the end of dinner.

"No, I didn't hear," Ari said, masking his surprise.

"She is. She has given her notice to Dr. Lieberman. She is taking the Clement girl with her. I knew she would run at the first sign of real trouble."

"Why shouldn't she go?" Ari said. "She is an American and the girl is what she came to Palestine for."

"She never had any use for us," Jordana snapped.

"That's not true," David said in defense.

"Don't always take her side, David."

"She is a nice woman," Sarah Ben Canaan said, "and I like her. Many times she passed this way and visited with me. She was very good to those children and they love her."

"She is better gone," Jordana persisted. "It is a shame she is taking the girl with her, but she has the child so spoiled now one would not think she was a Jewish girl."

Ari stood up and walked from the cottage.

"Why must you make it a point to hurt Ari?" Sarah said angrily. "You know what he feels for her and she is a fine person."

"He is well rid of her," Jordana said.

"And who are you to judge a man's heart?" Barak said.

David took Jordana's hand. "You promised we would take a horseback ride."

"You are on her side too, David."

"I like Kitty Fremont. Come, let's go for that ride."

Jordana strode from the room and David followed.

"Let them go, Sarah," Barak said. "David will calm her down. I am afraid our daughter is jealous of Mrs. Fremont as well she might be. Someday our girls may have the time to concentrate on being women."

Barak played with his tea, and his wife stood behind his chair and laid her cheek on his thick red hair. "Barak, you cannot go on like this. You must speak or you shall regret it to your grave."

He patted his wife's hand. "I will find Ari," he said.

Ari was near the orchard looking up into the hills at Gan Dafna when Barak came upon him.

"Does she matter that much, son?"

Ari shrugged.

"I rather liked her myself," Barak said.

"What is the difference? She comes from a world filled with silk stockings and perfume and she is going back to it."

Barak held his son's arm and they walked through their fields to the place where the Jordan River ran past their farm. They could see Jordana and David riding away and they could hear her laughter.

"You see, Jordana is over it already. How are things with the Palmach at Ein Or?"

"As they have always been, Father. Good boys and girls but too few of them and too little to fight with. We cannot expect to win a war against seven armies."

The sprinklers began whirling in the fields as the sun started its plunge behind the Lebanese hills near Fort Esther. The father and the son watched their fields for a long time. Each of them wondered if there would ever come a day when the only thing to worry about was the mending of a fence or the plowing of their land.

"Let's go back to the house," Ari said. "*Ema* is alone."

Ari turned to go. He felt his father's giant hand on his shoulder. He turned. His father's great head was bowed in sadness. "I leave for Geneva in two days. I leave with sorrow as I have never known. For fifteen years someone has been missing from our table. I have been a proud and stubborn man but I have paid the price of pride with torment. It is hell for me now. Ari, my son, do not let my brother Akiva hang at the end of a British rope."

CHAPTER SIXTEEN: Jerusalem seethed on the eve of the UNSCOP departure. In the Arab sector inflammatory oratory rang out to the wild chantings of Arab mobs. The city was split into fortified areas, cordoned off with barbed wire, and guarded by Tommies entrenched behind massed guns.

Ari Ben Canaan moved through Jerusalem, crossing from sector to sector to all of the known hangouts of Bar Israel, the Maccabee contact man. Bar Israel seemed to have disappeared. There had been no liaison between Maccabees and Haganah since the capture of Akiva and Little Giora. Ari was not without his sources of information, however, and he found out that Bar Israel was living in a room in the El Katamon district.

Ari went directly to the room and unceremoniously shoved the door open. Bar Israel was engaged in a chess game. He looked up, saw Ari, and returned to studying the chess board.

"Get out," Ari ordered the other player. He shoved the man through the door and closed it. "You knew damned well I was looking for you."

Bar Israel shrugged and lit a cigar. "You left fifty love letters all over Jerusalem."

"Then why didn't you contact me? I've been in Jerusalem for twenty-four hours."

"You've made your dramatic entrance. Now what do you want?"

"Take me to Ben Moshe."

"We aren't playing with you boys any more. We have an aversion to Haganah commanders learning our headquarters."

"You're not talking to a Haganah commander. You are talking to Ari Ben Canaan, the nephew of Akiva."

"Ari, I trust you personally but orders are orders."

Ari snatched Bar Israel out of his chair, spilling the chess board to the floor. He held the little Oriental by the lapels and shook him as though he were a weightless sack. "You are going to take me to Ben Moshe or I am going to snap your neck."

Ben Moshe sat at his desk at Maccabee headquarters in the Greek colony. Beside him stood Nahum Ben Ami. The two men glared angrily at the bewildered Bar Israel and Ari Ben Canaan.

"We all know Ari," Bar Israel whimpered. "I took a chance."

"Get out," Ben Moshe snarled at the sweating man. "We will settle with you later. Now that you are here, Ben Canaan, what do you want?"

"I want to know what you plan to do about Akiva and the boy?"

"Do? Why nothing, of course. What can we do?"

"You are a liar!" Ari said.

"Whatever we do it is none of your damned business," Nahum said.

Ari smashed his fist on the desk so hard it splintered the top. "It is my business! Akiva is my uncle!"

Ben Moshe remained icy. "We have had enough co-operation with traitors."

Ari leaned forward until his face was inches from Moshe's. "I hate your guts, Ben Moshe, and I hate yours, Nahum Ben Ami. But I am not leaving until I know your plans."

"You are asking for a bullet through your brain."

"You shut up, Nahum, or I'll dismantle you," Ari said.

Ben Moshe took off his glasses, wiped them, and put them back on. "Ari, you have such a pleasant way of persuasion," he said. "We are going into the Acre jail and take Akiva and Little Giora out."

"That is what I thought. When?"

"The day after tomorrow."

"I am going with you."

Nahum started to protest but Ben Moshe held up his hand to be quiet.

"You give your word the Haganah does not know about you being here?"

"You have it."

"What is his word?" Nahum said.

"I take the word of a Ben Canaan."

"I still do not like it," Nahum said.

"That is too bad then. You know what this means of course, Ari. We have mobilized our greatest strength. You have been in the Acre jail . . . you know what it is like. If we can do this thing it will break the British backs."

"Acre is an all-Arab city. The jail is the toughest stronghold they have in Palestine. Let me see your plans."

Ben Moshe opened the desk and took out a sheaf of blueprints. Everything in the Acre area had been covered: there was a layout of the town, the exterior approaches to the prison, the escape roads. The diagrams of the prison's interior were perfect as far as Ari could judge. They must have been drawn up by people who had been prisoners. The guard stations, the arsenal, the main communications center were all pinpointed on the maps.

Ari studied the timetables of the attack. They were masterpieces. Heavy explosives, grenades, and land mines, all manufactured by the Maccabees, were ingeniously employed.

"What do you think, Ari?"

"Everything is perfect—up to a point. I see how you are going to get in and get them outside but the escape from Acre"—Ari shook his head—"this will never work"

"We cannot hide conveniently at the nearest *kibbutz*," Nahum Ben Ami snapped.

"We know the chance of complete escape is very slim," Ben Moshe agreed.

"It is not very slim. It is nil. Of course I know you Maccabees pride yourselves on being dead heroes. Unless you set up better getaway plans, that is what you're going to become."

"I know what he is going to suggest," Nahum said. "He will suggest we co-operate with the Haganah and the *kibbutzim* . . ."

"That is exactly what I am going to suggest. If you don't you'll have a lot of new martyrs. Ben Moshe, you are brave but you are not crazy. As the matter stands now you have possibly a two-per-cent chance. If you allow me to set up more complete escape plans your chances will become fifty-fifty."

"Watch him," Nahum said, "he talks too slickly."

"Go on, Ari."

Ari spread the master map out on the desk. "I suggest that you take an extra ten or fifteen minutes inside the prison and use that time to free every prisoner in the place. They will scatter in twenty directions and force the British to chase them all and thereby cut the British strength."

Ben Moshe nodded.

"Now, our own groups should also break up into small units and each unit head out a different way from Acre. I will take Akiva with me and you will take the boy."

"Go on," Nahum Ben Ami said. As he listened he realized Ari was making sense.

"For my route I will break for Kfar Masaryk. There I will change transportation to throw them off and use back roads to go up to Mount Carmel south of Haifa. I have trusted friends in the Druse village of Daliyat el Karmil. The British won't even begin to look up there."

"It sounds good," Nahum said. "The Druses can be trusted . . . better than some Jews I know."

Ari ignored the insult. "The second unit carrying Dov Landau will go up the coast road to Nahariya and split. I can arrange sanctuary in a half dozen *kibbutzim* in the area. I suggest that Landau be taken to Mishmar *kibbutz* on the Lebanese border. I was there at the building of Mishmar; the area is filled with caves. Your brother David was with me at Mishmar in the second world war. We have used it for years as a hiding place for our leaders. Landau will be absolutely safe there."

Ben Moshe sat like a statue, looking over his plans. Without these hiding places he knew he had no more than a dramatic suicide mission. With Ari's help, there was a chance. Could he risk co-operation?

"Go on, Ari . . . set up your escape routes. I do this only because your name is Ben Canaan."

D-Day minus four.

Four days separated Akiva and Little Giora from a rope. The UNSCOP flew out of Lydda to Geneva. Palestine felt the deathly tense, foreboding calm. The Arab demonstrations stopped. Maccabee raids stopped. The city was an armed camp with British plain-clothes men flooding the area.

D-Day minus three.

A last-ditch appeal from the Prime Minister of Great Britain was turned down by Akiva and Little Giora.

D-Day.

Market day in Acre. At daybreak Arab crowds converged

424

on the city from twenty Galilee villages. The market areas were packed with donkeys and carts and produce. The roads were filled with travelers.

Oriental and African Jews, members of the Maccabees dressed as Arabs, drifted into Acre with the influx of the market-day throngs. Each man and woman carried a few sticks of dynamite, caps, wires, detonators, grenades, or small arms under their long dress. The Maccabees dispersed and mingled in the market stalls near the prison and throughout the jammed bazaar.

Eleven o'clock. H-Hour minus two.

Two hundred and fifty Maccabee men and fifty Maccabee women in Arab dress were now dispersed in Acre.

Eleven-fifteen. H-Hour minus one forty-five.

The guard changed inside the Acre jail. Four inside Maccabee collaborators stood by.

Eleven-thirty. H-Hour minus one-thirty.

Outside Acre at Napoleon's Hill, a second unit of Maccabees assembled. Three truckloads of men dressed as British soldiers drove into Acre and parked along the sea wall near the prison. The "soldiers" quickly broke up into four-man units and walked through the streets as though on security patrol. There were so many other soldiers about that this hundred new people received no attention.

High noon. H-Hour minus one.

Ari Ben Canaan drove into Acre in a staff car dressed as a British major. His driver parked on the sea wall on the west side of the prison. Ari walked out on the big rampart at the north end of the sea wall and leaned against a rusted old Turkish cannon. He lit a cigarette and watched the waves lap against the sea wall below him. The foam swirled around the mossy green rocks worn flat by the waters.

Twelve-five. H-Hour minus fifty-five minutes.

The shops of Acre closed one by one for the two-hour midday break. The sun was getting hot and it blazed down on the Arabs in the coffeehouses, who began to doze as the mournful wails of Radio Cairo blared. The British troops were stifled and groggy in the heat.

Twelve ten. H-Hour minus fifty minutes.

A Moslem caller climbed the long spiral stairs of the minaret beside the Mosque of El Jazzar. The caller cried out in the stillness and the Mohammedans gathered in the courtyard and inside the huge white-domed house of prayer and knelt in the direction of the holy city of Mecca.

Twelve-twelve. H-Hour minus forty-eight minutes.

The Maccabees moved toward their assembly points as the heat beat both Arabs and British soldiers into lethargy.

In groups of twos and threes they moved without apparent

purpose through the narrow dung-filled alleys to the assembly points.

Group one gathered at the Abu Christos—Father of Christ —Café. The café sat on the bay and the coffee drinkers watched the Arab boys dive from the rocks for a *grush*. They could see the entire sweep of the bay and Haifa at the far end.

A second large group came together at the mosque. They knelt at the outer fringes of the huge courtyard and joined the Arabs in prayer.

The third unit went to the Khan, a large square that had been used for more than a hundred years as a caravan resting and trading place. They mingled with the camels and the donkeys and the hundreds of market-day Arabs who lay on the ground and rested.

Group four met on the docks by the fishing fleet.

The fifth group assembled at the Land Gate on the sea wall.

At the same time the hundred Maccabees disguised as British soldiers moved for their positions. They had a greater freedom of movement; they went to house tops and blocked alleyways and roads so that they commanded every possible entrance and exit to Acre jail.

Outside of Acre the final unit of Maccabees got into position. These were people with no disguise. They planted land mines and stationed themselves on the highways with machine guns to stop British reinforcements from getting into Acre.

Twelve forty-five. H-Hour minus fifteen minutes.

The soldiers blocking off the jail were in position. The units on the highway outside Acre were in position.

The striking force, the two hundred and fifty disguised as Arabs, moved out of their assembly points in small groups and converged on the attack point.

Ben Moshe and Ben Ami reached the spot first. They watched their people converging. They looked over the roof tops and saw their soldiers in place. They looked at the prison where one of the four "inside" helpers signaled that all was ready.

Ari Ben Canaan walked to the edge of the rampart and flicked his cigarette out and walked quickly toward the attack point. The driver drifted along behind him in the car.

The attack point was the Hamman El-Basha, a hundred-and-twenty-year-old Turkish public bathhouse. The bathhouse, built by El Jazzar, was attached to the south wall of the Acre jail. In the rear of the bathhouse there was a courtyard used for sunning. A single stairway led up to the roof of the bathhouse and right to the prison wall. The Maccabees had discovered that from their various guard posts inside the prison the British could see every possible approach

426

and detect every possible movement around the jail—except one place: the bathhouse and the south wall, and here was where they would strike.

One o'clock. H-Hour.

The city of Acre was burned into somnolence by the sun.

Ben Moshe, Ben Canaan, and Ben Ami drew deep breaths and gave the signal. The raid of the Acre jail was on.

Ari Ben Canaan led the spearhead of fifty men. They went into the bathhouse and through it quickly to the courtyard in the rear. His group carried sticks of dynamite.

The Arabs sitting in the steaming rooms looked on in utter amazement. Terror seized them and in a second the bathhouse was a confusion of wet scrambling Arabs. A second force moved in and jammed the bathers into one steamflooded room so they could not escape and give an alarm.

Outside, Ben Moshe received the signal that Ari had reached the courtyard and all the Arabs were trapped.

In the courtyard at the rear of the bathhouse Ari's men raced up the steps, crossed the roof to set their dynamite charge against the south wall of the prison. The explosives and caps and wires came out from under their clothing and the charge was fixed with speed and efficiency. They retreated to the cover of the courtyard and lay flat.

One-fifteen.

An ear-shattering explosion shook Acre. The air was filled with flying rocks. It took a full two minutes for the dust to settle and reveal a huge breach in the jail wall.

With the explosion, the four inside men carried out their assignments. The first threw a grenade on the switchboard, stopping all phone operation. The second grenaded the main switch box, cutting the electricity and, with it, the alarm system. The third man seized the turnkey, and the fourth man rushed to the breach to direct the incoming Maccabees.

Ari's men poured into the prison. The first objective of half his force was to get the arsenal. In a few moments they were all equipped with heavy arms.

The second section of Ari's force cut off the main guard barracks so that these troops could not get out as reinforcements.

At intervals of one minute, Ben Moshe outside fed ten- and twenty-man units into the prison. Each group knew exactly where to hit. Guards were gunned from their positions and the Maccabees tore through the ancient passageways with Sten guns blazing and grenades blasting away obstacles. They fanned out, snatched their objectives, and with the precision of meticulous planning they held the interior of the Acre jail six minutes after the wall had been broken.

Outside the walls the covering force dug in and waited for

a counterattack from the British garrison. The troops and plain-clothes men already in the city were stopped by the Maccabees who controlled the entrances from roof tops and alleyways.

When all two hundred men were inside the jail they turned to smashing open the cell doors and freeing the prisoners. The escapees, Arabs and Jews alike, were ushered to the breach in the wall and soon they were running in every direction through Acre.

Ari led five men with the captured turnkey to the death cells and the hanging room. The turnkey began to open the door. Inside the four guards who kept constant watch on the condemned pair began to fire at the iron door. Ari waved the others back, slapped a magnetic mine on the door, and ducked back. The door was ripped from its hinges. Ari stepped into the doorway and hurled a grenade inside and the guards fled to the hanging room.

The party quickly entered, pinned down the guards, and opened the cell doors. Akiva and Dov Landau were rushed from the prison, across the bathhouse roof, and through the bathhouse to the outside.

Dov Landau was pulled aboard a truck filled with men. Ben Moshe waved to them to move out and the truck sped off toward Nahariya. Two minutes later the staff car pulled up and Ari led Akiva into it and they fled in a different direction.

Ben Moshe blew a whistle signal for the Maccabees to begin the withdrawal operations. It was a mere twenty-one minutes since the blast of the wall.

Confused units of the British garrisons attempted to converge on Acre jail. They were stopped by land mines, roadblocks and cross fires. Inside Acre disorganized British units were trying to chase the three hundred freed inmates.

The truck with Dov Landau raced up the coast road. It had been spotted by the British and was now trailed by a motor force that outnumbered its complement ten to one. The truck pulled into the Jewish town of Nahariya. Nahum Ben Ami fled with Dov toward the Lebanese border *kibbutz* of Ha Mishmar while the rest of the force deployed as a rear guard to stall the pursuers. These Maccabees managed to hold the British long enough to allow Nahum Ben Ami to lead Dov to safety, but it was a suicide action: all seventeen men and women of the rear guard were killed.

Akiva and Ari were in the back seat of the staff car. The driver and another Maccabee sat in front. They sped from the Acre area along an inland road toward the *kibbutz* Kfar Masaryk. At Napoleon's Hill, a Maccabee roadblock waved them down and told them to get off the main road, which was mined against British counterattack. This group was holding off two British companies trying to break through to Acre.

Ari made a quick decision.

"Driver. Can you drive through the fields here and get past that British unit?"

"We'll find out."

They careened off the road and banged and rattled through a field to encircle the area of action. They managed to get past the two British companies and turned again for the highway. A dozen soldiers chased after the car, firing as they ran. Just as the car touched the road again it swerved under the impact of a hail of bullets. Ari grabbed Akiva and held him down on the floor. The whine of bullets was all around them. The wheels of the car spun furiously, digging in the dirt for more traction. The driver threw the car into reverse as more bullets ripped into it. Two soldiers with submachine guns were almost on them. Ari fired through the back window. One of the soldiers dropped. The second opened up with a deadly burst of fire. Ari could see the red flames spit from the mouth of his gun.

Akiva shrieked.

Another burst spewed from the soldier's gun.

Ari fell on top of Akiva just as the car regained the road and raced away.

"Are you all right back there?"

"We've both been hit."

Ari pulled himself up and examined his right leg. He felt the inside of his leg. It was numb. The bullet had lodged deep. There was no bad bleeding or great pain, only a burning sensation.

He knelt and rolled Akiva over and ripped his bloody shirt open. Akiva's stomach was a gaping wound.

"How is he?"

"Bad . . . very bad."

Akiva was conscious. He pulled Ari close to him.

"Ari," he said, "am I going to make it?"

"No, Uncle."

"Then get me to some hidden place . . . you understand."

"I understand," Ari said.

The escape car reached Kfar Masaryk where a dozen *kibbutzniks* stood by ready to hide the car and provide a truck to continue the escape. Akiva was gory and unconscious by the time they pulled him from the car. Ari took a moment to pour sulfa into his wounded leg and put a pressure bandage on it. The two Maccabees with him pulled him aside.

"The old man is not going to make it if we go any farther. He must stay here and receive medical treatment."

"No," Ari said.

"Are you mad?"

"Now listen to me, you two. He has no chance to live. Even if he did the British would find him here. If we leave him and he dies here it will be known all over Palestine. No one but us must know that Akiva did not escape. The British must never know he is dead."

The two Maccabees nodded their understanding. They jumped into the front of the truck and Ari got into the rear with his uncle. Ari's leg was beginning to hurt.

The truck streaked south below Haifa. It ascended the narrow roads working up the side of Mount Carmel. Ari held his unconscious uncle in his lap as they bounced on the dirt roads and swayed around treacherous turns, sending up a trail of dust and jolting them unmercifully. Higher and higher into Mount Carmel they drove until they were in the territory where only the Druses lived in isolation.

Akiva opened his eyes. He tried to speak but he was unable to. He recognized Ari and he smiled and then sagged in Ari's arms.

The truck pulled into a clump of brush a mile before the Druse mountain village of Daliyat el Karmil. Mussa, a Druse Haganah soldier, waited with a donkey cart.

Ari crawled from the truck. He rubbed his leg. He was drenched with the blood of Akiva.

Mussa rushed to him.

"I'm all right," Ari said. "Get Akiva. He is dead."

The tired old body of Akiva was carried from the truck to the cart.

"You two men are Maccabees. You are not to reveal Akiva's death to anyone but Ben Moshe or Nahum. Now get the truck down from here and get it cleaned. Mussa and I will bury my uncle."

The truck sped away.

Ari got on the donkey cart. It bypassed the village and moved to the highest point on Mount Carmel, the south ridge. At twilight they entered a small forest that held the altar of the greatest of all the Hebrew prophets, Elijah. It was on this ground that Elijah had proved the power of God against Jezebel's priests of Baal.

The altar of the prophet Elijah looked down on the Jezreel Valley. The valley below stood as an eternal reminder that the land had not been forgotten.

Mussa and Ari scratched out a shallow grave near Elijah's altar.

"Let's get that red suit off of him," Ari said.

The British hanging clothes were removed and Akiva was rolled into his grave and it was filled up and the spot covered with branches. Mussa returned to the cart to wait for Ari.

Ari knelt for a long time over Akiva's grave. Yakov Rabinsky had been born in anger and he had died in sorrow. After so very many years of torment, he could at last find peace. He could find here a peace that had avoided him in life and he could sleep eternally looking down upon the land of the Jews. Someday, Ari thought, all the world will know where Akiva sleeps and it will be a shrine of all Jews.

"Goodbye, Uncle," Ari said. "I didn't even get a chance to tell you that your brother forgives you."

Ari stood up and began to sway. Mussa rushed over to him as he cried out in pain and pitched to the ground in a faint.

CHAPTER SEVENTEEN: Kitty and Dr. Lieberman were both glum as she went over some business in his office.

"I wish I knew the words that would make you stay," Dr. Lieberman said.

"Thanks," Kitty said. "Now that the time is here I feel very empty. I didn't realize how attached I had become to Gan Dafna. I was up most of the night going through these files. Some of these youngsters have made remarkable progress in light of their histories."

"They will miss you."

"I know. And I will miss them. I'll try to get everything up to date in the next few days. There are a few special cases I'd like to go over with you personally."

"Yes, of course."

Kitty stood up to leave.

"Be sure to get to the dining room a half hour early tonight."

"I would prefer it if they didn't. I don't think the occasion calls for a going-away party."

The little hunchback held up his hands. "Everyone insisted. What could I do?"

Kitty walked to the door and opened it.

"How is Karen?"

"Pretty badly upset. She has been since she saw Dov at the prison. I had a bad night with her last night when we heard about the Acre jail raid. Maybe she will learn soon whether or not he escaped. That poor child has been through enough suffering for a lifetime. It may take a while, Dr. Lieberman, but I am going to make her very happy in America."

"I wish it were in my heart to tell you that I think you are wrong for leaving us. I cannot say that."

Kitty left his office and walked down the corridor thinking about the news that had electrified the world. The Maccabees had lost twenty men and women killed and another fifteen were captured. No one knew how many wounded were in hiding. Ben Moshe had been killed. It seemed like a high price to pay for two lives—until one considered that they were not just any two lives. The raid had been a crushing blow to what was left of British morale and British desire to remain in Palestine.

Kitty stopped before Jordana's door. She hated the idea of confronting Jordana. She knocked.

"Yes?"

Kitty entered. Jordana looked up from her desk coldly.

"I was wondering, Jordana . . . Do you happen to know if Dov Landau made his escape yesterday? I mean, with Karen's attachment to the boy it would make her feel much better if . . ."

"I don't know."

Kitty started to leave, then turned at the last second. "Was Ari on the raid?"

"Ari doesn't give me a list of his raids."

"I thought you might know."

"How should I know? It was a Maccabee raid."

"You people have ways of obtaining information about things you want to learn."

"If I knew I wouldn't tell you, Mrs. Fremont. You see, I want nothing to stand in the way of your catching your plane out of Palestine."

"It would be much nicer if we could part friends but it doesn't look as though you are even going to give me a chance for that."

She turned quickly and left the office and walked out to the main door. Kitty could hear whooping and cheering coming from a football game on the athletic field. Out on the center green some of the younger children played tag and some of the older ones lay on the lawn studying.

The flowers never stopped blooming at Gan Dafna, Kitty reflected, and the air was forever filled with their scent.

Kitty walked down the steps of the administration building and crossed the green, past the trenches. She stopped by the statue of Dafna. This time she did not feel jealous of Ari's dead sweetheart. She looked down on the Huleh as Dafna always looked down on it and she felt a sudden twinge of loneliness.

"Shalom, Giveret Kitty," some youngsters called to her as they ran past. One of them ran up to her and threw his arms around her waist, and she mussed his hair and sent him along.

As she walked to the hospital she felt very depressed. Leaving Gan Dafna was going to be more difficult than she had thought.

In her office she began to go through her files, discarding some, sorting others.

It was strange, she thought; she had not felt this loss in leaving the orphanage in Salonika. Kitty never really tried to become a "friend" of the Jews at Gan Dafna. Why was it all catching up to her at this moment?

Perhaps it was because it was the end of an adventure. She would miss Ari Ben Canaan and she would think about him for a long time, maybe forever. But in time things would become sane and organized again and she would be able to give Karen all those things in life she wanted for the girl. There would be good times and wonderful vacations together and Karen would start her dancing lessons again. In time, the picture of Ari Ben Canaan would grow dim as would the memory of Palestine.

It was natural to feel badly, Kitty reasoned. There is a certain regret in leaving any job and moving from place to place.

She began reading through her personal notes on some of "her" children. Were they impersonal objects of prescribed therapies or were they little lost human beings who were dependent upon her? Did she have the right to take them up and just drop them, or did she have a further duty to them beyond her own personal desires?

Kitty quickly shut her mind to this line of thought. She opened her desk drawer and took out her passport. Karen's British passport was beside her own. There were two tickets —Departure, Lydda—Destination, New York.

Mark Parker was coming in from the Orient to meet them in San Francisco. Dear Mark . . . was there ever a more devoted friend? Mark would help Kitty get situated around San Francisco. Kitty loved the Bay Area. They could live in Marin County over the Golden Gate Bridge or in Berkeley near the university. They would be near the theater and ballet and the wonderland of San Francisco.

Kitty shut her desk drawer.

She picked up the files again and started to replace them in the cabinet. Of course it was right for her to go . . . of course it was. Even Dr. Lieberman said so. What did she owe these children? It was a job; nothing more, nothing less.

Kitty closed the drawer to the file cabinet and sighed. Even as she justified it to herself, the shadow of doubt began to creep into her mind. Was she really doing this for Karen or was she going because of her own selfish love for the girl?

Kitty turned and gasped! An Arab was standing in the doorway. He was dressed oddly. He wore an ill-fitting western suit of pin-striped worsted. On his head was a red fez bound in white cloth that gave his head a square look. His black mustache was enormous and waxed to fine points.

"I did not mean to frighten you," the Arab said. "I may come in?"

"Certainly," Kitty said, surprised to hear him speak in English.

She surmised that he was from a nearby village and that someone was sick.

The Arab entered and closed the door behind him.

"You are Mrs. Fremont?"

"Yes."

"I am Mussa. I am a Druse. You know of the Druses?"

She knew vaguely that they were an Islamic sect that lived in villages on Mount Carmel, south of Haifa, and that they were loyal to the Jews.

"Aren't you a long way from home?"

"I am Haganah."

Kitty sprang to her feet instinctively. "Ari!" she said.

"He hides in my village of Daliyat el Karmil. He led the raid at Acre. He asks that you come to him."

Kitty's heart pounded wildly.

"He has been badly wounded," Mussa said. "You will come?"

"Yes," she said.

"Do not take medicine. We must be cautious. There are many British roadblocks and if they find medicine they will be suspicious. Ari says to get the truck filled with children. Tomorrow there is a Druse wedding. We tell the British we are bringing the children to the ceremony. I have a truck. Get fifteen children right away and have them pack bedrolls."

"We will be ready in ten minutes," she said, and rushed out for Dr. Lieberman's office.

It was eighty kilometers from Gan Dafna to Mussa's village, mostly over narrow mountain roads of northern Galilee. The dilapidated truck made slow progress.

The children in the back, delighted with the unexpected holiday, sang at the top of their voices as the truck chugged through the hills. Only Karen, sitting in the front cabin with Kitty, knew the real nature of the journey.

Kitty pumped Mussa for information. All she was able to ascertain was that Ari had received a leg wound twenty-four hours ago, was unable to walk, and was in great pain. He knew nothing of Dov Landau and said nothing of the death of Akiva.

In spite of the instructions, Kitty had packed a small first-aid kit of sulfa, bandages, and iodine, which would appear innocent enough in the glove compartment.

434

She had known real deep fear only twice in her life. She knew fear in Chicago in the waiting room of the polio wing of the Children's Hospital during the three days and three nights of Sandra's crisis. She knew fear once again as she waited in the Dome Hotel for news of the hunger strike on the *Exodus*.

She knew fear now. She was oblivious to the children's singing or to Karen's efforts to keep her calm. She was dazed with anxiety.

She closed her eyes and her lips moved and she said the words to herself over and over . . . "Whoever this God is who watches Israel, keep Ari alive . . . please, let him be alive."

An hour passed and two and three.

Kitty's nerves had brought her to a state of near-exhaustion. She laid her head on Karen's shoulder and closed her eyes.

The truck rattled into the turn at Kfar Masaryk, using the roads that Ari had taken in his escape from Acre. As they moved toward Mount Carmel the roads came alive with troops.

They were stopped at a roadblock.

"These children from Gan Dafna. We have wedding at Daliyat tomorrow."

"Out, everyone," the British ordered.

They combed the truck. All the bedrolls were untied and searched thoroughly; two of them were ripped open with knives. The underneath of the truck was searched and the spare tire torn off the rim. The motor was looked over and the children were searched. The shakedown took nearly an hour.

A second British search took place at the foot of Mount Carmel. Kitty was played out by the time Mussa began to drive up the winding turns along the sides of Mount Carmel.

"All Druse villages are built very high places. We are small minority and need high places to defend against Moslem attacks," Mussa said; "we will be in Daliyat in few minutes."

Kitty pulled herself together quickly as they approached the outskirts and slowed in the narrow streets.

Daliyat el Karmil seemed to sit on the roof of the world.

It was sparkling white and clean in comparison to the filth and decay of most Arab villages. Most of the men wore mustaches and many wore western clothing. Their headdresses were somewhat different from those of other Arabs, but the most dramatic difference was the carriage of dignity and outward pride and the look which suggested that they could be fierce fighters.

The women were exceedingly handsome and the children

were bright-eyed and sturdy. The women were dressed in wild colors with white cloths over their heads.

Daliyat teemed with hundreds of visitors. They had come for the wedding from all the Carmel Druse villages, and in addition there were Jews from the *kibbutz* and as far away as Haifa.

The truck inched past the village reception house where solid lines of male guests gathered to congratulate the groom and the village elders. Alongside the reception house a veranda was built over the hillside. It held a twenty-five-yard-long table filled with fruits and rice and curried lamb and wines and brandies and stuffed marrows. The women, balancing dishes of food on their heads, kept a steady stream moving to and from the table.

Mussa stopped the truck beyond the reception house. A half dozen villagers came up to greet the children. The children unloaded the back of the truck and marched off with their bedrolls to their camping area to set up their camp and then return to join the festivities.

Mussa, Kitty, and Karen drove on down the center street. Here, Druse dancers wearing silver silk shirts and multi-colored embroidered skullcaps were in the middle of a wild performance. They were lined up, each with his hands on the next man's shoulders. Keeping the line straight, they continuously bounced from the ground, holding their bodies rigid, using only their feet as springs. In front of the line the finest Druse dancer in Palestine, a man named Nissim, went through wild gyrations with one knife in his teeth and a pair of knives in his hands.

Nearby, at the sanctuary, a verse maker told a story by calling out extemporaneous chants. Each line of the chant was repeated by a hundred men around him. As his story unfolded, each new line was repeated louder and louder, and as he came toward the end of his legend half the men drew pistols and fired them into the air.

Mussa turned the truck off the main street and took a narrower street down a steep incline. He jammed the transmission into low gear and held his foot on the brake as the vehicle slid down.

At the bottom of the grade, Mussa stopped the truck. The next road was too steep to attempt. The three of them got out quickly. Kitty took the small first-aid kit and followed Mussa down past a block of houses until they were far from the frenzied town activity.

At the last house in the village they stopped. It was closely guarded by a small band of fierce-looking armed Druse men.

Mussa held the door open. Kitty took a deep breath and

entered. Inside another pair of guards stood before an inner door. She turned to Karen.

"Stay here. I'll call you if I need you. Mussa, come in with me please."

The bedroom was almost dark, and it was chilly because of the altitude and the concrete floors. Kitty heard a groan. She walked quickly to the window and threw the shutters open, admitting a stream of light.

Ari lay on a double bed with a brass headboard. His fists were clenched around two of the rungs, which he had bent out of shape as he writhed in agony. Kitty threw the cover from him. His clothes and the mattress were dark with blood.

"Help me take his pants off," Kitty ordered.

Mussa straightened up with amazement.

"Never mind," she said. "Just stand out of my way. I'll tell you when I need you."

She carefully ripped away his trousers and examined him. His color seemed good and his pulse was relatively strong. She compared the two legs. The bad one did not seem to be unduly swollen nor did it appear that he had lost an excessive amount of blood.

Kitty's manner was brisk efficiency now that she knew Ari was alive and did not appear to be in critical danger.

"Mussa, bring me some soap and water and some clean towels. I want to take a closer look at the wound."

She washed her hands and wiped around the wound carefully. His thigh was discolored and the blood oozed from the puffy spot where the bullet had entered.

Ari fluttered his eyes open. "Kitty?"

"Yes, I'm here."

"Thank God."

"What have you done for this thing?"

"I put some sulfa on it yesterday. I had a pressure bandage but it didn't seem to be bleeding too much."

"I'm going to poke around. It's going to hurt."

"Go ahead." He grunted and broke out in a cold sweat as she felt the lump. He gripped the brass rungs and shook the bed. Kitty took her hand away quickly. Ari trembled for three minutes. She wiped his face with a wet towel.

"Can you talk to me, Ari?"

"It's going away," he said. "It comes and goes. This is a lot of fuss I'm making for a leg wound. Did your Cook County training include this sort of thing?"

Kitty smiled that he should remember. "Oh, every once in a while somebody's husband caught the boy friend in the act and he was dumped at the emergency door."

"What is it?"

"I can't say for sure. Bullets do funny things. There's no accounting for the way they twist. Your pulse and breathing are good, no shock. Your leg isn't swollen except around the immediate area of the wound."

"What does that mean?"

"I would say it means you haven't had an internal hemorrhage. The bullet missed a main artery. I can't see any infection, either. I'd say you were rather lucky . . . although I'm worried about this pain you're having."

"I've been passing out every few hours," he said.

"Hold on. I want to feel around again."

Ari braced himself but was only able to take the probing for a few seconds. He cried out and bolted up to a sitting position and then gasped and sank down.

"The sonofabitch is killing me!"

He clutched the sheets and rolled over on his face and shook.

He convulsed in pain for ten minutes, then fell limp. "Kitty . . . what is it? . . . for God's sake, I can't take much more . . ."

"Were you able to walk at all after you were hit?"

"Yes . . . what is it, Kitty? Why should it hurt like this?"

She shook her head. "I'm not a doctor. I can't say for sure. I may be all wrong."

"Tell me what you do know," he gasped.

"All right, this is what I think. The bullet entered your outer thigh and hit the bone. It didn't break your leg or you couldn't walk and it didn't pass to the inside of your thigh or it probably would have got an artery."

"What is it?"

"I think it hit the bone and either chipped or splintered it. That's one of the things that is hurting you. My guess is that the bullet ricocheted back toward the surface. It may be lodged against a nerve."

"What's going to happen?"

"It has to come out. That pain is either going to kill you or paralyze you. You can't take a trip down the mountain. It may start all sorts of things going . . . a hemorrhage, God knows what. You'll have to get a doctor up here in the next few hours—or you're going to be in very bad trouble. That bullet has to come out."

Ari looked over to Mussa. Kitty turned and looked at the Arab and then quickly to Ari.

"There are wounded men from yesterday's raid hiding all over the Galilee," Mussa said. "Every Jewish doctor in Palestine is being watched right now. If I try to bring one back up here for Ari, he is certain to be followed."

She stared from one to the other again and stood up and

lit a cigarette. "Then you'd better give yourself up and get this taken care of right away."

Ari nodded to Mussa and the Arab walked from the room. "Kitty," he called.

She walked to the side of the bed. He reached out and took her hand. "They'll hang me. It's up to you."

Her throat went dry. She pulled away and leaned against the wall and tried to think. Ari was calm now and his eyes were fixed on her.

"I can't. I'm not a doctor."

"You've got to."

"There is nothing to work with . . ."

"You've got to."

"I can't . . . I can't. Don't you see it will be so painful . . . it might put you into shock. Ari . . . I'm frightened."

She slumped into a chair. She thought of Ari's leading the raid and knew he was right about his fate if the British were to find him. She thought of Dov—and how Karen had felt. She knew that she was his only hope; to do nothing was equally courting death. She bit her clenched fingers and stood up quickly. There was a bottle of brandy on the dresser. She took it to him.

"Start drinking this. When this bottle is empty, we'll get you another one. Get drunk . . . get as drunk as you can, because I'm going to hurt you like hell."

"Thanks, Kitty . . ."

She opened the door quickly.

"Mussa!"

"Yes."

"Where can we get some medical supplies?"

"At the Yagur *kibbutz*."

"How long will it take to get a man there and back?"

"Getting him there there is no trouble. Coming back . . . he must not use the roads so he cannot take a car. By foot in these mountains will take many hours . . . maybe not even till late tonight."

"Look, I'll write you a list of things that I will want. You get a man to that *kibbutz* as fast as you can."

Kitty considered. The messenger might get back tonight and he might not get back at all. A *kibbutz* dispensary might or might not have anesthetics but she could not take the chance of waiting. She wrote a note for two liters of plasma, vials of penicillin, morphine, dressings, a thermometer, and some other instruments. Mussa dispatched one of the guards to Yagur.

"Karen, I'm going to need your help but it is going to be very rough."

"I can do anything."

"Good girl. Mussa, do you have anything at all in the way of medicine?"

"A few things, not much."

"Very well. We'll make do with what we have in that first-aid kit. Do you have a flashlight and . . . perhaps some unused razor blades or a very sharp small knife?"

"Yes, we can get that."

"All right, fine. I want the razor blades and the knife boiled for a half hour."

Mussa turned and issued the order.

"Now put some blankets on the floor. The bed is too springy. He will have to be braced solidly. When we move him to the floor, Karen, you get those dirty linens off and change the bed. Mussa, get her some clean sheets."

"Is there anything else?" Mussa asked.

"Yes, we will need six or eight men in here to move him and to hold him still."

Everything was made ready. Blankets were laid out on the floor. Ari was drinking steadily. Four of the Druses moved him as gently as possible to the floor. Karen quickly took off the bloody sheets and remade the bed. The blades and knife were brought in. Kitty scrubbed her hands and washed the wound area and painted it with iodine. She waited until the brandy had Ari mumbling incoherently, then placed a pillow beneath his head and placed a handkerchief in his mouth for him to bite on.

"All right," she said, "I'm ready. Hold him down and let's get going."

One man held Ari's head, two men held each arm, two held the good leg and one held the bad one. The eight Druses had Ari pinned solidly to the floor. Karen stood at the edge of the group with the flashlight, brandy, and the meager supplies at hand. Kitty got on her knees and knelt close to the wound. Karen turned the flashlight on it.

Kitty took a razor blade in her fingers and motioned the men to get ready. She pressed the blade against his thigh and lined up her stroke. With one quick hard motion she slit deeply into his flesh and opened it in a two-inch cut over the bullet hole. Ari shook violently. Mucus poured from his nose, and his eyes ran with tears of agony. The men strained to hold him.

Karen saw the blood leave Kitty's lips and her eyes started to roll. She grabbed Kitty's hair and pulled her face up and poured brandy down her throat. Kitty gagged a second and caught herself and took another drink. Ari's eyes rolled back into his head. He fell into blessed unconsciousness.

Karen turned the light on the incision once again. With one hand Kitty held the skin apart. With her other thumb and

440

third finger she dug into his flesh and felt around for the bullet. Her fingernail rubbed the hard object. With a final exertion of strength she gripped it and wiggled it loose from his leg.

She sat on the floor and held the bullet up and looked at it and began laughing. All the Druse men started laughing too. Kitty sobbed half hysterically.

"Mussa," Karen said, "get him back on the bed quickly. Don't let anything touch that wound."

Karen helped Kitty to her feet and sat her down in a chair. She pried the bullet from her hands and wiped them clean. The girl moved over to Ari and poured sulfa powder into the wound and laid a bandage over the top of it lightly. Then she sponged Ari down. Kitty remained crumpled and sobbing.

Karen ordered everyone from the room and poured another drink for Kitty and left.

Kitty sipped the brandy and walked over to Ari and felt his pulse. She pried his eyes open and watched his color.

Yes . . . he was going to come through all right . . .

She laid her head on his chest. "Ari . . . Ari . . . Ari . . . Ari . . ." she whispered between sobs.

CHAPTER EIGHTEEN: Ari remained in excruciating pain. The medicines failed to arrive. Kitty was unable to leave him for a second. Several times she had to call Mussa for men to keep Ari from thrashing around and endangering the open wound.

Up the hill in the center of the village the dancing and chanting and hilarity continued. The bride, who had been hidden all day, was taken from seclusion. The groom, dressed in a cutaway coat and top hat, mounted a horse and rode to her through a flower-strewn lane flanked with rifle-bearing Druse men.

After the ceremony many of the Jewish visitors, with the children from Gan Dafna, lit a campfire and there were more songs and a *hora*. There was Hebraic dancing to the tambour and flute and the Druse dancers, too, took their turn in the center ring.

Karen remained constantly in the outside room. She came in to spell Kitty for intervals during the long night. Morning found both of them exhausted from the lack of sleep and the prolonged tension. Kitty sat at the edge of the bed and sprang up each time Ari groaned or moved.

By morning the medicines still had not arrived.

"You had better take the children back to Gan Dafna,"

Kitty told Mussa. "Is there anyone else here who speaks English?"

"Yes, I will have him stay here."

"Good. Can you get another bed set up or a couch or something for me to rest on? I'll have to remain right here for some time."

"It will be arranged."

Kitty went into the next room where Karen dozed on a bench. She brushed the girl's cheek gently. Karen sat up and rubbed her eyes. "Is he all right?"

"No. He is in very bad pain. I want you to go back to Yad El with the children this morning."

"But, Kitty . . ."

"Don't argue. Tell Dr. Lieberman I have to stay here until I can get things under control."

"We are supposed to leave Palestine the day after tomorrow."

Kitty shook her head. "Cancel our flight. We can make new travel arrangements later. I have to stay here until they can get someone else up here to take care of him properly. I don't know how long it's going to be."

Karen embraced Kitty and turned to leave.

"Karen. Get to Safed, will you, and tell Bruce Sutherland where I am. Ask him if he will come to Haifa to meet me. Tell him to stay at the largest hotel. I'll find it, whatever it is. Have him bring some clothes for me."

By noon the hundreds of celebrants began drifting away from Daliyat el Karmil. The Druses left for their mountaintop villages and the Jews went back to the *kibbutz* and to Haifa. Mussa took the truckload of children back toward Gan Dafna.

When they were all gone, the Druses relaxed the heavy guard around Ari. The English-speaking Druse stood by in the next room.

Kitty Fremont was alone with him in this strange place. In this first moment of quiet the full impact of these events hit her. She stood over his bed and looked at him.

"God Almighty," she whispered. "What have I done?" All the months of fighting him, all the carefully built-up resistance, collapsed in that mad second that had sent her rushing to his side. At this moment she feared this power that Ari held over her.

Late in the evening the messenger arrived with medicines from Yagur *kibbutz*. He had been working his way through the mountains and hiding for long periods of time. British patrols were everywhere looking for the wounded from the Acre jail raid.

Kitty quickly administered a liter of plasma to Ari and filled him with penicillin as insurance against the infection

442

that she feared must be inevitable under the circumstances of the operation. She redressed the open wound and injected morphine to ease the murderous pain.

For the next two days and nights Kitty kept Ari under morphine sedation to block off the pain. She watched his progress from minute to minute. The incision was beginning to bind together. There appeared to be no great crisis. Ari was awake only for brief moments, during which he took some nourishment, but when he was awake he was too torpid to realize what was taking place around him. The Druse villagers marveled at Kitty's nursing efficiency and stamina. The women were particularly pleased with the way she snapped out orders to the men.

By the time Kitty knew Ari was safe, that time was the only requirement, she had become uncertain and filled with anxiety: the question of leaving Gan Dafna was in her mind again.

She pondered again her right to leave the children of Gan Dafna who needed her. Where was the line between professionalism and humanity? And what of Karen? Was Karen coming to America only out of fear of losing Kitty?

Of the thoughts that weighed on Kitty the worst was a factor she could no longer rationalize. Once before she had been draw into this strange group of people against her will: on Cyprus she had resolved not to work for them—and then she saw Karen. Now, it appeared to be a repetition: on the eve of her departure she was pulled back to Ari. Was this a coincidence or was her fate being shaped by a higher power? As much as her basic common sense resisted the fantastic idea, it kept haunting Kitty. She feared the power of Palestine.

Ari made swift progress under Kitty's ministrations. He was a remarkable man, Kitty reflected. The pain that he had borne could have killed an ordinary human being. By the end of the fourth day she had reduced the morphine sharply. She had also discontinued the use of penicillin, certain that the wound was healing and would not become infected.

Ari awoke on the fifth morning hungry, eager to shave and clean up, and in a cheerful frame of mind. As Ari emerged in renewed vitality, Kitty went into a shell. She adopted an icy, impersonal, clinical attitude. She snapped orders like a sergeant major, prescribing the next week's plans as though he were a complete stranger.

"I hope by the end of this week to have you completely off drugs. I want you to start exercising the leg and give it as much motion as possible. However, you must be very careful about putting too much strain on the incision. It isn't stitched."

"How long before I'll be able to walk?"

"I can't say without an X ray. I am inclined to think the bone was just cracked and not chipped. If there was a chip you would still be in severe pain. However, I can safely say that you aren't going anywhere for at least a month."

Ari whistled under his breath as she pulled the sheet up around him.

"I'm going out for a walk," she said. "I'll be back in a half hour."

"Kitty. Just a moment. I . . . uh . . . look, you've been very kind. You've watched over me like an angel. Since this morning you have seemed angry. Is there something wrong? Have I done something?"

"I'm tired, I'm worn out. I've been up for five nights. I'm sorry I can't do a song and dance for you."

"That's not it. There's something more. You're sorry you came here, aren't you?"

"Yes, I am," she said softly.

"Do you hate me?"

"Hate you, Ari? Haven't I made it quite obvious how I feel about you? Please, I'm tired . . ."

"What is it? Tell me?"

"I despise myself for caring for you. . . . Is there anything else you want to know?"

"You can be a terribly complicated woman, Kitty Fremont."

"I suppose I am."

"Why do you and I always have to confront each other with our guards up, ready to swing . . . ready to run?"

Kitty regarded him steadily for a moment. "Maybe because I don't live by your simple, uncluttered standards of I-like-you-and-you-like-me-so-let's-go-to-bed. Page four forty-four of the Palmach manual: boys and girls should not indulge in coyness. Women of Palestine, be forthright. If you love him, sleep with him."

"We aren't hypocrites."

"I'm not so advanced in my thinking as Jordana or your immortal Dafna."

"Stop it," Ari snapped. "How do you dare to imply that my sister and Dafna were—tramps? Jordana has loved only one man in her life. Is it wrong to give her love when she does not know if either of them will be alive at the end of the week? Don't you think I would have preferred to live in peace at Yad El with my Dafna than have her killed by Arab gangs?"

"I don't live my life as a noble mission. It is very simple with me, Ari. I have to be needed by the man I love."

444

"Let's quit this," Ari said. "Haven't I made it plain to you that I needed you?"

Kitty laughed shortly with bitterness. "Yes, you needed me, Ari. You needed me on Cyprus to smuggle forged papers out of Caraolos and you needed me again . . . to pull a bullet out of you. It is remarkable, that mind of yours. Even half dead and rolling in pain you could figure out all the angles. You could plot out the course . . . fill the truck up with children to avoid suspicion. You didn't need me, Ari. You needed a candidate to get through the British roadblocks.

"I'm not blaming you," she continued. "I am the number-one damned fool. We all have our crosses to bear and I guess you are mine. I just can't take it with the straight-faced unconcern of a *sabra*."

"Does that make it necessary to treat me like an animal?"

"Yes . . . because that's what you are. You're a mechanical animal, too infested with the second coming of the Israelites to be a human being. You don't know the meaning of giving love. You know only fighting. Well, I'm fighting *you*, Brother Ben Canaan, and I'm going to beat you, and I'm going to forget you, in spades."

Ari remained silent as she walked to the bed and stood over him with tears of anger welling in her eyes. "Some bright day you're really going to need someone and it's going to be a terrible thing because you don't have the capacity to truly ask for help."

"Why don't you take that walk?" he said.

"I'm taking it and I'm going to keep on walking. Good Nurse Fremont is through. Somebody from the Palmach will come up to take care of you in a few days. You'll live till then."

She spun around and opened the door.

"Kitty, this great vision of man you have . . . what do you want?"

"I want a man who knows what it is to cry. I feel sorry for you, Ari Ben Canaan."

Kitty left Daliyat el Karmil the same morning.

CHAPTER NINETEEN: Bruce Sutherland had been waiting for Kitty at the Zion Hotel in Haifa for two days. It seemed to her that she had never been happier to see anyone. After dinner Sutherland drove up to Har Hacarmel, the Jewish sector of the city which was spread on the slopes of Mount Carmel.

They went into a night club which was built with a view of Panorama Road, where the city below, the harbor, and the sweep of the bay could be seen to Acre and beyond it, to the hills of Lebanon.

"How's the girl?"

"Much better, thank you, Bruce. I do appreciate your coming." She looked at the view. "I came up here to Har Hacarmel the first night I was in Palestine. Ari brought me up. I think our conversation had something to do with living with tension."

"The Jews here have learned to live under the gun the way you Americans live with baseball. It's made them a hard lot."

"This place has got me so I can't think straight any more. The more I try to reason, the more I am trapped by sentiment and unexplainable forces. I've got to get out of here before it swallows me up."

"Kitty, we know that Dov Landau is safe. He is hiding up at Mishmar. I haven't told Karen yet."

"I guess she's got to know. Bruce, what's going to happen here?"

"Who knows?"

"You think the UN will give in to the Arabs?"

"There will be a war."

There was a fanfare at the bandstand. A master of ceremonies came out and told a few stories in Hebrew and then introduced a tall, handsome *sabra* youth. The young man wore the traditional white shirt opened at the throat and he had a black mustache and a small chain was around his neck with a Star of David pendant. He strummed a guitar and sang a song of passionate patriotism about the Jews coming back to their Promised Land.

"I must know what is going to happen at Gan Dafna."

"The Arabs can raise an army of fifty thousand Palestinians and perhaps twenty thousand irregulars from over the border. There was a chap named Kawukji who led irregulars in the '36-'39 riots. He's already busy getting another gang of cutthroats together. It is easier to get arms to the Arabs than to the Jews . . . they have friendly territory all around them."

"And the rest of it, Bruce?" Kitty demanded.

"The rest of it? Egypt and Iraq both have armies of around fifty thousand men. There will be some Saudi Arabian troops in the Egyptian Army. Syria and Lebanon will put another twenty thousand men on the field. Trans-Jordan has the Arab Legion . . . crack soldiers with the latest arms. According to present-day definitions the Arabs do not have first-class

446

armies; none the less they have many modern units with artillery, armament, and aircraft."

"You advised the Haganah, Bruce. What did you tell them?"

"I told them to form a defense line between Tel Aviv and Haifa and try to hold that strip of territory. Kitty, the other side of the picture is not pretty. The Jews have four or five thousand Palmach troops and a paper army of fifty thousand in the Haganah, but they only have ten thousand rifles. The Maccabees can put a thousand men out, no more, with light arms. They have no artillery, their air force is three Piper Cubs, and their navy is those illegal-immigrant runners tied up at Haifa. The Jews are outnumbered in soldiers forty to one, in population a hundred to one, in equipment a thousand to one, and in area five thousand to one. The Haganah has turned down my advice and the advice of every military man who has told them to pull in to a tight defense line. They are going to fight it out at every *moshav*, every *kibbutz*, every village. That means Gan Dafna, too. Do you want to hear any more?"

Kitty's voice was shaky. "No . . . I've heard enough. Isn't it strange, Bruce? One night when I was up on Mount Tabor with those young Palmach people I had the feeling that they were invincible . . . the soldiers of God. Firelight and moonlight does things to me."

"It does to me too, Kitty. Everything I've ever learned in my life in the service tells me that the Jews cannot win. Yet when you see what they have done with this land you are not a realist if you do not believe in miracles."

"Oh, Bruce . . . if I only could believe that way."

"What an army these Jews have! Boys and girls without guns, without rank and uniform, and without pay. The Palmach commander is all of thirty years of age and his three brigade commanders are all under twenty-five. But there are things no military man counts that the Arabs must reckon with. The Jews are willing to lose every man, woman, and child to hold what they have. How much blood are Arabs willing to pay?"

"Can they win? Do you really believe it?"

"Call it divine intervention, if you will, or maybe . . . let us say that the Jews have too many Ari Ben Canaans."

Kitty returned to Gan Dafna the next day. She was surprised to find Jordana Ben Canaan awaiting her in her office. The redheaded *sabra* girl was ill at ease.

"What do you want, Jordana?" Kitty asked coolly. "I'm going to be very busy."

447

"We learned what you did for Ari," Jordana mumbled awkwardly, "and I want to tell you how grateful I am."

"It seems that your intelligence system is getting information through again. I am sorry I had to delay my departure."

Jordana blinked but did not answer.

"Don't take this personally," Kitty said; "I would have done the same for a wounded dog."

Kitty made plans to leave. Then Dr. Lieberman induced her to remain an extra few weeks. Extra personnel had been brought in and needed training to handle a hundred more children who had been smuggled into the country by Aliyah Bet. Housing was being put up as quickly as possible. Many of the new children were in bad shape, having been in DP camps for more than two years.

Once more she made her travel plans. Soon there were but two days left before she and Karen were to depart from Gan Dafna and Palestine.

At the end of August in the year 1947 the UNSCOP announced its majority and minority plans from Geneva. Each of the plans called for partition into separate Arab and Jewish entities with Jerusalem to be an international territory. There was no doubt as to the moral issue, for the United Nations Special Committee on Palestine called for the immediate immigration of six thousand Jews a month from the DP camps in Europe and the resumption of land sales to Jews.

The Jews had begged that the Negev Desert be added to their state. The Arabs had millions of square miles of undeveloped wastelands. The Jews wanted this small piece of a few thousand square miles in the hope that they could redeem it. The United Nations committee agreed.

Weary from a half century of heartbreak and sellout, the Yishuv Central and World Zionists announced acceptance of the compromise. The partitioned area, even with the Negev Desert, was an abortion of a state. It was, in fact, three strips of territory linked together by narrow corridors, resembling a chain of sausages. The Arabs had three strips of territory, larger in area, also linked by corridors. The Jews lost their eternal city, Jerusalem. They kept the Sharon and the parts of the Galilee they had pulled out of swamplands. The Negev was wasteland. What was the use of fighting it further? It was a monstrosity but they accepted.

The Jews answered.

So did the Arabs. The partition would mean war, they said. Despite the Arab threats, the UNSCOP resolved to present

448

the partition plan to the General Assembly of the United Nations in New York in mid-September.

Every last detail had been taken care of. Again it was the eve of departure for Kitty and for Karen. At dawn Bruce Sutherland would drive them to the Lydda airport, and in the evening they would fly out to Rome. The heavy trunks had already been shipped ahead by boat. The cottage was ready to be vacated.

Kitty sat at her desk in her office with the final folders to be put away into the files. All that she had to do was to put them in the cabinet, close the drawer, and walk out of the door—forever.

She opened the first folder and picked up the top paper and looked at her notes.

MINNA (SURNAME UNKNOWN), AGE 7. Minna was born in Auschwitz concentration camp. Neither of her parents is known. We presume she is Polish. She was smuggled into Palestine by Aliyah Bet around the first of the year. When she was brought to Gan Dafna she was physically very weak and sick and showed many disturbances . . .

ROBERT DUBUAY, AGE 16. French nationality. Robert was found at the Bergen-Belsen concentration camp by British troops. Robert was thirteen years of age at the time and weighed fifty-eight pounds. The boy had previously been an eyewitness to the death of his mother, father, and a brother. A sister, who later was a suicide, had been forced into prostitution with German soldiers. Robert shows signs of hostility and . . .

SAMUEL KASNOWITZ, AGE 12. Estonian nationality. No known family survived. Samuel was hidden in the basement of a Christian family until he was forced to flee into a forest where he lived alone for two years . . .

ROBERTO PUCCELLI, AGE 12. Italian nationality. No known family survived. Liberated at Auschwitz. We found him permanently crippled in his right arm as a result of beatings . . .

MARCIA KLASKIN, AGE 13. Rumanian nationality. No known family. Found at Lachau . . .

HANS BELMAN, AGE 10. Dutch nationality. No known family. Found at Auschwitz. Hidden by Christians . . .

The files went on and on. "No survivors."

". . . this child has the dream so prevalent with those children at Auschwitz. She dreams she is packing a suitcase. This we know is a symbol of death, for suitcases were always

449

packed the night before inmates were transferred to the Birkenau gas chambers."

"The dream of smelling smoke is symbolic of the smell of burning flesh from the crematoriums."

Bedwetting.

Overt hostility.

Nightmares.

Belligerence.

Kitty looked at a copy of the letter she had once written to Harriet Saltzman.

My dear friend:

You have asked my opinion of the common denominator, and the reason we are able to get such quick recoveries and dynamic results from those children who are borderline psychopaths. Well, I think you know that answer far better than I. You gave it to me the first time I saw you in Jerusalem. The wonder drug is called "Eretz Israel." The spirit is so strong here it seems unnatural. They desire only to live and fight for their country. I have never seen such energy or drive among adults, much less children . . .

Kitty Fremont closed the files.

She stood up and looked around the office for several moments, then quickly snapped off the light and closed the door behind her.

She stopped outside the building for a moment. Halfway up the hill toward Fort Esther she saw a campfire. The Gadna children, the ten- and twelve- and fourteen-year-old soldiers would be singing and dancing a *hora.*

She shined her flashlight on the ground and crossed the green. New trenches had been dug. Larger bomb shelters were being installed by the children's houses.

The statue of Dafna stood its vigil.

"*Shalom, Giveret* Kitty," a group of youngsters shrilled as they raced to the recreation hall.

She opened her cottage door. The suitcases were all lined up near the door and marked with tags. The room was denuded of the personal little touches that she and Karen had put into it.

"Karen. Are you here, dear?"

There was a note on the kitchen table.

Dear Kitty:

The gang wanted to have a farewell campfire. I won't stay out too late. Love.

Karen

450

Kitty lit a cigarette and paced the room restlessly. She closed the draperies to shut off the view of the lights on the valley floor. She found herself holding the curtains which her children had made for her. Ten of them had already left Gan Dafna to go to the Palmach, that sad little army of the Jews.

It was stifling inside. She walked to the porch. The air was scented with rose blooms. Kitty walked down the dirt path between the rows of cottages all set inside little lawns and hedges and trees. She came to the end of the path and started to go back but was attracted by the light in Dr. Lieberman's cottage.

Poor old fellow, Kitty thought. Both his son and daughter had left the university and were in the Negev Brigade of the Palmach, so far away. She walked to the door and knocked. The housekeeper, as old and as quaint as Dr. Lieberman, led her to his study. The little hunchback was engrossed in translating some ancient Hebraic on a piece of pottery. A soft background of a Schumann symphony played on the radio. Dr. Lieberman looked up and saw Kitty and set his magnifying glass down.

"*Shalom*," Kitty said.

He smiled. She had never greeted him before in Hebrew. "*Shalom*, Kitty," he said. "It is such a nice word for good friends to use to say good-by."

"*Shalom* is a beautiful word and it is also a nice way for good friends to say hello."

"Kitty . . . my dear . . ."

"Yes, Dr. Lieberman . . . *Shalom* . . . I am staying at Gan Dafna. This is where I belong."

BOOK 4

Awake in Glory

Be merciful unto me, O God, be merciful unto me,
for my soul trusteth in thee: yea, in the shadow of
thy wings will I make my refuge, until these calamities
are overpast.

He shall send from heaven, and save me; he reproach-
eth him that would swallow me up ... God shall
send forth his mercy and his truth.

My soul is among lions: and I lie even among them
that are on fire, even the sons of men, whose teeth are
spears and arrows, and their tongue a sharp sword.

They have prepared a net for my steps; my soul is
bowed down: they have digged a pit before me,
into the midst whereof they are fallen, themselves...
Awake up, my glory ... I will rouse the dawn ...

The Fifty-Seventh Psalm of David

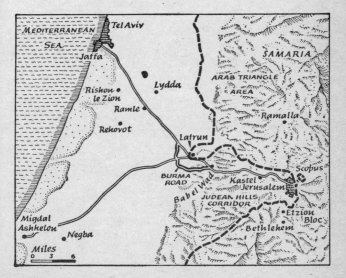

CHAPTER ONE

AUTUMN 1947
UNITED NATIONS
FLUSHING MEADOW, NEW YORK

The six-thousand-year-old case of the Jewish people was placed before the conscience of man.

Chaim Weizmann of the World Zionists and elder statesman Barak Ben Canaan led a twelve-man delegation to Flushing Meadow for the showdown. This delegation, seasoned by years of frustration and adversity, held no illusions.

An informal headquarters was established in Dr. Weizmann's mid-Manhattan apartment. The delegates were assigned to the task of getting votes. Weizmann took as his personal job the alerting of Jews throughout the world to bring attention and pressure upon their governments.

Barak Ben Canaan worked quietly behind the scenes. It was his job to keep abreast of the hourly shifts in strength, analyze and plug up weak spots, maneuver and reassign his men to meet any sudden changes, and spearhead the committee-room debates.

After initial parliamentary jockeying, the Palestine partition went on the agenda.

The Arabs went into Lake Success sure of victory. They had obtained UN membership for the Moslem state of Afghanistan and the medieval feudal kingdom of Yemen, bringing the Arab-Moslem bloc to eleven votes in the General Assembly. These latter were nations who had sat out World War II in silence and declared war against Germany in the last moment to qualify for the United Nations membership. The Yishuv, which had contributed so richly to the Allied cause, had no vote.

The Arabs used the eleven votes to dangle as bait before delegates from smaller nations. In exchange for a vote against partition, they offered their votes as a bribe to those who aspired to some of the lush jobs in the UN.

The Arabs also took full advantage of the cold war that existed between the two giants, the United States and the Soviet Union, deftly playing off one against the other. From the start it was obvious that passage of partition would need the blessing of both of these nations. Russia and the United States had never before joined on an issue and it appeared little likely that they would do it now.

To win partition a two thirds majority was needed. The Yishuv had to get twenty-two votes merely to offset the eleven of the Arab-Moslem bloc. From that point on they had to obtain two votes to each one the Arabs obtained. Mathematically the Arabs needed only a half dozen additional votes to eliminate partition. With their oil as an additional bargaining factor, it would be an easy matter.

The non-Arab world press generally favored partition. Moreover, Jan Smuts of South Africa and the great liberal, Jan Masaryk of Czechoslovakia, were out on the front of the battle lines. The Danes, the Norwegians, and a few others could be counted upon to the end. Sentiment for partition was strong, but sympathy would not be enough.

Then the Big Four powers, the mighty ones, abandoned the Yishuv.

France, who had been overtly friendly to illegal immigration, suddenly reverted to caution. Arabs in the French colonies of Morocco, Algeria, and Tunisia were rumbling with unrest. A French vote for partition could well trigger an explosion among them.

The Soviet Union had different reasons. For over two decades Zionism had been outlawed. The Russians set out upon a program to erase Judaism by a slow abrasive process. While on paper they granted religious freedom, it was nonexistent in reality. There was no Jewish press, theater, school or community life. Synagogues were limited; there was but one in all of Moscow. No member of a synagogue was allowed membership in the Communist party. By these means the Russians hoped to eliminate Judaism in the new generations. Zionism and the partition of Palestine could serve to remind the Russian Jews that they were Jews, and partition was therefore opposed. With the Soviet Union went the powerful Slav bloc.

The position of the United States was the most disheartening setback the Yishuv suffered. The President, the press and people were sympathetic, but international politics put the United States officially into an equivocal position.

To support partition meant splitting the cornerstone of the Western world by breaking the Anglo-American solidarity. Great Britain still dominated the Middle East; American foreign policy was linked to Britain's. To vote for partition was publicly to rebuff Britain.

More than this, the United States faced a greater threat. If partition was voted, the Arabs threatened war. If war came, the United Nations would be bound to enforce peace, and the Soviet Union or her satellites would put troops into the Middle East as part of an international force. This was America's greatest fear and the reason she chose to hedge on partition.

Of the four major powers, Great Britain struck the most

deadly blows against partition. When the British turned the mandate question over to the United Nations they thought that the United Nations could not reach a solution and that Britain would therefore be asked to remain in Palestine. Then UNSCOP went to Palestine, investigated, and reached a decision that censured British rule. Moreover, the world had learned that England's hundred-thousand-man army had not been able to cope with the determined Jews of the Haganah, Palmach, Maccabees and Aliyah Bet, a terrible blow to British prestige.

Britain had to maintain her position of power in the Middle East and to do so she had to save face with the Arabs by scuttling partition. Britain played on America's fear of Russian troops getting into the Middle East by announcing that she would withdraw her garrison by August of 1948. Further, she would not use her force in Palestine to enforce a United Nations decision. Thus checkmating the United States, Britain caused the Commonwealth countries to abstain from voting and applied pressure to those small European countries who were tied to her economically.

The rest of the picture was equally black for the Yishuv. Belgium, Holland, and Luxembourg bowed before British pressure. Other small countries whom the Yishuv had counted upon began to balk.

The position of the Asian countries was variable. They changed their minds and shifted their votes hourly. However, it appeared that the Asians would side with the Arabs as a gesture to the Western powers of their eternal hatred of colonial imperialism, and as evidence of their purchase of the Arab theme that the Jews were representatives of the West in a part of the world where they did not belong.

Greece had an intense dislike for the Arabs but a hundred and fifty thousand Greek nationals lived in Egypt. Egypt made painfully clear the fate of this minority if the Greeks voted for partition.

Ethiopia had little love for Egypt but was tied to her geographically and economically.

Romulo of the Philippines stood against partition.

The Colombians were overtly anti-Jewish.

The Central and South American countries held one third of the United Nations' fifty-seven votes. Most of these countries were completely removed from the issue and neutral. The Yishuv wanted Jerusalem as the capital of their state; they felt that without Jerusalem a Jewish state would be a body without a heart. The South and Central American countries were predominantly Catholic. The Vatican wanted Jerusalem internationalized. If the Yishuv pressed for Jerusalem there was a risk of losing this vital bloc of votes.

But the Yishuv continued to labor, hoping for the miracle which was obviously needed. Throughout September and October, Dr. Weizmann and Barak Ben Canaan were an inspiration to the delegation. They never despaired at the frequent reversals and were never stampeded into errors in strategy.

The greatest weapon the Yishuv had was truth. It was the truth that the neutral UNSCOP had found in Palestine: the truth that Palestine was a tyranny-ridden police state; the truth, seen through the thin veil of Arab deception, of the Arab failure to advance culturally, economically, and socially from the Dark Ages; the truth apparent in the Jewish cities that had sprung from sand and the Jewish fields that had been made to grow from desolation; the truth of industry and ingenuity; the truth—implicit in the DP camps—of the humanity of the Jewish case.

Granados of Guatemala, Lester Pearson of Canada, Evatt of Australia, Masaryk of Czechoslovakia, Smuts of South Africa, Fabregat of Uruguay, and a lot of little men from little nations would not let the truth die at Flushing Meadow.

Finally, in November of that autumn of 1947, "The Miracle of Lake Success" began to unfold.

First came a cautiously worded statement from the United States in favor of the "principle" of partition.

Then came a move that rocked the world. After outlawing Zionism for over two decades, the Soviet Union made one of its startling reversals and announced itself as favoring partition. The news was released after a secret caucus of the Slav bloc; Vishinsky orated in impassioned tones of the rivers of Jewish blood shed and the justice of a Jewish homeland.

Behind this humanitarian mask the Russians had made a shrewd political maneuver. First, they openly mistrusted the Arabs. They realized that the Arab anger was merely a verbal expedient; Russia could vote for partition today and buy the Arabs back tomorrow. Meanwhile the Soviet strategy was to brand Great Britain a tyrant, at the same time making a move that could possibly lead to a Russian foothold in the Middle East. Russia knew that if she voted for partition the United States had to follow suit or lose face around the world as a friend of justice. This in turn meant a break in Anglo-American solidarity. Finally, the Soviet Union stood to gain tremendous prestige value from its "humanitarian" proclamation. And so, inadvertently, the Yishuv suddenly found a strange bedfellow.

As the two great powers made their carefully worded statements for partition, the halls of the United Nations were filled with rumors that cropped up every hour.

The mammoth chess game went on. In the dramatic maneuverings Granados and Pearson became key figures. After much labor these two succeeded in the momentous achievement of closeting the United States and the Soviet Union in a meeting. They emerged from their conference with an electrifying joint statement of definite support of partition.

The Arabs girded for a last-ditch fight to keep the partition resolution from reaching the floor of the General Assembly. Soon it became apparent that a test vote would take place: to get the resolution to the General Assembly only a majority vote was needed, but this vote would indicate the strength of both sides. The vote came and the move passed and the resolution went to the General Assembly—but the roof caved in on the Yishuv. The count was twenty-five in favor, thirteen against, and seventeen abstentions, with two absent. If the same line-up held on the final vote for partition, the Yishuv would not get its needed two thirds majority. France, Belgium, Luxembourg, The Netherlands, and New Zealand had abstained. Paraguay and the Philippines were absent.

The Arabs saw that many "sure" partition votes had abandoned the Yishuv, and the Jews did not have the required number. Confident that they could bag an extra vote or two, the Arabs now switched tactics and pressed for the showdown on the assembly floor.

WEDNESDAY, NOVEMBER 27, 1947

The final debates raged. The Yishuv delegation sat in its special section of the General Assembly looking like men prepared for the executioner. The jolt of the test vote had shaken them to the core. As the arguments continued, their prospects turned darker by the hour.

Greece, expected to abstain out of friendship to the United States, declared openly against partition, fearing what the Egyptians would do to their nationals.

The Philippines, expected to follow the United States, reversed again.

Haiti was suddenly without instructions. Liberia went back on the fence and Siam crossed back to the Arabs.

It was "Black Wednesday" for the Jews.

As the day wore on, the friends of the Yishuv employed a desperation move to talk the clock out and stall the vote. The next day would be American Thanksgiving Day and a holiday. It offered twenty-four precious hours to muster the needed votes. The filibuster went on until an adjournment was called.

The Yishuv delegation assembled quickly in a caucus room. Everyone spoke at once.

"Quiet!" Barak roared. "We have twenty-four hours. Let's not panic."

Dr. Weizmann came into the room excitedly. "I have received a message from Paris that Léon Blum is personally interceding to get the French vote. Feeling for partition is running very high in Paris." It was cheering news, for the former Jewish premier of France was still a powerful voice.

"Can't we appeal to the United States to get Greece and the Philippines into line?"

The delegate who worked with the Americans shook his head. "Truman has issued absolute orders that the United States is not to pressure any delegation. They won't budge from that position."

"What a time to become honorable."

The phone rang. Weizmann lifted the receiver. "Good . . . good," he said. He held his hand over the mouthpiece. "Shmuel from downtown. Good . . . good . . . *Shalom.*" He replaced the phone. "The Ethiopians have agreed to abstain," he announced. Ethiopia, under pressure from her neighbor Egypt, had been expected to vote against partition. The abstention decision showed great courage on the part of Haile Selassie.

A newspaperman close to the Yishuv delegation knocked on the door and entered. "I thought you fellows would like to know that there has been a revolution in Siam and the Siamese delegate has been discredited." A yell of happiness went up at this Arab loss of another vote.

Barak made a quick run down of the roll call of nations—he knew it by heart—and calculated the vote shifts.

"How does it look, Barak?"

"Well, if Haiti and Liberia go with us and France comes in and we don't lose any more ground, we may just squeeze through."

It was still too close for comfort. Grimly and tensely they talked over the final assignments. They could not afford to lose a single vote at this stage.

There was a knock on the door and their champion, Granados of Guatemala, entered. There were tears in his eyes.

"The President of Chile has just sent personal instructions for his delegation to abstain. The delegation has resigned in protest."

"Impossible!" Dr. Weizmann cried. "The President is the honorary chairman of the Chilean Zionists."

The stark reality, the naked hopelessness of the situation crashed down on all of them. Who knew what pressure had been brought to bear on the President of Chile? Who knew where the screws would be turned in the next twenty-four hours?

The gavel rapped. The General Assembly of the United Nations was ordered into session.

"We shall have a roll call of nations on the partition resolution. A two thirds majority is needed for passage. Delegates will answer in one of three ways; for, against, or abstain."

A solemn quiet fell over the great hall.

"Afghanistan."

"Afghanistan votes against."

The Yishuv had lost the first vote. Barak marked it on a pad.

"Argentina."

"The government of Argentina wishes to abstain."

"We have to cut the abstentions down," Barak whispered; "they could kill us."

"Australia."

Everyone leaned forward as Evatt got to his feet with the first vote of a British Commonwealth nation.

"Australia votes in favor of partition," Evatt said.

A buzz of speculation went up. Weizmann leaned close to Barak's ear. "Do you think it might be a trend in the Commonwealth?"

"We'll just have to count them one at a time . . . we can't tell."

"Belgium."

"Belgium votes for partition."

Another buzz arose in the great hall. A few days earlier Belgium had abstained on the test vote. At the last minute Spaak had defied British pressure.

"Bolivia."

"Bolivia votes for partition."

"Brazil."

"Brazil favors partition."

The South American countries were sticking. A vital vote was coming up with the next call. If the Soviet Union had a double cross up its sleeve, the world would know it now, for a satellite, White Russia, was next.

"Byelorussia."

"White Russia votes for partition."

In unison the Jews breathed a sigh of relief. The Slav bloc was going to come in. The signs were bright.

"Canada."

Lester Pearson arose and spoke firmly. "Canada votes for partition." The second of the Commonwealth countries had gone against Great Britain.

"Chile."

Another delegate arose in place of the chief who had resigned in protest to his orders to abstain. "Chile has been ordered to abstain," he said slowly.

"China."

China, jockeying to become the dominant power in Asia, feared to go against the Moslems of India and Pakistan.

"China abstains."

It was a setback for the Yishuv.

"Costa Rica."

The Costa Rican delegate had been approached by the Arabs who tried to bribe his vote by a promise to support him for an important United Nations post. He stood and looked at the Egyptian delegation.

"Costa Rica votes in favor of partition."

The man who would not be bought sat down smiling.

"Cuba."

"Cuba votes against partition."

This came as a complete and unexpected shock to the Yishuv.

"Czechoslovakia."

"Czechoslovakia votes for partition," Jan Masaryk said.

"Denmark favors partition."

"The Dominican Republic favors partition."

"Egypt."

"Egypt votes against and will not be bound by this outrage!"

The gavel rapped and order came about slowly, following the Egyptian's angry outburst.

"Ecuador."

"Ecuador votes for."

"Ethiopia."

"Ethiopia . . . abstains."

It was a bombshell! The faces of all the Arab delegates turned to the Ethiopian with stunned expressions. The Syrian delegate shook his fist angrily.

"France."

The first of the big powers, reluctant France had its turn. Parodi came to his feet slowly. An abstention by France could prove disastrous for the Yishuv. Had Blum and the French people succeeded?

"The Republic of France votes *for* partition," Parodi said in a voice filled with satisfaction.

An expectant murmur went up. It was the first excited awareness that the miracle might actually take place!

"Guatemala."

Granados, the champion of partition, spoke. "For," he said.

"Greece."

"Greece votes against partition."

In the last moment the Greeks had bowed to Egyptian blackmail.

"Haiti."

Haiti was a key vote that had suddenly been left without instructions in the last two days. "The government of Haiti has just sent instructions for this delegation to vote in favor of partition."

"Honduras."

"Honduras wishes to abstain."

"Iceland."

"Iceland votes for partition." The world's oldest republic had worked to make the world's newest republic.

"India."

"India votes against partition."

"Iran."

"Iran votes against."

"Iraq."

"Iraq votes against and we will never recognize the Jews! There will be bloodshed over this day. We vote against!"

"Lebanon."

"Lebanon votes *against* partition," Malik said.

"How does the vote stand?" Weizmann asked Barak.

"Fifteen for, eight against, and seven abstentions."

It was not too encouraging. So far the Jews were running one vote shy of their two thirds, and the deadly abstentions were piling up.

"What do you think, Barak?"

"We will know when they come to the next three South American countries."

"I think we shall have to start pulling away. We are near the halfway mark and we show no decided strength," Weizmann said.

"Liberia."

"Liberia votes for partition."

"Luxembourg."

Another small country under duress in the British economic sphere.

"Luxembourg votes for partition."

And again the British had been directly rebuked. The Yishuv now stood one vote over two thirds.

"Mexico."

"Mexico abstains."

The entire Yishuv delegation winced.

"Netherlands."

"The Netherlands votes for partition."

"New Zealand."

"New Zealand votes for."

"Nicaragua . . . for."

"Norway . . . for."

"Pakistan votes against partition."

The pivot votes were coming up. "If we get over the next four I think we are in," Barak said shakily.

"Panama."

"The Republic of Panama favors partition."

"Paraguay."

"Paraguay has just received new instructions not to abstain . . . instead, Paraguay votes for partition."

"Peru."

"Peru favors partition."

"Philippines."

For a breathless second the world stood still. Romulo had been called away from Flushing Meadow. The alternate stood up.

"The Philippines votes *for* partition!"

A roar went up! The members of the Jewish delegation looked to each other with dazed expressions.

"Dear God," Barak said, "I think we have made it."

"Poland."

"Poland votes in favor of partition."

The Jews were beginning to pull away. Poland had paid its small indemnity for the years of persecution.

Siam was not represented.

"Saudi Arabia."

The white-robed Arab screamed out against partition in a hate-filled voice.

"Sweden."

"Sweden is for partition."

And now the Arabs had their backs to the wall as they went into the last ditch.

"Syria, *against!*"

"Turkey votes *against* partition."

Barak scanned the balance of the roster quickly. The Arabs still had a breath of life. They now had twelve votes with one more certain. If some last-minute change came through it could upset everything.

"Ukraine."

"For."

"Union of South Africa."

"For."

"Union of Soviet Socialist Republics."

Vishinsky got to his feet. "The Union of Soviet Socialist Republics votes for partition."

"The United Kingdom of Great Britain."

The hall became silent. The British delegate got to his feet and looked around the room ashen-faced. At this awesome moment he stood alone. The Commonwealth nations had deserted. France had deserted. The United States of America had deserted.

"His Majesty's Government wishes to abstain," the Englishman said in a shaken voice.

"The United States of America."

"The United States of America votes for partition."

It was all over. The reporters scrambled for their phones to flash the news around the world as the last vote was cast. Yemen gave the Arabs their thirteenth vote. Yugoslavia abstained in deference to a large Moslem minority. Professor Fabregat of Uruguay and the delegate of Venezuela gave the partition plan its thirty-second and thirty-third votes.

In Tel Aviv pandemonium broke loose.

In the final analysis, the Jewish victory was crushing. The Arabs had thirteen votes, and eleven of these were Arab or Moslem nations. The twelfth was a vote coerced from the Greeks. The thirteenth vote, Cuba, represented the only nation on the face of the earth that the Arabs were able to convince by force of argument.

Those men who had won this battle at Flushing Meadow and had seen the miracle unfold were realists. The Jews in Tel Aviv celebrated only for the moment. Ben Gurion and the leaders of the Yishuv knew that even a greater miracle would have to take place to win independence for the Jewish state, as the cry "Perish Judea!" arose like thunder on Arab lips.

CHAPTER TWO

KUWATLY, PRESIDENT OF SYRIA: *We live or die with Palestine!*

AL KULTA NEWSPAPER, CAIRO: *Five hundred thousand Iraqis prepare for this holy war. 150,000 Syrians will storm over the Palestine borders and the mighty Egyptian army will throw the Jews into the sea if they dare to declare their state.*

JAMIL MARDAM, SYRIAN PREMIER: *Stop talking, my brother Moslems. Arise and wipe out the Zionist scourge.*

IBN SAUD, KING OF SAUDI ARABIA: *There are fifty million Arabs. What does it matter if we lose ten million people to kill all the Jews? The price is worth it.*

SELEH HARB PASHA, MOSLEM YOUTH: *Unsheath your swords against the Jews! Death to them all! Victory is ours!*

SHEIK HASSAN AL BANNAH, MOSLEM BROTHERHOOD: *All Arabs shall arise and annihilate the Jews! We shall fill the sea with their corpses.*

AKRAM YAUYTAR, MUFTI SPOKESMAN: *Fifty million Arabs shall fight to the last drop of blood.*

HAJ AMIN EL HUSSEINI, MUFTI OF JERUSALEM: *I declare a holy war, my Moslem brothers! Murder the Jews! Murder them all.*

AZZAM PASHA, SECRETARY GENERAL OF THE ARAB LEAGUE: *This will be a war of extermination, and momentous massacre which will be spoken of like the Mongolian Massacres.*

Other Arab leaders and the Arab press and radio spoke out in equally appropriate words in answer to the United Nations' partition of Palestine.

On December 1, 1947, one day after the UN vote, Dr. Khalidi of the Arab Higher Committee in Palestine called a general strike in which inflamed mobs broke out in wild rioting. They crossed into the Jewish commercial center of Jerusalem and burned and looted while British troops stood by idly.

In Aleppo and Aden and throughout the Arab world, other mobs, goaded by their leaders, tore into Jewish ghetto quarters with murder, rape, and plunder in their hearts.

Instead of forming an international police force to fill the gap, the United Nations bogged down in the formation of committees and in endless talk. The body seemed to want to believe that partition was going to be enforced without dependence on a single gun.

The Jews were more realistic. A Jewish state had been given an unalterable basis of legality, but if the Jews intended to declare the statehood after the British left, they would have to face the Arab hordes alone.

Could a half million ill-armed people hold back a flood of fifty million hate-crazed Arabs? They would not only have to face the Arabs inside Palestine, all around them on a hundred fronts, but the regular national armies as well.

Chaim Weizmann set out to organize the world Zionist groups to launch fund-raising campaigns for the purchase of arms.

Barak Ben Canaan remained at Lake Success to head the Yishuv delegation and battle out the details of partition and look for arms support.

The great question became, "Would the Jews declare their independence?"

The Arabs had no intention of waiting until May to find out. Although they held their regular armies back, they went about raising various "Armies of Liberation" who were alleged volunteers, and they got mountains of arms in to the Palestine Arabs.

466

Haj Amin el Husseini, the Nazi agent, was back in business. He set up headquarters in Damascus. Money for the Palestine "volunteers" was extorted from Arabs all over the Middle East. Kawukji, the brigand who had served the Mufti in the 1936-39 riots, was again commissioned "generalissimo." Kawukji had been forced to flee Iraq when his part in the coup to deliver Iraq to the Germans was discovered. He spent the period of the war in Germany, acquired a wife there, and along with the Mufti had been pardoned from trial as a war criminal by the British.

Kawukji's agents scoured the stink holes of Damascus, Beirut, and Bagdad recruiting the dregs of humanity, thieves, murderers, highway robbers, dope runners, and white slavers, which he picturesquely dubbed the "Forces of the Yarmuk," after a battle the Arabs had won centuries before. These Kawukji "volunteers" were trained by other "volunteers," officers from the Syrian Army. Almost immediately Kawukji's forces began slipping over the Lebanese, Syrian, and Jordan borders into Palestine Arab villages. The main base was set up in Nablus, in a predominantly Arab area in Samaria, north of Jerusalem.

In the meantime, the Jews remained arms-starved. The British continued to blockade the Palestine coast. They even refused to allow immigrants to come from the Cyprus detention camps, where Aliyah Bet agents were speeding military training.

Yishuv agents searched the world desperately for arms.

Then came the devastating announcement that the United States had declared a "plague on both houses" by an arms boycott of the Middle East. This boycott, reminiscent of the boycott of the Spanish people fighting Mussolini and Hitler, actually worked for the Arabs, who could obtain all the arms they wished.

As the battle lines were drawn, the Yishuv Central confronted the blunt fact that it had only the Palmach of some four thousand fighters fully armed and trained. The Maccabees could raise only another thousand men and could be counted upon only for limited co-operation.

Avidan did have a few things working in his favor. He had several thousand reserves in the Haganah who had been combat trained by the British in World War II. He had settlement defense which had been organized for twenty years, and he had a good intelligence system. On the other side, the Arabs had a staggering superiority of manpower and arms, daily augmented by the continual infiltration of Kawukji's bloodthirsty irregulars. The Arabs had at least one excellent commander in Abdul Kadar, a cousin of the Mufti.

As if the Jews did not have enough to contend with, there

was the additional factor of the British. Whitehall was hopeful that the Yishuv would send out a mercy call, dropping the partition idea and asking the British to remain. But the Jews would not ask for help on these terms.

In theory, as they withdrew the British were to give the Taggart forts to the side with the greatest population in each area. But as they pulled back from sector after sector the British commander often turned these key places over to the Arabs when they should have gone to the Jews.

Former Nazi soldiers began appearing in the ranks of the "Forces of the Yarmuk" and other "liberation volunteers." For the first time in its existence, the Haganah took off its wraps as the Jews called for a general mobilization.

It was not long until the first shots were heard. In the Huleh Valley, Arab villagers, along with irregulars, fired on the communal settlements of Ein Zeitim, Biriya, and Ami Ad, but the attacks were little more than sniping actions and were repulsed.

Each day activity increased. There were constant ambushes on the roads so that soon Jewish transport, the lifeline of the Yishuv, was in danger any time it came near or passed through an Arab village.

In the cities the action was even more violent. In Jerusalem the air was filled with flying debris of bomb blasts. The Arabs fired from the sacred walls of the Old City, and the city was divided into battle zones with communications between sections made only on risk of death. In the streets between Tel Aviv and Jaffa sniper posts and barricades appeared.

In Haifa the worst so far of the fighting took place. In retaliation for Maccabee raids the Arabs rioted at the refinery where both Jews and Arabs worked and more than fifty Jews were killed.

Abdul Kadar was able to organize the Arabs in a manner that Kawukji and Safwat in the north could not do. Kadar, working around Jerusalem, formulated a master plan, based on the realization that neither the Palestine Arabs nor the irregulars were organized and skilled enough to carry out sustained attacks. Kadar also realized that the Jews would hang on desperately to every settlement and make the Arabs bleed. He needed easy victories to encourage his people. Kadar settled upon two tactics. First, he would isolate the Jewish settlements and starve them out. Second, he would step up his hit-and-run attacks on transport.

Kadar's strategy proved effective. The Arabs had freedom of movement while the Jews were forced to maintain tight positions. Day by day more Jewish settlements fell under siege.

Abdul Kadar centered his efforts on Jerusalem. The road from Tel Aviv to Jerusalem ran through the perilous Judean mountains and was dotted with Arab villages which commanded several key heights. Kadar wanted to cut off and starve out the hundred-thousand Jews in New Jerusalem. It would be a vital blow to the Yishuv.

To combat the effort, the Yishuv used makeshift armored cars to conduct large-scale convoys. These convoys were vulnerable, and the road to Jerusalem became littered with wrecked vehicles. Inside Jerusalem shortages developed, people had to move about in armored buses and children played inside sniper range.

With Arab strength growing daily in new arms and irregulars and no relief in sight for the Jews, Abdul Kadar was content to play a waiting game through the winter, then lop off the frozen and starved settlements one by one in the springtime.

The Yishuv leaders appealed to the British to patrol the Jerusalem-Tel Aviv road, on the grounds of the inhumanity of starving out a civilian population. The British refused.

This quick Arab action, under a good leader, set the Yishuv down in the initial gambit. The Haganah gave orders to turn every *kibbutz* and *moshav* into a miniature Tobruk. The Jews had paid in blood for their land and if the Arabs were going to take it, it would also have to be in blood.

The battle of the roads opened the first phase of the war. The decision of whether or not to declare independence still hung in the balance.

Ari Ben Canaan made a slow recovery from his wound. This posed a problem for Avidan, who wanted Ari to command one of the three Palmach Brigades. These included Hanita Brigade—the Spearhead—which covered the Galilee, the Hillmen in Judea, and the Desert Rats in the south.

The Palmach commanders from brigade level on down were young men in their twenties, often headstrong, who considered themselves an elite corps. The backbone of the Palmach consisted of boys and girls from the *kibbutzim.* They were communal in nature, even in military structure. Often they were politically opposed to the Yishuv Central and as often as not they resented Haganah authority.

Ari Ben Canaan was mature for his age. He could appreciate the necessity of grasping over-all strategy and carrying out orders instead of waging a private war. Submission to authority as part of a team made him desirable as a Palmach commander, but Ari was simply not yet strong enough to carry the burden. Each brigade covered a vast area in rugged terrain. The Palmach lived under the crudest of conditions. Ari's leg was still too weak.

Avidan instead assigned Ari as Haganah commander to one of the vital places of Palestine, Ari's own Huleh Valley. His command extended from the northern edge of the Sea of Galilee, included Safed, and continued up the valley in a fingerlike jut of land that pressed between the Lebanese and Syrian borders. Slightly south, a third Arab country, Trans-Jordan, bordered it at the Yarmuk River.

Ari's area was one of the chief crossing places for Kawukji's irregulars. If all-out war came and the regular Arab armies invaded Palestine, the Huleh Valley was certain to be one of the first objectives. The Arabs would attempt a junction of converging forces there, and if they took the Huleh they would use it as a base from which to capture the entire Galilee and to cut the Jews in half by striking between Haifa and Tel Aviv.

There were a dozen or more long-established *kibbutzim* and a few *moshavim* and villages in Ari's area, including his own Yad El, where the tough pioneer farmers could well handle the irregulars and Palestine Arabs. The settlements on the valley floor were close enough together to make it difficult for the Arabs to use their isolation and siege tactics.

The hills on the Lebanese border presented another problem. Here Fort Esther was the key. According to British agreement, Fort Esther was to be turned over to Ari because the Huleh was predominantly Jewish. With Fort Esther in Haganah hands, Ari could maintain excellent control of the border.

Ari's headquarters were in the centrally-located *kibbutz* of Ein Or—the Fountain of Light—which his uncle Akiva had helped establish. He had a few hundred Palmach troops from the Spearhead Brigade; he had David, Zev Gilboa, and Joab Yarkoni as aides. The Haganah organization in each of his settlements was strong: one hundred per cent subscribed in personnel quota and well trained.

The lack of arms was what plagued him, as it plagued the Yishuv all over Palestine. Every day settlement commanders harassed him for guns. He had none, Avidan had none.

There were two glaring weak spots in Ari's area: Gan Dafna and Safed. Ari felt that he would be able to protect the children's village once Fort Esther was turned over to him. So long as the road to Gan Dafna through Abu Yesha stayed open, the village was not in danger.

Safed was a headache. In fact no commander in Palestine had a larger headache. When the Jews made the decision to hold every settlement at any cost there were a few exceptions considered "untenable." Safed was one of the exceptions.

The city was an island in a sea of forty thousand Arabs in surrounding villages. Inside Safed the Jews were outnumbered twelve to one. Most of Safed's Jews were the Cabalists who knew nothing about fighting. In all, the Haganah in Safed had but two hundred able-bodied fighters to face more than two thousand Arabs and irregulars.

The Mufti had made Safed one of his first goals. Several hundred heavily armed irregulars had infiltrated and waited only for British withdrawal.

From the standpoint of interior strategy, the Jews were in even worse position. All three key points in the city would be in the hands of the Arabs: a police station right over the Jewish sector, the acropolis atop the town, and the Taggart fort on Mount Canaan would all be turned over to the Arabs.

In arms the Arabs had enough to carry on a war for months. he Jews had forty rifles, forty-two homemade Stens, one machine gun, and one mortar, plus a few hundred homemade grenades. They could arm less than a hundred men.

Safed appeared so obviously indefensible that the British even pled with Ari to let them evacuate the Jews.

Remez, the hotel owner and Haganah commander, paced back and forth before Ari's desk. Sutherland sat quietly in a corner and puffed a cigar.

"Well?" Ari asked at last.

Remez leaned on the desk. "We want to stay in Safed, Ari. We want to fight it out to the last man. We have decided."

"Good. I am glad."

"Give us more arms."

Ari leaped to his feet angrily. Twenty times a day he heard "give us more arms."

"Sutherland, you pray to Christ; you pray to Confucius, Remez; and I'll pray to Allah. Maybe rifles will rain down on us like manna from heaven."

"Do you trust Major Hawks?" Sutherland asked, speaking of the British commander in the area.

"Hawks has always been a friend," Ari answered.

"All right, then," Sutherland said, "perhaps you'd better listen to him. He guarantees British protection if you evacuate Safed. Otherwise, he guarantees there will be a massacre after he pulls his troops out."

Ari blew a long breath. "Did Hawks say when he is leaving?"

"No, he doesn't know yet."

"So long as Hawks remains in Safed we are relatively safe. The Arabs won't try too much with him around. Perhaps the situation will change for the better before he pulls out."

"Hawks may have his heart in the right place but his own

471

commanders are tying his hands," Sutherland said.

"The Arabs have already started sniping at us and are attacking our convoys," Remez said.

"So . . . ? Are you now going to run at the first shot?"

"Ari." Remez looked at him levelly. "I was born in Safed. I have lived there all my life. Even to this day I can still hear the chanting from the Arab quarters that we heard in 1929. We didn't know what it meant until we saw those crazed mobs pouring into our sector. They were our friends—but they were insane. I can see those pitiful Cabalists being dragged into the streets to have their heads cut off. I was only a boy then. We heard the Arabs chanting again in 1936 . . . we knew what it meant that time. For three years we ran and cowed in the old Turkish fort every time a loud noise came from the Arab section. We want to stay this time. We aren't going to run again. Not even the old ones. This time they won't have it easy, believe me . . . but, Ari, there is a limit to what can be asked of us."

Ari regretted having spoken sharply to Remez. Yes, the decision to remain in Safed took tremendous courage. "Go on back, Remez. Try to keep things calm. You can count on Major Hawks to keep it from getting out of control. In the meantime I'll give you a priority on everything I get."

When they were gone Ari sat down and gritted his teeth. What could he do? Perhaps he would be able to send fifty Palmach troops when the British left. It was little better than nothing. What could anyone do? There were two hundred Safeds all over Palestine. Fifty men here, ten men there. If Kawukji, Safwat and Kadar knew how desperate the situation was they would be making frontal assaults all over Palestine. There just wasn't enough ammunition to stop sustained and determined attacks. Ari feared that the first time the Arabs tried one and learned how meager the Jews' arms were, it would become a stampede.

David Ben Ami came in from an inspection tour of the northernmost settlements.

"*Shalom*, Ari," David said. "I met Remez and Sutherland on the road. Remez looks a little green around the gills."

"He has plenty of reason. Well, did you find anything interesting?"

"The Arabs have started sniping at Kfar Giladi and Metulla. Kfar Szold fears the Syrian villagers may try something. Everyone is dug in, all defenses built around the children's houses. They all want arms."

"Arms . . . what else is new? Where is the sniping coming from?"

"Aata."

"Good old Aata," Ari said. "When the British leave it's

472

going to be my first objective. When I was a boy they tried beating me up when I went to get the grain milled. They've been looking for a fight ever since. It is my guess that half of Kawukji's men are crossing over through Aata."

"Or Abu Yesha," David said.

Ari looked up angrily. David knew it was a sore point. "I have reliable friends in Abu Yesha," Ari said.

"Then they must have told you the irregulars are infiltrating through there."

Ari did not answer.

"Ari, many times you have told me that my weakness is allowing sentiment to cloud my judgment. I know how close you are to those people, but you've got to go up there and make the muktar understand."

Ari got up and walked away. "I'll have to talk to Taha."

David picked up the dispatches from Ari's desk, scanned them, and dropped them. He paced beside Ari, then stood looking out of the window in the direction of Jerusalem. A wave of moroseness washed over him.

Ari slapped him on the shoulder. "It will work out."

David shook his head slowly. "Things are getting desperate in Jerusalem," he said in a doleful monotone. "The convoys are having more and more trouble getting through. If this keeps up they will be starving in another few weeks."

Ari knew how the siege of his beloved city was affecting David. "You want to go to Jerusalem, don't you?"

"Yes," David said, "but I don't want to let you down."

"If you must, of course I'll relieve you."

"Thanks, Ari. Will you be able to manage?"

"Sure . . . as soon as this damned leg stops acting up. See here, David . . . I don't want you to leave."

"I'll stay until you are fit."

"Thanks. By the way, how long since you've seen Jordana?"

"Weeks."

"Why don't you go up to Gan Dafna tomorrow and look over the situation? Stay up there a few days and take a real good look."

David smiled. "You have such a nice way of persuasion."

There was a knock on the door of Kitty's office.

"Come in," she said.

Jordana Ben Canaan entered. "I would like a word with you if you are not too busy, Mrs. Fremont."

"Very well."

"David Ben Ami is going to come up and inspect the defenses this morning. We would like to have a staff meeting afterwards."

"I'll be there," Kitty said.

"Mrs. Fremont. I want to speak to you before the meeting. As you know, I am the commander here and in the future you and I will have to work in close co-operation. I wish to express the opinion that I have complete confidence in you. In fact, I consider it fortunate for Gan Dafna that you are here."

Kitty looked at Jordana curiously.

"I believe," Jordana continued, "that it would be good for the morale of the entire village if we set our personal feelings aside."

"I believe you are right."

"Good. I am glad we have an understanding."

"Jordana . . . just what is our situation here?"

"We are not in too much immediate danger. Of course, we will all feel better about things when Fort Esther is turned over to the Haganah."

"Suppose something goes wrong and the Arabs get Fort Esther? And . . . suppose the road through Abu Yesha is closed."

"Then the prospects become very unpleasant."

Kitty arose and paced the room slowly. "Please understand that I don't want to interfere in military matters, but looking at it realistically—we may fall under siege."

"There is that possibility," Jordana said.

"We have many babies here. Can't we talk over plans to evacuate them and some of the younger children?"

"Where shall we evacuate them to?"

"I don't know. A safer *kibbutz* or *moshav*."

"I don't know either, Mrs. Fremont. A 'safer *kibbutz*' is merely a term of relativity. Palestine is less than fifty miles wide. We have no safe *kibbutz*. New settlements are falling under siege every day."

"Then perhaps we can get them to the cities."

"Jerusalem is almost cut off. The fighting in Haifa and between Tel Aviv and Jaffa is the most severe in Palestine."

"Then . . . there is no place?"

Jordana did not answer. She did not have to.

CHAPTER THREE

CHRISTMAS EVE, 1947

The ground was sticky with mud and the air was crisp and the first snow of the winter floated down on Gan Dafna. Kitty walked quickly over the green toward the lane of cottages. Her breath formed little clouds.

"*Shalom, Giveret* Kitty," Dr. Lieberman called.

"*Shalom,* Doctor."

She raced up the steps and into the cottage, where it was warm and Karen had a steaming cup of tea waiting.

"Brrr," Kitty said, "it's freezing outside."

The room was cheerful. Karen had decorated it with pine cones, ribbons, and imagination. She had even got permission to cut down one of the precious little trees, which she had filled with tufts of raw cotton and paper cutouts.

Kitty sat down on the bed, kicked off her shoes, and put on a pair of fur-lined slippers. The tea tasted wonderful.

Karen stood by the picture window and watched the snow fall. "I think that the first snow falling is the most beautiful thing in the world," Karen said.

"You won't think it's so beautiful if the fuel ration gets any worse."

"I've been thinking about Copenhagen and the Hansens all day. Christmas in Denmark is a wonderful thing. Did you see the package they sent me?"

Kitty walked up to the girl, put her arm around her shoulders, and bussed her cheek. "Christmas makes people nostalgic."

"Are you terribly lonesome, Kitty?"

"Since Tom and Sandra died Christmas has been something I wanted to forget—until now."

"I hope you are happy, Kitty."

"I am . . . in a different way. I have learned that it is impossible to be a Christian without being a Jew in spirit. Karen, I've done things all my life to justify something missing in myself. I feel, for the first time, that I am able to give without reservation or hope of compensation."

"Do you know something? I can't ever tell the others because they wouldn't understand, but I feel very close to Jesus here," Karen said.

"So do I, dear."

Karen looked at her watch and sighed. "I must eat early. I have guard duty tonight."

"Bundle up. It's very cold outside. I'll work on some reports and wait up for you."

Karen changed into bulky, warm clothing. Kitty knotted the girl's hair and held it in place while she put on the brown stocking-like Palmach cap so that it covered her ears.

Suddenly there came a sound of voices singing from outside.

"What on earth is that?" Kitty asked.

"It is for you," Karen smiled. "They have been practicing in secret for two weeks."

Kitty walked to the window. Fifty of her children stood outside the cottage holding candles in their hands, singing a Christmas carol.

Kitty put on her coat and walked out on the porch with Karen. Behind the children she could see the lights of the valley settlements over two thousand feet below. One by one the cottage doors opened with curious onlookers. She did not understand the words but the melody was very old.

"Merry Christmas, Kitty," Karen said.

Tears fell down Kitty's cheek. "I never thought I would live to hear 'Silent Night' sung in Hebrew. This is the most beautiful Christmas present I have ever had."

Karen was assigned to a post in the outer trenches beyond Gan Dafna's gates. She walked out of the village and down the road to a point where the earthworks commanded a view of the valley floor.

"Halt!"

She stopped.

"Who is there?"

"Karen Clement."

"What is the pass word?"

"*Chag sameach.*"

Karen relieved the guard, jumped down in the trench, put a clip of bullets into the chamber of the rifle, closed the bolt, and put on her mittens.

It was nice standing guard, Karen thought. She looked through the tangle of barbed wire toward Abu Yesha. It was nice being alone out here with nothing to do but think for four hours and look down on the Huleh Valley. Karen could hear the faint voices of the children floating over the quiet winter air from Kitty's cottage. It was a most wonderful, wonderful Christmas.

Soon the voices were still and it was very silent all about. The snowfall thickened, building a white carpet over the mountainside.

Karen heard movement in the trees behind her. She turned quietly and squinted in the darkness. She sensed something alive moving about. She froze and watched. Yes! Something was there in the trees! A shadow . . . perhaps it is a hungry jackal, she thought.

Karen flicked the safety catch off her rifle, put it to her shoulder, and sighted it. The shadow moved closer.

"Halt!" her voice snapped out.

The figure stopped.

"What is the password?"

"Karen!" a voice called out.

"Dov!"

She climbed from the trench and ran through the snow toward him and he ran toward her and they fell into each other's arms.

"Dov! Dov! I can't believe it is you!"

They jumped down into the trench together and she strained in the darkness to make out his face.

"Dov . . . I don't know what to say . . ."

"I got here an hour ago," he said. "I waited outside your cottage until you left for guard duty. Then I followed you here."

Karen looked around, startled. "It isn't safe! You'll have to hide from the British!"

"It's all right now, Karen, it's all right. The British can't hurt me any more."

Her fingers trembled as she felt him in the darkness. "Dov, you're cold. You haven't even a sweater on. You must be freezing."

"No . . . no . . . I'm fine."

The snow fell into the trench and suddenly the moon appeared and they could see each other.

"I've been hiding at the caves outside Mishmar."

"I know."

"I . . . I thought you were in America."

"We couldn't go."

"I guess you wonder what I'm doing here. Karen . . . I . . . want to come back to Gan Dafna but I took some watches and rings when I left and I guess they think I'm a thief."

"Oh no, Dov. As long as you are safe and alive that is all that matters."

"You see . . . I'll pay everyone back."

"It doesn't matter. No one is angry with you."

Dov sat in the trench and lowered his head. "All the time I was in the Acre prison and all the time I was in the caves I thought to myself. I thought: Dov, no one is mad at you. It's just Dov that's mad . . . mad at himself. When I saw you in Acre I said then . . . I said I didn't want to die any more, I didn't want to die and I didn't want to kill anyone."

"Oh, Dov . . ."

"Karen . . . I never really had another girl. I . . . I just said that to make you go away."

"I know."

"Did you really know it all along?"

"I made myself believe that, Dov, because I wanted to believe you cared for me."

"That is what is so wonderful about you, Karen. You can make yourself believe things and make me believe them too. I

477

wanted to come back to Gan Dafna and make you proud of me. I wanted to make you proud even though I thought you would be gone."

Karen lowered her eyes.

"I'll do anything for you," he whispered.

She reached up and touched his cheek. "Dov, you are so cold. Please go to my cottage. You can tell Kitty everything. She understands about us. Just as soon as I get off guard duty we will go see Dr. Lieberman together. Be careful. The password is Happy Holiday."

"Karen. I have thought so much about you all the time. I won't ever do anything wrong or anything that would hurt you."

"I know that."

"Could I kiss you?"

"Yes."

Their lips brushed with a frightened searching.

"I love you, Karen," Dov said, and ran off toward the gates of Gan Dafna.

"International law," Barak Ben Canaan said angrily to the United States delegate, "is that thing which the evil ignore and the righteous refuse to enforce."

Conversation, no matter how well put, made little difference any longer. If the Jews declared their independence on May 15 they would have to face seven Arab armies alone.

Kawukji's irregulars and the Palestine Arabs under the command of Safwat and Kadar increased their activities.

The year 1948, the year of decision, came into being.

Through the first few months the Arabs became bolder and the tempo of the fighting increased as the British dismantled their huge military establishment and pulled back from position after position.

THE GALILEE

Irregulars lay siege to *kibbutz* Manara high in the hills on the Lebanese border. A half dozen other isolated Jewish positions were cut off.

The Arabs launched five straight attacks on Ein Zeitim— the Fountain of the Olives—but each attack was beaten back.

Syrian villagers began to fight. They crossed the Palestine border and attacked the northern Jewish outpost settlements of *kibbutz* Dan and Kfar Szold. Major Hawks, the British commander, dispatched forces to help drive the Syrians back over the border.

Arabs from Aata, helped again by Syrian villagers and irregulars, attacked Lahavot Habashan—the Flames of the Beshan—Mountains.

478

Ramat Naftali, named for one of the tribes of ancient Israel, was hit.

Arab activity in Safed increased as the Arabs waited for Major Hawks to withdraw. The blockade against the Jews was beginning to tell as food and water shortages developed in the Cabalist city. Convoys were getting through to Jewish quarters only when the British helped.

HAIFA

The key port of Palestine was a major objective of both sides. For the time, the dock area stayed in British hands, as it was essential for British withdrawal.

In Haifa the Jews had one of their few superior positions in Palestine, in Har Hacarmel above the Arab sector. The British commander, openly pro-Arab, continued to force the Jews out of strategic positions they had won.

Maccabees rolled barrel bombs down the slopes of Carmel into the Arab area and the Jews managed to ambush a huge Arab arms convoy from Lebanon and kill the Arab commander.

All normal business between the two sectors ceased. Amin Azaddin, an officer of the Arab Legion, arrived to assume command of the ever increasing irregular force.

The British held the Jews in check to allow the Arabs to build enough strength to launch an attack up Har Hacarmel.

THE SHARON

This central plain, scene of the great Crusader battles, was the most thickly settled Jewish area. It faced the most heavily populated Arab area of Samaria known, from its shape, as the "Triangle." Although both sides remained poised, this sector remained relatively quiet.

TEL AVIV-JAFFA

A battlefield appeared between the adjoining cities. Street fighting and patrols continued around the clock. The Maccabees took their place in the center of the Haganah lines. Raids on both sides were constant. The Arabs used a minaret as an observation and sniping post and the position of the intervening British troops prevented the Jews from attacking it.

THE SOUTH

In the sprawling Negev Desert the Jewish settlements were few and widely separated. The Arabs had two large bases, Beersheba and Gaza, of the fame of Samson. The Arabs were able to put a deadly siege on the settlements and slowly starve them. Each Jewish settlement managed to hold but the Arabs were bold in this area and the pressure steadily increased. The Jewish air force was born. It consisted of two Piper Cubs for liaison contact. Another Piper Cub flew into besieged Jerusalem. These Pipers carried out their first bombing missions by throwing grenades out of their windows.

JERUSALEM

Abdul Kadar tightened his grip on the throat of Jewish Jerusalem. The Bab el Wad, that tortuous and vulnerable road through the Judean hills, was shut tight. The Jews were able to get through only by organizing large convoys and then at heavy price. The British steadfastly refused to keep the roads open.

Outside of Jerusalem to the south, the Jews had four isolated settlements in the Hebron Hills on the road to Bethlehem. These four settlements, manned by Orthodox Jews, were known as the Etzion group. Their position was as bad and vulnerable as Safed's. The Etzion group was completely shut off from Jewish Palestine. To make matters worse, the Trans-Jordan Arab Legion, under the thin disguise of being British troops, blocked the road from Jerusalem to these settlements.

Inside Jerusalem the food and water shortages had become critical. Bombings, sniping, armored-car travel, and open warfare were the order of the day.

The fury reached a peak when a Red Cross convoy from the Hadassah Medical Center on Mount Scopus was ambushed by the Arabs and seventy-seven unarmed Jewish doctors were massacred and their bodies hacked to pieces. Again British troops took no action.

Zev Gilboa reported to Ari's office for the task of receiving Fort Esther from the British.

"We are all ready to go," Zev said.

"Good. You may as well drive on up to the fort. Major Hawks said he would turn the place over at fourteen hundred. Say, what's this I hear about you and Liora having another baby?"

"That's right."

"I'll have to stop giving you weekends off if you can't keep out of trouble." Ari smiled.

Zev ran outside, jumped into the cab of the truck, kicked off the brakes, and drove out of Ein Or *kibbutz*. Twenty Palmach boys and girls rode along to man Fort Esther. Zev drove over the main artery and then took the mountain roads toward the Lebanese border and Fort Esther.

Zev thought about his last visit to his *kibbutz*, Sde Shimshon—the Field of Samson. Liora had told him that they were expecting another child. What wonderful news! Zev was a shepherd when he wasn't on duty . . . but that seemed long ago. How grand it would be to take his sons out with him and laze on the hillsides around watching the flock . . .

He switched off thoughts like these; there was much work to do. When Fort Esther was turned over he had to relieve the siege of *kibbutz* Manara and start dispatching patrols along the border to cut down the flow of irregulars.

The big concrete blockhouse dominated the entire Huleh Valley. It would certainly be a relief to raise the Star of David over the fort.

The gang in the back began to sing as the truck spun around the sharp turns on the mountain road. Zev checked his watch. It was fifteen minutes until the appointed time. He turned the truck around the last turn. The huge square building appeared on the horizon a few miles away. Below him, Zev could see the white cluster of Abu Yesha in the saddle of the hill and the green plateau of Gan Dafna above it.

As he drove within a few hundred yards of Fort Esther, he sensed something strange. He slowed down and looked out of the window. If the British were withdrawing it was odd that there was no activity about. Zev looked up to the concrete watch and gun tower. His eye caught the flag of Kawukji's irregulars on the tower just as a burst of gunfire erupted from Fort Esther.

Zev slammed on the brakes and pulled over to the side of the road.

"Scatter!"

His troops dived for cover. The truck went up in flames. Zev quickly pulled his people back out of firing range, assembled, and began to double-time down the mountain toward Ein Or.

When Ari received the news that Fort Esther had been turned over to the Arabs he rushed to Safed immediately to the Taggart fort on Mount Canaan.

He went directly into the office of the British area commander, Major Hawks, a heavy-set man with dark features. Hawks was haggard from lack of sleep when the angry Ben Canaan entered.

"You Judas!" Ari snarled.

"It wasn't my fault," Hawks said in a half whine. "You've got to believe me."

"No, I can't believe it. Not from you."

Hawks held his head in his hands. "Last night at ten o'clock I got a call from headquarters in Jerusalem. They ordered me to pull my men out of Fort Esther immediately."

"You could have warned me!"

"I couldn't," Hawks mumbled. "I couldn't. I'm still a soldier, Ben Canaan. I . . . I didn't sleep all night. This morning I called Jerusalem and begged them to let me go back to Fort Esther and take it back."

Ari glared at the man in contempt.

"Whatever you think of me is probably right."

Ari continued to stare.

"All right, have it your way . . . there was no excuse."

"It's your life, Hawks. I guess you're not the first soldier who swallowed his conscience."

"What's the use of talking? What's done is done."

"This may make you a good soldier, Hawks, but I feel sorry for you. You're the one who has to live with the siege of Gan Dafna on his conscience, provided you've still got one."

Hawks turned pale.

"You're not going to leave those children on the mountain . . . you've got to take them away!"

"You should have thought about that. Without Fort Esther we've got to hold Gan Dafna or lose the whole Huleh Valley."

"Look, Ari . . . I'll convoy the children to safety."

"They have no place to go."

Ari watched Hawks beat his fists on the table and mumble under his breath. He had turned Gan Dafna into a suicide position. There was no use of berating him further. The man was obviously sick over what he had been forced to do.

On his way over, Ari's brain had been busy on a scheme, risky at best, but a long gamble that might save the key position of Gan Dafna.

He leaned over Hawks's desk. "I'm going to give you a chance to undo part of the damage."

"What can I do now, Ben Canaan?"

"As area commander it is completely within your rights to come up to Gan Dafna and advise us to evacuate."

"Yes, but . . ."

"Then do it. Go up to Gan Dafna tomorrow and take fifty trucks up with you. Put armor in front and behind you. If anyone asks you what you are doing, tell them you intend to evacuate the children."

"I don't understand. Are you going to evacuate?"

"No. But you leave the rest to me. You just come up with the convoy."

Hawks did not press to know what Ari had in mind. He followed the instructions and took a fifty-lorry convoy to Gan Dafna, escorted by half tracks and armored cars. The half-mile-long procession moved from the Taggart fort through six Arab villages on the way to the Huleh. It drove up the mountain road, through Abu Yesha, in plain sight of the irregulars in Fort Esther. The convoy arrived around noon at Gan Dafna. Major Hawks went through the motions of advising Dr. Lieberman to quit the place; the latter, on Ari's advice, officially refused. After lunch, the convoy left Gan Dafna and returned to its base in Safed.

In the meanwhile Ari "confided" to some of his Arab friends at Abu Yesha that Major Hawks had left tons of arms —from machine guns to mortars—at the village.

"After all," Ari said in greatest confidence, "Hawks has been a known friend of the Jews and he was privately doing something to compensate for the Arab occupation of Fort Esther."

The story was planted. Within hours the rumor had spread throughout the area that Gan Dafna was impregnable. The children were armed to the teeth. This story was lent weight by the fact that there was no evacuation of the children: the Arabs knew the Jews would get the children out if there were great danger.

Ari made a visit to Abu Yesha, once the "might" of Gan Dafna had been established and proved a checkmate.

He went to see his old friend Taha the muktar in the stone house by the stream. No matter how strained feelings were, a man must be made welcome in the house of an Arab. It was an age-old custom, but despite Taha's going through the motions of hospitality Ari felt a coldness he had never known before from Taha.

The two men shared a meal and spoke small talk. When Ari felt that enough ceremony had been served he turned to the purpose of his visit.

"The time has come," Ari said, "that I must know your feelings."

"My feelings these days are of little concern."

"I am afraid that I must talk now as the Haganah commander of the area, Taha."

"I gave you my word that Abu Yesha would remain neutral."

Ari stood up from the table and looked Taha directly in the eye and spoke words harsh to an Arab ear.

"You have given your word but you have broken it," he said.

Taha looked at him with a flash of anger.

"We happen to know that Kawukji's men have been passing through Abu Yesha in droves."

"And what do you expect of me?" Taha snapped. "Shall I ask them to please stop coming? I didn't invite them."

"Neither did I. Look, my friend . . . there was once a time when you and I didn't speak to each other this way."

"Times change, Ari."

Ari walked to the window and looked out at the mosque

483

by the opposite side of the stream. "I have always loved this spot. We knew many happy days in this room and by that stream. Do you remember the nights that you and I camped out there?"

"That was a long time ago."

"Maybe I've got a long memory. We used to talk about it during the riots, how ridiculous it was for everyone else to fight. We took blood vows to be eternal brothers. Taha . . . I was up all of last night thinking of what I was going to say today. I began remembering all the things that you and I have done together."

"Sentimentality does not become you, Ari."

"Neither does having to threaten you. Mohammed Kassi and the men in Fort Esther are the same kind of men who murdered your father while he was kneeling at prayer. The minute the British leave the area he is going to come down from Fort Esther and get you to block the road to Gan Dafna. If you let him, he'll shove rifles in the hands of your people and order you to attack Yad El."

"And just what do you expect of me?"

"And what do you expect of me?" Ari countered.

A stony silence ensued.

"You are the muktar of Abu Yesha. You can rally your people just as your father did. You've got to stop doing business with the irregulars."

"Or what?"

"Or you will be treated as an enemy."

"*Or what?* Ari?"

"You are going to bring on the destruction of Abu Yesha."

Neither Ari nor Taha quite believed Ari's words. Ari was tired; he walked up to the Arab and put his hand on Taha's shoulder.

"Please," Ari said, "help me."

"I am an Arab," Taha said.

"You are a human being. You know right from wrong."

"I am a *dirty Arab!*"

"It is you who thinks that of himself."

"Are you going to tell me I am your brother?"

"You always have been," Ari said.

"If I am your brother, then give me Jordana. Yes, that is right . . . give her to me and let me take her to my bed. Let her bear my children."

Ari's fist shot out and crashed against Taha's jaw. The Arab was sent sprawling to his hands and knees. He sprang up and instinctively unsheathed the dagger from his waist sash and came at Ari.

Ari stood rigidly, making no move to defend himself. Taha

raised the knife, then froze and turned and threw it from him. It clattered over the stone floor.

"What have I done?" Ari whispered. He walked toward Taha with an expression that begged forgiveness.

"You have told me everything that I need to know. Get out of my house, Jew."

CHAPTER FOUR: A terrible turn had taken place at Flushing Meadow. Anticipating the necessity of armed intervention to back up partition, and fearing the Russian position as part of an international force, the United States announced its intention to abandon its stand for partition.

The Yishuv launched a desperate campaign to change the American defeatist attitude. In the middle of these important maneuvers, Barak Ben Canaan received an urgent cable to report at once to France. Because of the urgency of the work at Flushing Meadow, Barak was puzzled by the order, but he left immediately by plane.

He was met by two Yishuv agents. Barak had been called to take part in highly secret negotiations of a vital arms deal. The Yishuv calculated that with the turn of events at Flushing Meadow, arms were the most urgent immediate need, and Barak one of the most able men for such business. It was their friend, Jan Masaryk of Czechoslovakia, who provided the information on sources of weapons in a half dozen European countries.

After several weeks of confidential and ticklish parleying the deals were closed. The problem now became getting the arms into Palestine, still under British blockade.

The first step was to acquire an airplane large enough to haul the arms. In Vienna an Aliyah Bet agent found an obsolete, surplus American Liberator bomber, which was purchased under the name of Alpine Charter Flights, Inc.

Next they had to find a crew; six men, four South African Jews and two American Jews who had flown during the war, were picked and sworn to secrecy.

Finally, the most difficult task was to create a secret airfield in tiny Palestine undetected by the British. An abandoned British fighter-plane base in the Jezreel Valley was selected. It lay in an all-Jewish area and offered the maximum chance of the Liberator's being able to get in and out again.

Meanwhile the assembly of the arms inside Europe was carried out with the same secrecy that hid the true identity of the Alpine Charter Flights, Inc.

It was a race against time. Two weeks would be needed before the first load of arms could leave Europe. The question was whether or not it would be too late.

So far, miraculously, not a single settlement had fallen, but the Jewish convoys were being ripped to pieces. Water lines to the Negev Desert settlements had been cut. In some places the settlers were subsisting on potato peelings and olives.

The focal point of the struggle was Jerusalem, where the isolation-and-starvation tactics were beginning to pay off. The Bab el Wad from Tel Aviv was littered with the wreckage of burned-out trucks. Only occasional huge convoys, mounted at crippling cost of men and matériel, staved off disaster in Jerusalem.

For the first time in the history of Jerusalem, the city was violated by artillery fire, from Kawukji's irregulars.

Kawukji, Safwat, and Kadar urgently needed a victory. The Palestine Arabs were becoming uneasy over the failure of Arab predictions of "great victories."

It was Kawukji, the self-styled generalissimo of the Mufti's "Forces of the Yarmuk," who decided to grab off the honor of capturing the first Jewish settlement. He picked his target carefully, having no wish to try a nut too tough to crack the first time out.

Kawukji picked what he believed to be a soft spot: Tirat Tsvi—the Castle of the Rabbi Tsvi—was elected for the distinction of being the first Jewish settlement to fall. The *kibbutz* of Tirat Tsvi was made up of Orthodox Jews, many of whom were concentration camp "graduates." The *kibbutz* stood in the southern section of the Beth Shean Valley, located there purposely to neutralize an otherwise completely Arab area. South of the *kibbutz* was the "triangle," the all-Arab area of Palestine. Within shooting distance stood the borders of Jordan. Slightly north, the hostile Arab city of Beth Shean completed the cutoff of the *kibbutz*.

Tirat Tsvi was one of the Jewish outposts that guarded the Jordan Valley farther to the north.

Kawukji was delighted with his choice of Tirat Tsvi. The religious Jews of the *kibbutz* would crumple before the first massed attack. The brigand assembled hundreds of Arabs at the Nablus base in the Triangle and marched up for the attack.

Kawukji announced his victory in advance; it was published even before he made an attack. When he did move his troops into position, the Arab women from Beth Shean came to the edge of the battlefield and waited with sacks and containers to rush up after the troops and plunder the *kibbutz*.

The attack came with a cloudy dawn. The Jews had one hundred and sixty-seven men and women of fighting age on the battle line, in trenches, and behind rough barricades facing the Arab position. The children were hidden in the centermost building of the *kibbutz*. The defenders had no armament heavier than a single two-inch mortar.

A bugle blew. Arab Legion officers with drawn swords led the charge. The irregulars behind them poured over the open fields in a massed frontal assault calculated to overrun the *kibbutz* by sheer weight of numbers.

The Jews waited until the Arab force was within twenty yards, then on signal they cut loose with a tremendous volley. Arabs went down like mown wheat.

The impetus of the Arab charge carried forward a second, third, and fourth headlong wave. The Jews continued their disciplined fire, blasting each rush as the leaders' feet touched *kibbutz* ground.

The field was littered with Arab dead and the wounded screamed, "We are brothers! Mercy, in the name of Allah!"

The rest scrambled back out of range and began a confused retreat. Kawukji had promised them easy victory and plunder! He had told them this bunch of Orthodox Jews would flee at the sight of them! They had not reckoned on such a fight. The Arab women on the outskirts of the battle began to flee too.

The Arab Legion officers herded the running irregulars together and stopped the retreat only by firing at them. The leaders reorganized their men for another rush at the *kibbutz*, but the irregulars' hearts were no longer in their effort.

Inside Tirat Tsvi the Jews were in bad trouble. They did not have enough ammunition left to hold off another charge if Arabs came in strong and hard. Moreover, if the Arabs changed strategy and tried a slow attack with flanking movement the Jews could not contain it. They hastily organized a desperation tactic. Most of the ammunition was given to twenty sharpshooters. The rest dropped back to the children's house and prepared for a last-ditch fight with bayonets, clubs, and bare hands. Through field glasses they watched the Arabs mass and saw that there were enough troops left to overrun the *kibbutz*.

The Arabs came over the field more slowly this time, with some of the Legion officers behind the troops forcing them on at gun point.

Suddenly the heavens opened up in an unexpected downpour. Within minutes the open field was turned into a deep and bogging mud. The Arab charge, instead of gaining momentum, began to wallow, just as the Canaanite chariots had done against Deborah.

As the first Legion officers reached the *kibbutz*, the sharp-shooters picked them off. Kawukji's noble "Forces of the Yarmuk" had had enough for the day.

Kawukji was in a rage over the Tirat Tsvi debacle. He had to have a victory quickly to save face. This time he decided to go after big game.

The road between Tel Aviv and Haifa was more important to the Yishuv from a purely strategic standpoint than the road to Jerusalem. If the Tel Aviv-Haifa line could be cut, the Arabs could sever the Jewish dispositions, splitting the Galilee away from the Sharon. There were Arab villages on the main highway which forced the Jews to use alternate interior roads to maintain transportation between the two cities. On one of the vital alternate roads was *kibbutz* Mishmar Haemek—the Guardpost of the Valley. Mishmar Haemek became Kawukji's goal in the ambitious move to separate Tel Aviv from Haifa.

This time Kawukji determined not to repeat the mistakes of Tirat Tsvi. He massed more than a thousand men and moved them into the hills surrounding the *kibbutz*, together with ten 75mm. mountain guns.

With Mishmar Haemek ringed, Kawukji opened a brutal artillery barrage. The Jews had one machine gun with which to answer back.

After a day of the pounding, the British called a truce, entered the *kibbutz*, and advised the Jews to pull out. When they refused the British left, washing their hands of the affair. Kawukji learned from the British that the Jews were relatively weak inside the *kibbutz*. What he did not know, because of his lack of an intelligence system, was that the Emek Valley was alive with men in training for the Haganah. During the second night two entire battalions of Haganah, all armed with rifles, slipped into the *kibbutz*.

On the third day, Kawukji mounted the attack.

Instead of walking into a frightened and cowering *kibbutz*, he ran into two battalions of eagerly waiting and trained men. Kawukji's offense was smashed.

He rallied his men and tried a slow sustained move. It was equally unsuccessful. He mounted more attacks, but with each the irregulars showed less inclination to fight. They straggled forward halfheartedly and pulled back whenever resistance stiffened.

Toward the end of the day, Kawukji lost control of his troops. They began to walk out of the battle area.

Inside the *kibbutz*, the Jews witnessed the development and poured out after the Arabs. Here was a completely unexpected turn. The Arabs were so startled at the sight of Jews charging that they all fled, with the Haganah literally at their heels. The running fight surged back miles, to Megiddo, site of a hundred battles through the ages. Here, on the historic fighting ground of Armageddon, the Jews completely broke Kawukji's forces. The carnage stopped only when the British stepped in and forced a truce.

The Jews had won their first real victory of the War of Liberation.

In the Jerusalem corridor the Hillmen Brigade of the Palmach performed titans' work to keep the road open. This gang of teen-agers, with commanders in their twenties, patrolled the deep gorges and wilds of Judea, making fierce hit-and-run raids on Arab villages in conjunction with convoy runs. They frequently worked around the clock until they were numb with exhaustion, yet they could always be goaded on to one more patrol, one more raid, one more hike through the fierce country.

"In this wadi King David also lived as a guerrilla fighter!" The bloodshot eyes of the Palmach youngsters recorded fatigue as they roused to still another effort.

"Remember, you are fighting at the place where Samson was born!"

"In this valley David met Goliath!"

"Here Joshua made the sun stand still!"

At night the Bible was read to the exhausted warriors as a source of inspiration for the superhuman efforts the next day would call forth. Here, in Kadar's territory, the fighting was hard and constant and the Arabs had confidence behind a strong leader.

An enormous convoy mustered in Tel Aviv for another all-out effort to save Jerusalem. The Hillmen Brigade's job was to take the Arab village of Kastel, built on a Crusader fort dominating one of the main heights of the highway.

The storming of Kastel became the first Jewish offensive action in the War of Liberation. The brigade made a sheer-guts attack, crawling up the treacherous incline under cover of friendly darkness. They reached the peak of the Kastel bloodied and weary but threw themselves into hand-to-hand combat and threw the Arabs out.

Kastel lifted the flagging spirits of the Yishuv. Following the victory, the huge convoy from Tel Aviv battled every inch of the way through the Bab el Wad, slogged on through to New Jerusalem, and again brought vital relief to the beleaguered Jews.

Kawukji summoned Mohammed Kassi, the Huleh commander of the irregulars, from Fort Esther to headquarters in Nablus.

Kawukji was frantic for a victory. For months he had been writing communiqués boasting of triumph after triumph. As the "general" of the Mufti, Kawukji had nourished the dream of commanding an Arab army that spread from the borders of Turkey to the Rock of Gibraltar. He blamed "British intervention" as the reason he had been unable to win a Jewish settlement. When the British pulled out of the Huleh area he had no alibi left.

Kawukji kissed Mohammed Kassi on both cheeks in the accustomed style and they spoke at great lengths of their glorious victories. Kassi told of how he had "conquered" Fort Esther, and Kawukji described how he had weakened Tirat Tsvi and Mishmar Haemek with brilliant probing tactics.

"I have received a message from his Holiness, the Mufti in Damascus," Kawukji said. "On May 15, the day after the British terminate the mandate, Haj Amin el Husseini will make a triumphant return to Palestine."

"And what a magnificent day that shall be for all of Islam," Mohammed Kassi nodded.

"His Holiness has selected Safed as his temporary capital until the Zionists are completely exterminated. Now that the dear friend of the Jews, Major Hawks, is gone from Safed, we will have it within a week."

"I am delighted to hear such news!"

"However," Kawukji continued, "Safed will not be truly safe and fit for the return of his Holiness so long as a single Jew remains in the Huleh Valley. They hold a dagger in our backs. We must erase them."

Mohammed Kassi turned slightly pale.

"The Huleh, I believe, is in your command, my brother. I want you to capture Gan Dafna at once. As soon as Gan Dafna falls we will have the rest of the Huleh Zionists by the throat."

"Generalissimo, let me assure you that each and every one of my volunteers is a man filled with the courage of a lion and is dedicated to the noble cause of crushing Zionism. They have all vowed to fight to the last drop of blood."

"Good. They are costing us almost a dollar a month in pay alone."

Kassi stroked his beard and held up his forefinger with its large jeweled ring. "However! It is well known that Major Hawks left three thousand rifles, a hundred machine guns, and dozens of heavy mortars at Gan Dafna!"

Kawukji sprang to his feet.

"You cringe before children!"

"I swear by Allah's beard that the Jews have sent in a

490

thousand Palmach reinforcements. I have seen them with my own eyes."

Kawukji slapped Mohammed Kassi twice across the face. "You will lay open Gan Dafna, you will level it to the ground, and you will wash your hands in their blood or I will set your carcass out for the vultures!"

CHAPTER FIVE: Mohammed Kassi's first move was to send a hundred of his men into Abu Yesha. Immediately some of the villagers went down to *kibbutz* Ein Or to report the fact to Ari. Ari knew that the people of Abu Yesha were predominantly with the Jews. He waited for them to act.

The Arabs of Abu Yesha resented the presence of the irregulars. They had been neighbors of the people of Yad El for decades; their homes had been built by the Jews. They were not angry and had no desire to fight and they looked to Taha, their muktar, to rally them and eject Kassi's men.

Taha kept a strange silence, speaking neither for nor against the coming of the irregulars. When the elders of Abu Yesha urged him to unite the people, Taha refused to discuss the matter. His silence sealed the fate of Abu Yesha, for the fellaheen were helpless without leadership. They quietly submitted to the occupation.

Kassi was quick to capitalize on Taha's passive acquiescence. Day by day his men became bolder and more unruly as Taha continued his silence. The road to Gan Dafna was cut. There was anger in Abu Yesha but it was no more than grumbling on an individual level. Then four Abu Yesha Arabs were caught by the irregulars running food up to Gan Dafna. Kassi had them killed, decapitated, and their heads put on display in the village square as a warning. From that point on Abu Yesha was completely subdued.

Ari had guessed wrong. He had felt sure that the people of Abu Yesha would force Taha to take a stand, especially with the safety of Gan Dafna at stake. Their failure to act and the closing of the road put him in a terrible position.

The road shut, Kassi's ponderous mountain guns began an around-the-clock shelling of Gan Dafna from Fort Esther.

The Jews had trained for this sort of thing at Gan Dafna from the day the place was opened. Everyone knew his job. They switched onto emergency footing quickly and quietly.

All children over the age of ten were assigned to an active part in the village defense. The water tank had been sand-bagged and the power generators, medical supplies, arsenal, and food stores had been installed underground.

Life went on as usual in the dank bunkers. School classes, dining, games, and all routine functions continued below the ground. Sleeping quarters were shelf-like bunks in dormitories built inside sections of twelve-feet-diameter concrete water pipes which had been sunk deeply into the earth and covered with yards of dirt and sandbags.

Whenever the shelling outside stopped, the children and staff came out from the bunkers to play, stretch their cramped muscles, and to take care of the lawns and gardens.

Within a week the staff had made it seem that the whistling shells and explosions were merely another minor unpleasantness of daily living.

Down at Ein Or *kibbutz*, Ari faced the problem. All the settlements must depend on their own defense systems, but Gan Dafna held six hundred children and stood in the most vulnerable place, there beneath Fort Esther. There was enough food for a month, and the water supply would be ample if the tank was not hit. Fuel would become a problem. It was extremely cold during the nights in the mountains and Ari knew that Dr. Lieberman would rather freeze than cut down the precious trees for burning. Communications from Gan Dafna were maintained by blinker light to Yad El; the telephone line had been cut. The children's village was so completely cut off that the only way it could be reached was by a dangerous and grueling climb up the west face of the mountain, more than two thousand feet, which had to be negotiated by night.

The communication and supply problem, however, was not Ari's main worry. The fear of a massacre was. He could not guess how long it would be until the "armed might" myth of Gan Dafna would be exploded.

By shaking down his entire command, Ari was able to come up with a dozen Spanish rifles of late 1880 vintage, twenty-three homemade Sten guns, and an obsolete Hungarian antitank weapon with five rounds of ammunition.

Zev Gilboa and twenty Palmach reinforcements were ordered to deliver the new equipment. Zev's patrol were to be human pack mules. The antitank gun had to be dismantled and carried in pieces. The patrol moved out under cover of dark, and through one entire night they climbed up the sheer west slope of the mountain.

At one critical point they passed within a few feet of Abu Yesha's boundary, through a three-hundred-yard draw which had to be negotiated by crawling a few inches at a time. They could see, hear, and smell Kassi's irregulars.

The sight of Gan Dafna was a saddening one. Many of the buildings showed artillery hits, and the lovely center green had been chopped to pieces. The statue of Dafna had been

492

knocked from its pedestal. Yet the morale of the children was amazingly high, and the security system was completely effective. Zev was amused by the sight of little Dr. Lieberman coming out to greet the patrol with a pistol strapped to his waist. Sighs of relief greeted the coming of the twenty Palmach reinforcements.

Kassi continued the bombardment for ten more days. The mountain guns knocked down the buildings one by one. Gan Dafna drew its first casualties when a shell exploded near the entrance of a shelter and killed two children.

But Kawukji wanted action. Kassi tried two or three half-hearted probes. Each time his men were ambushed and killed, for Zev had extended Gan Dafna defenses to the very gates of Fort Esther. Palmach boys and girls hid out near both the fort and Abu Yesha to watch every Arab move.

Meanwhile, a courier came to Ari from Haganah headquarters in Tel Aviv. Ari called his settlement commanders together at once. A high decision had been made in Tel Aviv regarding the children in border settlements. It was recommended that all children be moved into the Sharon-Tel Aviv area close to the sea where the situation was not so critical and where every home, *kibbutz* and *moshav* was ready to receive them. One could read between the lines: the situation had become so bad that the Haganah was obviously thinking of eventual evacuation of the children by sea to save them from massacre if the Arabs broke through.

It was not an order; each *kibbutz* and *moshav* had to make the decision for itself. On the one hand, the farmers would fight more fiercely with their children close by. On the other hand, massacre was a horrible specter to contemplate.

The evacuation of the children was a doubly painful thing for these pioneers, for it became symbolic of further retreat. Most of them had fled from former horror to come to this place and their farms were the last line of retreat. Beyond Palestine there was no hope.

Each settlement made its decision. Some of the older and longer-established places simply refused to let their children go. Others vowed they would all stand and die together: they did not want their children to know the meaning of retreat. Others in the mountains already isolated and undergoing hardships managed to bring children out for removal.

Gan Dafna was everyone's responsibility.

Ari's spies reported that Kawukji was bringing unbearable pressure on Mohammed Kassi to make an assault on Gan Dafna. Food was getting low in the village and fuel was all but gone. The water tank had sprung several leaks from near hits. The hardship of bunker life was wearing down the community, although there were no complaints.

The commanders in the Huleh Valley agreed that the younger children had to be taken out of Gan Dafna. The question was—how! A truce would involve a double danger: first, Kassi would never recognize it; second, it would be a costly show of weakness to the Arab commander. If Ari tried a convoy through the roads or an outright attack on Abu Yesha he would have to pull out and mass his entire Huleh strength—then he could be only half certain of success. It was not merely a matter of winning or losing a battle. To lose would lead to the death of the children.

As so many times before, Ari was called upon to evolve a desperation measure to counter crushing odds. And because there was no choice, again he conceived a fantastic plan, this one more daring than anything he had ever tried in his life.

After organizing the details of his scheme, Ari left David to mobilize a task force and he set out for Gan Dafna. The climb up the mountainside was painful every inch of the way. His leg throbbed constantly and collapsed several times during the night. He was able to compensate for the handicap by his intimate knowledge of the route, for he had climbed it a dozen times as a boy. He reached Gan Dafna at dawn and immediately called a meeting of the section heads at the command post bunker. Zev, Jordana, Dr. Lieberman, and Kitty Fremont were among them.

"There are two hundred and fifty children here under the age of twelve," Ari said without introduction or preface. "They will be evacuated tomorrow night."

He looked at the dozen surprised faces.

"A task force is now assembling at Yad El *moshav*," he continued. "Tonight, four hundred men from every settlement in the Huleh will be led up the west face of the mountain by David Ben Ami. If everything goes according to plan and they are not discovered they should be here by daybreak tomorrow. Two hundred and fifty of the men will each carry a child down the mountain tomorrow night. The balance, a hundred and fifty men, will act as a guard force. I may add that the guard force will be carrying all the heavy automatic weapons in the Huleh Valley."

Ari's listeners in the bunker stared at him as though he were insane. There was no sound or movement for a full minute.

Finally Zev Gilboa stood up. "Ari, perhaps I did not understand you. You actually plan to carry two hundred and fifty children down the mountain at night?"

"That is correct."

"It is a treacherous trip for man by himself in daylight,"

Dr. Lieberman said. "Carrying a child down at night—some of them are certain to fall."

"That is a risk that has to be taken."

"But Ari," Zev said, "they must pass so close to Abu Yesha. It is certain that Kassi's men will detect them."

"We will take every precaution to see that they are not detected."

Everyone began to protest at once.

"Quiet!" Ari snapped. "This is not a forum. You people here are not to speak of this to anyone. I want no panic. Now, get out of here, all of you. I have a lot of work to do."

The shelling from Fort Esther was particularly heavy during the day. Ari worked with each section head in turn to complete the smallest details of the evacuation and to work out a minute-by-minute timetable.

Each of those dozen people who knew of the scheme went around with hearts heavy with apprehension. A thousand things could go wrong. Someone could slip and cause a panic . . . the Arab dogs in Abu Yesha would hear them or smell them and bark . . . Kassi would discover the move and attack all the settlements in the Huleh realizing they were without their heavy weapons . . .

Yet they knew that there was little else that Ari could do. In a week or ten days Gan Dafna would reach a desperation level anyhow.

As evening approached, David Ben Ami, with the task force in Yad El, sent out a coded blinker message that he would be on the way with the darkness.

Throughout that second night, the four hundred volunteers pushed their way up the mountain and appeared on the outskirts of Gan Dafna before daybreak in a state of exhaustion from the climb and the tension. Ari met them outside the village and hid them in the woods. He did not want them spotted by Kassi's men, nor did he want any wild speculation inside Gan Dafna.

They remained in the woods through the entire day. At ten minutes to six in the evening, exactly forty minutes before the sun was to set, the operation went into full effect.

The children to be evacuated were fed at exactly five minutes to six and a sleeping powder was put in each child's milk. By a quarter after six the children were put into their bunks in the water-pipe shelters beneath the ground. They were led in group singing until they dropped off into a deep drugged slumber.

At six thirty-two the sun set behind Fort Esther.

At six-forty Ari called a meeting of the entire staff outside of the children's bunkers.

"You will all pay strict attention," he said sternly. "In a few minutes we are going to begin the evacuation of the younger children. Your name will be called and you will be given an assignment. Everything has been worked out on a tight schedule and any variation of it could endanger the lives of the children and their escorts as well as yourselves. I want no discussion or questions. Any failure to co-operate will be dealt with drastically."

At six forty-five Jordana Ben Canaan set out a guard around Gan Dafna consisting of the rest of the children. The guard was four times normal strength to make certain there would be no Arab infiltration that might discover the movements inside Gan Dafna. Zev Gilboa and his twenty Palmach troops attached to Dafna pushed out toward the hills on a special covering mission.

As soon as the security around Gan Dafna was reported tight, twenty-five of the Gan Dafna staff went into the bunkers to dress the sleeping children in their warmest clothing. Kitty moved from child to child to make certain that each one had been properly drugged by the sleeping powder. A thick strip of adhesive tape was placed over each child's mouth so that he could not cry out in his sleep. By seven thirty the unconscious children were dressed and ready. Ari then brought the task force from its hiding place in the woods.

A chain line was formed from the bunkers, and the sleeping little bodies handed out one by one. Improvised strap rigs had been sewn together to form a makeshift saddle seat for the back of the men so that the children could be carried like packs. This would allow each man to have both hands free for his rifle and the climb.

By eight-thirty, the two hundred and fifty men and their small slumbering loads stood a final check to see that the children were strapped in securely. Then the line moved out to the main gate where the protecting force, a hundred and fifty men with automatic weapons, stood ready. With Ari leading the way, they pushed off over the edge of the drop down the side of the mountain. One by one the men and the children dropped down, until the last of them disappeared into the night.

Those left behind stood at the gates of Gan Dafna in silence. There was nothing to do now but wait until morning. They began drifting back toward their bunkers, where they would spend the sleepless night in silence, trembling with fear for the children and for the fate of this strange convoy.

Kitty Fremont stood alone by the main gate for more than an hour after they had gone. She stared vacantly into the darkness.

"It is going to be a very long night," a voice said behind her. "You might as well get in out of the cold."

Kitty turned. Jordana stood next to her. For the first time since they had met, Kitty was actually glad to see the red-headed *sabra*. She had been developing a growing admiration for Jordana since her decision to stay. Jordana was perhaps the one person most responsible for keeping Gan Dafna calm. The girl had instilled the young Gadna troops with an infectious confidence; they behaved like spirited battle veterans. During all the ordeals since the closing of the road, Jordana had remained contained and efficient. It was quite a load for a young woman not yet twenty, but Jordana had that quality of leadership that made those around her feel secure.

"Yes, it's going to be a very long night," Kitty said.

"Then we can keep each other company," Jordana said. "I will tell you a secret. I have a half bottle of brandy hidden in the command-post bunker. I think that tonight would be a perfect time to finish it. Why don't you wait for me at my bunker? I have to bring in the guards. I'll be back in a half hour."

Kitty didn't move. Jordana took her arm. "Come on," she said gently, "there is nothing we can do now."

Kitty had been sitting nervously and smoking cigarette after cigarette until Jordana finally got back to the command post. Jordana took the brown Haganah stocking cap from her head, and her long scarlet tresses fell to her shoulders. She alternately held her cheeks and rubbed her hands together to drive out the cold. The brandy was hidden in a loosely filled place in the dirt wall. She took it out and wiped off the bottle and poured Kitty and herself a stiff drink.

"*Le chaim,*" Jordana said, taking a sip. "That is good."

"How long will it be before they pass near Abu Yesha?"

"That won't be until after midnight," Jordana answered.

"I have been telling myself over and over that they are going to come through all right. Then I begin thinking of the thousands of things that can go wrong."

"It is impossible not to think about it," Jordana said, "but it is in the hands of God now."

"God? Yes, He does special things here," Kitty said.

"If you don't get religion in Palestine, I doubt that you'll get it anywhere," Jordana said. "I cannot remember the time that we have not lived on faith. We actually have little else to sustain us."

Coming from Jordana Ben Canaan, the words sounded strange, yet—not strange at all. On the surface Jordana did not appear to harbor a deep faith . . . but what else could give her the power to exist under this constant tension if it were not faith?

"Kitty," Jordana said suddenly, "I have a confession to make to you. I have wanted very much for us to become friends."

"Why is that, Jordana?"

"Because I have learned something from you . . . something I have been very wrong about. I have watched you work here with the children and I know what you did for Ari. When you decided to stay I realized something . . . I realized that a woman like you can have just as much courage as . . . our kind of people. I used to believe that to be feminine was a sign of weakness."

"Thank you, Jordana," Kitty smiled weakly, "but I'm afraid I could use a little of your brand of faith or courage or whatever it is right now. I feel as though I'm ready to fall apart."

Kitty lit a cigarette and Jordana poured her another brandy.

"I have been thinking . . ." Jordana said. "You would be good for Ari."

Kitty shook her head. "We are, as the saying goes, two nice people not made for each other."

"That is unfortunate, Kitty."

Kitty looked at her watch. She knew from the discussions that the long column of men would now be approaching the first of the almost straight drops. With the children, they would use ropes easing each man's descent, one by one. It was a thirty-five-foot plunge. From there they would have to slide in loose dirt for a hundred yards.

"Tell me about yourself and David," Kitty said quickly.

Jordana's eyes lit up. "Ah, my David . . . my gentle, wonderful David."

"Where did you first meet?"

"At the Hebrew University. I met him the second day I was there. I saw him and he saw me and we fell in love at that very moment and we have never fallen out of it."

"That's the way it was with my husband and me," Kitty said.

"Of course it took me all that first term to let him know he was in love with me."

"It took me longer than that." Kitty smiled.

"Yes, men can be a bother about such things. But by summer he knew very well who his woman was. We went out on an archaeological expedition together into the Negev Desert. We were trying to find the exact route of Moses and the ten tribes in the Wildernesses of Zin and Paran."

"I hear it's pretty desolate out there."

"No, actually there are ruins of hundreds of Nabataean

498

cities. The cisterns still have water in them. If you run in luck you can find all sorts of antiquities."

"It sounds exciting."

"It is, but it's terribly hard work. David loves digging for ruins. He feels the glory of our people all around us. Like so many others . . . that is why the Jews can never be separated from this land. David has made wonderful plans. After the war we are both going to return to the university. I will go for my master's degree and David his doctorate, and then we shall excavate a big, big Hebrew city. He wants to open Hazor, right here in the Huleh. Of course, these are only dreams. That takes lots of money . . . and peace." Then she laughed ironically. "Peace, of course, is merely an abstract word, an illusion. I wonder what peace is like?"

"Perhaps peace would be dull for you."

"I don't know," Jordana said, with a trace of tiredness in her young voice. "Just once in my life I would like to see how human beings live a normal life."

"Will you travel?"

"Travel? No. I do what David does. I go where David goes. But, Kitty, I would like to go out once. All my life I have been told that all life begins and ends in Palestine. But . . . every once in a while I feel strangled. Many of my friends have gone away from Palestine. It seems that we *sabras* are a strange breed made for fighting. We cannot adjust to living in other places. They all come back to Palestine sooner or later—but they grow old so quickly here." Jordana cut herself short. "It must be the brandy," she said. "As you know, *sabras* can't drink at all."

Kitty smiled at Jordana and felt her first compassion for the girl. She snuffed out her cigarette and looked at her watch again. The minutes were dragging.

"Where would they be now?"

"Still being lowered down that first cliff. It will take at least two hours to get them all down."

Kitty sighed weakly and Jordana stared into space.

"What are you thinking?"

"About David . . . and children. That first summer on the desert we found a graveyard more than four thousand years old. We managed to uncover a perfect skeleton of a little child. Perhaps it died trying to find the Promised Land. David looked at the skeleton and cried. He is like that. His heart is sick day and night over the siege of Jerusalem. I know he is going to try to do something foolish. I know it. . . . Why don't you lie down, Kitty? It is going to be a long time before we know anything."

Kitty finished her brandy and stretched back on the cot

499

and closed her eyes. In her mind she saw that long line of men being lowered by rope with the sleeping children dangling from their backs. And then she saw flinty-eyed Arab irregulars lurking near the column, spying on their moves—waiting for them to get close and into a trap.

It was impossible to sleep.

"I think I'll go over to Dr. Lieberman's bunker and see how they're doing."

She put on a wool-lined jacket and walked outside. There hadn't been any shelling all evening. An alarming thought came: perhaps Mohammed Kassi knew something and had moved most of his men out of Fort Esther. She did not like it. The moon was far too bright. The night was far too clear and quiet. Ari should have waited until a foggy night to move the children. Kitty looked up the hill and made out the outlines of Fort Esther. They must have seen, she thought.

She entered one of the faculty bunkers. Dr. Lieberman and the rest of the staff all sat on the edge of their cots staring blankly, numb with tension. Not a word was spoken. It was so morbid she could not stand it and she went outside again.

Both Karen and Dov were standing sentry duty.

She returned to the command-post bunker to find that Jordana had gone.

She stretched out on the cot again and covered her legs with a blanket. The vision of the men inching down the mountainside came to her once more. The day had left her spent. She began to doze. The hours passed.

Midnight—one o'clock. Kitty thrashed about on the cot. Her brain was filled with nightmare. She saw the horde of Kassi's men charging out at the column, shrieking, with their sabers glinting. The guards were dead and the Arabs had taken all the children and dug a huge pit for them. . . .

Kitty bolted up on the cot in a cold sweat with her heart pounding madly. She shook her head slowly and trembled from head to foot. Then a sound reached her ears. She cocked her head and listened. Her eyes widened in terror!

It was a sound of distant gunfire!

She staggered to her feet. Yes! It was gunfire . . . coming from the direction of Abu Yesha! It was no dream! The column had been discovered!

Jordana entered the bunker just as Kitty rushed for the door.

"Let me go!" she shrieked.

"Kitty, no, no . . . !"

"They're killing my babies! Murderers! Murderers!"

Jordana exerted all her strength to pin Kitty to the wall but Kitty was wild. She lashed out and tore from Jordana's grasp. The *sabra* girl grabbed her, spun her around, and smashed her across the shoulders, sending her to the floor sobbing.

"Listen to me! That gunfire you hear is Zev Gilboa and the Palmach making a diversionary attack. They are hitting the opposite side of Abu Yesha to draw Kassi's men away from the convoy."

"You're lying!"

"It is true, I swear it. I was told not to say anything until just before the attack. I came here and saw you asleep and went to warn the others."

Jordana knelt down and helped Kitty to her feet and led her to the cot. "There is a little brandy left. Drink it."

Kitty swallowed it, half gagging to force it down. She brought herself under control.

"I am sorry that I struck you," Jordana said.

"No . . . you did the right thing."

Jordana sat beside Kitty and patted her hand and massaged the back of her neck. Kitty weakly lay her head on Jordana's shoulder and cried very softly until she had cried herself out. Then she stood up and put on her heavy clothing.

"Karen and Dov will be coming off guard soon. I'll go to my bunker and make them some tea."

The hours of darkness dragged on and on—a night without end. Out in the blackness the men crawled on their bellies past Abu Yesha while the Palmach made its raid on the other side of the village, and then they plunged quickly down . . . down . . .

Two o'clock. Three o'clock. By now the waiters, even Jordana Ben Canaan, sat drained and empty, in a dazed silence. At five-fifteen they came out of the bunkers. The morning was icy. A thin, slick frost covered the center green. They all walked out of the main gate to that point where the lookout post hung over the edge of the mountain.

The darkness faded from the land and the lights in the valley went off one by one as a musty gray dawn revealed the floor far below.

The sentry looked through the field glasses for some sign of life down the mountain. There was nothing.

"Look!"

The sentry pointed. All of them stared toward the Yad El *moshav*, where dots and dashes blinked out from a signal light.

"What does it read? What does it mean?"

"It says . . . X1416 . . ."

For a moment there was confusion. The message was repeated—X1416.

"They are safe!" Jordana Ben Canaan said. *"But lift thou*

up thy rod, and stretch out thine hand over the sea, and divide it: and the children of Israel shall go on dry ground through the midst of the sea. Exodus: fourteen, sixteen." She smiled exultantly at Kitty.

CHAPTER SIX: Four days after the younger children of Gan Dafna had been evacuated a series of reports filtered in to Ari. His settlement commanders were forwarding information that Arab pressure was lessening. When he learned from friends in Abu Yesha that Kassi had withdrawn half of the hundred men in the village and ordered them back to Fort Esther, Ari knew that the attack on Gan Dafna would come any day.

Ari took twenty more Palmach troops, the last that could be spared anywhere in the Galilee, and once again made the mountain climb to Gan Dafna to assume personal command.

He had forty Palmach troops in all, around thirty staff and faculty members capable of fighting, and Jordana's Gadna youngsters, some two hundred in number. His arsenal showed one hundred and fifty antiquated rifles or homemade Sten guns, two machine guns, a few hundred homemade grenades, mines, and fire bombs, and the obsolete Hungarian antitank gun with its five rounds of ammunition.

Intelligence reports indicated that, opposing him, Mohammed Kassi had eight hundred irregulars with unlimited ammunition and artillery support, plus perhaps another several hundred Arabs from Aata and other hostile villages along the Lebanese border.

Ari's supply of ammunition was critical. He knew that when the attack did come it had to be broken immediately. His one advantage was knowledge of the enemy. Mohammed Kassi, the Iraqi highway robber, had no formal military training. He was recruited by Kawukji on the promise of adventure and loot. Ari did not consider Kassi's men a particularly brave lot, but they could be whipped into a frenzy; if they ever got the upper hand during battle they would become murderous. Ari planned to use Arab ignorance and lack of imagination as his allies. He banked his defensive plan on the presumption that Kassi would try a direct frontal assault in the straightest and shortest line from Fort Esther. The frontal attack had been the history of Arab irregulars' tactics since he began fighting them as a boy. He stacked his defenses in one place.

The key spot in Ari's defense was a ravine that led like a funnel into Gan Dafna. If Ari could get Kassi to come into the ravine he had a chance. Zev Gilboa kept patrols in the rocks and brush right outside Fort Esther to observe the Arab movements. He had confirmed the fact that Kassi was massing men.

Three days after Ari arrived at Gan Dafna, a young runner came into his command post with the news that Kassi's men, nearly a thousand strong, had left the fort and were starting down the hill. Within two minutes the "black alarm" was sounded and every man, woman, and child at Gan Dafna took his post and stood by.

A deep saddle in the mountains could cover Kassi's men until they arrived at a knoll directly over Gan Dafna, some six hundred yards from the north side of the village and two hundred yards from the critical ravine which led in like a funnel.

Ari's men dug in to their prepared positions, became silent, and waited.

Soon heads began popping up on the knoll. Within minutes the point was swarming with irregulars. They stopped their progress and stared down at the ominously quiet village. The Arab officers were suspicious of the silence. Not a shot had been fired by either side.

In the watch and gun tower atop Fort Esther, Mohammed Kassi looked through powerful field glasses and smiled as he saw his horde of men poised atop Gan Dafna. Since the Jews had not fired at them his confidence grew that his men would be able to overrun the place. A cannon fired from the fort as a signal for the attack to begin.

In Gan Dafna they could hear harangues and conversation in Arabic as officers shouted at their men. Still no one moved down from the knoll. The quiet from the village baffled them. More of them began to scream and point down at the village. Their curses and their anger rose in hysterical crescendo.

"They're trying to work themselves into a heroic lather," Ari said.

The disciplined forces of the Jews showed neither their faces nor their guns, though each man found it hard to remain controlled under the chilling abuse of the Arabs.

After twenty minutes of ranting there was a sudden eruption from the knoll as irregulars poured down with unearthly shrieks, sabers and bayonets flashing a steel silhouette against the sky.

The first phase of Ari's defense would now receive a test. Each night he had sent patrols out to plant homemade land mines which could be detonated from inside Gan Dafna. The mines formed a corridor and were so placed to compress the Arabs toward the middle of the ravine.

Zev Gilboa, in the forwardmost position, waited until the

Arab charge was in full fury. When the horde of men reached the mine field, Zev held up a green flag. Inside Gan Dafna, Ari set off the charges.

Twenty mines, ten on each side, blew up at once. The roar shook the mountainside. The mines exploded on the fringe of the mob, which immediately squeezed together and rushed right down the funnel of the ravine.

On the sides of the ravine Ari had placed his forty Palmach troops, the two machine guns, and all the grenades and fire bombs in the arsenal. As the Arabs passed directly under them the Palmach opened up a cross-fire with the two guns and turned the ravine into a gory turkey shoot. Flames erupted from the fire bombs and turned dozens of the irregulars into human torches, while the Palmach hurled a torrent of grenades among them.

In addition the Palmach set off strings of firecrackers, while from loud-speakers in the trees came a recording of bombing explosions. The continued din of the real and artificial arms was deafening and terrifying.

Inside Fort Esther, Mohammed Kassi frantically called for artillery to clean off the sides of the ravine. The excited Arab gunners opened fire and landed half of their shells among their own men. Finally they managed to silence one Palmach machine gun.

The advance Arab force had been cut down like cordwood, but still they poured in. They had been stimulated to such frenzy that their thrust was now that of men insane with fear.

The second machine gun stopped firing when its barrel burned out. The Palmach quit its position on the sides of the ravine and dropped back into Gan Dafna before the unabated onslaught. The Arabs' rush came to within a hundred yards of the village in disorganized knots of screaming men. David Ben Ami had the cover off the barricaded and sandbagged Hungarian antitank gun. The projectiles had been modified and each of the five rounds now contained two thousand shotgun pellets. If the gun worked properly it would have the effect of a battery of men firing at once.

The leading bunched mass of maddened Arabs rolled to within fifty yards . . . forty . . . thirty . . . twenty . . .

The sweat poured down David Ben Ami's face as he sighted the gun at point-blank range.

Ten yards . . .

"Fire one!"

The ancient antitank gun bounced off the ground and spewed pellets into the faces of the chargers. Bloodcurdling shrieks mingled with smoke, and through it, as he swiftly reloaded, David glimpsed piles of men lying dead or wounded

504

within yards of the gun and others staggering back in blind shock.

The second wave came in behind the first.

"Fire two!"

The second wave went down in slaughter.

"Fire three!"

The barrel blew off the gun and she was finished, but she had done her work. In three shots the buckshot canister sprays had dropped nearly two hundred men. The momentum of the drive was halted.

A last assault was tried. A hundred Arabs again reached the edge of Gan Dafna, to be met by a broadside from Jordana Ben Canaan's entrenched Gadna youths.

Bewildered and bleeding, the Arab survivors now scrambled back up the death-filled ravine. As they retreated, Zev Gilboa yelled out for the Palmach troops to follow him. The shepherd led his forty fighters after several hundred running Arabs. He chased them back up the knoll and continued to pursue them.

Ari looked through his field glasses.

"The God-damned fool!" Ari yelled, "he's going to try to take Fort Esther. I told him to stop at the knoll."

"What's the matter with Zev?" David grunted between his teeth.

"Come on," Ari cried. "Let's see if we can stop him."

Ari issued hasty orders for Jordana to have the Gadna children pick up the Arab arms in the field and pull back into Gan Dafna.

His plan had paid off. In less than fifteen minutes he had dissipated the strength of his defense, but nearly half Kassi's troops lay dead or wounded.

When Mohammed Kassi saw his men run back up toward the fort, confusion broke out. Zev Gilboa was twenty-five yards out ahead of the rest of the Palmach when it happened. Arab gunners from Fort Esther began firing toward their own retreating men in order to stop the pursuing Palmach. Some of the Arabs managed to get inside Fort Esther. Those too close to the pursuing Jews were shut out and fired on. Zev had passed the outer accordions of barbed wire only forty yards from the fort.

"Cover!" he screamed at his troops. He threw himself flat and fired his Sten gun at the fort until the Palmach fell back out of range. Seeing that his attack was futile, Zev turned and tried to crawl back down the hill. A barrage of bullets came from the fort and he was hit. He stood up and ran and again he was hit, and this time he fell into the barbed wire and became entangled. He was unable to move.

The Palmach had dug in and were preparing to go up to

try to bring Zev out when Ari and David crawled up to them.

"It's Zev. He's out there tangled up in the wire."

Ari looked out from behind a large rock. He was a hundred yards away from Zev across an open field. There were some places he could find cover behind large rocks, but close to Zev he would be fully exposed.

Suddenly the firing from Fort Esther stopped and it became very still.

"What's going on?" David asked.

"They're using Zev for bait. They see he can't move and they hope we'll try to get up there and get him."

"Those bastards. Why don't they shoot him and get it over with?"

"Can't you see, David? He's lost his rifle. They're going to wait until we leave and try to take him alive. They're going to take it out on him for all the men they lost today."

"Oh, my God," David groaned. He jumped out from cover but Ari grabbed him and threw him back.

"Somebody give me a pair of grenades," Ari said. "Good. David, take the troops back into Gan Dafna."

"You're not going up there by yourself, Ari . . ."

"Do what I order, damn you!"

David turned quietly and signaled to start a withdrawal. He looked back to see Ari already scuttling up the hill toward Zev.

The Arabs watched Ari move up. They knew someone would try to get the wounded man. They would wait until he got close enough and try to wound him too; then the Jews would send another man up . . . and another.

Ari got up, sprinted, and dived behind a rock. The Arabs did not shoot.

Then he crawled again until he got to cover twenty yards from where Zev was tangled in the wire. Ari guessed that the Arabs would wait until he actually reached Zev and was an unmissable target.

"Get back . . . !" Zev called. "Get back!"

Ari peeked around the boulder. He could see Zev clearly. The blood was spurting from his face and stomach. He was completely trapped in the wire. Ari looked up to Fort Esther. He could see the sun glint off the barrels of rifles trained on Zev.

"Get back!" Zev shouted again. "My guts are hanging out. I can't last ten minutes . . . get back!"

Ari slipped the hand grenades from his belt.

"Zev. I'm going to throw you some grenades!" he called in German. Ari locked the pins in so they could not explode. He stood up quickly and threw both grenades to the boy. One landed just beside him.

506

Zev picked up the grenade and held it close to his torn stomach.

"I've got it . . . now get back!"

Ari ran down the hill quickly, catching the Arabs off guard; they had been expecting him to come up after Zev. When they opened fire he was out of range and making his way toward Gan Dafna.

Zev Gilboa was alone now and the life was oozing from him. The Arabs waited for a half hour, watching for a trick, expecting a Jew to come up after him. They wanted him alive.

The gates of Fort Esther opened. Some thirty Arabs emerged and trotted down to surround Zev.

Zev twisted the pin out of the grenade, held it next to his head and let the spoon fly off.

Ari heard the blast and stopped. He turned chalky white and his bad leg folded up under him. The insides of him shook; then he continued crawling down to Gan Dafna.

Ari sat in the command-post bunker alone. His face was waxen, and only the trembling of his cheek muscles showed there was life in him. His eyes stared dully from black-ringed sockets.

The Jews had lost twenty-four people: eleven Palmach boys, three Palmach girls, six faculty members, and four children. There were another twenty-two wounded. Mohammed Kassi had lost four hundred and eighteen men killed and a hundred and seventy wounded.

The Jews had taken enough weapons to make it likely that Kassi would never try another attack on Gan Dafna. But the Arabs still held Fort Esther and controlled the road through Abu Yesha.

Kitty Fremont entered the bunker. She too was on the brink of exhaustion. "The Arab casualties have all been removed to Abu Yesha except those you wanted for questioning."

Ari nodded. "How about our wounded?"

"Two of the children don't look as though they'll make it. The rest will be all right. Here . . . I brought you some brandy," Kitty said.

"Thanks . . . thanks . . ."

Ari sipped and remained quiet.

"I brought Zev Gilboa's things over to you. There isn't very much here . . . a few personal things."

"A *kibbutznik* doesn't have very much of his own. Everything, including his life, belongs to something else," he said, with a trace of irony.

"I liked Zev," Kitty said. "He was telling me last night how he looked forward to tending his sheep again. Anyhow . . . his wife may want these things. She's having another baby, you know."

"Zev was a damned fool!" Ari snarled. "He had no business trying to take that fort."

Ari picked up the handkerchief filled with Zev's meager articles. "Liora's a good girl. She's tough. She'll come through it." Ari threw the belongings into the kerosene stove. "I'll have a hard time replacing him."

Kitty's eyes narrowed. "Is that what you were thinking . . . you'd have a hard time replacing him?"

Ari stood up and lit a cigarette. "You don't grow men like Zev on trees."

"Is there nothing you cherish?"

"Tell me, Kitty. What did your husband's commander do when he was killed at Guadalcanal? Did he hold a wake for him?"

"I thought this was a little different, Ari. You've known Zev since he was a boy. That girl, his wife, is a Yad El girl. She was raised two farms away from yours."

"What do you want me to do?"

"Cry for that poor girl!"

For a second Ari's face twisted and his lips trembled and then his features sat rigidly. "It is nothing new to see a man die in battle. Get out of here. . . ."

CHAPTER SEVEN: The siege of Safed had begun exactly one day after the partition vote of November 29, 1947. When the British left Safed in the spring of 1948, as expected, they handed the three key spots over to the Arabs: the police station looking right down on the Jewish quarter, the acropolis commanding the entire city, and the Taggart fort on Mount Canaan just outside town.

Safed was shaped like an inverted cone. The Jewish quarter occupied a slice of about one eighth of the cone, so that the Arabs were above, below, and on both sides of them. The Jews had only two hundred half-trained Haganah men. Their refusal of evacuation and their decision to fight to the last man was in the spirit and tradition of the ancient Hebrews. The Cabalists of Safed, the least capable among the Jews of defending themselves, had been a primary target for the Mufti's riots. They had faced slaughter from Arab mobs before and they had cringed. Now they had made up their minds that they would stand and die. The Jewish quarter, jammed into the narrow twisting lanes, sustained an amazing spirit.

508

One day after the British left, Ari slipped Joab Yarkoni into the Jewish quarter of Safed with thirty Palmach boys and twenty Palmach girls. A wild celebration marked their arrival. It was the Sabbath and Yarkoni's troops were exhausted from travel through hostile country and they were hungry. For the first time in centuries, the Cabalists broke the Sabbath by cooking a hot meal for the reinforcements.

Kawukji, wanting to secure Safed as the temporary capital for the Mufti, ordered the irregulars to overrun the Jewish quarter. The Arabs tried a few sorties and were thrown back out; they soon realized that they would take the quarter only by a house-by-house, room-by-room fight. They reconsidered and returned to sniping and siege tactics.

The Jews were commanded by Remez and Joab Yarkoni. Brigadier Sutherland had left his villa on Mount Canaan to become the only guest of Remez's resort hotel. He was called upon for advice now and then but conceded that the Jews were doing quite well enough without his help.

Remez took on as his first task the clearing of a definite field of fire. The Arab and Jewish quarters were jammed up against each other, making it easy for Arab patrols to slip through and spread his already thin defensive strength. He wanted space between his forces and the Arabs. Yarkoni took a crew into the Arab quarters, seized a dozen borderline houses, and began shooting from them. Then he withdrew. Each time the Arabs came back, Yarkoni would again attack and take the same borderline houses. Finally the Arabs dynamited the houses to keep the Jews from using them. It was exactly what Remez wanted: it created the space between the two sectors to give the Jews better visibility and easier defense.

With this accomplished Remez and Yarkoni devised the second tactic. Yarkoni set out to harass the Arabs around the clock. Each day he sent three or four Palmach patrols into the Arab sector to move through the maze of alleys or over the roof tops. His patrols would suddenly make a sharp hit-and-run attack, each time at a different place. Whenever the Arabs concentrated their men in one strong point, the Jews were informed of it by spies and thus knew exactly where to strike and what spot to avoid. Like a jabbing boxer the daylight patrols kept the Arabs off balance.

But it was the night patrols of the Palmach that drove the Arabs into a frenzy. Yarkoni had lived in Morocco and he knew his enemy. The Arab was a superstitious man, with an unnatural fear of the dark. Yarkoni used the darkness like extra troops. The Palmach night patrols, merely by shooting off firecrackers, kept the Arab population in a panic.

Remez and Yarkoni admitted that their tactics were desperation measures. They were not strong enough to do real damage to the enemy, and the sheer weight of Arab numbers, position, and arms began to grind them down. A lost Palmach or Haganah soldier could not be replaced. Food was almost as difficult to replace. Ammunition was so critical that fines were levied against any Haganah or Palmach soldier who wasted a bullet.

Even as they were being worn down, the Jews held every inch of their quarter, and the amazing spirit never flagged. A single radio receiver was by now their only daily contact with the outside world, yet schools continued on schedule, the small newspaper never skipped an edition, and the pious did not miss a minute of synagogue. Letters got out by the patrols were fixed with hand-drawn stamps and were honored throughout Palestine by the Yishuv.

The siege carried on through the winter and the spring. Finally one day Yarkoni met with Sutherland and Remez to face bitter reality. The Jews had lost fifty of their best fighting men, they were down to their last twelve bags of flour, and they did not have ammunition to last five days. Yarkoni did not even have firecrackers for his patrols. The Arabs had sensed this weakness and were becoming bolder.

"I promised Ari that I wouldn't bother him with our troubles but I am afraid I must get to Ein Or and talk to him," Yarkoni decided. The same night he slipped out of Safed and went to Ari's headquarters.

Joab reported in full on the Safed situation. He concluded, "I hate to bother you, Ari, but in another three days we are going to have to start eating rats."

Ari grunted. The stand at Safed had been an inspiration to the entire Yishuv. It was more than a strategic position now, it was another invaluable symbol of defiance. "If we could win Safed we could crush Arab morale in the whole Galilee."

"Ari, every time we have to fire a bullet, we must go into a debate about it."

"I have an idea," Ari said. "Come with me."

Ari set up an emergency night patrol to get at least some supplies of food into Safed and then took Joab to the ordnance shed. In an inner room he showed the Moroccan a strange-looking contraption of cast iron, nuts, and bolts.

"What the hell is it?" Joab asked.

"Joab, you are looking at a *Davidka*."

"A Davidka?"

"Yes . . . a Little David, handcrafted by Jewish genius."

Joab scratched his jaw. In some respects one might say it did appear to be a weapon—of a sort. Yet . . . nothing quite like it existed anywhere else, Joab was sure.

"What is it supposed to do?"

"I am told that it shoots mortar shells."

"How?"

"Damned if I know. We haven't experimented yet. I have a report from Jerusalem saying that it has been very effective."

"For the Jews or Arabs?"

"Joab, I'll tell you what I'm going to do. I've been saving this weapon for the proper situation. It's yours, take it to Safed."

Joab walked around the odd piece of machinery. "The things we have to resort to to win a war," he mumbled.

The night patrol carrying emergency rations into Safed also brought along the Davidka and thirty pounds of ammunition. As soon as he arrived, Joab called the Haganah and Palmach leaders together, and through the rest of the night they traded ideas on how the thing was supposed to work. Ten people were present and ten opinions were given.

At last someone thought of sending for Brigadier Sutherland. He was awakened at the hotel and half dragged to headquarters. He stared at the Davidka in disbelief.

"Only a Jew could concoct something like this," he concluded.

"I hear it was very effective in Jerusalem," Joab apologized.

Sutherland played with all the levers and handles and switches and sights and in the next hour they evolved a firing procedure which might—or might not—work.

The next morning the Davidka was carried to a clearing and pointed in the general direction of the Arab-held police station and some nearby houses the Arabs used as sniping posts.

The Davidka's ammunition was no less strange in appearance than the Davidka. It was shaped like a mallet, of which the head was an iron cylinder filled with dynamite equipped with detonators. The thick handle allegedly fit down the mortar tube. On firing, the handle was supposed to be thrust out with such force that it would hurl the whole unbalanced load of dynamite at the target. Sutherland had visions of the thing flying for a few feet and exploding in front of them.

"If that warhead merely falls out of the end of the tube—as I confidently expect," Sutherland said, "we are likely to lose the entire Jewish population of Safed."

"Then I suggest we rig up a long line so we can fire it from a safe distance," Remez said.

"How do we aim it?" Yarkoni asked.

"Aiming this monstrosity isn't going to do much good. Just point it in the general direction and pray for the best."

The chief rabbi and many of the Cabalists and their wives gathered around the Davidka and carried on a lengthy debate on whether or not it meant doomsday for all of them. Finally the chief rabbi said special benedictions over the weapon and asked the Messiah kindly to spare them for they had indeed been very good in keeping the laws.

"Well, let's get it over with," Remez said pessimistically.

The Cabalists backed to safety. Firing caps were stuffed down the tube and one of the shells was lifted and the long handle placed inside. The cylinder of dynamite balanced over the end of the tube threateningly. A long line was attached to the firing mechanism. Everyone took cover and the earth stood still.

"Let her go," Yarkoni ordered in a shaky voice.

Remez jerked and a strange thing happened. The Little David fired.

The handle hissed out of the tube and the bucket of dynamite arched and spun, handle over bucket, up the hill. As it hurled through the air, growing smaller and smaller, it made a hideous swishing sound. It crashed into some Arab houses near the police station.

Sutherland's mouth hung open.

Yarkoni's mustache went from down to up.

Remez's eyes popped out.

The old Cabalists stopped praying long enough to look in astonishment.

The shell exploded like a thunderclap, shaking the town to its foundations. It seemed as though half the hillside must have been blown away.

After moments of stunned silence there was an eruption of shouting and hugging and kissing and praying and jubilation.

"By jove . . ." was all Sutherland could say. "By jove . . . !"

The Palmachniks formed a *hora* ring and danced around the Little David.

"Come on, come on. Let's fire another round!"

In the Arab quarters they could hear the Jews cheering, and the Arabs knew why. The very sound of the flying bomb in itself was enough to frighten one to death, to say nothing of the explosion. No one, Palestinian Arabs or irregulars, had bargained for anything like this; each time the Little David fired, a scene of havoc followed. The Arabs quaked in terror as the Jews revenged some of the hundred years of torment.

Joab Yarkoni got word to Ari that the Davidka had the Arabs in a turmoil. Ari sensed an opportunity and decided on a risky attempt to exploit it. He took a few men from each settlement and was able to scrape together two companies of Haganah. He got them into Safed at night with more ammunition for the Davidka.

Swish . . . *whoom!*

512

The bucket of bolts and its hissing bomb was devastating the town. Swish . . . *whoom!*

The third day after the Davidka had come to Safed the skies opened and it poured rain. Ari Ben Canaan then made the greatest bluff of the war that counted bluffs as part of the arsenal. He had Remez call all the Arab spies together and he gave them a briefing.

"In case you didn't know, brothers"—Ari addressed them in Arabic—"we have a secret weapon. I am not at liberty to disclose the nature of the weapon but I might say that you all know that it always rains after a nuclear blast. Need one say more?"

Within minutes the spies spread the word that the Little David was a secret weapon. Within an hour, every Arab mouth in Safed had repeated the appalling news: *the Jews have the atom bomb!*

Swish . . . whoom! The Little David roared and the rain turned to a deluge and the panic was on. Inside of two hours the roads out of Safed were clogged with fleeing Arabs.

Ari Ben Canaan led the Haganah on an attack with three hundred men. The attack was more spontaneous than calculated and Ari's men were thrown off the acropolis by irregulars and a handful of angry Safed Arabs. He lost heavily, but the Safed population continued to run.

Three days later, with Safed nearly empty of Arab civilian population and with hundreds of the irregulars deserted, Ari Ben Canaan, Remez, and Joab Yarkoni led a better planned, three-pronged attack and took the acropolis.

The tables were turned. The Jews were on the high ground above the Arab police station. Now those who had for decades tormented and murdered the Cabalists in wild mobs had their chance to stand and fight, but they fled in the face of the Jewish wrath. The police station fell and Ari immediately headed outside of the town to block off the huge Taggart fort on Mount Canaan, the strongest of the Arab positions. When he arrived he was astounded to discover that the Arabs had abandoned the Taggart fort, a position it would have been impossible to take. With the fort in his hands, the conquest of Safed was complete.

The victory of Safed was staggering. The vulnerable position thought impossible to defend had not only been defended but the defenders had conquered the city—with a few hundred fighters and a weird weapon called the Little David.

There were many theories and much discussion on just how this victory came about. Even the Cabalists of Safed were split on the subject. Rabbi Haim of the Ashkenazim or

European school was quite certain of divine intervention as foretold in Job:

When he is about to fill his belly, God shall cast the fury of his wrath upon him, and shall rain it upon him while he is eating. He shall flee from the iron weapon . . .

Rabbi Meir of the Sephardic or Oriental school disputed Haim and was just as certain of divine intervention as described in Ezekiel:

Thy walls shall shake at the noise . . . he shall enter into thy gates, as men enter into a city wherein is made a breach . . . thy strong garrisons shall go down to the ground.

Bruce Sutherland returned to his villa on Mount Canaan. The Arabs had desolated it. They had trampled his lovely rose garden to the earth and they had stolen everything including the doorknobs. It did not matter to Sutherland, for it would all be rebuilt again. He and Yarkoni and Remez walked out to his rear patio and looked over the valley to Safed. They drank a lot of brandy and they began to chuckle.

Neither they nor anyone else was aware of it yet, but the stampede of Safed's population had opened a new and tragic chapter—it began the creation of Arab refugees.

Somewhere in the Galilee, an obsolete Liberator bomber piloted by a volunteer crew of South Africans and Americans looked to the earth for a pair of blue flares.

The flares were spotted and they landed the bomber blind, with only a few flashlights marking the airfield. The plane bumped harshly over a pitted runway and skidded to a stop. The motors were cut quickly.

Swarms of people engulfed the plane and emptied it of its cargo, the first shipment of modern arms. Rifles, machine guns, mortars, and hundreds of thousands of rounds of ammunition were snatched from its waist and tail sections and its converted bomb bays.

The working parties stripped the Liberator clean in minutes. They loaded up a dozen trucks, which scattered in as many different directions. In a dozen *kibbutzim* Gadna youths stood ready to clean the weapons and get them out to the embattled settlements. The plane was turned and made a hair's-breadth take-off and flew back to Europe to get another load of arms.

In the morning British troops came to investigate Arab complaints that they had heard an airplane landing in the area. The British were unable to find a single trace of a plane and were certain the Arab imagination was being carried away again.

By the time the fourth and fifth shipment of arms arrived, the Jews began to roll up victories. Tiberias on the Sea of

Galilee had fallen to the Jews. The huge Gesher Taggart ort was grabbed by the Jews and held off repeated attacks y Iraqi irregulars.

With the fall of Safed, the Jews launched their first co-rdinated offensive, Operation Iron Broom, to sweep Galilee clean of hostile villages. Iron Broom was led by machine-gun-bearing jeeps which blazed into the villages and stam-eded the Arabs. Safed had started a crack in Arab morale hat gave Iron Broom a psychological jump.

With a score of local victories behind them and the knowl-dge that they could mount a successful offensive, the Haga-ah went after the vital port of Haifa.

The Haganah swept down the slopes of Mount Carmel in a four-pronged attack, each action aimed at an Arab strong oint. The Arab troops, consisting of home guards, Syrian, Lebanese, and Iraqi irregulars, mounted a strong defense and were at first able to contain the battle. The British, who still controlled the dock area, called truce after truce o stop the Jewish offenses, and at times took away hard-won vantage points.

The Arabs continued to hold well against the steady Jew-sh pressure. Then, as the fighting reached a peak, the Arab commander and his entire staff slipped out and quietly fled. Arab resistance became demoralized and collapsed entirely. Again the British called a truce as the Jews swept into the Arab quarters.

At that point a fantastic event took place. The Arabs sud-denly announced, to the general astonishment, that the entire population wished to leave. The procedure followed the curious pattern of Safed and many of the villages. It was a strange spectacle to see whole Arab populations stampeding for the Lebanese border, with no one pursuing them.

Acre, an all-Arab city crammed with refugees, fell to the Haganah after a halfhearted and feeble defense that lasted only three days. The infection spread to the Arab city of Jaffa, where the Maccabees held the center of the line and launched an attack which took this oldest port in the world—and the Arabs of Jaffa fled.

In the Jerusalem corridor, Abdul Kadar succeeded in driv-ng the Jews from the vital height of the Kastel, but the Haganah and Palmach came right back and threw the Arabs ff in turn. Kadar rallied his people for still another attempt on the Kastel, and in this try he was killed. The loss of their one good commander was a further severe blow to the de-moralized Arabs.

May 1948 came into being. The British had only two more weeks left to complete their evacuation and give up the man-date.

515

On the borders, the revengeful armies of Syria, Yemen, Lebanon, Trans-Jordan, Egypt, Saudi Arabia, and Iraq stood poised to cross and crush the conquering Jews.

The hour of decision—to declare statehood or not to declare statehood—was at hand.

CHAPTER EIGHT: Between November of 1947 and May of 1948, the Yishuv had staged a spectacular show by successfully fighting against overwhelming odds with little more than nothing. During that period of time the Jews had converted the Haganah from an underground defense unit into the nucleus of a real army. They had trained new troops and staff men and organized tactical schools, operations, supply and transport and the hundreds of other things that marked the conversion from guerrilla fighting to organized warfare.

The first air force of grenade-throwing Piper Cub pilots had grown to include a few Spitfires manned by Jews who had flown with the American, British, and South African air forces. The Navy had begun with the rickety immigration runners and now had a few corvettes and PT boats.

From the beginning the Jews had appreciated the importance of administration, intelligence, and command. Each day they gained in experience and their victories brought confidence. They had shown they could organize and coordinate small-scale efforts: the convoys to Jerusalem, Operation Iron Broom, and other local actions.

They had met the challenge and triumphed. Yet they knew that they had only fought a small war, against an enemy who did not have a tremendous desire to fight. The Arabs had little organization or leadership and no stomach for sustained fighting. The Arab debacle proved that it took more than slogans to give a man the stamina and courage to put his life on the block.

The planeloads of small arms had helped to save the Yishuv. As the hour of decision came near the reality came with it that these arms would have to face regular armies with tanks, artillery, and modern air forces.

Those who believed that the Arab countries were bluffing soon got a rude awakening as the Arab Legion of Trans-Jordan wantonly violated every concept of honor. The Legion operated in Palestine as a British police force. This "British police force" began open action against the isolated Etzion Group settlements on the Bethlehem Road.

The four villages in the Etzion group were manned by Orthodox Jews who chose to stay and fight, as did every

516

settlement in the Yishuv. Led by British officers, the Trans-Jordan Arab Legion shelled the four settlements without mercy and completely cut them off from outside help.

Kibbutz Etzion was the first target of the Legion. After blasting the *kibbutz* apart, the Legion attacked the siege-weary, half-starved settlement. The Orthodox Jews of *kibbutz* Etzion held fast until their last round of ammunition had been fired and only then did they surrender. Arab villagers who had followed the Legion rushed into the *kibbutz* and massacred almost all the survivors. The Legion made an attempt to stop the slaughter but when it was over only four Jews had survived.

The Haganah immediately appealed to the International Red Cross to supervise the surrender of the other three Etzion group settlements, which were also close to being out of ammunition. Only this move prevented mass murder there, too.

In the Negev Desert near the Dead Sea, the Arab Legion of Trans-Jordan attacked again.

This time they hit a *kibbutz* that the Jews had built in the lowest and hottest place on the earth. It was called Beth Ha-Arava—the House in the Wilderness. In the summertime it was one hundred and twenty-five degrees in the shade. When the Jews came to this place no living thing had grown in the alkaline soil in all of history. They washed the soil down, acre by acre, to free it of salts, and by this pains-taking process and through the creation of spillways, dams, and cisterns to trap the rainfall, they built a modern farm.

With the nearest Jews a hundred miles away and facing unbeatable odds, Beth Ha-Arava surrendered to the Arab Legion, and as the people walked from the House in the Wilderness the Jews set a torch to it and burned their houses and fields which had been built with inhuman toil.

And so, the Arabs had got their victories at last—Beth Ha-Arava—the House in the Wilderness—and the blood-stained conquest of the Etzion group.

On the night of May 13, 1948, the British High Commis-sioner for Palestine quietly left embattled Jerusalem. The Union Jack, a symbol here of the misuse of power, came down from the staff—forever.

MAY 14, 1948

In Tel Aviv the leaders of the Yishuv and the world Zion-ists met in the house of Meier Dizengoff, the founder and first mayor of the city. Outside the house, Sten-gun-bearing guards kept back anxious crowds.

In Cairo, in New York, in Jerusalem, and in Paris and

London and Washington they turned their eyes and ears to this house.

"This is Kol Israel—the Voice of Israel," the announcer said slowly from the radio station. "I have just been handed a document concerning the end of the British mandate which I shall now read to you."

"Quiet! Quiet!" Dr. Lieberman said to the crowd of children who had gathered in his cottage. "Quiet!"

"The Land of Israel," the voice over the radio said, "was the birthplace of the Jewish people. Here their spiritual, religious, and national identity was formed. Here they achieved independence and created a culture of national and universal significance. Here they wrote and gave the Bible to the world."

Bruce Sutherland and Joab Yarkoni stopped the chess game in Remez's hotel and, with Remez, listened raptly.

"Exiled from the Land of Israel, the Jewish people remained faithful to it in all the countries of their dispersion, never ceasing to pray and hope for their return and the restoration of their national freedom."

In Paris, the static on the radio increased and drowned out the voice as Barak Ben Canaan and the Yishuv agents frantically twisted the dials and beat on the receiver.

"Impelled by this historic association, Jews strove throughout the centuries to go back to the land of their fathers and regain their statehood. In recent decades they returned in their masses. They reclaimed the wilderness, revived their language, built cities and villages, and established an ever-growing community with its own economic and cultural life. They sought peace, yet were prepared to defend themselves. They brought the blessings of progress to all inhabitants . . ."

In Safed, the Cabalists listened in hope of words to fulfill the ancient prophecies. In the Jerusalem corridor the dog-tired Palmach fighters of the Hillmen Brigade listened, and in the isolated and besieged settlements of the blistering Negev Desert they listened.

". . . right was acknowledged by the Balfour Declaration of November 2, 1917, and reaffirmed by the mandate of the League of Nations, which gave explicit international recognition . . ."

David Ben Ami rushed into the commander's office at Ein Or *kibbutz*. Ari held his finger to his lips and pointed to the radio.

". . . the recent holocaust which engulfed millions of Jews in Europe proved anew the need . . ."

Sarah Ben Canaan listened at Yad El and she remembered the first time she had seen Barak ride into Rosh Pinna on a white Arab steed with his great red beard flowing down on his tunic.

". . . re-establishment of the Jewish state, which would open the gates to all Jews and endow the Jewish people with equality of status among the family of nations . . ."

Dov and Karen held hands quietly in the dining hall and listened to the loud-speaker.

"In the second world war the Jewish people in Palestine made their full contribution to the struggle. . . . On November 29, 1947, the General Assembly of the United Nations adopted a resolution requiring the establishing of a Jewish state in Palestine . . . the right of the Jewish people to establish their independent state is unassailable. It is the natural right of the Jewish people to lead, as do all other nations, an independent existence as a sovereign state.

"We hereby proclaim the establishment of the Jewish state in Palestine, to be called the State of Israel."

Kitty Fremont felt her heart leap—Jordana smiled.

"The State of Israel will be open to immigration to Jews from all countries of their dispersion; will promote the development of the country for the benefit of all its inhabitants; will be based on the principles of liberty, justice, and peace as conceived by the prophets of Israel; will uphold the full social and political equality of all its citizens, without distinction of religion, race, or sex; will guarantee freedom of religion, conscience, education, and culture; will safeguard holy places of all religions; and will loyally uphold the principles of the United Nations Charter . . .

". . . In the midst of wanton aggression, we yet call upon the Arab inhabitants of the State of Israel to preserve the ways of peace and play their part in the development of the state, on the basis of full and equal citizenship and due representation in all its bodies and institutions . . .

". . . we extend our hand in peace and neighborliness to all the neighboring states and their peoples, and invite them to co-operate . . .

". . . With trust in Almighty God, we set our hand to this declaration at this session of the Provisional State Council, on the soil of the homeland, in the city of Tel Aviv, on this Sabbath eve, the fifth of Iyar 5708, the fourteenth day of May 1948."

After two thousand years, the State of Israel was reborn.

Within hours, through President Harry Truman, the United States became the first of the nations of the world to recognize the State of Israel.

Even as the crowds in Tel Aviv danced the *hora* in the streets, Egyptian bombers took off en route to the city to destroy it and the armies of the Arab world crossed the frontiers of the infant state.

CHAPTER NINE: As the individual Arab armies violated the borders of Israel they boasted of immediate victory and began to issue glorious communiqués giving vivid descriptions of imaginary triumphs. The Arabs revealed that they had a "master plan" for throwing the Jews into the sea. If a master plan existed there was no master commander, for each Arab country had its own idea of who should run the armies and each Arab country had its own idea of who should rule Palestine afterward. Bagdad and Cairo both claimed leadership of the Arab world and of a "greater Arab state"; Saudi Arabia claimed leadership as the country which held the sacred cities of Mecca and Medina; Jordan aspired to Palestine as part of the mandate; Syria had never dropped the claim that Palestine was the southern part of an Ottoman province. And so—the "united" Arabs attacked.

NEGEV DESERT

A much-heralded Egyptian aggressive force came from bases in the Sinai through Arab-held Gaza along the coast. The first of two Egyptian columns, backed by tanks, armored cars, artillery, and modern aircraft, moved along the coastal road which followed the railroad due north to the Jewish provisional capital of Tel Aviv. The Egyptians were confident the Jewish settlements would break and run before their awesome, overwhelming power.

At the first *kibbutz*, Nirim, the Egyptians made a headlong rush and were hurled out. At the second and third settlements along the way they met the same stiff resistance. This shocking bit of business caused the Egyptian staff to reevaluate the situation. They decided to bypass these tougher spots and continue on up the coast. However, they ran the danger of overextending their supply lines and leaving their rear open for attack from these Jewish pockets: it was mandatory that they stop and fight in certain key places.

Egyptian artillery pounded the settlements to the ground and Egyptian planes bombed and raked them. After furious encounters the Egyptians captured three settlements. The majority of the settlements held and were bypassed.

The most vital strategic settlement in the Egyptian line of march was *kibbutz* Negba—Gate of the Negev—which was located near the intersection of the north road to Tel Aviv and a lateral road that ran inland. This was one of the places that the Egyptians had to capture.

Less than a mile from *kibbutz* Negba stood the Taggart fort of Suweidan—the Monster on the Hill. Suweidan had been handed over to the Arabs by the British. From the fort they were able to shell *kibbutz* Negba to rubble. Negba did not own a gun which could reach the fort.

The farmers of Negba realized the importance of their vital junction to the invaders. They also knew they were not invincible. They knew what to expect; nevertheless, they made the decision to stay and fight. As the guns from Suweidan knocked down every last building and the water ration was reduced to a few drops a day and the subsistence fell to starvation level, Negba continued to hold. Assault followed assault, and each time the Jews threw the Egyptians back. During one Egyptian attack led by tanks, the Jews were down to their last five rounds of antitank ammunition and they knocked out four tanks. For weeks Negba held the Egyptians at a stalemate. It refused to be taken. It fought as the ancient Hebrews of Masada had fought, and Negba became the first symbol of the defiance of the new state.

The Egyptian coastal column left huge forces in Suweidan and continued on up the coast. They moved dangerously close to Tel Aviv.

At Isdud, only twenty miles from Tel Aviv, the Israelis stiffened their defenses. As quickly as arms could be unloaded at the docks, they were rushed to Isdud, along with green new immigrants, to block the Egyptian column.

The Egyptians called a halt to regroup, resupply, and probe in preparation for a final thrust which would take them into Tel Aviv.

The second half of the Egyptian invasion force wheeled inland to the Negev Desert. As they advanced unmolested through Arab cities of Beersheba and Hebron and Bethlehem, Radio Cairo and the Egyptian press hailed "victory after victory."

It was intended that this second column join in the "glorious" conquest of Jerusalem by attacking from the south simultaneously with an attack of the Arab Legion. However, the Egyptians decided not to share the credit and went after Jerusalem by themselves.

Massing at Bethlehem, they assaulted Ramat Rahel—the Hill of Rachel—a *kibbutz* outpost defending the southern approach to New Jerusalem, the place where Rachel once wept for the exiled children of Israel.

The farmers of Ramat Rahel held under the Egyptian attack until they could hold no longer and they fell back slowly into Jerusalem. At the southern outskirt of the city they were met by Haganah reinforcements and they regrouped and roared back into their *kibbutz* and threw the Egyptians out and chased them to Bethlehem.

JERUSALEM

When the British left Jerusalem, the Haganah moved quickly to seize the sections where the British had been and to launch attacks on sections which held Kawukji's irregulars. The fighting consisted of street-to-street engagements, with Gadna children serving as runners and men in business suits leading attacks.

The second objective of the Haganah was to take an Arab suburb which separated the Jews on Mount Scopus from the Jews in New Jerusalem. With this done, a decision had to be made. The Jews were now in a position to win the Old City of Jerusalem. With the Old City in their hands they would have a solid strategic front. Without the Old City they were vulnerable. International politics, the fear of damage to the holy places, and great outside pressures made them decide to leave the Old City alone, although inside the walls was a quarter of several thousand pious Jews.

The Jews abandoned a lookout post in the tower of an Armenian church inside the Old City, at the request of the monks. The moment the Jews left, the irregulars grabbed the same place and refused to leave. Despite this fact, the Jews felt that the Arabs would not dare to attack the Old City, sacred to three religions, and would follow the example set by the Jews in this holiest ground in the world.

The Haganah then became faced with the final bit of treachery. Glubb Pasha, British commander of the Arab Legion, had given solemn promise that the Legion would be returned to Jordan when the British evacuated. But when the British left Jerusalem, the Arab Legion rushed to that city in open violation of the promise. The Legion attacked and was able to gain back part of what the Haganah had taken earlier. The suburb linking New Jerusalem with Mount Scopus had been given to the Maccabees to defend; they lost it to the Legion, thus isolating the forces on Scopus. Then Glubb ordered the Arab Legion to attack the Old City!

The Jews had no illusions left after their years of dealing with the Arabs, but this attack on the most sacred shrine of mankind was the nadir. There was nothing to stop the Legion but a few thousand ultra-Orthodox Jews who would not raise a finger in their own defense. The Jews rushed as much of the Haganah as they could spare into the Old City, and the Haganah was followed by several hundred angry Maccabee volunteers. Once inside the Old City there was no escape for their forces.

522

JERUSALEM CORRIDOR

The road from Jerusalem to Tel Aviv continued to bear the hardest fighting of the war. The Hillmen of the Palmach had cleared a half dozen heights in the Judean hills. The Kastel was firmly in their hands and they had assaulted and won the Comb, Suba, and enough key places to open the tricky and vulnerable Bab el Wad.

Then the blackest blot on the Jewish record occurred. The Maccabees were given the high Arab village of Neve Sadij to hold. In a strange and inexplicable sequence of events a panic broke out among Maccabee troops and they opened up a wild and unnecessary firing. Once started it could not be stopped. More than two hundred Arab civilians were massacred. With the Neve Sadij massacre the Maccabees, who had proved so valuable, had fixed a stigma on the young nation that it would take decades to erase.

Although the Hillmen Brigade had opened the Bab el Wad, the British made it more convenient for the Arabs to blockade Jerusalem by handing the Legion the Taggart fort of Latrun. Latrun, once a British political prison at one time or another graced by all the leaders of the Yishuv, sat squarely on a junction in the road, blocking the entrance to the Bab el Wad.

Latrun, therefore, became the most important objective of the Israelis. In a desperation plan to capture the fort a special brigade was formed. Most of it consisted of Jewish immigrants freed from Cyprus internment or from the DP camps. The officers were equally unequipped for a major operation. Quickly armed and trained, this brigade was moved into the corridor and a night attack on Latrun was tried. It was ill-planned and badly executed. The disciplined Arab Legion threw it back.

The brigade tried two more attacks on Latrun on succeeding nights with equal lack of success. Then the Palmach Hillmen Brigade, badly overextended by the attempt to cover the long stretch of the Bab el Wad to Jerusalem, nevertheless made an attack on Latrun and almost, but not quite, succeeded in taking the place.

An American army colonel, Mickey Marcus, who used the code name of Stone, had joined the Israeli Army. Now he was sent to the corridor, where his tactical and organizational experience was desperately needed. His efforts there began to bear fruit. In a short time he had reorganized the transportation and amplified the mechanized jeep-cavalry which the Israelis had used in Iron Broom. Marcus was mainly concerned with quickly forming a well-trained and well-led unit capable of carrying out a strategic movement on the Latrun

523

bottleneck. He was close to attaining this objective when another tragedy befell Israel: Marcus was killed.

Jerusalem remained sealed off.

HULEH VALLEY—SEA OF GALILEE

The Syrian Army swept into Palestine from the eastern side of the Sea of Galilee and the Jordan River in several columns, led by tanks and supported by aircraft.

The first Syrian column chose as its objective the three oldest collective settlements in Palestine: the bloc consisting of Shoshanna, the birthplace of Ari Ben Canaan, and Dagania A and Dagania B, where the Jordan flowed into the Galilee.

The Jews were so short of men in that area that they daily drove trucks back and forth from Tiberias to these settlements to make the Syrians believe they were bringing in reinforcements and arms.

The farmers at the Shoshanna bloc had so little to fight with that they sent a delegation up to see Ari Ben Canaan. The Shoshanna bloc was actually outside his command, but they hoped to appeal to a sentimental regard for his birthplace. Ari's hands were full, however, with Kassi at Gan Dafna and at Safed and with another of the Syrian columns. He told the delegation that only one thing might save them—anger. He advised them to make Molotov cocktails and to let the Syrians get inside the villages. If anything could raise the Jews to an inspired defense, it would be the sight of Arabs on their beloved soil.

The Syrians went after Dagania A first. The Haganah commanders ordered the defenders to hold their fire until the tanks leading the attack penetrated to the center of the village houses. The sight of Syrian tanks on their rose gardens enraged the *kibbutzniks* to the point where they loosed their barrage of fire bottles with deadly accuracy from a distance of a few feet and gutted the lead tanks. The Syrian infantry which followed the tanks was no match for the farmers. They fled under the wrath of the Jews and would not return.

The second Syrian column attacked farther to the south in the Jordan-Beth Shean valleys. They managed to win Shaar Hagolan and *kibbutz,* Massada—where the Yarmuk flowed. When the Jews counterattacked, the Syrians burned the villages to the ground, looted everything that could be carried off, and fled. At the Gesher fort, taken earlier by the Haganah, the Jews held and they held at the rest of their Jordan-Beth Shean settlements.

The third column came over the Jordan River in Ari Ben Canaan's area of the Huleh Valley. They overwhelmed and captured Mishmar Hayarden—the Guardpost of the Jordan.

Then they regrouped for the thrust that would carry them into the center of the Huleh to link up with Kawukji's irregulars on the Lebanese side. But Yad El, Ayelet Hashahar, Kfar Szold, Dan, and the rest of the tough settlements stiffened and held, patiently enduring the artillery fire which they could not return, then fighting like tigers when the Syrians came within rifle shot. At Ayelet Hashahar a rifleman actually managed to bring down a Syrian airplane, the credit for which was taken by every *kibbutznik* in the settlement.

Across the way, the Lebanese pawed at the Jewish settlements in the hills and at Metulla. The Lebanese, mostly Christian Arabs, had some leaders who were sympathetic to Zionism, and these people had little desire to fight. They entered the war mainly out of fear of reprisal from other Arab nations and to make a "show of unity." The first time they ran into stiff resistance the Lebanese seemed to vanish as a fighting force.

Ari had successfully blocked a junction of Arab forces in the Huleh. When he received a new shipment of arms he moved quickly to the offensive. He evolved a "defense-offense" plan: those settlements not under direct pressure organized offenses and took objectives rather than sitting and waiting for an attack. By this method Ari was able to keep the Syrians completely off balance. He was able to shift arms and men to the hard-pressed places and ease their burden. He built up his communications and transportation so that the Huleh became one of the strongest Jewish areas in Israel. The only major objective left for him was Fort Esther.

The entire Syrian invasion sputtered. It had turned into a fiasco except for Mishmar Hayarden and one or two smaller victories. The Syrians chose to concentrate their efforts on a single *kibbutz* to make up for their losses. Ein Gev, on the eastern shore of the Sea of Galilee, the home of the winter concerts, was the objective.

The Syrians dominated high hills on three sides of the *kibbutz*. The sea was the fourth side. The Syrians held the columnar mountain of Sussita—the Horse—the ancient Roman city which looked right down into the *kibbutz*. Ein Gev was completely cut off from contact except by boat at night from Tiberias across the lake.

As Syrian guns shelled the *kibbutz* without respite the Jews were forced to live underground. There they kept up their schools, a newspaper, and even their symphony orchestra practice. Each night they came out of the bunkers and tended their fields. The endurance of Ein Gev was matched only by the stand at Negba in the Negev Desert.

Every building in the *kibbutz* was blown to pieces. The

525

Syrians burned the fields. The Jews did not have a weapon capable of firing back. They were subjected to brutal punishment.

After weeks of this pounding the Syrians made their assault, sweeping down from their high ground in numbers of thousands. Three hundred *kibbutzniks* of fighting age met the charge. They fired in disciplined volleys, and snipers picked off the Syrian officers. The Syrians rallied time and again and pressed the Jews back to the sea. But the defenders would not yield. There were twelve rounds of ammunition left to them when the back of the Syrian attack was broken.

Ein Gev had held and with it the Israeli claim to the Sea of Galilee.

SHARON, TEL AVIV, THE TRIANGLE

A large bulge of land in Samaria anchored by the all-Arab cities of Jenin, Tulkarm and Ramallah formed the "Triangle." Nablus, the early base for Kawukji's irregulars, became the chief base of the Iraqi Army. The Iraqis had made an ill-fated attempt to cross the Jordan River into the Beth Shean Valley but were badly beaten, then had settled down in Arab Samaria.

Opposite the Triangle on the west was the Sharon Valley. It was a vulnerable area—the Jews held only a narrow neck of land along the Tel Aviv-Haifa highway, ten miles inside from the Triangle front to the sea. If the Iraqis could make the break-through they could cut Israel in half.

The Iraqis, however, showed an aversion to combat. When the Jews made badly organized attempts on the Triangle city of Jenin, the Iraqi officers fled, and only the fact that their troops were chained in their positions kept them from running away. The thought of attacking the thickly settled Sharon Valley was distasteful; the Iraqis wanted no part of it.

Tel Aviv itself suffered several air raids from the Egyptians before antiaircraft equipment arrived to ward off further attacks. In the Arab press, however, there were at least a dozen reports of Tel Aviv being completely leveled by Egyptian bombers.

The Jews managed to get a few planes into operation and scored one big air victory by driving away an Egyptian cruiser which had come to shell Tel Aviv.

WESTERN GALILEE

After six months Kawukji's irregulars were yet to take their first Jewish settlement. Kawukji moved his headquarters to the predominantly Arab area of central Galilee, around Nazareth. Here he waited for that junction with the Syrians, Lebanese, and Iraqis which never came. There were many Christian Arabs in the Nazareth area who wanted nothing to do with the war and repeatedly requested of Kawukji that he remove himself from the Nazareth Taggart fort.

Most of the western Galilee had been cleaned out before the invasion of the Arab armies. Haifa had fallen to the Jews and the Hanita Brigade's Iron Broom had done away with many hostile villages. With the fall of Arab Acre, the Jews held everything up to the Lebanese border. The Galilee was free of the enemy except for Kawukji in the center.

The advertised "master plan" of the Arabs had become a complete fiasco. The infant Jewish state had borne and blunted the first shock of invasion. Over the world military experts shook their heads in disbelief. The Jews had fought a civil war on a hundred fronts; they had won out over fantastic odds on a dozen more fronts against regular troops.

The Arab victories could be measured. The greatest success had been scored by the Legion which continued to hold Latrun, the key to the Jerusalem blockade. The rest of the Arab armies combined had captured but a handful of settlements and no cities or towns. They had managed to get to within striking distance of Tel Aviv.

Arms poured into Israel, and every day the Jewish military establishment improved. On the day the Israelis declared statehood six new settlements broke ground and throughout the invasion immigrants built more communities. Nation after nation recognized the State of Israel.

Ein Gev and Negba and the hundred other settlements which would not give up, the Palmachniks, who fought for days without food and water, the new immigrants who rushed to the battle lines, the ingenuity employed in place of guns, the raw courage which made extraordinary heroism a commonplace—all these stopped the Arabs.

There was more. Divine inspiration, the destiny foretold by the ancient prophets, the heritage of a people who had fought for their freedom before, the tradition of King David and Bar Giora and Bar Kochba, strength and faith from an unseen source—these, too, stopped the Arabs.

CHAPTER TEN: Barak Ben Canaan had concluded several arms negotiations as well as several diplomatic missions in Europe. He had been sick with anxiety and begged to be allowed to return to Israel. Now past his eightieth year, he had begun to slow up considerably, although he would not admit it.

He arrived in Naples to catch a ship home. There he was

met by Israelis who had a headquarters in the city. Most of them were Aliyah Bet agents now working on dissolving the DP camps in Italy as fast as ships could be procured. The manpower of the DP camps was urgently needed in Israel. Those of military age were rushed to training centers as quickly as they landed. A great part of the rest was sent out to build defensive border settlements.

Barak's arrival was the signal for a gathering, and the midnight oil burned in Israeli headquarters. Over many drinks of brandy everyone wanted to hear and rehear Barak's story of the "Miracle of Lake Success" and of the secret arms deals which he had just concluded.

Then talk turned to the war. There was general dejection over the siege of Jerusalem; news had come through that another attempt to capture Latrun had failed. No one knew how much longer the hundred thousand civilians could hold out.

Around two o'clock in the morning the conversation turned to the private little war the Israelis were having right in Naples over a ship named the *Vesuvius*, a four-thousand-ton Italian motor ship. The *Vesuvius* had been chartered by the Syrians to carry arms to Tyre. The cargo, purchased all over Europe, included ten thousand rifles, a million rounds of ammunition, a thousand machine guns, a thousand mortars, and a variety of other weapons.

A month ago the *Vesuvius* was ready to sail from Naples. The Israelis learned of the ship and cargo from a friendly Italian customs official, and the night before her scheduled departure Israeli skin divers swam along the waterfront, dived beneath the ship, and fixed magnetic mines to her sides. The mines blew three nice holes in the *Vesuvius's* sides but failed to set off the explosives as they had hoped. The ship did not fully sink, but partly submerged at her berth. From that point on the *Vesuvius* became the center of an involved cat-and-mouse game.

Syrian Colonel Fawdzi, in charge of the multimillion dollar cargo, had the ship raised, dry-docked, and the holes repaired. He brought fifty Arab students from Rome and Paris to guard the area and replaced the twelve-man crew with Arabs. Only the captain and his first and second officers were Italians from the chartering company. The captain, however, could not have disliked the pompous Colonel Fawdzi more and secretly agreed to help the Israelis, provided they promised not to damage his ship again. Again they got word that the *Vesuvius* was ready to sail.

The Israelis could not allow the arms to reach Tyre—but how to stop the ship? They had promised both the Italian officials and the captain that they would not blow her up in the harbor. Once on the high seas the Israeli Navy, consisting of three corvettes, could never find the *Vesuvius*.

Barak Ben Canaan was impressed by the importance of the situation and intrigued by the kind of knotty problem he had faced and solved many times before. Once again he conceived the inconceivable. By dawn he had worked out the details of another of his fantastic plots.

Two days later the *Vesuvius* moved out of the Naples harbor and, as it did, the Italian second officer was relieved of radio duty as an extra precaution by Fawdzi. Radio contact, however, was not necessary to the plotters. The Israelis knew the exact instant the *Vesuvius* left. The ship had barely cleared the harbor area when an Italian customs cutter raced for her with its bull horn blasting.

Fawdzi, who knew no Italian, rushed up to the steering room and demanded to know from the captain what it all meant.

The captain shrugged. "Who knows?"

"Hello, *Vesuvius*," the loud-speaker boomed. "Stand by to be boarded!"

A Jacob's ladder was dropped and twenty men wearing uniforms of the Italian customs service quickly boarded from the cutter.

"I demand to know the meaning of this!" Colonel Fawdzi screamed.

The leader of the boarding party, a giant of a man with a great red and white beard, who bore a remarkable resemblance to Barak Ben Canaan, stepped forward and spoke to Fawdzi in Arabic: "We have information that one of your crew set a time bomb in one of the holds," he said.

"Impossible," Fawdzi shouted.

"We happen to know he was bought out by the Jews," the leader asserted sincerely. "We must clear the harbor area before the ship explodes."

Fawdzi became confused. He had no intention of being blown up with the *Vesuvius*, nor did he like the idea of going out of the harbor with this strange gang of Italian "customs officials" aboard. On the other hand, he could not show cowardice by demanding to be taken off the ship.

"You will line up your crew," the man with the big beard said. "We will find the culprit and he will tell us where he has planted the bomb."

The Arab crew was assembled and taken into the gallery for "questioning," and while they were being questioned the *Vesuvius* passed outside of the three-mile limit and the customs' cutter returned to Naples. The disguised Aliyah Bet agents then produced pistols and locked up Fawdzi and the

Arab crew. Later that day, when they had made further distance, the crew was given a compass, a map, and a rowboat and set adrift. Colonel Fawdzi was kept aboard in his cabin. The Israelis took over as crew of the ship as it raced for open sea.

Thirty-six hours later, the *Vesuvius* was met by two corvettes flying skull and crossbones. The corvettes tied up on either side of the motor ship, removed the cargo and crew, and sped off after smashing the radio. The *Vesuvius* then returned to Naples.

Colonel Fawdzi foamed with rage and demanded a full investigation of the high-seas piracy. The Italian customs service, accused by the Arabs of lending the Jews a cutter and uniforms, said it knew nothing about the matter. All cutter movement was clearly logged for anyone to see. The Arab crew followed Arab practice of never admitting failure and twelve different stories came from the twelve men. Other officials of the Italian government assumed that if there was any piracy, they certainly were not aware of it, for the captain of the ship and the first and second officers swore that the Arab crew deserted because they found out the hold held explosives.

Soon a corps of lawyers had the affair so twisted up with contradictory stories that it was impossible to unscramble the facts. The Israelis in Naples added the final touch of confusion by planting the story that it was actually a Jewish ship stolen by the Arabs and that Fawdzi was a Jewish spy.

Colonel Fawdzi took the only course open. He faked an elaborate suicide and disappeared, never to be heard of again —apparently to the regret of nobody.

Two days after the transfer of arms, the corvettes, now flying the Star of David, brought Barak home in a triumphant entry to Israel.

CHAPTER ELEVEN: Ari Ben Canaan received orders to report to Tel Aviv. Headquarters was located in a pension in Ramat Gan. Ari was surprised at the sight of it. The Star of David flew atop the building and uniformed guards of the new army of Israel were everywhere. Identification passes were demanded by the security police before entry was permitted. Outside the headquarters were a hundred jeeps and motorcycles, and there was a military bustle and briskness all about.

Inside, the big switchboard rang constantly. Ari was led through the operations room where huge blown-up maps pinpointed the battle lines and the message center where a battery of radios communicated with the front lines and the settlements. As Ari looked around him he reflected that it was a far cry from the mobile one-desk headquarters of the Haganah.

Avidan, the former head of the Haganah, had given up official command to the young leaders in their mid-twenties and early thirties who had had experience as British officers or were seasoned, as Ari was, in long years of Arab fighting. Avidan now acted in the capacity of liaison between the Army and the provisional government, and although he held no official post he was still a power in general policy as "commander emeritus."

He greeted Ari warmly. It was difficult for Ari to tell if Avidan was tired or had just awakened, or if he was morose or happy, for Avidan always wore the same solemn expression. As they went into his office he ordered all telephone calls or other interruptions withheld.

"This is quite a fancy store you have here," Ari said.

"Not much like the old days," Avidan agreed. "It is hard for me to get over it myself. I drive up here many mornings thoroughly expecting the British to sweep down and throw us all into Acre jail."

"None of us expected you to retire yourself."

"This army and running a big war is a young man's job. Let me argue policy in my old age."

"How goes the war?" Ari asked.

"Jerusalem . . . Latrun. There is our problem. We won't be able to hold out too much longer inside the Old City. God knows how long the New City can stand it if we don't get through to them soon. Anyhow . . . you've certainly done a job for us in your district."

"We've been lucky."

"Safed wasn't luck and neither are those magnificent children at Gan Dafna luck. Don't be modest, Ari. We've got children under siege at Ben Shemen too . . . the Iraqis won't dare take a try at them. Ari, Kawukji is still in the central Galilee . . . we want to get rid of the bastard. That's why I asked you to come down here. I want to extend your command and I want you to take charge of the operation. In a matter of a few weeks we should be able to get a battalion of men up there to you, along with some new stuff."

"How do you figure it?"

"If we take Nazareth I think we've got it all. We'll have the whole Galilee then, all the roads from east to west."

"What about the Arab villages in the area?"

"Mostly Christian, as you know. They've already sent delegations down here to see us. They've asked Kawukji to leave. At any rate, they're not interested in fighting."

"Good."

"Before we proceed with the planning of this operation we want you to secure your area completely, Ari."

"Fort Esther?" Ari asked.

Avidan nodded.

"I need artillery to take Fort Esther—I wrote you that. At least three or four Davidkas."

"Why don't you ask for gold?"

"Look, there are two border villages guarding the approaches to Fort Esther. I just can't get at the place without some long-range pieces."

"All right, I'll send them up to you." Avidan stood up abruptly and began pacing the room. Behind him was a large map of the fighting zones. Ari had felt strangely all along about Avidan calling him to Tel Aviv. He had felt there was more to it than the planning of a new operation and he knew that Avidan was leading up to it now.

"Ari," the bald-headed block of a man said slowly, "you were ordered to capture Abu Yesha two weeks ago."

"So that's why you called me down here."

"I thought it would be best if you and I talked it over before it gets kicked around like a football in general staff."

"I sent you a report that I didn't feel Abu Yesha was a threat to us."

"We think differently."

"As area commander, I believe I'm in the best position to judge."

"Come off it. Abu Yesha is a base for Mohammed Kassi. It's an entry point for the irregulars and it blocks the road to Gan Dafna."

Ari stiffened and looked away.

"You and I have known each other too long for equivocation."

Ari was silent for a moment. "I've known the people in Abu Yesha since I was old enough to walk and talk," he said. "We've celebrated weddings together. We've gone to funerals together. We built their houses and they gave us land to make Gan Dafna."

"I know all that, Ari. Dozens of our settlements are faced with the same thing. We happen to be fighting for our lives. We didn't invite the Arab armies to invade us."

"But I know those people," Ari cried; "they aren't enemies. They're just plain decent farmers who want nothing more in life than to be left alone."

"Ari!" Avidan said sharply. "We have Arab villages who have shown the courage to resist Kawukji and the Arab armies. The people in Abu Yesha made their own decision. It is wishful thinking for you to say it is not hostile. It has to go . . ."

532

"Go to hell," Ari said and got up to leave.

"Don't go," Avidan said quietly. "Please don't go." The big farmer now actually did appear tired. His shoulders sagged. "We've begged the Palestine Arabs a thousand times to stay out of this fight. No one wants to drive them from their homes. Those villages that have shown loyalty have been left alone. But the others have left us no choice. They are used as arsenals and training camps and as bases to attack our convoys and starve our settlements. A hundred thousand civilians are starving in Jerusalem now because of them. We talked about this thing for weeks. We have no choice but to kill or be killed."

Ari walked to the window and lit a cigarette. He stared moodily out of the window. Avidan was right and he knew it. The Jewish settlements had not been given the same choice the Arab had been given. With the Jews it was stand and die . . . fight to the last bullet and be massacred.

"I could easily put another man up in your command to take Abu Yesha. I don't want to do it that way. If you feel morally incapable of doing this then I give you the choice of asking for a transfer from your area."

"To what? Another Abu Yesha by another name?"

"Before you give an answer . . . I have known you since you were a baby. You have been a fighter since you were fifteen years old. We haven't enough men of your caliber. In all those years I've never known you to disobey an order."

Ari turned from the window. His face was lined with worry, sadness, and resignation. He sagged into the chair. "I will do what has to be done," he whispered.

"Get together with operations," Avidan said softly.

Ari shook his head and walked to the door.

"By the way, you are Colonel Ben Canaan, now."

Ari gave a short sarcastic laugh.

"I am sorry, believe me, I'm sorry," Avidan said.

Colonel Ari Ben Canaan, his executive officer and his adjutant, Majors Ben Ami and Joab Yarkoni, mapped out Operation Purim for the capture of Fort Esther and the removal of Abu Yesha as an Arab base. It would be the final securing of the Huleh Valley.

The artillery that Avidan had promised never arrived, but Ari really didn't expect it. He brought the faithful Little David mortar from Safed and rounded up fifty rounds of ammunition.

Frontal attack from Gan Dafna on Fort Esther was ruled out without the artillery. Kassi still had some four hundred men in the area and superior arms at Fort Esther plus better strategic position. Ari also knew that Kassi's men would give a better account of themselves fighting a defensive battle inside the concrete barricade.

Ari had three Arab villages to worry about. Abu Yesha was the first on the road to Fort Esther. High up in the mountains on the Lebanese border a pair of villages flanked the entrances to Fort Esther. Kassi had men stationed in both of these. Ari planned his battle to get around to the rear of Fort Esther. In order to do it he had to get past the two flanking villages.

The move on Fort Esther was planned to involve three columns. Ari took the first unit out. At darkness, they went up the mountainside by goat trails to the Lebanese border with the Davidka and its ammunition. His objective was to get near the first of the mountain villages. The going would be hard and tricky. He had to swing wide and travel many extra miles to be able to get at their rear without detection. He had the mountain, the darkness, and the weight of the mortar and ammunition to contend with. Thirty-five men and fifteen girls carried one round of ammunition each. Another fifty men acted as cover.

Ari's leg still gave him trouble but he pushed his column up the mountain in a brutally paced forced march. They had to make their objective by daylight or the whole operation would fail.

They reached the top of the mountain at four o'clock in the morning, exhausted. But there could be no rest now. They continued at a murderous pace along the mountaintop toward the first village. They swung wide of it and made a rendezvous with a patrol from a friendly Bedouin tribe which was acting as a watch on the village. The Bedouins advised Ari the area was clear.

Ari raced his outfit into the ruins of a small Crusader castle two miles past the village. As dawn began to break they scrambled for cover and collapsed into a heap of weariness. All day they stayed hidden, with the Bedouins standing guard.

The next night the two other columns moved out from Ein Or headquarters. Major David Ben Ami led his men up the face of the mountain on the now familiar route into Gan Dafna. He reached the village by daylight and went into hiding in the woods.

The final column led by Major Joab Yarkoni traced Ari's steps in the wide circular route on the goat trails. His men were able to move faster because they did not have the weight of the Davidka and its ammunition. However they had a greater distance to travel as they had to pass the first village where Ari hid, pass Fort Esther and get near the second of the villages. Again the Bedouins met Yarkoni's column on the mountaintop and led them undetected to their objective.

At nightfall of the second day Ari sent the Bedouin leader to the near village with a surrender ultimatum. Meanwhile Ari moved his men out of the Crusader fort and crept close to the village. The muktar and some eighty of Kassi's soldiers thought it was a bluff: no Jews could have got up the mountains and behind them without detection. The Bedouin returned to Ari with the report that the village needed convincing, so Ari had two rounds of the Davidka fired.

Two dozen of the mud huts were blown to pieces. The Arabs were convinced. With the second mortar shot the officers of the irregulars were leading a stampede across the Lebanese border and an array of white flags was going up. Ari acted quickly. He dispatched a small part of his column into the village to guard it and sped on to the second village where Yarkoni had already opened an attack.

Twenty minutes and three Davidka rounds after Ari arrived, the village fell and another hundred of Kassi's men fled to Lebanon. The awesome Little David had again done its job of inflicting terror and destruction. The two villages had fallen so quickly that Fort Esther was completely unaware of it. They assumed the distant sound of the Davidka shells and the firing were their own men firing for pleasure.

At dawn of the third day, David Ben Ami moved his column out of hiding at Gan Dafna and set up an ambush outside Abu Yesha where Kassi had another hundred men. With Ben Ami's men in position to cut off reinforcements from Abu Yesha, Ari and Yarkoni's forces moved to the rear of Fort Esther. When the Little David opened fire Kassi had only a hundred men in the fort. The rest were in Lebanon or Abu Yesha. Round after round of the buckets of dynamite swished and sputtered through the air and exploded against the concrete blockhouse. Each round came a little closer to the mark, the iron rear gate. By the twentieth round, the gate was blown off its hinges, and the next five rounds fell into the courtyard of the fort.

Ari Ben Canaan jumped off with the first wave of attackers, who crawled forward on their bellies beneath machine-gun fire and intermittent blasts of the Davidka.

The actual damage to Fort Esther was superficial, but the noise and the sudden swiftness of the attack was too much for Kassi and his dubious warriors. They made a feeble defense, waiting for reinforcements to come. The only reinforcements left moved out of Abu Yesha and walked right into David Ben Ami's trap. Kassi saw it through his field glasses. He was cut off. The Jews were at the rear gate. The white flag of surrender went up over Fort Esther.

Yarkoni took twenty men into the fort, disarmed the Arabs and sent them packing to Lebanon. Kassi, now quite docile, and three of his officers were led to the jail as the Star of David was raised over the fort. Ari took the rest of the men down the road to where David had set the ambush. They were ready for the final phase of the end of Abu Yesha as an Arab base.

The people of Abu Yesha had seen and heard the fighting. They knew, surely, their village was next. Ari sent a truce team in to give those who were left twenty minutes to evacuate or face the consequences. From his vantage point he could see many of his lifelong friends trudging out of Abu Yesha toward the hills of Lebanon. Ari felt sick in his stomach as he saw them go.

A half hour passed and then an hour.

"We had better start," David said to him.

"I . . . I want to make sure they are all out."

"No one has left for a half hour, Ari. Everyone is out who is coming out."

Ari turned and walked away from his waiting troops. David followed him. "I'll take command," David said.

"All right," Ari whispered.

Ari stood alone on the mountainside as David led the men down to the saddle in the hill where Abu Yesha nestled. He was pale as he heard the first sounds of gunfire. David deployed the men as they approached the outskirts. A clatter of machine-gun and small-arms fire went up. The Jews dropped and crawled forward in a squad-by-squad advance.

Inside Abu Yesha a hundred Arabs led by Taha had chosen to make a determined stand. The fight for the village was a rare situation for this war; the Jews had superior numbers of men and arms. A withering barrage of automatic fire was followed by a rain of grenades on the forward Arab positions. The first Arab machine gun was knocked out, and as the defenders fell back the Jews gained a foothold in the town itself.

David Ben Ami conducted the battle by sending out patrols to move street by street, house by house, to clean out pockets of resistance. The going was slow and bloody; these were houses built of stone, not mud, and those who remained fought it out hand to hand.

The day wore on. Ari Ben Canaan did not move from his position on the mountainside. The constant sound of gunfire and the bursts of grenades and even the screams of men reached his ears.

The Arabs of Abu Yesha fell back from position after position as the relentless attack cut off any co-ordination between groups or individuals. Finally all those left were squeezed into one street on the edge of town. More than seventy-five Arabs had been killed fighting to the end in the most dramatic defense the Arabs had made of one of their villages. It was a tragic fight; neither the Jews nor the Arabs wanted it.

The last eight men were pushed into the last stronghold, the fine stone house of the muktar which stood near the stream across from the mosque. David called for the Davidka. The house was blown to pieces. The last eight men, including Taha, were killed.

It was nearly dark when David Ben Ami walked up the road to Ari. David was battle weary.

"It is all over," David said.

Ari looked at him glassy-eyed but did not speak.

"There were nearly a hundred of them. All dead. We lost . . . fourteen boys, three girls. Another dozen wounded are up at Gan Dafna."

Ari did not seem to hear him. He started to walk down the hill toward the village.

"What is going to become of their fields?" Ari whispered. "What will become of them . . . where will they go . . . ?"

David grabbed Ari's shoulder.

"Don't go down there, Ari."

Ari looked at the little sea of flat roofs. It was so quiet.

"Is the house by the stream . . ."

"No," David said. "Try to remember it as it was."

"What will become of them?" Ari said. "They are my friends."

"We are waiting for the order, Ari."

Ari looked at David and blinked his eyes and shook his head slowly.

"I must give it then," David said.

"No," Ari whispered, "I shall give it." He looked at the village for the last time. "Destroy Abu Yesha," Ari said.

CHAPTER TWELVE: David slept in Jordana's arms.

She held his head tightly against her breast. She could not sleep. Her eyes were wide, staring into the darkness.

Ari had given her leave from Gan Dafna so the two of them could travel to Tel Aviv together and have a weekend alone. After tomorrow, the Lord only knew how long it would be before she saw him again, if ever. Jordana had known in her heart all along that David would volunteer for such a mission. Since the beginning of the siege he had been eating his heart out for Jerusalem. She saw that distant look of sadness and pain each time she looked into his eyes.

He stirred in his sleep. She kissed his forehead gently and

ran her fingers through his hair and he smiled in his sleep and became still once more.

It would not be right for a *sabra* girl to tell her lover she was ill with worry for him. She must only smile and encourage him and conceal the fear in her heart. She felt weak with apprehension and she pressed him close to her body and wanted to hold him for a night without end.

It had begun the day partition was voted. The next day the Higher Arab Committee called for a general strike which erupted into the savage burning and plunder of the Jewish commercial center of Jerusalem. While the Arab mobs ran wild, British troops stood by.

The siege of the city began almost immediately with Abdul Kadar using Arab villages along the highway to blockade the Jewish convoys from Tel Aviv. While the titanic battles in the corridor raged for the heights, the Kastel and the other villages, the Jews in Jerusalem were frozen, hungry, and thirsty, and under direct cannonading from Kawukji and Kadar. While the Palmach Hillmen fought to keep the road open, the Yishuv organized the convoys which slugged their way along the Bab el Wad until the Judean hills were littered with wreckage.

Inside the city the fighting started with bombings and ambushes and erupted into full-scale war. The Haganah cleared a huge field of fire from King David Hotel to the Old City wall where the irregulars massed and the wreckage was called Bevingrad. The commander of the Haganah in Jerusalem was saddled with problems beyond mere military matters. He was burdened by a huge civilian population that had to be fed and protected in a situation of siege. He was further burdened by the fact that a large part of his population, ultra-Orthodox and fanatical Jews, not only refused to fight, but obstructed the efforts of the Haganah to protect them. In ancient Israel the commander of Jerusalem had been plagued by the same problems. In the siege against the Romans the fall of Jerusalem was hastened by a division of strength by the Zealots, and it led to a Roman massacre of 600,000 Jews. On that occasion the Jews had held out against the Romans for three years; it was unlikely that they could do it again.

In addition to the problem of the ultra-Orthodox and fanatics who refused to fight, the Maccabees only co-operated part of the time and were frequently concerned with carrying on a private war. When they did support the Haganah, it was not with particular distinction. The Hillmen Brigade of the Palmach was overextended and overworked in the Judean hills and quite reluctant to take orders from the Haganah commander of Jerusalem. It added up to a desperate situation in which the Haganah commander could do no right.

Beautiful Jerusalem became battle scarred and bloody. The Egyptians attacked from the south and shelled the city and bombed it from the sky. The Arab Legion used the sacred walls of the Old City as a stockade. Casualties mounted to the thousands. Again uncommon valor and ingenuity were the keynotes of the Jews' defense. Again the Davidka mortar did yeoman's work. It was moved from place to place to make the Arabs think there were many of them.

Outside Jerusalem, when the Arab Legion took Latrun fort they promised to keep the water pumping station open so that the civilian population would have enough to drink. Instead the Arabs blew up the pumping station and cut off the water supply. Cisterns two and three thousand years old were known to exist under Jerusalem. The Jews located them, tore the covers from them and discovered that, as if by a miracle, they still held water. Until emergency pipelines could be built, these ancient cisterns were all that kept the Jews from dying of thirst.

The days passed into weeks and the weeks into months and still Jerusalem held out. Every home became a battlefield. Men, women, children daily girded to battle with a spirit of defiance that would never be conquered.

David Ben Ami's heart ached for Jerusalem. The siege was on his mind all day and all night.

He opened his eyes.

"Why aren't you sleeping?" he asked Jordana.

"I have enough time for sleeping when I am away from you," she answered.

He kissed her and told her that he loved her.

"Oh, David . . . my David."

She wanted to beg him not to ask for this mission. She wanted to cry out and tell him that if anything happened to him there could be no life for her. But she held her tongue as she knew she must. One of his six brothers had died at *kibbutz* Nirim fighting the Egyptians and another was dying from wounds received in a convoy to relieve besieged Negba in the Negev Desert. David's brother Nahum of the Maccabees had chosen to go into the Old City.

David heard the rapid beating of Jordana's heart.

"David, love me . . . love me," she pleaded.

In the Old City of Jerusalem, the Arab mobs surged in behind the Legion to destroy a score of synagogues and holy places, and they pillaged and looted every Jewish house that fell.

The pious ones and their Haganah and Maccabee defenders were squeezed back and back until they held only two buildings, one of them the Hurva Synagogue. It could only be a matter of days before they were all wiped out.

Jordana was awakened by the light of day. She stretched and purred with contentment, for her body was pleased with love. She reached out for David. He was not there.

Her eyes opened with alarm and then she saw him standing over her. David, for the first time, was dressed in the uniform of the army of Israel. She smiled and lay back on the pillows and he knelt beside her and touched her hair, which was a scarlet disarray.

"I have been watching you for an hour. You are very beautiful when you sleep," he said.

She reached out and opened her arms and drew him close and kissed him.

"*Shalom*, Major Ben Ami," she whispered in his ear, and kissed it softly.

"Darling, it's late. I have to be going," he said.

"I'll get dressed right away," she said.

"Why don't I just go right now by myself? I think it will be better this way."

Jordana felt her heart stop. For a fraction of a second she meant to seize him, then she quickly masked her shock and smiled.

"Of course, darling," she said.

"Jordana . . . Jordana . . . I love you."

"*Shalom*, David. Go quickly . . . please."

She turned her face to the wall and felt his kiss on her cheek and then she heard the door closing.

"David . . . David," she whispered. "Please come back to me."

Avidan drove with Major Ben Ami to the flat that Ben Zion, the chief of operations, kept near headquarters. General Ben Zion, a man of thirty-one, was also a Jerusalemite. His aide, Major Alterman, was present when they arrived.

They exchanged greetings and condolences for the death of David's brother at Nirim.

"Avidan tells us you have something of interest," Alterman said.

"Yes," David answered slowly. "Ever since the partition vote, the 'lament of the exiles' has been running through my mind, night and day, 'If I forget thee, O Jerusalem.' "

Ben Zion nodded. He shared David's feeling for Jerusalem. His wife, his children, and his parents were there.

David continued. "We control the road fairly well up to

Latrun. Beyond Latrun, in the Bab el Wad, the Palmach had cleared most of the heights."

"We all know that Latrun is our greatest stumbling block," Alterman said crisply.

"Hear him out," Ben Zion snapped.

"I have been thinking . . . I know that area around Latrun like my mother's smile. I have been going over the ground in my mind, inch by inch, for nearly six months. I am absolutely certain Latrun can be bypassed."

There was a stunned silence for a moment.

"Just what do you mean?" Ben Zion asked.

"If you draw an arc around Latrun from road to road, it is sixteen kilometers."

"But this sixteen kilometers is merely a line on the map. There is no road. Those hills are wild and impassable."

"There is a road," David said.

"David—what on earth are you talking about?" Avidan demanded.

"Over part of the way there is an ancient Roman road. It is two thousand years old and it is completely covered by brush and slide and washout, but it is there. The bed runs through the wadis for about eight kilometers. I know as surely as I stand here that I can follow the wadis for the balance of the distance."

David walked to the wall map and drew a semicircle around Latrun, linking the roads.

Avidan and Ben Zion stared for several moments. Alterman looked cynical. Avidan, who had already heard some of the plans from Ari Ben Canaan, was critical.

"David," Avidan said coldly, "say you are able to find this alleged Roman road and suppose you are able to find a goat path through the wadis—what then? You are still a long, long way from relieving the siege of Jerusalem."

"What I propose," David said without hesitation, "is that we build another road atop the Roman road and eliminate the need for capturing Latrun by going around it."

"Come now, David," Ben Zion said. "According to the route you have drawn on the map we will have to build this road right under the noses of the Arab Legion at Latrun."

"Exactly," David said. "We don't need much more than a trail. Just enough to accommodate the width of a single truck. Joshua made the sun stand still at Latrun. Perhaps we can make the nights stand still. If one task force builds from the Jerusalem end and another from Tel Aviv and we work quietly by night, I know we can complete the bypass in a month. As for the Arab Legion, you know damned well that Glubb won't bring them out of Latrun to fight. He is keeping them where they are safe from open battle."

"We aren't so sure of that," Alterman said. "He may fight for the road."

"If Glubb wasn't afraid of committing the Legion to battle, then why hasn't he attacked from the Triangle and tried to cut Israel in half?"

It was a question no one could answer. It could only be assumed that David was right. The opinion of the staff was that Glubb was overextended and had no intention of fighting beyond the areas of Jerusalem, the corridor, and Latrun. Besides, the Israelis would welcome the chance to meet the Legion in the field.

Ben Zion and Avidan sat quietly and mulled over David's proposal.

"What do you want?" Ben Zion said at last.

"Give me a jeep and one night to drive through."

Avidan was worried. In the early days of Haganah, it pained him every time he drew a casualty. It was like losing a son or daughter. In a small, close-knit community like the old Yishuv, each loss was a personal tragedy. Now, with the war, the Jews had casualties in the thousands and for a small country it was a devastating number. Most of them were the cream of the nation's youth, men and women. No nation, no matter how large or small, had David Ben Amis to spare, Avidan thought. It seemed like a suicide task that David was taking upon himself. Maybe David only thought he knew of a route into Jerusalem because he wanted to believe that one existed.

"A jeep and twenty-four hours . . ." David pleaded.

Avidan looked at Ben Zion. Alterman shook his head. What David wanted to do was impossible. The burden of Jerusalem weighed every heart, it was the life beat, the very breath of Judaism, yet . . . ; Ben Zion wondered if it had not been madness to try to hold the city from the very beginning.

David's parents had suffered enough, Avidan thought. One brother dead and another wounded and a third the leader of the Maccabees suicide squad inside the Old City walls.

David looked from one to the other frantically. "You must give me a chance!" he cried.

There was a knock on the door. Alterman took a communiqué and handed it to Ben Zion. The blood drained from the face of the operations chief. He handed the paper to Avidan. None of them remembered Avidan's ever losing his composure, but now his hand trembled as he read and tears welled in his eyes.

His voice quivered. "The Old City has just surrendered."

"No!" Alterman cried.

David sagged into a chair.

Ben Zion's fists clenched and he gritted his teeth. "Without

542

Jerusalem there is no Jewish nation!" he cried. He turned to David. "Go up to Jerusalem, David . . . go up!"

When Moses led the tribes of Israel to the shores of the Red Sea he asked for a man with such faith in the power of God that he would be the first to jump into the sea. Nahshon was the name of the man who came forward. "Nahshon" became the code name of David Ben Ami's venture.

At darkness David left the town of Rehovot south of Tel Aviv and drove toward Judea. At the foothills, near Latrun, David turned off the road into the wilderness, into the steep rock-filled hills and the gorges and wadis. David Ben Ami was driven by an obsession, but his passion was tempered by his appreciation of the gravity of the mission and controlled by his infinite knowledge of the land around him.

The jeep twisted and banged and rebelled against the torture which no mechanical thing was made to take. In compound low gear David drove slowly and cautiously as he came very close to Latrun. The danger of meeting a Legion patrol was great.

His eyes and instincts sharpened as he saw the fort in the distance. He inched the vehicle down a treacherous slope, in search of the Roman road buried under centuries of debris. He followed the contours of washed-down dirt and rocks, and at the junction of two wadis he stopped and dug up some rocks. Their size and texture assured him that the road was there. Once he had established the general direction of the pathway of Roman legions he was able to move along it more quickly.

David Ben Ami swept in a circle around Latrun, pushing himself and his vehicle without mercy. Many times he cut the motor and sat in frozen silence to listen for an imagined enemy sound. Many times he crawled on his belly in the darkness to feel out the route through the dry, rocky wadis. Those sixteen kilometers were the longest David had ever known. The night passed too quickly for him and with its passing the danger of an Arab patrol increased.

At dawn, Ben Zion and Avidan were drowsy from a night of waiting and filled with apprehension. They now knew the folly of David's attempt; they felt in their hearts that they would never see him again.

The phone rang. Avidan lifted the receiver and listened.

"It is the coding room," Avidan said. "They have just received a message from Jerusalem."

"What is it?"

"I358."

They dashed for the Bible. Ben Zion emitted a long sigh of

relief as he read, "Isaiah: thirty-five, eight: *And an highway shall be there . . . no lion shall be there, nor any ravenous beast shall go up thereon . . . but the redeemed shall walk there . . ."*

Nahshon had arrived in Jerusalem! David Ben Ami had found a bypass of Latrun. Jerusalem still had a chance.

Thousands of volunteers in Jerusalem were sworn to secrecy. They poured out of the city to claw a road through the wilderness along the route that David had found. David returned to Tel Aviv where a second corps of volunteers worked at the opposite end to link up with the Jerusalem people.

The two task forces hid by day and built by night, right under the noses of the Arab Legion at Latrun. They toiled in feverish silence, carrying away by hand each bagful of dirt. Through the wadis and ravines, along the ancient Roman road, the two forces inched toward each other. David Ben Ami asked for permanent transfer to Jerusalem and got it.

Jordana had had a case of nerves ever since she had left David in Tel Aviv. She returned to Gan Dafna where there was a tremendous amount of work to be done rebuilding the wrecked village. Most of the buildings had been hit by artillery fire. The younger children who had been evacuated were now returned. Kitty's cottage had not been too severely damaged so Jordana moved in with her and Karen. The two women had developed a fast friendship. Jordana found herself able to confide in Kitty the things which she could not tell others for fear of showing weakness.

Kitty was fully aware of Jordana's state when she returned from Tel Aviv, though Jordana tried to mask it with an outward show of gruffness. On an evening two weeks after she had parted from David she sat with Kitty in the dining room, having a late snack and tea. As Kitty chatted, Jordana suddenly became pale and stood up quickly and ran from the room. Kitty followed her outside and reached her just as Jordana slumped to the ground. Kitty caught her and supported her, half leading and half carrying Jordana to her office. She stretched the *sabra* on the cot and forced some brandy into her.

It was ten minutes before Jordana came fully around. She sat up in a daze. Kitty made her put her head down. When she had regained her senses Jordana shook her head with disbelief.

"What happened?" Kitty asked.

"I don't know. Nothing like that has ever happened to me. I was listening to you and all of a sudden I couldn't hear you or see you. It turned dark and a cold chill passed through me."

"Go on . . ."

"I . . . I heard David shriek . . . it was horrible."

"Now you listen to me, young lady. You've been so tensed up you're ready to explode. I want you to take a few days' rest. Go down to Yad El with your mother . . ."

Jordana sprang to her feet. "No!" she said.

"Sit down!" Kitty barked.

"It's nonsense. I am behaving shamefully."

"You are acting quite normally. You wouldn't get yourself into such a state if you would let off a little steam and a few tears occasionally and not try to hold it all inside you."

"David would be so disgusted with me if he knew I was carrying on so."

"Oh, stop it, Jordana. Damn your *sabra* pride. I'm giving you a sedative and I want you to go right to bed."

"No!" Jordana said and ran from the room.

Kitty gave a sigh of resignation. What did you do with a girl who felt that any show of emotion would be construed as a weakness. Years of tension and struggle had built a thick skin on the *sabras*. Their pride was fierce beyond comprehension.

Three days after the incident Kitty came into her cottage one evening after sending Karen over to Dov's. Jordana was working on reports. Kitty sat down before the desk. Jordana looked up and smiled, then turned grave as she saw the expression on Kitty's face. Kitty took the pen from her hand.

Neither of them spoke for several moments.

"David is dead," Jordana said.

"Yes."

"How did it happen?" Jordana said in an emotionless monotone.

"Ari phoned a few minutes ago. The details are not clear. It seems that he organized a band of some Palmach, some Maccabees, some Haganah. It was not authorized . . . apparently David had been looking at the walls of the Old City and it was more than he could stand. They made an attack to try to win back the Old City. They conquered Mount Zion . . ."

"Go on," Jordana said.

"They didn't have a chance. It was a suicide mission."

Jordana did not move or even blink her eyes.

"What can I do? What can I say?" Kitty said.

The girl stood up and held her chin high. "Don't worry about me," she said in a clear voice.

If Jordana Ben Canaan had tears for her David, no one ever saw them. She disappeared with her grief into the ruins of Abu Yesha. She sat neither moving nor eating nor drinking for four days and four nights. She returned to Gan

Dafna. As Ari had done with his sweetheart, Jordana never mentioned David's name again.

One night, a month from the time David Ben Ami found the way to Jerusalem, the "Burma Road," the bypass of Latrun, was completed. A convoy rushed through and the siege of Jerusalem was over for all time.

Until that moment no one had known for certain if Israel would live. In the magic instant when the workers from Jerusalem shook hands with the workers from Tel Aviv, the Jews had won their War of Liberation.

CHAPTER THIRTEEN: There were many months of the bitterest and most bloody fighting ahead, but the opening of the "Burma Road" gave the Jews a spiritual lift at a time it was sorely needed.

After the Jews had stopped the first invasion of the Arab armies, the Security Council of the United Nations was able to effect a temporary truce. Both sides welcomed it. The Arabs obviously had to shake up their commands and reorganize. They had lost face in the eyes of the world by failure to overrun the country. The Israelis wanted the time to get in more weapons and increase their operational strength.

The Provisional Government did not have complete control of the situation, for the co-operation of the Palmach, the ultra-Orthodox, and the Maccabees was still a matter of degrees. The Palmach, to their credit, gave up their elite corps and joined the army of Israel en masse, when faced with expulsion from the fighting fronts for failure to take orders from the central command. The Maccabees likewise made up special Maccabee battalions in the Israeli Army, but insisted on their own officers. But nothing could change the unyielding attitude of the fanatics who continued to wait for the Messiah in an absolute literal interpretation of the Bible.

Just as unification of these elements appeared a reality, a tragic event occurred to alienate the Maccabees forever. Maccabee sympathizers in America had purchased a large amount of needed arms and a cargo plane which had named the *Akiva.* Along with the arms, they had several hundred volunteers ready to join the special Maccabee battalions. Under truce conditions, neither side was supposed to rearm nor reinforce any position. Both Arabs and Jews ignored this UN dictate. Both sides secretly moved arms and men around in their build-ups of strength.

The existence of the *Akiva* became known by Israeli people in Europe. The Provisional Government demanded that the

Akiva and its arms be turned over to it. Israel was one nation now, fighting a single war, they argued, and, after all, the Maccabee battalions were part of the army of Israel. The Maccabees objected. They wanted to keep their identification and they argued that the arms were specifically purchased for use of their members.

The government brought up the question of violation of the truce. If the Provisional Government handled the entry of the *Akiva* the chances of getting the arms in secretly were a hundred per cent better than if the Maccabees tried on their own. The Maccabees countered by claiming that they did not have to recognize the truce order for they were independent of a central command. So the bitter squabble raged, with the Provisional Government asserting that there could be but one central authority and the Maccabees claiming otherwise.

The *Akiva* took off from Europe with its first load of arms and volunteers. The government, which sorely needed both the arms and the men, was forced to order the Maccabees to make the plane return without landing. The Maccabees were enraged at this order.

As the *Akiva* reached Palestine, in defiance of the edict, the airdrome was filled with government officials, Maccabees, and United Nations observers. The government radioed the plane a final warning to return to Europe. The *Akiva* refused. The Provisional Government ordered fighter planes up and the *Akiva* was shot down.

Fighting erupted between army and Maccabee troops. In anger the Maccabees withdrew their battalions from the army. Both sides hurled names and charges and countercharges until all justice in the "*Akiva* incident" was buried under a welter of insults and accusations. The bitterness created in Maccabee ranks was permanent.

The incident did prove to be a final clearing of the air. During the years of the British mandate the Maccabees had been a factor in making the British quit by their constant goading. Once the British were gone, terror tactics lost their usefulness and the Maccabees appeared unable to accept the discipline that a field army required. Thus their value as a fighting force was seriously qualified. Their one great victory had been at Jaffa, a city of crushed morale. In other places they had failed. Their massacre at the village of Neve Sadij remained as the one great black mark against the Jews. The Maccabees were activists with great individual courage but by their very nature they rebelled against authority. After the *Akiva* incident they remained as an angry, defiant, political group whose basic tenet was that force conquered all problems.

For a month talks went on with both sides. Count Bernadotte and his American aide, Ralph Bunche, working for the United Nations, were unable to bring the sides together. They could not break down in a month what had been building for three decades. Kawukji, in central Galilee, had been constantly violating the truce. Now the Egyptians broke faith by resuming fighting before the truce deadline was up.

It was a great mistake, for it triggered a new Israeli campaign. If the world's military experts had been amazed by the ability of the Jews to withstand the invasion, they were stunned as the army of Israel went on the offensive.

The new phase of the war opened with the Israel air force bombing Cairo, Damascus, and Amman as a warning for the Arabs to quit similar attacks on Tel Aviv and Jerusalem. The Arabs did not bomb Jewish cities from the air again. Israeli corvettes carried the fight to the enemy by shelling Tyre, in Lebanon, one of the key ports for the entry of arms.

At Ein Gev *kibbutz* on the Sea of Galilee, the farmers, who had been under siege for months and who had broken a Syrian attack, now struck back. In a bold night maneuver, they climbed the Sussita mountain and threw the Syrians from it.

In the central Galilee, Ari Ben Canaan went after Kawukji and Nazareth. By pushing his troops to the limit of their endurance and by making brilliant use of his equipment he completely outmaneuvered and outfought the irregulars. The Mufti's personal general took a sound licking and lost Nazareth. With the fall of Nazareth the hostile Arab villages in the central Galilee collapsed and Kawukji led a flight to the Lebanese border. The Israelis commanded the entire Galilee and all its roads.

In the Bab el Wad and the Jerusalem corridor the Hillmen Brigade widened the way and began moving south toward Bethlehem.

In the Negev Desert, the Israelis held the Egyptians in a stalemate. Samson once set fire to the tails of a thousand foxes and turned them loose on the Philistine fields. Now lightning jeep units with machine guns, called "Samson's Foxes," made fierce attacks on Egyptian supply lines and Arab villages. The terrible siege of Negba *kibbutz* was lifted.

It was in the Sharon Valley facing the Triangle that the Israelis scored their most spectacular success. Using the jeep units to the fullest and led by the former Hanita Brigade of the Palmach, the Jews swept into Lydda and Ramle, Arab towns that had harassed the road to Jerusalem. They captured the Lydda airdrome, the largest field in Palestine, and then swung into the Samarian Triangle to develop a maneuver to encircle Latrun. On the way they brushed aside the Iraqi forces and relieved the siege of another children's village,

Ben Shemen. Just as encirclement of Latrun was near accomplishment the Arabs, in unison, screamed for a second truce. All the Israeli victories had been scored in ten days.

As Bernadotte and Bunche conducted the second truce talks, the Arab world was frantic. Abdullah of Trans-Jordan was the first to see the handwriting on the wall. He went into secret negotiations with the Provisional Government and agreed to keep the Legion sitting and out of action. This would permit the Jews to turn their full attention to the Egyptians. In exchange, the Jews agreed not to go after the Old City or the Legion-dominated Samarian Triangle.

Again the brigand Kawukji broke the truce by attacking from Lebanon. As the second truce ended, "Operation Hiram," named for the Lebanese King in the Bible, blew Kawukji and the Mufti's dreams into smoke, once and for all. The Israeli Army swept over the Lebanese border on the heels of the shattered and fleeing irregulars. Lebanese villages showed an array of white flags of surrender. With Kawukji banished, the Jews pulled back to their own borders, although there had been little to stop them from going clear to Beirut and Damascus.

With the Galilee clear, the Sharon quiet, and a promise to Abdullah not to attack Jordan-held positions, the army turned its full attention on the Egyptians.

Meanwhile the Arab world scrambled to explain away the series of Israeli successes. Abdullah of Trans-Jordan publicly blamed Iraq for the Arab failure: Iraq had failed to attack from the Triangle to cut the Jews in half and had generally made themselves look ridiculous. Iraq, which dreamed of ruling a Greater Arab Nation in its "Fertile Crescent" scheme blamed their overextended supply lines. The Syrians were the most vocal of all: they blamed the Americans and Western imperialism. The Saudi Arabians, who fought in the Egyptian Army, blamed nearly everyone, each Arab country in turn. The Egyptians blamed Trans-Jordan for selling out by Abdullah's agreement with the Jews. However, one of the most spectacular by-products of the War of Liberation was the manner in which the Egyptian press and radio translated Egyptian disasters as victories. So far as the Egyptian public was concerned, their troops were winning the war. The Lebanese and the Yemenites kept very quiet. They were not too interested in the fighting to begin with.

The myth of Arab unity exploded as the Jews continued to administer defeats on the combined Arab strength. The former kisses, handshakes, and vows of eternal brotherhood changed to knife pulling, haranguing, and, finally, political assassination. Abdullah was eventually murdered by Moslem fanatics as he came from prayer in the Mosque of Omar in the Old City. Farouk was thrown out of Egypt by a clique of militarists who spoke the pages of an Arab *Mein Kampf*. Intrigue and murder, the old Arab game, raged at full force.

In the Negev Desert, the army of Israel, now balanced and co-ordinated, brought the war into its closing stages. Suweidan, the Monster on the Hill which had tormented the Negba *kibbutz*, fell. It was at Suweidan that the Egyptians showed their greatest valor.

A bypassed Egyptian pocket at Faluja, which had been under Jewish siege, was later evacuated under truce talks. One of its Egyptian officers was a young captain later to lead the overthrow of Farouk. His name was Gamal Abdel Nasser.

The pride of the Egyptian Navy, the cruiser *Farouk*, had tried to shell a Jewish position a few hours before one of the truces to gain a tactical advantage. It was sunk by Israeli motorboats filled with dynamite which were driven out in the water, set, and rammed into the cruiser's sides.

Beersheba—the Seven Wells, the city of Father Abraham —fell in the autumn of 1948 to a surprise Israeli attack. The Egyptians dug in and built a deep and stacked defense for a stand below Beersheba. The defenses seemed impenetrable. Again the Jews called upon their intimate knowledge of the land. They found a Nabataean path, thousands of years old, which allowed them to encircle the Egyptian defenses and attack from the rear.

From then on it was a rout. The army of Israel lashed out after the fleeing Egyptians. They bypassed the Gaza area and crossed into the Sinai itself.

The Lord has mingled a spirit of perverseness in the midst of her; and they have caused Egypt to go astray in every work thereof, as a drunken man staggereth in his vomit. Neither shall there be for Egypt any work which head or tail, palm branch or rush, may do. In that day shall the Egyptians be like unto women; and they shall tremble and fear because of the shaking of the Hand of the Lord of Hosts, which he shaketh over them.

The words of Isaiah had come true!

At the Suez Canal, the British became alarmed at the Egyptian debacle and the possibility of Israeli penetration near the canal. They demanded that the Jews stop or face the British Army. In warning, the British sent Spitfire fighters into the sky to gun the Israelis. It seemed only fitting somehow that the last shots of the War of Liberation were against the British. The Israeli Air Force brought down six British fighter planes. Then Israel yielded to international pressure by letting the

Egyptians escape. The shattered Egyptian Army regrouped and with fantastic audacity marched into Cairo and staged a "victory parade."

The War of Liberaton became history!

For months there had been truce talk. For centuries there would be arguments over how it all happened. Experts were confounded and realists were confused.

The Arab people of Palestine had long ago accepted the return of the Jews and were prepared to live in peace and benefit from the progress which had been brought after a thousand sterile years. These people simply did not want to fight and never had. They were betrayed by leaders who were first to run in the time of danger. Their courage was mob frenzy. They were confused by catch phrases they did not understand, much less believe in. They were victimized by racist polemics and filled with a fear of a militant "Zionism" that never existed. Arab leaders exploited their ignorance for their own willful purposes.

Some of the Arabs and their armies fought with valor. Most of them did not. They had been promised easy victories, loot, and rape. They had bolstered each other with a false illusion of Arab unity. Obviously, the "cause" was not so great it was worth bleeding for.

There never was a question of the Jews' willingness to die for Israel. In the end they stood alone and with blood and guts won for themselves what had legally been given them by the conscience of the world.

And so—the Star of David, down for two thousand years, shone from Elath to Metulla, never to be lowered again.

The aftermath of the War of Liberation involved one of the most widely discussed and thorniest dilemmas of the century —the Arab refugee problem. More than a half million Palestine Arabs had fled from their homes to neighboring Arab states. All discussions of the disposition of these people became bogged down in furious arguments, accusations, confusion, nationalism, and incrimination. The issue became so involved and mired that it turned into a political time bomb.

Barak Ben Canaan was called upon once more to serve his country. The government of Israel asked him to make a complete study of this apparently insolvable situation. He made a painstaking investigation and his findings filled several hundred pages. In a short summary, Barak shed light on what appeared to be a hopelessly confused problem.

SUMMARY OF THE ARAB REFUGEE SITUATION

The most publicized afterevent of the War of Liberation

has been the Palestine Arab refugee problem. It has become the most potent political weapon in the Arab arsenal.

The Arabs have gone to great lengths to describe the plight of these war victims and to keep the refugee camps as working models to demonstrate to the world Jewish cruelty. Indeed, those who visit these wretched souls are certain to be touched by their plight.

The Arabs would have the world believe that the Palestine Arab refugee is unique. Nothing could be further from the truth. Every war man has waged has created refugees, homeless and displaced people. Today in Europe and Asia, five years after the end of World War II, displaced people number in the tens of millions. This is the very nature of war.

Had the Arab leaders obeyed the decision of the highest international tribunal and adhered to the law, there would have been no Arab refugee problem. The refugees came as a direct result of a war of aggression waged by the Arabs to destroy the people of Israel.

The Arabs created the Palestine refugee problem themselves. After the November 1947 partition vote the Yishuv of Palestine begged the Palestine Arabs to remain calm, friendly, and to respect the unassailably legal rights of the Jewish people.

Despite wanton aggression the State of Israel, in its Declaration of Independence, held out its hand in friendship to its Arab neighbors, even at the moment her borders were being violated.

The avowed intention of murdering the Jewish people and completely destroying the State of Israel was the Arab answer to law and friendship.

Strangely, most of the Palestine Arabs fled even before the invasion. Jaffa, Haifa, and the Galilee created most of the refugees while the fighting was comparatively light.

The first reason for this was that the Palestine Arabs were filled with fear. For decades racist leaders had implanted the idea of mass murder in their minds. These leaders played on the illiteracy, superstition, and fanatical religious devotion of the fellaheen. These leaders never cared for the fellaheen but only for their own personal ambitions. They completely betrayed the people. Blind fear and ignorance caused the first flight of the Arabs. Was this fear founded upon fact? No! At one place, Neve Sadij, there was an unforgivable massacre of innocent people. Otherwise, the Arabs who remained in Palestine were completely unmolested. No Arab village which remained at peace was harmed in any way by the Israelis.

In regard to Neve Sadij we might add that this one example of Jewish excess—in the heat of war, one must remember—

552

pales beside the record of scores of Arab-led massacres in over a three-decade period of nominal peace.

The second major cause of the refugee situation comes from the absolutely documented fact that the Arab leaders wanted the civilian population to leave Palestine as a political issue and a military weapon.

The Arab generals planned an annihilation of the Jewish people. They did not want a large Arab civilian population present to clutter their operational freedom.

The politicians wanted to prove Jewish inhumanity by pointing to the Arab refugees "forced" from their homes. Lastly, the actual fighting helped create part of the refugee situation. Those few Arab villages which fought against the State of Israel were attacked and the Arabs driven from them. No apologies have to be made for this.

Documented proof exists that the Arabs were promised they could return to their homes on the heels of Arab victories to loot the destroyed State of Israel. No one can question Arab hostility toward Israel since the war. They have blockaded the Suez Canal in violation of international agreement, they have boycotted business, blackmailed foreign firms, raided border settlements, and constantly threatened to come back for a second attempt to destroy Israel. In the light of this it is inconceivable that Israel could even consider resettlement of a hostile minority, pledged to destroy the State. We come now to the most horrible of all the facts concerning the Arab refugees. The Arab nations do not want these people. They are kept caged like animals in suffering as a deliberate political weapon. In Gaza, to cite one example, the roads are mined and patrolled so that these refugees cannot reach Egypt.

The United Nations has established a fund of two hundred million dollars for resettlement of the Palestine refugees. There is much lush, fertile, and empty land in the seven million square miles of the Arab world. The Tigris-Euphrates Valley, one example, has some of the richest unused land in the world. It is inhabited by a handful of Bedouins. This section alone could take not only the half million but ten million others as well.

Not one penny of the resettlement money has been used. On the other hand, Israel, an unfertile land whose seven thousand square miles are half desert, has taken in more than a half million Jewish refugees from Arab countries and stands ready to take in that number again.

The Arabs argue that the Palestine refugees themselves do not want to be resettled but want their farms in Palestine back. This is sheer nonsense. The Arabs have cried crocodile tears over the great love these poor fellaheen have for their lost homes.

The fact is, the Palestine fellaheen were victimized by men who used them as a tool, deserted them, and are victimizing them again. Kept penned up, fed with hatred, they are being used to keep Arab hatred of Israel at the boiling point.

If the Arabs of Palestine loved their land, they could not have been forced from it—much less run from it without real cause. The Arabs had little to live for, much less to fight for. This is not the reaction of a man who loves his land.

A man who loves his land, as the Arabs profess, will stand and die for it.

The Arabs tell the world that the State of Israel has expansionist ideas. Exactly how a nation of less than a million people can expand against fifty million is an interesting question.

The Arab people need a century of peace.

The Arab people need leadership, not of desert sheiks who own thousands of slaves, not of hate-filled religious fanatics, not of military cliques, not of men whose entire thinking is in the Dark Ages. The Arab people need leaders who will bring them civil liberties, education, medicine, land reforms, equality.

They need leaders with the courage to face the real problems of ignorance, illiteracy, and disease instead of waving a ranting banner of ultranationalism and promoting the evil idea that the destruction of Israel will be the cure for all their problems.

Unfortunately, whenever an enlightened Arab leader arises he is generally murdered. The Arabs want neither resettlement of the refugees, alleviation of their plight, nor do they want peace.

Israel today stands as the greatest single instrument for bringing the Arab people out of the Dark Ages.

Only when the Arab people get leadership willing to grasp the hand extended in friendship will they begin to solve the problems which have kept them in moral and physical destitution.

BARAK BEN CANAAN

554

BOOK 5

With Wings as Eagles

> *A voice crieth in the wilderness, Prepare ye the way of the Lord, make straight in the desert a highway for our God.*
>
> *They that wait upon the Lord shall renew their strength; they shall mount up with wings as eagles.*
>
> Isaiah

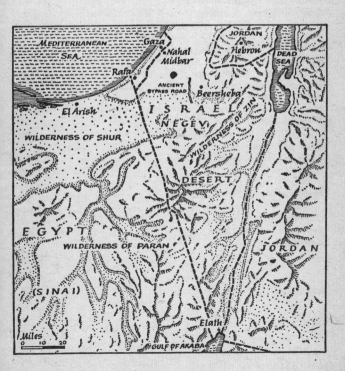

CHAPTER ONE:

NOME, ALASKA
LATE 1948

The entire flying stock of the Arctic Circle Airways consisted of three army-surplus cargo ships purchased on credit by Stretch Thompson.

Stretch had served in Alaska during the war. He had won renown as a young man with a fertile mind and unlimited imagination when it came to devising means of avoiding honest labor. The nights were long in Alaska and they gave Stretch Thompson much thinking time. Most of his thinking time was devoted to exploiting the untapped riches of Alaska and avoiding honest labor. The longer the nights became, the more Stretch stretched—and thought. And one night he hit it.

Crabs!

The entire coast was lined with virgin beds of Alaskan king crabs, some sixteen inches in diameter. Why, with a little enterprise he could train the American public to drool for king crabs. In a year he would make them a delicacy equal to Maine lobsters, Maryland terrapin, or cherry-stone clams. He could fly the giant crustaceans down to the United States packed in ice. Eager dealers would snap them up. He would be rich. He would be known as Stretch Thompson, the King Crab King.

Things did not work out exactly as Stretch had planned. It appeared that the human race was not advanced enough for his king crabs. The cost of a plane, gas, and a pilot seemed, somehow, always to come out to more than what he could get for his crabs. None the less, Stretch was not a man to say die. With deft bookwork and glib tongue he kept the creditors off his back and he did have an airline, such as it was. With bailing wire, spit, and chewing gum he was able to keep the three crafts of Arctic Circle aloft. Just when things looked the darkest, along came a pay load to keep him in business.

Stretch's one bit of continued good luck was his chief, and sometimes only, pilot, Foster J. MacWilliams, known as "Tex" for the usual obvious reason. Foster J. had flown the Hump during the war and was, as Stretch put it, "The best goddam chief pilot any goddam airline ever had." Such was Foster J. MacWilliams' prowess that no one in Nome would bet against his setting down a C-47 on the tail end of an iceberg in the middle of a blizzard—drunk. In fact, on various occasions Stretch tried to raise enough money to make the bet worth while but something always happened . . . either the blizzard slackened or Foster couldn't get drunk enough.

557

MacWilliams was a tramp. He liked flying. He didn't like the fancy stuff of flying over set routes or with a schedule or with first-class craft. Too dull. The risks of flying Arctic Circle suited him fine.

One day MacWilliams came into the shack at the end of the runway which served as office, operations headquarters, and home for Stretch Thompson.

"Goddam, Stretch," he said, "it's colder than a well digger's ass out there."

Stretch had the look on his face of the proverbial canary-filled cat. "Foster," he said, "how'd you like to go to a warmer climate and get *all* of your pay in one bundle?"

"You always did have a gruesome sense of humor."

"I kid you not, Tex. You'll never guess . . ."

"What?"

"Guess."

Foster shrugged. "You sold the airline."

"That's right."

Foster's mouth dropped open. "Who'd buy this pile of crap?"

"I didn't ask their life history. I found out their check was good and that was all she wrote."

"Well, I'll be a sad bastard. That's fine, Stretch, because I'm getting tired of this chicken kacky up here, anyhow. How much you figure you owe me?"

"With the bonus I'm giving you, about four grand."

Foster J. MacWilliams whistled. "That will buy a lot of first-class tail. I can stay drunk and laid from here to South America. That's my next stop, Stretch. I'm going to latch onto one of them South American outfits. I hear they pay big dough hauling dynamite over the Andes."

"There's a hitch . . ." Stretch said.

"I figgered as much."

"We got to deliver the three planes to the new owners. I hired two boys to run the number one and two ships over . . . I can't find another one."

"You mean I'm the only one fool enough to fly the number three ship. Well, that's all right. Where do I deliver it?"

"Israel."

"Where?"

"Israel."

"Never heard of it."

"I was just looking for it on the map, myself, when you came in."

Stretch Thompson and Foster J. MacWilliams searched high and low on the world map. After a futile half hour Tex shook his head. "Stretch, I think somebody gave you the rub."

They went into Nome and asked around the bars where

558

Israel might be. One or two people had heard something or the other about it. Stretch was beginning to perspire in the cold when someone suggested they get the librarian up.

"It's Palestine!" the irate librarian said, "and midnight is no time to pound on my door."

After another search on the map they finally located it.

Foster shook his head. "Goddam, Stretch," he said. "It's smaller than a big iceberg. I'm liable to fly right over it."

Three weeks later, Foster J. MacWilliams landed the number three plane of Arctic Circle Airways at Lydda airdrome. Stretch Thompson had flown over a week earlier and was there to meet him. Foster was ushered into an office which bore the words: PALESTINE CENTRAL AIRWAYS, S. S. THOMPSON, GENERAL MANAGER.

Foster J. MacWilliams smelled a rat.

"How was the trip, old buddy? I'm sure glad to see you."

"Just fine. Now if you'll give me my back pay, old buddy, I'll just shuffle off to Paris. I got my hooks on a real goer and a month before I hitch a ride to Rio D."

"Sure, sure," Stretch said. "Got the check right here in the safe."

Stretch watched Foster MacWilliams' eyes bug out. "Four thousand, five hundred and no zero zero's!"

"The extra five bills is to prove that Stretch Thompson ain't no hog," Stretch said.

"You're a big man . . . always said that."

"Y' know, Tex, this here is an interesting place. Just about everybody around here is a Jew. Been here a week and I can't get used to it."

Foster was reluctant to ask why Stretch was here—but he did.

"Name on the door tells the story. Palestine Central Airways. I thought of the name myself. You see, these guys here haven't had too much experience running a first-class line, so they induced me to stay. First thing I told 'em . . . boys, I said . . . if you want a first class operation, you have to have a first-class chief pilot and I got the best goddam chief pilot any goddam airline . . ."

"I'll see you around," Foster said, standing up quickly.

"What's the fire?"

"I'm on my way to Paris."

"I got a deal for you."

"Not interested."

"Do me the courtesy of listening."

"I'll listen but I'm not buying. I'm going to Paris if I got to swim there."

"Here's the pitch. Like I said, everybody around here is

559

a Jew. They bought out the old Arctic Circle so's they could haul more Jews in. Man, I hear they got them stashed everywhere in the world, and they all want in. All we got to do is bring the bodies in. Can't you see it? Every load a pay load. Cash on the line . . . per head. This is dream stuff, Tex boy. Stick with me and you'll be bathing in it. You know me, Tex . . . I ain't no hog."

"I know what I'll be bathing in. I'll drop you a card from Rio D."

"O.K., Foster . . . been nice knowing you."

"Now, don't get mad, Stretch."

"Who's mad, who's mad?"

"We've had our times in Nome."

"Sure . . . sure . . . swell times. I froze my butt off."

"Well, put her there," Foster said. Stretch shook his hand half-heartedly.

"Now, what's the matter, Stretch? You act like I'm putting a knife in your ribs."

"Going to level with you, Foster. I'm in trouble. We got a hot flash that a bunch of these Jews are sitting around and waiting to be picked up at a place called Aden. I had some pilots but they chickened out on me."

"That's tough titty. You don't con me. I'm going to Paris."

"Sure," Stretch said. "Go to Paris. If I was you I'd go too. I don't blame you. Those other pilots ran like striped apes when they heard there was danger of the Arabs firing on them."

Foster was on his way out. He stopped and turned around.

"You're right, Foster. No use getting your brains blown out. This is a real rough run . . . even rougher than flying the Hump or running dynamite over the Andes."

Foster J. MacWilliams licked his lips. Stretch went into some more dramatics but he knew that the bait had been swallowed.

"Tell you what I'm gonna, Stretch. I'll make this run for you just to help you off a spot. By the time I'm back you'd better gotten your hooks on some pilots. Just one run. Now where the hell is this Aden?"

"Damned if I know."

"Well, let's get a map and look for it."

As Foster J. MacWilliams, American tramp pilot for Palestine Central, nee Arctic Circle, took off from Lydda airdrome he opened a twentieth-century fantasy out of the pages of the *Arabian Nights*.

He flew toward the British protectorate of Aden at the bottom of the Arabian Peninsula, moving right down the Red Sea.

The story actually began three thousand years before

560

Foster's time in ancient Sheba. In the time of the Queen of Sheba, the southern part of the Arabian Peninsula was a land of richness. The people had learned the art of constructing spillways and dams and cisterns to trap and conserve water and, with it, created a garden.

After the Queen of Sheba had made her visit to Solomon, some of Solomon's people left Israel to go to Sheba to establish trade routes through the desert, along the Red Sea, and begin a colony. These Jews came to Sheba in Biblical times, hundreds of years before even the fall of the First Great Temple.

For centuries the Jews in Sheba prospered. They colonized well with their own villages; they integrated into the complexities of tribal life. They became leaders of the court and the most prominent of citizens.

Then came the horrible years when the sands slowly and cancerously ate away the fertile land; the wadis dried and the rains disappeared into parched earth. Man and beast wilted and withered under the unmerciful sun, and the fight to conquer thirst was the fight for life itself. Fruitful Sheba and the neighboring states broke up into jealous and hate-filled tribes which warred upon each other constantly.

When Islam first swept the world, the Jews of the ancient religion were given respect and freedom in their ways. Mohammed himself wrote the laws, which all Moslems were to follow, prescribing the kindly treatment of Jews.

This equality of the Jews was short-lived. As in all Moslem lands, all citizens other than Moslems became scorned as infidels. In their own way the Arabs had grudging respect for the Jews, and in their own way granted them a reasonable amount of tolerance. Arab massacres of Jews were never the calculated genocide of Europe, but rather the flaring of a sudden spark of violence. The Arabs had become too busy plotting against each other to be much concerned with the docile little Jews in the land now known as Yemen; centuries of suppression had removed any warlike qualities.

As in all Arab lands, these Jews lived as second-class citizens. There were the usual repressive laws, unequal taxation, persecutions, and denial of the civil rights given to Moslems. The degree of persecution varied with the particular ruler in the particular area.

A standing rule forbade Jews' raising their voices before a Moslem, building a house higher than a Moslem, touching a Moslem, or passing a Moslem on the right side. A Jew must not ride a camel, for the mount would put his head higher than a Moslem's. In a land where the camel was the chief mode of transportation, this was a severity. Jews lived in *mellahs,* Oriental versions of ghettos.

561

The world moved on and progressed. Time stood still in Yemen. It remained as primitive as the jungle and as remote and inaccessible as Nepal or Outer Mongolia. No hospital existed in Yemen, no school or newspaper or printing press or radio or telephone or highway.

It was a land of desert and vicious mountains linked only by the paths of camel caravans. Hidden cities nestled in twelve-thousand-foot ranges surrounded by hundreds of thousands of square miles of complete waste. Illiteracy was nearly a hundred per cent. Backward, forsaken, wild and uncharted, some of its boundaries were never defined.

Yemen was ruled by an Imam, a relative of Mohammed, and the personal representative of Allah, the Merciful, the All-Compassionate. The Imam of Yemen was an absolute ruler. He controlled the life of every subject. He controlled the gold and the single crop of coffee. He answered to no cabinet. He provided no civil or social services. He held power by dexterously balancing tribal strength, being continually occupied in crushing one tribe or aiding another among the hot desert feuds and the raging jealousies. He kept hostile tribes under control by kidnaping their people and holding them as hostages. He kept hundreds of slaves. He sat in cross-legged pompousness and dispensed justice according to his whim, ordering the noses of prostitutes cut off and the hands of thieves amputated. He scorned civilization and did all in his power to keep it from penetrating his kingdom, although he was forced to yield occasionally from fear of his powerful Saudi Arabian neighbor to the north who dabbled in international intrigue.

Part of the Imam's fear of civilization derived from civilization's desire to subjugate his land. Despite its remoteness it was located in a corner of the world that formed a gateway to the Orient through the Red Sea. Time and again Yemen became a battlefield as colonial expansionists set covetous eyes on it.

The Imam traditionally assumed the role of benevolent despot toward the Jews. So long as the Jews remained subservient they were given some protection. The Imam was cautious: the Jews were the finest artisans and craftsmen of the land. Their generations passed down the arts of silversmithing, jewelry making, minting, leatherwork, carpentry, shoemaking, and a hundred other trades which most Arabs had not mastered. The latter either farmed or comprised the roving Bedouin bands. Thus skill brought the Jews some measure of protection.

That the Jews of Yemen remained Jews was incredible. For three thousand years these people had no contact with the outer world. Their lives would have been much easier had they taken up Islam. Yet the Yemenite Jews kept the Torah, the Laws, the Sabbath, and the holidays through the centuries of isolation. Many of the Jews were illiterate in Arabic but all of them knew Hebrew. There were no presses; all holy books were written by hand with great accuracy and passed down through the generations.

Direct pressure was often brought to bear to make them convert from Judaism to Islam, but they resisted. When the Imam began to abduct orphans and convert them, the Jews embraced the practice of immediately marrying orphans no matter what their age. There were cases of children only a few months old becoming husbands or wives.

In physical appearance, in dress, in action, and in spirit the present-day Yemenite Jews could have been mistaken for ancient prophets. As in Biblical days, they still practiced multiple marriage. They believed in the evil eye, in ill winds and a variety of demons, against which they wore protective amulets. Their belief in the Bible was absolutely literal.

During the years, the Yemenite Jews never stopped looking toward Jerusalem. They waited through the centuries in patience and devotion for Him to send the word for them to "go up." From time to time small groups or individuals managed to get out of Yemen, and they returned to Palestine and established a small community there.

And then, the word came, as the prophets had declared it would!

Yemen declared war upon Israel after the Israeli Declaration of Independence and sent a token force to fight in the Egyptian Army. This action apprised the Jews of the fact that Israel had been reborn. Their rabbis told them it was the message from God. King David had returned to Jerusalem! Their long wait would come to an end! The Haham —the Wise Ones—told them to rise and go up to the Promised Land on wings of the eagle!

When the first stir of this Yemenite exodus reached the ears of those in Israel, the War of Liberation still raged. Little was known of the number of the Yemenites, of how to get them out, or what to do with them.

The chief Haham went to the Imam and petitioned the All-Merciful to allow the Jews to leave. There were a number of political and economic reasons why the Imam felt it was better to keep the Jews. The rabbi intimated that the Imam had better reacquaint himself with the chapters of Exodus in the Old Testament.

The Imam sat cross-legged in his harem and thought for several days. The rabbi had made his point. The thought of the Ten Plagues was in the Imam's heart. Not long before the chief rabbi had petitioned him a typhoid epidemic had wiped out a quarter of his population. He decided that it was a warning from Allah.

The Imam agreed that the Jews could leave with the condition that all property was left to him, a head tax was paid, and several hundred artisans and craftsmen stayed as hostages to teach the Moslems.

The Jews of Yemen left behind their fields and their homes. They packed what they could carry and began a trek through the wild and murderous mountains, the searing sun, and the vast wastelands scourged by hundred-mile-an-hour winds.

They walked toward the border of the Western Protectorate, this gentle little people with olive skins and delicate features. They were turbaned and wore the same kind of long striped robes that were worn in the palace of Solomon. The women from Sa'na were dressed in black gowns with white fringe and they carried their babies in slings on their backs. They trudged along in the fulfillment of a prophecy, easy prey to the Arab tribes who took their meager possessions as toll for the passage.

The protectorates along the Arabian Peninsula consisted of a complex of large and small Arab kingdoms, sheikdoms and Bedouin tribes which skirted the shores from the Red Sea along the Gulf of Aden on through to the Arabian Sea and Persian Gulf. The British controlled the area by a hundred different treaties which paid tribute in arms or money to the tribes for oil rights. In turn, the British attempted to keep the feuds down and give protection and passage.

The key place in this holding was the Crown Colony of Aden in the Western Protectorate. The port of Aden was a passageway between East and West, settled by Greeks, British, Arabs, and Jews, and a blend of oriental filth, Asiatic exoticness, British rigidity, traces of industrial progress, and the wildness of a port of call. It was at once an exciting and disgusting place.

The port of Aden was the goal of the Yemenite exodus. At first the British did not quite know what to do with these people pouring in over their border in caravans that seemed right out of the Bible. They were still at odds with the Jews over the mandate, yet they could feel no hatred for the Yemenites. The British gave conditional approval to the Yemenites to enter and establish camps, provided the Israelis came down and got them out.

They were tragic figures as they came from Yemen, dressed in rags, filthy and half dead from starvation and thirst. Almost all their possessions had been stolen from them by the Arabs. But each man still carried his Bible and each village still carried the Holy Torah of the synagogue.

A hasty camp was set up at Hashed near the port of Aden. The Israelis covered the border between the Western Protectorate and Yemen. As soon as there was news of another group arriving, they rushed transport to the border to bring them to Hashed. There was a shortage of personnel and supplies at Hashed. The organization badly lagged behind the needs of the numbers coming through.

The immigration people faced the additional difficulty of having to deal with a semiprimitive people. The Yemenites could not comprehend things like water taps, toilets, or electric lights. This was a community who had suddenly caught up with almost three thousand years of progress in hours. Motor vehicles, medicine, western dress, and a thousand things were strange and awesome to them. It was a frightening experience.

The women shrieked as doctors and nurses tried to remove their lice-filled rags to exchange them for clean clothing. They refused to have their bodies examined for sores and diseases, and rebelled against shots and vaccinations. There was a continuous fight against the workers who tried to remove temporarily the infants who badly needed treatment for malnutrition.

Fortunately there was a partial solution that kept the workers and doctors from complete frustration. The camp workers, mostly Israelis with an intimate knowledge of the Bible, quickly learned to go to the Yemenite rabbis with appropriate Biblical passages, and thereby nearly anything could be accomplished. So long as it was written in "the Book," the Yemenites would accede.

The Hashed camp grew, and reports along the Western Protectorate frontier told of more Yemenites coming. Under agreement with the British, the Israel Provisional Government had to get them out of Aden. So Arctic Circle Airways became Palestine Central and Foster J. MacWilliams unwittingly answered an age-old prophecy by dropping from the sky with the first of the great "eagles."

The arrival of the plane created tremendous excitement. The first group picked up their Torah and their water bottles and were removed to the airport. They saw the eagle and nodded their heads knowingly: God had sent it as He said He would. But when they were asked to board, they refused. The rabbi in the group remembered it was the Sabbath. A terrible argument ensued. The Hashed camp chief explained that thousands of people were waiting to get to Israel and it was unfair to hold up the eagle for even a day. No amount of arguing could make them break the Sabbath. They sat adamantly under the wings of the eagle and refused to

565

budge. After three thousand years of waiting, they could wait one more day.

Foster J. MacWilliams took one look at these strange creatures, listened to the arguments in the gobbledygook lingo, uttered a short oath to Stretch Thompson and went into town and got very intoxicated.

He was awakened the next morning and carted to the airport with a horrible throbbing hangover from mixing Greek ouzo, rice wine, and Scotch. He watched the Yemenites carrying their water bottles and their Torah aboard the plane.

"Jesus H. Christ," Foster commented on the procession.

"Captain MacWilliams," a voice said behind him. He turned and faced a tall, well-shaped *sabra* who introduced herself as Hanna. She was in her mid-twenties and wore the traditional blue of a *kibbutz* and had sandals on her feet. "I will be flying with you and taking care of the passengers."

At that point the trip started to become interesting to Foster. Hanna was unconcerned that he was looking her over very carefully. "Do you have any particular instructions? I mean this is our first experiment."

"Hell, no. Just keep them gooks out of the pilot's cabin. Of course, *you* are welcome to come in . . . any time. And call me 'Tex.'"

Foster was watching the loading. The line of Yemenites seemed endless. "Hey! What's the score? How many of them do you think that plane will hold?"

"We have a hundred and forty listed."

"What! You crazy? We won't get that thing into the air. Now, Hanna, you just run up there and tell whoever is putting those people on to take half of them off."

"Captain MacWilliams," the girl pleaded, "they are very light people."

"So are peanuts light. That don't mean that I can haul a billion of them."

"Please. I promise you won't have any trouble with them."

"You're damned right I won't. We'll all be dead at the end of the runway."

"Captain MacWilliams. Our situation is desperate. The British have ordered us to get them out of Aden. They are pouring over the border by the hundreds every day."

Foster grumbled and studied the weight charts. The Israeli workers nearby held their breath as he calculated. He made the mistake of looking up into Hanna's eyes. He refigured, cheated a bit, and reckoned with luck the old ship could rev up enough steam to get up in the air. Once up, he'd keep her up . . . somehow. "Hell, leave them in," he said, "this is my first and last trip, anyhow."

566

The camp director handed him the final manifest. A hundred and forty-two Yemenites were packed into the craft. Hanna got the food and supplies aboard and he climbed up the ladder.

The stench hit his nostrils!

"We didn't have time to bathe them all," Hanna apologized. "We didn't know when you were coming."

He poked his head in the main cabin. It was jammed tight with the little people. They sat cross-legged and frightened on the floor. The smell was horrible.

Foster stepped in and closed and locked the door. Whereupon the unventilated hundred-and-twenty-degree heat began to work on the odors. He worked his way forward an inch at a time. By the time he reached the pilot's cabin he was an interesting shade of green. He threw the window open to get air but instead got a blast of heat. He ran up the engines and as he taxied down the runway he held his head out of the window and vomited. He continued retching as he gunned the plane down the runway and barely lifted at the last inch. He sucked a lemon as he fought for altitude, and finally, with the coming of cooler air, his stomach came under control.

It was choppy and the plane bounced badly as he tried to get height. He "turned the corner" at the Strait of Bab el Mandeb and beelined up the center of the Red Sea with Saudi Arabia on one side and Egypt on the other.

Hanna came in and she, too, was green. "Can't you make this plane stop bouncing?" she said. "They're all throwing up in there."

Foster shut off the heat in the main cabin. "Get in there and open the air vents. I'll try to get a little higher. The cold air will straighten them out."

His head throbbed from the hangover. Why did he ever let Stretch Thompson talk him into this?

In another half hour, Hanna returned. "They're all complaining that they are freezing . . . so am I."

"You got your choice—if I turn on the heat they'll start vomiting again."

"Let them freeze," Hanna mumbled, and returned to her passengers.

In a few moments she ran into the cabin shrieking and screaming in Hebrew.

"Speak English!"

Hanna pointed to the main cabin. "Fire . . . they've started a fire to keep warm."

The plane was on automatic pilot and Foster tore out, throwing bodies to right and left. A small fire was going in the middle of the floor. He stamped it out in a rage and went to Hanna, who sagged limply by the compartment door.

"Do you know how to talk to these people?"

"Yes . . . Hebrew . . ."

Foster shoved the intercom microphone into her hands. "Now you tell them the next one who moves out of his place is going for a swim in the Red Sea!"

The Yemenites had never heard a loud-speaker before. When they heard Hanna's voice they all began pointing to the ceiling and, terrified, they cried and cringed.

"What the hell's the matter with them? What did you tell them?"

"They've never heard it before. They think it's God commanding them."

"Good. Don't tell them no different."

Things went fairly well for the next few hours. There were a few minor incidents, nothing bad enough to endanger the plane. Foster had just begun to relax when he heard another loud commotion from the main cabin. He closed his eyes. "Dear Lord," he sighed, "I'll be a good Christian from now on. Just let this day end."

Hanna returned.

"I'm afraid to ask," Foster mumbled.

"Tex," she said, "you are the godfather of a baby boy."

"What!"

"We've just had a birth."

"No . . . no . . . no!"

"It's all right," Hanna said. "Giving birth is a very routine matter with them. Mother and son are resting well."

He closed his eyes and gulped.

Nothing more happened for an hour—suspiciously, Foster thought. The little people got used to the sound of the engines of the "eagle" and began to doze off one by one, tired from their ordeal. Hanna brought a bowl of hot broth to Foster and they began to laugh over the events of the day. Foster asked Hanna a lot of questions about the Yemenites and the war.

"Where are we now?"

Foster, pilot, co-pilot, navigator, and radio operator, looked up at the map. "We'll be turning the corner pretty soon and go up the Gulf of Akaba. On the way down I was able to see the battle lines in the desert."

"I hope the war will be over soon."

"Yeah, war's rough. Say, how in hell did you ever get roped into a job like this? Whatever they pay you, it's worth double."

Hanna smiled. "I don't get paid for this."

"Don't get paid?"

"No. I was sent here. I may go out with these people to build a settlement or I may continue this run."

"I don't dig you at all."

568

"It is rather hard to explain. Sometimes outside people don't understand how we feel. Money means nothing to us. Getting these people into Israel means everything. Sometime I'll explain it better."

Foster shrugged. A lot of strange things were happening. Well, it didn't matter, he thought. It was worth the ride, but once on a run like this was enough.

After a while he pointed ahead. "That's Israel," he said. Hanna ran to the microphone.

"What the hell you doing!"

"Please let me tell them, Tex. They've been waiting for this moment for . . . thousands of years."

"They're liable to tear the plane apart!"

"I promise . . . I'll make them stay calm."

"Well . . . go on."

He set the automatic pilot again and went back to make sure they didn't blow the plane up. Hanna made the announcement.

A fantastic scene of jubilation broke out. Crying, singing, laughing, praying. Whoops of joy—dancing—hugging.

"My God," Foster marveled, "they didn't make this much fuss when we beat Georgia Tech in the Cotton Bowl."

A Yemenite woman took his hand and kissed it. He pulled away and returned to the controls. They continued cheering and singing all the way to Lydda. As the plane touched the end of the runway the din rose above the sound of the engines.

Foster watched them pour out of the plane, fall on their knees, and kiss the ground of Israel, weeping.

"Good-by, Tex," Hanna said. "I am sorry you are leaving, but have a good time in Paris."

Foster J. MacWilliams came slowly down from the plane. He looked at the scene of bustle. Ambulances and buses stood by. There were dozens of girls like Hanna mingling among the little Yemenites, calming them and joining in their joy. Foster froze at the bottom of the steps and a strange new feeling churned inside him.

He did not even see Stretch Thompson rush out for him.

"Good go, Foster baby! How'd the crate hold up?"

"Huh?"

"I said, how'd she fly?"

"Like an eagle."

A half dozen officials from immigration pumped Foster's hand and pounded his back.

"How'd they behave?"

"Was it a routine flight?"

Foster shrugged. "Routine," he said, "just routine."

Stretch led Foster away from the scene of jubilation. Foster stopped and looked back for a second and Hanna waved to him and he waved back.

"Well, Foster, you can go to Paris now. I've got my crews in and we dug up another plane."

"If you're in a jam, Stretch, I *could* take one more run. But it would be my last."

Stretch scratched his head. "I don't know . . . Well, maybe I can sign you on for one run—to try out the new ship." Hooked! Stretch said in glee to himself. I got the bastard hooked!

It was the beginning to Operation Magic Carpet.

Stretch Thompson, the erstwhile King Crab King, brought in rough-and-ready American flyers who had flown the Berlin airlift. Each new pilot and crew in turn became obsessed with the mission of bringing the Yemenites to their Promised Land.

Many times the planes were almost ready to come apart. Yet, no craft was ever lost, despite being overworked and underserviced. The pilots on Magic Carpet began to believe that the planes were being divinely sustained so long as they carried Yemenites.

Foster J. MacWilliams never did get to Paris. He flew the Aden run until all the Yemenites were evacuated and then he went on to Operation Ali Baba, the airlift of the Iraqi Jews from Bagdad. Foster worked longer and harder hours than any pilot in the history of aviation. As soon as his ship would land at Lydda with a load of immigrants, he would grab a few hours sleep right at the airport while his plane was being serviced. As soon as the plane was ready, he flew out again. In the next few years Foster flew four hundred missions covering millions of miles and bringing in nearly fifty thousand Jews to Israel.

He kept swearing that each trip was his last, right up to the time he married Hanna and took an apartment in Tel Aviv.

Magic Carpet was the beginning. They came from the hinterlands of Kurdistan and Iraq and Turkey.

A warlike lost tribe of Jews in Hadhramaut in the Eastern Protectorate fought their way to Aden.

They poured out of the displaced persons camps in Europe.

Jews came to Israel from France and Italy and Yugoslavia and Czechoslovakia and Rumania and Bulgaria and Greece and Scandinavia.

Across the breadth of northern Africa they arose from the *mellahs* of Algeria and Morocco and Egypt and Tunisia.

In South Africa, the wealthy Jewish community and the most ardent Zionists in the world went to Israel.

570

They came from China and India where they had settled three thousand years before.

They came from Australia and Canada and England.

They came from the Argentine.

Some walked through burning deserts.

Some flew on the rickety craft of the airlift.

Some came in jam-packed holds of cattle freighters.

Some came in deluxe liners.

They came from seventy-four nations.

The dispersed, the exiles, the unwanted came to that one little corner of the earth where the word Jew was not a slander.

CHAPTER TWO: The trickle became a stream and then a deluge of humanity.

The exodus soon doubled, then began to triple, the population of Israel. The economy, ruptured by war, buckled under the flood of immigrants. Many came with little more than the clothes they were wearing. Many were old and many were ill and many were illiterate, but no matter what the condition, no matter what the added burden, no Jew was turned away from the doors of Israel.

It was not a melting pot, it was a pressure cooker, for they came from every corner of the earth and had lived under every variety of circumstance.

Tent cities and ugly corrugated-tin-shack villages sprang up to blot the landscape from the Galilee to the Negev. Hundreds of thousands of people lived "under canvas," in makeshift hovels, breaking down the medical, educational, and welfare facilities.

Yet there was an attitude of optimism all over the land. From the moment the downtrodden set foot on the soil of Israel they were granted a human dignity and freedom that most of them had never known, and this equality fired them with a drive and purpose without parallel in man's history.

Every day new agricultural settlements sprang up. The immigrants went out to attack the wastes and the desert with the same fervor that the early pioneers had shown in rolling back the swamps.

Cities and towns seemed to spring up from the earth.

South Africans and South Americans and Canadians poured money into industry. Factories were built until the manufacturing potential reached one of the highest levels in Africa or Asia. General scientific, medical, and agricultural research reached an advanced stage.

Tel Aviv expanded into a bustling metropolis of a quarter of a million people, and Haifa grew into one of the most important ports on the Mediterranean. In both cities, heavy industry sprang up. New Jerusalem, the capital and educational center of the new nation, expanded into the hills.

Chemicals, drugs, medicines, mining, engineering, shoe and clothing manufacturing—the list grew into thousands of items. Cars were assembled and buses were built. Tires were made and airstrips laid down, and a network of highways spanned the nation.

Housing, housing, housing—people needed homes, and the concrete and steel skylines pushed farther into the suburbs almost by the hour. The sound of the hammer, the music of the drill, the concrete mixer, the welding torch never stopped in Israel!

The arts flourished. Bookstores lined Herzl Street and Allenby Road. In every *kibbutz* and in every home and in every *moshav* shelves were filled with books written in a dozen languages. Musicians, painters, writers put this dynamic new society into words and on canvas and into melody.

From Metulla to Elath, from Jerusalem to Tel Aviv there was the electrifying feel and smell of one huge boom town.

Yet life was brutally hard. Israel was a poor and unfertile country and every single advance was made with sweat. Workers labored exhausting hours for little pay. Those out in the settlements fighting the soil toiled under nearly unbearable conditions. All the citizens were taxed to the breaking point to pay for the new immigrants pouring in. Clawing, bleeding, conquering with their bodies and minds, they made the tiny nation live and grow.

A national airline took to the skies.

A merchant marine flying the Star of David began to sail to the corners of the earth.

The people forged ahead with a determination that captured the heart of the civilized world. Young Israel stood out as a lighthouse for all mankind, proving what could be done with will power and love. No one in Israel worked for comfort in his own lifetime: it was all for tomorrow, for the children, for the new immigrants coming in. And in the wake of this drive, the tough young *sabra* generation emerged a generation never to know humiliation for being born a Jew.

Israel became an epic in the history of man.

The Negev Desert composed half the area of Israel. It was for the most part a wilderness, with some areas which resembled the surface of the moon. This was the wilderness of Paran and Zin where Moses wandered in search of the Promised Land. It was a broiling mass of denuded desolation where the heat burned down at a hundred and twenty-five degrees over the endless slate fields and deep gorges and canyons. Mile after mile of the rock plateaus would not give life to so much as a single blade of grass. No living thing, not even a vulture, dared penetrate.

The Negev Desert became Israel's challenge. The Israelis went down to the desert! They lived in the merciless heat and they built settlements on rock. They did as Moses had done: they brought water from the rocks, and they made life grow.

They searched for minerals. Potash was pulled from the Dead Sea. King Solomon's copper mines, silent for eternities, were made to smelt the green ore again. Traces of oil were found. A mountain of iron was discovered. The northern entrance to the Negev, Beersheba, became a boom town with a skyline springing up on the desert overnight.

The greatest hope of the Negev was Elath, at the southern tip on the Gulf of Akaba. When Israeli troops arrived at the end of the War of Liberation it consisted of two mud huts. Israel had the dream of making a port here with a direct route to the Orient, someday when the Egyptians lifted the blockade of the Gulf of Akaba. They built in preparation for that day.

It was here in the Negev Desert that Colonel Ari Ben Canaan volunteered for duty after the War of Liberation. He was assigned the task of learning every inch of this vital place hemmed in by three sworn enemies, Egypt, Jordan, and Saudi Arabia.

Ari took troops over the killing slate fields and through the wadis in places where no human was meant to travel. He devised training so brutally hard that few armies of the world could duplicate it. All officer candidates were sent to Ari to receive some of the most severe physical testing human beings could stand.

Ari's permanent troops became known as "the Beasts of the Negev." They were a raw, spirited breed of desert rats who hated the Negev while they were in her and longed for her when they were away. Twenty parachute drops, hundred-kilometer forced marches, road-gang labor, hand-to-hand combat were all part of the experiences that made the Beasts of the Negev men among men. Only the toughest could qualify. The army of Israel gave no medals for bravery—one soldier was considered as brave as the next—but those who wore the shield of the Beasts of the Negev were held in special awe.

Ari's base was Elath. He watched it grow into a town of a thousand hardy pioneers. Water was piped in and the copper mines went into full operation. Paths grew to roads as the Jews worked to strengthen their southern foothold.

There were whispers about the strangeness of Colonel Ben

Canaan. He never seemed to laugh, rarely to change his hard expression. There seemed to be a sorrow and longing gnawing at him, forcing him to push himself and his troops too, almost beyond human endurance. He refused to come out of the desert for two long years.

Kitty Fremont had become known as "the Friend," a title hitherto conferred only upon P. P. Malcolm, the founder of the Night Raiders. After the War of Liberation, Kitty involved herself in immigration work and soon was the chief trouble shooter for the Zion Settlement Society.

In January of 1949 at the beginning of Magic Carpet, Kitty had been asked to leave Gan Dafna and go to Aden to organize the medical facilities in the children's compound of the Hashed camp. Kitty proved a wizard at the chore. She brought order out of chaos. She was firm in her orders, yet tender in her treatment of the youngsters who had walked from Yemen. In a matter of months she had become a key official in the Zion Settlement Society.

From Aden she went directly to Magic Carpet at Bagdad, an airlift operation twice the size of the Yemenite airlift. Then with things under control in Iraq she rushed to Morocco, where tens of thousands of Jews poured out of the *mellahs* of Casablanca to go "up" to Israel.

She went from place to place as the *aliyahs* of the exodus formed. She made hasty flights to the European DP camps to break bottlenecks and she scoured Europe to find personnel and supplies. When the high point of the flood receded, Kitty was recalled to Jerusalem, where the Zion Settlement Society assigned her as an official in Youth Aliyah.

She had helped bring the youngsters in. Now she went at the job of getting them integrated into the complex society of Israel. Villages like Gan Dafna were the answers, but they were too few for the numbers arriving. The older ones received an education from the army of Israel, which became the greatest single integration instrument in the country, among other things teaching every new soldier to read and write Hebrew.

Kitty Fremont by now spoke a fluent Hebrew. She was at home flying in with Foster MacWilliams and a load of tubercular children, or visiting a border *kibbutz*. "Shalom, Giveret Kitty," was a password in a hundred places which held her children.

And then something happened that Kitty found both heartwarming and heartbreaking at once. Kitty began to see the infants of the older youths she had known at Gan Dafna who had married and gone to the settlements. Some of them had been her babies in the camp in Cyprus and on the *Exodus*, and now they had children of their own. Kitty had watched the machinery of Youth Aliyah grow until it could handle any emergency. She had helped set up the administration and train the people, from the first harrowing trials of inexperience to the point where they constituted a smooth-functioning organization. Now Kitty Fremont suddenly realized, with heavy heart, that her work was done. Neither Karen nor Israel would need her, and she decided she should leave forever.

CHAPTER THREE: Barak Ben Canaan reached his eighty-fifth year.

He retired from public life and was content to worry about running his farm at Yad El. It was what he had longed for for half a century. Even at his great age Barak remained a powerful man, mentally alert and physically able to put in a full day's work in his fields. His enormous beard was almost fully white, but there were still traces of the old red flame in it and his hand still had a grip of steel. The years after the War of Liberation gave him great contentment. He had time, finally, to devote to himself and Sarah.

His happiness, however, was qualified by the unhappiness of Jordana and Ari. Jordana did not get over the death of David Ben Ami. She was wild and restless. She had traveled in France for a while and she plunged into a few unsatisfying affairs that ended in bitterness. At last she returned to Jerusalem, David's city, and went back to the university, but there was an eternal emptiness about her.

Ari had banished himself to the Negev. Barak knew the reason for Ari's exile, but he was unable to reach his son.

It was just after his eighty-fifth birthday that Barak developed stomach pains. For many weeks he said nothing about them. As he thought of it, he was entitled to a few aches and pains. A nagging cough followed the pains, impossible to conceal from Sarah. She insisted he see a doctor but Barak made light of it. Whenever he did promise, he generally found reason to put off a visit to the doctor.

Barak received a call from Ben Gurion asking if he and Sarah would come to Haifa for the celebration of the third Independence Day and sit in the reviewing stand. It was a singular honor for the old man and he said he would come. Sarah used the occasion of the trip as a lever to make Barak promise to get a full examination. They left for Haifa five days before the celebration. Barak went into the hospital to undergo a complete physical check-up. He stayed in the hospital until the day of Independence eve.

"What did the doctors say?" Sarah asked.

Barak laughed. "Indigestion and old age. They gave me some pills."

Sarah tried to press the issue.

"Come on, old girl. We are here to celebrate Independence Day."

Crowds had been pouring into Haifa all day. They hitchhiked, drove, and came by plane and train. The city was bulging with humanity. All day long people stopped by Barak's hotel room to pay their respects to him.

In the evening a torchlight parade of youth groups started the celebrations. They passed in review before the green at the City Hall on Har Ha-Carmel and after the usual speeches there was a fireworks display from Mount Carmel.

The entire length of Herzl Street was packed with tens of thousands of people. Loud-speakers played music and every few yards *hora* rings formed. Herzl Street was a riot of whirling feet and music and color. Barak and Sarah joined the *hora* rings and danced to riotous applause.

Barak and Sarah were invited as guests of honor to the Technical Institute where the "Brotherhood of Fire," the Palmach fighters during the riots, had gathered. They lit a huge bonfire and Yemenites danced and Druse Arabs danced and a lamb was roasted and Arab coffee was brewed and a chorus sang oriental and Biblical songs. All over the campus of the Technical Institute boys and girls from the settlements slept in each other's arms. The "Brotherhood of Fire" danced and sang until daybreak.

Sarah and Barak returned to their hotel to freshen up, and even at daybreak the dancing was still going on in all the streets. Later in the day they drove in an open car along the parade route, to thunderous cheers, and went to the reviewing stand alongside the President.

Carrying banners like the ancient tribes, New Israel marched past Barak—the Yemenites, now proud and fierce soldiers and the tall strong *sabra* boys and girls and the flyers from South Africa and America and the fighters who had come from every corner of the world. The elite paratroops in their red berets and the border guards in green marched by. Tanks rumbled and planes roared overhead. And then Barak's heart skipped a beat as the ovation rose in a new crescendo and the bearded, leathery Beasts of the Negev saluted the father of their commander.

After the parade there were more speeches and parties and celebrations. When Barak and Sarah left for Yad El two days later, dancers were still whirling in the streets.

No sooner had they reached their cottage at Yad El than Barak broke into a long, wracking spasm of coughing, as though he had been holding it in by main strength during the celebrations. He sagged into his big chair, exhausted, as Sarah brought him some medicine.

"I told you it would be too much excitement," she admonished. "You should start acting your age already."

Barak's mind was on the tanned, rough youngsters marching in the parade. "The army of Israel . . ." he mumbled.

"I'll make some tea," she said, fondly mussing his hair.

Barak took her wrist and pulled her down on his lap. She rested her head on his shoulder and then looked at him questioningly, and he turned his eyes away.

"Now that the celebrations are through," Sarah said, "tell me what the doctors really told you."

"I never have been able to lie to you very well," he said.

"I won't make a fuss, I promise."

"Please understand that I am ready," Barak said. "I think I have known it all along."

Sarah uttered a short cry and bit her lip.

Barak nodded slowly. "You had better send for Ari and Jordana."

"Cancer?"

"Yes."

"How long?"

"A few months . . . a few wonderful months."

It was hard to think of Barak as anything but a giant. Now, in the succeeding weeks, his age showed frightfully. The flesh had melted from his powerful frame and he was bent with age and his complexion had turned sallow. He was in great pain but he hid the fact and adamantly refused to be moved to a hospital.

His bed was arranged by a window so that he could spend his days looking out upon his fields and up the hills to the border of Lebanon. When Ari arrived he found Barak here, gazing with sadness toward the place where Abu Yesha no longer existed.

"*Shalom, abba,*" Ari said embracing Barak. "I came as quickly as I could."

"*Shalom,* Ari. Let me look at you, son. It has been so long . . . over two years. I thought you might be at the celebrations with your troops."

"The Egyptians have been acting up at Nitzana. We had to make a reprisal."

Barak studied his son. Ari was bronzed from the Negev sun and looked as powerful as a lion.

"The Negev agrees with you," he said.

"What is all this nonsense *ema* tells me?"

"Don't feel obligated to cheer me up, Ari. I am ancient enough to die gracefully."

577

Ari poured some brandy and lit a cigarette while Barak continued to study him. Tears welled in the old man's eyes.

"I have been happy these days, except for you and Jordana. If I could only go and know I am leaving you content."

Ari sipped his brandy and turned his eyes away. Barak took his son's hand.

"They tell me you could be chief of staff of the army of Israel someday, if you would choose to come out of the desert."

"There is work to be done in the Negev, Father. Someone has to do it. The Egyptians are forming *fedayeen* gangs of murderers to cross the border and raid our settlements."

"But you are not happy, Ari."

"Happy? You know me, Father. I'm not given to making demonstrations of happiness like new immigrants."

"Why have you shut yourself off from me and your mother for two years?"

"I am sorry about that."

"You know, Ari, for the first time in my life, these past two years, I have had the luxury of being able just to sit and think. It is wonderful for a man to be able to meditate in peace. And in these last few weeks I have had even more time. I have thought of everything. I know that I have not been a good father. I have failed you and Jordana."

"Come, Father . . . I won't listen to such nonsense. Don't get sentimental on me."

"No, there's truth in what I say. It seems now I see so clearly. You, and Jordana, and I . . . the little time I have been able to give you . . . and Sarah. Ari, for a family this is wrong."

"Father . . . please. No son has had the love and the understanding that I have. Perhaps all fathers believe they could have done more."

Barak shook his head. "When you were a small boy, you were a man. You stood beside me and worked these swamps when you were twelve. You have not needed me since I put a bull whip in your hands."

"I don't want to hear any more of this. We live in this country for what we can do for tomorrow. It is the way you had to live and the way I live now. I won't let you torment yourself. We had to live this way because we have never had a choice."

"That is what I try to tell myself, Ari. I say what else? A ghetto? A concentration camp? Extermination ovens? I say anything is worth this. Yet, this freedom of ours . . . the price is so high. We cherish it so fiercely that we have created a race of Jewish Tarzans to defend it. We have been

578

able to give you nothing but a life of bloodshed and a heritage of living with your back to the sea."

"No price is too great for Israel," Ari said.

"It is—when I see sadness in my son's eyes."

"You didn't take David Ben Ami from Jordana. It is the price of being born a Jew. Is it not better to die for your country than to die the way your father died, at the hands of a mob in a ghetto?"

"But the sadness of my son is my fault, Ari." Barak licked his lips and swallowed. "Jordana has become a great friend of Kitty Fremont."

Ari started at the mention of her name.

"She has become a saint. She visits us when she is in the Huleh. It is too bad you haven't seen her."

"Father . . . I . . ."

"Don't you think I see the hunger in that woman's eyes for you? Is this the way a man gives love, by hiding in the desert? Yes, Ari! Let's have it all out now. You've run and hidden from her. Say it. Say it to me and say it to yourself."

Ari got off the edge of the bed and walked away.

"What is this terrible thing in your heart that keeps you from going to this woman and telling her your heart breaks for her?"

Ari felt his father's burning gaze at his back. He turned slowly with his eyes lowered. "She told me once I would have to need her so badly that I would have to crawl."

"Then crawl!"

"I cannot crawl! I don't know how! Can't you see, Father . . . I can never be the man she wants."

Barak sighed sadly. "And that is where I have failed you, Ari. You see, I would have crawled to your mother a million times. I would crawl to her because I need her in order to live. She is my strength. God help me, Ari, I have been a party to the creation of a breed of men and women so hard they refuse to know the meaning of tears and humility."

"She once said that to me," Ari whispered.

"You have mistaken tenderness for weakness. You have mistaken tears for dishonor. You have made yourself believe that to depend on another person is to retreat. You are so blind that you cannot give love."

"So, I cannot do what I cannot do," Ari cried.

"And I am sorry for you, Ari. I am sorry for you and I am sorry for myself."

The next day Ari carried his father in his arms to his car and drove him to Tel Hai, to the very spot at which he and his brother Akiva had crossed to Palestine more than half a century before.

The graves of the Guardsmen were there at Tel Hai, the first Jews to bear arms at the turn of the century in a roving defense of Jewish settlements against Bedouins. It was as a Guardsman, Barak was remembering, that he had met Sarah at Rosh Pinna.

The stones of the dead formed two lines, and there were a dozen plots waiting for those Guardsmen still alive. Akiva's remains had been removed from Elijah's Point to this place of honor. The plot next to Akiva was reserved for Barak.

Ari carried his father beyond the graves to where the huge stone statue of a lion stood looking down upon the valley, the symbol of a king protecting the land. On the base of the statue they read the words: "IT IS GOOD TO DIE FOR ONE'S COUNTRY."

Barak looked down at the valley. Settlements were everywhere. A town was springing up below them with thousands of new settlers. The father and the son lingered at Tel Hai until darkness fell and they watched the lights go on, ringing the valley with a fortress of determination. Yad El—the Hand of God—stood in their center. A settlement of tough new youngsters had just broken ground at Gonen far below; they lived in tents just a few yards from the Syrian border. The lights of Gonen went on too.

"It is good to have a country to die for," Barak said.

Ari carried his father down from the hill.

Two days later Barak Ben Canaan died in his sleep and he was taken back to Tel Hai and buried next to Akiva.

CHAPTER FOUR: In the last stages of the War of Liberation, Dov Landau joined the army of Israel and took part in Operation Ten Plagues against the Egyptians. His bravery in the storming of Suweidan won him a field commission. For several months he stayed in the desert as one of Colonel Ben Canaan's Beasts of the Negev. Ari recognized the boy's obvious talents and sent him north for tests. The army then asked Dov to go to the Technical Institute at Haifa and study specialized courses for the ambitious water projects being planned for the redemption of the Negev. Dov proved to be a brilliant scholar.

He had completely burst out of his former darkness. Now he was warm and filled with humor and showed uncommon understanding for those people who suffered. Still rather slight in stature, with sensitive features, Dov had become a handsome young man. He and Karen were deeply in love.

The young romance was plagued with constant separations, uncertainty and of course the eternal tension. The land was in a turmoil and so were they; each had his separate serious duties. It was an old story in Israel, it was the story of Ari and Dafna and the story of David and Jordana. Each time they saw each other the desire and the frustration grew. Dov, who worshiped Karen, became the stronger of the two.

When he reached his twenty-first birthday he was a captain in the corps of engineers and was considered one of the most promising officers in his field. His time was spent studying at the Technical Institute and at the Weizmann Research Institute at Rehovot.

Karen left Gan Dafna after the War of Liberation and also went into the Army. There she continued nurses' training. She had gained valuable experience in working with Kitty and was able to finish her basic training quickly. Nursing suited Karen. She wanted someday to follow in Kitty's footsteps and specialize in caring for children. She was stationed in a hospital in the Sharon. It was convenient, for she was able to hitch a ride to Jerusalem to Kitty when Kitty was there and to get to Haifa frequently to see Dov.

Karen Hansen Clement grew from a beautiful girl into a magnificent woman. She was striking perfection, with the tenderness and kindness which had characterized her youth following her into maturity.

In the depths of Kitty's mind the thought sometimes rose that Karen might come with her to America, but it was pure wishful thinking. In more realistic moments she knew that Karen did not need her. She had done her job for the girl just as she had done it for Israel. Karen was a part of Israel now, too deeply rooted to be torn away. And Kitty knew that she did not need Karen now. Once she believed she would never be able to part from the girl. But that void, the emotional starvation in Kitty, had been filled by years of unselfish devotion to "her children."

Kitty not only knew she could leave Karen, but she dared hope that normalcy and true happiness awaited her somewhere, sometime, again.

No, for Karen and herself, Kitty had no fears about leaving Israel. But there was one fear—a fear for Israel itself.

The Arabs sat at Israel's borders, licking their wounds and waiting for that day they would pounce on the little nation and destroy her in their much-advertised "second round."

The Arab leaders handed their masses guns instead of plowshares. Those few who saw the light of Israel and wanted to make peace were murdered. The old harangues poured from the Arab press, from its radio, its leaders, and from the Moslem pulpits.

The Arab people, already bled dry by willful men, were

bled even dryer to pay for hundreds of millions of dollars in arms.

The refugee situation was distorted so as to be made insolvable.

Nasser, the one-time army captain who sat in the pocket at Faluja under siege, inflamed the Arab world like a would-be Hitler.

The Suez Canal was blocked by Egypt to Israeli ships and ships of other nations bringing cargo to Israel, in violation of international law.

The Gulf of Akaba was blockaded to keep the Jews from operating a port at Elath.

The Legion of Jordan blatantly ignored the truce agreement whereby Jews were to have free access to Old Jersusalem for worship at their holiest shrine, the Wall of Solomon's Temple.

All Arab nations refused to recognize the existence of Israel; all Arab nations swore to destroy Israel.

Then came the most vicious move. The Arabs, mainly the Egyptians in the Gaza Strip, organized *fedayeen* gangs for the purpose of murdering Israelis. These gangs crossed the border nightly to kill, to burn fields, to cut water-pipe lines, to destroy. Tormented Palestine refugees were used in these gangs, goaded by hate-spewing leaders.

Israel, with all of her other burdens, had to adopt an axiom of reality: "When Hitler said he was going to exterminate the Jews, the world did not believe him. When the Arabs say it, we in Israel believe them."

Military training in Israel was compulsory for girls as well as for boys. They learned at early ages to handle arms. All men received training one month out of each year until the age of forty-five. Israel became the most efficiently organized and largest—in proportion to population—standing militia in the world.

The notorious *fedayeen* continued to commit atrocity after atrocity. They reached a new depth by the bombing of children's houses on the border settlements.

At last Israel had no choice but reprisal. The army of Israel swore to kill ten for one. Unfortunately, reprisal seemed to be the only language that the Arabs understood, the only thing that might stop them.

One of the defensive measures used by Israel was the creation of Nahal. Nahal was a militarized intensification of settlements in strategic places. Many youth groups of boys and girls went into the army to take their training as a unit. After basic training they were sent out to the borders to build combined farming and defensive settlements. To build a wall of flesh on the Israeli borders was a partial answer to

582

fedayeen terror. The settlements of these youngsters in their late teens were only yards from the frontier; they lived in the jaws of the enemy.

The conditions on the frontier were brutal. The pay rate of the young soldier-farmer was thirty dollars a year. Death lay on one side of them, unfertile land on the other. Yet— still another of the nation's miracles—Israel's youth volunteered to spend their entire lives in border settlements. They went quietly and without heroics. Like Jordana and Ari and David and Joab and Zev . . . it was their job. They lived with no thought of material gain for themselves, but only of Israel and tomorrow.

The toughest of these frontiers was the Gaza Strip, the finger of land which was left jutting into Israel as an aborted border at the end of the war. Ancient Gaza, where Samson had lifted the gates, had new gates now, the gates of the Palestine refugee camps. The victimized Arabs were allowed to wallow in listlessness and become wards of world charity while they were pumped full of hatred by Egyptian administrators. Gaza was the principal base and training ground of the Egyptian sponsored *fedayeens*.

It was in this place, less than ten kilometers from the enemy nest, that twenty-two boys and sixteen girls came to build a Nahal settlement.

It was named Nahal Midbar—the Stream in the Desert.

Among the sixteen girls was their nurse, Karen Hansen Clement.

Dov had finished his studies at the Weizmann Institute and was transferred to a water project in the Huleh Valley. He achieved a five-day leave before reporting to his new post so he could hitch a ride to Nahal Midbar to see Karen. They had been separated for six weeks, since she had left with her group.

It took Dov all day to travel to the remote spot in the Negev Desert. A dirt path branched off the main road along the Gaza Strip and ran some four kilometers to the settlement.

Most of Nahal Midbar was still canvas. Only a dining shack, a tool shed, and a pair of guard towers had been built. The water tank and the irrigation pipes were nearly in. Those few buildings stood in the center of a wind-swept, bleak and desolate, sun-baked corner that seemed to be the end of the earth. It was, indeed, on the brink of nowhere. On the horizon could be seen the sinister outline of Gaza. Emplacements of barbed wire and trenches faced the enemy.

The first *dunams* of land were under the plow. Dov stopped at the gate and observed for a moment. Nahal Midbar was depressing. Then, suddenly it turned in his sight into the most magnificent garden on earth, for he saw Karen running toward him from her hospital tent.

"Dov! Dov!" she cried, and raced over the bare brown knoll and flung herself into his waiting arms and they held each other tightly, their hearts pounding in excitement and joy with the feel of each other.

They held hands as Karen took Dov to the water tank; he washed his sweaty face and took a long drink. Then Karen led him away from the settlement to a path which led beyond the knoll where some Nabataean ruins stood. It was the forward outpost, right on the border marker, and the favorite meeting place of the single boys and girls.

Karen gave a signal to the guard that she would take the watch and the guard left knowingly. They picked their way through the ruins until they came to the enclosure of an ancient temple and there they waited until the guard was out of sight. Karen peered out at the field through the barbed wire. Everything was quiet.

They both leaned the rifles they carried against the wall and embraced and kissed.

"Oh, Dov! At last!"

"I've almost died from missing you," he said.

They kissed again and again ignoring the burning midday desert sun, ignoring everything but each other. Dov led her to a corner and they sat on the earthen floor, Karen lying in his arms, and he kissed her and caressed her and she closed her eyes and purred with happiness.

And then his hands became still and he just gazed lovingly.

"I have some wonderful news," he said.

She looked up. "What could be more wonderful than this minute?"

"Sit up," he commanded teasingly.

"What is it, Dov?"

"You know about me being transferred to the Huleh Project?"

"Yes, of course."

"Well, I was called in yesterday. They want me to stay up there until the end of the summer only . . . then they want me to go to America for advanced studies! The Massachusetts Institute of Technology!"

Karen blinked her eyes.

"America? To study?"

"Yes . . . for two years. I could hardly wait to get here and tell you."

She forced herself to smile—quickly. "How wonderful, Dov. I am so proud. Then you will be going in about six or seven months."

"I didn't give them an answer," he said. "I wanted to talk it over with you."

"Two years isn't forever," Karen said. "Why, by the time you get back the *kibbutz* will all be built up. We'll have two thousand *dunams* under cultivation and a library and a children's house full of babies."

"Wait a minute . . ." Dov said. "I'm not going to America or anywhere else without you. We will get married right now. Of course, it will be difficult in America. They can't give me much of an allowance. I'll have to work after classes but you can study nursing and work too . . . we'll make it."

Karen was very quiet. She looked out and saw the rise of Gaza in the distance and the guard towers and the trenches.

"I can't leave Nahal Midbar," she whispered. "We have only started here. The boys are working twenty hours a day."

"Karen . . . you've got to take leave."

"No, I can't, Dov. If I go it makes it that much harder on everyone else."

"You've got to. I'm not going without you. Don't you understand what this means? I'll come back here in two years and I'll know everything there is to know about water tables and drilling and pipes. It will be perfect. We'll live in Nahal Midbar together and I'll be working around close by in the desert. The *kibbutz* will have my salary. Karen . . . I'll be worth fifty times the value I am now to Israel."

She stood up and turned her back to him. "It's *right* for you. It's important for you to go to America. I'm more important here, now."

Dov turned pale and his shoulders sagged. "I thought I would make you happy . . ."

She faced him. "You know you have to go and you know I have to stay."

"No, dammit! I can't be away from you for two years! I can't even take it for two days any more." He stood and seized her in his arms and covered her mouth with kisses and she returned kiss for kiss and both of them cried, "I love you" over and over and their cheeks were wet with perspiration and tears and their hands felt for each other's bodies and they slipped to the floor.

"Yes! Now!" she cried.

Dov sprang to his feet and stood trembling. He clenched his fists tightly. "We've got to stop this."

It was still except for Karen's soft sobbing. Dov knelt behind her. "Please don't cry, Karen."

"Oh, Dov, what are we going to do? It is just as though I'm not living when you are away. And now, every time we see each other it ends up the same way. When you leave me I am sick with wanting you for days."

"It's just as hard on me," he said. "It's my fault. We'll be more careful. Nothing is going to happen until we marry."

He helped her to her feet.

"Don't look at me that way, Karen. I don't want to ever hurt you."

"I love you, Dov. I'm not ashamed or afraid of wanting you."

"I'm not going to do what's wrong for you," he said.

They stood still, eyes shining with love and bodies taut with insistence.

"We had better go back to the *kibbutz*," Karen said at last, with desolation in her voice.

Kitty had traveled over most of Israel and she had seen the most rugged of the settlements. She knew when she traveled to Nahal Midbar that it was the brink of hell. Yet in spite of preparing herself for the worst her heart sank at the sight of Nahal Midbar, a bake furnace planted in the path of angry Arab hordes.

Karen showed Kitty around with obvious pride over what had been accomplished in three months. There were a few new wooden shacks, a few more *dunams* of land plowed, but it was a heartbreaking sight. It represented boys and girls working agonizing hours during the day and standing guard during the night.

"In a few years," Karen said, "there will be trees and flowers everywhere, if we can only get enough water."

They walked out of the sun into Karen's hospital tent and each had a drink of water. Kitty looked through the tent flap. Barbed wire and trenches. Out in the fields, boys and girls worked in the sun while others walked behind them with rifles, guarding them. One hand on the sword and one on the plow. That was the way they rebuilt the walls of Jerusalem. Kitty looked at Karen. The girl was so young and so lovely. In a few years in this place she would age before her time.

"So you are really planning to go home. I can hardly believe it," Karen said.

"I told them I want to take a year's leave. I have been terribly homesick lately. And now, with you gone . . . well, I just want to take things easy for a little while. I may come back to Israel, I am not sure."

"When will you leave?"

"After Passover."

"So soon? It will be dreadful with you gone, Kitty."

"You are a grown woman now, Karen. You have a life of your own."

"I can't think of it with you away."

"Oh, we'll write. We will always be close. Who knows,

after living in this volcano for four years, I may find the rest of the world too dull for me."

"You must come back, Kitty."

Kitty smiled. "Time will tell. How is Dov these days? I hear he has finished school."

Karen avoided telling Kitty that Dov had been asked to go to America, for she knew Kitty would take Dov's side.

"They sent him to the Huleh Lake. They are planning a project to dig channels and lower the whole lake into the Sea of Galilee and reclaim it for farmland."

"Dov has become a very important young man. I hear tremendous things about him. Will he be able to get here for Passover?"

"It doesn't look like it."

Kitty snapped her fingers. "Say! I have a splendid idea. Jordana has asked me to come to Yad El for Passover and I promised I would. Dov is working close by. Why don't you come up to Yad El?"

"I really should stay at my *kibbutz* for Passover."

"You'll be here for many Passovers. It will be a farewell present to me."

Karen smiled. "I'll come."

"Good. Now, how is that young man of yours?"

"Fine . . . I guess," Karen muttered glumly.

"Did you have an argument?"

"No. He won't argue with me. Oh, Kitty, he is so damned noble sometimes I could scream."

"I see," Kitty said raising her eyebrows. "You are quite the grown-up woman of eighteen."

"I just don't know what to do. Kitty . . . I . . . I go crazy thinking about him and then every time we see each other he gets noble. They . . . may send him away. It may be two years before we can get married. I think I'm going to break open."

"You love him very much, don't you?"

"I could die for wanting him. Is it terrible for me to talk this way?"

"No, dear. To love someone that way is the most wonderful thing in the world."

"Kitty . . . I want so much to love him. Is that wrong?"

Was it wrong? Kitty remembered standing over a bed and implying to Ari that Jordana was a tramp for the moments she had stolen with David Ben Ami. Was that wrong? How many times she had regretted her words. David had been dead for three years and Jordana still grieved deeply. Even with that tough shell of *sabra* aggressiveness she would take a broken heart to her grave. Was it wrong? How many to-morrows would Dov and Karen have? That angry host of people beyond the barbed wire—would they let them live?

Karen . . . her precious baby . . .

"Love him, Karen," Kitty said. "Love him with all the love that is in you."

"Oh . . . Kitty!"

"Yes, dear. Love him."

"He is so afraid."

"Then help him not to be afraid. You are his woman and that is the way it should be."

Kitty felt empty inside her. She had given her Karen away forever. She felt Karen's hand on her shoulder.

"Can't *you* help Ari?"

Kitty's heart skipped a beat at the mention of his name. "It is not love when one person loves and the other doesn't."

They were both silent for a long time. Kitty went to the tent flap and looked outside. The flies swarmed around her. She spun around quickly and faced Karen. "I can't go without telling you I am sick about your coming to this place."

"The borders must be defended. It is easy enough to say let the other fellow do it."

"Nahal Midbar is three months old. Already you have a boy and a girl in your graveyard, murdered by *fedayeen*."

"We don't think of it that way, Kitty. Two are lost but fifty more have joined Nahal Midbar and another fifty have come to build a settlement five kilometers away—because we came here. In a year we will have a children's house and a thousand *dunams* of land under cultivation."

"And in a year you will begin to grow old. You will work eighteen hours a day and spend your nights in the trenches. All that you and Dov will ever have out of this is a single room eight by ten feet. Even the clothes on your back won't belong to you."

"You are wrong, Kitty. Dov and I will have everything."

"Including a quarter of a million kill-crazy Arabs at your throats."

"We cannot be angry at those poor people," Karen said. "They sit there day after day, month after month, locked up like animals, watching our fields grow green."

Kitty sagged down in a cot and buried her face in her hands.

"Kitty . . . listen . . ."

"I can't."

"Please . . . please listen. You know that even when I was a little girl in Denmark I asked myself why I was born a Jew. I know the answer now. God didn't pick us because we were weak or would run from danger. We've taken murder and sorrow and humiliation for six thousand years and we have kept faith. We have outlived everyone who has tried to destroy us. Can't you see it, Kitty? . . . this little land was chosen for us because it is the crossroads of the world, on the edge of man's wilderness. This is where God wants His people to be . . . on the frontiers, to stand and guard His laws which are the cornerstones of man's moral existence. Where else is there for us to be?"

"Israel stands with its back to the wall," Kitty cried. "It has always stood that way and it always will . . . with savages trying to destroy you."

"Oh no, Kitty, no! Israel is the bridge between darkness and light."

And suddenly Kitty saw it all, so clearly . . . so beautifully clear. This then was the answer. Israel, the bridge between darkness and light.

CHAPTER FIVE: One night above all other nights is the most important for a Jew and that is the religious holiday of Passover. The Passover is celebrated in memory of the deliverance from bondage in Egypt. The Egyptians, the original oppressors, had become the symbol of all the oppressors of all the Jews throughout all the ages.

The high point occurs on the eve of Passover when the Seder—the Feast of Liberation—is held to give thanks for freedom and to offer hope for those who do not have it. For the exiles and the dispersed, before the rebirth of Israel the Seder always ended with the words: ". . . *next year in Jerusalem.*"

The Haggadah, a special book of prayers, stories, and songs for Passover, parts of which were written three thousand years ago, is read. The story of the Exodus from Egypt is recited by the head of the house.

The Seder was the high moment of the year. The woman of the house had to prepare for it for a month. All dirt had to be chased. Special Passover foods and decorations had to be prepared. All over Israel half-frantic preparations for the Seder took place. In the communal settlements the Seder table would hold hundreds. Other homes had small and simple Seders. As the eve of Passover drew near, the air of anticipation of the great feast grew and grew to a bursting point.

The Seder this year at the Ben Canaan cottage at Yad El was to be a relatively small affair. None the less, Sarah had to carry out the prescribed traditions and rituals to the letter. It was a labor of love and she would not be robbed of it. The cottage, inside and out, was made spotless. On the day of the feast the rooms were filled with enormous Galilee roses. The Menorah—the ritual candlesticks—had been polished to a dazzling gleam. Tens of dozens of special Passover cookies and candies had been made. All the special foods had been prepared and Sarah herself was dressed in her finest.

On the day of Passover Eve, Kitty and Sutherland drove from his villa to Yad El.

"The idea of your leaving Israel is wretched," Sutherland grumbled. "Can't make myself get on to it."

"I've given it a lot of thought, Bruce. It is best. In America we always say, 'leave them laughing.' "

"Do you really feel that immigration has passed its peak?"

"Well, let's say the first flood is over. There are many small communities of Jews, like the Poles, locked in Europe who want to get out. We suspect the roof may fall in on the Jews in Egypt at any time. But the main thing is that we have personnel and facilities for any emergencies."

"You mean for little emergencies," Sutherland said. "What about the giants?"

"I don't understand."

"The United States has six million Jews and the Russians have four. What of them?"

Kitty thought deeply. "Most of those few Jews who have come from the United States are either one of two things; they are either idealists of the old pioneer days or neurotics seeking a false haven. I do not believe that the day will ever come that American Jews must come to Israel because of fear or persecution. If the day does come, I do not want to be alive to see it. As for the Russians, there is a strange and haunting story that not many people know."

"You have me curious," Sutherland said.

"Well, you know that they have tried to integrate the Jews by swallowing them up in theories and in evolution. They have tried to make them lose their identity by letting the old ones die out and indoctrinating the young ones from birth. Of course you know that anti-Semitism still rages in Russia."

"I've heard."

"It was on the last high holy days that this fantastic thing happened. It proved that the Soviets have failed miserably. The ambassador from Israel went to the only synagogue they permit in Moscow. After thirty years of silence, thirty thousand Jews appeared on the streets just to see and touch the ambassador! Yes, there will be a great *aliyah* from Russia someday."

The story struck Sutherland deeply and he was silent. It was the same old story, the concept that arose so often in his mind: . . . *the Jew never loses his identity*. And . . .

590

there comes that day of truth when he must stand and declare himself. He thought of his own beloved mother . . .

They turned from the main road into the Yad El *moshav*. Sarah Ben Canaan rushed from the cottage to meet them. There were hugs and holiday greetings.

"Are we the first here?"

"Dov has arrived. Come in already, come in . . . come in."

Dov met them at the door. He shook Sutherland's hand and embraced Kitty warmly. She held him off at arm's length. "*Major* Dov Landau! You get better-looking every time I see you."

Dov blushed.

Sutherland was examining Sarah's roses in the living room with a trace of envy.

"Where is everybody?" Kitty asked.

"Jordana went to Haifa last night. She said she would be back early," Sarah said.

"Karen wrote me that she would leave Nahal Midbar the day before," Dov said. "That would be yesterday. She's allowing plenty of time to get here. She may have stayed over at Haifa last night. Anyhow, she may have to hitch a ride beyond Safed."

"Don't fret," Sutherland said. "She'll be here in time for the Seder."

Kitty was disappointed that Karen had not arrived but made no point of it before the others. Transportation was terrible, especially on a holiday. "Is there anything I can help you with?" she asked Sarah.

"You can sit down and take life easy. Already there have been a dozen calls for you from the *moshav* office. Your children all over the Huleh know you are coming. They said they would be dropping in during the day before the Seder." Sarah rushed off to her kitchen.

Kitty turned to Dov. "I hear some very good reports about you, Dov."

The boy shrugged.

"Don't be modest. I understand you're planning a Jordan water project."

"If the Syrians let us, which they won't. Funny, Syria and Jordan stand to benefit from it ten times more than we do. But so long as it puts an extra ounce of water into Israel, they are against it."

"What is the problem?" Sutherland asked.

"We have to change the course of the Jordan a few kilometers. The Arabs say we are doing it for defensive reasons, even though we welcome their observers. Oh well, we will work it out."

591

Dov took a deep breath. He was obviously preoccupied and Sutherland sensed that Dov wanted to talk privately to Kitty, so he drifted to the far end of the room and absorbed himself in the shelves of books.

"Kitty," Dov said. "I wanted to talk to you about Karen before she gets here."

"Yes, Dov, of course."

"She is very stubborn."

"I know. I was at Nahal Midbar a few weeks ago. We had a long talk."

"Did she tell you that I have a chance to study in America?"

"She didn't tell me but I knew, anyhow. You see, I've been in Israel so long I've developed my own spy system."

"I don't know what to do. She is loyal to her *kibbutz*. I am afraid she will refuse to leave. I . . . I just can't leave her for two years."

"I'll work on her," Kitty smiled. "She is weakening by the moment. You'll see, Dov. Everything is going to work out fine."

The front door was flung open and Jordana, her red hair flowing, held open her arms.

"*Shalom,* everybody," she called.

Kitty embraced her.

"*Ema!*" Jordana called. "Come here. I have a surprise for you!"

Sarah rushed in from the kitchen just as Ari walked through the door.

"Ari!"

She reached for her handkerchief and simultaneously burst into happy tears and embraced him. "Ari! Oh, Jordana, you are a devil with red hair! Why didn't you tell me Ari was coming!"

"Well, I figured that you might have made enough for an extra mouth at the table," he said, hugging his mother.

"You devils!" Sarah said, shaking her finger at them, and dabbing at her eyes. "Let me look at you, son. Ari, you look tired. You are working too hard."

They embraced again and laughed.

Then Ari saw Kitty Fremont.

The room turned awkwardly quiet as both of them stared long and hard. Jordana, who had carefully arranged the meeting, looked from one to the other.

Kitty stood up slowly and nodded her head. "*Shalom,* Ari," she said softly.

"*Shalom,*" he whispered.

"Make yourselves at home," Jordana said, grabbing her

mother's arm quickly and leading her back to the kitchen.

Dov shook Ari's hand. "*Shalom*, Brigadier Ben Canaan," he said. Kitty watched Dov. The young man's eyes brimmed with admiration, seeing Ari as the almost legendary leader of "the Beasts."

"*Shalom*, Dov. You are looking fine. I hear you are going to bring water down to us in the desert."

"We will try very hard, Brigadier."

Sutherland and Ari shook hands.

"I received your letter, Sutherland, and I will be delighted to have you visit us at Elath any time."

"I am terribly keen to see the Negev first hand. Perhaps we can arrange a time."

"Fine. And how does your garden grow?"

"Well, I must say, your mother's roses are the first I've found to envy. I say, old boy, I'm not letting you get back to Elath without spending an afternoon at my villa."

"I shall try."

Again an awkward silence fell as Bruce Sutherland looked from Ari to Kitty. She had not taken her eyes from Ari. Sutherland walked over to Dov quickly and led him from the room. "Now, Major Landau, you've got to tell me just how you chaps plan to drop the Huleh Lake into the Sea of Galilee. That's a bit of doing . . ."

Ari and Kitty were alone.

"You look well," Kitty said at last.

"And you."

And there was silence between them once more.

"I . . . uh . . . how is little Karen? Is she coming?"

"Yes, she will be here. We are expecting her at any time."

"Would you . . . would you like to take a walk? It is quite fresh outside."

"Yes, why don't we?" Kitty said.

They walked wordlessly past the fence and along the edge of the fields and past the olive orchard, until they came to the Jordan River. The rebirth of springtime was in the smell and the sight of everything. Ari lit two cigarettes and handed Kitty one.

She was even more beautiful than the memory he held of her.

Kitty became aware of Ari's fixed gaze.

"I . . . am really quite ashamed of myself. I have never been to Elath. The commander at Beersheba has offered to fly me down a half dozen times. I should see it, I suppose."

"The water and the mountains are quite beautiful."

"Is the town growing?"

"It would be the fastest-growing town in the world if we

593

could break the blockade and open her as a port to the Orient."

"Ari," Kitty said seriously, "what is the situation down there?"

"What it has always been . . . as it will always be."

"The *fedayeen* gangs are getting worse, aren't they?"

"Those poor devils aren't our real worry. They're massing to overrun the entire Middle East from Sinai. We're going to have to hit them first if we expect to survive." Ari smiled. "My boys tell me we should cross the border and find Mount Sinai and give the Ten Commandments back to God . . . it's all caused us enough trouble."

Kitty stared at the bubbling stream for a long time. She sighed unevenly. "I am sick with worry over Karen. She is on the Gaza Strip . . . Nahal Midbar."

"Nasty place," Ari muttered. "But they are tough youngsters. They'll make out."

Yes, that is the way that Ari would answer, Kitty thought.

"I hear you are returning to America."

Kitty nodded.

"You've become a woman of renown."

"More of a curiosity," Kitty said.

"You're modest."

"I'm sure Israel will survive without me."

"Why are you leaving?"

"You saw Dov . . . Major Dov Landau now. He's a fine young man. Karen is being left in good hands. I don't know . . . maybe I just don't want to wear out my welcome. Maybe I still don't fully belong here. Maybe I'm homesick. There are lots of reasons and no reasons. Anyhow, I just want a year to take off and spend the time thinking—just thinking."

"Perhaps you are doing a wise thing. It is good for a person to think without the pressures imposed by daily living. It was a luxury my father was denied until his last two years."

Suddenly they seemed to run out of words to say.

"We had better start back for the house," Kitty said. "I want to be there when Karen arrives. Besides, I am expecting visits from some of my children."

"Kitty . . . a moment, please."

"Yes?"

"Let me say that I am grateful for the friendship you have given Jordana. You have been good for her. I have been worried about this restlessness of hers."

"She is a very unhappy girl. No one can ever really know how much she loved that boy."

"When will it end?"

"I don't know, Ari. But I have lived here so long that I

have become a cockeyed optimist. There will be happiness again for Jordana, someday."

The unspoken question—the unasked words—hung between them. Would there be happiness for her . . . and for him, someday, too?

"We had better go back," Kitty said.

All through the morning and afternoon Kitty's children came from Gan Dafna and from a dozen Huleh settlements to see her. The people of Yad El came to see Ari. There was a constant flow of traffic through the Ben Canaan house. They all remembered the first time they had seen Kitty, aloof and awkward. Now she spoke to them in their language and they all looked up to her in admiration.

Many of her children had traveled a long distance to spend a few minutes with her. Some showed off new husbands or wives. Almost all of them were in the uniform of the army of Israel.

As the afternoon passed, Kitty became concerned at the failure of Karen to appear. Several times Dov went out to the main road to look for a sign of her.

By late afternoon all the visitors had left to get ready for their own Seders.

"Where the devil is that girl?" Kitty snapped, expressing her worry in annoyance.

"She's probably just a little way off," Dov said.

"The least she could have done was to phone and let us know she was delayed. It isn't like Karen to be thoughtless," Kitty said.

"Come now, Kitty," Sutherland said, "you know it would take an act of Parliament to put a phone call through today."

Ari saw Kitty's discomfort. "Look . . . I'll run down to the *moshav* office and put in a priority call to her *kibbutz.* Perhaps they know where she planned to stay en route and we can track her down."

"I would appreciate that very much," Kitty said.

Not long after Ari had left Sarah came in and announced that the Seder table was ready for everyone's inspection. This was her moment of triumph after a month of labor. She opened the door to the dining room and the guests self-consciously tiptoed in with a chorus of "ohs" and "ahs." It was a table indeed fit for a Feast of Liberation.

All the silver and dishes glistened. They were used only once a year, on this holiday. The silver candlesticks shone in the center of the table. Next to the candlesticks sat a huge ornate sterling-silver goblet which was called "Elijah's cup." It was set there and filled with wine to welcome the prophet. When he came to drink from the cup he came as the forerunner of the Messiah.

Special wine and silver goblets were at each place, to be filled four times during the Seder for the four promises of God: to bring forth, deliver, redeem, and take the Children of Israel. The wine symbolizing joy would also be sipped during the recounting of the Ten Plagues against Pharaoh, and when the Song of Miriam, of the closing of the Red Sea on Pharaoh's army, was sung.

At the head seat there was a pillow, so that the teller of the story of the Exodus might relax. In ancient times only free men relaxed, while slaves were made to sit rigid.

And in the center near the candlesticks sat the gold Seder dish holding the symbolic foods. There was matzos, the unleavened bread to remind them that the Children of Israel had to leave Egypt so quickly their bread was unleavened. There was an egg to symbolize the freewill offering, and water cress for the coming of spring, and the shank of lamb bone to recall the offerings to God in the Great Temple. There was a mixture of nuts and diced apples and *maror*, bitter herbs. The first symbolized the mortar the Egyptians forced them to mix for brick building, and the herbs recalled the bitterness of bondage.

Sarah shooed them all out and they returned to the living room. As they entered, it was Jordana who saw Ari first. He leaned in the doorframe, pale and with a dazed expression in his eyes. Now they all stared at him. He tried to speak but couldn't, and as a moment passed they all knew at once.

"Karen! Where is she!" Kitty demanded.

Ari's jaw trembled and he lowered his head.

"Where is she!"

"Karen is dead. She was murdered last night by a gang of *fedayeen* from Gaza."

Kitty let out an anguished shriek and slumped to the floor.

Kitty blinked her eyes open. Bruce and Jordana knelt near her. The remembrance hit her and her eyes bulged and she turned and sobbed, "My baby . . . my baby . . ."

She sat up slowly. Jordana and Sutherland were in a stupor of shock. They looked haggard and numb with grief.

"Karen is dead . . . Karen is dead . . ."

"If I could only have died for her," Jordana cried.

Kitty struggled to her feet.

"Lie down, dear . . . please, lie down," Sutherland said.

"No," Kitty said, "no . . ." She fought clear of Sutherland. "I must see Dov. I must go to him."

She staggered out and found Dov sitting in the corner of another room, hollow-eyed and his face contorted with pain. She rushed to him and took him in her arms.

"Dov . . . my poor Dov," Kitty cried.

Dov buried his head in her bosom and sobbed heart-brokenly. Kitty rocked him and they cried together, until darkness fell upon the Ben Canaan cottage and no one had any tears left.

"I'll stay with you, Dov . . . I'll take care of you," Kitty said. "We will get through this, Dov."

The young man stood up shakily. "I will be all right, Kitty," he said. "I'm going on. I'll make her proud of me."

"I beg you, Dov. Don't go back to the way you were because of this."

"No," he said. "I thought about it. I cannot hate them, because Karen could not hate them. She could not hate a living thing. We . . . she said we can never win by hating them . . ."

Sarah Ben Canaan stood at the door. "I know we are all broken," she said pitifully, "but we should go on with the Seder."

Kitty looked to Dov and the boy nodded.

They walked in tragic procession toward the dining room. Jordana stopped Kitty outside the door.

"Ari sits alone in the barn," Jordana said. "Will you go to him?"

Kitty walked from the cottage. She saw the lights of the other houses of the *moshav*. The Seder had begun in them. At this very moment, fathers were telling their families the age-old story of the Exodus as it had always been told by fathers and would be told for eternities to come. It began to drizzle and Kitty walked faster, toward the flickering lantern light from the barn. She entered and looked around. Ari sat with his back to her on a bale of hay. She walked up behind him and touched his shoulder.

"Ari, the Seder is about to begin."

He turned and looked up at her and she stepped back as though from a physical blow. She was shocked by Ari's face, distraught with a suffering that she had never seen in a human being. Ari Ben Canaan's eyes were filled with anguish. He looked at her but he did not seem to see her. He turned and hid his face in his hands and his shoulders sagged with defeat.

"Ari . . . we must have the Seder . . ."

"All my life . . . all my life . . I have watched them kill everyone I love . . . they are all gone now . . . all of them."

The words came from profound depths of an unbearable despair. She was awed and half frightened by the almost tangible emotion that tortured the now-strange figure before her.

"I have died with them. I have died a thousand times. I am empty inside . . . I have nothing left."

"Ari . . . Ari . . ."

"Why must we send children to live in these places? This

597

precious girl . . . this angel . . . why . . . *why* did they have to kill her too . . . ?"

Ari staggered to his feet. All the strength and power and control that made him Ari Ben Canaan was gone. This was a tired and beaten hulk. "Why must we fight for the right to live, over and over, each time the sun rises?"

The years of tension, the years of struggle, the years of heartbreak welled up in one mighty surge. Ari lifted his pain-filled face to heaven and raised his fists over his head. "God! God! Why don't they let us alone! *Why don't they let us live!*"

And his powerful shoulders drooped and his head hung to his chest and he stood and trembled.

"Oh, Ari . . . Ari!" Kitty cried. "What have I done to you! Why didn't I understand? Ari, my darling . . . what you must have suffered. Can I ever be forgiven for hurting you?"

Ari was exhausted, drained. He walked along the edge of a stall. "I am not myself," he mumbled. "Please do not let the others know about this."

"We had better go in. They are waiting for us," Kitty said.

"Kitty!"

He walked toward her very slowly until he stood before her looking down into her eyes. Slowly he sank to his knees and put his arms around her waist and laid his head against her.

Ari Ben Canaan wept.

It was a strange and terrible sound to hear. In this moment his soul poured out in his tears and he wept for all the times in his life he had dared not weep. He wept with a grief that was bottomless.

Kitty pressed his head tightly against her body and stroked his hair and whispered words of comfort.

"Don't leave me," Ari cried.

Ah, how she had wanted to hear those words! Yes, she thought, I will stay, this night and for a few tomorrows, for you need me now, Ari. But even as you show tears and humility for the first time in your life, you are ashamed of them. You need me now but tomorrow . . . tomorrow you will be Ari Ben Canaan again. You will be all the strong, defiant Ari Ben Canaans who inure themselves to tragedy. And then . . . you will no longer need me.

She helped him to his feet and dried his tears. He was weak. Kitty put his arm over her shoulder and held him tightly. "It is all right, Ari. You can lean on me."

They walked from the barn slowly. Through the window they could see Sarah lighting the candles and reciting a bene-diction.

He stopped and released her and straightened himself up, standing tall and strong again.

Already, so soon, he was Ari Ben Canaan again.

"Before we go in, Kitty, I must tell you something. I must tell you I never loved Dafna as I love you. You know what kind of a life you must share with me."

"I know, Ari."

"I am not like other men . . . it may be years . . . it may be forever before I can ever again say that my need for you comes first, before all other things . . . before the needs of this country. Will you be able to understand that?"

"I will understand, always."

Everyone entered the dining room. The men put on skull caps.

Dov and Jordana and Ari and Kitty and Sutherland and Sarah. Their hearts were bursting with sorrow. As Ari walked toward the head of the table to take Barak's place, Sutherland touched his arm.

"If you would not be offended," Sutherland said, "I am the oldest male Jew present. May I tell the Seder?"

"We would be honored," Ari said.

Sutherland walked to the head of the table, to the place of the head of the family. Everyone sat down and opened his copy of the Haggadah. Sutherland nodded to Dov Landau to begin.

Dov cleared his throat and read. *"Why is this night different from all other nights of the year?*

"This night is different because we celebrate the most important moment in the history of our people. On this night we celebrate their going forth in triumph from slavery into freedom."

ABOUT THE AUTHOR

LEON URIS, born in Baltimore in 1924, left high school to join the Marine Corps. In 1950, Esquire magazine bought an article from him—and it encouraged him to begin work on a novel. The result was his acclaimed bestseller *Battle Cry*. *The Angry Hills*, a novel set in war-time Greece, was his second book. As a screen writer and then newspaper correspondent, he became interested in the dramatic events surrounding the rebirth of the state of Israel. This interest led to *Exodus*, his monumental success which has been read by millions of people. From one of the episodes in *Exodus* came *Mila 18*, the story of the heroic uprising of Jewish fighters in the Warsaw Ghetto. *Exodus Revisited*, a work of nonfiction, presents the author's feeling for the land and the people of Israel. Mr. Uris is also the author of *Armageddon, Topaz, QB VII, Trinity* and (with his wife, Jill) *Ireland: A Terrible Beauty*—all sensational bestsellers.

At present, Leon and Jill Uris live in Aspen, Colorado.